VINTAGE R🌀SE MYSTERIES
MYSTERIES

LUCKY ME

DONNA SHELTON

VINTAGE R🌻SE
MYSTERIES

SADDLEBACK
EDUCATIONAL PUBLISHING
www.sdlback.com

ISBN: 978-1-68021-759-9
eBook: 978-1-64598-066-7

Printed in the United States
25 23 23 22 21   2 3 4 5 6

THE HISTORY OF THE
VINTAGE ROSE ANTIQUE SHOP

The story begins with a sorcerer named Ervin Legend. He had a talent for making money. While traveling, Ervin bought items all over the world. He would have called himself a collector. Others might say hoarder. Once he grew tired of things, he sold them for a profit. "One man's junk is another man's treasure," he used to say.

Eventually, Ervin wanted to settle down. His home was in Scarecrow, California. But he needed somewhere to put all of his things. Ervin opened the Vintage Rose Antique Shop in 1912. It was a place to keep his collections. His wife, Visalia, inspired the shop's name. She loved roses and kept them in vases all over the shop. "Roses mask the smell of old things," she would say.

After the shop opened, Ervin kept traveling. He collected pieces to sell from all over. In 1949, Ervin and Visalia went to Cairo, Egypt. While there, the couple disappeared. Nobody knows what happened to them. Some say Ervin's love of sorcery might have been to blame. He may have looked into something he shouldn't have.

Family members took over the shop. None were quite like Ervin, though. Without his passion, the business began to fail. His sister believed it was cursed.

In 1979, the Legends put the shop up for sale. Rose Myers bought it. She was odd, like Ervin. Her passion for old things was like his. "Everything has a story," she would say, with a twinkle in her eye. From a young age, Rose had looked for bargains. She would resell things for a profit. Buying the Vintage Rose was her dream come true. The place was old. It was filled with odd treasures. Plus, Rose was part of the name of the store. It seemed like this was meant to be.

Rose ran the shop for 40 years. When she passed away, it closed. The business had been left to her nephew, Evan Stewart. He was Rose's closest living relative. The Stewart family moved to Scarecrow. They reopened the shop in 2019.

Today, the shop still holds many treasures. Collectors come from all over. Some have purchased these mysterious relics. Are they magical? Do they watch over the store? We may never find out. Or will we?

CHAPTER 1

NEW DAY

Everything in my life is new. My family just moved over spring break. We're living in a new house in a new city. I have a new neighborhood and a new school. All my clothes are new too. Sometimes I don't even recognize myself. This feels like someone else's life.

At least we stayed in the same state. We moved from Sunnyside, California, to Scarecrow. So far, the cities don't seem that different. Both have shopping centers and parks. I guess the biggest difference is that the houses in Scarecrow are bigger and older. Also, the weather in Scarecrow always seems to be overcast. It wasn't like that in Sunnyside.

My family spent spring break at home, settling into the new house. Most of the time we were unpacking boxes and putting furniture together. I didn't go outside or look for anyone my age to hang out with.

Other than unpacking, I watched movies on Syfy. I'm a Syfy geek and proud of it. It's not something that makes me a lot of friends. But that's okay. Usually I don't mind being alone.

Now that spring break is over, reality is setting in. I'm going to be the new girl at school. Today is my first day. Part of me is nervous, but another part of me doesn't care.

I grab my backpack. Mom said she put something special inside. All I see is a brown paper bag with my lunch. There's nothing *special* about a sack lunch. Maybe she put money in it so I can buy a hot lunch at school.

After slinging my backpack over my shoulder, I grab my phone. There's no way I could survive without this.

"Bye, Mom!" I shout while heading out the door. Ready or not, here I come.

"Bye, Ana! Have a good day!"

I'm taking the bus to school. Being trapped on a bus with 50 strangers is basically my worst nightmare. It seems like I always get stuck next to a weird kid. But there's no other option. Mom's car is in the shop and Dad is already at work. At least my phone is with me. YouTube, Instagram, and my music will keep me company.

At the end of our street, a group of kids stands on the corner. That's where the bus is supposed to pick us up. A few look at me as I walk toward them. Most are on their phones and don't pay any attention to me. I put in my earbuds, and they all fade away.

CHAPTER 2

MEAN GIRLS

The bus pulls up and screeches to a stop. Its door squeaks open. I let all the other kids go ahead of me. When I step onto the bus, a chunky blond woman in a blue uniform is sitting in the driver's seat. She sees me and smiles.

"Good morning!" She looks like she might jump out of her seat and hug me. "You must be the new student!"

Everyone on the bus is now staring at me. I remove one earbud.

"Yeah, I'm Ana," I say in a low voice. Hopefully she will get the hint and lower her voice too.

"I'm Barbara," she says loudly. "It's nice to meet you, sweetheart."

Sweetheart? Ugh! This lady is too friendly.

I smile and hurry down the aisle. There's an open seat in the back. Tossing my bag down, I duck into it and turn on some music. Lately I've been into the band

Broken Bones. Their newest album plays loudly in my earbuds.

At the next stop, only a few kids get on. Two of them are pretty girls. Everyone moves out of their way to let them through. It must be nice to be so pretty that people move out of your way when you walk. These girls stare at their phones like me, but they aren't using them to hide from people.

When they walk up to me, it seems like they want to sit down. These girls are tall, and their clothes are so cool. Their hair and makeup are perfect. When they smile, their teeth are so white, they almost look fake. Do they really want to sit with *me*?

"Hi. Are you new?" the blond with the brightest teeth asks.

I smile. "Yeah, I just moved here from—"

"We don't care." She waves her hand to silence me. "You're in our seat. Please move."

"Oh."

This is embarrassing. I should have known that they didn't want to sit with me. Suddenly my short brown hair, plain face, T-shirt, and jeans feel so boring.

The closest available seat is next to a boy who is staring out the window. He has his earbuds in too. For a moment, I wonder what he's listening to. Then I decide it doesn't matter. All I want is for this day to be done. The boy quietly moves over when I plop down next to him.

As the bus lurches forward, I look back at the blond girl as she talks with her friend. Nobody has ever been so politely rude to me before.

The kid next to me now is tall and skinny with black-rimmed glasses. His glasses are so thick and heavy, he keeps having to push them back up on his nose. Like me, the boy is trying to hide behind his phone. Does he even realize I'm sitting here?

CHAPTER 3

NEW FRIEND

The bus makes a few more stops. There seem to be more kids than this bus can hold. People squeeze into seats that are already full. We're all staring at our phones.

I look back at the two pretty girls. No one tries to squeeze in with them. Maybe they're mean to everyone. They seem to be in their own bubble.

The boy next to me says something. At first I don't hear him because my music is too loud.

"What?" I ask, turning down the volume without removing my earbuds.

"Don't worry about Heather and Sasha." He's looking down at his feet. For a second, I'm not sure who he's talking to.

"You're talking to me, right?"

"I'm not talking to myself." Finally, the boy looks at me. He doesn't take out his earbuds either. "Heather is the one who made you move. They don't let anyone sit back there. Don't take it personally."

It's hard to tell if he's trying to be nice or just making small talk. Maybe he's being politely mean like the girls. Reading people is not what I'm best at. I'm much better at avoiding them.

"Are they always mean?" I ask.

"More like entitled."

I nod, hugging my backpack to my belly.

"My name is Ana."

"I'm Nate."

"What are you listening to?"

"Death in Summer," he says. "Their new songs are sick."

"That's cool," I say. "I stopped listening to them after their second album. All their songs started to sound the same."

"Yeah, I know. These new songs are really good though," he says. "You should give them another chance. I like Broken Bones a lot too. They're on my playlist."

"That's what I'm listening to right now." I smile. It might be the first time I've smiled since we moved.

The truth is that I was kind of mad about moving here. I did sixth and most of seventh grade at Sunnyside

Middle School. Then my dad switched jobs. He started making more money. We had been renting a house, but my parents decided they wanted to buy one instead. Scarecrow is closer to Dad's work, and the houses are less expensive. That's how we ended up here. Leaving my friends wasn't a big deal because, well, I didn't really have that many. But my family had been in Sunnyside my whole life. Starting over somewhere new was not in my plans.

"Cool," Nate says. His delayed reaction snaps me out of my wandering thoughts.

Nate seems shy like me. Maybe we can be friends.

Finally, I see Scarecrow Middle School. It's a large, white stone building with huge windows. This school is a lot bigger than Sunnyside Middle School.

The bus driver pulls into the parking lot and stops behind the other buses. I hang back with Nate as all the kids squeeze into the main aisle. They're pushing forward to get off the bus. We wait for the mean girls to go ahead before we get up.

When Nate and I get off the bus, I take my earbuds out and try to move away from the crowd. Three more buses pull in behind ours. Kids file out. Others climb out of cars. Some ride up on their bikes and skateboards.

One guy is yelling at a girl he just dropped off. He keeps calling her Twig. She quickly walks past me. Her face is getting redder by the minute. Loud music blares from his car as he drives away.

There must be over 500 kids here. Most of them are looking at their phones. The ones who aren't seem to stare at me as if I'm an alien. Suddenly, I feel so alone in a world of strangers.

This is only my second time at the school. The first time was when Mom brought me here to register. That was during spring break, when the school was empty. Everything looks different now that it's full of people.

"Do you know where you're going?" Nate asks.

I realize Nate has been standing next to me the whole time. He has taken out his earbuds too. Digging into my pocket, I pull out a folded paper. This is my schedule. Nate looks at it and points toward my first class. It's algebra in room 14 with Mr. Nash.

"Come on. I'll show you where it's at."

When I registered, the lady in the office said she could assign me a class buddy on my first day. It would be another student to help me find my classes. But that sounds embarrassing. I'd rather walk with Nate.

Kids swarm around us as I follow Nate inside. I try

not to get lost. We walk to my first class. Nate stands by the door.

"Good luck, Ana," he says. "See you later." I watch as he walks away, disappearing into the mass of students.

CHAPTER 4

STABBED IN THE BACK

In my first class, I find a seat toward the back. After tucking my backpack under my chair, I look around at the other students. Most of them have their school tablets out. None of them seem to be working on algebra. Some are watching videos. Others play games. I take out the tablet they gave me at registration last week and turn it on.

The two mean girls from the bus, Heather and Sasha, are sitting next to the window. As they talk, the girls lean in and look back at me. They're probably talking about me. This is great. First period hasn't even started and I already have enemies.

Our teacher walks in just as the bell rings. Mr. Nash is an older man with a long beard and big glasses. His plaid button-down shirt is tucked into his jeans.

"Good morning and welcome back," he says. "I hope you enjoyed spring break. All of you missed me, I'm sure."

15

I think he's joking. Usually when someone tells a joke, you can hear it in their voice. But his voice is flat and dull. If he's smiling, his beard is covering it up.

Mr. Nash sits at his desk. Papers are piled all over it. He starts typing on his computer. His notes appear on the white board for the whole class to see. They also show up on our tablets. As he types, he says everything out loud. Listening to his voice makes me sleepy. It's no wonder a bunch of students just play games on their tablets.

"Hey," a voice whispers behind me.

Is someone talking to me? I don't turn around.

"Hey," the voice says again.

Something sharp pokes me in the back. When I turn around, I see a red-haired boy whose face is covered in freckles. He is staring at the teacher.

I face the front again. What was that all about?

There's another poke to my back. I quickly turn around. The red-haired boy is hiding a pencil under his desk.

"What do you want?" I whisper to him.

"I didn't do anything," he says, making an innocent face.

It's hard to tell whether he's being playful or mean. But he's getting on my nerves.

I turn my attention back to Mr. Nash. Then I feel the pencil poke me again, harder this time.

"Stop it!" I hiss. "What's your problem?"

"What's *your* problem?" he says.

I turn around, biting my lip. Is he picking on me because I'm the new kid? It would be just my luck to pick a seat in front of a bully.

There's another poke. Without thinking, I turn around, grab the pencil out of his hand, and throw it across the room. It bounces off the window and hits Heather in the head.

Half the kids gasp. The other half laugh. Everyone looks at me. I look at Heather. Her face is red. She picks up the pencil and breaks it in half.

"I will end you," she says to me from across the room.

All I can do is stammer. "But I . . . he . . . it just . . ."

Mr. Nash hushes the room. "Young lady," he says to me. "Take a walk to the principal's office."

"But—"

"Now."

The boy behind me laughs quietly. There's no use in arguing with the teacher. I pack up my stuff. Then I walk out the door with my head down. Could this day get any worse?

CHAPTER 5

MOM'S SURPRISE

Standing in the empty hall, I look around. How can I go to the principal's office when I don't know where it is?

After wandering around for a few minutes, I find another student. She shows me to the principal's office. But his secretary tells me he's not there.

I wait in the office for a good 20 minutes. Finally, a tall man with a bushy mustache and big hands comes in. This is Principal Legend. At least he is interested in hearing my side of the story before judging me. We talk until the bell rings. Then he tells me to stay out of trouble and sends me on my way.

Getting to my second class feels like swimming upstream. There are so many kids, and they all seem to be headed in the opposite direction. I manage to make it to P.E. right as the bell rings.

I go into the girls' locker room to get changed. After finding my locker, I put on my gym clothes.

My next task is to stuff my school clothes and backpack into my locker. They won't fit.

Most of the students have bigger lockers. Mine is small. This was probably the only one left so late in the year.

No amount of shoving helps me close the locker door. It looks like I'm taking my backpack to the gym with me. I'll figure out what to do with it later.

When I walk out of the locker room, a bunch of students are gathered by the door. Heather is there. It feels like her eyes are on me. I pretend not to see her. She's making me nervous.

The school gym looks just like the one at Sunnyside. It has a shiny floor and new wood bleachers against the walls.

Someone calls my name. It's Nate, the boy from the bus. He waves me over. I'm happy to see a friendly face. Luckily, he's standing far away from Heather. I walk over to him.

Just then, the P.E. teachers walk in. Everyone gets quiet.

Mr. Dan is a thick, bald man with a whistle hanging around his neck. Ms. Lin is younger with short, dark hair.

"Good morning!" Mr. Dan says. He scans the sea

of students in front of him. "Hopefully you all had a nice spring break. Is everybody as excited as I am to be back?"

Some kids laugh. Most just groan. Do all the teachers at this school try to be funny?

"Today, you will pick out jerseys for our volleyball unit. Teams will be based on your jersey color. We'll start tomorrow."

There are more groans. If all we're doing today is picking jerseys, why did we have to dress out at all?

Mr. Dan ignores the scattered groans. He starts telling us what we will do in gym until the end of the year.

While listening, I notice my mouth feels dry. I rummage through my backpack. There must be some gum in here. In a pocket, my hand grazes something small and furry. What is that?

I look inside. It's . . . a mouse!

Without thinking, I scream and toss my bag to the floor.

Mr. Dan comes over.

"What's the problem?"

"A mouse! In my bag!" I screech.

Some girls scream and scramble away from me. Nate looks at me like I'm crazy.

Mr. Dan walks over to my bag and picks it up. He looks inside. Then he reaches in and pulls the small furry thing out.

"You're safe," he says, handing it to me. "A rabbit's foot won't hurt you." Mr. Dan chuckles and walks away.

Nate leans over and looks at it.

"Those are supposed to bring good luck," Nate says. "I think yours is broken."

"Yeah. Me too." My face feels hot. This is so embarrassing.

CHAPTER 6

FIERCE FOOT

Everyone walks ahead to pick out their jerseys, but I stay behind. I'm staring at the furry brown object in my hand. A rabbit's foot is supposed to bring good luck. Maybe this one isn't working because I don't believe in it.

This must be the special thing Mom said she put in my bag. She's the one who believes in this stuff, not me. She knocks on wood for good luck and avoids black cats like the plague. One time she broke a mirror, which is supposed to bring seven years of bad luck. Mom spent hours in the yard looking for a four-leaf clover to reverse it.

Those things have always seemed silly to me. But I could use a little luck right now. It would be nice to believe in the luck of a rabbit's foot. How can a foot be lucky though? It wasn't lucky for the rabbit it came from.

I rub the soft brown fur with my finger. It's

comforting in a way. The feeling reminds me of one Christmas when I was little. Dad got me a teddy bear. It had big, soft feet. When I rubbed them, the bear laughed.

The memory makes me think of Dad. He's always gone on business trips or working really late. We never know when he'll be home. I barely see him anymore. Working hard is how he got his new job. But I wish he didn't work so much.

I'm still rubbing the rabbit's foot. Through the fur, I feel four white claws. Their sharpness surprises me.

Suddenly, the claws close around my finger. They are poking into my skin.

What kind of rabbit's foot is this? I suck in my breath, trying not to scream. There have been enough embarrassing moments already today.

First I shake my hand to try to get it off. The claws feel like fishhooks in my skin. They don't budge. I have to grab the foot with my other hand and pull it off. After throwing it on the gym floor, I look at my finger. Drops of blood rise up from four tiny holes.

I stare at the rabbit's foot on the floor. What just happened? Did that foot come alive?

My mind is racing. There's no way a rabbit's foot could come alive! Maybe it's a trick rabbit's foot. It must have some kind of button in it that I accidentally pushed.

I stick my finger in my mouth. It's gross, but bleeding all over the gym floor would be worse. Going to the nurse is not an option either. How would I explain what happened? The office staff has seen me enough today as it is.

When my finger stops bleeding, I pick the foot up off the floor and look it over. It's not moving. The thing isn't alive. I tuck it into my pocket and go to pick out my jersey.

CHAPTER 7

EAT DIRT

I'm one of the last kids to get a jersey. The only one left in my size is black. It's number 13. Mom would not like this at all.

When the bell rings, I don't leave the locker room right away. Hopefully Heather will leave first. The thought of facing her again is painful.

While stalling, I pull out my phone and look up the meaning of a rabbit's foot. A bunch of websites come up. One says the foot is supposed to give people courage in tough times. Another says that since rabbits live underground, they can talk with spirits of the dead. None of them sound very convincing to me. People like Mom believe a lot of weird stuff though.

Finally, I walk out of the girl's locker room. Heather seems to be gone. That's a relief.

Nate comes up to me. "Two more classes until lunch," he says.

"Good. My stomach is growling."

We start walking. The hall is crowded with students. Out of nowhere, Heather and Sasha step in front of me.

"I didn't forget about you," Heather says. She looks angry.

Nate starts to talk. "Heather, look—"

"I'm not talking to you, loser." She flips her hair and points at me.

"It was an accident," I say.

"You coming here was the accident." Sasha crosses her arms over her chest.

Students stop in the hall to stare. They're whispering and waiting for something to happen. A few take out their phones. If something goes down, they want to post it to social media.

"I wish you would eat dirt!" I say.

As the words leave my mouth, something moves in my pocket. It feels like an animal is biting me. I grab at my pocket and realize the rabbit's foot is in it. Quickly, I pull it out, grimacing in pain. The claws actually pierced the fabric of my jeans and dug into my skin.

Sasha tries to say something. Then she chokes. Her eyes bug out and she starts coughing. She grabs her throat. As her eyes water, her face gets redder and redder.

"What's wrong with you?" Heather says to her

friend. She seems more annoyed than concerned. People around us laugh.

Sasha coughs again, hard this time. Black dirt sprays from her mouth into Heather's face. Her friend screams and wipes it off. The whole hallway explodes in laughter. I look around and see phones everywhere. This video is going viral for sure.

"What is wrong with you?" Heather screams at Sasha and stomps away.

Sasha spits out the last of the dirt on the floor.

"I'm sorry!" Sasha coughs again and follows her friend.

I look at Nate, speechless. My eyes feel like they're going to pop out of my head. Down the hall, a teacher yells for everyone to break it up and get to class.

"How did that happen?" I ask Nate.

"Maybe she ate dirt for breakfast." He laughs as he starts to walk away. "You are going to be *so* popular after this."

I roll my eyes. "Ha! I *wish* I were popular."

The rabbit's foot moves in my hand and the claws pierce my skin.

"Ow!" I screech, pulling it out with my other hand. What is up with this thing?

Blood drips from my hand. It really hurts. Nobody

else seems to notice though. Everyone is heading to their classes. I have no idea where my next class is. This day can't end soon enough.

CHAPTER 8

POPULAR ME

After putting the rabbit's foot in my back pocket, I pull out my schedule. Then I walk up to a group of girls.

"Excuse me. Can you tell me where Mrs. Walker's class is?"

One girl looks at me and smiles. She turns and gives a big grin to the other girls in the group.

"Science? Yes. We're going there now. Walk with us."

I breathe a sigh of relief. Maybe there are some nice girls at this school after all.

As we walk to class, the girls talk to me. They're so friendly. At the same time, I notice that other students are stopping to look at me. Some even smile and wave. A few say hi. Suddenly everyone seems to like me. I feel like the most popular girl in school.

This is weird. Is it all because I stood up to Heather and Sasha?

31

Then I think about the rabbit's foot. Could it really be giving me good luck?

In science class, I sit near the girls who walked with me. They keep asking how I made Sasha spit up dirt. One of the girls even shows me the video. It already has hundreds of views.

Mrs. Walker welcomes me to class. Then she says there's an open-note quiz today. All the notes are on Mrs. Walker's page on the school website. I use them and get an *A* on a quiz I never even studied for! Later, the teacher gives me a homework pass coupon for answering a question correctly. It was a lucky guess.

After science, I go to Mr. Nguyen's English class. English is my favorite subject. Not only does Mr. Nguyen seem cool, but he also tells jokes that are actually funny. My day really seems to be turning around.

It's finally time for lunch. In the lunchroom, I'm not sure where to sit. Nate isn't there yet. I choose an empty table and pull out my lunch. Mom packed me a peanut butter and jelly sandwich, chips, and an apple. There's some money too. It's enough to get a bottle of water and some cheesecake bites.

Within five minutes, my table is full. Everyone wants to sit with me. After I mention that I like the cheesecake bites, everyone gives me theirs. I'm not sure what's going on, but all the attention feels pretty good.

The only person I expected to sit with is Nate, but he still isn't around. At least I kind of know him. We like the same bands. He was nice to me before anyone else was.

While scanning the room for Nate, I see Heather and Sasha. They're sitting together, but they're not even talking to each other. All they do is look at their phones. Why are they so mean? How am I going to get through the rest of the school year with them hating me? I wish I could be more popular than them so that maybe they would want to be friends with me.

"Ouch!" I scream and jump out of my seat. Something bit my butt!

"Are you okay, Ana?" one of the girls at my table asks.

Then I remember the rabbit's foot. I reach into my back pocket and pry the claws out of my backside. There's a sensation of wetness when I touch my pants. It must be blood. This rabbit's foot is too weird. Can it somehow hear my thoughts?

"Yeah, something poked me." I don't want to say what it was.

Sitting back down, I shove the rabbit's foot into my backpack. It can't hurt me from there.

When I look around, no one is laughing. Their faces just look concerned. This is really strange. *I* would be laughing at me if I were them. What's going on?

After lunch, Heather and Sasha come up to me. I brace myself for a fight.

"Hey, Ana!" Heather smiles, blinding me with her white teeth. "Sorry for the misunderstanding earlier. Forgive me?"

What misunderstanding? This has got to be a trick.

"Anyway—there's a pool party at my house after school. I would love it if you could come."

My mind is racing. A few hours ago, she wanted to "end me," and now she's inviting me to a party. Is this the rabbit's foot at work? If the popular girls want to hang out with me, does that make me popular too?

"Um . . ." I start. "You're not mad about what happened earlier?" I still can't believe she's serious.

"Mad? You're the most popular girl in school. How can I be mad at you?"

Now my mind is racing. Is this a setup? I'm actually deathly afraid of water and don't know how to swim. Does she somehow know? Maybe she wants to get me alone and drown me in her pool.

There's no way she could know that, though. Is it possible that this rabbit's foot is granting all my wishes? The idea defies logic, but so does this whole day.

"Please come!" Sasha says. "We'll have so much fun."

"O . . . kay," I squeak out. Who knows if I'll actually go, but it feels like I can't say no.

"I can't wait!" Heather smiles and takes out her phone. "What's your number so I can text you my address?"

The rest of the day is more of the same. Everyone is unbelievably nice to me. I feel popular for the first time in my life. None of it makes sense, but it's a great feeling. Part of me keeps expecting someone to come out and say I'm on TV and everyone is messing with me.

CHAPTER 9

JUST MY LUCK

When I get home, Mom asks how my day went.

"It was great, actually. I'm making friends."

"That's wonderful, honey! Sounds like my surprise worked."

She's talking about the rabbit's foot. I pull it out of my bag and follow Mom into the kitchen.

"About that—where did you get it?"

"At a neat little store in town. It's called the Vintage Rose Antique Shop. I thought you could use some luck on your first day."

Today wasn't all great. But things did seem to turn around after I found the rabbit's foot. Could that weird furry thing really be why? I shake my head. There's no such thing as a lucky rabbit's foot. In fact, this one seems cursed. It keeps clawing me and making me bleed. The more I think about it, nothing about today has seemed real at all.

I toss the rabbit's foot on the counter. The thought

of carrying a piece of a rabbit around with me all day grosses me out.

"Ana, can you get the milk out of the refrigerator please?" Mom is making dinner.

I open the fridge. It's jam-packed with food. The milk is toward the back. As I reach for it, stuff gets pushed aside. Then a bowl of eggs falls out. The glass bowl shatters on the floor. Every egg breaks wide open.

"Oh no!" I look at Mom.

"Ana, watch out for the glass. I'll get some paper towels."

I reach in farther and grab the milk. When I pull it out, the carton snags a bottle of orange juice. It falls out and hits the floor. The lid pops off and juice pours out everywhere.

"Seriously?"

I quickly close the door so nothing else can fall out. Then I try to take one big step over the mess so I can set the milk on the counter. But the juice has spread farther than I thought. My foot slips, and both legs go out from under me. The next thing I know, my body hits the floor hard.

Lying on my back, I wonder what just happened. The slimy eggs and orange juice are soaking through my clothes. Milk is pouring out of the carton into my hair. This feels so gross!

"What happened?" Mom is standing over me with a roll of paper towels. "Are you hurt?"

"Just my pride."

"Don't move. I'm going to get you some towels."

I couldn't move if I tried.

When Mom comes back with the towels, she helps me up. I'm covered in eggs, orange juice, and milk. There might be some broken glass stuck to me too. Mom tries to pat me dry.

"Go take a shower. I'll clean this up."

I start to walk slowly out of the kitchen.

"Oh, Ana!"

When I turn around, Mom hands me the rabbit's foot.

"This might not have happened if you kept this on you."

Is she serious? I take the foot and rub it. It's true that everything was going great when it was in my pocket. Once I took it out, bad things happened. But there's no way the foot is lucky. This must be a coincidence.

As I'm about to go upstairs, the front door slams shut. I run into the living room to see who it is.

"Dad?" Just before hugging him, I remember how messy I am. "You're home early."

"Hi, pumpkin." He drops his briefcase by the door. Then he checks his texts. Dad is always on his phone. He's vice president of sales for a huge heating and cooling company.

After a moment, he looks at me. "What happened to you?"

Mom comes into the room and gives him a hug.

"I didn't expect you home until eight."

"Yes, I know." There's a smile on his face, but he looks sad.

"Is something wrong?" Mom asks.

"We can talk about it later. I'm just glad to be home."

Standing there looking at Dad, I remember my wish in gym class today. I wished Dad didn't work so much. Now he's home early. Everything I wished for today has come true. When the rabbit's foot wasn't in my pocket, disaster struck.

A drop of milk slides down my forehead. Is this thing a blessing or a curse?

CHAPTER 10

TAKING CHANCES

Upstairs, I put the rabbit's foot on the sink next to the shower. I had better keep it close just in case. The shower feels amazing, and I manage not to slip and break my neck on the slick tile. Afterward, I put my robe on and slide the rabbit's foot in the pocket. It seems best not to take any chances.

My phone rings. A number I don't recognize shows on the screen. Usually I don't answer calls from unknown numbers, but something tells me to answer this one.

"Hello?"

"Hi, Ana! It's Heather. What's up, girlfriend?"

It takes me a second to remember that I gave Heather my number. I'm at a loss for words. One of the most popular girls in school is calling *me*!

"Hey . . . you. What's up?"

"Do you want to come over and hang by the pool? Sasha is coming too."

The pool? Now I remember her saying something about a pool party. That would be fun if I weren't terrified of water. But I don't want her to know I can't swim. Maybe I can hang out by the pool without actually going in the water.

"Yeah. That sounds great." The words come out of my mouth before I realize what I'm saying.

"Yay! I texted you my address. See you later!"

After hanging up, I sit on my bed and check my texts. Sure enough, Heather sent me her address. She included a bunch of smiley face emojis too.

Then reality hits me. I just agreed to go to a pool party. But I hate the water. If I do go in a pool, I stay in the shallow end and hold onto the edge.

My fear of water started when I was seven. Mom took me to a nearby pool. I tried to do a cannonball like all the other kids. It looked so fun when they did it. As soon as my head went under and there was nothing solid to grab onto, I panicked and started sucking in water. After that, I didn't want to be in a pool ever again.

There's another problem. Do I even have a swimsuit that fits?

After digging through a drawer, I find a one-piece, solid black swimsuit. It's snug, but it will work. I put a T-shirt and shorts on over the suit. Then I shove the rabbit's foot into the pocket of my shorts. That furry chunk of luck is coming too. Having friends is new to me, and I need all the luck I can get.

CHAPTER 11

POOL PARTY

As usual, it's overcast in Scarecrow today. It feels odd to be going to a pool party in this sort of weather. The longtime residents of this town are probably used to it though. Not every place can be bright like Sunnyside, I guess.

Mom drops me off at Heather's house. She lives in the neighborhood behind the school. To kids like me, it's known as the "rich neighborhood." All the houses are large and fancy. Some of them look like mansions. The wide green yards are perfectly kept. Shiny new cars are parked in all the driveways.

Heather lives in a huge, beige two-story house at the end of the street. The attached garage makes it look even bigger. As we pull up, I notice that the garage door is open. Little kids ride bicycles in the driveway. One almost runs into me as I walk up. Two women are sitting in chairs in the garage, watching the kids and talking. One of them looks like an older version of Heather. This has to be her mom.

I walk up to them. "Hi, I'm Ana. Is Heather here?"

"She's in back by the pool." She points to the side of the house. "Go out and through the gate."

I go around the garage and see a big, black iron gate that leads to the backyard. A bunch of kids are running around back there. They're laughing and hitting each other with pool noodles. A tall man in a Hawaiian shirt makes food on a grill.

Heather and Sasha are sitting on the edge of the pool. They're splashing their feet in the water. Both of them hold their phones. I go through the gate and get their attention.

"Ana!" Sasha shouts. "You made it!"

I smile. My stomach does nervous flip-flops, and I feel out of place. But I don't want it to show.

"Get your suit on!" Heather says as she gets up and runs over to me. "I'll show you where you can change."

She loops her arm in mine and leads me to a little hut. It's a changing room. A bench and a chair are inside. My suit is under my clothes, but I need a minute to breathe. I close the door and take off my shirt and shorts. Then I hang them over the bench. *You can do this,* I tell myself.

There is no pocket in my bathing suit for the rabbit's foot. I panic. What will happen if I'm too far away from it? I guess I'm about to find out.

I walk out and sit with Heather and Sasha on the edge of the pool. It feels a little cool with the overcast weather, but I don't complain. My feet dangle in the water like theirs. I have my phone too. So far, so good.

"Don't mind the kids," Heather says. "It's my little cousin's birthday party. She's seven. Such a big deal, right?"

Sasha laughs.

I smile and watch the kids as they crawl out of the pool and grab drinks from a cooler. Sitting here with my feet in the water feels good. It helps that I can't fall down since I'm already on my butt.

Suddenly, a scream comes from the changing hut. Then a young girl runs out while waving something in the air.

"Who did this?" The girl is screaming and almost in tears.

"Marina, what's your problem?" Heather says. Then she turns to me and Sasha. "That's my little cousin. She's *such* a drama queen."

Heather snaps a picture of Marina. She and Sasha

look at the picture and crack up. Then Heather starts editing it.

"Let's make a meme. What should it say?" she asks both of us.

Marina stomps over to us and shoves something in Heather's face. Heather and Sasha scream. They jump up and run away from the small, brown furry object. It's my rabbit's foot.

CHAPTER 12

BUNNY KILLER

Who did this?" Marina demands to know.

"It's mine. Give it here." I set down my phone and hold out my hand.

"You!" Her face is full of anger. "Why would you cut a bunny's foot off? You're a monster!"

I stand up and adjust my swimsuit. This thing is so tight, it's going to leave marks on my skin.

Marina shoots daggers at me with her eyes. Lowering my voice, I talk to her calmly. Arguing with a seven-year-old during her birthday party seems rude.

"I know what it looks like. But someone gave it to me. It's a good-luck charm. The rabbit was dead before I got it. Can you please give it back?"

"No!" Marina stands her ground. "I'm going to bury it. It needs a funeral."

Oh, no she's not!

Lunging forward, I try to grab it from her. My bare foot lands on something sharp. It's a rock. The pain makes me instantly jump back. Sasha is standing behind me. I slam into her, knocking her into the pool. We both scream as water splashes everywhere.

"That's what you get!" Marina shouts.

Heather steps up to her cousin. "Give my friend her rabbit's foot back and you won't get hurt."

"If you touch me, I'll tell my mom."

"Give it to me or I'll cut your foot off and give it to Ana as a replacement."

Marina's face is so red, it looks like she might explode. She and Heather are having a staring contest.

Sasha crawls out of the pool behind me. She holds up her phone. "You're lucky my phone is water-resistant!" Sasha barks. "Otherwise you would have—"

"The rabbit needs its foot back! She's a murderer!"

"You can't put it back on once it's taken off, you twerp!" Heather shouts.

"You want it?" Marina holds the foot up and looks at me. "Go get it!"

She throws the rabbit's foot into the pool. Heather lunges toward her and Marina runs off, yelling for her mom.

My heart jumps into my throat. Is a rabbit's foot water-resistant?

"Ugh!" I groan, watching the foot floating in the middle of the pool.

Part of me wants to jump in after it, before anything bad happens. But I don't want to drown.

CHAPTER 13

CANNONBALL

The rabbit's foot feels so far away. It's only a few feet, but it might as well be miles.

Panic rises in my body. Maybe there's a pool net or something I can use to fish it out. I turn around to look and accidentally bump into Sasha again. She loses her balance. As she's falling, she grabs for me but I lean out of the way. Sasha screams as she splashes back into the water.

"Sorry! Again!" I yell out to her. "Uh . . . while you're in there, can you get my rabbit's foot? Please?" It's a bad time to ask, but I'm desperate.

At first Sasha looks mad. Then Heather shouts, "Not if I get it first!"

She cannonballs into the pool. Both girls swim for the rabbit's foot. They are laughing at their new game.

"Got it!" Heather holds up the soggy foot in triumph.

I breathe a huge sigh of relief. Maybe I can avoid getting in the pool after all.

"Yay! Thank you."

Now Heather is waving the rabbit's foot in the air. "Come and get it, girl."

"Come on, Ana. Cannonball!" Sasha shouts.

Panic sets in again. They want me to do a cannonball into the pool? The scene plays out in my mind. I see myself jumping in and realizing there is nothing to hold onto. Then my mouth and nose fill with water. Once they realize I can't swim, how long will it take for them to rescue me?

"Okay." It's my voice, but I feel like someone else is talking.

My brain is saying, *Not okay. Do not do this.*

I walk around the edge of the pool, trying to buy time. Somehow I have to come up with the courage to jump in or an excuse not to.

"Jump in, Ana!" Heather yells.

"Yeah, join us!" Sasha chimes in.

With a fake smile on my face, I back away to get a running start. My brain is screaming for me not to do it. I can run away and beg Mom to homeschool me. Then I would never have to see these girls again. The other option is to jump in, panic, and drown.

"Okay, here I come!"

I begin to run. Maybe the luck of the rabbit's foot will save me.

"Girls," an angry voice behind me says. "What did you do to Marina?"

The voice stops me in my tracks. One of the women from the garage is walking toward us. It must be Marina's mom.

"She was being a brat, Aunt Sue," Heather says. "She was taking our things and throwing them into the pool."

It's sort of true.

"Well, pool time is over. Come inside and eat."

"Oh, come on! Ana didn't even get to swim."

Aunt Sue looks at me.

"It's okay. We can eat first. I'm *starving*."

You're not supposed to swim for at least an hour after eating, right? This will give me plenty of time to hang out and then come up with an excuse to go home.

The girls crawl out of the pool. Heather hands me the rabbit's foot back as I give them towels. I'm not letting this thing out of my sight again.

CHAPTER 14

NOT SO FUN

After eating, we join in on singing "Happy Birthday" to Marina. We have a slice of cake and watch her open presents. Then Heather suggests we go up to her room. I'm relieved not to be going back out to the pool.

Heather's bedroom is much bigger than mine. Her king-size bed is covered in pillows. She even has matching bedding and curtains. This room looks like it belongs in a celebrity's Instagram post.

We all gather on the huge bed. Heather says she wants to show me something on her phone. This is really exciting. I've always wondered what popular kids do on their phones. They seem to spend so much time looking at them. Whatever they're looking at must be truly magical. Now that I'm suddenly popular, I'm about to find out what it is.

I sit on one side of Heather. Sasha sits on the other. We can both see her screen. She opens Instagram and starts scrolling through a list of people.

"Let's have some fun," Heather says.

"Do that one!" Sasha says, pointing. "He's such a nerd."

I look at the profile picture. The boy has short hair and a chubby face. His smile shows his slightly crooked teeth. Next to the picture is the name "otterpop927." Heather clicks on the picture and taps a button to send him a message.

"Who is that?" I ask.

"Wesley Otter," Sasha answers. "This kid picks his nose and eats it in class. And he smells *so* bad. Last year someone filled his locker with deodorant samples. When he opened it, they poured out all over the hallway. It was the funniest thing ever!" Heather and Sasha laugh.

"Let's mess with him," Heather says.

I notice that her username is "beachlvr416." Her profile picture shows a girl on the beach. It's taken from behind so you can see her hair, but not her face. Scarecrow isn't near any beaches. But maybe Heather really likes going to the beach on vacation?

She starts typing a message.

beachlvr416

hi! gr8 pic! 🐨

otterpop927

thx. do i know u?

beachlvr416

no but I want to know u. wanna hang out sometime? 😏

Heather and Sasha are smiling and giggling. I don't understand what they're up to. Didn't they just say this kid was a nerd? But now they want to hang out with him?

otterpop927

sure. want to see a movie? 🍿

beachlvr416

lol! just kidding! I'm way 2 good for a nerd like u!

They fall back on the bed, laughing. I'm trying to figure out what is so funny. Is this what popular girls are always doing on their phones? This isn't magical at all. It just seems mean.

"Come on, Ana!" Sasha says. "Pick someone to message. We have fake accounts just for this. It's fun."

"No, thanks."

"Do you want to go back in the pool?" Heather asks.

My phone vibrates. A notification says someone started following me on Instagram. I look at the profile and see that it's Nate. After quickly following him back, I have an idea.

"Hey, sorry, but I have to go."

"No! You just got here." Heather gives me a sad face.

"My mom texted me. She wants me to come home. Sorry." I pretend to be disappointed.

"Okay. Text me later," Heather says.

"Me too," Sasha adds. She must have forgotten that I don't have her number.

My mom said to call her for a ride home, but I decide to walk instead. It gives me time to think.

Having friends like this is new to me. I feel like such an outsider. At the same time, it's nice to be included. These girls' version of fun is not the same as mine though. Maybe I like the idea of their friendship more than the actual friendship itself. The whole thing is so confusing.

I decide I can't give up after one day. Tomorrow could be better. Even if the friendship doesn't work out, it's good to get to know different people.

When I get home, I go up to my room. My bedroom looks sad compared to Heather's. One lonely pillow sits on my twin bed. I have had the same Hello Kitty comforter for years. The rainbow curtains are old and faded. Nothing in my room matches. This has never bothered me before, but it does now. Suddenly my room is so depressing.

I take out the rabbit's foot and examine it. The fur is dry now. While rubbing it, I whisper, "I wish I had a bedroom like Heather's."

Then it happens again. The claws dig into my finger. I forgot how much this hurts.

"Ouch!" I yelp.

With my other hand, I pull the claws off. My finger bleeds from four tiny holes. Why did I do that?

CHAPTER 15

FOLLOW ME

When I come downstairs the next morning, Dad is sitting at the kitchen table. He's in his pajamas drinking coffee and reading the news on his tablet. This is weird. Usually he has left for work by now. I'm happy to see him, but something seems off.

"Hey, Dad. What are you up to today?" I ask.

"Hopefully finding a good-paying job," he mumbles.

"What?"

"I lost my job, pumpkin," he says. "That's why I came home early yesterday."

My jaw drops. Yesterday I wished Dad could spend more time with me. Then he came home early because he lost his job. Is this my fault? I touch the pocket of my shorts where the rabbit's foot is tucked away.

Mom walks into the room. "Ana, you better get going," she says. "The bus is coming in five minutes."

63

"Okay." I grab my bag and head for the door. "See you later. Good luck, Dad!"

The bus pulls up just as I get to the corner. After getting on, I look for Nate. He takes his earbuds out when he sees me.

"Hey," I say, sitting down next to him.

"Hi. Thanks for following me back. I didn't think you would."

"Why?"

He shrugs.

"I stalked your Instagram," Nate says. "We have a lot in common."

"You're not supposed to *tell me* you stalked my posts." I laugh. "It's okay though. I stalked yours too." Nate and I start talking about music again.

At the next stop, Heather and Sasha get on the bus. They walk toward the back while looking at their phones. It seems like they don't see me, but then Sasha tugs at my shoulder as she walks by.

"Come sit with us," she says.

"Oh, that's okay. I'm fine here."

"Come on, girl!" Sasha grabs my arm and pulls me up. "You're with *us* now."

I look at Nate and mouth, "Sorry."

Sasha drags me to the back of the bus with her and

Heather. When we sit down, Nate looks back at me. I raise my hand to wave him over. Heather grabs my hand and pulls it down.

"What are you doing?" she says.

"I want him to sit with us."

"No. He's way beneath you."

Beneath me? I look at her and Sasha. They're both shaking their heads. It feels like I have to choose between them and Nate. Is this what it's like to hang out with popular girls? Do they get to decide who else I can be friends with?

Nate smiles at me as he walks up.

"Keep going, nerd," Heather says. She doesn't even look up from her phone.

Nate's face gets red. I don't know what to say. Then he walks back to his seat without saying anything.

That was so mean of her! I'm about to jump up and go back to sit with Nate. Then Heather starts talking.

"So my mom said I could redo my bedroom. Ana, do you want my old bed set?"

She has my attention.

"I'm getting all new stuff." Heather turns her phone screen toward me. She has used an app to show how her new bed set will look in her room. It's so fancy.

"You can have my sheets and pillows and stuff. I'm even getting a new mattress and frame. Take the old ones if you want."

"Okay, yeah, thanks," I say, trying not to sound too eager. Of course I want it all.

Getting what I wished for should make me happy. So why do I keep looking at the back of Nate's head and feeling like I betrayed him?

CHAPTER 16

TAKE A SEAT

Mr. Nguyen lets us out of class five minutes before the bell. I get to the lunchroom early. Heather and Sasha aren't there yet. Neither is Nate. After buying some cheesecake bites, I sit down at an empty table and pull out my lunch. Then I take out my phone.

As I'm scrolling Instagram, a tray drops on my table. I look up. There's the boy in the profile picture from yesterday at Heather's house. His hair is messed up. There are stains on his shirt. But the chubby face and crooked teeth are the same. It's definitely Wesley Otter.

For a moment, I panic inside. He looks grumpy. Why is he sitting across from me? Does he somehow know I was with Heather yesterday when she messaged him?

"This is my table," he grunts.

I glance at his tray. It holds a soda and a brown paper lunch bag. The bag looks like it has been used a thousand times.

"Hey. How's it going?" I smile. After what Heather and Sasha did to him, I want to show him some kindness. "Is it okay if I sit here?"

He just stares at me. His blank, wide-eyed look is creeping me out. I scan the lunchroom and see that other students are starting to file in. Some are watching us.

"Wesley Otter has a dollar!" one boy shouts in a nasally voice. Others around him laugh. Then they join in the chant.

"Wesley Otter has a dollar! Wesley Otter has a dollar!"

"Hey, Wesley!" another boy says. "You got your soda today! Sharing it with the new girl?" Then he makes a high-pitched *ooh* sound. The other kids erupt in laughter.

Wesley's face turns bright red. He looks down at his tray. It seems like more kids are teasing him *because* I'm sitting with him. The only thing I can think to do is leave him alone.

Nate is sitting at a table near the window now. There are a couple of other kids with him. They're on their phones, and they look just as nerdy as he does. But that doesn't bother me.

I walk over to Nate's table. "Hi," I say, getting his attention.

Hopefully he'll invite me to sit down. But I wouldn't blame him if he didn't. He's probably still mad at me after what happened on the bus this morning. *I'm* even mad at me about that.

"Hey, Ana." He barely looks at me.

"Sorry about this morning," I say.

"Forget about it," he says.

The other two boys just stare at me. It feels like I've interrupted something.

"Look," I say, putting my lunch on the table and sitting down across from Nate. "I feel really bad about the bus. That wasn't cool."

Nate doesn't seem angry. I'm pretty sure his feelings are hurt though. Why did I let Heather and Sasha treat him that way? What is wrong with me?

Then Nate looks at me and smiles. "It's okay," he says. "We're still friends, right?"

"Right." I smile back at him.

"Hey, why were you sitting with Wesley Otter?"

"I wasn't. Well, not on purpose. My class got out early so I just sat at that table, and then . . ." I shrug as my voice trails off. "What does 'Wesley Otter has a dollar' mean, anyway?"

Nate rolls his eyes. "Wesley never has much money, but sometimes he has a dollar to buy a drink or whatever. Those kids always tease him about it. It's messed up."

I nod but don't really know what to say. Then Nate and his friends start talking about a science project they're working on together. After that, they talk about the show *Strange Brain*. It's on the Syfy channel. The show examines how people's minds work. I've only watched it a few times, but Nate and his friends make me want to watch it more. There is something so comfortable about sitting at this table. It feels like I belong here.

Then I hear a voice behind me.

"Ana!" Heather shouts. "Why are you sitting at the *nerd* table?"

My peace is suddenly shattered. I look behind me. Heather and Sasha are standing there. They each have one hand on their hip and their phone in the other.

Nate and I lock eyes. Then Sasha grabs my lunch and Heather grabs my arm and pulls me up.

"You should be sitting with *us*!" Heather scolds me as she drags me over to their table. "You're *our* friend, not theirs." Part of me wants to argue with her, but I really do want to get her bedroom set after school.

I used to think that being friends with popular girls would be awesome. But it's not. At least it's not with these two. All they care about are their phones and bullying people. We don't have anything in common. Sure, I'm sitting with the cool kids, but I don't feel cool at all.

CHAPTER 17

NOT SO BAD

After school, I go to Heather's house. Her mom has her new room put together already. She also has the old bedroom set packed up for me. I hang out until Mom and Dad come to get me and my new bed.

When we put my bedroom together, it looks like a smaller version of Heather's room. For the first time in my life, everything matches. This is awesome! I take a picture and post it on Instagram.

"Wow!" Mom takes it all in. "Your room looks better than ours."

"I can't wait to sleep in it tonight."

"You're a lucky girl." She winks at me and walks away. Dad follows her.

My hand touches the pocket with the rabbit's foot in it. "Yeah, I guess I am."

I take the rabbit's foot out and hold it as I sit on the bed. It seems like every time something good happens, something bad happens too. First I wished for Dad to be home more. He came home, but only because he lost his job. Then I wanted to be popular and for Heather to be my friend. All of a sudden I'm popular, and Heather wants to hang out with me. But she and Sasha are not nice people. We have nothing in common.

There's only one person I have anything in common with, and that's Nate. But they won't let me hang out with him.

My phone vibrates. It's a text from Heather. She wants me to come over and go swimming tomorrow. A feeling of dread fills my body.

Then it hits me. The friendship I wished for isn't the one I want. Instead, I want the friendship with the quiet kid on the bus.

I ignore Heather's message and tuck the rabbit's foot under one of my eight pillows. Sinking into my new bed, I fall asleep playing on my phone.

Sirens screeching past the house wake me up. It's still dark outside. Red lights flash through my window. I get up and go downstairs.

Mom is standing at the front door.

"What's going on?" I ask her.

"There's a fire down the street."

"Which house?"

"Not sure. I'm going to walk down there and see."

"I'll go with you."

After putting on our shoes, we walk down the street. Two fire trucks, an ambulance, and three police cars block the road. A crowd is starting to gather around the emergency vehicles.

Smoke billows out of the house at the end of the block. It's the poorest house in the neighborhood. The faded green paint was peeling, shutters were falling off, and the roof had been patched in many places. Now the whole thing seems to be collapsing in on itself as the firefighters spray it with water.

"What happened?" Mom asks one of the neighbors.

"The Otters' house caught fire. Everyone got out. They're all okay."

"The Otters' house? Does Wesley live here?" I ask.

"Yeah. The family has been on this block for years."

I didn't realize Wesley lived down the street from me. Looking around, I see him sitting on the curb with his parents and little sister. They are all wrapped in blankets from the fire department.

"That poor family," Mom says. Then she turns to me. "Come on, honey. Let's get back. It's cold."

"I'm glad they're okay," I say.

"Me too."

Back in my new room, I snuggle into the expensive blankets on my huge bed. Where will Wesley and his family be sleeping tonight? The thought makes me sad.

Comparing my life to Wesley's, it's not half-bad. Since Mom gave me the rabbit's foot, I've been wishing for things I thought would make me happy. But they haven't. If anything, they have caused more problems. A part of me wants to get rid of the foot. At the same time, I'm afraid of what might happen if it's gone. How do I get rid of this thing without my luck running out?

CHAPTER 18

LUCKY YOU

At school the next day, I'm a little shocked to see Wesley. A house fire should have gotten him some time off school. But maybe he's here because he has nowhere else to go.

Whatever the reason, it's good he's here. This morning an idea came to me.

I walk into the lunchroom with a purpose, doing a big circle around Heather and Sasha. There's no time to deal with them right now. Something more important is on my agenda.

Wesley is sitting alone at the same table as yesterday. He is wearing the same clothes too. I go up to him.

"Sorry about your house," I say.

He looks up at me, chewing, with a Pop-Tart in his hand. Those wide blank eyes won't scare me away today.

"Here's something for you. Maybe it can help."

I put a scratch-off lotto ticket and a quarter on the

77

table in front of him. He shoves the rest of the Pop-Tart into his mouth. Then he takes the scratch-off ticket and looks it over without speaking. It seems Wesley Otter is a man of few words.

When he picks up the quarter, I put my hand in my pocket and make a wish. As he scratches away at the numbers, the claws of the rabbit's foot dig into my finger. At least this time the pain will help somebody else.

Wesley is done scratching. His expression changes. He drops the quarter and holds the ticket in both hands. Then he looks at me with big eyes and an open mouth.

"I won," he says quietly at first.

Soon he is shouting. "I won! I won!"

I smile and laugh. It worked!

Wesley breaks into a happy dance. Everyone in the lunchroom stares at him. Some students take video with their phones.

After a few minutes, he stops and looks at me. "Why?" he asks.

"Because you deserve some good luck."

He takes the ticket and runs out of the lunchroom. My guess is that he's running straight to his parents with the ticket. After all, they're the only ones who can cash it.

I pull my hand out of my pocket and pry the foot off my finger. That's the last time I do that.

After getting my lunch tray, I look around the room. Heather and Sasha are sitting at their usual table. Heather glares at me as I walk up to them.

"Why don't you go sit with your boyfriend?" she says.

"My boyfriend?"

"Yeah," Sasha says. "Wesley Otter has a dollar."

Okay, so we're back to this. What did I ever see in these two? Shaking my head, I find an empty table and sit. Then Nate sits down across from me.

"Someone told me you gave Wesley a winning lottery ticket," he says. "That was really cool. I've never seen Wesley smile."

"He deserves for something good to happen to him."

"How much did he win?"

I shrug. "I'm probably better off not knowing." A small part of me wishes I had kept the winning ticket for myself, but Wesley needs it more.

"Where did you get the ticket? You have to be 18 to buy those. How'd you know it would be a winner?"

"I found it this morning on the way to school. It was just pure luck."

Nate doesn't need to know about the rabbit's foot and how it has to break my skin for the good luck to happen.

All this luck is making me sore. There probably isn't enough blood left in my finger to make another wish. Somehow I have to figure out how to get rid of my lucky rabbit's foot without getting hurt.

"Do you want to come over tomorrow morning?" Nate asks. "*Sharknado* marathon starts at ten."

"Sure! I've only seen the first four." Those movies are some of my favorites. Spending a Saturday watching them with Nate sounds awesome.

"Four? There are six of them now!"

"Fantastic! I'll be there." My smile is so big, my face hurts.

CHAPTER 19

INSIDE THE BAG

According to every horror movie on Syfy, cursed objects must be destroyed. My internet searches lead to articles that say the same thing. Usually it's best to burn these objects. But I'm too afraid to destroy the rabbit's foot. What if it doesn't work? There's no going back and un-burning it. Will my luck be bad for the rest of my life?

Finally, I decide to take it back to the store where Mom got it. She isn't happy that I'm returning her gift. I convince her that the rabbit's foot did its job for me, and now someone else deserves a chance with it. This excuse seems to satisfy her. She even says she's proud of me for thinking of others. All I'm really doing is thinking about me, but she doesn't have to know that.

After school, Mom drives us to town. She browses in a clothing boutique while I go into the Vintage Rose Antique Shop. It's small and dusty. Clutching a paper bag with the rabbit's foot in it, I walk straight up to the front counter.

The cashier turns and looks at me. I think I've seen her at school. She's the girl that guy was calling "Twig" when he dropped her off. Who would name their kid that? Hopefully it's a nickname.

"I would like to return this, but I don't have the receipt," I say, setting the bag on the counter.

"Sorry, but all returns need to have a . . ." the girl starts to say. Then she looks inside the bag and her face changes. "Just a minute."

The girl bends down and disappears behind the counter. Peeking over, I see her pull a ratty blue book out of her backpack. She quickly flips through the pages, reads one, and slams it shut.

"Okay, this can be returned without a receipt. I just have to give you five dollars for it. That's our policy with certain items returned without a receipt."

"Oh, don't worry about it. I don't want the money." Who knows what Mom paid for the rabbit's foot in the first place? Getting rid of it is worth more than a few bucks to me anyway.

"You need to take the money," the girl says. Her face is serious. She opens the register and pulls out a five-dollar bill, holding it out to me. "To seal the deal."

I get the feeling she knows something about the rabbit's foot, but she's not telling me. Should I ask her about it? Maybe it's better not to know.

We stare at each other for a moment. Then I take the money and she takes the paper bag with the foot inside. She picks it up with two fingers, like she doesn't want to touch it.

The deal is done. It's a relief to think about going back to my normal life, before the rabbit's foot. Not having to worry about claws in my skin and wishes that backfire will be nice.

Saturday morning, I pack up Heather's bedroom set and give it to Mom. She loves it more than I do. Luckily we didn't get rid of my old bed yet. I put my old, mismatched sheets back on it. The room looks shabby again, but that's okay.

As I'm hanging up my old rainbow curtains, Mom knocks on the door.

"I talked to the neighbors down the street," she says. "The Otters won the lottery. Can you believe that? They're talking about buying a house in the neighborhood behind your school."

"Wow. That's great news." I pretend to be surprised.

That scratch-off ticket must have been worth a lot of money if they're planning to move to Heather's neighborhood. Why didn't I think of that wish for myself? Maybe if we had won the lottery, Dad wouldn't have to look for a new job. It's too late now. Hopefully, some good luck that doesn't have anything to do with a rabbit's foot will come my way soon.

"Yes, it is great news," Mom says. "Hey, let's go shopping this weekend. You need some new curtains and a bed set. We can't buy expensive ones like your friend's, but you deserve something nice."

"That sounds good. By the way, Heather isn't my friend anymore."

"Oh? What happened?"

"We just didn't click."

"I'm sorry to hear that."

"It's okay. I have another friend named Nate. He's cool." I grab my phone to check the time. "That reminds me—I should get going! There's a *Sharknado* marathon on in ten minutes. We're watching it at Nate's house."

Mom smiles. "That sounds fun. Have a good time!"

Nate lives on the next block. I grab a bottle of water and a bag of microwave popcorn on my way out the door. For the first time since we moved to Scarecrow, it feels like it's going to be a good day.

CHAPTER 20

THE GOOD AND THE BAD

Watching the *Sharknado* marathon with Nate is great. We have so much in common. The same things make us laugh. It's nice to finally have a friend I click with.

Heather and Sasha don't text me all day. This is a relief. Maybe I'm not popular anymore, but that's okay with me.

When I get home from Nate's, Mom and Dad are sitting in the living room. The TV is off. Their faces are serious.

"Hi, Ana," Dad says. "Your mom and I have news."

Suddenly I'm worried that getting rid of the rabbit's foot really did bring me bad luck.

"Is everything okay?" I ask.

"My old boss called today. He offered me a new position."

"That's good, right?"

"Yes, it is. But . . ." He looks over at Mom.

"But what?"

"The new position means I'll be traveling a lot more."

My heart sinks. Dad's news should make me happy, but it means he'll be home even less. Now I'm really regretting giving Wesley Otter that lottery ticket.

The rabbit's foot is gone. Why does it seem like every good thing that happens is still followed by something bad?

"I liked having you home more."

"I'm sorry, pumpkin."

"Can't you find a job where you don't have to travel so much?"

"I know this doesn't seem fair. But this new position pays a lot more money. That's going to benefit our whole family."

"Why does it matter how much money you make when you're never home?"

Anger bubbles up inside me. It's not just that I'm mad. My feelings are hurt too.

"It won't be like this forever, Ana. I told my boss I wanted more time with my family. He agreed to give me extra vacation days in the summer. We can finally plan one of those trips we've talked about."

This makes me feel a bit better. A real summer vacation sounds awesome.

Dad is doing his best. I give him a little smile. Then my phone buzzes. Nate is texting me.

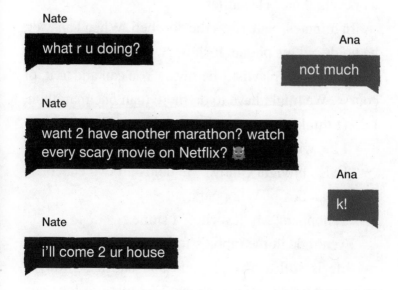

Nate
what r u doing?

Ana
not much

Nate
want 2 have another marathon? watch every scary movie on Netflix? 👹

Ana
k!

Nate
i'll come 2 ur house

Hanging out with Nate will take my mind off Dad's news. I guess it will be okay. At least we don't have to move again.

"Nate's coming over," I tell my parents. "We're going to watch a bunch of scary movies."

"That's great!" Mom says, smiling.

"You promise you aren't mad about my new job?" Dad asks.

"Well, I understand why you have to take it. And I'm already thinking of where we can go on vacation. Hawaii? The Grand Canyon? Disneyland?"

Dad laughs. "That's the spirit. Everything will work out, Ana." He smiles.

In minutes, Nate rings the doorbell. When I answer, he holds out his phone. It shows a list of movie titles.

"Here's my playlist," he says. "You can add to it, of course. We might have to do more than one marathon. I don't think we can watch everything today."

"Fine with me!" I say. "Let's make some popcorn."

"I also brought candy." He holds up two chocolate bars and a box of Whoppers.

"Whoppers! My favorite!" I smile.

Even though the rabbit's foot is gone, it seems like my life is still a mix of good and bad luck. Maybe that's just how life is. For now, I'm going to focus on the good.

VINTAGE R🌀SE MYSTERIES

THE SECRET ROOM
978-1-68021-758-2

LUCKY ME
978-1-68021-759-9

VCR FROM BEYOND
978-1-68021-760-5

NEW PAINTING
978-1-68021-761-2

CALL WAITING
978-1-68021-762-9

WWW.SDLBACK.COM/VINTAGE-ROSE-MYSTERIES

the American Compensation Association **and the**
International Foundation of Employee Benefit Plans**.**

American Compensation Association

The American Compensation Association (ACA) is a not-for-profit organization of more than 20,000 members engaged in the design, implementation, and management of employee compensation and benefits programs. Members include practitioners, consultants, and academicians from all levels of human resources in a wide variety of industries.

Founded in 1955, ACA is governed by a Board of Directors elected from the membership. ACA promotes and sponsors research activities, training events, certification programs, and a variety of educational and informational publications.

American Compensation Association
14040 N. Northsight Blvd.
Scottsdale, AZ 85260-3601
Telephone: (602) 951-9191
Fax: (602) 483-8352
E-mail: custservice@acaonline.org
World Wide Web: http://www.acaonline.org

STRATEGIC
COMPENSATION

STRATEGIC COMPENSATION

A Human Resource Management Approach

Joseph J. Martocchio

Institute of Labor and Industrial Relations
University of Illinois at Urbana-Champaign

PRENTICE HALL
Upper Saddle River, N.J. 07458

Acquisitions Editor: Natalie Anderson
Development Editor: Trish Taylor
Associate Editor: Lisamarie Brassini
Editorial Assistant: Crissy Statuto
Editor-in-Chief: James Boyd
Director of Development: Steve Deitmer
Marketing Manager: Sandra Steiner
Production Editor: Louise Rothman
Production Coordinator: Renee Pelletier
Managing Editor: Dee Josephson
Manufacturing Buyer: Kenneth J. Clinton
Manufacturing Supervisor: Arnold Vila
Manufacturing Manager: Vincent Scelta
Senior Designer: Ann France
Design Director: Patricia Wosczyk
Interior Design: Nicole Leong
Cover Design: Maureen Eide
Composition: Rainbow Graphics, Inc.
Cover Art/Photo: Phil Foster

Copyright © 1998 by Prentice-Hall, Inc.
A Simon & Schuster Company
Upper Saddle River, New Jersey 07458

Library of Congress Cataloging-in-Publication Data
Martocchio, Joseph J.
    Strategic compensation : human resource management
  approach / Joseph J. Martocchio.
        p.   cm.
    Includes bibliographical references and index.
    ISBN 0-13-440983-3 (hardcover)
    1. Compensation management.   I. Title.
HF5549.5.C67M284   1998
658.3′22—dc21   96-50312
                                                      CIP

Prentice-Hall International (UK) Limited, London
Prentice-Hall of Australia Pty. Limited, Sydney
Prentice-Hall Canada, Inc., Toronto
Prentice-Hall Hispanoamericana, S.A., Mexico
Prentice-Hall of India Private Limited, New Delhi
Prentice-Hall of Japan, Inc., Tokyo
Simon & Schuster Asia Pte. Ltd., Singapore
Editora Prentice-Hall do Brasil, Ltda., Rio de Janeiro

Printed in the United States of America

10 9 8 7 6 5 4 3 2

To those who have been my advocates throughout the years

and

three of the gentlest giants whom I have had the privilege to know:
Elsa, Otis, and Mr. Worf

TABLE OF CONTENTS

PREFACE

A company's success in the marketplace is as much a function of the way business practitioners manage employees as it is a function of company structure and financial resources. Compensating employees represents a critical human resource management practice: Without sound compensation systems, companies would not be able to attract and retain the best-qualified employees.

Compensation systems can promote companies' competitive advantages when properly aligned with strategic goals. Likewise, compensation practices can undermine competitive advantages when designed and implemented haphazardly. The title of this book, *Strategic Compensation: A Human Resource Management Approach*, reflects the importance of employees as a key element of strategic planning.

The purpose of this book is to provide a solid understanding of the art of compensation practice and its role in promoting companies' competitive advantages. Students will be prepared best to assume the role of competent compensation strategist if they possess a solid understanding of compensation practices. Thus, we examine the context of compensation practice, the criteria used to compensate employees, compensation system design issues, employee benefits, and contemporary challenges that compensation professionals will face well into the twenty-first century.

About this book

This book contains 14 chapters, lending itself well to courses offered in 10-week quarters or 15-week semesters. The chapters are organized into five parts:

- ☆ Part 1: Setting the Stage for Strategic Compensation
- ☆ Part 2: Bases for Pay
- ☆ Part 3: Designing Compensation Systems
- ☆ Part 4: Employee Benefits
- ☆ Part 5: Contemporary Strategic Compensation Challenges

Course instructors on a 10-week schedule might consider spending two weeks on each part. Course instructors on a 15-week schedule might consider spending one week on each chapter.

Each chapter contains a chapter outline, learning objectives, discussion questions, and list of key terms. In addition, each chapter includes two features. The "Reflections" features prompt students to recognize the deeper or not-so-obvious implications of compensation practices. The "Flip Side of the Coin" features point out the paradox of particular compensation issues.

This textbook is well suited to a variety of students including community college students, undergraduates, and master's degree students. In addition, the book was prepared for use by all business students regardless of their majors. Both human resource management majors and other majors (accounting, finance, general management, international management, marketing, and organizational behavior) will benefit equally well from *Strategic Compensation*. After all, virtually every manager, regardless of functional area, will be involved in making compensation decisions.

Available teaching and learning aids

The teaching and learning accessories are designed to promote a positive experience for both instructors and students.

STUDY GUIDE WITH COMPUTER CASEBOOK The study guide, prepared by David Oakes, a graduate student at the University of Illinois, will help students prepare for quizzes or tests. It includes key learning points, a sample of multiple-choice questions, and fill-in-the-blank questions. Included with the study guide is a computer casebook.

Brian Pianfetti and Mona Shannon, graduate students at the University of Illinois, designed this casebook to provide students opportunities to apply the concepts they learned in the textbook. Learning modules that correspond to the chapters in *Strategic Compensation* should promote students' appreciation of the strategic planning that underlies compensation decisions and enhance their analytic thinking skills. These case exercises can be used on IBM-compatible personal computers.

INSTRUCTOR'S RESOURCE MANUAL The instructor's resource manual, designed by Professor Matthew J. Stollak, Visiting Professor of Human Resource Management at Ohio University, contains learning objectives, chapter outlines, discussion questions, and supplemental descriptions of compensation in practice.

TRANSPARENCY MASTERS *Strategic Compensation* contains approximately 150 figures with illustrations and tables. Most of these have been re-drawn using PowerPoint and reproduced as one-color transparency masters at the end of the Instructor's Manual. They are also available in full color on disk.

TEST ITEM FILE Professor Matthew J. Stollak prepared multiple-choice and short essay test questions. Each chapter contains 25 to 40 multiple-choice questions and 5 to 10 short essay questions. The test item file contains the answers to the multiple-choice questions and suggested answers for the short essay questions. The test item file is also available in a Windows format. Prentice Hall's custom test allows manipulation of questions and easy test preparation.

TAKE IT TO THE NET Students can find World Wide Web exercises to complement *Strategic Compensation* at www.prenhall.com/stratcomp. These exercises were developed by Angela Cruz, who possesses certification as a compensation professional by the American Compensation Association.

Acknowledgments

Many individuals made valuable contributions to this first edition. I am indebted to the reviewers who provided thoughtful remarks on the prospectus and chapter drafts during the development of this textbook: Peggy Anderson, University of Wisconsin-

Whitewater, Whitewater, WI; Ed Arnold, Auburn University, Montgomery, AL; Don Ashbaugh, University of Northern Iowa, Cedar Falls, IA; Dave Balkin, University of Colorado-Boulder, Boulder, CO; Alison Barber, Michigan State University, East Lansing, MI; John Deckop, Temple University, Philadelphia, PA; Dan Farrell, Western Michigan University, Kalamazoo, MI; Dan Gallagher, James Madison University, Harrisonburg, VA; Luis Gómez-Mejía, Arizona State University, Tempe, AZ; Russell Kent, Georgia Southern University, Statesboro, GA; Sue Malcolm, Robert Morris College, Pittsburgh, PA; Margaret Mitchell, Central Connecticut State University, New Britain, CT; Jonathan Monat, California State University at Long Beach, Long Beach, CA; Jim Morgan, California State University-Chico, Chico, CA; Barbara Nassell, University of North Texas, Denton, TX; Craig Russell, University of Oklahoma, Norman, OK; Amit Shah, Frostburg State University, Frostburg, MD; Cynthia Simerly, Lakeland Community College, Kirtland, OH; Michael Stevens, University of Texas-El Paso, El Paso, TX; Tom Stone, Oklahoma State University, Stillwater, TX; Lee Till, Southwest Texas State University, San Marcos, TX; Steve Thomas, Southwest Missouri State University, Springfield, MO; and Fraya Wagner, Eastern Michigan University, Ypsilanti, MI.

I thank the following individuals at the University of Illinois: Margaret Chaplan, Katie Dorsey, Jerry Ferris, Emily Gleichman, and Mona Shannon. Margaret Chaplan, a labor librarian, provided invaluable assistance by sharing her wealth of knowledge and offering appropriate challenges on particular issues. Katie Dorsey, a library clerk, also offered excellent reference assistance and graciously retrieved information from the library during my recovery from knee surgery. Jerry Ferris, my faculty colleague, shared his expertise about human resources with me and cheered me on when I felt snowed under with work. Emily Gleichman was my competent research assistant during the latter part of the project. Mona Shannon, also my research assistant, produced the indexes.

At Prentice Hall, I thank the following individuals for their guidance, expertise, and high standards: Natalie Anderson, Steve Deitmer, Ann France, Stephanie Johnson, Margo Quinto, Louise Rothman, Crissy Statuto, Sandra Steiner, and Trish Taylor.

Joseph J. Martocchio

INTRODUCTION

Strategic Compensation contains 14 chapters divided into five parts. An introduction to each part follows.

Part 1: Setting the stage for strategic compensation

☆ Chapter 1: Compensation: A Component of Human Resource Systems

☆ Chapter 2: Strategic Compensation: Attaining a Competitive Advantage

☆ Chapter 3: Contextual Influences on Compensation Practice

Virtually all U.S. employees receive monetary compensation and nonmonetary compensation (for example, paid vacations) in exchange for the work they perform in companies. Compensation serves many functions to employees, including the means to recognize their contributions to the company, meet economic necessity (for example, making car payments to the bank), establish lifestyle (for example, owning a speed boat), and achieve social status goals (for example, living in a 4,000-square-foot home in an exclusive neighborhood rather than a 1,700-square-foot home in a mediocre neighborhood).

U.S. companies develop compensation programs to reward employees, and these programs represent one component among several human resource management practices. In addition, well-designed compensation systems serve a strategic role by promoting companies' success in highly competitive markets in which technological change constantly influences how employees perform their jobs and the skills and knowledge they must possess to perform their jobs successfully. Compensation professionals do not develop strategies or practices in a vacuum. They must recognize three contextual influences: laws, unions, and market factors.

We explore those issues in Part 1. Chapter 1 introduces the compensation concept and the relationships between compensation and other human resource management practices. Chapter 2 addresses the strategic role of compensation. Chapter 3 examines the contextual influences on compensation practices with which compensation professionals must be familiar.

Part 2: Bases for pay

☆ Chapter 4: Traditional Bases for Pay: Seniority and Merit

☆ Chapter 5: Incentive Pay

☆ Chapter 6: Pay-for-Knowledge and Skill-Based Pay

Most U.S. companies recognize employees' contributions by periodically awarding increases to base pay. *Basis for pay* represents the factors that supervisors and managers consider periodically to increase employees' base pay levels.

We explore seniority and merit pay in Chapter 4. Seniority and merit pay bases represent traditional bases for pay in companies. Nowadays, a limited set of companies use seniority pay. Companies that use seniority pay award permanent base pay increases to employees as they accumulate years of service on the job. Presumably, more-senior employees have developed higher skill proficiencies and possess greater knowledge than employees with less seniority and so are expected to perform better.

Merit pay programs award permanent base pay increases to employees according to supervisors' judgments of employees' past performance. Sound merit pay programs rest largely on the quality of performance appraisal mechanisms. Thus, we review key performance appraisal concepts and practices.

In Chapter 5, we take up the topic of incentive pay, also known as variable pay. Incentive pay rewards employees on the extent to which they successfully attained a predetermined work objective. In contrast to merit pay programs, incentive pay plans communicate to employees explicit work goals and the amount of monetary reward in advance. Incentive pay increases are usually one-time payments rather than permanent increases to base pay.

Pay-for-knowledge and skill-based pay, which we address in Chapter 6, result in permanent base pay increases. As the terms imply, employees receive additional compensation for successfully acquiring job-related knowledge and skills. Pay-for-knowledge and skill-based pay differ from merit and incentive pay in an important way: Pay-for-knowledge and skill-based pay reward employees for the promise of better future performance; employees receive additional compensation upon successfully acquiring new job-relevant knowledge and skills that they have not necessarily applied yet on the job. On the other hand, incentive and merit pay recognize promised fulfilled, that is, demonstrated job performance.

Part 3: Designing compensation systems

☆ Chapter 7: Building Internally Consistent Compensation Systems

☆ Chapter 8: Building Market-Competitive Compensation Systems

☆ Chapter 9: Building Pay Structures That Recognize Individual Contributions

The best-laid compensation strategies are doomed to failure unless compensation professionals design compensation programs with three important objectives in mind: internal consistency, market competitiveness, and recognition of individual contributions. Although these practices are not incompatible with each other, such practical constraints as limited financial resources keep compensation professionals from maximizing all three objectives. Thus, they must balance these objectives with compensation strategies.

Internally consistent compensation systems (Chapter 7) clearly define the relative value of each job among all jobs within a company. This ordered set of jobs represents the job structure or hierarchy. Employees with greater qualifications, more responsibilities, and more-complex job duties should receive higher pay than employees with lesser qualifications, fewer responsibilities, and less-complex job duties. Internally consistent job structures formally recognize differences in job characteristics and thereby enable compensation managers to set pay accordingly.

Market-competitive pay systems (Chapter 8) represent companies' compensation policies that fit the imperatives of competitive advantage. Market-competitive pay systems play a significant role in attracting the best qualified employees.

Pay structures assign different pay rates for jobs of unequal worth *and* provide the framework for recognizing differences in individual employee contributions (Chapter 9). No two employees possess identical credentials, nor do they perform the same jobs equally well. Companies recognize these differences by paying individuals according to their credentials, knowledge, or job performance.

Part 4: Employee benefits

☆ Chapter 10: Legally Required Benefits

☆ Chapter 11: Discretionary Benefits

In Chapters 10 and 11 we examine basic fringe compensation components in strategic compensation programs. Traditionally, most employers did not regard employee benefits as having any strategic value. Our discussion indicates that employee benefits do have strategic value.

In Chapter 1, we define *fringe compensation*, also referred to as *employee benefits*, as any variety of programs that provide for pay for time-not-worked, employee services, and protection programs. Providing employee benefits is costly to employers. Companies' fringe compensation costs often amount to more than one-third of total compensation expenditures.

We review legally required benefits in Chapter 10. Legally required benefits are protection programs that attempt to promote worker safety and health, maintain family income streams, and assist families in crisis. Legally required benefits do not *directly* meet the imperatives of competitive strategy. However, legally required benefits may contribute *indirectly* to competitive advantage by enabling individuals to participate in the economy.

In Chapter 11, we examine a variety of common discretionary benefits. Discretionary benefits fall into three broad categories: protection programs, pay for time-not-worked, and services. Protection programs provide family benefits, promote health, and guard against income loss caused by catastrophic factors such as unemployment, disability, or serious illness. Pay for time-not-worked provides employees time off with pay, such as vacation. Services provide enhancements to employees and their families, such as tuition reimbursement and daycare assistance. Management can use discretionary benefit offerings to promote particular employee behaviors that have strategic value.

Part 5: Contemporary strategic compensation challenges

☆ Chapter 12: International Compensation

☆ Chapter 13: Compensating Executives

✱ Chapter 14: Compensating the Flexible Work Force: Contingent Employees and Flexible Work Schedules

Part 5 addresses the most prominent contemporary strategic compensation challenges, indicated in the chapter titles above. Although compensation professionals have dealt with these issues in the past, their strategic importance has increased dramatically in recent years. In addition, these challenges will remain important well into the twenty-first century.

International compensation programs have strategic value. U.S. businesses continue to establish operations in foreign countries. The establishment of operations in Pacific Rim countries, Eastern European countries, and Mexico is on the rise. Several factors have contributed to the expansion of global markets. These include such free trade agreements as the North American Free Trade Agreement, the unification of the European market, and the gradual weakening of communist influence in Eastern Europe and Asia. Likewise, foreign companies have greater opportunities to invest in the United States. As a result, U.S. companies must compensate U.S. employees who work overseas as well as foreign employees working for U.S. companies at foreign posts and in the United States. These compensation systems differ from domestic U.S. compensation systems in key ways.

Compensating executives has strategic value. After all, executives are the top-level leaders in U.S. corporations. It is essential that companies be able to attract and retain the most-talented leaders. Executives of U.S. companies are among the highest-paid employees in the world. Not surprisingly, therefore, executive compensation has come under intense and widespread scrutiny. The controversy centers on (1) whether executives deserve to earn as much as they do, particularly in light of rampant company downsizing, and (2) whether they deserve as much as they do when company performance is lackluster.

Changing business conditions have led to an increase in contingent workers (that is, employees whose relationship with the company is of known limited duration) and workers following flexible work schedules (that is, permanent employees whose work week schedules differ from the standard eight-hour days for five consecutive days) in the United States. Likewise, the complexities of employees' personal lives—dependent children and elderly relatives, dual-career couples, disabilities—make working standard eight-hour days for five consecutive days every week difficult. As a result, many companies have had to develop compensation programs that address the needs of contingent workers and workers on flexible schedules.

CHAPTER

ONE

Compensation: A component

of human resource systems

CHAPTER OUTLINE

In this chapter, you will learn about

1. Basic compensation concepts and the context of compensation practice
2. Compensation professionals' goals within a human resource department
3. How compensation professionals accomplish their goals
4. How compensation professionals relate to various constituencies
5. The changing compensation environment and five assumptions that underlie this book

AUTOPART is a manufacturer of windshield wiper assemblies, which they sell to the Big Three automobile manufacturers—Chrysler, Ford, and General Motors. AUTOPART employs 3000 professional and nonprofessional workers. Of the total work force, 1750 are line employees who manufacture the windshield wiper assemblies. This segment of the work force is represented by a union. Most of the remaining 1250 employees are professional, administrative, and clerical staff members in accounting, marketing, human resources, and office administration.

Maria Sanchez is AUTOPART's Compensation Director. It's Friday, around 6 P.M., and Maria is preparing to go home. She looks over her calendar for the upcoming week to decide which files she will bring home to review. Here are the highlights of Maria Sanchez's upcoming work week.

Monday, 9 A.M.: Maria will meet with Bill Schultz, the Manager of Recruitment and Selection. They plan to discuss the highlights of the new compensation plan and how to incorporate the compensation plan's selling points into the recruiting plan. In addition, they will discuss the updated starting pay rates for new employees.

Monday, 2 P.M.: Anne Larsen, Director of Performance Appraisals, and Maria will talk about how to better align performance appraisal methods with the merit pay system for professional employees.

Tuesday, all day: Maria and top management officials will meet with union representatives to discuss the possibility of introducing an incentive pay system for union workers.

Wednesday, breakfast: Maria will meet with AUTOPART's Chief Executive Officer to brief him on how a new incentive pay system is expected to substantially reduce administrative costs.

Wednesday, 10 A.M.: Maria and Sam Smithlow, Training Director, will review the adequacy of the existing training programs to support the current pay-for-knowledge program.

Wednesday, 3 P.M.: AUTOPART's Benefits Manager will meet with Maria to review the cost-benefit analysis of alternative vacation plans.

Thursday, all day: Maria will meet with her six compensation professional staff members to review their goals for the next year's compensation program.

Friday morning: Maria will lead a seminar for all department managers on AUTOPART's revised leave policy under the *Family and Medical Leave Act of 1993*.

Exploring and defining the compensation context

The compensation function is just one component of a company's human resource systems.

The vignette illustrates that the compensation function does not operate in isolation. To the contrary, the compensation function is just one component of a company's human resource systems. In addition, compensation professionals interact with members from various constituencies, including union representatives and top executives. We will explore these ideas in more detail after we have introduced some fundamental compensation concepts.

What is compensation?

Compensation represents both the intrinsic and extrinsic rewards employees receive for performing their jobs. **Intrinsic compensation** reflects employees' psychological mind sets that result from performing their jobs. **Extrinsic compensation** includes both monetary and nonmonetary rewards. Organizational development professionals promote intrinsic compensation through effective job design. Compensation professionals are responsible for extrinsic compensation. Thus, we study extrinsic compensation in this book. Although our focus is on extrinsic compensation, let's take a moment to briefly explore the intrinsic compensation concept.

INTRINSIC COMPENSATION Intrinsic compensation represents employees' critical psychological states that result from performing their jobs. **Job characteristics theory** describes these critical psychological states. According to job characteristics theory, employees experience enhanced psychological states (that is, intrinsic compensation) when their jobs rate high on five core job dimensions: skill variety, task identity, task significance, autonomy, and feedback.[1] Jobs lacking in these core characteristics do not provide much intrinsic compensation. Exhibit 1-1 illustrates the influence of core job characteristics on intrinsic compensation and subsequent benefits to employers.

- ✮ **Skill variety.** The degree to which the job requires the person to do different tasks and involves the use of a number of different skills, abilities, and talents.

- ✮ **Task identity.** The degree to which the job is important to others, both inside and outside the company.

- ✮ **Task significance.** The degree to which the job has an impact on the lives or work of other people.

- ✮ **Autonomy.** The amount of freedom, independence, and discretion the employee enjoys in determining how to do the job.

- ✮ **Feedback.** The degree to which the job or employer provides the employee with clear and direct information about job outcomes and performance.

What are some examples of these critical psychological states, or intrinsic compensation? According to job characteristics theory, jobs that demand skill variety, task identity, and task significance lead to an employee's perceiving his or her work as meaningful. Jobs that provide autonomy lead to an employee's feeling responsible for outcomes of work. Jobs that convey feedback enhance employees' knowledge of the actual results of their work activities, or how well they have performed. Ultimately, the benefits of these core characteristics to employers are increased job performance, lower absenteeism and turnover, and higher employee satisfaction.

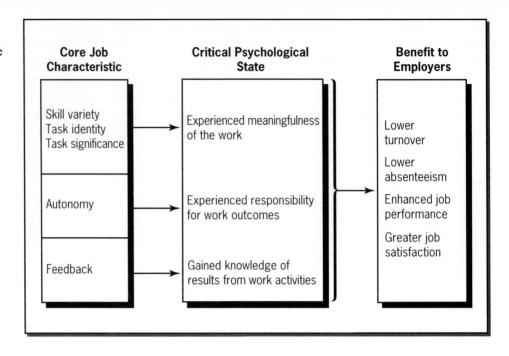

Core Job Characteristic	Critical Psychological State	Benefit to Employers
Skill variety Task identity Task significance	Experienced meaningfulness of the work	Lower turnover Lower absenteeism
Autonomy	Experienced responsibility for work outcomes	Enhanced job performance
Feedback	Gained knowledge of results from work activities	Greater job satisfaction

EXTRINSIC COMPENSATION Extrinsic compensation includes both monetary and non-monetary rewards. Compensation professionals establish monetary compensation programs to reward employees according to their job performance levels or for learning job-related knowledge or skills. As we discuss shortly, monetary compensation represents **core compensation.** Nonmonetary rewards include protection programs (for example, medical insurance), paid time off (for example, vacations), and services (for example, daycare assistance). Most compensation professionals refer to nonmonetary rewards as **employee benefits** or **fringe compensation.**

The meaning of money

National culture creates the context for the meaning of money to individuals in different countries.[2] Our focus here is on U.S. culture. We consider the impact of other national cultures on the meaning of money in Chapter 12.

U.S. culture emphasizes instrumentality. Employees strive for high levels of performance when they believe that better performance leads to greater pay. Money derives importance from what it can buy. Greater amounts of money enable people to buy more things. What things do people buy? We buy (or rent) housing, utilities, food, clothing, transportation, and entertainment.

Money also is instrumental to how people feel. Employees' accumulation of wealth may increase their sense of security.[3] Investing money wisely provides a "nest egg" for retirement and necessary financial resources in the event of a "rainy day."

Money symbolizes achievement. For example, many sales professionals' earnings depend upon how much they sell. As earnings increase, so does money's symbolic value as a measure of professional achievement.

Money also defines social relationships within and outside the workplace. Social status in society often depends on individuals' wealth. Annual salary is a strong indicator of status within and outside companies. Earnings level typically indicates rank in the company hierarchy. Earnings usually influence where people can afford to live

Exhibit 1-2
Some Meanings of Money

- A reward for work well done
- A means to support oneself and one's family
- A status symbol—the more you make, the more status you have in the company and in society
- Payment for doing a job—never as much as is deserved
- A paycheck and benefits such as paid vacation and health insurance
- Security
- A trap—the more you make, the more you spend, so the more you need
- A symbol of professional achievement
- Payment for doing a job regardless of how well the job was done
- A means of classifying people (as low-income, middle-income, or high-income)
- A company's obligation to employees

in their communities. In the greater Los Angeles area, living in Brentwood or Beverly Hills denotes greater social status than living in less affluent parts of the Los Angeles metropolitan area. Other signs of status include a season subscription to the opera, membership in an exclusive country club, or a lakeside vacation home.

Ultimately, the meaning of money is unique to individuals. Exhibit 1-2 contains a sample listing of the various meanings of money to many people I have asked over the years.

Core compensation

There are six types of monetary, or core, compensation. The elements of base pay and the five types of base pay adjustments are listed in Exhibit 1-3.

BASE PAY Employees receive **base pay,** or money, for performing their jobs. Base pay is recurring; that is, employees will continue to receive base pay as long as they remain in their jobs. Companies disburse base pay to employees in either one of two forms: hourly pay (wage) or salary. An employee's **wage,** or **hourly pay,** is compensation for each hour worked. A **salary** is compensation for job performance, regardless of the actual number of hours worked. Companies measure salary on an annual basis. The *Fair Labor Standards Act* (Chapter 3) established criteria for awarding hourly pay or salary.

Exhibit 1-3
Elements of Core Compensation

BASE PAY
• Hourly pay
• Annual salary

HOW BASE PAY IS ADJUSTED OVER TIME
• Cost-of-living adjustments
• Seniority pay
• Merit pay
• Incentive pay
• Pay-for-knowledge and skill-based pay

Companies typically set base pay amounts for jobs according to the level of skill, effort, or responsibility required to perform the jobs and the severity of the working conditions. Compensation professionals refer to skill, effort, responsibility, and working conditions as **compensable factors** because they influence pay level (Chapters 3 and 7). Courts of law use these four compensable factors to determine whether jobs are equal in administering the *Equal Pay Act of 1963* (Chapter 3). Compensation professionals use these compensable factors to help meet three pressing challenges, which we introduce later in this chapter and discuss in more detail in later chapters: internal consistency (Chapter 7), market competitiveness (Chapter 8), and recognizing individual contributions (Chapter 9).

Over time, employers adjust employees' base pay to recognize increases in the cost of living, differences in employees' performance, or differences in employees' acquisition of job-related knowledge and skills. We discuss these core compensation elements next.

COST-OF-LIVING ADJUSTMENTS (COLAs) **Cost-of-living adjustments,** or **COLAs,** are periodic base pay increases that are based on changes in prices, as indexed by the consumer price index (CPI). COLAs enable workers to maintain their purchasing power and standards of living by adjusting base pay for inflation. COLAs are most common among workers represented by unions. Union leaders fought hard for these improvements to maintain the memberships' loyalty and support (Chapter 3). Many employers use the CPI to adjust base pay levels for newly hired employees (Chapter 9).

SENIORITY PAY *Seniority pay* systems reward employees with periodic additions to base pay according to employees' length of service (Chapter 4). These pay plans assume that employees become more valuable to companies with time and that valued employees will leave if they do not have a clear idea that their salaries will increase over time.[4] This rationale comes from **human capital theory,**[5] which states that employees' knowledge and skills generate productive capital known as **human capital.** Employees can develop such knowledge and skills from formal education and training, including on-the-job experience. Over time, employees presumably refine existing skills or acquire new ones that enable them to work more productively. Thus, seniority pay rewards employees for acquiring and refining their skills as indexed by seniority.

MERIT PAY *Merit pay programs* assume that employees' compensation over time should be determined, at least in part, by differences in job performance[6] (Chapter 4). Employees earn permanent increases to base pay according to their performance. This system rewards excellent effort or results, motivates future performance, and helps employers retain valued employees.

INCENTIVE PAY *Incentive pay,* or *variable pay,* rewards employees for partially or completely attaining a predetermined work objective. Incentive pay is defined as compensation, other than base wages or salaries, that fluctuates according to employees' attainment of some standard based on a preestablished formula, individual or group goals, or company earnings[7] (Chapter 5).

PAY-FOR-KNOWLEDGE AND SKILL-BASED PAY *Pay-for-knowledge* plans reward managerial, service, or professional workers for successfully learning specific curricula (Chapter 6). *Skill-based pay,* used mostly for employees who do physical work, increases these workers' pay as they master new skills (Chapter 6). Both skill- and knowledge-based pay programs reward employees for the range, depth, and types of skills or knowledge they are capable of applying productively to their jobs. This feature distinguishes pay-for-knowledge plans from merit pay, which rewards employees' job performance. Said another way, pay-for-knowledge programs reward employees for their *potential* to make meaningful contributions on the job.

"Fringe" compensation, or employee benefits

Earlier, we noted that fringe compensation represents nonmonetary rewards. Fringe compensation, or employee benefits, includes any variety of programs that provide for pay for time not worked, employee services, and protection programs. Fringe compensation can be divided into two categories. The U.S. government requires that most employers provide particular sets of benefits to employees. We refer to these as legally required benefits (Chapter 10). In addition, companies offer other benefits on a discretionary basis. We refer to these as discretionary benefits (Chapter 11). Exhibit 1-4 on page 8 lists the major legally required and discretionary benefits.

LEGALLY REQUIRED BENEFITS The U.S. government established programs to protect individuals from catastrophic events such as disability and unemployment. **Legally required benefits** are protection programs that attempt to promote worker safety and health, maintain family income streams, and assist families in crisis. The key legally required benefits are mandated by the *Social Security Act of 1935,* various state workers' compensation laws, and the *Family and Medical Leave Act of 1993*. All provide benefits to employees and their dependents.

DISCRETIONARY BENEFITS **Discretionary benefits** fall into three broad categories: protection programs, pay for time-not-worked, and services. **Protection programs** provide family benefits, promote health, and guard against income loss caused by catastrophic factors such as unemployment, disability, or serious illnesses. Not surprisingly, **pay for time-not-worked** provides employees time off with pay, such as vacation. **Services** provide enhancements to employees and their families, such as tuition reimbursement and daycare assistance.

Compensation professionals' goals within a human resource department

Understanding compensation professionals' goals requires that we understand the role of human resources within companies and specific human resource (HR) practices. In addition, we need to know something about the particular HR functions.

How human resource professionals fit into the corporate hierarchy

Line function and staff function broadly describe all employee functions. **Line employees** are directly involved in producing a company's goods or delivering its services. Assembler, production worker, and sales employee are examples of line jobs. **Staff functions** support the line functions. Human resource management and accounting are examples of staff functions. Human resource professionals are staff employees

Exhibit 1-4
*Elements of Fringe
Compensation*

LEGALLY REQUIRED BENEFITS

Social Security Act of 1935

- Unemployment insurance
- Retirement insurance
- Benefits for dependents
- Disability benefits
- Medicare

State compulsory disability laws (Workers' Compensation)

Family and Medical Leave Act of 1993 (12 weeks of annual unpaid leave)

DISCRETIONARY BENEFITS

Protection Programs

- Income protection programs
- Health protection programs

Pay for time-not-worked

- Holidays
- Vacation
- Sick leave
- Personal leave
- Jury duty
- Funeral leave
- Military leave
- Cleanup, preparation, travel time

Services

- Employee assistance programs (EAPs)
- Family assistance programs
- Tuition reimbursement
- Transportation services
- Outplacement assistance
- Wellness programs

because they offer a wide variety of support services for line employees. In a nutshell, HR professionals promote the effective use of all employees in companies. Effective use means attaining work objectives that fit with the overall mission of the company. Human resource professionals design and implement a variety of HR practices that advance that objective. Besides compensation, these other HR practices include:

- ✩ Recruitment
- ✩ Selection

☆ Performance appraisal

☆ Training

☆ Career development

☆ Labor-management relations

☆ Employment termination

☆ Managing human resources within the context of legislation

RECRUITMENT **Recruitment** entails identifying qualified job candidates and promoting their interest in working for a company. Specifically, HR professionals form a pool of qualified job candidates for the available job openings. They may identify candidates from among current employees, or they may search for candidates outside the company. Also, HR professionals promote qualified candidates' interest in the company as a possible place of employment. Human resource professionals use open houses, job fairs, informational interviews, and current employees' testimonies to promote interest among prospective employees.

SELECTION **Selection** is the process HR professionals employ to hire qualified candidates for job openings. Human resource professionals' main responsibilities include determining which candidates have the required skills, abilities, and relevant work experience to perform the available jobs well. They rely on the results of interviews, reference checks, and candidates' performance on employment tests to make this determination.

PERFORMANCE APPRAISAL **Performance appraisal** describes employees' past performance and serves as a basis to recommend how to improve future performance. Human resource professionals determine the focus of performance appraisal, and they select the appropriate techniques from among trait systems, comparison systems, behavioral systems, and goal-oriented systems. *Trait systems* ask raters to evaluate each employee's traits, such as appearance, dependability, cooperation, initiative, or creativity. *Comparison systems* evaluate a given employee's performance against the performance of other employees. Employees are ranked from the best performer to the poorest performer. *Behavioral systems* rate employees on the extent to which they display successful job performance behaviors. In contrast to trait and comparison methods, behavioral methods rate objective job behaviors. With *goal-oriented systems,* supervisors and employees jointly determine performance objectives against which supervisors judge employees' performance.

TRAINING **Training** is a planned effort to facilitate employees' learning of job-related knowledge, skills, or behaviors. Effective training programs lead to desired employee learning, which translates into improved future job performance. **Continuous learning**[8] philosophies underlie most training efforts in companies. Progressive companies encourage employees to continuously develop their skills, knowledge, and abilities through formal training programs.

CAREER DEVELOPMENT **Career development** is a cooperative effort between employees and their employers to promote rewarding work experiences throughout employees' work lives. Human resource professionals develop and administer these initiatives. Well-designed career development programs represent win-win opportunities for employers and employees alike. Besides leading to fruitful work experiences for employees, career development programs contribute to companies' success by developing highly skilled and motivated work forces.

LABOR-MANAGEMENT RELATIONS **Labor-management relations** involves a continuous relationship between a company's HR professionals and a particular group of employees—members of a labor union and its bargaining unit. Since the passage of the *National Labor Relations Act of 1935 (NLRA)* (Chapter 3), the U.S. government requires employers to enter into good-faith negotiations with labor union representatives over the terms of employment including compensation, working hours, working conditions, and supervisory practices. Workers join unions to influence employment-related decisions, especially when they are dissatisfied with job security, wages, benefits, and supervisory practices. The **collective bargaining agreement** describes the terms of employment reached between management and the union.

EMPLOYMENT TERMINATION **Employment termination** takes place when an employee's agreement to perform work is terminated. Employment terminations are voluntary or involuntary. The HR department plays a central role in managing involuntary employment terminations. Employees initiate **voluntary terminations,** and they do so to work for other companies or to begin their retirements. Companies initiate **involuntary terminations** for a variety of reasons including poor job performance, insubordination, violation of work rules, reduced business activity due to sluggish economic conditions, or plant closings. **Discharge** is involuntary termination for poor job performance, insubordination, or gross violation of work rules. **Layoff** describes involuntary termination under sluggish economic conditions or for plant closings. In the case of layoffs, HR professionals typically provide outplacement counseling to help employees find work elsewhere.

MANAGING HUMAN RESOURCES WITHIN THE CONTEXT OF LEGISLATION Human resource professionals are responsible for managing personnel within the context of legislation. A multitude of laws protect employees' rights in the workplace. Employment laws protect employees against potential employer abuses including illegal employment practices on the basis of age, race, sex, color, religion, national origin, or disability. Human resource professionals maintain records, develop nondiscriminatory policies, and monitor employment decisions to guard against illegal discrimination.

How the compensation function fits into HR departments

Human resource practices do not operate in isolation. Every HR practice is related to others in different ways. Let's consider the relationships between compensation and each of the HR practices we just reviewed.

COMPENSATION, RECRUITMENT, AND SELECTION Job candidates choose to work for particular companies for a number of reasons including career advancement opportunities, training, reputation for being a "good" place to work, location, and compensation. Companies try to spark job candidates' interest by communicating the positive features of the core and fringe compensation programs. As we discuss in Chapter 8, companies use compensation to compete for the very best candidates. In addition, companies may offer such inducements as one-time signing bonuses to entice high-quality applicants. It is not uncommon for signing bonuses to amount to as much as 10 percent of starting annual salaries. Signing bonuses are useful when the supply of qualified candidates falls short of companies' needs.

COMPENSATION AND PERFORMANCE APPRAISAL Accurate performance appraisals are key to effective merit pay programs. For merit pay programs to succeed, employees must know that their efforts meeting production quotas or quality standards will lead to pay raises. Job requirements must be realistic, and employees must be prepared to meet job goals with respect to their skills and abilities. Moreover, employees must perceive a strong relationship between attaining performance standards and being given pay increases. Merit pay systems require specific performance appraisal approaches, as noted previously. Administering successful merit pay programs depends as much on sound performance appraisal practices as on the compensation professionals' skill in designing and implementing such plans.

COMPENSATION AND TRAINING Successful pay-for-knowledge plans depend upon a company's ability to develop and implement systematic training programs. When training is well designed, employees should be able to learn the skills needed to increase their pay, as well as the skills necessary to teach and coach other employees at lower skill levels. Companies implementing pay-for-knowledge typically increase the amount of classroom and on-the-job training.[9] Pay-for-knowledge systems make training necessary rather than optional. Accordingly, companies that adopt pay-for-knowledge systems must ensure that all employees have equal access to the needed training for acquiring higher-level skills.

COMPENSATION AND CAREER DEVELOPMENT Most employees expect to experience career development within their present companies. Employees experience career development in two different ways. Some employees will change the focus of their work: for example, from supervisor of payroll clerks to supervisor of inventory clerks. This change represents a lateral move across the company's hierarchy. Others will maintain their focus, assuming greater responsibilities. This change illustrates advancement upward through the company's hierarchy. Advancing from payroll clerk to manager of payroll administration is an example of moving upward through a company's hierarchy. Employees' compensation will change to reflect career development.

COMPENSATION AND LABOR-MANAGEMENT RELATIONS As we discussed previously, collective bargaining agreements describe the terms of employment reached between management and the union. Compensation is a key topic. Unions have fought hard for general pay increases and regular COLAs[10] to promote members' standards of living. In Chapter 3, we will review the role of unions in compensation, and Chapter 4 discusses how unions have traditionally bargained for seniority pay systems. More recently, unions are willing to incorporate particular incentive pay systems. For example, unions appear to be receptive to the use of behavioral encouragement plans (Chapter 5) because it is in both employees' and employers' best interests to improve worker safety and to minimize absenteeism.

COMPENSATION AND EMPLOYMENT TERMINATION Earlier, we distinguished between involuntary and voluntary employment terminations. In the case of layoffs, a type of involuntary termination, companies may choose to award severance pay. **Severance pay** usually includes several months' pay after termination and, in some cases, continued coverage under the employers' medical insurance plan. Often, employees rely on severance pay to meet financial obligations while searching for employment.

In the case of voluntary terminations, companies sponsor pension programs. **Pension programs** provide income to individuals throughout their retirement (Chapter 11). Sometimes, companies use early retirement programs to reduce work force size and trim compensation expenditures. **Early retirement programs** contain incentives designed to encourage highly paid employees with substantial seniority to

Early Retirement Incentives Backfire

Companies use early retirement programs to lower their compensation costs in the long run by trimming the size of their work forces. But some unexpected problems may result.

As we discussed, companies offer senior employees early retirement packages as an incentive to leave before their planned retirements. That is, early retirement should be optional. Unfortunately, some senior employees may view their company's early retirement incentives as coercive attempts to force them out of their jobs. There are documented cases in which senior employees sued their employers and successfully convinced juries that they were wrongfully forced out of their companies. The judges required those companies to pay substantial compensatory damages to the plaintiffs; the companies' objectives to save compensation costs were thwarted.

Another unexpected problem is that more employees than were anticipated might accept early retirement incentives, leading to severe understaffing. In addition, it is often the best-qualified employees who take the incentives rather than employees with modest job performance. Better qualified employees probably have more or better job alternatives. To add insult to injury, it is quite possible that those "early retirees" will take positions with competing companies.

---

retire earlier than planned. These incentives expedite senior employees' retirement eligibility and increase retirement income. In addition, many companies include continuation of medical benefits.

COMPENSATION AND LEGISLATION Employment laws establish bounds of acceptable employment practices as well as employee rights. Federal laws that apply to compensation practices are grouped according to four themes, which we address in Chapter 3:

- ☆ Income continuity, safety, and work hours
- ☆ Pay discrimination
- ☆ Accommodating disabilities and family needs
- ☆ Prevailing wage laws

Exhibit 1-5 lists the major laws for each theme that influence compensation practice.

The government enacted income continuity, safety, and work-hours laws (for example, the Fair Labor Standards Act of 1938) to stabilize individuals' income when they became unemployed because of poor business conditions or workplace injuries and to set pay minimums and work-hour limits for children. The civil rights movement of the 1960s led to the passage of key legislation (for example, the Equal Pay Act of 1963 and the Civil Rights Act of 1964) designed to protect designated classes of employees and to uphold their individual rights against discriminatory employment decisions, including matters of pay. Congress enacted legislation (for example, the Pregnancy Discrimination Act of 1978, the Americans with Disabilities Act of 1990, and the Family and Medical Leave Act of 1993) to accommodate employees with disabilities and pressing family needs. Prevailing wage laws (for example, the Davis-Bacon Act of 1931) set minimum wage rates for companies that provide paid services—such as building maintenance—to the U.S. government.

Exhibit 1-5
Laws That Influence Compensation

INCOME CONTINUITY, SAFETY, AND WORK HOURS

Minimum wage laws—Fair Labor Standards Act of 1938

Minimum wage

Overtime provisions

Portal-to-Portal Act of 1947

Equal Pay Act of 1963

Child labor provisions

Work Hours and Safety Standards Act of 1962

McNamara-O'Hara Service Contract Act of 1965

PAY DISCRIMINATION

Equal Pay Act of 1963

Civil Rights Act of 1964, Title VII

Bennett Amendment (1964)

Executive Order 11246 (1965)

Age Discrimination in Employment Act of 1967 (amended in 1978, 1986, 1990)

Executive Order 11141 (1964)

Civil Rights Act of 1991

ACCOMMODATING DISABILITIES AND FAMILY NEEDS

Pregnancy Discrimination Act of 1978

Americans with Disabilities Act of 1990

Family and Medical Leave Act of 1993

PREVAILING WAGE LAWS

Davis-Bacon Act of 1931

Walsh-Healey Public Contracts Act of 1936

The compensation department's main goals

Compensation professionals promote effective compensation systems by meeting three important objectives—internal consistency (Chapter 7), market competitiveness (Chapter 8), and recognizing individual contributions (Chapter 9).

INTERNAL CONSISTENCY *Internally consistent compensation systems* clearly define the relative value of each job among all jobs within a company. This ordered set of jobs represents the job structure, or hierarchy, of the company. Companies rely on a simple, yet fundamental, principle for building internally consistent compensation systems: Employees with greater qualifications, more responsibilities, and more-complex job duties should receive higher pay than employees with lesser qualifications, fewer responsibilities, and less complex job duties. Internally consistent job structures formally recognize differences in job characteristics, and, in so doing, enable compensation managers to set pay accordingly.

Compensation professionals use job analysis and job evaluation to achieve internal consistency. *Job analysis* is a systematic process for gathering, documenting, and analyzing information in order to describe jobs. Job analyses describe job content or duties, worker requirements, and, sometimes, the job context or working conditions.

Compensation professionals use *job evaluation* to systematically recognize differences in the relative worth among a set of jobs and establish pay differentials accordingly. Whereas job analysis is almost purely descriptive, job evaluation partly reflects the values and priorities that management places on various positions. On the basis of job content differences (that is, job analysis results) and firm priorities, managers establish pay differentials for virtually all positions within the company.

MARKET COMPETITIVENESS *Market-competitive pay systems* represent companies' compensation policies that fit with companies' business objectives. Market-competitive pay systems play a significant role in attracting and retaining the best-qualified employees. Compensation professionals build market-competitive compensation systems on the basis of the results of strategic analyses and compensation surveys.

A *strategic analysis* entails an examination of a company's external market context and internal factors. Examples of external market factors include industry profile, information about competitors, and long-term growth prospects. Internal factors encompass financial condition and functional capabilities—for example, marketing and human resources. Strategic analyses permit business professionals to see where they stand in the market in light of external and internal factors.

Compensation surveys involve the collection and subsequent analysis of competitors' compensation data. Compensation surveys traditionally focused on competitors' wage and salary practices. Most recently, fringe compensation is also a target of surveys because benefits are a key element of market-competitive pay systems. Compensation surveys are important because they enable compensation professionals to obtain realistic views of competitors' pay practices. Compensation professionals would have to use guesswork to build market-competitive compensation systems in the absence of compensation survey data.

RECOGNIZING INDIVIDUAL CONTRIBUTIONS *Pay structures* represent pay rate differences for jobs of unequal worth *and* the framework for recognizing differences in employee contributions. No two employees possess identical credentials, nor do they perform the same jobs equally well. Companies recognize these differences by paying

---

 **REFLECTIONS**

Balancing Compensation Objectives

Ultimately, compensation professionals must balance external market considerations with internal consistency objectives. In practice, compensation professionals judge the adequacy of pay differentials by comparing both market rates and pay differences among jobs within their companies.

Compensation professionals consult with the top HR official and chief financial officer when discrepancies arise, particularly if company pay rates are generally lower than the market rates. After carefully considering the company's financial resources and the strategic value of the jobs in question, these individuals decide whether to adjust pay rates for the jobs that have below-market values.

---

individuals according to their credentials, knowledge, or job performance. When completed, pay structures should define the boundaries for recognizing employee contributions. Well-designed structures should promote the retention of valued employees.

Pay grades and pay ranges are structural features of pay structures. *Pay grades* group jobs for pay policy application. Human resource professionals typically group jobs into pay grades based on similar compensable factors and value. These criteria are not precise. In fact, no single formula determines what is sufficiently similar in terms of content and value to warrant grouping into a pay grade. Pay ranges build upon pay grades. *Pay ranges* include midpoint, minimum, and maximum pay rates. The minimum and maximum values denote the acceptable lower and upper bounds, respectively, of pay for the jobs contained within particular pay grades.

How compensation professionals relate to various constituencies

The HR department provides services to constituencies within and outside the company. These include:

* ★ Employees
* ★ Line managers
* ★ Executives
* ★ Unions
* ★ U.S. government

The success of HR departments depends on how well they serve various constituencies.[11] "Each constituency has its own set of expectations regarding the personnel department's activities; each holds its own standards for effective performance; each applies its own standards for assessing the extent to which the department's activities meets its expectations; and each attempts to prescribe preferred goals for the subunit or presents constraints to its sphere of discretion. Multiple constituencies often compete directly or indirectly for the attention and priority of the personnel department."[12] Our focus is on some of the ways compensation professionals serve these constituencies.

The success of HR departments depends on how well they serve various constituencies.

Employees

As we discussed earlier, successful pay-for-knowledge programs depend upon a company's ability to develop and implement systematic training programs. Compensation professionals must educate employees about their training options and how successful training will lead to increased pay and advancement opportunities within the company. These professionals should not assume that employees will necessarily recognize the opportunities unless they are clearly communicated. Written memos and informational meetings conducted by compensation professionals and HR representatives are effective communications media.

Discretionary benefits provide protection programs, pay for time-not-worked, and services. As compensation professionals plan and manage fringe compensation programs, they should keep these functions in mind. Probably no single company expects its fringe compensation program to meet all these objectives. So compensation professionals, as representatives of company management, along with union representatives, must determine which objectives are the most important for their particular work forces.

Line managers

Compensation professionals use their expert knowledge of the laws that influence pay and benefits practices (Chapter 3) to help line managers make sound compensation judgments. For example, the Equal Pay Act of 1963 (with a few exceptions, which are discussed in Chapter 3) prohibits sex discrimination in pay for employees performing equal work. Thus, compensation professionals should advise line managers to pay the same hourly pay rate or annual salary for men and women hired to perform the same job.

Line managers turn to compensation professionals for advice about appropriate pay rates for jobs. Compensation professionals oversee the use of job evaluation (Chapter 7) to establish pay differentials among jobs within a company. In addition, compensation professionals train line managers how to properly evaluate jobs.

Executives

Compensation professionals serve company executives by developing and managing sound compensation systems. Executives look to compensation professionals to ensure that the design and implementation of pay and benefits practices comply with pertinent legislation (Chapter 3). Violation of these laws can lead to substantial monetary penalties to companies. Also, executives depend on compensation professionals' expertise to design pay and benefits systems that will attract and retain the best-qualified employees. As we discuss in Chapter 2, employees play a major role in companies' success.

Unions

As noted earlier, collective bargaining agreements describe the terms of employment reached between management and the union. Compensation professionals are responsible for administering the pay and benefits policies specified in collective bargaining agreements. Mainly, they ensure that employees receive COLAs and seniority pay increases on a timely basis.

U.S. government

The U.S. government requires that companies comply with all employment legislation. Compensation professionals apply their expert knowledge of pertinent legislation to design legally sound pay and benefits practices. In addition, since the passage of the Civil Rights Act of 1991 (Chapter 3), compensation professionals apply their expertise to demonstrate that alleged discriminatory pay practices are a business necessity. Thus, as we discuss in Chapter 3, compensation professionals possess the burden of proof to demonstrate that alleged discriminatory pay practices are not in fact discriminatory.

The changing compensation environment: five assumptions that underlie this book

Five assumptions guided the development of this book. They are:

- ☆ Compensation systems are in a state of transition.
- ☆ Compensation practices can be used as a strategic tool.
- ☆ Incremental change is needed.

- ✪ Current practices of meeting market pay rates regardless of overall company strategy need to be replaced by pay-for-performance initiatives.
- ✪ Controlling benefits costs requires changing the "entitlement" mentality.

Compensation systems in a state of transition

Compensation systems are in a state of transition right now, changing from the fairly rigid, hierarchical systems developed after World War II to ones that reflect more-cooperative, horizontal structures. Team- and group-based incentive compensation programs reflect greater cooperative approaches to work. Fewer hierarchical levels have led to flatter, horizontal organizational structures. Companies have had to change because of increased global competition, increased attention to company shareholder values, and increased product differentiation in the market place.

Compensation practices as a strategic tool

Strategic compensation initiatives try to capture those structural changes in companies. Both line and staff managers at many levels are trying to make compensation systems reflect individual contributions more accurately. In addition, these professionals pay more than lip service to the benefits of teams by endorsing team- and group-based incentive programs.

Incremental change

Businesses would probably like to implement such changes overnight. In practical terms, change to compensation systems is incremental. We have moved away from such traditional pay practices as seniority and other non-performance-based pay methods to practices that include base pay plus pay-for-performance and knowledge- or skill-based pay. Specifically, these performance-based pay systems include incentive pay (Chapter 5) and broadbanding (Chapter 9). Pay-for-knowledge and skill-based pay reward employees for acquiring job-related knowledge and skills (Chapter 6). These changes are incremental because employees retain base pay regardless of performance. Moving to pay-at-risk, a system in which employees could earn less for below-average performance, would be a radical change.

Current practices of meeting market pay rates regardless of overall company strategy

In reality, many companies find pay-for-performance too difficult to figure out. So companies often fashion pay amounts after the competition, and they award across-the-board "merit" increases that stingily resemble COLAs. Many companies would benefit from systematically examining their pay practices and beliefs rather than relying solely on external market factors to set pay rates. Such examinations should include job analysis and evaluation. Accurate job analyses and job evaluations underlie many pay-for-performance initiatives, including merit pay, broadbanding, and incentive programs.

Controlling benefits costs and changing the "entitlement" mentality

In the current employment environment, controlling rising benefits costs requires that companies examine employees' traditional "entitlement" mentalities as well. For too many years, companies have awarded benefits to employees regardless of employees'

> *Compensation systems are in a state of transition right now, changing from the fairly rigid, hierarchical systems developed after World War II to ones that reflect more-cooperative, horizontal structures.*

performance or the cost impact of these benefits on company performance. Companies need to take a closer look at benefits costs and ways to minimize employees' entitlement beliefs.

Summary

This chapter introduced basic compensation concepts and the context of compensation practice, compensation professionals' goals within a human resources department, how compensation professionals accomplish their goals, how compensation professionals relate to various constituencies, the changing compensation environment, and five assumptions that underlie this book. We distinguished between intrinsic and extrinsic compensation, noting that our focus is on extrinsic compensation. Then we reviewed the relationships between compensation and other HR practices as well as how compensation professionals serve several constituencies, pointing out that compensation professionals do not function in a vacuum. Compensation professionals focus on internal and external pay differentials among jobs and on creating pay structures that recognize employees for their particular contributions. We concluded with five assumptions that underlie this book, all of which recognize that compensation practice is in a state of flux.

Students of compensation should keep the following in mind: Compensation systems are changing. Change creates many exciting challenges for those who wish to work as compensation professionals. This book highlights those challenges.

Discussion questions

1. Define compensation.
2. Presumably, five core job characteristics promote intrinsic compensation. Give examples of jobs that you believe rate highly on these core job characteristics. Explain your answer.
3. Are the three main goals of compensation departments equally important, or do you believe that they differ in importance? Give your rationale.
4. Discuss what money means to you. Has the discussion of the meaning of money in this chapter influenced your views? How?
5. Describe your reaction to the following statement: "Compensation has no bearing on a company's performance."

Key terms

intrinsic compensation
extrinsic compensation
jobs characteristics theory
core compensation

employee benefits
fringe compensation
base pay
wage

hourly pay
salary
compensable factors
cost-of-living adjustments (COLAs)
human capital theory
human capital
legally required benefits
discretionary benefits
protection programs
pay for time-not-worked
services
line employees
staff functions
recruitment
selection

performance appraisal
training
continuous learning
career development
labor-management relations
collective bargaining agreement
employment termination
voluntary terminations
involuntary terminations
discharge
layoff
severance pay
pension programs
early retirement programs

Endnotes

[1] J. R. Hackman and G. R. Oldham, Motivation through the design of work: Test of a theory, *Organizational Behavior and Human Performance* 16 (1976):250–279.

[2] T. A. Mahoney, The symbolic meaning of pay, *Human Resource Management Review* 1 (1991):179–192.

[3] D. Rush Finn, The meanings of money: A view from economics, *American Behavioral Scientist* 35 (1992):658–668.

[4] N. J. Cayer, *Public personnel administration in the United States* (New York: St. Martin's Press, 1975).

[5] G. Becker, *Human capital* (New York: National Bureau of Economic Research, 1975).

[6] C. Peck, *Pay and performance: The interaction of compensation and performance appraisal,* Research Bulletin No. 155 (New York: The Conference Board, 1984).

[7] C. Peck, *Variable pay: Nontraditional programs for motivation and reward* (New York: The Conference Board, 1993).

[8] J. Rosow and R. Zager, *Training—The competitive edge* (San Francisco: Jossey-Bass, 1988).

[9] G. D. Jenkins Jr. and N. Gupta, The payoffs of paying for knowledge, *National Productivity Review* 4 (1985):121–130.

[10] R. H. Ferguson, *Cost-of-living adjustments in union management agreements* (Ithaca, N.Y.: Cornell University Press, 1976).

[11] J. Pfeffer and G. Salancik, *The external control of organizations: A resource dependence perspective* (New York: Harper & Row, 1978).

[12] A. S. Tsui, Personnel department effectiveness: A tripartite approach, *Industrial Relations* 23 (1984):187.

CHAPTER

TWO

Strategic compensation: Attaining a competitive advantage

CHAPTER OUTLINE

LEARNING OBJECTIVES

In this chapter, you will learn about

1. A historical perspective on compensation, from an administrative function to a strategic function
2. The difference between strategic and tactical compensation
3. Two competitive strategies that companies pursue, cost leadership and differentiation
4. Factors that influence companies' competitive strategies and compensation practices
5. Evaluating the effectiveness of compensation strategies

Until 1978, the U.S. government regulated domestic airline operations. Government regulation minimized competition among airlines by heavily influencing airfares and maintaining control over access to air routes. As a result, airfares were generally much higher (controlling for inflation) before 1978 than they are today. Also, consumers had few choices about which airline to fly. The government limited the number of different airlines for each air route.

Since government deregulation of the U.S. airline industry, competition among airlines has increased dramatically for at least three reasons. First, airlines have substantially greater choice about which routes to fly. Second, airlines have full authority to set their own airfares, enabling them to compete for passengers on the basis of price. Third, government deregulation has made it easier for new airlines to form and for existing airlines to grow without governmental control over air routes.

Although consumers have benefited from government deregulation of the airline industry, the airlines have had difficulties maintaining profitability. In recent years, many airline industry analysts have attributed dismal financial performance to low airfares, particularly deeply discounted airfares offered during intense fare wars. Although enplanements (that is, a measure of passenger volume) increased as a result of these fare wars, airlines found it difficult to cover operating expenses. Consequently, some airlines entered bankruptcy protection (for example, America West Airlines) while others went out of business (for example, Eastern Airlines).

Deregulation has had a major impact on compensation practices. The airline industry was among the highest-paying industries before deregulation. Since then, airlines have attempted to contain compensation costs to promote positive financial performance. For example, United Airlines implemented a two-tier pay structure in 1994. Two-tier pay structures (Chapter 9) reward both temporary and permanent newly hired employees less than established employees. United Airlines paid newly hired reservation agents and other nonunion, lower-level employees less pay and fewer benefits than current nonunion employees. In 1994, Southwest Airlines pilots signed a 10-year contract with the Southwest Airlines Pilots Association that swaps up to 14 million shares of company stock for a five-year freeze in their salaries. Other airlines reduced compensation costs through layoffs and hiring freezes.

This brief account of the U.S. airlines industry illustrates the role compensation practices may have on companies' performance in competitive markets. As we discuss shortly, many companies choose to compete on the basis of costs. After deregulation, airlines generally lowered airfares to increase passenger loads on popular air routes. Increases in passenger loads often did not offset the exorbitant costs required to successfully run airlines—routine maintenance, jet fuel, fees to maintain access at airports, and compensation and benefits. Therefore, airlines sought other ways to reduce total costs while not compromising passenger safety or service quality. Modifications to compensation practices in the airline industry contributed to cost reductions.

A historical perspective on compensation: The road toward strategic compensation

Agriculture and small family craft businesses were the bases for the U.S. economy before the 1900s. The turn of the twentieth century marked the beginning of the Industrial Revolution in the United States. During the Industrial Revolution, the economy's transition from agrarian and craft businesses to large-scale manufacturing began. Increasingly, individuals were becoming employees of large factories instead of self-employed farmers or small business owners. This shift from the agricultural sector to the industrial sector promoted the beginnings of the field of human resource management.[1]

The factory system gave rise to divisions of labor based on differences in worker skill, effort, and responsibilities. The growth in the size of the workplace necessitated practices to guide such activities as hiring, training, setting wages, handling grievances, and terminating workers. At the time, practitioners referred to these activities as personnel administration practices, which is the predecessor of modern human resource management (HRM) practices.

The early personnel (and compensation) function emphasized labor cost control and management control over labor. Many employers instituted so-called scientific management practices to control labor costs and welfare practices to maintain control over labor. Scientific management practices gave rise to individual incentive pay systems (Chapter 6). Welfare practices represent the forerunner of modern discretionary employee benefits practices (Chapter 11).

Scientific management practices promoted labor cost control by replacing inefficient production methods with efficient production methods. Factory owners used time-and-motion studies and job analysis to meet that objective. **Time-and-motion studies** analyzed the time it took employees to complete their jobs. These studies literally focused on employees' movements and the identification of the most-efficient steps to complete jobs in the least amount of time.[2] As discussed in Chapter 1, *job analysis* is a systematic process for gathering, documenting, and analyzing information in order to describe jobs. At the time, employers used job analysis to classify the most efficient ways to perform jobs.

How did scientific management methods influence compensation practices? Scientific management methods gave rise to the use of piecework plans (Chapter 5). Under piecework plans, an employee's compensation depends on the number of units she or he produces over a given period. Specifically, these plans reward employees on the basis of their individual hourly production against an objective output standard, determined by the pace at which manufacturing equipment operates. For each hour, workers receive piecework incentives for every item produced over the designated production standard.

The early personnel (and compensation) function emphasized labor cost control and management control over labor.

Welfare practices were generous endeavors undertaken by some employers, motivated in part to minimize employees' desires to seek union representation, to promote good management, and to enhance worker productivity. **Welfare practices** were "anything for the comfort and improvement, intellectual or social, of the employees, over and above wages paid, which is not a necessity of the industry nor required by law."[3] Companies' welfare practices varied. For example, some employers offered facilities such as libraries and recreational areas; others offered financial assistance for education, home purchases, and home improvements. In addition, employers' sponsor of medical insurance coverage became common. The use of welfare practices created the need for the administration of them. Welfare secretaries served as an intermediary between the company and its employees, and they were essentially a predecessor of human resource professionals.[4]

Apart from management initiatives, the U.S. government also contributed to the evolution of compensation practice. The U.S. government instituted major legislation aimed at protecting individual rights to fair treatment in the workplace. Most often, fair treatment means making employment-related decisions according to job performance: for example, awarding higher merit pay increases for the better performers. We introduced some of these laws in Chapter 1, and we address all of them in Chapter 3. Federal laws that apply to compensation practices are grouped according to four themes:

* ★ Income continuity, safety, and work hours
* ★ Pay discrimination
* ★ Accommodating disabilities and family needs
* ★ Prevailing wage laws

Federal laws led to the bureaucratization of compensation practice.

Federal laws led to the bureaucratization of compensation practice. Personnel and compensation administrators took the lead in developing and implementing employment practices that upheld the myriad federal employment laws. These professionals also maintained records, creating documentation in the event of legal challenges to employment practices. In short, compensation professionals were largely administrators who reacted to government regulation.

Personnel administration was transformed from a purely administrative function to a competitive resource in many companies during the 1980s.

Since the early 1980s, compensation professionals began designing and implementing compensation programs that contribute to companies' competitive advantage.[5] Personnel administration was transformed from a purely administrative function to a competitive resource in many companies during the 1980s.

Competitive advantage describes a company's success. Specifically, competitive advantage refers to a company's ability to maintain market share and profitability over a sustained period of several years. Employers began to recognize that employees are key resources necessary for the company's success, particularly in changing business environments characterized by rapid technological change and intense business competition from foreign countries. Employers' recognition that employees represent an important resource led to the view of employees as human resources. In line with this view, companies design human resource management practices to promote competitive advantage.

As technology leads to the automation of more tasks, employers combine jobs and confer broader responsibilities on workers. For example, the technology of advanced automated manufacturing, such as that used in the automobile industry, began doing the jobs of people, including the laborer, the materials handler, the operator-assembler, and the maintenance person. Nowadays, a single employee performs all of these tasks in a position called "manufacturing technician." The expanding range of tasks and responsibilities in this job demands higher levels of reading, writing, and computation skills than did the jobs that it replaced, which required strong hand-to-eye coordination. Most employees must possess higher levels of reading skills than before because they must be able to read the operating and troubleshooting manuals (when problems arise) of automated manufacturing equipment that is based on computer technology. Previously, manufacturing equipment had a relatively simple design, based on simple mechanical principles such as pulleys, and it was easy to operate.

Increased global competition has forced companies in the United States to become more productive. Now, more than ever, companies must provide their employees with leading-edge skills and encourage them to apply their skills proficiently to sustain competitive advantage. Evidence clearly shows that workers in other countries are better skilled and able to work more productively than U.S. employees[6] (Chapter 6).

Compensation practices contribute to competitive advantage by promoting more-productive and highly skilled work forces.[7] Well-designed merit pay programs (Chapter 4) reinforce excellent performance by awarding pay raises commensurably with performance attainments. The use of incentive pay practices (Chapter 5) is instrumental in changing the prevalent entitlement mentality U.S. workers have toward pay and in containing compensation costs by awarding one-time increases to base pay once work objectives have been attained. Pay-for-knowledge and skill-based pay programs (Chapter 6) are key to providing employees the necessary knowledge and skills to use new workplace technology effectively. Management can use discretionary benefit offerings (Chapter 11) to promote particular employee behaviors that have strategic value. For instance, when employees take advantage of tuition reimbursement programs, they are more likely to contribute to the strategic imperatives of product or service differentiation and cost reduction objectives.

> *Compensation practices contribute to competitive advantage by promoting more-productive and highly skilled work forces.*

Strategic versus tactical compensation

Business professionals make two kinds of decisions—strategic decisions and tactical decisions. Briefly, strategic decisions guide the activities of companies in the market. Tactical decisions support the fulfillment of strategic decisions. Business professionals apply these decisions to companies' functions including manufacturing, engineering, research and development, management information systems, human resources, and marketing. For example, HR professionals make strategic compensation decisions and tactical compensation decisions. Exhibit 2-1 shows the relationship between strategic decisions and tactical decisions.

Strategic management entails a series of judgments, under uncertainty, that companies direct toward achieving specific goals.[8] Companies base strategy formulation on environmental scanning activities (Chapter 8). Discerning threats and opportunities is the main focus of environmental scanning. Strategic management is an inexact process because companies distinguish between threats and opportunities on the basis of interpretation. Threat suggests a negative situation in which loss is likely and over which an individual has relatively little control. An opportunity implies a positive situation in which gain is likely and over which an individual has a fair amount of control.[9]

Exhibit 2-1
Relationship between strategic and tactical decisions

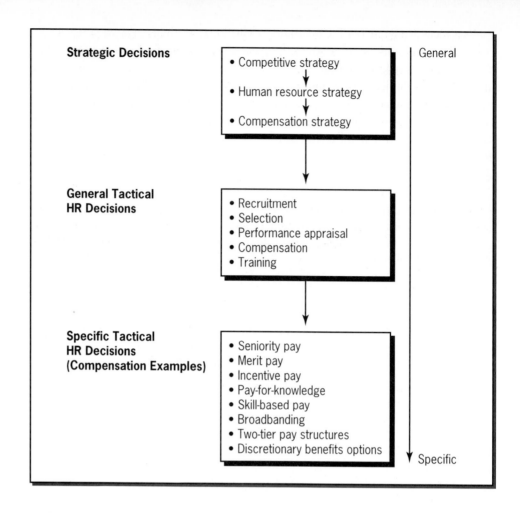

Strategic Decisions
- Competitive strategy
- Human resource strategy
- Compensation strategy

General

General Tactical HR Decisions
- Recruitment
- Selection
- Performance appraisal
- Compensation
- Training

Specific Tactical HR Decisions (Compensation Examples)
- Seniority pay
- Merit pay
- Incentive pay
- Pay-for-knowledge
- Skill-based pay
- Broadbanding
- Two-tier pay structures
- Discretionary benefits options

Specific

For example, Lufthansa has been reducing costs. In 1992, the German airline announced its first loss in 20 years—$315 million in 1991. Lufthansa's revenues of $11 billion, its more than 50,000 employees, and its 200 jets made it one of Europe's largest airlines. However, rising interest rates and the deregulation of the airline industry in Europe were threats to Lufthansa's profitability.[10] Rising interest rates increased the costs to borrow money for jet purchases. As had the U.S. airlines after deregulation, European airlines faced greater competition from other airlines, forcing them to compete for passengers on the basis of cost. Lowering airfares to contain costs compromised Lufthansa's profitability.

J. C. Penney, one of America's largest retailers, lost sales during the early 1990s when the economic recession and Gulf War led to lower consumer spending. At the time, Penney had expanded its selection of higher-priced goods, which consumers generally chose not to buy. J. C. Penney turned this threat into an opportunity by adopting a competitive strategy of lower prices and higher quality, contributing to substantially improved sales.[11] Since then, the company has kept current fashions and respected brand names while reorienting itself as a moderately priced merchant. In addition, J. C. Penney expanded the team of quality inspectors for its private-label goods, which account for the vast majority of sales and usually yield higher margins than the average for national brands. Further, Sears's decision to shut down its catalog business has presented a rare opportunity for Penney's to expand its mail order business.

Exhibit 2-2 contains brief descriptions that illustrate threats and opportunities in four industries—missiles, mainframe computers, video cassettes, and bicycles.

Strategic decisions support business objectives. Companies' executives communicate business objectives in competitive strategy statements. **Competitive strategy** refers to the planned use of company resources—technology, capital, and human resources—to promote and sustain competitive advantage. According to Jack Welch,

Exhibit 2-2
Threats and Opportunities in Sample Industries

MISSILES

Defense cutbacks and continued decline in the aerospace industry have curtailed demand in the missile segment. With the end of the cold war, Pentagon officials began shifting priorities away from nuclear weaponry and toward missile systems that will provide enhanced strategic conventional capability. New weapons programs in missiles and space will focus on U.S. ability to deter or win regional, nonnuclear conflicts.

MAINFRAME COMPUTERS

Mainframe computers, once the workhorses of the computing world, are being challenged by a rising tide of new, competitive technologies. On one end is the strong demand for cheaper, less-powerful systems that are inexpensive to operate and can be placed directly under the control of individual users. That demand has resulted in the rapid rise of sales of personal computers and workstations. At the opposite end of the user spectrum are the supercomputers. These have become the dominant systems used by many researchers and scientists. Mainframes generally have not been capable of providing the advanced scientific operations that they need. Mainframe firms have responded by making computers more available to individuals via networks and more capable of advanced scientific uses through the attachment of vector processors. At the same time, companies have continued to make rapid advances in disk-storage capacity and processing performance.

VIDEO CASSETTES

The video cassette business includes both rentals and sales. With ownership of video cassette players approaching saturation of U.S. television households, the growth of cassette sales and rentals is shrinking because buyers of VCR players tend to rent fewer tapes after the first year of ownership. The growth of cassette sales will be further stunted by the popularity of other video delivery systems such as cable television and pay-per-view. The largest potential challenger to video cassettes is pay-per-view or video-on-demand television. Viewers potentially benefit from the convenience of telephoning their program requests and receiving movies on home screens instead of traveling to the video store.

BICYCLES

The slowed growth in U.S. demand for bicycles is due to two factors. First, bicycles generally are a discretionary purchase, so changes in real disposable personal income can significantly affect trends of bicycle sales. Consumers have been reluctant to make discretionary purchases for fear of job losses and another recession in the overall U.S. economy. Second, consumers began purchasing a new type of bicycle, the mountain bike. Consumers replaced their old lightweight bicycles with mountain bikes faster than they would normally replace a bicycle. Prior to the mountain bike, consumers replaced their lightweight bikes about once every three years. Since the advent of the sturdier mountain bikes, consumers tend to replace their bikes less frequently.

Source: U.S. Department of Commerce, *U.S. industrial outlook* (Washington, D.C.: U.S. Department of Commerce, 1994).

General Electric Corporation's (GE) Chief Executive Officer, each GE business (for example, consumer appliances, aircraft engines) will be number one or two in their markets. The time horizon for strategic decisions may span in excess of two years.

Human resource strategies specify the particular use of HR practices to be consistent with competitive strategy. One of GE's HR strategies is to provide managers with increased problem-solving responsibility. General Electric promotes this strategy in at least two ways: First, Jack Welch reduced the number of decision-making levels by flattening GE's organizational structure. Welch coined the term *delayering* to describe GE's initiative. Second, GE's *workout* program provides managers from different functions the opportunities to meet off site to find creative solutions to business problems.

Strategic decisions support business objectives. Companies' executives communicate business objectives in competitive strategy statements.

Compensation strategies describe the use of compensation practices that support human resource and competitive strategies. General Electric's use of broadbanding (Chapter 9, and described briefly later in this chapter) is consistent with flattening organizational hierarchies.

Tactical decisions support competitive strategy. Human resource professionals make tactical decisions to specify policy for promoting competitive advantage. Developing compensation programs, recruitment plans, and methods to reduce turnover among excellent performers are just a few examples of general HR tactical decisions. Specific compensation tactics include establishing base pay levels, seniority pay, merit pay, incentive pay, pay-for-knowledge, skill-based pay programs, broadbanding, two-tier pay structures, and discretionary benefits programs. The time horizon for tactical decisions is suited to meet the imperatives of competitive strategy.

Tactical decisions support competitive strategy.

Competitive strategy choices

COST LEADERSHIP **The cost leadership strategy,** or **lowest-cost strategy,** focuses on gaining competitive advantage by being the lowest-cost producer of a good or service within the marketplace, while selling the good or service at a price advantage relative to the industry average. Lowest-cost strategies require aggressive construction of efficient-scale facilities and vigorous pursuit of cost minimization in such areas as operations, marketing, and human resources.

United Parcel Service (UPS) is an excellent illustration of an organization that pursues a lowest-cost strategy because its management successfully reduced operations costs. Specifically, UPS has gained a competitive advantage through the elimination of wasteful steps in the parcel delivery process. For example, UPS managers have accompanied couriers on their routes to determine whether they work inefficiently. To do so, these observers literally counted couriers' motions, steps, and time to complete parcel pickups and deliveries. Couriers receive feedback on how to improve their efficiency by reducing unnecessary steps (that is, the number of parcels picked up or delivered for a specified period).

DIFFERENTIATION Companies adopt **differentiation** strategies to develop products or services that are unique. Differentiation can take many forms, including design or brand image, technology, features, customer service, and price. Differentiation strategies lead to competitive advantage through building brand loyalty among devoted consumers. Because brand-loyal consumers are less sensitive to price increases, companies can invest in research and development initiatives to further differentiate themselves from competing companies.

The Iams Company, a cat and dog food manufacturer, successfully pursues a differentiation strategy based on brand image and price premiums. The company offers two dog food lines. Iams is a superpremium line that is nutritionally well balanced for dogs and uses quality ingredients. Eukanuba is an ultrapremium line that contains more chicken and vital nutrients than the Iams line and OmegaCOAT® Nutritional Science (fatty acids that promote shiny and healthy coats). Together, Iams and Eukanuba appeal to a substantial set of dog owners. The Iams Company distinguishes Eukanuba from Iams, claiming that Eukanuba is "the best you can do for your dog." The Eukanuba slogan is the company's basis for brand image.

Besides brand image, the Iams Company also differentiates its Eukanuba line by charging a price premium. This price premium has enabled the Iams Company to be an innovator in canine nutrition by investing heavily in product research and development. For example, the Iams Company was the first to offer a Eukanuba puppy formula to nutritionally support balanced muscular and skeletal development of large and giant breed dogs.

Tactical decisions that support the firm's strategy

As noted earlier, human resource tactics and tactics in other functional areas support a company's competitive strategy. Compensation and HR professionals can orchestrate HR and other functional tactics to promote competitive strategy. In addition, HR practices support competitive advantage through energizing key employee roles.

TACTICS IN OTHER FUNCTIONAL AREAS Companies must determine which functional capabilities are most crucial to maintaining competitive advantage. Again, functional capabilities include manufacturing, engineering, research and development, management information systems, human resources, and marketing. Rapid advances in medical science are moving toward less-invasive surgical procedures that require special surgical instruments. One noteworthy example is arthroscopic surgery. Arthroscopes enable surgeons to perform knee and shoulder surgeries without invasive surgical openings. Competitive advantage in this industry depends largely on researching, developing and manufacturing, leading-edge surgical instruments for these new, less-invasive surgical procedures.

Companies such as McDonald's Corporation rely on marketing savvy to remain competitive. McDonald's has had the reputation of catering to young children. McDonald's recent introduction of the Arch Deluxe™ hamburger represents the corporation's attempt to increase sales and market share by identifying with an older crowd: "The Arch Deluxe™ is the hamburger with the grown-up taste."

EMPLOYEE ROLES ASSOCIATED WITH COMPETITIVE STRATEGIES Human resource professionals must decide which employee roles are instrumental to the attainment of competitive strategies.[12] Knowledge of these required roles should enable HR professionals to implement HR tactics that encourage their enactment of these roles. Of course, compensation professionals are responsible for designing and implementing compensation tactics that elicit strategy-consistent employee roles.

For the lowest-cost strategy, the imperative is to reduce output costs per employee. The desired employee roles for attaining a lowest-cost strategy include repetitive and predictable behaviors, a relatively short-term focus, primarily autonomous or individual activity, high concern for quantity of output, and a primary concern for results.[13] The UPS example illustrated the attainment of most of these behaviors. Compensa-

Human resource professionals must decide which employee roles are instrumental to the attainment of competitive strategies.

tion practices can encourage UPS couriers to repeat these behaviors regularly and consistently by rewarding them for efficiency.

The key employee roles for differentiation strategies include highly creative behavior, a relatively long-term focus, cooperative and interdependent behavior, and a greater degree of risk taking.[14] Compared with lowest-cost strategies, successful attainment of differentiation strategies depends on employee creativity, openness to novel work approaches, and willingness to take risks. In addition, differentiation strategies require longer time frames to provide sufficient opportunity to yield the benefits of these behaviors. The Iams Company's success is based in large part on its innovations in canine nutritional formulas. Compensating research scientists to find creative solutions is key to this company's competitive advantage.

TACTICS IN THE HR DEPARTMENT, ESPECIALLY COMPENSATION SPECIALTIES We discuss the appropriateness of the following compensation tactics for lowest-cost and differentiation competitive strategies in subsequent chapters after becoming knowledgeable about the particulars:

- ✯ Seniority pay (Chapter 4)
- ✯ Merit pay (Chapter 4)
- ✯ Incentive pay (Chapter 5)
- ✯ Pay-for-knowledge and skill-based pay (Chapter 6)
- ✯ Base pay levels (Chapter 8)
- ✯ Broadbanding (Chapter 9)
- ✯ Two-tier pay structures (Chapter 9)
- ✯ Legally required benefits (Chapter 10)
- ✯ Discretionary employee benefits (Chapter 11)

Factors that influence companies' competitive strategies and compensation practices

Several factors influence a company's choice of competitive strategies and compensation tactics. These include national culture, organizational culture, and organizational and product (or service) life cycle. Exhibit 2-3 lists the particular dimensions of these influences on competitive strategy and compensation tactics.

National culture

National culture refers to the set of shared norms and beliefs among individuals within national boundaries who are indigenous to that area. National culture increasingly has become an important consideration in strategic compensation. As we touch upon briefly, national culture influences the effectiveness of various forms of pay as motivators of proficient employee behavior. U.S. managers responsible for managing compensation programs abroad may find that cultural differences reduce the effectiveness of U.S. compensation practices. This problem is particularly troublesome given the rise in U.S. companies' presence in foreign countries. Foreign offices or plants of multinational corporations tend to employ local nationals who may not un-

Exhibit 2-3

Influences on Competitive Strategy

NATIONAL CULTURE

- Power distance
- Individualism-collectivism
- Uncertainty avoidance
- Masculinity-femininity

ORGANIZATIONAL CULTURE

- Traditional organizational hierarchy
- Flatter organizational structures
- Team orientation

ORGANIZATIONAL AND PRODUCT LIFE CYCLE

- Growth
- Maturity
- Decline

---

derstand U.S. culture. In the People's Republic of China, native Chinese who work for U.S.-Chinese joint venture companies are not accustomed to performance-based pay: The Communist influence in China led to need-based pay programs.

Compensation experts maintain that understanding the normative expectations of different national cultures should promote competitive advantage.[15] Thus, it is important to be familiar with differences in national culture and to understand how those differences may influence the effectiveness of alternative pay programs. Geert Hofstede, a renowned researcher of national culture, categorizes national culture along four dimensions—power distance, individualism-collectivism, uncertainty avoidance, and masculinity-femininity.[16] This categorization of variations in national culture facilitates a discussion of how they may affect compensation tactics.

Compensation experts maintain that understanding the normative expectations of different national cultures should promote competitive advantage.

Power distance is the extent to which people accept a hierarchical system or power structure in companies. Status differentials between employees and employers are typical in high power distance cultures. Cultures that highly value power distance are likely to have compensation strategies that reinforce status differentials among employees, perhaps using visible rewards that project power. For example, Venezuela, the Philippines, and Arab nations rate high on power distance. Where power distance is not a dominant value, compensation strategies probably endorse egalitarian compensation tactics as well as participatory pay programs. Australia, Sweden, and the Netherlands rate low on power distance.

Individualism-collectivism is the extent to which individuals value personal independence or group membership. Individualist cultures place value on personal goals, independence, and privacy. Collectivist cultures favor social cohesiveness and loyalty to such groups as coworkers and families. Individualist cultures adopt compensation strategies that reward individual performance as well as acquisition of skill or knowledge. In collectivist societies, employers reward employees on the basis of group performance and individual seniority to recognize the importance of employees' affiliation with groups. Shortly, we contrast the U.S. and Japanese cultures, which exemplify individualism and collectivism, respectively.

Uncertainty avoidance represents the method by which society deals with risk and instability for its members. Fear of random events, value on stability and routines, and risk aversion are hallmarks of high uncertainty avoidance. Italy and Greece are examples of countries that rate high on uncertainty avoidance. On the other hand, welcoming random events, valuing challenge, and seeking risk characterize low uncertainty avoidance. Where uncertainty avoidance is high, employers probably use bureaucratic pay policies, emphasize fixed pay as more important than variable pay, and bestow little discretion to supervisors in distributing pay. Where uncertainty avoidance is low, employers probably use incentive pay programs and grant supervisors an extensive amount of latitude in pay allocation. Singapore and Denmark rate low on uncertainty avoidance.

Masculinity-femininity refers to whether masculine or feminine values are dominant in society. Masculinity favors material possessions. Femininity encourages caring and nurturing behavior. The compensation strategies of masculine cultures are likely to contain pay policies that allow for inequities by gender as well as paternalistic benefits for women in the form of paid maternity leave and day care. Mexico and Germany possess masculine national cultures. In contrast to those of masculine cultures, the compensation strategies of feminine cultures may encourage job evaluation regardless of gender composition as well as offer perquisites on bases other than gender. Finland and Norway possess feminine national cultures.

In sum, national culture is a complex phenomenon that is related to differences in compensation practices. Hofstede provides a useful framework for describing the dimensions of national culture. Next, we contrast the national cultures of the United States and Japan to illustrate the influence of national culture on compensation practices. The individualism-collectivism dimension characterizes the differences between U.S. and Japanese culture.

U.S. CULTURE U.S. culture is a good example of individualism and, as noted in Chapter 1, it emphasizes instrumentality. Employees strive for high levels of performance when they believe that better performance leads to greater pay. Money derives importance from what it can buy, the sense of security it creates, as a sign of achievement, and its definition of personal relationships. As we discuss throughout this book, with few exceptions, most compensation practices in U.S. companies reward individual performance (that is, merit pay and incentive pay) or individuals' acquisition of job-relevant knowledge or skills (that is, pay-for-knowledge and skill-based pay).

JAPANESE CULTURE Japan's national culture is collectivist. Influenced by the Zen, Confucian, and Samurai traditions, the predominant values of Japanese culture are social cooperation and responsibility, an acceptance of reality, and perseverance.[17] People hold dear membership in groups. Duty to group needs prevails over each individual's needs and personal feelings. Failure to meet group needs results in personal shame because society disapproves of individuals who do not hold group interests in high esteem.

These principles apply to all aspects of Japanese life including employment. Traditionally, employers have highly valued employees' affiliation, and they have taken personal interest in employees' personal lives as well as work lives. The value placed on group membership leads employers to care about the well being of their employees' families because families are important groups in Japan. Employers generally award base pay to meet families' needs and also on the basis of seniority to honor affiliation as employees.

Compared with North Americans, the Japanese are more likely to produce at high levels because of the values that they embrace rather than because of what is in it for them.[18] This contrast holds implications for compensation tactics in these two countries. Traditionally, compensation professionals designed U.S. compensation systems to reward individual performance. Also, the time orientation tends to be short-term—typically one year or less.[19] In Japan, compensation professionals design pay systems to reward employees' loyalty and to meet the personal needs of the individual because Japanese employers value employees' affiliation with their companies. Japanese compensation systems focus on the long term, changing as employees' needs change throughout their work lives.

Organizational culture

Organizational culture is an organization's system of shared values and beliefs that produce norms of behavior.[20] These values are apparent in companies' organizational

THE FLIP SIDE OF THE COIN

Japanese Lifetime Employment Possibly Short-Lived

The globalization of the economy influences business activity worldwide. For example, economic recessions threaten companies' profitability because of weak consumer confidence. Weak consumer confidence leads to reduced spending, thus, lackluster company revenue and profits.

Most U.S. and Western European companies respond to economic recession by cutting total cost expenditures. Often, compensation costs are targeted for cuts. U.S. and Western European companies usually reduce compensation costs in various ways, including withholding pay increases, reducing base pay and benefits, or through hiring freezes or employee layoffs. Layoffs are common. In fact, newspapers report companies' plans for layoffs almost on a daily basis.

In Japan, lifetime employment has been a national ideal for decades, making layoffs an undesirable course of action. Presently, there appear to be two schools of thought regarding the appropriateness of layoffs. Japanese traditionalists argue against layoffs: Layoffs represent a breach of the long-standing lifetime employment ethic. In addition, traditionalists argue that maintaining employment will lead to greater

- cooperation among employees to improve productivity
- companies' investments in employee training based on the belief that employees will not leave to take jobs with the competition
- research and development activities because companies will feel more confident that trade secrets will not leak to the competition

Advocates of change argue that Japanese companies should adopt layoff policies to reduce compensation costs. In addition, advocates of change maintain that Japanese companies should avoid large staffing levels. Some Japanese companies are managing staffing levels (and avoiding layoffs) through early retirement offerings and lower hiring rates.

and work structures. Also, organizational culture influences human resource systems designs including compensation.

TRADITIONAL HIERARCHY The traditional design of U.S. companies emphasizes efficiency, decision making by managers, and dissemination of information from the top of the company to lower levels. Exhibit 2-4 illustrates a traditional organizational hierarchy. The company's executive vice president is the intermediary for the company's chief executive officer and the vice presidents of the functional areas. Within the functional areas, the decision making flows downward from the vice presidents to managers of specialties within the functions.

For example, a company's top executives recognize the need to motivate employees to learn new skills associated with changing workplace technology. As discussed in Chapter 1, systematic training programs and pay-for-knowledge programs go hand in hand. Thus, the executive vice president communicates the strategic imperative for developing a pay-for-knowledge program to the vice presidents of training and compensation. In turn, these vice presidents charge their directors and managers with the responsibility of developing such programs. The managers identify the major design considerations of pay-for-knowledge programs (Chapter 9). Exhibit 2-5 lists these main considerations.

Seniority pay (Chapter 4) and such pay-for-performance programs as merit pay (Chapter 4) fit best with traditional hierarchical structures. Seniority pay programs create hierarchies based on length of time in a job. Under seniority systems, employees performing the same jobs may receive markedly different pay. Likewise, merit pay programs create hierarchies. The use of narrower pay grades (that is, pay grades that contain relatively few jobs) tend to promote hierarchy. As we discussed in Chapter 1, pay grades group jobs for pay policy application, and pay ranges indicate acceptable minimum and maximum pay rates for each pay grade. In addition, we discussed that compensation professionals group jobs into pay grades based on such compensable factors as skill, effort, responsibility, and working conditions. In general, minimum and maximum pay rates increase as the level of compensable factors (for example, greater skill) increases.

FLATTENING THE ORGANIZATION Although traditional hierarchical organizational structures still are prevalent, many companies' structures are flattening, becoming less bureaucratic.[21] Many companies have recognized the need to move to an adaptive, high-involvement organizational structure. In the adaptive organizational structure, employees are in a constant state of learning and performance improvement.[22] Employees are free to move wherever they are needed in the company. Employees, managers, vendors, customers, and suppliers work together to improve service quality and to create new products and services. Line employees are trained in multiple jobs, communicate directly with suppliers and customers, and interact frequently with engineers, quality experts, and employees from other functions.

Broadbanding represents the increasing organizational trend toward flatter, less hierarchical corporate structures that emphasize teamwork over individual contributions alone.[23] Broadbanding uses only a few, large salary ranges spanning levels within the organization previously covered by several pay grades. Thus, HR professionals place jobs that were separated by one or more pay grades in old pay structures into the same band under broadbanding systems, minimizing hierarchical differences among jobs. Exhibit 2-6 illustrates the broadbanding concept.

Exhibit 2-4
Traditional Organizational Structure

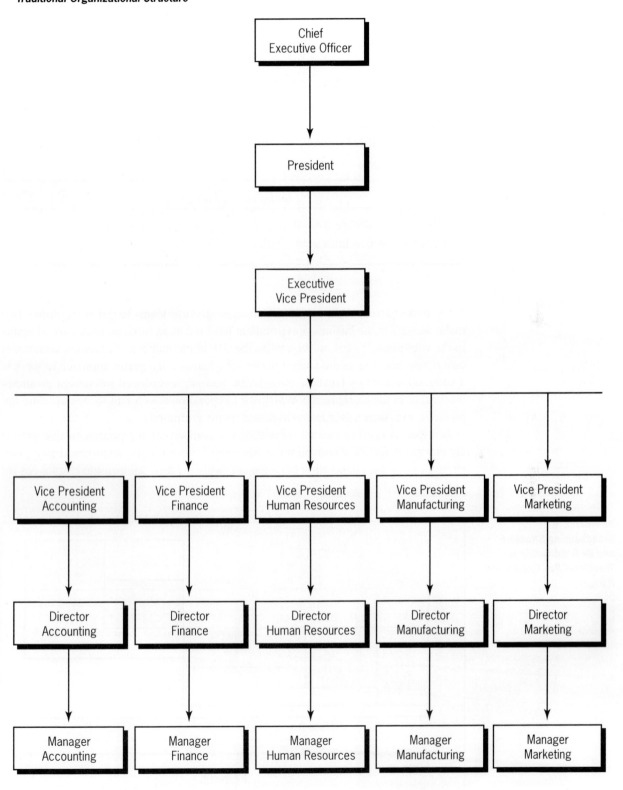

Exhibit 2-5
Designing Pay-for-Knowledge Programs

ESTABLISHING SKILL BLOCKS

- Skill type
- Number of skills
- Grouping of skills

TRANSITION MATTERS

- Skills assessment
- Aligning pay with the knowledge structure
- Access to training

TRAINING AND CERTIFICATION

- In-house or outsourcing training
- Certification and recertification

TEAM ORIENTATION U.S. employers increasingly use teams to get work done. Two main changes in the business environment have led to an increase in the use of teams in the workplace.[24] First, in the 1980s, the rise in the number of Japanese companies conducting business in the United States was dramatic. The team approach to work is a common feature of Japanese companies. Second, team-based job design promotes innovation in the workplace.[25] Whirlpool Corporation uses teams to manufacture appliances, and Saturn uses teams to manufacture automobiles.

Companies need to change individualistic compensation practices so that groups are rewarded for their collaborative behavior.[26] Accordingly, team-based pay plans should emphasize cooperation between and within teams, compensate employees for

Exhibit 2-6
Broadbanding Structure and Its Relationship to Traditional Pay Grades and Ranges

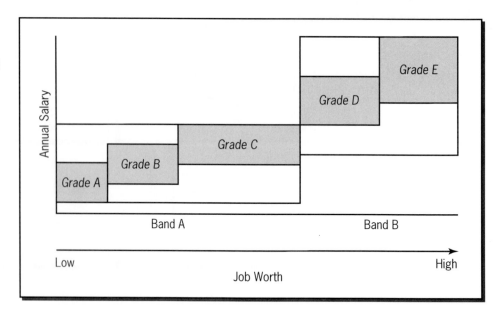

additional responsibilities they often must assume in their roles as members of a team, and encourage team members to attain predetermined objectives for the team.[27]

Team-based organizational structures encourage team members to learn new skills and assume broader responsibility than is expected of them under traditional pay structures that are geared toward individuals. Employees who work in teams must initiate plans for achieving their teams' production goals. Usually, a pay plan for teams emphasizes cooperation, rewarding its members for the additional responsibilities they must take on and skills and knowledge they must acquire. Chapter 5 (incentive pay) addresses the design of team incentive pay plans. Chapter 6 shows how skill-based pay plans and knowledge-based pay can address these additional responsibilities.

Organizational and product life cycles

Many business professionals set competitive strategies on the basis of organizational and product life cycles. **Organizational and product life cycles** describe the evolution of companies and products in terms of human life cycle stages. Much as people are born, grow, mature, decline, and die, so do companies, products, and services. Business priorities including HR vary with life cycle stage.[28] In particular, life cycle stage influences the choice of competitive strategies and such specific HR strategies as compensation.

Many business professionals set competitive strategies on the basis of organizational and product life cycles.

GROWTH PHASE Differentiation strategies are most appropriate for companies in the growth phase. In competitive markets, newcomers must distinguish themselves from the established competitors in ways that appeal to prospective consumers and clients. Failure to do so will create competitive disadvantages. After all, why purchase a product or service from a new, unknown company when you can get exactly the same thing from a well-known company?

Companies that provide services on the Internet are growth companies. The Internet is a single network that connects millions of computers around the world. The number of computers connected to the Internet has grown exponentially—from 562 computers in 1983 to well over 2 million computers in 1994.[29] Likewise, the amount of information on the Internet has grown exponentially. There does not appear to be a foreseeable slowdown in the expansion of the Internet. Excite, Incorporated; Infoseek Corporation; and the McKinley Group are examples of growth companies that provide services on the Internet. These companies offer "search engines" that enable individuals to systematically locate, identify, and edit material on the Internet on the basis of key words and concepts. Research and development is a key focus as these companies continually develop new software to increase search capabilities.

Growth companies experience cash demands to finance capital expansion projects (for example, new buildings, manufacturing equipment, or enhanced telecommunications services). These companies also strive to employ the best-qualified employees for key positions. Often, getting the most talented executives and professional employees requires exorbitant expenditures on compensation, discounting labor cost containment strategies.[30] As a result, growth companies tend to emphasize market-competitive pay systems over internally consistent pay systems.

Not all core compensation tactics are appropriate for growth companies. Long-term incentive programs with annual or longer goals for professionals and executives are suitable. Rewarding engineers' innovations in product design requires a long-term orientation: It takes an extended amount of time to move through the series of steps required to bring the innovation to the marketplace—patent approval, manufacturing, and market distribution. The incentives that executives receive are based on long-term horizons because their success is matched against the endurance of their companies over time (Chapter 13). Lucrative long-term incentive awards may be able to maintain key employees' commitment to growth objectives over time.

Core compensation tactics for staff (for example, compensation specialist) and lower-level line employees (for example, first-line supervisors) typically consist of base pay, periodically increased with modest merit awards. Base pay levels usually are consistent with external market pay rates. Although these employees are not directly responsible for company growth, they do contribute by offering consistency in the product manufacturing or service delivery processes. In some cases, growth companies may set base pay levels somewhat below external market rates to maximize cash flow for research and development activities or marketing campaigns. As we discuss in Chapter 9, setting base pay too low may make it difficult for companies to recruit and retain well-qualified employees.

Growth companies tend to keep discretionary benefits offerings to a minimum. As we discuss in Chapter 11, discretionary benefits represent a significant fiscal cost to companies. In 1994, U.S. companies spent an average $11,506 per year per employee to provide discretionary benefits.[31] Such discretionary benefits accounted for approximately one-third of employers' total payroll costs (that is, the sum of core compensation and all fringe compensation costs). For too many years, companies have awarded benefits to employees regardless of employees' performance or the cost impact of these benefits on company performance. Growth companies cannot afford expenditures that do not contribute directly to growth objectives.

MATURITY Lowest-cost strategies are most appropriate for mature companies. Products and services have fully evolved within the constraints of technology. Mature companies strive to maintain or gain market share. Efficient operations are paramount to striking a balance between cost containment and offering the best possible quality products or services.

Southwest Airlines is an exemplar of a mature company that successfully pursues a lowest-cost strategy. Several features of Southwest's operations account for its success as a low-cost, yet safe and reliable airline. Southwest does not offer as many nonstop flight arrangements as its competitors. For example, flying from New Orleans to Indianapolis may require three separate flights—New Orleans to Houston, Houston to St. Louis, and St. Louis to Indianapolis. By offering shorter flights, Southwest is able to more easily fill their planes, increasing cost efficiency. Southwest also saves money by using an open seating policy on its flights. This open seating policy frees up reservationists' time for booking additional reservations. Southwest further contains costs because there is no need to issue paper boarding passes. Instead, gate agents hand passengers plastic boarding cards that flight attendants collect upon boarding. These plastic boarding cards are used again for future flights. Finally, Southwest Airlines manages costs by not offering full meal services on its flights.

Mature companies usually have large, well-developed internal labor markets. Internal labor markets are pools of skills and abilities from among a company's current work force. As companies mature, employees presumably become more skilled and able to make greater contributions to the attainment of companies' goals. Management can capitalize on internal labor markets through the implementation of career development programs. Current excellent performers may receive promotions, leaving mainly entry-level job openings available to external candidates.

As we discuss in Chapter 6, pay-for-knowledge and skill-based pay programs are suitable for companies that pursue lowest-cost strategies. Both programs are instrumental to developing internal labor markets. In the short run, pay-for-knowledge and skill-based pay programs may undermine the imperatives of lowest-cost strategies because of the associated training costs. However, productivity enhancements and increased flexibility should far outweigh the short-run costs.

Other core compensation programs may be appropriate for lowest-cost strategies as well. Logically, base pay rates should be set below the market average to contain costs. However, compensation professionals must recommend pay rates that strike a balance between efficiency mandates and the need to retain valued employees. Often, setting base pay to meet market averages strikes this balance when it is augmented with incentive pay. Lowest-cost strategies demand reduced output costs per employee. As we discussed in Chapter 1, incentive pay fluctuates according to employees' attainment of some standard based on a preestablished formula, individual or group goals, or company earnings.[32] Merit pay systems are most appropriate only when the following two conditions are met: Pay increases are commensurate with employee productivity, and employees maintain productivity long after receiving permanent increments to base pay.

DECLINE Companies in decline experience diminishing markets and, subsequently, poor business performance. Several factors can result in decline including limited financial resources and changes in consumer preferences. Business leaders can respond to decline in either of two ways. They can allow decline to continue until the business is no longer profitable. Alternatively, business leaders may choose to make substantial changes that reverse decline. A company's response to decline determines whether lowest-cost or differentiation strategies are most appropriate.

Differentiation strategies become the focus when companies choose to redirect activities toward distinguishing themselves from the competition by modifying existing products or services in some creative way or by developing new products or services. American Express Corporation differentiated itself in response to the declining market for its charge cards (see "Reflections").

Lowest cost strategies are most appropriate when companies allow decline to continue to business closure. The era of small, family-owned furniture stores is coming to an end as large discount furniture stores take hold. This trend is the result of two factors. First, small, family-owned furniture stores generally charge substantial price premiums (anywhere from 200 to 300 percent more than the suggested manufacturers' prices). Large discount stores usually price furniture well below suggested manufacturers' rates—anywhere from 30 to 80 percent below. Second, showroom space is quite limited in family-owned stores relative to the large discount stores. As a result, the family-owned businesses display far less furniture, giving the consumer fewer options from which to choose. These factors make it virtually impossible for family-owned furniture stores to compete. Many of these small business owners choose to go out of business. Upon making this decision, these businesses adopt lowest-cost strategies in which they offer deep discounts to sell remaining inventories as quickly as possible. Although profit margins are lower under these circumstances, business owners are more likely to minimize losses by eliminating sooner such overhead expenses as rent, utilities, insurance, and compensation.

JVC and American Express Reinvent Themselves

Technological advances and changing consumer preferences have contributed to companies' decline. As we discussed earlier, a company can choose to allow the decline to continue until the business is no longer viable, or it can respond by reinventing itself. The Victor Company (JVC) and American Express Company are just two examples of reinvention.

The consumer electronics industry manufactures such products as stereos, video cassette recorders, and television sets. JVC invented the video cassette recorder during the 1970s using analog technology. Since then, the company's success was based on making improvements to the product (for example, from two-head to four-head models that produce higher-quality graphic resolution) and sales. Most recently, the consumer electronics industry is undergoing a tremendous shift from analog to digital technology. JVC has responded to this technological shift by developing digital versions of the video cassette recorder. Besides advanced graphics resolution, video cassette recorders based on digital technology permit the storage of substantially more information on compact disks than conventional tape media. In addition, digital video cassette recorders will permit individuals to store enormous amounts of information downloaded from the Internet at rapid rates.

Changes in preferences have led consumers to choose credit cards over charge cards. These changes created problems for the American Express Company, which is well known for charge cards. Charge card agreements require card holders to pay balances in full, typically on a monthly basis. Credit cards are based on revolving debt. Credit card holders have the option to pay balances in full, typically on a monthly basis, without paying interest charges. Alternatively, credit card holders may pay only a small percentage (usually, 5 percent or less) every month, but they pay to the credit card companies interest on remaining balances.

Credit card purchases are consistent with the trend in U.S. consumer purchasing patterns of "spend now," but "pay much later." The American Express Company has lost considerable market share and revenue because of this trend in consumer purchasing patterns. In response to changing consumer preferences, the American Express Company began offering a unique credit card in 1996—the Optima True Grace Card®. The Optima True Grace Card® is unique because it permits card holders to avoid paying interest on new purchases for 25 days even if they have an account balance. Virtually all other credit cards offer grace periods on purchases only if card holders' balances are zero. In addition, the American Express Company is using telephone sales techniques to aggressively market this credit card to current American Express charge card customers.

Evaluating the effectiveness of compensation strategies

Evaluating the effectiveness of compensation strategies is important. Compensation professionals can use evaluation information to justify continued use of effective strategies or to modify ineffective strategies. In the short run (for example, less than two years), compensation professionals analyze whether compensation strategies lead to desired employee behavior. In the long run (for example, at least two years), compensation professionals team up with top management accounting and finance officials to analyze whether employee behaviors influence the company's performance.

Our focus in this section is on the short-run evaluations because these fit well within the domain of HR practice. Although, ultimately, business leaders associate strategic analyses with company performance, it would be impossible to attribute company performance to any HR practice without short-run evaluations. Specifically, it is not possible to determine whether compensation strategies are effective (that is, improve company performance) unless we know whether the strategies first stimulated desired employee behaviors.

Short-run evaluations are based on:

☆ Measuring employee performance: vital information

☆ Performance appraisal

☆ Periodic compensation system review: Is it doing what we want it to do?

> *It is not possible to determine whether compensation strategies are effective (that is, improve company performance) unless we know whether the strategies first stimulated desired employee behaviors.*

Measuring employee performance: Vital information

Job analysis lies at the heart of performance measurement. As noted in Chapter 1, job analysis is almost purely a descriptive procedure that identifies job content. Job content describes job duties and tasks as well as such pertinent factors as skill, effort, responsibility, and working conditions (compensable factors) needed to perform the job adequately. Said another way, job content refers to the actual activities that employees must perform in the job.

Job descriptions summarize a job's purpose and list the tasks, duties, and responsibilities, as well as the skills, knowledge, and abilities necessary to perform at a minimum level. Effective job descriptions generally explain:

☆ What the employee must do to perform the job

☆ How the employee performs the job

☆ Why the employee performs the job in terms of its contribution to the functioning of the company

☆ Supervisory responsibilities, if any

☆ Contacts (and purpose of these contacts) with other employees inside or outside the company

☆ The skills, knowledge, and abilities the employee should have or must have to perform the job duties

☆ The physical and social conditions under which the employee must perform the job

Performance appraisals

Effective performance appraisals drive effective merit pay and incentive programs. The standards by which employee performance is judged should be linked to the competitive strategies a company is using. For example, each member of a product development team that is charged with the responsibility of marketing a new product might be given pay increases if certain sales goals are reached.

> *Effective performance appraisals drive effective merit pay and incentive programs. The standards by which employee performance is judged should be linked to the competitive strategies a company is using.*

Merit pay systems require specific performance appraisal approaches (Chapter 4). Administering successful merit pay programs depends as much on the supervisor's appraisal approach as on the professional's skills in designing and implementing such plans.

Companies use incentive pay to reward individual employees, teams of employees, or overall companies on the basis of their performance. Incentive pay plans are not limited solely to production or nonsupervisory workers. Many incentive plans apply to other categories of employees including sales professionals, managers, and executives. Typically, management relies on business objectives to determine incentive pay levels. Most automobile sales professionals receive incentive awards based on the attainment of three objectives:

- ✩ Number of automobiles sold
- ✩ Number of extended manufacturers' warranties sold
- ✩ Quality of customer service based on an independent assessment by market research companies

Management then communicates these planned incentive levels and performance goals to automobile sales professionals. Whereas merit pay performance standards aim to be measurable and objective, incentive levels tend to be based on even more objective criteria such as quantity of items an employee produces per production period or market indicators of a company's performance, for example, an increase in market share for the fiscal year. Moreover, supervisors communicate the incentive award amounts that correspond to objective performance levels in advance. On the other hand, supervisors generally do not communicate the merit award amounts until after they offer subjective assessments of employees' performance.

Employers who adopt pay-for-knowledge or skill-based pay programs must ensure that employees are applying the skills they have learned to jobs in the workplace. To ensure this transfer of theoretical knowledge and skills to actual performance, companies that use pay-for-knowledge and skill-based pay systems often combine them with pay-for-performance programs such as merit or incentive pay.[33] Thus, not all companies award increases to employees solely on the basis of whether they completed training successfully. As we discuss in Chapter 6, some companies that use pay-for-knowledge programs defer awarding pay increases until after employees have successfully applied their knowledge or skills to the job.

Periodic compensation system review: Is it doing what we want it to do?

Periodic review of compensation system effectiveness is important. For obvious reasons, excellent performers will generally have greater job alternatives than mediocre or poor performers. Effective compensation systems should minimize voluntary quits of exemplary performers by awarding pay commensurably with performance and meeting employees' needs with discretionary benefits programs.

Sound pay-for-knowledge and skill-based pay programs reward employees for successfully learning pertinent knowledge and skills. The selection of training topics is key to ensure that employees learn appropriate knowledge and skills.

Technological advances are likely to change the structure of jobs. Compensation professionals must adopt the appropriate job analysis techniques to accurately describe job duties, tasks, and performance standards.

TURNOVER RATES Turnover rates represent the frequencies of employment termination. **Employment termination** takes place when employees' agreement to perform work is ended. Employment terminations are voluntary or involuntary. Human resource professionals look to turnover rates as a symptom of possible problems. Usually, excessive turnover rates indicate possible problems. Judgments about whether turnover rates are excessive depend upon company size and industry. The Bureau of National Affairs *Quarterly Report on the Employment Outlook, Job Absence and Turnover* provides detailed information about turnover rates by company size and industry.

Human resource professionals want to minimize dysfunctional turnover rates. **Dysfunctional turnover** occurs whenever high-performing employees voluntarily terminate their employment, particularly when these high-performing employees take jobs in competitor companies. Human resource professionals must identify the causes of dysfunctional turnover before they can effectively reduce its occurrence.

Exit interviews provide HR professionals an opportunity to learn why employees have chosen to quit their jobs. Exhibit 2-7 shows the main factors that encourage employee turnover. For example, when general economic conditions are positive, high performers will probably have more job alternatives. Compensation professionals can use exit interviews to ascertain whether compensation practices have contributed to dysfunctional turnover.

Employees often blame poor pay and benefits for their resignations.[34] Three specific reasons related to core compensation can contribute to dysfunctional turnover. First, competitors offer substantially higher pay. Second, managers award pay increases on factors other than performance, such as politics. This practice raises questions about the procedural and distributive fairness of pay systems. As applied to compensation, **procedural fairness** refers to employees' beliefs about the appropriateness of the policies and practices used to determine pay and pay-increase amounts. **Distributive fairness** refers to employees' beliefs about the appropriateness of the actual pay and pay-increase amounts. Employees are more likely to leave when they believe that the compensation system lacks procedural and distributive fairness.

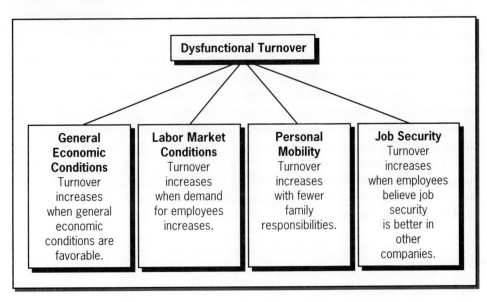

Exhibit 2-7
Factors That Lead to Dysfunctional Turnover

Third, employees perceive the job to require more effort and responsibility than actually is the case. Consequently, employees do not perceive that they are receiving sufficient compensation for their contributions.

Discretionary benefits also can contribute to dysfunctional turnover.[35] Well-designed discretionary benefits accommodate the needs of a diverse work force. As we discuss in Chapter 11, companies choose between offering one standard set of benefits to all employees or a flexible benefits program that permits each employee to have some control over the kinds of discretionary benefits coverage. For example, with an increase of dual-career couples with children, there becomes a strong need for some form of child care for preschool-aged children. However, not all employees require child care because they do not have children or their children are old enough not to require this kind of supervision. If a company were to offer a standard fixed plan of discretionary fringe compensation, then only one segment of the work force would benefit—those with very young children. Employees not needing child care assistance would be receiving a benefit of no value to them. In effect, the entire value of the benefits program would be reduced for those employees. On the other hand, a company that did not offer child care, could expect higher rates of absenteeism and turnover as employees with young children struggled to cope with child care. In either case, a standard benefits plan would not be helpful. However, a flexible plan would enable employees to receive benefits that are useful to their situation, minimizing the possible problems just mentioned. In the long run, accommodating the diverse needs of the work force has strategic value by minimizing dysfunctional turnover.

TRAINING TOPICS As we discussed, short-run evaluations examine whether employees exhibited behaviors consistent with compensation strategy. It is possible that failure to do so was a result of insufficient skills or knowledge. Human resource and compensation professionals should regularly monitor the skills and knowledge requirements of jobs, particularly if technological advances require new skills and knowledge. For example, the technology used to establish communications systems has evolved from analog to fiber optics. Northern Telecom developed and implemented training to increase field technicians' knowledge of fiber optics technology. Staying abreast of the new technology should help Northern Telecom technicians serve their clients more effectively.

ADJUSTING JOB ANALYSES AND PERFORMANCE STANDARDS Existing job analysis methods and performance standards may become obsolete as new technology changes how employees perform their jobs. Human resource professionals must adopt appropriate job analysis methods to accurately describe changing performance standards. Earlier, we discussed how the technology of advanced automated manufacturing in the automobile industry expanded the range of tasks and responsibilities, demanding higher levels of reading, writing, and computation skills than its predecessor, which required employees to possess strong hand-to-eye coordination. Today, these employees must have higher levels of reading skills than before because they must be able to read the operating and troubleshooting manuals of automated manufacturing equipment.

Summary

This chapter reviewed the strategic role of compensation in attaining competitive advantage. We reviewed the evolution of compensation from an administrative function to a strategic function, distinguished between lowest cost and differentiation, two competitive strategies companies pursue, and discussed the factors that influence competitive strategies and compensation practices—national culture, organizational culture, and organizational and product life cycle. We concluded with a discussion of compensation system evaluation. As competition increases, compensation professionals must meet the imperatives of competitive strategy by skillfully choosing compensation practices to promote the attainment of competitive advantage.

Discussion questions

1. Discuss what strategic compensation means to you.
2. Review the descriptions in Exhibit 2-2. Identify the threats and opportunities conveyed in them. For each industry, find at least one example (newspapers or business periodicals are excellent sources) that illustrates how these threats and opportunities are affecting companies. Discuss your examples in class.
3. Identify two companies: one that you believe pursues a lowest-cost strategy and another that pursues a differentiation strategy. Relying on personal knowledge, company annual reports, or articles in newspapers and business periodicals, discuss these companies' competitive strategies.
4. Discuss what tactical compensation means to you.
5. Identify three products or services with which you are familiar. Discuss whether these are in growth, maturity, or decline stages.
6. Identify and discuss other factors (besides the ones reviewed in this chapter) compensation professionals may use to conduct short-run evaluations of compensation strategies.

Key terms

scientific management
time-and-motion studies
welfare practices
competitive advantage
strategic management
strategic decisions
competitive strategy
human resource strategies
compensation strategies

tactical decisions
cost leadership strategy
lowest-cost strategy
differentiation
national culture
power distance
individualism-collectivism
uncertainty avoidance
masculinity-femininity

organizational culture
organizational and product life
  cycles
employment termination

dysfunctional turnover
procedural fairness
distributive fairness

Endnotes

[1] J. N. Baron, F. Dobbin, and P. D. Jennings, War and peace: The evolution of modern personnel administration in U.S. industry, *American Journal of Sociology* (1986): 350–383.

[2] H. S. Person, The new attitude toward management, in H. S. Person, ed., *Scientific management in American industry* (New York: Harper & Brothers, 1929).

[3] U.S. Bureau of Labor Statistics, *Welfare work for employees in industrial establishments in the United States,* Bulletin No. 250 (Washington, D.C.: U.S. Government Printing Office, 1919), pp. 119–123.

[4] H. Eilbirt, The development of personnel management in the United States, *Business History Review* 33 (1959):345–364.

[5] J. Pfeffer, Producing sustainable competitive advantage through the effective management of people, *Academy of Management Executive* 9 (1995):55–69.

[6] A. P. Carnevale, and J. W. Johnston, *Training in America: Strategies for the nation* (Alexandria, Virg.: National Center on Education and the Economy and The American Society for Training and Development, 1989).

[7] Pfeffer, Producing sustainable competitive advantage through the effective management of people.

[8] C. A. Lengnick-Hall and M. L. Lengnick-Hall, *Interactive Human Resource Management and Strategic Planning* (New York: Quorum Books, 1990).

[9] J. E. Dutton and S. E. Jackson, The categorization of strategic issues by decision makers and its links to organizational action, *Academy of Management Review* 12 (1987): 76–90.

[10] I. Reichlin and A. Rothman, Even Lufthansa is carrying too much baggage, *Business Week,* September 7, 1992, p. 80.

[11] W. Zellner, Penney's rediscovers its calling (good quality at lower prices), *Business Week,* April 5, 1993, pp. 51–52.

[12] R. S. Schuler and S. E. Jackson, Linking competitive strategies with human resource management practices, *Academy of Management Executive* 1 (1987):207–219.

[13] Ibid.

[14] Ibid.

[15] L.R. Gòmez-Mejìa and T. Welbourne, Compensation strategies in a global context, *Human Resource Planning* 14 (1991):29–41.

[16] G. Hofstede, *Culture's consequences* (Newbury Park, Calif.: Sage, 1980).

[17] V. Terpstra and K. David, *The cultural environment of international business,* 3rd ed. (Cincinnati: South-Western Publishing, 1991).

[18] J. P. Muczyk and R. E. Hastings, In defense of enlightened hardball management, *Business Horizons,* July/August, 1985, pp. 23–29.

[19] R. L. Heneman, *Merit pay: Linking pay increases to performance ratings* (Reading, Mass.: Addison-Wesley, 1992).

[20] L. Smircich, Concepts of culture and organizational analysis, *Administrative Science Quarterly* 28 (1983):339–358.

[21] S. Marcus, Delayering: More than meets the eye, *Perspectives* 3 (1991):22–26.

[22] J. Rosow and R. Zager, *Training—The competitive edge* (San Francisco: Jossey-Bass, 1988).

[23] H. H. Risher and R. J. Butler, Salary banding: An alternative salary-management concept, *ACA Journal* 2 (Winter 1993/94): 48–57.

[24] S. E. Jackson, Team composition in organizational settings: Issues in managing an increasingly diverse work force, in S. Worchel, W. Wood, and J. A. Simpson, eds., *Group process and productivity* (Newbury Park, Calif.: Sage, 1992), pp. 138–173.

[25] R. M. Kanter, When a thousand flowers bloom: Structural, collective, and social conditions for innovation in organizations, in B. M. Staw and L. L. Cummings, eds., *Research in organizational behavior,* vol. 10 (Greenwich, Conn.: JAI Press, 1988), pp. 169–211.

[26] S. Worchel, W. Wood, and J. A. Simpson, (eds.), *Group process and productivity* (Newbury Park, Calif.: Sage, 1992).

[27] J. Kanin-Lovers and M. Cameron, Team-based reward systems. *Journal of Compen-*

sation and Benefits, January–February, 1993, pp. 55–60.

[28] R. S. Schuler, Strategic human resource management and industrial relations, *Human Relations* 42 (1989):157–184.

[29] D. E. Comer, *The Internet book* (Englewood Cliffs, N.J.: Prentice Hall, 1995).

[30] J. R. Galbraith, Strategy and organizational planning, *Human Resource Management* 22 (1983):63–77.

[31] U.S. Chamber of Commerce, *Employee benefits 1995 edition: Survey data from benefit year 1994* (Washington, D.C.: U.S. Chamber of Commerce Research Center, 1995).

[32] C. Peck, *Variable pay: Nontraditional programs for motivation and reward* (New York: The Conference Board, 1993).

[33] J. R. Schuster and P. K. Zingheim, *The new pay: Linking employee and organizational performance* (New York: Lexington Books, 1992).

[34] P. W. Hom and R. W. Griffeth, *Employee turnover* (Cincinnati: South-Western College Publishing, 1995).

[35] Ibid.

CHAPTER

THREE

Contextual influences on compensation practice

CHAPTER OUTLINE

In this chapter, you will learn about

1. Compensation and the social good
2. Various laws that influence private sector companies' and labor unions' compensation practices
3. Contextual influences on the federal government's compensation practices
4. Labor unions' influence on companies' compensation practices
5. Market factors' impact on companies' compensation practices

As competition increased in the textile industry, the original concern of the mill owners for their employees gave way to stricter controls that had nothing to do with the well-being of the workers. Employers reduced wages, lengthened hours, and intensified work. For a work day from 11.5 to 13 hours, making up an average week of 75 hours, the women operatives were generally earning less than $1.50 a week (exclusive of board) by the late 1840s, and they were being compelled to tend four looms, whereas in the 1830s they had taken care of only two. . . . [The manager] ordered them [the female textile workers] to come before breakfast. "I regard my work-people just as I regard my machinery. So long as they can do my work for what I choose to pay them, I keep them, getting out of them all I can." [1]

> Anne Brown, the claims department manager of a small insurance company, said to Bill Smith, the human resource manager, "I'm sick and tired of having secretaries who just don't work out. The quality of their work is not very good, nor are they reliable—they are frequently absent or late. They are limiting my ability to maintain timely and accurate claims processing." Bill replied, "You get no argument from me. It's been nearly impossible to recruit top-quality secretarial candidates ever since ABC Automobile Parts Company established a manufacturing facility across town. After all, ABC's secretaries earn nearly 40 percent more than our secretaries."

The preceding quotations illustrate three major contextual influences on companies' compensation practices. The first quotation captures the inherent conflict between employers and employees: employers' profit maximization objective and employees' desire for equitable and fair treatment. This conflict gave rise to the first two contextual influences that we will review in this chapter, federal protective legislation and labor unions.

The second quotation represents a third contextual influence: market forces. In particular, this quotation illustrates a potential consequence of interindustry compensation differentials—the inability to recruit top-quality employees. We will address these differentials later in the chapter.

Compensation promotes the social good by enabling citizens to actively participate as consumers in the economy. But conflicting goals among employees, employers, and government can threaten the social good.

Compensation and the social good

The term *social good* refers to a booming economy, low levels of unemployment, progressive wages and benefits, and safe and healthful working conditions. Compensation promotes the social good by enabling citizens to actively participate as consumers in the economy. But conflicting goals among employees, employers, and government can threaten the social good. Exhibit 3-1 illustrates the relationships among employ-

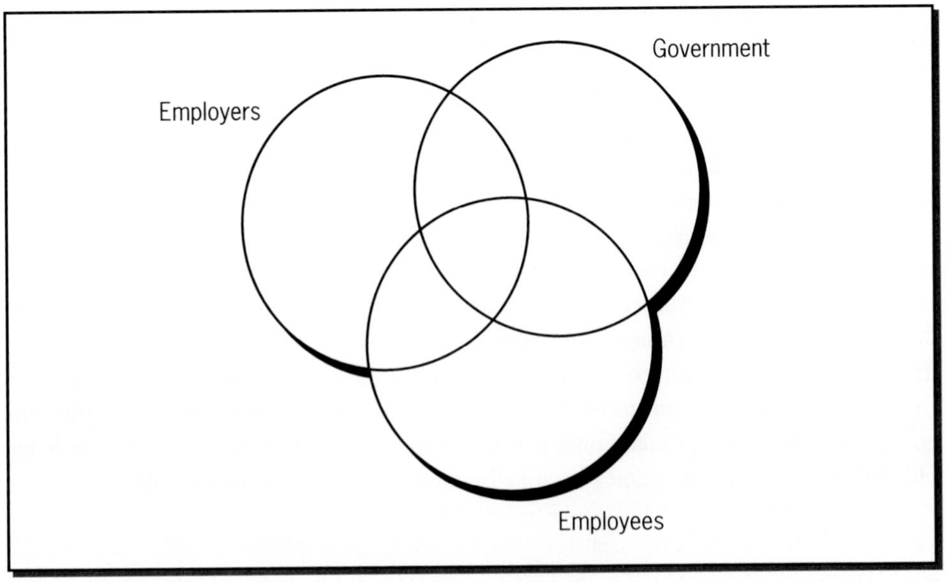

Exhibit 3-1
**Employers', Employees',
and Government's Goals**

ees', employers', and government's goals.[2] The overlapping areas represent the mutual goals between any two or all three groups. The nonoverlapping areas represent unique goals that can undermine the social good.

Employees, employers, and government do share some common goals. Each group wants a booming economy. Employers' profits and demand for their products and services tend to be high within booming economies. Employees prosper because unemployment is low, and they tend to have confidence in the future, which leads to higher spending. Higher income tax revenues enable the government to fund programs—for example, national defense—and government employees' compensation packages.

Employees' goals

Employees' fundamental goal is to attain high wages, comprehensive benefits, safe and healthful work conditions, and job security. Before the 1930s, employees did not possess the right to negotiate with their employers over terms and conditions of employment. As a result, many workers were subjected to poor working conditions, low pay, and excessive work hours[3]—as illustrated by the first opening quotation. Unemployment was employees' main alternative to enduring these conditions. Today, employment legislation and labor unions protect workers' rights and status. Thus, employer abuses are much less prevalent than before the passage of legislation and the rise in labor unions. Nevertheless, employers still maintain the fundamental profit maximization objective, which necessitates legal and labor union impacts.

Employers' goals

The employers depicted in Exhibit 3-1 are private sector companies. Private sector employers strive to increase profits, market shares, and returns on investment. These employers expect workers to be as productive as possible and to produce the highest quality products or services. The majority of U.S. civilian employees work under this objective. In 1994, 83 percent of all U.S. civilian employees worked for private sector businesses.[4]

Government's goals

The government's ultimate goal is to promote the social good without extensive involvement in private sector employers' operations. It must operate as both an employer and consumer to achieve the social good. In 1994, the government employed 17 percent—nearly 20 million employees—of all U.S. civilian employees to ensure national security and legal compliance.[5]

In addition, the government is both a buyer and consumer of the products and services that private sector companies produce. The federal government's expenditures on such items have increased tremendously—from $500 billion in 1980 to $1.5 trillion in 1995.[6] The government uses energy to run its buildings, and it engages in contracts with private sector companies for a multitude of goods and services ranging from building construction to multimillion-dollar defense systems. For example, the government relies on private construction companies for erecting new and repairing old buildings and on companies such as Lockheed for defense armaments.

Employment laws that influence compensation practices

The federal constitution forms the basis for employment laws.

Employment laws establish bounds of acceptable employment practices as well as employee rights. The federal constitution forms the basis for employment laws. The following section and three amendments of the Constitution are most applicable:

Article I, Section 8. The Congress shall have Power . . . To regulate Commerce with foreign Nations, and among the several States, and with the Indian Tribes. . .

First Amendment. Congress shall make no law respecting an establishment of religion, or prohibiting the free exercise thereof; or abridging the freedom of speech, or of the press; or the right of the people peaceably to assemble, and to petition the Government for a redress of grievances.

Fifth Amendment. No person shall . . . be deprived of life, liberty, or property, without due process of law . . .

Fourteenth Amendment, Section 1 . . . No state shall make or enforce any law which shall abridge the privileges or immunities of citizens of the United States; nor shall any State deprive any person of life, liberty, or property without due process of law; nor deny any person within its jurisdiction the equal protection of the laws.

The United States government is organized at three levels roughly defined by geographic scope:

★ Federal

★ State

★ Local

A single **federal government** oversees the entire United States and its territories. The vast majority of laws that influence compensation were established at the federal level. Next, individual **state governments** enact and enforce laws that pertain exclusively to their respective regions, for example, Illinois and Michigan. Finally, **local governments** enact and enforce laws that are most pertinent to smaller geographic regions, for example, Champaign County in Illinois and the city of Los Angeles. Many of the federal laws have counterparts in state and local legislation. State and local legislation may be concurrent with federal law, or it may exist in the absence of similar federal legislation. Federal law prevails wherever state or local laws are inconsistent with federal legislation.

The federal government has three branches:

☆ Legislative

☆ Executive

☆ Judicial

Congress creates and passes laws within the legislative branch. The **executive branch** enforces the laws of various quasilegislative and judicial agencies and through executive orders. The President of the United States possesses the authority to establish **executive orders** that influence the operation of the federal government and companies that are engaged in business relationships with the federal government. The judicial branch is responsible for interpreting the laws. The U.S. Supreme Court, which consists of nine life-appointed justices, is the forum for these interpretations.

Federal laws that apply to compensation practices are grouped according to key themes:

☆ Income continuity, safety, and work hours

☆ Pay discrimination

☆ Accommodating disabilities and family needs

☆ Prevailing wage laws

Income continuity, safety, and work hours

Three factors led to the passage of income continuity, safety, and work hours legislation: the Great Depression, the move from family businesses to large factories, and divisions of labor within factories. During the **Great Depression,** which took place during the 1930s, scores of businesses failed, and most workers became chronically unemployed. Government enacted key legislation designed to stabilize individuals' income when they became unemployed because of poor business conditions or workplace injuries. The *Social Security Act of 1935 (Title IX)* provided temporary income to workers who became unemployed through no fault of their own. Workers' compensation programs granted income to workers who were unable to work because of injuries sustained while on the job. Supporting workers during these misfortunes promoted the well-being of the economy: These income provisions enabled the unemployed to participate in the economy as consumers of essential goods and services. We will defer a more detailed discussion of the Social Security Act of 1935 and workers' compensation laws until Chapter 10 because these laws represent legally required employee benefits.

Second, the main U.S. economic activity before the twentieth century consisted of agriculture and small family businesses that were organized along craft lines. Workers began to move from their farms and small family businesses to capitalists' factories for employment. The character of work changed dramatically with workers' moves to factories. Individuals' status changed from owners to employees. This status change meant that individuals lost control over their earnings and working conditions.

Third, the factory system also created divisions of labor characterized by differences in skills and responsibilities. Some workers received training; others did not.

Workers with higher skills and responsibilities did not necessarily earn larger wages than workers with lower skills and responsibilities. Paying some workers more than others only increased costs, which factory owners avoided whenever possible.

In sum, factory workers received very low wages, and the working conditions were often unsafe. Factory workers received low wages and worked in unsafe conditions because factory owners sought to maximize profits. Offering workers high wages and providing safe working conditions would have cut into factory owners' profits. These conditions led to the passage of the **Fair Labor Standards Act of 1938.** The FLSA addresses major abuses that intensified during the Great Depression and the transition from agricultural to industrial enterprises. These include substandard pay, excessive work hours, and the employment of children in oppressive working conditions.

FAIR LABOR STANDARDS ACT OF 1938 The FLSA addresses three broad issues:

- ✮ Minimum wage
- ✮ Overtime pay
- ✮ Child labor provisions

The Department of Labor enforces the FLSA.

Minimum wage The purpose of the minimum wage provision is to ensure a minimally acceptable standard of living for workers. The original minimum wage was $0.25 per hour. Since the act's passage in 1938, the federal government has raised the minimum wage several times. The most recent minimum wage increase, to $5.15 per hour, was signed into law in August of 1996. The change from $0.25 per hour to $5.15 per hour represents a 1,960 percent minimum wage increase! Unfortunately, most minimum wage earners cannot sustain a minimally acceptable standard of living because the costs of goods and services have increased at a much greater rate.

Let's look at some examples.[7] Consider both the minimum wage increase and the cost-of-living increase between 1983 and 1993. The minimum wage was $3.35 per hour in 1983, and $4.25 in 1993, representing a 27 percent increase. At first glance, it appears that purchasing power increased by 27 percent over this 10-year period. That conclusion would be correct if the prices of goods and services did not increase between 1983 and 1993. But the cost of living increased dramatically during this period. In 1993, one dollar, on average, purchased only 70 percent as much as it could in 1983. Said another way, the purchasing power of the dollar eroded by 30 percent between 1983 and 1993. Inflation outpaced the value of the dollar.

The increase in cost of living relative to the increase in minimum wage is devastating when we consider the federal government's annual poverty threshold. The **poverty threshold** represents the minimum annual earnings needed to afford housing and other basic necessities. An individual who was earning the 1993 minimum wage of $4.25 had an annual income of $8,840 ($4.25 per hour × 40 hours per week × 52 weeks). The annual poverty threshold in 1993 for single individuals (that is, unmarried without any dependents) was $7,363. In 1993, a single person's minimum wage income exceeded the poverty threshold by a mere $1,500.

The picture for individuals with dependents is even bleaker. Let's consider an individual who supports a family of three on minimum wage earnings. This individual's minimum wage income fell below the 1993 poverty threshold—$11,522—by more

The change from $0.25 per hour to $5.15 per hour represents a 1,960 percent minimum wage increase! Unfortunately, most minimum wage earners cannot sustain a minimally acceptable standard of living because the costs of goods and services have increased at a much greater rate.

The Minimum Wage Debate

Over the years, there have been several heated debates in Washington, D.C., about the merits of raising the minimum wage. Some oppose a minimum wage hike. Others support a minimum wage increase. Opponents believe that raising the minimum wage would lead to higher unemployment rates: Increasing the minimum wage would raise companies' costs, cutting into profits. Companies would increase prices to offset the higher costs. However, the price increases may be high enough to reduce consumers' demand for these companies' products and services. In turn, business activity would decrease, necessitating layoffs. Extremists have argued that the government should abolish the minimum wage altogether, allowing market forces to determine its level.

Advocates argue for a higher minimum wage—a living wage—to provide unskilled workers a better standard of living. They believe that government intervention is essential to achieving that goal: Most minimum wage earners possess low skill levels, so their job alternatives are limited. The combination of low skill levels and limited alternatives restricts their ability to bargain with employers for higher wages.

In addition, most minimum wage earners reside in large cities such as Boston and Los Angeles, where the cost of living is much higher than the national average. Consequently, these minimum wage earners require such government subsidies as food stamps to afford basic necessities. Thus, advocates of a higher minimum wage call for a living wage that would greatly reduce the need for government subsidies.

than $2,600. Exhibit 3-2 illustrates the difference between annual minimum wage earnings and annual poverty thresholds based on a family of three for selected years. These figures indicate that minimum wage earnings became less adequate over time as the annual poverty threshold rose. As an aside, the income status of minimum wage earners worsens with additional dependents.

YEAR	FEDERAL MINIMUM HOURLY WAGE	ANNUAL MINIMUM WAGE EARNINGS (hourly min. wage × 40 hr/week × 52 weeks) A	ANNUAL POVERTY THRESHOLD (family of three) B	DIFFERENCE A – B
1980	$3.10	$6,448	$6,565	–$ 117
1986	$3.35	$6,968	$8,737	–$1,769
1989	$3.35	$6,968	$9,885	–$2,917
1990	$3.80	$7,904	$10,419	–$2,515
1992	$4.25	$8,840	$11,186	–$2,346
1994	$4.25	$8,840	$11,542	–$2,702

Exhibit 3-2
Differences between Annual Minimum Wage Earnings and Annual Poverty Thresholds for Selected Years

Source: U.S. Department of Commerce, *Statistical abstracts of the United States*, 115th ed. (Washington, D.C.: U.S. Government Printing Office, 1995).

Specific FLSA exemptions permit employers to pay some workers less than the minimum wage. Students employed in retail or service businesses, on farms, or in institutions of higher education may be paid less than the minimum wage with the consent of the Department of Labor. With explicit permission from the Department of Labor, employers can pay less than the minimum wage for trainee positions or to prevent a reduction in the employment of mentally or physically disabled individuals. Exhibit 3-3 lists the six factors that define trainees.

Overtime provisions The FLSA requires that employers pay workers at a rate equal to time and one-half for all hours worked in excess of 40 hours within a seven-day period. For example, a worker's regular hourly rate is $10 for working 40 hours or less within a seven-day period. The FLSA requires the employer to pay this employee $15 per hour for each additional hour worked beyond the regular 40 hours within this seven-day period.

There are some general exceptions to this rule: Negotiated overtime pay rates contained within collective bargaining agreements prevail over the one and one-half time rule. In health care facilities, a base work period is 80 hours during 14 consecutive days rather than 40 hours during seven consecutive days. Workers in health facilities receive overtime base pay for each hour worked over 80 within a 14-day period.

The overtime provisions and basic exceptions are based on employees' working set hours during fixed work periods. However, many employees work irregular hours that fluctuate from week to week (Chapter 14). A Supreme Court ruling *(Walling v. A. H. Belo Corp.)*[8] requires that employers guarantee fixed weekly pay when the following conditions prevail:

☆ The employer typically cannot determine the number of hours employees will work each week, and

☆ The work week period fluctuates both above and below 40 hours per week

Overtime work becomes necessary when employees cannot meet higher than normal work loads during the standard work week. Often, overtime pay is typically more cost effective than hiring additional permanent employees: Companies pay a fixed amount to provide employees fringe benefits. In other words, benefits costs generally do not increase with the number of hours worked. Overtime practices increase wage costs. However, hiring additional permanent workers leads to higher total wage and

---

Exhibit 3-3
Six Defining Factors of Trainee for the FLSA

- The training, even though it includes actual operation of the employers' facilities, is similar to that which would be provided in a vocational school.
- The training is for the benefit of the trainee.
- The trainee does not displace regular employees but works under closer supervision.
- The employer providing the training gains no immediate advantage from the trainees' activities; on occasion, the employer's operation may in fact be hindered.
- The trainee is not guaranteed a job at the completion of the training.
- The employer and the trainee understand that the employer is not obligated to pay wages during the training period.

Source: J.E. Kalet, *Primer on wage and hour laws* (Washington, D.C.: Bureau of National Affairs, 1987).

fixed fringe benefits costs. Awarding existing employees overtime pay also is less expensive than hiring temporary workers. Temporary workers may be less productive in the short run because they are not familiar with specific company work procedures.

The overtime provision does not apply to all jobs. In general, administrative, professional, and executive employees are **exempt** from the FLSA overtime and minimum wage provisions. Exhibit 3-4 describes criteria that exempt executive, administrative, and professional jobs from this act. Most other jobs are nonexempt. **Nonexempt** jobs are subject to the FLSA overtime pay provision.

Classifying jobs as either exempt or nonexempt is not always clear-cut. In *Aaron v. City of Wichita, Kansas,*[9] the city contended that its fire chiefs were exempt as executives under the FLSA because they spent more than 80 percent of their work hours managing the fire department. The fire chiefs maintained that they should not be exempt from the FLSA because they do not possess the authority to hire, fire, authorize shift trades, give pay raises, or make policy decisions. The court offered several criteria to determine whether these fire chiefs were exempt employees, including the:

✯ Relative importance of management as opposed to other duties

✯ Frequency with which they exercised discretionary powers

✯ Relative freedom from supervision

✯ Relationship between their salaries and wages paid to other employees for similar nonexempt work

---

Exhibit 3-4
FLSA Exemption Criteria for Executive, Administrative, and Professional Employees

EXECUTIVE EMPLOYEES

- Primary duties include managing the organization
- Regularly supervise the work of two or more full-time employees
- Authority to hire, promote, and discharge employees
- Regularly use discretion as part of typical work duties
- Devote at least 80 percent of work time to fulfilling the previous activities

ADMINISTRATIVE EMPLOYEES

- Perform nonmanual work directly related to management operations
- Regularly use discretion beyond clerical duties
- Perform specialized or technical work, or perform special assignments with only general supervision
- Devote at least 80 percent of work time to fulfilling the previous activities

PROFESSIONAL EMPLOYEES

- Primary work requires advanced knowledge in a field of science or learning, including work that requires regular use of discretion and independent judgment, or
- Primary work requires inventiveness, imagination, or talent in a recognized field or artistic endeavor

Source: 29 Code of Federal Regulations, Sec. 541.3. 29; Sec. 541.1.

On the basis of these criteria, the court determined that the City of Wichita improperly exempted fire chiefs from the FLSA overtime pay provisions.

The federal government broadened the scope of the FLSA twice since 1938 through the passage of two acts:

✯ Portal-to-Portal Act of 1947

✯ Equal Pay Act of 1963

The **Portal-to-Portal Act of 1947** defines the term *hours worked* that appears in the FLSA. Exhibit 3-5 lists the compensable activities that precede and follow the primary work activities. For example, time spent by state correctional officers caring for police dogs at home is compensable under the FLSA *(Andrews v. DuBois).*[10] The care of dogs, including feeding, grooming, and walking is indispensable to maintaining dogs as a critical law enforcement tool; it is part of officers' principal activities; and it benefits the Corrections Department. However, the district court in Massachusetts ruled that time spent by state correction canine handlers transporting dogs between home and correctional facilities is not compensable under FLSA.

The Equal Pay Act of 1963 prohibits sex discrimination in pay for employees performing equal work. We will discuss the Equal Pay Act of 1963 later in this chapter.

Child labor provisions The FLSA child labor provisions protect children from being overworked, working in potentially hazardous settings, and having their education jeopardized because of excessive work hours. The restrictions vary by age:

✯ Children under age 14 usually cannot be employed.

✯ Children ages 14 and 15 may work in safe occupations outside school hours, or their work does not exceed three hours on a school day (18 hours per week while school is in session). When school is not in session, as in the summer, children cannot work more than 40 hours per week.

✯ Children ages 16 and 17 do not have hourly restrictions; however, they cannot work in hazardous jobs: for example, jobs that require the use of heavy industrial equipment or involve exposure to harmful substances.

WORK HOURS AND SAFETY STANDARDS ACT OF 1962 The **Work Hours and Safety Standards Act of 1962** covers all laborers and mechanics who are employed by contractors who meet the following criterion: Federal loans or grants fund part or all of

Exhibit 3-5
Compensable Activities That Precede and Follow Primary Work Activities

- The time spent on the activity was for the employee's benefit.
- The employer controlled the amount of time spent.
- The time involved is categorized as "suffered and permitted," meaning that the employer knew the employee was working on incidental tasks either before or after the scheduled tour of duty.
- The time spent was requested by the employer.
- The time spent is an integral part of the employee's principal duties.
- The employer has a union contract with employees providing such compensation, or, as a matter of custom or practice, the employer has compensated the activities in the past.

the contracts. The act requires that contractors pay employees one and one-half times their regular hourly rate for each hour worked in excess of 40 hours per week.

MCNAMARA-O'HARA SERVICE CONTRACT ACT OF 1965 The **McNamara-O'Hara Service Contract Act of 1965** applies to all contractors who employ service workers. The term *contractor* refers to companies doing business with the United States. For this act, service employees work in recognized trades or crafts other than skilled mechanical or manual jobs. Plumbers and electricians are recognized trades workers. The act contains two main provisions: First, all contractors must pay at least the minimum wage as specified in the FLSA. Second, contractors holding contracts with the federal government that exceed $2,500 in value must pay the local prevailing wages. In addition, contractors must offer fringe compensation equal to the local prevailing benefits.

Pay discrimination

The civil rights movement of the 1960s led to the passage of key legislation designed to protect designated classes of employees and to uphold their rights individually against discriminatory employment decisions. Some of these laws, such as the Civil Rights Act of 1964, apply to all employment-related decisions (recruitment, selection, performance appraisal, compensation, and termination). Other laws, such as the Equal Pay Act of 1963, apply specifically to compensation practices. These laws limit employers' authority over employment decisions.

The civil rights movement of the 1960s led to the passage of key legislation designed to protect designated classes of employees and to uphold their rights individually against discriminatory employment decisions.

EQUAL PAY ACT OF 1963 Congress enacted the **Equal Pay Act of 1963** to remedy a serious problem of employment discrimination in private industry: "Many segments of American industry have been based on an ancient but outmoded belief that a man, because of his role in society, should be paid more than a woman even though his duties are the same." [11] The Equal Pay Act of 1963 is based on a simple principle. Men and women should receive equal pay for performing equal work.

The Equal Employment Opportunity Commission (EEOC) enforces the Equal Pay Act of 1963. The EEOC possesses the authority to investigate and reconcile charges of illegal discrimination. The act applies to all employers and labor organizations. In particular,

> No employer . . . shall discriminate within any establishment in which such employees are employed, between employees on the basis of sex by paying wages to employees in such establishment at a rate less than the rate at which he pays wages to employees of the opposite sex . . . for equal work on jobs the performance of which requires equal skill, effort, and responsibility, and which are performed under similar working conditions (29 USC 206, Section 6, (d))

The Equal Pay Act of 1963 pertains explicitly to jobs of *equal* worth. Companies assign pay rates to jobs according to the levels of skill, effort, responsibility, and working conditions. Skill, effort, responsibility, and working conditions represent compensable factors. The U.S. Department of Labor's definitions of these compensable factors are listed in Exhibit 3-6.

How do we judge whether jobs are equal? The case *EEOC v. Madison Community Unit School District No. 12* [12] sheds light on this important issue. The school district paid female athletic coaches of girls' sports teams less than it paid male athletic coaches of boys' teams. The judge concluded:

FACTOR	DEFINITION
Skill	Experience, training, education, and ability as measured by the performance requirements of a job
Effort	The amount of mental or physical effort expended in the performance of a job
Responsibility	The degree of accountability required in the performance of a job
Working conditions	The physical surroundings and hazards of a job, including dimensions such as inside versus outside work, heat, cold, and poor ventilation

Source: U.S. Department of Labor, *Equal pay for equal work under the Fair Labor Standards Act* (Washington, D.C.: U.S. Government Printing Office, December 31, 1971).

The jobs that are compared must be in some sense the same to count as "equal work" under the Equal Pay Act of 1963; and here we come to the main difficulty in applying the Act; whether two jobs are the same depends on how fine a system of job classification the courts will accept. If coaching an athletic team in the Madison, Illinois school system is considered a single job rather than a [collection] of jobs, the school district violated the Equal Pay Act prima facie by paying female holders of this job less than male holders. . . . If on the other hand coaching the girls' tennis team is considered a different job from coaching the boys' tennis team, and if coaching the girls' volleyball or basketball team is considered a different job (or jobs) from coaching the boys' soccer team, there is no prima facie violation. So the question is how narrow a definition of job the courts should be using in deciding whether the Equal Pay Act is applicable.

We can get some guidance from the language of the Act. The Act requires that the jobs compared have "similar working conditions," not the same working conditions. This implies that some comparison of different jobs is possible. . . . Since the working conditions need not be "equal," the jobs need not be completely identical. . . .

Above the lowest rank of employee, every employee has a somewhat different job from every other one, even if the two employees being compared are in the same department. So, if "equal work" and "equal skill, effort, and responsibility" were taken literally, the Act would have a minute domain. . . .

The courts have thus had to steer a narrow course. The cases do not require an absolute identity between the jobs, but do require substantial identity.

Pay differentials for equal work are not always illegal. Pay differentials between men and women who are performing equal work are acceptable where

such payment is made pursuant to (i) a seniority system; (ii) merit system, (iii) a system which measures earnings by quantity or quality of production; or (iv) a differential based on any other factor other than sex: *Provided,* that an employer who is paying a wage rate differential . . . shall not . . . reduce the wage rate of any employee. (29 USC 206, Section 6, (d))

As an aside, **comparable worth** is the subject of an ongoing debate in American society that differs from the issues addressed in the Equal Pay Act of 1963. The debate centers on the pervasive pay differentials between men and women who perform comparable, but not equal, work.[13] In a nutshell, jobs held predominantly by women are paid at substantially lower rates than jobs held predominantly by men that require comparable skill, effort, responsibility, and working conditions. Researchers have compared female-dominated jobs with male-dominated jobs: for example:

- ✯ Nurses and tree trimmers
- ✯ Clerical workers and parking lot attendants
- ✯ Clerk typists and delivery van drivers

These comparisons showed that female-dominated jobs are paid about the same as male-dominated jobs that require comparable skill, effort, responsibility, and working conditions. Comparable-worth advocates maintain that employers should pay employees holding predominantly female jobs the same as employees holding predominantly male jobs if these jobs require comparable skills, effort, responsibility, and working conditions.

Two compensation practices have played a large role in fueling the comparable-worth debate: job evaluation (Chapter 7) and companies' reliance on market rates for setting pay (Chapter 8). We will revisit the comparable-worth debate in Chapter 8 after covering job evaluation and compensation survey practices.

CIVIL RIGHTS ACT OF 1964 The **Civil Rights Act of 1964** is a comprehensive piece of legislation. **Title VII** of the Civil Rights Act is the most pertinent to compensation. Legislators designed Title VII to promote equal employment opportunities for underrepresented minorities. According to Title VII:

It shall be an unlawful employment practice for an employer—

(1) to fail or refuse to hire or to discharge any individual, or otherwise to discriminate against any individual with respect to his compensation, terms, conditions, or privileges of employment, because of such individual's race, color, religion, sex, or national origin; or

(2) to limit, segregate, or classify his employees or applicants for employment in any way which would deprive or tend to deprive any individual of employment opportunities or otherwise adversely affect his status as an employee, because of such individual's race, color, religion, sex, or national origin. (42 USC 2000e-2, Section 703)

The courts have distinguished between two types of discrimination covered by Title VII: disparate treatment and disparate impact. **Disparate treatment** represents intentional discrimination, occurring whenever employers intentionally treat some workers less favorably than others because of their race, color, sex, national origin, or religion. Applying different standards to determine pay increases for blacks and whites may result in disparate treatment. For example, awarding pay increases to blacks according to seniority and to whites according to performance may lead to disparate treatment, particularly if blacks have significantly less seniority than whites.

Disparate impact represents unintentional discrimination. It occurs whenever an employer applies an employment practice to all employees, but the practice leads to unequal treatment of protected employee groups. Awarding pay increases to male and female production workers according to seniority could lead to disparate impact if females had less seniority, on average, than men.

Title VII applies to companies with 15 or more employees, employment agencies, and labor unions. Title VII excludes employees of the U.S. government. The EEOC enforces the Civil Rights Act.

BENNETT AMENDMENT The **Bennett Amendment** is a 1964 amendment to Title VII that allows employees to charge employers with Title VII violations regarding pay only when the employer has violated the Equal Pay Act of 1963. The Bennett Amendment was necessary because lawmakers could not agree on the answers to the following questions:

- ✯ Does Title VII incorporate both the Equal Pay Act of 1963's equal pay standard and the four defenses for unequal work [(i) a seniority system; (ii) a merit system, (iii) a system which measures earnings by quantity or quality of production; (iv) a differential based on any other factor other than sex]? or,

- ✯ Does Title VII include only the four Equal Pay Act of 1963 exceptions?

Some lawmakers believed that Title VII incorporates the equal pay standard (that is, answering Yes to the first question and No to the second question). Other lawmakers believed that Title VII did *not* incorporate the equal pay standard (that is, answering No to the first question and Yes to the second question). If Title VII did not incorporate the equal pay standard, then employees could raise charges of illegal discrimination (on the basis of race, religion, color, sex, or national origin) for unequal jobs.

EXECUTIVE ORDER 11246 **Executive Order 11246** extends Title VII standards to contractors holding government contracts worth more than $10,000 per year. In addition, Executive Order 11246, signed into law in 1965, imposes additional requirements on contractors with government contracts worth more than $50,000 per year and who have 50 or more employees. These contractors must develop written plans each year—affirmative action plans. Contractors specify in affirmative action plans goals and practices that they will use to avoid or reduce Title VII discrimination over time.

AGE DISCRIMINATION IN EMPLOYMENT ACT OF 1967 (AMENDED IN 1978, 1986, 1990) Congress passed the **Age Discrimination in Employment Act of 1967 (ADEA)** to protect workers age 40 and older from illegal discrimination. This act provides protection to a large segment of the U.S. population known as the baby boom generation, or "baby boomers." The baby boom generation was born roughly between 1942 and 1964, representing a swell in the American population. Some members of the baby boom generation reached age 40 in 1982. By the year 2004, all members of the baby boom cohort will be at least age 40.

A large segment of the population will probably continue to work beyond age 65, the "traditional" retirement age, because many fear that Social Security retirement income (Chapter 10) will not provide adequate support. The U.S. Census Bureau predicts that individuals aged 65 and over will increase from about 32 million in 1992 (12.6 percent of the population) to about 70 million (20.7 percent of the population) by 2030.[14] Thus, the ADEA should be extremely relevant for some time to come.

The ADEA established guidelines prohibiting age-related discrimination in employment. Its purpose is "to promote the employment of older persons based on their ability rather than age, to prohibit arbitrary age discrimination in employment, and to help employers and workers find ways of meeting problems arising from the impact of age on employment."[15] The ADEA specifies that it is unlawful for an employer:

(1) to fail or refuse to hire or to discharge any individual or otherwise discriminate against any individual with respect to his compensation, terms, conditions, or privileges of employment, because of such individual's age;

(2) to limit, segregate or classify his employees in any way which would deprive or tend to deprive any individual of employment opportunities or otherwise adversely affect his status as an employee, because of such individual's age; or

(3) to reduce the wage rate of any employee in order to comply with this Act. (29 USC 623, Section 4)

The ADEA applies to employee benefits practices as well:

Any employer must provide that any employee aged 65 or older, and any employee's spouse aged 65 or older, shall be entitled to coverage under any group health plan offered to such employees under the same conditions as any employee, and the spouse of such employee, under age 65. (29 USC 623, Section 4, paragraph (g)(1))

The ADEA also sets limits on the development and implementation of employers' "early retirement" practices, which many companies use to reduce their work force. Most early retirement programs are offered to employees who are at least 55 years of age. These early retirement programs are permissible when companies offer them to employees on a voluntary basis. Forcing early retirement upon older workers represents age discrimination *(EEOC v. Chrysler).*[16]

The **Older Workers Benefit Protection Act (OWBPA)**—the 1990 amendment to the ADEA—placed additional restrictions on employers' benefits practices. Under particular circumstances, employers can require older employees to pay more for health care insurance coverage than younger employees. This practice is permissible when older workers collectively do not make proportionately larger contributions than the younger workers.[17] Moreover, employers can legally reduce older workers' life insurance coverage only if the costs for providing insurance to them is significantly greater than the cost for younger workers. Further, the OWBPA enacts the **equal benefit or equal cost principle:** Employers must offer benefits to older workers that are equal to or more than the benefits given to younger workers with one exception. The OWBPA does not require employers to provide equal or more benefits to older workers when the costs to do so are greater than for younger workers.

The ADEA covers private employers with 20 or more employees, labor unions with 25 or more members, and employment agencies. The EEOC enforces this act.

EXECUTIVE ORDER 11141 **Executive Order 11141** was signed into law in 1964. It prohibits federal contractors from discriminating against employees on the basis of age.

CIVIL RIGHTS ACT OF 1991 Congress enacted the **Civil Rights Act of 1991** to overturn several Supreme Court rulings. Perhaps most noteworthy is the reversal of *Atonio v. Wards Cove Packing.*[18] The Supreme Court ruled that plaintiffs must indicate which employment practice created disparate impact, and they must demonstrate how the employment practice created disparate impact. Since the passage of the Civil Rights Act of 1991, employers must show that the challenged employment practice is a business necessity. Thus, the Civil Rights Act of 1991 shifted the burden of proof from employees to employers.

Two additional sections of the Civil Rights Act of 1991 apply to compensation practice. The first feature pertains to seniority systems. As we discuss in Chapter 4, public sector employers make employment decisions on the basis of employees' seniority. For example, public sector employers award more vacation days to employees with higher seniority than to employees with lower seniority. The Civil Rights Act of 1991 overturns the Supreme Court's decision in *Lorance v. AT&T Technologies,*[19] which allowed employees to challenge the use of seniority systems only within 180 days from the system's implementation date. Now, employees may file suits claiming

Affirmative Action Doesn't Break Glass Ceiling

The purpose of affirmative action is to promote the employment of individuals who are protected under the Civil Rights Act of 1964. Many companies began using affirmative action plans over 30 years ago. Although great strides have been made in promoting the employment of women and underrepresented minorities, affirmative action has not benefited everyone. In 1991, the **Glass Ceiling Act** was enacted under **Title II** of the Civil Rights Act of 1991. The term *glass ceiling* describes the artificial barriers that prevent qualified minority men and women from advancing to and reaching their full career potentials in the private sector. The Glass Ceiling Act established the Glass Ceiling Commission—a 21-member bipartisan body appointed by President Bush and Congressional leaders and chaired by the Secretary of Labor. The Committee was charged with the following responsibilities:

- To conduct a study of opportunities for, and artificial barriers to, the advancement of minority men and all women into management and decisionmaking positions in U.S. businesses

- To prepare and submit to the President of the United States and Congress written reports containing the findings and conclusions resulting from the study and the recommendations based on those findings and conclusions

The Glass Ceiling Commission completed its deliberations in 1995 and found that three artificial barriers continue to limit the advancement of minorities and women. Those barriers are described in Exhibit 3-7.

Exhibit 3-7

Glass Ceiling Barriers: The Glass Ceiling Commission's Major Findings

---

Societal barriers that may be outside the direct control of business

- The supply barrier related to educational opportunity and attainment
- The difference barrier as manifested in conscious and unconscious stereotyping, prejudice, and bias related to gender, race, and ethnicity

Internal structural barriers within the direct control of business

- Outreach and recruitment practices that do not seek out or reach or recruit minorities and women
- Corporate climates that alienate and isolate minorities and women
- Pipeline barriers that directly affect opportunity for advancement (initial job placements, lack of mentoring, lack of management training, lack of career development, counterproductive behavior and harassment by colleagues)

Governmental barriers

- Lack of vigorous, consistent monitoring and law enforcement
- Weaknesses in the formulation and collection of employment-related data that make it difficult to ascertain the status of groups at the managerial level and to disaggregate the data
- Inadequate reporting and dissemination of information relevant to glass ceiling issues

---

Source: Federal Glass Ceiling Commission, *Good for business: Making full use of the nation's human capital* (Washington, D.C.: U.S. Government Printing Office, March, 1995).

discrimination either when the system is implemented or whenever the system negatively affects them.

A second development addresses the geographic scope of federal job discrimination. Before the Civil Rights Act of 1991, the U.S. Supreme Court *(Boureslan v. Aramco)*[20] ruled that federal job discrimination laws do not apply to U.S. citizens working for U.S. companies in foreign countries. Since the act's passage, U.S. citizens working overseas may file suit against U.S. businesses for discriminatory employment practices.

The Civil Rights Act of 1991 provides coverage to the same groups protected under the Civil Rights Act of 1964. The 1991 act also extends coverage to Senate employees and political appointees of the federal government's executive branch. The EEOC enforces the Civil Rights Act of 1991. Since the passage of the 1991 act, the EEOC helps employers avoid discriminatory employment practices through the Technical Assistance Training Institute.

Accommodating disabilities and family needs

Congress enacted the Pregnancy Discrimination Act of 1978, the Americans with Disabilities Act of 1990, and the Family and Medical Leave Act of 1993 to accommodate employees with disabilities and pressing family needs. These laws protect a significant number of employees: In 1992, 54 percent of employed women (nearly 2,000,000 women) gave birth to at least one child.[21] The preamble to the Americans with Disabilities Act states that it covers 43,000,000 Americans. Many employees will benefit from the Family and Medical Leave Act as they need substantial time away from work to care for newborns or elderly family members. Two trends explain this need. First, many elderly and seriously ill parents of the employed baby boom generation depend on their children. Second, both husbands and wives work full-time jobs now more than ever before, necessitating extended leave to care for newborns or children who become ill.

Congress enacted the Pregnancy Discrimination Act of 1978, the Americans with Disabilities Act of 1990, and the Family and Medical Leave Act of 1993 to accommodate employees with disabilities and pressing family needs.

PREGNANCY DISCRIMINATION ACT OF 1978 The **Pregnancy Discrimination Act of 1978 (PDA)** is an amendment to Title VII of the Civil Rights Act of 1964. The PDA prohibits disparate impact discrimination against pregnant women for all employment practices. Employers must not treat pregnancy less favorably than other medical conditions covered under employee benefits plans. In addition, employers must treat pregnancy and childbirth the same way they treat other causes of disability. Further, the PDA protects the rights of women who take leave for pregnancy-related reasons. The protected rights include:

 ✮ Credit for previous service

 ✮ Accrued retirement benefits

 ✮ Accumulated seniority

AMERICANS WITH DISABILITIES ACT OF 1990 The **Americans with Disabilities Act of 1990 (ADA)** prohibits discrimination against individuals with mental or physical disabilities within and outside employment settings including public services and transportation, public accommodations, and employment. It applies to all employers with 15 or more employees, and the EEOC is the enforcement agency. In employment contexts, the ADA:

prohibits covered employers from discriminating against a "qualified individual with a disability" in regard to job applications, hiring, advancement, discharge, compensation, training or other terms, conditions, or privileges of employment. Employers are required to make "reasonable accommodations" to the known physical or mental limitations of an otherwise qualified individual with a disability unless to do so would impose an "undue hardship." [22]

Title I of the ADA requires that employers provide "reasonable accommodation" to disabled employees. Reasonable accommodation may include such efforts as making existing facilities readily accessible, restructuring jobs, and modifying work schedules. Every "qualified individual with a disability" is entitled to reasonable accommodation. A qualified individual with a disability, however, must be able to perform the "essential functions" of the job in question. Essential functions are those job duties that are critical to the job.

Let's apply these principles to an example. Producing printed memoranda is a key activity of a clerical worker's job. Most employees manually keyboard the information using a word processing program to generate written text. In this case, the essential function is producing memoranda using word processing software. However, manual input represents only one method to enter information. Information input based on a voice recognition input device is an alternative method for entering information. If a clerk develops crippling arthritis, the ADA may require that the employer make reasonable accommodation by providing the clerk with a voice recognition input device.

FAMILY AND MEDICAL LEAVE ACT OF 1993 The **Family and Medical Leave Act of 1993 (FMLA)** aimed to provide employees with job protection in cases of family or medical emergency. The basic thrust of the act is guaranteed leave, and a key element of that guarantee is the right of the employee to return either to the position he or she left when the leave began or to an equivalent position with the same benefits, pay, and other terms and conditions of employment. We will discuss this act in greater detail in Chapter 10 because compensation professionals treat such leave as a legally required benefit.

Prevailing wage laws

DAVIS-BACON ACT OF 1931 The **Davis-Bacon Act of 1931** establishes employment standards for construction contractors holding federal government contracts valued at more than $2,000. Covered contracts include highway building, dredging, demolition, and cleaning, painting, and decorating public buildings. This act applies to laborers and mechanics who are employed on-site. Contractors must pay wages at least equal to the prevailing wage in the local area. The U.S. Secretary of Labor determines prevailing wage rates on the basis of compensation surveys of different areas. In this context, "local" area refers to the general location where work is performed. Cities and counties represent local areas. The "prevailing wage" is the typical hourly wage paid to more than 50 percent of *all* laborers and mechanics employed in the local area. The act also requires that contractors offer fringe benefits that are equal in scope and value to fringe compensation that prevails in the local area.

WALSH-HEALEY PUBLIC CONTRACTS ACT OF 1936 The **Walsh-Healey Public Contracts Act of 1936** covers contractors and manufacturers who sell supplies, materials, and equipment to the federal government. Its coverage is more extensive than that of the Davis-Bacon Act. The Walsh-Healey Public Contracts Act of 1936 applies to both construction and nonconstruction activities. Also, this act covers all of the contractors' employees except office, supervisory, custodial, and maintenance workers who do any work in preparation for the performance of the contract. The minimum contract amount that qualifies for coverage is $10,000 rather than the $2,000 amount under the Davis-Bacon Act of 1931.

The Walsh-Healey Act of 1936 mandates that contractors with federal contracts meet guidelines regarding wages and hours, child labor, convict labor, and hazardous working conditions. Contractors must observe the minimum wage and overtime provisions of the FLSA. In addition, this act prohibits the employment of individuals younger than 16 and convicted criminals.

Contextual influences on the federal government as an employer

As we discussed previously, federal government employees do not receive protection under Title VII, ADEA, and the Equal Pay Act of 1963. Shortly after the passage of these acts during the 1960s, the President of the United States and Congress enacted executive orders and laws to prohibit job discrimination and promote equal opportunity in the federal government. These executive orders and laws apply to employees who work within:

☆ Military service (civilian employees only)

☆ Executive agencies

☆ Postal Service

☆ Library of Congress

☆ Judicial and legislative branches

Exhibit 3-8 a summarizes these key executive orders and laws. We already discussed the FMLA because it applies to private sector employers as well.

Exhibit 3-8
Executive Orders and Laws Enacted to Protect Federal Government Employees

- **Executive Order 11478** prohibits employment discrimination on the basis of race, color, religion, sex, national origin, handicap, and age (401 *FEP Manual* 4061).

- **Executive Order 11935** prohibits employment of nonresidents in U.S. civil service jobs (401 *FEP Manual* 4121).

- The **Rehabilitation Act** mandates that federal government agencies take affirmative action in providing jobs for individuals with disabilities (401 *FEP Manual* 325).

- The **Vietnam Era Veterans Readjustment Assistance Act** applies the principles of the Rehabilitation Act to veterans with disabilities and veterans of the Vietnam War (401 *FEP Manual* 379).

- The **Government Employee Rights Act of 1991** protects U.S. Senate employees from employment discrimination on the basis of race, color, religion, sex, national origin, age, and disability (401 *FEP Manual* 851).

- The **Family and Medical Leave Act of 1993** grants civil service employees, U.S. Senate employees, and U.S. House of Representative employees a maximum 12-week unpaid leave in any 12-month period to care for a newborn or a seriously ill family member (401 *FEP Manual* 891).

Labor unions as contextual influences

Since the passage of the **National Labor Relations Act of 1935 (NLRA),** the federal government requires employers to enter into good-faith negotiations with workers over the terms of employment. Workers join unions to influence employment-related decisions, especially when they are dissatisfied with job security, wages, benefits, and supervisory practices.

Since the 1950s, the percentage of U.S. civilian workers represented by unions declined steadily to 17.4 percent in 1994.[23] As we will discuss shortly, union representation will probably continue to decline in the future. This decline may be attributed to the reduced influence of unions. Whatever the reason, 17.4 percent of the U.S. civilian work force stands for a large number of workers—nearly 20 million.

National Labor Relations Act of 1935

The purpose of the NLRA was to remove barriers to free commerce and to institute equality of bargaining power between employees and employers. Employers denied workers the rights to bargain collectively with them on such issues as wages, work hours, and working conditions. Consequently, employees experienced poor working conditions, substandard wage rates, and excessive work hours. Section 1 of the NLRA declares the policy of the United States to protect commerce

> by encouraging the practice and procedure of collective bargaining and by protecting the exercise by workers of full freedom of association, self-organization, and designation of representatives of their own choosing for the purpose of negotiating the terms and conditions of employment.

Sections 8(a)(5), 8(d), and 9(a) are key provisions of this act. Section 8(a)(5) provides that it is an unfair labor practice for an employer "to refuse to bargain collectively with the representatives of his employees subject to the provisions of Section 9(a)."

Section 8(d) defines the phrase "to bargain collectively" as the "performance of the mutual obligation of the employer and the representative of the employees to meet at reasonable times and confer in good faith with respect to wages, hours, and other terms and conditions of employment."

Section 9(a) declares:

> Representatives designated or selected for the purposes of collective bargaining by the majority of employees in a unit appropriate for such purposes, shall be the exclusive representatives of all the employees in such unit for the purposes of collective bargaining in respect to rates of pay, wages, hours of employment, or other conditions of employment.

The National Labor Relations Board (NLRB) oversees the enforcement of the NLRA. The President of the United States appoints members to the NLRB for five-year terms.

Compensation issues in collective bargaining

Union and management negotiations usually center on pay raises and fringe benefits.[24] Unions fought hard for general pay increases and regular cost-of-living adjustments (COLAs).[25] COLAs represent automatic pay increases that are based on changes in prices, as indexed by the consumer price index (CPI). COLAs enabled workers to maintain their standards of living by adjusting wages for inflation. Union leaders fought hard for these improvements to maintain the memberships' loyalty and support.

Unions generally secured high wages for their members through the early 1980s. In fact, it was not uncommon for union members to earn as much as 30 percent more than their nonunion counterparts. Unions also improved members' fringe compensation. Most noteworthy was the establishment of sound retirement income programs.[26]

Unions' gains also influenced nonunion companies' compensation practices. In a phenomenon known as a *spillover effect,* many nonunion companies offered similar compensation to their employees. Why? Management of nonunion firms hoped to reduce the chance that employees would seek union representation.[27]

Unions' influence has declined since the 1980s for three key reasons. First, union companies demonstrated consistently lower profits than nonunion companies.[28] As a result, management has been more reluctant to agree on large pay increases because these represent costs that lead to lower profits. Second, drastic employment cuts have taken place in various industries including the highly unionized automobile and steel industries.[29] Technological advances and foreign competition have contributed to these declines. Automated work processes in both the automobile and steel industries made many workers' skills obsolete. Foreign competition dramatically reduced market share held by domestic automobile manufacturers and steel plants. Third, foreign automobile manufacturers produced higher quality vehicles than U.S. automobile manufacturers. Although the foreign-made cars were more expensive, U.S. consumers were willing to pay higher prices in exchange for better quality.

As a result of the changing business landscape, unions tempered their stance in negotiations with management. Many unions focused more heavily on promoting job security than on securing large pay increases. This stance is known as **concessionary bargaining.** Exhibit 3-9 displays the decline in annual negotiated pay increases for se-

	1970	1975	1980	1985	1990	1992	1994
All industries							
First year	11.9	10.2	9.5	2.3	4.0	2.7	2.0
Contracts with COLA	NA	12.2	8.0	1.6	3.4	2.7	2.7
Contracts without COLA	NA	9.1	11.7	2.7	4.4	2.7	1.8
Over life of contract	8.9	7.8	7.1	2.7	3.2	3.0	2.3
Contracts with COLA	NA	7.1	5.0	2.5	1.9	2.5	2.5
Contracts without COLA	NA	8.3	10.3	2.8	4.0	3.1	2.3
Manufacturing							
First year	8.1	9.8	7.4	0.8	3.7	2.6	2.4
Over life of contract	6.0	8.0	5.4	1.8	2.1	2.6	2.3
Nonmanufacturing							
First year	15.2	10.4	10.9	3.3	4.3	2.7	1.8
Over life of contract	11.4	7.8	8.3	3.3	4.0	3.0	2.3

Exhibit 3-9
Major Collective Bargaining Settlements: Average Percent Changes in Wage Rates Negotiated, 1970 to 1994

Source: U.S. Department of Commerce, *Statistical abstracts of the United States,* 115th ed. (Washington, D.C.: U.S. Government Printing Office, 1995).

lected years between 1970 and 1994. The average pay increase declined from 15.2 percent in 1970 to 1.8 percent in 1994. During the 1980s, concessions were most prevalent in small companies, in high-wage companies, and in companies with a small percentage of employees covered by unions.[30]

Market influences

In competitive labor markets, companies attempt to attract and retain the best individuals for employment partly by offering lucrative wage and benefits packages. Unfortunately, some companies were unable to compete on the basis of wage and benefits, as illustrated in the second chapter-opening quotation. Indeed, there are differences in wages among industries. These differences are known as interindustry wage or compensation differentials. Exhibit 3-10 displays the average weekly earnings in various industries for selected years between 1980 and 1994. Construction and manufacturing establishments paid the highest wages throughout this period; retail trade and service companies paid the lowest wages.

Interindustry wage differentials can be attributed to several factors, including the industry's product market, the degree of capital intensity, and the profitability of the industry.

Interindustry wage differentials can be attributed to several factors, including the industry's product market, the degree of capital intensity, and the profitability of the industry.[31] Companies that operate in product markets where there is relatively little competition from other companies tend to pay higher wages because these companies exhibit substantial profits. This phenomenon can be attributed to such factors as higher barriers to entry into the product market and an insignificant influence of foreign competition. Government regulation and extremely expensive equipment represent entry barriers. The U.S. defense industry and the public utilities industry have high entry barriers and no threats from foreign competitors.

Capital-intensity—the extent to which companies' operations are based on the use of large-scale equipment—also explains pay differentials between industries. The amount of average pay varies with the degree of capital-intensity. On average, capital-intensive industries (for example, manufacturing) pay more than industries that are less capital-intensive (service industries). Service industries are not capital-intensive,

Exhibit 3-10
Average Weekly Earnings by Industry Group, 1980 to 1994

INDUSTRY	1980	1985	1990	1993	1994
Construction	$397	$520	$603	$647	$666
Manufacturing	$368	$464	$526	$552	$570
Transportation, public utilities	$351	$450	$505	$540	$554
Wholesale trade	$267	$351	$411	$448	$460
Mining	$235	$299	$345	$374	$385
Finance, insurance, real estate	$210	$289	$357	$406	$424
Services	$191	$257	$319	$351	$360
Retail trade	$147	$175	$194	$210	$216

Source: U.S. Department of Commerce, *Statistical abstracts of the United States*, 115th ed. (Washington, D.C.: U.S. Government Printing Office, 1995).

and most have the reputation of paying low wages. The operation of service industries depends almost exclusively on human resources rather than on physical equipment such as casting machines or robotics. Retail sales and the myriad "1-900" phone lines are just two examples of service businesses.

Finally, companies in profitable industries tend to pay higher compensation, on average, than companies in less profitable industries. Presumably, employees in profitable industries receive higher pay because their skills and abilities contribute to the company's success.

Summary

This chapter discussed the various contextual influences on compensation practice, including laws, labor unions, and market forces. These contextual influences pose significant challenges for compensation professionals. Aspiring compensation professionals must be familiar with the current contextual influences and anticipate impending ones. For example, most companies must adjust in order to accommodate workers with disabilities.

Discussion questions

1. Identify the contextual influence that you believe poses the greatest challenge to companies' competitiveness, and identify the contextual influence that poses the least challenge to companies' competitiveness. Explain your rationale.

2. Copy three job descriptions of your choice from the *Dictionary of Occupational Titles*. On the basis of our discussion of the Americans with Disabilities Act, suggest how you would modify these jobs to accommodate legally blind employees and hearing-impaired employees.

3. Should the government raise the minimum wage? Explain your answer.

4. Do unions make it difficult for companies to attain competitive advantage? Explain your answer.

5. Select one of the contextual influences presented in this chapter. Identify a company that has dealt with this influence, and conduct some research on the company's experience. Be prepared to present a summary of the company's experience.

Key terms

federal government	Fair Labor Standards Act of 1938
state governments	poverty threshold
local governments	*Walling v. A.H. Belo Corp.*
executive branch	exempt
executive orders	nonexempt
Great Depression	*Aaron v. City of Wichita, Kansas*

Portal-to-Portal Act of 1947
Andrews v. DuBois
Work Hours and Safety Standards
  Act of 1962
McNamara-O'Hara Service Contract
  Act of 1965
Equal Pay Act of 1963
*EEOC v. Madison Community Unit
  School District No. 12*
comparable worth
Civil Rights Act of 1964
Title VII
disparate treatment
disparate impact
Bennett Amendment
Executive Order 11246
Age Discrimination in Employment
  Act of 1967 (ADEA)
EEOC v. Chrysler
Older Workers Benefit Protection
  Act (OWBPA)
equal benefit or equal cost principle

Executive Order 11141
Civil Rights Act of 1991
Atonio v. Wards Cove Packing
Lorance v. AT&T Technologies
Boureslan v. Aramco
Glass Ceiling Act
glass ceiling
Title II
Pregnancy Discrimination Act of
  1978 (PDA)
Americans with Disabilities Act of
  1990 (ADA)
Title I
Family and Medical Leave Act of
  1993 (FMLA)
Davis-Bacon Act of 1931
Walsh-Healey Public Contracts Act
  of 1936
National Labor Relations Act of
  1935 (NLRA)
concessionary bargaining
capital-intensity

Endnotes

[1] F. R. Dulles and M. Dubofsky, *Labor in America: A history,* 4th ed. (Arlington Heights, Ill.: Harlan Davidson, 1984), p. 72.

[2] J. T. Dunlop, *Industrial relations systems,* rev. ed. (Boston: Harvard Business School Press, 1993).

[3] Dulles and Dubofsky, *Labor in America,* 4th ed.

[4] U.S. Department of Commerce, *Statistical abstracts of the United States,* 115th ed. (Washington, D.C.: U.S. Government Printing Office, 1995).

[5] Ibid.

[6] Ibid.

[7] Data for the examples in this section are from U.S. Department of Commerce, *Statistical abstracts of the United States,* 115th ed.

[8] *Walling v. A.H. Belo Corp.,* 316 U.S. 624 1942, 2 WH Cases 39 (1942).

[9] *Aaron v. City of Wichita, Kansas,* 54 F. 3d 652 (10th Cir. 1995), 2 WH Cases 2d 1159 (1995).

[10] *Andrews v. DuBois,* 888 F. Supp. 213 (D.C. Mass 1995), 2 WH Cases 2d 1297 (1995).

[11] S. Rep. No. 176, 88th Congress, 1st Session 1 (1963).

[12] *EEOC v. Madison Community Unit School District No. 12,* 818 F.2d 577 (7th Cir. 1987), 28 WH Cases 105 (1987).

[13] P. England, *Comparable worth: Theories and evidence* (New York: Aldine De Gruyter, 1992).

[14] G. Spencer, Projection of the population of the United States, by age, sex, race, and Hispanic origin: 1992 to 2050. *Current population reports,* P-25, No. 1092. (Washington, D.C.: U.S. Government Printing Office, November, 1992).

[15] 401 *FEP Manual* 207.

[16] *EEOC v. Chrysler Corp.,* 652 F. Supp. 1523 (D.C. Ohio 1987), 45 FEP Cases 513.

[17] D. W. Myers, *Compensation management* (Chicago: Commerce Clearing House, 1989).

[18] *Atonio v. Wards Cove Packing Co.,* 490 U.S. 642, 49 FEP Cases 1519 (1989).

[19] *Lorance v. AT&T Technologies,* 49 FEP Cases 1656 (1989).

[20] *Boureslan v. Aramco,* 499 U.S. 244, 55 FEP Cases 449 (1991).

[21] U.S. Department of Commerce, *Statistical abstracts of the United States,* 115th ed.

[22] Bureau of National Affairs, Americans with Disabilities Act of 1990: Text and analysis, *Labor Relations Reporter* 134, No. 3 (1990).

[23] U.S. Department of Commerce, *Statistical abstracts of the United States,* 115th ed.

[24] T. R. Kochan, H. C. Katz, and R. B. McKersie, *The transformation of American industrial relations* (Ithaca, N.Y.: ILR Press, 1994).

[25] R. H. Ferguson, *Cost-of-living adjustments in union management agreements* (Ithaca, N.Y.: Cornell University Press, 1976).

[26] S. Allen and R. Clark, Unions, pension wealth, and age-compensation profiles. *Industrial and Labor Relations Review* 42 (1988):342–359.

[27] L. Solnick, The effect of the blue collar unions on white collar wages and benefits. *Industrial and Labor Relations Review* 38 (1985):23–35.

[28] D. G. Blanchflower and R. B. Freeman, Unionism in the United States and other advanced OFCD countries. *Industrial Relations* 31 (1992):56–79.

[29] Kochan, Katz, and McKersie, *The transformation of American industrial relations.*

[30] L. Bell, Union concessions in the 1980s: The importance of firm-specific factors. *Industrial and Labor Relations Review* 48 (1995):258–275.

[31] A. B. Krueger and L. H. Summers, Reflections on inter-industry wage structure, in K. Lang and J. S. Leonard, eds., *Unemployment and the structure of the labor market* (New York: Basil Blackwell, 1987), pp. 14–17.

CHAPTER

FOUR

Traditional bases for pay:
Seniority and merit

CHAPTER OUTLINE

Continued on next page

LEARNING OBJECTIVES

In this chapter, you will learn about

1. U.S. business traditional practice of setting employees' base pay on their seniority or longevity with the company
2. How seniority pay practices fit with the two competitive strategies, lowest-cost and differentiation
3. U.S. business traditional practice of setting employees' base pay on their merit
4. The role of performance appraisal in the merit pay process
5. Ways to strengthen the pay-for-performance link
6. Some possible limitations of merit pay programs
7. How merit pay programs fit with the two competitive strategies, lowest-cost and differentiation

Rewarding employees according to their performance has been the cornerstone of compensation practice in the United States for most of the twentieth century.

Rewarding employees according to their performance has been the cornerstone of compensation practice in the United States for most of the twentieth century. In the 1930s, employers assumed that workers with greater seniority or tenure on the job or with the company made greater contributions than employees with less seniority, presumably because the higher experience levels of senior employees enhanced their proficiency. This pay practice is known as seniority, or longevity, pay. Although the concept of pay-for-performance is not new, its meaning has evolved in response to greater pressures on companies to be more competitive.

Nowadays, management places greater emphasis on rewarding employees for demonstrated job performance because of such factors as increased global competition. That is, companies have quickly moved away from simply assuming that employees with greater seniority perform better than do employees with lower seniority. Rather, supervisors actively judge the level of employee performance, and they award higher pay raises to the better performers. This practice is known as merit pay, which represents the most common pay-for-performance method used in companies today.[1]

Seniority, or longevity, pay

Seniority pay, or **longevity pay,** systems reward employees with periodic additions to base pay according to employees' length of service. (Although the concepts of seniority and longevity pay are similar, there are some differences between them; the differences are described later in this chapter. Until then, the terms will be used interchangeably.) These pay plans assume that employees become more valuable to companies with time and that valued employees will leave if they do not have a clear idea that their salaries will progress over time.[2] This rationale comes from human capital theory,[3] which states that employees' knowledge and skills generate productive capital known as human capital. Employees can develop such knowledge and skills from formal education and training, including on-the-job experience. Over time, employees presumably refine existing skills or acquire new ones that enable them to work more productively. Thus, seniority pay rewards employees for acquiring and refining their skills as indexed by seniority.

Historical overview

A quick look back into U.S. labor relations history will help shed light on the adoption of seniority pay in many companies. President Franklin D. Roosevelt advocated policies designed to improve workers' economic status in response to severely depressed economic conditions that started in 1929. Congress instituted the National Labor Relations Act (NLRA) in 1935 to protect worker rights, predicated on a fundamental, but limited, conflict of interest between workers and employers. President Franklin D. Roosevelt and other leaders felt that companies needed to be regulated to establish an appropriate balance of power between the parties. The NLRA established a collective bargaining system nationwide to accommodate employers' and employees' partially conflicting and partially shared goals.

Collective bargaining led to **job control unionism,**[4] in which collective bargaining units negotiate formal contracts with employees and provide quasijudicial grievance procedures to adjudicate disputes between union members and employers. Union shops establish workers' rights and obligations and participate in describing and delineating jobs. In unionized workplaces, terms of collective bargaining agreements may determine the specific type of seniority system used, and seniority tends to be the deciding factor in nearly all job scheduling, transfer, layoff, compensation, and promotion decisions. Moreover, seniority may become a principal criterion for selecting one employee over another for transfer or promotion. Exhibit 4-1 illustrates the seniority pay program contained in the collective bargaining agreement between the United Auto Workers and the Ford Motor Company (dated September 15, 1993).

Political pressures probably drive the prevalence of public sector seniority pay. Seniority-based pay systems essentially provide automatic pay increases. Assessing employees' performance is usually a subjective evaluation made by a supervisor. Performance assessments tend to be subjective rather than objective (for example, production data including dollar volume of sales and units produced and human resource data including accidents and absenteeism) because accurate job performance measurements are very difficult to obtain. In contrast, employees' seniority is easily indexed; time on the job is a relatively straightforward and concrete concept. Implementing such a system that specifies the amount of pay raise an employee will receive according to his or her seniority is automatic. Politically, "automatic" pay adjustments protect public sector employees from the quirks of election-year politics.[5] In addition, the federal, state, and local governments can avoid direct responsibility for pay raises, so employees can receive fair pay without political objections.

Exhibit 4-1

*Seniority Pay Provision in
the Collective Bargaining
Agreement between United
Auto Workers and the Ford
Motor Company*

Employees hired or rehired on or after October 4, 1993, on classifications other than those in Appendix F (Skilled Trades) will be paid a hiring-in rate of 70% of the negotiated classification rate of the job to which they are assigned.

(i)   Upon completion of 26 weeks of employment such employees will receive an increase to 75% of the negotiated classification rate of the job to which they are assigned.

(ii) Upon completion of 52 weeks of employment such employees will receive an increase to 80% of the negotiated classification rate of the job to which they are assigned.

(iii) Upon completion of 78 weeks of employment such employees will receive an increase to 85% of the negotiated classification rate of the job to which they are assigned.

(iv) Upon completion of 104 weeks of employment such employees will receive an increase to 90% of the negotiated classification rate of the job to which they are assigned.

(v)   Upon completion of 130 weeks of employment such employees will receive an increase to 95% of the negotiated classification rate of the job to which they are assigned.

(vi) Upon completion of 156 weeks of employment such employees will receive the negotiated classification rate of the job to which they are assigned.

Source: From: Article IX, Section d (i)–(vi) of *Agreements between UAW and the Ford Motor Company,* Vol. 1, September 15, 1993.

Who participates?

Today, most unionized and public sector organizations continue to base salary on seniority or length of employee service. The total number of unionized employees and public sector employees is quite large. In 1994, unions covered nearly 17 million workers, and government (federal, state, and municipal) employed slightly more than 19 million workers.[6] Members of union bargaining units whose contract includes seniority provisions, usually rank-and-file as well as clerical workers, receive automatic raises based on the number of years they have been with the company. In the public sector—municipal, state, and federal government organizations—most administrative, professional, and even managerial employees receive such automatic pay raises.

Effectiveness of seniority pay systems

Virtually no systematic research has demonstrated these pay plans' effectiveness, nor is there any documentation regarding their prevalence. Seniority or longevity pay plans will likely disappear from for-profit companies in increasingly competitive markets. External influences necessitate a strategic orientation toward compensation. Such influences include increased global competition, rapid technological advancement, and skill deficits of new and current members of the work force. These influences will likely force companies to establish compensation tactics that reward employees for making tangible contributions toward companies' quests for competitive advantage and for learning job-relevant knowledge and skills. Seniority pay meets neither goal.

Public sector organizations face less pressure to change these systems because they exist to serve the public rather than to make profits. For example, the Internal Revenue Service is responsible for collecting taxes from U.S. citizens. Paying taxes to the federal government is an obligation of virtually all U.S. citizens. The amount of taxes each citizen pays is based on established tax code. The Internal Revenue Service is not in the business of finding new customers to pay taxes. It does not compete against any other businesses.

Design of seniority pay and longevity pay plans

Although seniority pay and longevity pay are similar, there are some important distinctions between them. The object of seniority pay is to reward job tenure or employees' time as members of a company explicitly through permanent increases to base salary. Employees begin their employment at the starting pay rate established for the particular jobs. At specified time intervals—as short as three months and as long as three years—employees receive designated pay increases. These pay increases are permanent additions to current pay levels. Over time, employees will reach the maximum pay rate for their jobs. Companies expect that most employees will earn promotions into higher paying jobs that have seniority pay schedules. Exhibit 4-2 illustrates a seniority pay policy for a junior clerk job and an advanced clerk job. Pay rates are associated with seniority. Presumably, when employees reach the top pay rate for the junior clerk position, they are qualified to assume the duties of the advanced clerk position.

Longevity pay rewards employees who have reached pay grade maximums and who are not likely to move into higher grades. State and local governments often use longevity pay as incentive to reduce employee turnover and to reward employees for continuous years of service. Longevity pay may take the form of a percentage of base pay, a flat dollar amount, or a special step increase based on the number of years the employee has spent with the organization.[7]

Federal employees are subject to longevity pay via the **General Schedule (GS),** which is shown in Exhibit 4-3. The General Schedule classifies federal government jobs into 15 classifications (GS-1 through GS-15) based on such factors as skill, education, and experience levels. In addition, jobs that require high levels of specialized education (for example, a physicist), have a significant influence on public policy (for

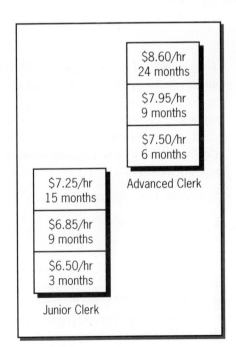

Exhibit 4-2
A Sample Seniority Policy for Junior and Advanced Clerk Jobs

$8.60/hr
24 months

$7.95/hr
9 months

$7.50/hr
6 months

$7.25/hr
15 months

$6.85/hr
9 months

$6.50/hr
3 months

Advanced Clerk

Junior Clerk

Exhibit 4-3
Base 1996 General Schedule Pay Scale
Annual Rates by Grade and Within-Grade Step Increases

	ONE	TWO	THREE	FOUR	FIVE	SIX	SEVEN	EIGHT	NINE	TEN
GS-1	12,384	12,797	13,208	13,619	14,032	14,274	14,679	15,089	15,107	15,489
GS-2	13,923	14,255	14,717	15,107	15,274	15,723	16,172	16,621	17,070	17,519
GS-3	15,193	15,699	16,205	16,711	17,217	17,723	18,229	18,735	19,241	19,947
GS-4	17,055	17,624	18,193	18,762	19,331	19,900	20,469	21,038	21,607	22,176
GS-5	19,081	19,717	20,353	20,989	21,625	22,261	22,897	23,533	24,169	24,805
GS-6	21,269	21,978	22,687	23,396	24,105	24,814	25,523	26,232	26,941	27,650
GS-7	23,634	24,422	25,210	25,998	26,786	27,574	28,362	29,150	29,938	30,726
GS-8	26,175	27,048	27,921	28,794	29,667	30,540	31,413	32,286	33,159	34,032
GS-9	28,912	29,876	30,840	31,804	32,768	33,732	34,696	35,660	36,624	37,588
GS-10	31,839	32,900	33,961	35,022	36,083	37,144	38,205	39,266	40,327	41,388
GS-11	34,981	36,147	37,313	38,479	39,645	40,811	41,977	43,143	44,309	45,475
GS-12	41,926	43,324	44,722	46,120	47,518	48,916	50,314	51,712	53,110	54,508
GS-13	49,856	51,518	53,180	54,842	56,504	58,166	59,828	61,490	63,152	64,814
GS-14	58,915	60,879	62,843	64,807	66,771	68,735	70,699	72,663	74,627	76,591
GS-15	69,300	71,610	73,920	76,230	78,540	80,850	83,160	85,470	87,780	90,090

Pay rates for Senior Level (SL) and Scientific & Professional (ST) positions range from $81,529 to $115,700. Senior Executive Service (SES) pay rates range from $92,900 to $115,700.

example, law judges), or require executive decision making are classified in separated categories: Scientific & Professional (ST) positions, Senior level (SL) positions, and the Senior Executive Service (SES) positions, respectively. The government typically increases all pay amounts annually to adjust for inflation.

Employees are eligible for 10 within-grade step pay increases. Presently, it takes employees 18 years to progress from step 1 to step 10. The waiting periods within steps are as follows:

☆ Steps 1–3: one year

☆ Steps 4–6: two years

☆ Steps 7–9: three years

The aging of the baby boom generation may make companies' use of seniority or longevity infeasible. Most individuals in the baby boom generation, born roughly between 1942 and 1964, are currently in the work force, and only a small segment of them are presently approaching retirement age. Companies that use seniority plans are likely to find the costs burdensome.

Advantages of seniority pay

Seniority pay offers some advantages to both employees and employers. Employees are likely to perceive that they are being treated fairly because they earn pay increases according to seniority, which is an objective standard. Seniority stands in contrast to subjective standards based on supervisory judgment. The inherent objectivity of seniority pay systems should lead to greater cooperation among coworkers.

Seniority pay offers two key advantages to employers. First, seniority pay facilitates the administration of pay programs. Pay increase amounts are set in advance, and employers award raises according to a pay schedule, much like the federal government's General Schedule. A second advantage is that employers are less likely to offend some employees by showing favoritism to others because seniority is an objective basis for making awards. The absence of favoritism should enable supervisors and managers to effectively motivate employees to perform their jobs.

Fitting seniority pay with competitive strategies

Seniority pay does not fit well with the imperatives of competitive strategies because employees can count on receiving the same pay raises for average and exemplary performance, and this fact represents the greatest disadvantage of seniority pay systems. Employees who make significant contributions in the workplace receive the same pay increases as coworkers who make modest contributions. In addition, employees receive pay raises without regard to whether companies are meeting their differentiation or cost goals. Employees clearly do not have any incentives to actively improve their skills or to take risks on the job, because they receive pay raises regardless of any initiatives.

So, in light of increased external pressures on companies to promote productivity and product quality, will seniority and longevity pay be gradually phased out? With the exception of companies that are shielded from competitive pressures—for example, public utilities—it is likely that companies that intend to remain competitive will set aside seniority pay practices. Although seniority pay plans reflect employees' increased worth, they measure such contributions indirectly rather than on the basis of tangible contributions or the successful acquisition of job-related knowledge or skills. Now, more than ever, companies need to be accountable to shareholders, and that accountability will require direct measurement of employee job performance.

> *Seniority pay does not fit well with the imperatives of competitive strategies because employees can count on receiving the same pay raises for average and exemplary performance, and this fact represents the greatest disadvantage of seniority pay systems.*

Merit pay

Merit pay programs assume that employees' compensation over time should be determined, at least in part, by differences in job performance.[8] Employees earn permanent merit increases based on their performance. The increases reward excellent effort or results, motivate future performance, and help employers retain valued employees.

Who participates?

Merit pay represents one of the most commonly used compensation methods in the United States. Various small-scale surveys of no more than a few hundred companies,[9] conducted by compensation consulting firms, academicians, and professional associations, do demonstrate that merit pay plans are firmly entrenched within U.S. business. Their popularity may result from the fact that merit pay fits well with U.S. cultural ideals that reward individual achievement.[10] Merit pay programs occur most often in the private "for-profit" sector of the economy rather than in the public sector organizations such as local and state governments.[11] Approximately 80 percent of private sector companies in the United States employ merit pay plans for virtually all employee groups, ranging from employees without supervisory responsibilities to executives.

Exploring the elements of merit pay

Managers rely on objective as well as subjective performance indicators to determine whether an employee will receive a merit increase and the amount of increase warranted. As a rule, supervisors give merit increases to employees on the basis of subjective appraisal of employees' performance.[12] Supervisors periodically review individual employee performance to evaluate how well each worker is accomplishing assigned duties relative to established standards and goals. Thus, as we discuss later in this chapter, accurate performance appraisals are key to effective merit pay programs.

For merit pay programs to succeed, employees must know that the efforts they expend to meet production quotas or quality standards will lead to pay raises. Job requirements must be realistic, and employees must be prepared to meet job goals with respect to their skills and abilities. Moreover, employees must perceive a strong relationship between attaining performance standards and pay increases.

Further, companies that use merit programs must ensure that funds needed are available to fulfill these promises to compensate employees. For now, we assume that adequate funding for merit pay programs is in place. In Chapter 9 (see "The Flip Side of the Coin"), we address the ramifications of insufficient budgets for funding merit pay programs.

Finally, companies should make adjustments to base pay according to changes in the cost of living or inflation before awarding merit pay raises. Merit pay raises should always reward employee performance, rather than representing adjustments for inflation. Inflation represents rises in the cost of consumer goods and services (for example, food, health care) that boost the overall cost of living. Over time, inflation erodes the purchasing power of the dollar. No doubt, you've heard the expression "it's harder to stretch a dollar these days." Employees are concerned about how well merit increases will raise purchasing power. Compensation professionals attempt to minimize negative inflationary effects by making permanent increases to base pay known as cost-of-living adjustments. We visit the issue of cost-of-living adjustments again in this chapter's "The Flip Side of the Coin" feature and in Chapters 8 and 9. For now, let's assume that inflation is not an issue. (As an aside, this principle also applies to seniority pay. Pay increases should reflect additional seniority after making specific adjustments for inflation.)

Compensation professionals should consider two factors—commitment from top management and the design of jobs—before endorsing the use of merit pay systems.

Although fairly common, merit pay systems are not appropriate for all companies. Compensation professionals should consider two factors—commitment from top management and the design of jobs—before endorsing the use of merit pay systems. Top management must be willing to reward employees' job performance with meaningful pay differentials that match employee performance differentials. Ideally, companies should grant sufficiently large pay increases to reward employees for exemplary job performance and to encourage similar expectations about future good work.

The amount of merit pay increase should reflect prior job performance levels, and it should motivate employees toward striving for exemplary performance. The pay raise amount should be meaningful to employees. The concept of **"just-meaningful**

pay increase" refers to the minimum pay increase that employees will see as making a meaningful change in compensation.[13] The basic premise of this concept is that a trivial pay increase for average or better employees is not likely to reinforce their performance or to motivate enhanced future performance. We take up the specifics of the just-meaningful pay increase concept in Chapter 9.

In addition to top management's commitment to merit pay programs, HR professionals must design jobs explicitly enough that employees' performance can be measured accurately. Merit programs are most appropriate when employees have control over their performance and conditions outside of the employees' control do not substantially affect their performance. Examples of conditions outside of employees' control that are likely to limit job performance vary by the type of job. For sales professionals, recessionary economic spells generally lead consumers to limit spending on new purchases because they anticipate the possibility of layoff. Certainly, sales professionals do not create recessionary periods, nor can they allay consumers' fears about the future. For production workers, regular equipment breakdowns will lead to lowered output.

Moreover, there must be explicit performance standards that specify the procedures or outcomes against which employees' job performance can be clearly evaluated. At Pratt & Whitney, HR professionals and employees worked together to rewrite job descriptions. The purpose was to define and put into writing the major duties of a job and to specify written performance standards for each duty to ensure that the job requirements provided a useful measurement standard for evaluation. The main performance standards included such factors as quality, quantity, and timeliness of work.

Exhibit 4-4 displays a job description for an animal keeper. The five duties describe the activities the job holder performs. Besides indicating the activities of an animal keeper, the duties convey standards against which the animal keeper's work can be compared. For example, the animal keeper's supervisor can monitor whether the animals receive fresh water and food.

Performance appraisal

Effective performance appraisals drive effective merit pay programs. Merit pay systems require specific performance appraisal approaches. Administering successful merit pay programs depends as much on supervisors' appraisal approach as on the professionals' skill in designing and implementing such plans.

Effective performance appraisals drive effective merit pay programs.

Types of performance appraisal plans

Performance appraisal methods fall into four broad categories:

- ✮ Trait systems
- ✮ Comparison systems
- ✮ Behavioral systems
- ✮ Goal-oriented systems

The four kinds of performance appraisal methods are described in turn.

TRAIT SYSTEMS **Trait systems** ask raters to evaluate each employee's traits or characteristics such as quality of work, quantity of work, appearance, dependability, co-

Exhibit 4-4
Sample Job Description:
Animal Keeper

JOB SUMMARY

This position is located in the Office of Animal Management, The Zoological Park, and is directly supervised by the Curator of the assigned unit.

The function of the animal keeper is to perform the described duties (below), most of which require specialized skills that result in the proper care, feeding, exhibition, and propagation of a collection of wild and exotic animals, many of which are endangered species. The keeper is also responsible for maintaining a presentable exhibit so that the animal may be shown to the public in an attractive setting.

All duties are performed in accordance with established policies and procedures of the Office of Animal Management. The incumbent is informed of any changes governing policies and procedures by the Animal Manager and/or Curator, who are available for consultation when new or unusual problems arise. Assignment areas will normally include any or all cages and enclosures in the assigned unit. The keeper receives technical supervision and daily work assignments from the Animal Manager of an assigned section of the unit.

DUTIES

1. Cleaning of animal enclosures, including hosing, sweeping, scrubbing, raking, and removal and disposal of manure, unconsumed food, and other refuse.
2. Maintenance of enclosure materials such as trimming and watering of plants, and cleaning and maintenance of perches, nest boxes, feed containers, and decorative materials, and provision of nesting and bedding material.
3. Feeding and watering of all animals, including measurement and preparation of feed items and prepared diets, placement in feed pans or other containers, and timely distribution and placement in animal enclosures.
4. Cleaning of service areas and of public areas adjacent to the animal enclosures.
5. Inspection of all animals at specific times to ensure security of animals in proper enclosures and to assure prompt reporting of illness or abnormal behavior.

PHYSICAL REQUIREMENTS AND CONDITIONS

This position requires considerable walking, standing, heavy lifting up to 100 pounds, stooping, and other types of physical effort and dexterity in moving and distributing animals, animal feed, cage materials, equipment, and in opening and closing cage doors and gates. Although safety measures are taken, there is always a hazard of injury in working with exotic and unpredictable animals.

Incumbent will be required to work both indoors and outdoors during all types of weather and may be required to work in areas that are hot, cold, dusty, odorous, or with high humidity, as well as in closed areas and cramped spaces.

operation, initiative, judgment, leadership responsibility, decision-making ability, or creativity. Appraisals are typically scored using descriptors ranging from unsatisfactory to outstanding. Exhibit 4-5 contains an illustration of a trait method of performance appraisal.

Trait systems are easy to construct and use and apply to a wide range of jobs. They are also easy to quantify for merit pay purposes. Increasingly, trait systems are becoming common in companies, such as Fleet Mortgage Group and L.L. Bean, that focus on the quality of interactions with customers. But this approach is not without

Exhibit 4-5
*A Trait-Oriented
Performance Appraisal
Rating Form*

Employee's Name: Employee's Position:

Supervisor's Name: Review Period:

INSTRUCTIONS: For each trait below, circle the phrase that best represents the employee.

1. Diligence
   - a. outstanding   b. above average   c. average   d. below average   e. poor

2. Cooperation with others
   - a. outstanding   b. above average   c. average   d. below average   e. poor

3. Communication skills
   - a. outstanding   b. above average   c. average   d. below average   e. poor

4. Leadership
   - a. outstanding   b. above average   c. average   d. below average   e. poor

5. Decisiveness
   - a. outstanding   b. above average   c. average   d. below average   e. poor

limitations. First, trait systems are highly subjective,[14] as they are based on the assumption that all supervisors' perceptions of a given trait are the same. For example, the trait "quality of work" may be defined by one supervisor as "the extent to which an employee's performance is free of errors." To another supervisor, quality of work might mean "the extent to which an employee's performance is thorough." Human resource professionals and supervisors can avoid this problem by working together in advance to clearly specify the definition of traits.

Another drawback is that systems rate individuals on subjective personality factors rather than on objective job performance data. Essentially, trait assessment focuses on employees rather than on the employees' job performance. Employees may simply become defensive rather than trying to understand the role that the particular trait plays in shaping their job performance and taking corrective actions.

COMPARISON SYSTEMS **Comparison systems** evaluate a given employee's performance against the performance of other employees. Employees are ranked from the best performer to the poorest performer. In the simplest form of comparison system, supervisors rank each employee and establish a performance hierarchy such that the employee with the best performance receives the highest ranking. Employees may be ranked on overall performance or on various traits.

An alternative approach, called a **forced distribution** performance appraisal assigns employees to groups that represent the entire range of performance. For example, three categories might be used: the best performers, moderate performers, and poor performers. A forced distribution approach, in which the rater must place a specific number of employees into each of the performance groups, can be used as the basis of a comparison system. Exhibit 4-6 displays a forced distribution evaluation form, with five performance categories, for the animal keeper job.

Many companies use forced distribution approaches to minimize the tendency for supervisors to rate most employees as excellent performers. This tendency usually arises out of supervisors' self-promotion motives. Supervisors often provide positive performance ratings to most of their employees because they do not want to alienate

Exhibit 4-6
A Forced Distribution Performance Appraisal Rating Form

INSTRUCTIONS: You are required to rate the performance for the previous 3 months of the 15 workers employed as animal keepers to conform with the following performance distribution:

- *15 percent* of the animal keepers will be rated as having exhibited poor performance.
- *20 percent* of the animal keepers will be rated as having exhibited below-average performance.
- *35 percent* of the animal keepers will be rated as having exhibited average performance.
- *20 percent* of the animal keepers will be rated as having exhibited above-average performance.
- *10 percent* of the animal keepers will be rated as having exhibited superior performance.

Use the following guidelines for rating performance. On the basis of the five duties listed in the job description for animal keeper, the employee's performance is characterized as:

- poor if the incumbent performs only one of the duties well.
- below-average if the incumbent performs only two of the duties well.
- average if the incumbent performs only three of the duties well.
- above average if the incumbent performs only four of the duties well.
- superior if the incumbent performs all five of the duties well.

---

them. After all, their performance as supervisors depends largely on how well their employees perform their jobs.

Forced distribution approaches have drawbacks. The forced distribution approach can distort ratings because employee performance may not fall into these predetermined distributions. Let's assume that a supervisor must use the following forced distribution to rate her employees' performance:

- ☆ 15 percent well below average
- ☆ 25 percent below average
- ☆ 40 percent average
- ☆ 15 percent above average
- ☆ 5 percent well above average

This distribution presents a problem to the extent that the actual distribution of employee performance is substantially different from this forced distribution. If 35 percent of the employees' performance was either above average or well above average, then the supervisor would be required to underrate the performance of 15 percent of the employees. On the basis of this forced distribution, the supervisor can rate only 20 percent of the employees as having demonstrated above-average or well above-average job performance. Ultimately, management-employee relationships suffer because workers feel that ratings are dictated by unreal models rather than individual performance.

A third comparative technique for ranking employees establishes **paired comparisons.** Supervisors compare each employee with every other employee, identifying the better performer in each pair. Exhibit 4-7 displays a paired comparison form. Upon completion of the comparison, the employees are ranked according to the number of times they were identified as being the better performer. In this example, Allen Jones

Exhibit 4-7
**A Paired Comparison
Performance Appraisal
Rating Form**

INSTRUCTIONS: Please indicate by placing an *X* which employee of each pair has performed most effectively during the past year. Refer to the duties listed in the job description for animal keeper as a basis for judging performance.

_X_	Bob Brown	_X_	Mary Green
___	Mary Green	___	Jim Smith
_X_	Bob Brown	___	Mary Green
___	Jim Smith	_X_	Allen Jones
___	Bob Brown	___	Jim Smith
_X_	Allen Jones	_X_	Allen Jones

is the best performer because he was identified most often as the better performer, followed by Bob Brown (identified twice as the better performer) and Mary Green (identified once as the better performer).

Comparative methods are best suited for small groups of employees who perform the same or similar jobs. They are cumbersome for large groups of employees or for employees who perform different jobs. For example, it would be difficult to judge whether a production worker's performance is better than a secretary's performance because the jobs are substantively different. The assessment of production workers' performance is based on the number of units they produce during each work shift, and secretaries' performance is based on the accuracy with which they type memos and letters.

As do trait systems, comparison approaches have limitations. They tend to encourage highly subjective judgments, and the chances for rater errors and biases are high. In addition, small differences in performance between employees may become exaggerated by using such a method if supervisors feel compelled to distinguish among levels of employee performance.

BEHAVIORAL SYSTEMS **Behavioral systems** rate employees on the extent to which they display successful job performance behaviors. In contrast to trait and comparison methods, behavioral methods rate objective job behaviors. When correctly developed and applied, behavioral models provide results that are relatively free of rater errors and biases. The three main types of behavioral systems are the critical incident technique (CIT), behaviorally anchored rating scales (BARS), and behavioral observation scales (BOS).

The **critical incident technique** (CIT)[15] requires job incumbents and their supervisors to identify performance incidents—on-the-job behaviors and behavioral outcomes—that distinguish successful performance from unsuccessful ones. The supervisor then observes the employees and records their performance on these critical job aspects. Usually, supervisors rate employees on how often they display the behaviors described in each critical incident. Exhibit 4-8 illustrates a CIT form for the animal keeper. Two statements represent examples of ineffective job performance (numbers 2 and 3), and two statements represent examples of effective job performance (numbers 1 and 4).

The CIT tends to be useful because this procedure requires extensive documentation that identifies successful and unsuccessful job performance behaviors by both the

Exhibit 4-8
A Critical Incidents
Performance Appraisal
Rating Form

INSTRUCTIONS: For each description of work behavior below, circle the number that best describes how frequently the employee engages in that behavior.

1. The incumbent removes manure and unconsumed food from the animal enclosures.

1	2	3	4	5
Never	Almost Never	Sometimes	Fairly Often	Very Often

2. The incumbent haphazardly measures the feed items when placing them in the animal enclosures.

1	2	3	4	5
Never	Almost Never	Sometimes	Fairly Often	Very Often

3. The incumbent leaves refuse dropped by visitors on and around the public walkways.

1	2	3	4	5
Never	Almost Never	Sometimes	Fairly Often	Very Often

4. The incumbent skillfully identifies instances of abnormal behavior among the animals, which represent signs of illness.

1	2	3	4	5
Never	Almost Never	Sometimes	Fairly Often	Very Often

employee and the supervisor. But the CIT's strength is also its weakness: Implementation of the CIT demands continuous and close observation of the employee. Supervisors may find the record keeping to be overly burdensome.

Behaviorally anchored rating scales (BARS)[16] are based on the critical incident technique, and these scales are developed in the same fashion with one exception. For the CIT, a critical incident would be written as "the incumbent completed the task in a timely fashion." For the BARS format, this incident would be written as "the incumbent could be expected to complete the task in a timely fashion." The designers of BARS write the incidents as expectations to emphasize the fact that the employee does not have to demonstrate the exact behavior that is used as an anchor in order to be rated at that level. Because a complete array of behaviors that characterize a particular job would take many pages of description, it is not feasible to place examples of all job behaviors on the scale. Therefore, experts list only those behaviors that they believe are most representative of the job the employee must perform. A typical job might have 8 to 10 dimensions under BARS, each with a separate rating scale. Exhibit 4-9 contains an illustration of a BARS for one dimension of the animal keeper job—cleaning animal enclosures and removing refuse from the public walkways. The scale reflects the range of performance on the job dimension from ineffective performance (1) to effective performance (7).

As do all performance appraisal techniques, BARS has its advantages and disadvantages.[17] Among the various performance appraisal techniques, BARS is the most highly defensible in court because it is based on actual observable job behaviors. In addition, the BARS method encourages all raters to make evaluations in the same way. Perhaps the main disadvantage of BARS is the difficulty of developing and maintaining the volume of data necessary to make it effective. The BARS method requires companies to maintain distinct appraisal documents for each job. As jobs change over time, the documentation must be updated for each job.

Another kind of behavior system, a **behavioral observation scale** (BOS),[18] displays illustrations of positive incidents (or behaviors) of job performance for various

Exhibit 4-9
A Behaviorally Anchored
Rating Scale for the
Cleaning Dimension of the
Animal Keeper Job

INSTRUCTIONS: On the scale below, from 7 to 1, circle the number that best describes how frequently the employee engages in that behavior.

7   The incumbent could be expected to thoroughly clean the animal enclosures and remove
| refuse from the public walkways as often as needed.

6
|

5   The incumbent could be expected to thoroughly clean the animal enclosures and remove
| refuse from the public walkways twice daily.

4
|

3   The incumbent could be expected to clean the animal enclosures and remove refuse from
| the public walkways in a sketchy fashion twice daily.

2
|

1   The incumbent could be expected to rarely clean the animal enclosures or remove refuse
    from the public walkways.

---

job dimensions. The evaluator rates the employee on each behavior according to the extent to which the employee performs in a manner consistent with each behavioral description. Scores from each job dimension are averaged to provide an overall rating of performance. The behavioral observation scale is developed in the same way as a BARS instrument, except that it incorporates only positive performance behaviors. The BOS method tends to be difficult and time consuming to develop and maintain. Moreover, in order to assure accurate appraisal, raters must be able to observe employees closely and regularly. Observing employees on a regular basis may not be feasible if supervisors are responsible for several employees.

GOAL-ORIENTED SYSTEMS **Management by objectives** (MBO) [19] is possibly the most effective performance appraisal technique because supervisors and employees determine objectives for employees to meet during the rating period, and the employees appraise how well they have achieved their objectives. Management by objectives is used mainly for managerial and professional employees. It typically evaluates employees' progress toward strategic planning objectives.

Together, employees and supervisors determine particular objectives tied to corporate strategies. Employees are expected to attain these objectives during the rating period. At the end of the rating period, the employee writes a report explaining his or her progress toward accomplishing the objectives and the employee's superior appraises the employee's performance-based accomplishment of the objectives.

Management by objectives can promote effective communication between employees and their superiors. On the down side, it is time consuming, requiring constant information flows between employees and employers. Moreover, its focus is only on the attainment of particular goals, often to the exclusion of other important outcomes. This drawback is known as a "results at any cost" mentality.[20] Historically, the role of automobile sales professionals was literally limited to making sales. Once these professionals and customers agreed on the price of a car, the sales professionals' work with customers was completed. Nowadays, automobile sales professionals remain in contact with clients for as many as several months following the completion of the sale. The purpose is to ensure customer satisfaction and build loyalty to the product and dealership by addressing questions about the vehicle's features and reminding clients about scheduled service checks.

Exploring the performance appraisal process

Performance appraisals represent a company's way of telling employees what is expected of them in their jobs and how well they are meeting those expectations. Typically, performance appraisals require supervisors to monitor employees' performance, complete a performance appraisal form about the employee, and hold a discussion with employees about their performance. Companies that use merit pay plans must assess employee job performance. The assessment serves as a basis for awarding merit pay raises. Awarding merit pay increases on factors other than job performance, but for three exceptions (discussed in Chapter 3), could lead some employees to level charges of illegal pay discrimination against the employer on the basis of the Equal Pay Act of 1963.

One such violation of the Equal Pay Act involves two female employees of Cascade Wood Components Company, which remanufactures lumber products.[21] The job in question was the sawyer job; a sawyer is responsible for cutting the best-grade wood segments, which will be manufactured into the highest grade lumber. Cascade awarded pay increases to male sawyers before awarding pay increases to more experienced female sawyers. The court found Cascade in violation of the Equal Pay Act because the higher pay raises awarded to the male sawyers could not be accounted for by commensurate differences in job performance, in seniority, in a merit system that measures earnings by quantity or quality of production, or on any factor other than sex.

Chapter 3 emphasized how U.S. civil rights laws protect employees from illegal discrimination based on age, race, color, religion, sex, national origin, or qualified disability. Since negative performance appraisals can affect an individual's employment status and related decisions such as pay levels and increases, promotions, and discharges, appraisals must be based on job-related factors and not on any discriminatory factors.

Legislation and court decisions have subjected performance appraisals to close scrutiny. In **Brito v. Zia Company**[22] the court found that the Zia Company violated Title VII when a disproportionate number of protected-class individuals were laid off on the basis of low performance appraisal scores. Zia's action was a violation of Title VII because the use of the performance appraisal system in determining layoffs was indeed an employment test. In addition, the court ruled that the Zia Company had not demonstrated that its performance appraisal instrument was *valid*. In other words, the appraisal did not assess any job-related criteria based on quality or quantity of work.

FOUR ACTIVITIES TO PROMOTE NONDISCRIMINATORY PERFORMANCE APPRAISAL PRACTICES Since the *Brito v. Zia Company* decision, court opinions and compensation experts suggest the following four points to ensure nondiscriminatory performance appraisal practices and to protect firms using merit pay systems if legal issues arise.[23] Nondiscriminatory performance appraisal systems are key to effective merit pay systems because they accurately measure job performance.

1. Conduct job analyses to ascertain characteristics necessary for successful job performance.

Companies must first establish definitions of the jobs and then discover what employee behaviors are necessary to perform the jobs. Job analysis is essential for the development of *content-valid* performance appraisal systems. Content validity displays connections between the measurable factors upon which the employee is being appraised and the job itself. For example, customer service associates' performance might be judged on the basis of courtesy and knowledge of the company's products or services, and these measures would be content-valid dimensions. Both measures are representative of and relative to the job. On the other hand, knowledge of the company's financial accounting practices would not be content-valid criteria of customer service associates' performance.

Human resource and compensation experts must review performance appraisal tools regularly to ensure that the tools adequately reflect the key behaviors necessary for effective job performance. Job holders, supervisors, and clients can often give the most relevant input to determine whether a performance appraisal system contains dimensions that are related to a particular job.

2. Incorporate these characteristics into a rating instrument. Although the professional literature recommends rating instruments that are tied to specific job behaviors (for example, behaviorally anchored rating scales), the courts routinely accept less sophisticated approaches such as simple graphic rating scales and trait ranges. Regardless of method, HR departments should provide all supervisors and raters with written definitive standards.

The examples given earlier about the animal keeper job indicate that effective performance appraisal instruments are based on explicitly written job duties conveyed in the job description.

3. Train supervisors to use the rating instrument properly. Raters need to know how to apply performance appraisal standards when they make judgments. The uniform application of standards is extremely important. In addition, evaluators should be aware of common rater errors, which are discussed later in this chapter.

4. Several cases demonstrate that formal appeal mechanisms and review of ratings by upper-level personnel help make performance appraisal processes more accurate and effective.

Allowing employees to voice their concern over ratings they believe to be inaccurate or unjust opens a dialogue between employees and their supervisors that may shed light on the performance appraisal outcomes. Employees may be able to point out instances of their performance that may have been overlooked in the appraisal process, or they may be able to explain particular extreme instances as the result of extraordinary circumstances. For example, an ill parent in need of regular attention is the reason for an employee's absence rather than an employee's deliberate breach of work responsibilities because the employee chose to relax at the beach.

SOURCES OF PERFORMANCE APPRAISAL INFORMATION Information for performance appraisal can be obtained from five sources:

★ Employee (that is, the individual whose job performance is being appraised)

★ Employee's supervisor

★ Employee's coworkers

☆ Employee's subordinates

☆ Employee's customers or clients

More than one source can provide performance appraisal information. Although supervisory input is the most common source of performance appraisal information, companies are increasingly calling on as many sources of information as possible to gain a more complete picture of employee job performance. Performance appraisal systems that rely on many *appropriate* sources of information are known as 360-degree performance appraisals.

Three criteria should be used to judge the appropriateness of the information source.[24] First, the evaluators should be aware of the objectives of the employee's job. Second, the evaluators should have occasion to frequently observe the employee on the job. Third, the evaluators should be capable of determining whether the employee's performance is satisfactory.

The use of 360-degree performance appraisals is on the rise in American businesses. Three main factors account for this trend. First, as companies downsize, the organizational structures are becoming less hierarchical. As a result, managers and supervisors are increasingly responsible for more workers. With responsibility for more employees, it has become difficult for managers and supervisors to provide sufficient attention to each employee throughout the appraisal period.

Second, the use of 360-degree performance appraisal methods is consistent with the increased prevalence of work teams in companies. At Digital Equipment Corporation, members of semiautonomous work teams communicate their work goals to the entire team. At the end of the designated appraisal period, team members' judge others' performance on the basis of the prior statement of work goals.

Third, companies are placing greater emphasis on customer satisfaction as competition for a limited set of customers increases. Nowadays, companies turn to customers as a source of performance appraisal information. For example, it is common for restaurants, furniture stores, moving companies, and automobile manufacturers to ask customers to complete short surveys designed to measure how well they were satisfied with various aspects of their interactions with the companies. Exhibit 4-10 illustrates a customer satisfaction survey from a major moving company.

ERRORS IN THE PERFORMANCE APPRAISAL PROCESS   Almost all raters make rating errors. **Rating errors** reflect differences between human judgment processes and objective, accurate assessments uncolored by bias, prejudice, or other subjective, extraneous influences.[25] Rating errors occur because raters must always make subjective judgments. Human resource departments can help raters minimize errors by carefully choosing rating systems and teaching raters to recognize and avoid common errors. Some major types of rater errors are[26]

☆ Bias errors

☆ Contrast errors

☆ Errors of central tendency

☆ Errors of leniency or strictness

Bias errors. **Bias errors** happen when the rater evaluates the employee on the basis of his or her negative or positive opinion of employees rather than on employees' actual

Exhibit 4-10
*Sample Customer
Satisfaction Survey*

BEFORE AND DURING YOUR MOVE:	YES	NO
1. Did our moving consultant help with packing and moving-day suggestions?	☐	☐
2. Were we on time?	☐	☐
3. Was our packing service satisfactory?	☐	☐
4. Were our moving personnel courteous?	☐	☐
5. Did your possessions arrive in good condition?	☐	☐
6. Would you recommend us to your friends?	☐	☐

Why did you choose us?

☐ Reputation   ☐ Contacted by salesperson

☐ Have used before   ☐ Recommended by friends

☐ Selected by employer ☐ Recommended by employer

☐ Contacted by telemarketer ☐ Other: _____

How can we better serve you?

_____

_____

_____

_____

performance. Supervisors may bias evaluation effects because of negative and positive halo effects, similar-to-me effects, and illegal discriminatory biases.

A manager biased by a **first-impression effect** might make an initial favorable or unfavorable judgment about an employee and then ignore or distort the employee's actual performance in accordance with that judgment. For instance, a manager expects that a newly hired graduate of a prestigious Ivy League university will be an exemplary performer. After one year on the job, this employee fails to meet many of the work objectives; nevertheless, the manager rates the job performance more highly because of the initial impression.

A **positive halo effect** or **negative halo effect** occurs when a rater generalizes employees' good or bad behavior on one aspect of the job to all aspects of the job. A secretary with offensive interpersonal skills is a proficient user of various computer software programs and he is an outstanding typist. The secretary's supervisor receives frequent complaints from other employees and customers. At performance appraisal time, the supervisor gives this employee an overall negative performance rating.

A **similar-to-me effect** refers to the tendency on the part of raters to judge favorably employees whom they perceive as similar to themselves. Supervisors biased by this effect rate more favorably employees whose attitudes, values, backgrounds, or interests are similar to their own. Employees whose children attend the same elementary school as their manager's children receive higher performance appraisal ratings than employees who do not have children. Similar-to-me errors and biases easily can lead to charges of **illegal discriminatory bias,** the fourth type of bias error, wherein a supervisor rates members of his or her race, gender, nationality, or religion more favorably than members of other classes.

Contrast errors Supervisors make **contrast errors** when they compare an employee with other employees rather than with specific, explicit performance standards. Such comparisons qualify as errors because other employees are required to perform only at minimum acceptable standards. Employees performing at minimally acceptable levels should receive satisfactory ratings, even if every other employee doing the job is performing at outstanding or above-average levels.

Errors of central tendency When supervisors rate all employees as average or close to average, they commit **errors of central tendency.** Such errors are most often committed when raters are forced to justify only extreme—high or low ratings—with written explanations. Therefore, HR professionals should require justification for ratings at every level of the scale and not just at the extremes.

Errors of leniency or strictness Raters sometimes place every employee at the high or low end of the scale regardless of actual performance. With a **leniency error,** managers tend to appraise employees' performance more highly than what it really rates compared with objective criteria. Over time, if supervisors commit positive errors, their employees will expect higher-than-deserved pay rates.

On the other hand, **strictness errors** occur when a supervisor rates employee performance less than what it compares against objective criteria. If supervisors make this error over time, employees may receive smaller pay raises than deserved, and employees may lower their effort and perform poorly. In effect, this error erodes employees' belief that effort varies positively with performance and that performance influences the amount of pay raises.

Strengthening the pay-for-performance link

Ultimately, companies who don't consider these possible limitations weaken the relationship between pay and performance. Human resource managers can employ a number of approaches to strengthen the link between pay and job performance.

Link performance appraisals to business goals

The standards by which employee performance is judged should be linked to the competitive strategy of the company.

The standards by which employee performance is judged should be linked to the competitive strategy of the company. For example, each member of a product development team that is charged with the responsibility of marketing a new product might be given merit increases if certain sales goals are reached.

Analyze jobs

Job analysis (Chapter 7) is vital to companies who wish to establish *internally consistent job structures.* Job descriptions (Chapter 7)—a product of job analyses—can be used by supervisors to create objective performance measures as discussed earlier. Job descriptions note the duties, requirements, and relative importance of the jobs within the company. Supervisors appraising performance can match employees' performance to these criteria. This approach may help reduce supervisors' arbitrary decisions about merit increases by clarifying the standards against which an employees' performance is judged.

Communicate

For merit pay programs to succeed, employees must clearly understand what they need to do to receive merit increases and what the rewards for their performance will be. Open communication helps employees develop reasonable expectations and encourages them to trust the system and those who operate it.

Establish effective appraisals

During performance appraisal meetings with employees, supervisors should discuss goals for future performance and employee career plans. If performance deficiencies are evident, the supervisor and employee should work together to identify possible causes and develop an action plan to remedy those deficiencies. The performance standards listed within job descriptions should serve as the guides for establishing performance targets. For example, ABC Company's job description for secretary specifies that the job incumbent be able to use one word processing software package proficiently. The supervisor should clearly explain what software usage proficiency means. Proficiency may refer to the ability to operate certain features of the software well, including the mail merge utility, the table generator, and the various outlining utilities, or proficiency may refer to the ability to operate *all* features of the software well.

Empower employees

Because formal performance appraisals are conducted periodically—maybe only once a year—supervisors must empower their employees to make performance self-appraisals between formal sessions.[27] Moreover, supervisors need to take on a coach's role to empower their workers.[28] As coaches, supervisors must ensure that employees have access to the resources necessary to perform their jobs. Supervisors-as-coaches should also help employees interpret and respond to work problems as they develop. Empowering employees in this fashion should lead to more self-corrective actions rather than reactive courses of action to supervisory feedback and only to the criticisms addressed in performance appraisal meetings.

Differentiate among performers

Merit increases should consist of meaningful increments. If employees do not see significant distinctions between top performers and poor performers, top performers may become frustrated and reduce their level of performance. When companies' merit increases don't clearly reflect differences in actual job performance, they may need to provide alternative rewards. For example, fringe compensation—additional vacation days, higher discounts on the company's product or service—can complement merit pay increases.

Possible limitations of merit pay programs

Despite merit pay systems' popularity, these programs are not without potential limitations that may lessen their credibility with employees. If employees do not believe in a merit pay program, the pay system will not bring about the expected motivational impacts. Supervisors, human resource managers, and compensation professionals must address eight potential problems with merit pay programs.

Merit Pay Equals Cost-of-Living Adjustment

Over time, the costs of consumer goods and services escalate. Thus, a given amount of money—employees' take-home pay—buys less. Some companies provide employees with cost-of-living adjustments in order to maintain their salaries' purchase power. If budgetary constraints permit and their competitive strategy warrants, companies may award employees merit pay increases in addition to cost-of-living adjustments. Some companies distinguish between these two kinds of pay increases; others do not. Rather than making this distinction, some companies simply claim to offer a merit pay increase to their employees. That claim is misleading and ineffective.

For example, let's assume that the inflation rate for the past year was 3 percent. A company announces that it will award a 5 percent merit pay increase to its exemplary performers. If the company offers a 5 percent raise only, then 3 percent covers the cost-of-living increase, and only 2 percent represents merit. If this hypothetical company were offering a genuine 5 percent merit increase, then it would award a total pay increase that equals 8 percent—3 percent to cover the cost-of-living increase and 5 percent to cover the merit portion.

Compensation professionals should be concerned about the implications of not identifying the components of pay raises to employees. Obviously, employees use their earnings to make purchases. Undoubtedly, employees are aware of price increases and understand that the "dollar doesn't stretch as far it used to." Thus, companies that do not distinguish between the merit and cost-of-living components of raises are likely to compromise their employees' trust and their motivation to perform well in the future.

Failure to differentiate among performers

Employees may receive merit increases even if their performance does not warrant them, because supervisors want to avoid creating animosity among employees. Therefore, poor performers may receive the same pay increase as exemplary performers, and poor performers may come to view merit pay increases as entitlements. Superior performers may question the value of striving for excellent performance.

Poor performance measures

Accurate and comprehensive performance measures that capture the entire scope of an employee's job are essential to successful merit pay programs.

Accurate and comprehensive performance measures that capture the entire scope of an employee's job are essential to successful merit pay programs. In most companies, employees' job performance tends to be assessed subjectively by the supervisors. And, merit pay programs rely on those supervisors' subjective assessment of employees' job performance. Unfortunately, developing performance measures for every single job is difficult and expensive.

Supervisors' biased ratings of employee job performance

As we discussed earlier, supervisors are subject to a number of errors when they make subjective assessments of employees' job performance. These errors often undermine the credibility of the performance evaluation process. Performance evaluation processes that lack credibility do little to create the perception among employees that pay reflects performance.

Merit Pay for *Non*performance

Merit increases have traditionally been permanent increases to employees' base pay.[29] Thus, companies carry merit pay increase expenses as long as employees remain employed. This design feature essentially rewards employees over time for some prior performance accomplishments, even though employer benefits have typically long since expired. Past exemplary performers can slack off and still enjoy high compensation based on past performance. On the other hand, newcomers who are capable performers must perform well for several years in order to reach the same pay level as longer-service employees.

Since the early 1980s, many companies began using an alternative kind of merit pay award known as the **merit bonus.** The merit bonus differs from the traditional merit pay increase in an important way. The merit bonus is not added to base pay as a permanent increment. Employees must earn the bonus each year. Companies that use merit bonuses find it less costly than companies that rely solely on permanent merit pay increases. In addition, employees who choose to slack off will be at a disadvantage because merit bonuses are not added as permanent increments to base pay.

Exhibit 4-11 illustrates the cost burden to companies that is associated with awarding permanent merit pay increases versus merit bonuses.

At the end of 1991, Angela Johnson earned an annual salary of $20,000.

YEAR	INCREASE AMOUNT	COST OF INCREASE (TOTAL CURRENT SALARY – 1991 ANNUAL SALARY)		TOTAL SALARY UNDER:	
		PERMANENT MERIT INCREASE	MERIT BONUS	PERMANENT MERIT INCREASE (% INCREASE × PREVIOUS ANNUAL SALARY)	MERIT BONUS (% INCREASE × 1991 ANNUAL SALARY)
1992	3%	$ 600	$ 600	$20,600	$20,600
1993	5%	$ 1,630	$ 1,000	$21,630	$21,000
1994	4%	$ 2,496	$ 800	$22,496	$20,800
1995	7%	$ 4,070	$ 1,400	$24,070	$21,400
1996	6%	$ 5,514	$ 1,200	$25,514	$21,200
1997	5%	$ 6,790	$ 1,000	$26,790	$21,000
1998	3%	$ 7,594	$ 600	$27,594	$20,600
1999	6%	$ 9,250	$ 1,200	$29,250	$21,200
2000	8%	$11,590	$ 1,600	$31,590	$21,600
2001	7%	$13,801	$ 1,400	$33,801	$21,400
Total increase amount		$63,335	$10,800		

Exhibit 4-11
The Costs of Permanent Merit Increases versus Merit Bonus Awards: A Comparison

Lack of open communication between management and employees

If managers cannot communicate effectively with employees, employees will not trust performance appraisal processes. Trust is difficult to build when decisions are kept secret and employees have no influence on pay decisions. Thus, merit pay decisions systems can cause conflict between management and employees. If mistrust characterizes the relationship between management and employees, then performance appraisals will mean little to employees and could even lead to accusations of bias. In an environment of secrecy, employees lack the information necessary to determine if pay actually links to job performance.

Undesirable social structures

Relative pay grades can reflect status differentials within a company: Employees with lucrative salaries are usually granted higher status than lesser-paid employees. Permanent merit increases may rigidify the relative pay status of employees over time.[30] Exhibit 4-12 shows the permanence of the relative pay difference between two jobs, each of which receives a 5 percent merit increase each year. Even though the two employees performed well and received "equal" merit increases in percentage terms, the actual salary differential prevails each year. Thus, when pay level is an indicator of status, permanent merit increases may reinforce an undesirable social structure. Lower-paid employees may resent never being able to catch up.

Factors other than merit

Merit increases may be based on factors other than merit, which will clearly reduce the emphasis on job performance. For example, supervisors may subconsciously use their employees' age or seniority as bases for awarding merit increases. Studies show that the extent to which supervisors like the employees for whom they are responsible determines the size of pay raises in a merit pay program.[31] In addition, company politics assumes that the value of an employee's contributions depends on the agenda, or goals, of the supervisor rather than on the objective impact of an employee's contributions to a rationally determined work goal.[32] For instance, an accounting manager wishes to use a certain accounting method. Top management wants to use a different one. The accounting manager believes that she can gain top management support by demonstrating that the accounting staff agrees with her position. The accounting man-

Exhibit 4-12
The Impact of Equal Pay Raise Percentage Amounts for Distinct Salaries

At the end of 1995, Anne Brown earned $50,000 per year as a systems analyst, and John Williams earned $35,000 per year as an administrative assistant. Each received a 5 percent pay increase every year until the year 2000.

	ANNE BROWN	JOHN WILLIAMS
1996	$52,500	$36,750
1997	$55,125	$38,587
1998	$57,881	$40,516
1999	$60,775	$42,542
2000	$63,814	$44,669

ager may give generally positive performance evaluations regardless of demonstrated performance to those who endorse her accounting methods.

Undesirable competition

Because merit pay programs focus fundamentally on individual employees, these programs do little to integrate workforce members.[33] Employees must compete for a larger share of a limited budget for merit increases. Competition among employees is counterproductive if teamwork is essential for successfully completing projects. Thus, merit increases are best suited for jobs in which the employee works independently, such as clerical positions and many professional positions in fields such as accounting.

Little motivational value

Notwithstanding their intended purpose, merit pay programs may not influence employee motivation positively. Employers and employees may differ in what they see as "large enough" merit increases to really motivate positive worker behavior. For example, increases diminish after deducting income taxes and contributions to Social Security, which sometimes amounts to more than 6 percent. If we assume that an employee receives a merit pay increase once a year, the difference in the employee's monthly paycheck may be negligible.

Linking merit pay with competitive strategy

As you will recall, in Chapter 2 we reviewed a framework for establishing a basis for selecting particular compensation tactics to match a company's competitive strategy. How do merit systems fit with the two fundamental competitive strategies—lowest-cost and differentiation? Ultimately, merit pay systems, when properly applied, can contribute to a company's meeting the goals of whichever strategy it chooses—lowest-cost or differentiation. However, the rationale for the appropriateness of merit pay systems differs according to the imperatives of the lowest-cost and differentiation competitive strategies.

Lowest-cost competitive strategy

Lowest-cost strategies require firms to reduce output costs per employee. Merit pay systems are most appropriate only when the following two conditions are met: (1) Pay increases are commensurate with employee productivity, *and* (2) employees maintain productivity levels over time. Unfortunately, factors outside companies' control may lead to lower employee productivity from time to time. Personal illness and shortage of raw materials for production are examples of factors that undermine employee productivity. Companies that typically experience such slowdowns are likely to find that merit pay systems run counter to cost containment goals.

Differentiation competitive strategy

A differentiation strategy requires creative, open-minded, risk-taking employees. Compared with lowest-cost strategies, companies that pursue differentiation strategies must take a longer-term focus to attain their preestablished objectives. Merit pay has the potential to promote creativity and risk taking by linking pay with innovative job accomplishments. However, objectives that are tied to creativity and risk taking must be established on a regular basis for merit pay to be effective under differentiation strategies. Granting merit pay raises for past performance would be tantamount to rewarding employees long after the impact of their past performance has subsided.

Summary

This chapter discussed the seniority pay and merit pay concepts. Companies should move away from rewarding employees solely on the basis of seniority and toward rewarding employees for measurable accomplishments. To be successful, merit pay programs must be founded on well-designed performance appraisal systems that accurately measure performance. In addition, rewards commensurate with past performance should be given. Perhaps the greatest challenge for companies is to ensure that employees are given the opportunity to perform at exemplary levels.

Discussion questions

1. Human capital theory has been advanced as a rationale underlying seniority or longevity pay. Identify two individuals you know who have performed the same job for at least two years. Ask them to describe the changes in knowledge and skills they experienced from the time they assumed their jobs to the present. Present your findings to the class.

2. Subjective performance evaluations are likely to involve several types of rater error, so objective measures seem a better alternative. Discuss when subjective performance evaluations might be better (or more feasible) than objective ratings.

3. Consider a summer job that you have held. Write a detailed job description for that job. Then develop a behaviorally anchored rating scale (BARS) that can be used to evaluate an individual who performs that job in the future.

4. This chapter indicates that merit pay plans appear to be the most common form of compensation in the United States. Although widely used, these systems are not suitable for all kinds of jobs. On the basis of your knowledge of merit pay systems, identify at least three jobs for which merit pay is inappropriate. Be sure to provide your rationale, given the information in this chapter.

5. Using the *Dictionary of Occupational Titles,* select three distinct jobs of your choice—a clerical job, a technical job, and a professional job. For each job, identify what you believe is the most appropriate performance appraisal method. Sketch a performance appraisal instrument for each of the three jobs you chose. Discuss the rationale for your choice of performance appraisal methods.

Key terms

seniority pay

longevity pay

job control unionism

General Schedule (GS)

merit pay programs

just-meaningful pay increase

trait systems

comparison systems

forced distribution

paired comparisons

behavioral systems

critical incident technique

behaviorally anchored rating scales

behavioral observation scale

management by objectives

Brito v. Zia Company

rating errors

bias errors

first-impression effect

positive halo effect

negative halo effect

similar-to-me effect

illegal discriminatory bias

contrast errors

errors of central tendency

leniency error

strictness errors

merit bonus

Endnotes

[1] R. L. Heneman, *Merit pay: Linking pay increases to performance* (Reading, Mass.: Addison-Wesley, 1992).

[2] N. J. Cayer, *Public personnel administration in the United States* (New York: St. Martin's Press, 1975).

[3] G. Becker, *Human capital* (New York: National Bureau of Economic Research, 1975).

[4] T. R. Kochan, H. C. Katz, and R. B. McKersie, *The transformation of American industrial relations* (Ithaca, N.Y.: ILR Press, 1994).

[5] Cayer, *Public personnel administration in the United States.*

[6] U.S. Department of Commerce, *Statistical abstracts of the United States,* 115th ed. (Washington, D.C.: U.S. Government Printing Office, 1995).

[7] R. C. Kernel and K. S. Moorage, Longevity pay in the States: Echo from the past or sound of the future? *Public Personnel Management* 19 (1990):191–200.

[8] C. Peck, *Pay and performance: The interaction of compensation and performance appraisal,* Research Bulletin No. 155 (New York: The Conference Board, 1984).

[9] L. R. Gòmez-Mejìa, D. R. Balkin, and R. L. Cardy, *Managing human resources* (Englewood Cliffs, N.J.: Prentice Hall, 1995).

[10] L. R. Gòmez-Mejìa, and T. Welbourne, Compensation strategies in a global context, *Human Resource Planning* 14 (1991):29–41.

[11] Heneman, *Merit pay.*

[12] G. P. Latham and K. N. Wexley, *Increasing productivity through performance appraisal* (Reading, Mass.: Addison-Wesley, 1982).

[13] L. A. Krefting and T. A. Mahoney, Determining the size of a meaningful pay increase, *Industrial Relations* 16 (1977):83–93.

[14] H. J. Bernardin and R. W. Beatty, *Performance appraisal: Assissing human behavior at work* (Boston: Kent Publishing, 1984).

[15] G. Fivars, The critical incident technique: A bibliography, *JSAS Catalog of Selected Documents in Psychology* 5 (1975):210.

[16] P. Smith and L. M. Kendall, Retranslation of expectations: An approach to the construction of unambiguous anchors for rating scales, *Journal of Applied Psychology* 47 (1963):149–155.

[17] Latham and Wexley, *Increasing productivity through performance appraisal.*

[18] G. P. Latham and K. N. Wexley, Behavioral observation scales for performance appraisal purposes, *Personnel Psychology* 30 (1977): 255–268.

[19] P. F. Drucker, *The practice of management.* (New York: Harper, 1954).

[20] Bernardin and Beatty, *Performance appraisal.*

[21] *Coe v. Cascade Wood Components,* 48 FEP Cases 664 (W.D. OR. 1988).

[22] *Brito v. Zia Co.,* 478 F. 2d 1200 (10th Cir. 1973), 5 FEP Cases 1207 (1973).

[23] G. V. Barrett and M. C. Kernan, Performance appraisal and terminations: A review of court decisions since *Brito v. Zia* with implication for personnel practices, *Personnel Psychology* 40 (1987):489–503.

[24] Latham and Wexley, *Increasing productivity through performance appraisal.*

[25] M. L. Blum and J. C. Naylor, *Industrial psychology: Its theoretical and social foundations* (New York: Harper & Row, 1968).

[26] Latham and Wexley, *Increasing productivity through performance appraisal.*

[27] Gòmez-Mejìa, Balkin, and Cardy, *Managing human resources.*

[28] R. D. Evered and J. C. Selman, Coaching and the art of management, *Organizational Dynamics* 18 (1989):16–33.

[29] C. Peck, *Variable pay: Nontraditional programs for motivation and reward* (New York: The Conference Board, 1993).

[30] M. Haire, E. E. Ghiselli, and M. E. Gordon, A psychological study of pay, *Journal of Applied Psychology Monograph* 5, No. 636 (1967): whole issue.

[31] R. L. Cardy and G. H. Dobbins, Affect and appraisal: Liking as an integral dimension in evaluating performance, *Journal of Applied Psychology* 71 (1986):672–678.

[32] K. R. Murphy and J. N. Cleveland, *Performance appraisal: An organizational perspective* (Boston: Allyn & Bacon, 1991).

[33] E. E. Lawler and S. G. Cohen, Designing a pay system for teams, *American Compensation Association Journal* 1 (1992):6–19.

CHAPTER

FIVE

Incentive pay

CHAPTER OUTLINE

Continued on next page

LEARNING OBJECTIVES

In this chapter, you will learn about

1. How incentive pay and traditional pay systems differ
2. Plans that reward individual behavior
3. A variety of plans that reward group behavior
4. The most broadly used corporatewide incentive plan, profit sharing
5. Considerations for designing incentive pay plans
6. How individual, group, and gain sharing incentive plans contribute to differentiation and lowest-cost competitive strategies

Incentive pay, or variable pay, rewards employees for partially or completely attaining a predetermined work objective. **Incentive pay,** or **variable pay** is defined as compensation, other than base wages or salaries, that fluctuates according to employees' attainment of some standard such as a preestablished formula, individual or group goals, or company earnings.[1]

Effective incentive pay systems are based on three assumptions:[2]

☆ Individual employees and work teams differ in how much they contribute to the company, not only in what they do but also in how well they do it.

☆ The company's overall performance depends to a large degree on the performance of individuals and groups within the company.

☆ To attract, retain, and motivate high performers and to be fair to all employees, a company needs to reward employees on the basis of their relative performance.

Much like seniority and merit pay approaches, incentive pay augments employees' base pay, but incentive pay appears as one-time payments.

Much like seniority and merit pay approaches, incentive pay augments employees' base pay, but incentive pay appears as one-time payments. Usually, employees receive a combination of recurring base pay and incentive pay, with base pay representing the greatest portion of core compensation. However, incentive pay is the only form of core compensation for many jobs, particularly in the sales fields.

Employees' earning potential under incentive pay systems is tremendous. Lincoln Electric Company, a manufacturer of welding machines and motors, is renowned for its use of incentive pay plans. At Lincoln Electric, production employees receive recurring base pay as well as incentive pay. The company determines incentive pay awards according to five performance criteria: quality, output, dependability, cooperation, and ideas. In 1995, each production worker earned incentive pay that averaged 56 percent of base pay, or nearly $20,000! Although there is an absence of survey data that document the average incentive payments, a 56 percent incentive payment is quite excellent.

Companies generally institute incentive pay programs to control payroll costs or to motivate employee productivity. Companies can control costs by replacing annual merit or seniority increases or fixed salaries with incentive plans that award pay raises only when the company enjoys a rise in productivity, profits, or some other measure of business success. Well-developed incentive programs base pay on performance, so employees control their own compensation levels. Companies can choose incentives to further company goals. For example, the management of Evart Products Company, which supplies automotive assembly plants with exterior signal lighting and other plastic products, decided to lower costs and improve quality by reducing the defect rate. Evart employees received incentive pay for substantially reducing the defect rate.

Contrasting incentive pay with traditional pay

In traditional pay plans, employees receive compensation based on a fixed hourly pay rate or annual salary. Annual raises are linked to such factors as seniority and past performance. Some companies use incentive pay programs that replace all or a portion of base pay in order to control payroll expenditures and to link pay to performance. Companies use incentive pay programs in varying degrees for different kinds of positions. Some compensation programs consist of both traditional base pay and incentive pay; others, usually sales jobs, offer only incentive pay: a case of full pay-at-risk.[3]

Traditional core compensation generally includes an annual salary or hourly wage that is increased periodically on a seniority or merit basis. Companies usually base pay rates on the importance they place on each job within their corporate structure and in the "going rate" that each job commands in similar companies. For example, Lincoln Electric determines the importance of the jobs within its job structure on the basis of job evaluation techniques. The five criteria on which Lincoln evaluates jobs are skill, responsibility, mental aptitude, physical application, and working conditions. Then Lincoln Electric surveys the pay rates of competitors, and it uses these data to set base pay rates.

As we discussed in Chapter 4, employees under traditional pay structures earn raises according to their length of service in the organization or supervisors' subjective appraisals of employees' job performance. Again, both merit pay raises and seniority pay raises are permanent increases to base pay. Although the annual percentage increase amounts usually total no more than a small percentage of base pay—nowadays, 1 to 5 percent is not uncommon—the dollar impact represents a significant cost to employers over time. Exhibit 5-1 shows the contrast in rate of compensation increase between a traditional merit compensation plan and an incentive plan.

Companies use incentive pay to reward individual employees, teams of employees, or the company overall for performance. Incentive pay plans are not limited solely to production or nonsupervisory workers. Many incentive plans apply to other categories of employees, including sales professionals, managers, and executives. Typically, management relies on business objectives to determine incentive pay levels. At Taco Bell, restaurant managers receive biannual bonuses based on the attainment of three objectives:[4]

- ✯ Target profit levels
- ✯ Quality of customer service based on an independent assessment by a market research company
- ✯ Store sales

Companies can control costs by replacing annual merit or seniority increases or fixed salaries with incentive plans that award pay raises only when the company enjoys a rise in productivity, profits, or some other measure of business success.

At the end of 1991, John Smith earned an annual salary of $35,000.

| | | COST OF INCREASE (TOTAL CURRENT SALARY – 1991 ANNUAL SALARY) | | TOTAL SALARY UNDER: | |
| | | PERMANENT MERIT INCREASE | INCENTIVE AWARD | PERMANENT MERIT INCREASE (% INCREASE × PREVIOUS ANNUAL SALARY) | INCENTIVE AWARD (% INCREASE × 1991 ANNUAL SALARY) |
YEAR	INCREASE AMOUNT				
1992	3%	$ 1,050	$ 1,050	$36,050	$36,050
1993	5%	$ 2,853	$ 1,750	$37,853	$36,750
1994	4%	$ 4,367	$ 1,400	$39,367	$36,400
1995	7%	$ 7,122	$ 2,450	$42,122	$37,450
1996	6%	$ 9,649	$ 2,100	$44,649	$37,100
1997	5%	$ 11,881	$ 1,750	$46,881	$36,750
1998	3%	$ 13,287	$ 1,050	$48,287	$36,050
1999	6%	$ 16,185	$ 2,100	$51,185	$37,100
2000	8%	$ 20,279	$ 2,800	$55,279	$37,800
2001	7%	$ 24,148	$ 2,450	$59,148	$37,450
Total increase amount		$110,821	$18,900		

Management then communicates these planned incentive levels and performance goals to restaurant managers. Whereas merit pay performance standards aim to be measurable and objective, incentive levels tend to be based on even more-objective criteria such as quantity of items an employee produces per production period or market indicators of a company's performance, for example, an increase in market share for the fiscal year. Moreover, supervisors communicate in advance the incentive award amounts that correspond to objective performance levels. In constast, supervisors generally do not communicate merit award amounts until after they have offered subjective assessments of employees' performance.

Incentive pay plans can be broadly classified in three categories:

☆ **Individual incentive plans.** These plans reward employees whose work is performed independently. Some companies have piecework plans, typically for their production employees. Under piecework plans, an employee's compensation depends on the number of units she or he produces over a given period.

☆ **Group incentive plans.** These plans promote supportive, collaborative behavior among employees. Group incentives work well in manufacturing and service delivery environments that rely on interdependent teams. In gain sharing programs, group improvements in productivity, cost savings, or product quality are shared by employees within the group.

INDIVIDUAL INCENTIVE PLANS

Quantity of work output

Quality of work output

Monthly sales

Work safety record

Work attendance

GROUP INCENTIVE PLANS

Customer satisfaction

Labor cost savings (base pay, overtime pay, benefits)

Materials cost savings

Reduction in accidents

Services cost savings (e.g., utilities)

COMPANYWIDE INCENTIVE PLANS

Company profits

Cost containment

Market share

Sales revenue

---

* **Companywide plans.** Current profit sharing plans tie employee compensation to a company's performance based on a short time frame, usually anywhere from a three-month period to a one-year period.

Exhibit 5-2 lists common performance measures used in individual, group, and companywide incentive plans.

Individual incentives

Individual incentive plans are most appropriate under three conditions. First, employees' performance can be measured objectively. Examples of objective performance measures include:

* **Number of units produced.** An automobile parts production worker's completion of turn signal lighting assembly

* **Sales amount.** A Mary Kay Cosmetics sales professional's monthly sales revenue

* **Reduction in error rate.** A word processor's reduction in keyboarding errors

Second, the use of individual incentive plans is appropriate when employees have sufficient control over work outcomes. Such factors as frequent equipment breakdowns and delays in receipt of raw materials limit employees' ability to control their performance levels. Employees are not very likely to be diligent when they encounter interference: Chances are good that employees who previously experienced interference will expect to encounter interference in the future. Employees' resistance threatens companies' profits because they will find it difficult to motivate them to work hard when problem factors are present.

Third, the use of individual incentive plans is appropriate when they do not create a level of unhealthy competition among workers that ultimately leads to poor quality. For example, a company may create unhealthy competition when it limits the number of incentive awards to only 10 percent of the employees who have demonstrated the highest levels of performance. If the company judges performance according to volume, then employees may sacrifice quality as they compete against each other to outmatch quantity. In addition, under an incentive plan that rewards quantity of output, those employees who meet or exceed the highest standard established by their employer may be subject to intimidation by workers whose work falls below the standard.[5] Unions may use these intimidation tactics to prevent plan standards from being raised.

Who participates?

According to a recent survey, 25 percent of 382 companies in the manufacturing, financial services, public utilities, diversified services (for example, health care and restaurants), and trade (for example, wholesale and retail trade) industries reported using individual incentives.[6] Of all the companies reporting use of individual incentives, companies in the financial service industry reported the greatest use (41 percent), and companies in the diversified services industry reported the least use (10 percent). Moreover, of the companies reporting use of individual incentives, 19 percent covered hourly employees only, 46 percent covered salaried employees, and 35 percent covered all employees with the exception of executives.

The same survey also indicated that companies do not use individual incentive plans as much as they once did. In fact, the use of individual incentive plans fell in all industries surveyed between 1990 and 1992. Forty-three percent of the companies surveyed used individual incentive plans in 1990. In 1992, only 10 percent of these companies used individual incentive plans. The utilities industry exhibited the smallest decline in the usage of individual incentive plans—from 19 percent in 1990 to 16 percent in 1992.

Partly, this decline can be explained by automation in the workplace, which has particularly affected production workers on assembly lines. Robots and other computerized machines perform tasks once done by workers. Today, assembly line automation negates the need for workers to manually package items once they come off the assembly line. Individual incentives do not work well given the interdependencies in modern production processes.[7]

Defining individual incentives

Individual incentive plans reward employees for meeting work-related performance standards such as quality, productivity, customer satisfaction, safety, or attendance. Any one of these standards or some combination may be used. Ultimately, a company should employ the standards that represent work that an employee actually performs. For instance, take the case of telemarketers. Customer satisfaction and sales-volume measures indicate telemarketers' performance. Tardiness would not be as relevant unless absenteeism were a general management problem.

Managers should also choose factors that are within the individual employee's control when they create individual performance standards. Further, employees must know about standards and potential awards before the performance period starts. When designed and implemented well, individual incentive plans reward employees on the basis of results for which they are directly responsible. The end result should be that excellent performers receive higher incentive awards than poor performers.

Types of individual incentive plans

There are four common types of individual incentive plans:

* ☆ Piecework

* ☆ Management incentive plans

* ☆ Behavior encouragement plans

* ☆ Referral plans

PIECEWORK PLANS In general, companies use one of two **piecework plans.**[8] The first, typically found in manufacturing settings, rewards employees for their individual hourly production as measured against an objective output standard determined by the pace at which manufacturing equipment operates. For each hour, workers receive piecework incentives for every item produced over the designated production standard. Workers also receive a guaranteed hourly pay rate regardless of whether they meet the designated production standard. Exhibit 5-3 illustrates the calculation of a piecework incentive.

Companies use piecework plans when the time to produce a unit is relatively short, usually less than 15 minutes, and the cycle repeats continuously. Piecework plans are usually found in manufacturing industries such as textile and apparel.

Quality is also an important consideration. Companies do not reward employees for producing defective products. In the apparel industry, manufacturers attempt to minimize defect rates because they cannot sell defective clothing for the same price

---

Exhibit 5-3
Calculation of a Piecework Award for a Garment Worker

Piecework standard: 15 stitched garments per hour

Hourly base pay rate awarded to employees when the standard is not met: $4.50 per hour. That is, workers receive $4.50 per hour worked regardless of whether they meet the piecework standard of 15 stitched garments per hour.

Piecework incentive award: $0.75 per garment stitched per hour above the piecework standard

	GUARANTEED HOURLY BASE PAY	PIECEWORK AWARD (NO. OF GARMENTS STITCHED ABOVE THE PIECEWORK STANDARD × PIECEWORK INCENTIVE AWARD)	TOTAL HOURLY EARNINGS
First hour	$4.50	10 garments × $0.75/garment = $7.50	$12.00
Second hour	$4.50	fewer than 15 stitched garments, thus piecework award equals $0	$ 4.50

as nondefective clothing. Selling defective clothing at a lower price reduces company profits.

The second type of piecework incentive plan establishes individual performance standards that include both objective and subjective criteria. Units produced represents an objective standard. Overall work quality is a subjective criterion that is based on supervisors' interpretations and judgments. For example, supervisors may judge customer service representatives' performance to be higher when sales professionals emphasize the benefits of purchasing extended product warranties than when sales professionals merely mention the availability and price of extended product warranties.

MANAGEMENT INCENTIVE PLANS **Management incentive plans** award bonuses to managers when they meet or exceed objectives based on sales, profit, production, or other measures for their division, department, or unit. Management incentive plans differ from piecework plans. Piecework plans base rewards on the attainment of one specific objective. Instead, management incentive plans often require multiple complex objectives. For example, management incentive plans reward managers for increasing market share or reducing their budgets without compromising the quality and quantity of output. The best-known management incentive plan is management by objectives (MBO).[9] In Chapter 4, MBO was presented as an outcome-oriented performance appraisal technique for merit pay systems. When MBO is used as part of a merit pay system, superiors make subjective assessments of managers' performance, and they use those assessments to determine permanent merit pay increases. When MBO is used as part of an incentive program, superiors communicate the amount of incentive pay managers will receive based on the attainment of specific goals.

BEHAVIOR ENCOURAGEMENT PLANS Under **behavior encouragement plans,** employees receive payments for specific behavioral accomplishments, such as good attendance or safety records. For example, companies usually award monetary bonuses to employees who have exemplary attendance records for a specified period. Behavioral encouragement plans are also applied to safety records. When applied to safety records, workers earn awards according to the attainment of lower personal injury or accident rates associated with the improper use of heavy equipment or hazardous chemicals. Exhibit 5-4 contains an illustration of a sample behavioral encouragement plan that rewards employees for excellent attendance. Employees can earn

Exhibit 5-4
A Sample Behavioral Encouragement Plan That Rewards Employee Attendance

At the end of each three-month period, employees with exemplary attendance records will receive monetary incentive awards according to the following schedule. Note that the number of days absent does not refer to such company-approved absences as vacation, personal illness, jury duty, bereavement leave, military duty, scheduled holidays, and educational leave.

NUMBER OF DAYS ABSENT	MONETARY INCENTIVE AWARD
0 days (perfect attendance)	$250
1 day	$200
2 days	$100
3 days	$ 50
4 days	$ 25

$250 for perfect attendance during a three-month period. With perfect attendance for an entire year, employees can earn $1,000!

Unions appear to be receptive to the use of behavioral encouragement plans because it is also in their best interest to promote worker safety and to minimize absenteeism; both labor and management often view absenteeism as a breach of the employment contract. For example, Erie Plastics implemented a labor-management team to help improve the safety of its workers. Employees earn monetary incentives based on individual improvement in weight control, cholesterol reduction, smoking cessation, lower absenteeism, and receiving annual health screenings.

REFERRAL PLANS Employees may receive monetary bonuses under **referral plans** for referring new customers or recruiting successful job applicants. In the case of recruitment, employees can earn bonuses for making successful referrals for job openings. A successful referral usually means that companies typically award bonuses only if hired referrals remain employed with the company in good standing beyond a designated period, often, at least 30 days. Referral plans rely on the idea that current employees' familiarity with company culture should enable them to identify viable candidates for job openings more efficiently than employment agencies could, since agents are probably less familiar with client companies' cultures. Because their personal reputations are at stake, employees usually are likely to make referrals only if they truly believe they are worthwhile.

> Unions appear to be receptive to the use of behavioral encouragement plans because it is also in their best interest to promote worker safety and to minimize absenteeism; both labor and management often view absenteeism as a breach of the employment contract.

Advantages of individual incentive pay programs

There are three key advantages of individual incentive pay plans. First, individual incentive plans can enhance the relationship between pay and performance. As discussed in Chapter 1, employees in the United States are motivated primarily by earning money. Employees will strive for excellence when they expect to earn incentive awards commensurate with their job performance.

Second, individual incentive plans promote an equitable distribution of compensation within companies. That is, the amount employees earn depends upon their job performance. The better they perform, the more they earn. Ultimately, equitable pay enables companies to retain the best performers. Paying higher performers more money sends a signal that the company appropriately values positive job performance.

A third advantage of individual incentive plans is the compatibility with individualistic cultures such as that in the United States. U.S. employees are socialized to make and be recognized for their individual contributions. Therefore, the national culture of the United States probably enhances the motivational value of individual incentive programs.

Disadvantages of individual incentive pay programs

Although individual incentive plans can prove effective in certain settings, these programs also have serious limitations. Supervisors, human resource managers, and compensation professionals should know about three potential problems with individual incentive plans.

First, individual incentive plans have the potential to promote inflexibility.[10] Since supervisors determine employee performance levels, workers under individual incentive plans become dependent on supervisors for setting work goals. If employees become highly proficient performers, they are not likely to increase their performance beyond the point at which their rewards no longer increase. For example, let's assume that management defines the *maximum* incentive award as $500 per month, which is awarded to employees whose productivity rates 15 percent above the performance standard. Employees who produce at a level greater than 15 percent above the production standard will not receive additional incentive pay besides the $500. With this design, employees would not be motivated to improve their performance beyond 15 percent.

Second, much as with merit pay systems, supervisors must develop and maintain comprehensive performance measures to properly grant incentive awards. Individual incentive programs pose measurement problems when management implements improved work methods or equipment. When such changes occur, it will take some time for employees to become proficient performers. Thus, because it will be difficult for companies to determine equitable incentive awards, employees may resist the new methods.

A third limitation of individual incentive plans is that they may encourage undesirable workplace behaviors when they reward only one or a subset of dimensions that constitute employees' total job performance. Let's assume that an incentive plan rewards employees for quantity of output. If employees' jobs address various dimensions such as quantity of output, quality, and customer satisfaction, employees may

REFLECTIONS

Culture Influences Incentive Pay Effectiveness

Are individual incentive programs appropriate for all companies worldwide? Initially, you might be tempted to answer Yes for two reasons. First, companies design individual incentive programs to promote workers' productivity. Second, all companies must improve workers' productivity in order to maintain competitiveness in the global marketplace. Although these reasons are indisputable, individual incentive programs may not be appropriate for all companies. Careful consideration of national culture should reveal why this is the case. The contrast in national culture between the United States and Japan provides a case in point.

The character of the United States national culture is individualistic. American workers tend to perform at high levels when they believe that there is a link between their effort and resultant performance and that this attendant performance leads to rewards that they consider important in the short term. Thus, individual incentive programs fit well with the individualistic values of the U.S. national culture.

In contrast to U.S. culture, Japan's national culture is characterized by a group orientation. Influenced by the Zen, Confucian, and Samurai traditions, the predominant values of Japanese culture are social cooperation and responsibility, an acceptance of reality, and perseverance.[11] In particular, an individual holds dear a membership in a group. Within the group, duty comes first, and a person must set aside personal feelings, especially if those feelings will hinder the fulfillment of one's duty. These principles fully apply to all aspects of life, including the workplace. Employees' affiliation with a company for an extended period tends to be at least as valuable as monetary compensation. Individual incentive programs clearly are not compatible with the character of Japanese culture.

focus only on the one dimension—in this case, quantity of output—that leads to incentive pay, neglecting the other dimensions.

Group incentives

U.S. employers increasingly use teams to get work done. Two main changes in the business environment have led to an increase in the use of teams in the workplace.[12] First, in the 1980s, the rise in prevalence of Japanese companies conducting business in the United States was dramatic, particularly in the automobile industry. A common feature of Japanese companies was the use of teams, which was seen as contributing to the superior quality of their products. General Motors' Saturn division is an excellent example of quality improvement based on teamwork. Second, team-based job design promotes innovation in the workplace.[13] At Rubbermaid, a manufacturer of such plastic household products as snap-together furniture and storage boxes, product innovation has become the rule since the implementation of project teams. Team members represent various cross-functional areas including research and development, marketing, finance, and manufacturing. Rubbermaid attributes the flourishing of innovation to the cross-fertilization of ideas that has resulted from the work of these diverse teams.

U.S. employers increasingly use teams to get work done. Two main changes in the business environment have led to an increase in the use of teams in the workplace.

Companies that use work teams need to change individualistic compensation practices so that groups are rewarded for their behavior together.[14] Accordingly, team-based pay plans should emphasize cooperation between and within teams, compensate employees for additional responsibilities they often must assume in their roles as members of a team, and encourage team members to attain predetermined objectives for the team.[15] Merit, seniority, and individual incentives do not encourage team behaviors and may potentially limit team effectiveness. Experts support the idea that traditional pay programs will undermine the ability of teams to function effectively.[16] This effect is probably because both merit- and seniority-based pay emphasize hierarchy among employees, which is incompatible with the very concept of a team.

Team-based organization structures encourage team members to learn new skills and assume broader responsibility than is expected of them under traditional pay structures that are geared toward individuals. Rather than following specific orders from a supervisor, employees who work in teams must initiate plans for achieving their team's production. Usually, a pay plan for teams emphasizes cooperation, rewarding team members for the additional responsibilities they must take on and for the skills and knowledge they must acquire. Chapter 6 shows how skill- and knowledge-based pay plans can address these additional responsibilities.

Defining group incentives

Group incentive programs reward employees for their collective performance rather than for each employee's individual performance. Group incentive programs are most effective when all group members have some impact on achieving the goal, even though individual contributions might not be equal. Boeing utilizes a team-based approach to manufacture its model 777 jumbo jet. Although more than 200 cross-functional teams contribute to the construction of each jet, the individual contributions of all the persons involved clearly are not equal. Installing the interior trim features such as upholstery is not nearly as essential to the airworthiness of each jet as are the jobs of ensuring the aerodynamic integrity of each aircraft.

Ultimately, well-designed group incentive plans reinforce teamwork, cultivate loyalty to the company, and increase productivity. For instance, at General Motor's Saturn division, each team is responsible for managing itself. Each team manages its own budget and determines who to hire. The renowned quality of Saturn automobiles has been attributed to the effective utilization of teams.

Companies use two major types of group incentive plans. In *team-based,* or *small group, incentive plans,* a small group of employees share a financial reward when a specific objective is met. In *gain sharing plans,* a group of employees, generally a department or a work unit, is rewarded for productivity gains.

Team-based, or small group, incentive plans

WHO PARTICIPATES? According to the survey cited earlier, 18 percent of the 382 companies in the manufacturing, financial services, public utilities, diversified services, and trade industries reported using group incentives.[17] Of all the companies reporting use of group incentives, companies in the financial services industry and manufacturing industries reported the greatest use (22 and 21 percent, respectively), and companies in the utilities and trade industries reported the least use (7 and 5 percent, respectively). Moreover, of the companies reporting use of group incentives, 24 percent covered salaried employees, and 19 percent covered all employees including salaried workers, with the exception of executives.

The survey also indicated that companies use group incentive plans more than they once did. In fact, the use of group incentive plans rose in all industries surveyed between 1990 and 1992 with the exception of the trade industry, which experienced a decline. The greatest increases in group incentive usage were found in the financial services industry (from 16 percent in 1990 to 22 percent in 1992) and in the manufacturing industry (from 13 percent in 1990 to 21 percent in 1992). As noted, only the trade industry experienced a decline in use of group incentives plans—from 19 percent in 1990 to 5 percent in 1992.

DEFINING TEAM-BASED, OR SMALL GROUP, INCENTIVE PLANS **Team-based incentives,** or **small group incentives,** are similar to individual incentives with one exception. Each group member receives a financial reward for the attainment of a group goal. The timely completion of a market survey report depends upon the collaborative efforts of several individual employees. For example, some group members design the survey; another set collects the survey data; and a third set analyzes the data and writes the report. It is the timely completion of the market survey report, not the completion of any one of the jobs that are required to produce it, that determines whether the group members will receive incentive pay.

There are many kinds of team incentive programs. Companies define these programs according to the performance criteria. Teams or groups may receive incentive pay based on a variety of criteria including customer satisfaction, safety records, quality, and production records. Although these criteria apply to other categories of incentive programs (individual, companywide, and group plans) as well, companies allocate awards to each worker on the basis of the group's attainment of predetermined performance standards.

Human resource managers must devise methods for allocating incentives to team members. Although the team-based reward is generated by the performance of the team, the incentive payments typically are distributed to members of the team individually. Human resource experts allocate rewards in one of three ways:

* Equal incentives payment to all team members

* Differential payments based on team member's contributions to the team's performance

* Differential payments determined by a ratio of each team member's base pay to the total base pay of the group

The first method, the *equal incentives payment approach,* reinforces cooperation among team members except when team members perceive differences in members' contributions or performance. The second method, the *differential incentive payments approach,* distributes rewards based to some extent on individual performance. Obviously, differential approaches can hinder cooperative behavior. Some employees may focus on their own performance rather than on the group's performance because they wish to maximize their income. In compromise, companies may base part of the incentive on individual performance, with the remainder based on the team's performance. The third disbursement method, *differential payments by ratio of base pay,* rewards each group member in proportion to his or her base pay. This approach assumes that employees with higher base pay contribute more to the company and so should be rewarded in accord with that worth.

Gain sharing

WHO PARTICIPATES? Eleven percent of the 382 companies that took part in the previously mentioned survey reported using gain sharing.[18] Of all the companies reporting the use of gain sharing, companies in the manufacturing industry and utilities industry reported the greatest use (17 and 11 percent, respectively), and companies in the trade and financial services industries reported the least use (5 and 4 percent, respectively). Moreover, of the companies reporting the use of gain sharing, 45 percent covered all employees with the exception of executives, 15 percent covered salaried employees with the exception of executives, and 23 percent covered hourly employees only. Further, the use of gain sharing plans remained steady between 1990 and 1992.

EXPLORING THE GAIN SHARING CONCEPT **Gain sharing** describes group incentive systems that provide participating employees with an incentive payment based on improved company performance whether it be for increased productivity, increased customer satisfaction, lower costs, or better safety records.[19] Gain sharing was developed so that all employees could benefit financially from productivity improvements resulting from the suggestion system (see following). Besides serving as a compensation tool, most gain sharing reflects a management philosophy that emphasizes employee involvement. The use of gain sharing is most appropriate where workplace technology does not constrain productivity improvements. For example, assembly line workers' ability to improve productivity may be limited. Increasing the speed of the conveyor belts may compromise workers' safety.

Most gain sharing programs have three components:[20]

* Leadership philosophy

* Employee involvement systems

* Bonus

The first component, *leadership philosophy,* refers to a cooperative organizational climate that promotes high levels of trust, open communication, and participation. The second component, *employee involvement systems,* drives organizational productivity improvements. Employee involvement systems use broadly based suggestion systems. Anyone can make suggestions to a committee, made up of both hourly and management employees, who oversee the implementation of the suggestion. This involvement system also may include other innovative employee involvement practices, such as problem-solving task forces.

The *bonus* is the third component of a gain sharing plan. A company awards gain sharing bonuses when its actual productivity exceeds its targeted productivity level. Usually, the gain sharing bonuses are based on a formula that measures productivity that employees perceive as fair and the employer believes will result in improvements in company performance. Employees typically receive gain sharing bonuses on a monthly basis.

Although many accounts of gain sharing use can be found in the practitioner and scholarly literature, no one has completed a comprehensive, soundly designed investigation of the effectiveness of gain sharing programs.[21] Meanwhile, gain sharing programs' success has been attributed to company cultures that support cooperation among employees.[22] Some gain sharing attempts have failed. Organizational, external environment, and financial information factors, such as poor communications within and across departments, highly competitive product markets, and variable corporate profits over time can hinder the effectiveness of gain sharing programs.[23] Poor communications will stifle the creativity needed to improve the efficiency of work processes when employees focus exclusively on their own work. Highly competitive product markets often require companies to make frequent changes to their production methods. A good example is the automobile industry, in which such changes occur each year with the introduction of new models. When companies make frequent or sudden changes, employees must have time to learn the new processes well before they can offer productive suggestions. Companies that experience variable profits from year to year are most likely not to use gain sharing because management sets aside as much excess cash as possible in reserves for periods when profits are down and excess cash is scarce.

The Scanlon, Rucker, and Improshare gain sharing plans are the most common forms of gain sharing used in companies, and they were also the first types of gain sharing plans developed and used by employers. In the early days of gain sharing, these plans were adopted wholesale. Today, employers generally modify one of these traditional plans to meet their needs, or they adopt hybrid plans.

THE SCANLON PLAN Joseph Scanlon first developed the gain sharing concept in 1935 as an employee involvement system without a pay element. The hallmark of the **Scanlon Plan** is its emphasis on employee involvement. Scanlon believed that employees exercise self-direction and self-control if they are committed to company objectives and that employees will accept and seek out responsibility if given the opportunity.[24] Current Scanlon plans include monetary rewards to employees for productivity improvements. Scanlon plans assume that companies will be able to offer higher pay for workers, generate increased profits for stockholders, and lower price for consumers.

Scanlon plan is a generic term referring to any gain sharing plan that has characteristics common to the original gain sharing plan devised by Joseph Scanlon. Scanlon plans have the following three components:[25]

☆ An emphasis on teamwork to reduce costs, assisted by management-supplied information on production concerns

☆ Suggestion systems that route cost-saving ideas from the work force through a labor-management committee that evaluates and acts on accepted suggestions

☆ A monetary reward based on productivity improvements to encourage employee involvement

Scanlon plan employee involvement systems include formal suggestion systems structured at two levels. *Production-level committees,* usually including a department foreman or supervisor and at least one elected worker, communicate the suggestion program and its reward features to workers. Production committee members encourage workers to make suggestions, help them formulate their suggestions, and formally record their suggestions for consideration. Production committees may also reject suggestions that are not feasible, but they must provide a written explanation of the reasons for the rejection to the worker who made the suggestion. Providing a written rationale under this circumstance is important because it helps employees understand *why* the suggestions were not feasible, and, thus, prevents discouraging workers from making suggestions in the future. After employees' suggestions have been fully implemented, they typically receive bonuses on a monthly basis.

The production committee forwards appropriate suggestions to a *companywide screening committee,* which also includes worker representatives. This committee reviews suggestions referred by the production committees, serves as a communications link between management and employees, and reviews the company's performance each month.

Actual gain sharing formulas are designed to suit the individual needs of the company.[26] Usually, formulas are based on the ratio between labor costs and *sales value of production* (SVOP).[27] The SVOP is the sum of sales revenue plus the value of goods held in inventory.

$$\text{Scanlon ratio} = \frac{\text{Labor costs}}{\text{SVOP}}$$

Small Scanlon ratios indicate that labor costs are low relative to SVOP. Companies definitely strive for lower ratios as Exhibit 5-5 illustrates. In addition, Exhibit 5-5 shows the calculation for a bonus distribution under a Scanlon plan.

THE RUCKER PLAN Similar to Scanlon's plan, the **Rucker Plan** was developed by Allan W. Rucker in 1933. Both Scanlon and Rucker plans emphasize employee involvement and provide monetary incentives to encourage employee participation. The main difference lies in the formula used to measure productivity. Rucker plans use a *value-added formula* to measure productivity. Value-added is the difference between the value of the sales price of a product and the value of materials purchased to make the product. The following example illustrates the concept of value added based on the sequence of events that eventually lead to selling bread to consumers. These events include growing the wheat, milling the wheat, adding the wheat to other ingredients to make bread, and selling the bread to consumers.

First, a farmer grows the wheat and sells it to a miller; the added value is the difference in the income the farmer receives for his wheat and the costs he incurred for seed, fertilizer, fuel and other supplies. The miller, in turn, buys the wheat from the farmer, mills it, and then

Exhibit 5-5
*Illustration of a
Scanlon Plan*

For the past three years, the labor costs for XYZ Manufacturing Company have averaged $44,000,000 per year. During the same three-year period, the sales value of XYZ's production (SVOP) averaged $83,000,000 per year. (As an aside, of the $83,000,000, $65,000,000 represents sales revenue, and $18,000,000 represents the value of goods held in inventory.) The Scanlon ratio for XYZ Manufacturing Company is:

$$\frac{\$44,000,000}{\$83,000,000} = 0.53$$

The ratio of 0.53 is the base line. Any benefits resulting from an improvement, such as an improvement in production methods that results in a reduction in labor costs, are shared with workers. In other words, when improvements lead to a Scanlon ratio that is lower than the standard of 0.53, employees will receive gain sharing bonuses.

The operating information for XYZ Manufacturing Company for the month March 1998 was as follows:

Total labor costs $3,100,000

SVOP $7,200,000

The Scanlon ratio, based on March 1998 information was

$$\frac{\$3,100,000}{\$7,200,000} = 0.43$$

The Scanlon ratio for March 1998 was less than the standard of 0.53, which was based on historical data. In order for there to be a payout, labor costs for March 1998 must be less than $3,816,000 (i.e., 0.53 × $7,200,000); $3,816,000 represents allowable labor costs for March 1998 based on the Scanlon standard established for XYZ Manufacturing.

In summary, the allowable labor costs for March 1998 were $3,816,000. The actual labor costs were $3,100,000. Thus, the savings $716,000 ($3,816,000 − $3,100,000) is available for distribution as a bonus.

---

sells it to a bakery. The difference in the cost of buying the wheat and the price it is sold for to the baker is the amount of "value" the miller "adds" in the milling processes. The same process is repeated by the baker, as the flour which was milled by the miller is mixed with other ingredients and is sold as bread either to the consumer or to a retailer who in turns sells it to the consumer. The baker "adds value" by blending in the other ingredients to the flour and baking the bread. If the bread is sold to the consumer through a retailer, then the retailer also "adds value" by buying the bread from the bakery, transporting it to a store convenient for the consumer, displaying the bread and selling it. The sum of all the added values from each step along the way equals the total contribution to the overall economy from the chain of events.[28]

The following ratio is used to determine whether bonuses will be awarded under a Rucker plan:

$$\text{Rucker ratio} = \frac{\text{(Value added)} - \text{(Costs of materials, supplies, and services rendered)}}{\text{Total employment costs of plan participants (wages, salaries, payroll taxes, and fringe compensation)}}$$

Exhibit 5-6
Illustration of a Rucker Plan

Last year, ABC Manufacturing Company generated net sales of $7,500,000. The company paid $3,200,000 for materials, $250,000 for sundry supplies, and $225,000 for such services as liability insurance, basic maintenance, and utilities. On the basis of these data, value added was $3,825,000 (i.e., net sales − costs of materials, supplies, and services rendered). For this example: $7,500,000 − ($3,200,000 + $250,000 + $225,000).

For the same year, total employment costs were $2,400,000, which includes hourly wages for nonexempt workers, annual salaries for exempt employees, payroll taxes, and all benefits costs. Based on the Rucker formula, the ratio of value added to total employment costs was 1.59. This ratio means that if there are to be bonuses, each dollar attributed to employment costs must be accompanied by creating at least $1.59 of value added.

The operating information for ABC Manufacturing Company for the month July 1998 was as follows:

Value added $670,000

Total employment costs $625,000

The Rucker ratio, based on July 1998 information was:

$$\frac{\$670,000}{\$625,000} = 1.07$$

The Rucker ratio for July 1998 is less than the standard of 1.59, which was based on historical data. In order for there to be a payout, value added for July 1998 must be more than the standard, which would be $1,065,300 (1.59 × $670,000). However, based on the Rucker ratio obtained for July 1998 (1.07), value added was only $716,900. Therefore, employees of ABC Manufacturing will not receive any gain sharing bonuses for July 1998 performance.

In contrast to the Scanlon ratio, companies prefer a larger Rucker ratio. A larger Rucker ratio indicates that value added is greater than total employment costs. Exhibit 5-6 illustrates the calculation for bonus distribution under the Rucker Plan.

IMPROSHARE   Invented by Mitchell Fein in 1973, **Improshare**—*im*proved *productiv*ity through *shar*ing—measures productivity physically rather than in terms of dollar savings as used in the Scanlon and Rucker plans. The programs aim to produce more products with fewer labor hours. Under Improshare, the emphasis is on providing employees with an incentive to finish products.

The Improshare bonus is based on a *labor hour ratio formula*. A standard is established by analyzing historical accounting data to estimate the number of labor hours needed to complete a product. Productivity is then measured as a ratio of standard labor hours and actual labor hours. Unlike the Rucker and Scanlon plans, employee participation is not a feature, and workers receive bonuses on a weekly basis.

Improshare plans feature a *buy-back provision*. Under this provision, a maximum productivity improvement payout level is placed on productivity gains. Any bonus money that is generated because of improvements above the maximum is placed in a reserve. If productivity improves to the point where the maximum is repeatedly exceeded, the firm buys back the amount of the productivity improvement over the maximum with a one-time payment to employees. This payment usually is equal to the amount in the reserve. The company then is permitted to adjust the standards so that a new ceiling can be set at a higher level of productivity. In unionized settings, management's discretion may be challenged by unions when union leadership be-

FEATURE	SCANLON	RUCKER	IMPROSHARE
Program goal	Productivity improvement	Productivity improvement	Productivity improvement
Basis for savings	Labor costs	Labor costs plus raw materials costs plus services costs (e.g., utilities)	Completing work at or sooner than production standard
Employee involvement	Required	Required	Not required
Type of employee involvement	Screening and production committees	Screening and production committees	Not applicable
Bonus payout frequency	Monthly	Monthly	Weekly

lieves that management is simply trying to exploit workers by making it more difficult for them to receive bonuses.

In summary, the Scanlon, Rucker, and Improshare plans are among the best-known kinds of gain sharing programs that are used by companies. The principle underlying these different plans is the same: A group incentive system provides all or most employees in a company with a bonus payment based on improved company performance. But the three plans rest on slightly different assumptions. Exhibit 5-7 details a comparison of these three plans.

Advantages of group incentives

The use of group incentive plans has two advantages for companies. First, companies can more easily develop performance measures for group incentive plans than for individual incentive plans. This is true because obviously there are fewer groups in a company than there are individuals. Thus, companies generally use fewer resources such as staff time to develop performance measures. In addition, judging the quality of the final product makes the most sense because companies must deliver high-quality products to maintain competitiveness. During the late 1970s and early 1980s, American automobile manufacturers (especially Chrysler Corporation) lost substantial market share to foreign automobile manufacturers (especially Honda and Toyota) because foreign auto makers marketed automobiles of substantially higher quality than did American auto makers. The trend did not change until the late 1980s, when American auto makers began to market high-quality vehicles.

Greater group cohesion is the second advantage associated with group incentive plans.[29] Cohesive groups are usually more effective in achieving common goals than are individuals focusing on specific tasks for which they are responsible. Undoubtedly, working collaboratively is in group members' best interest in order to maximize their incentive awards.

Disadvantages of group incentives

The main disadvantage of group incentive compensation is employee turnover. Companies' implementation of group incentive programs may lead to turnover because of the *free-rider effect*. Some employees may make fewer contributions to the group goals because they may possess lower ability, skills, or experience than other group members. In some groups, members may deliberately choose to put forth less effort, particularly if all group members receive the same incentive compensation regardless of individual contributions to the group goals. In any case, the free-rider effect initially leads to feelings of inequity among those who make the greatest contributions to the attainment of the group goal. Over time, members who make the greatest contributions will likely leave.

Group members may feel uncomfortable with the fact that other members' performance influences compensation level. Exemplary performers are more likely to feel this way when some other group members are not contributing equally to the attainment of group goals, and the lower performance of group members may lead to lower earnings for all members of the group. Discomfort with group incentive plans is likely to be heightened if incentive compensation represents the lion's share of core compensation.

Companywide incentives: Profit sharing

Two companywide incentive programs are employee stock ownership plans (ESOPs) and profit sharing plans. Employee stock ownership plans are best known as a major component of executive compensation plans. Discussion of ESOPs is deferred to Chapter 13, which addresses executive compensation. The focus here will be on profit sharing plans.

The use of companywide incentive plans can be traced to the nineteenth century. Companies instituted profit sharing programs to ease workers' dissatisfaction with low pay and to change their beliefs that company management paid workers substandard wages while earning substantial profits. Quite simply, management believed that workers would be less likely to challenge managerial practices if they were to receive a share of company profits.

As competitive pressures on companies increased, management sought methods to improve employee productivity. At the present time, companies use profit sharing to motivate employees to work harder for increased profits, primarily through increased productivity. Advocates of profit sharing programs believe that well-designed profit sharing programs link pay to profits. When pay is tied to profits, workers' and managements' interests will become more compatible as both strive toward increasing company profits.

At the present time, companies use profit sharing to motivate employees to work harder for increased profits, primarily through increased productivity.

Defining profit sharing plans

Profit sharing plans pay a portion of company profits to employees, separate from base pay, cost-of-living adjustments, or permanent merit pay increases. Two basic kinds of profit sharing plans are used widely today. First, **current profit sharing** plans award cash to employees, typically on a quarterly or annual basis. Second, **deferred profit sharing** plans place cash awards in trust accounts for employees. These trusts are set aside on employees' behalf as a source of retirement income. Apart from the time horizon, these plans differ with regard to taxation. Current profit sharing plans provide cash to employees as part of their regular core compensation; thus, these payments are subject to Federal income taxation when they are earned. Deferred profit sharing plans are not taxed until the employee begins to make withdrawals during retirement. Premature withdrawal of funds that were secured under a deferred compensation plan are subject to stiff tax penalties (up to 10 percent). The IRS (Internal Revenue Service) established this penalty to discourage employees from making premature withdrawals. Some companies offer deferred compensation as one kind of retirement program. We discuss deferred profit sharing plans in Chapter 11. The focus here will be on current profit sharing plans because employees receive cash compensation as a reward for on-the-job performance.

In the survey cited earlier, 21 percent of 382 companies in the manufacturing, financial services, public utilities, diversified services, and trade industries reported using current profit sharing plans. Of all the companies reporting use of current profit sharing, companies in the manufacturing industry, diversified services industry, and financial services industry reported the greatest use (24, 22, and 21 percent, respectively), and companies in the trade industry and utilities industry reported the least use (10 and 9 percent, respectively). Moreover, of the companies reporting use of current profit sharing programs, 53 percent covered all employees. Twenty-eight percent covered all employees with the exception of executives.[30] In general, two employee groups do not participate in companywide incentive plans: executives and hourly workers who are employed under a collectively bargained agreement that governs the terms of the employment relationship with the employer. Usually, executive-level employees do not participate in profit sharing plans because they participate in other incentive systems that are based on company profit levels, which we discuss in Chapter 13. Therefore, the reason for excluding executives from general profit sharing programs is to avoid "double dipping."

The survey also indicates that some industries have experienced an increase in the usage of current profit sharing while other industries have exhibited a decrease in usage.[31] Between 1990 and 1992, the use of profit sharing rose in the diversified services industry (from 14 to 22 percent) and in the financial services industry (from 19 to 21 percent). Companies in the trade industry experienced the greatest decline in profit sharing usage for the same period—from 14 to 10 percent. In general, these changes can be explained by the trends in profits. When profits increase, so does the prevalence of profit sharing plans; when profits decrease, so does the prevalence of profit sharing plans.

Calculating profit sharing awards

Human resource professionals determine the pool of profit sharing money with any of three possible formulas. A *fixed first-dollar-of-profits formula* uses a specific percentage of either pre- or posttax annual profits contingent upon the successful attainment of a company goal. For instance, a company might establish that the profit sharing fund will equal 7 percent of corporate profits but that payment is contingent on a specified reduction in scrap rates.

Second, other companies use a *graduated first-dollar-of-profits formula* instead of a fixed percentage. For example, a company may choose to share 3 percent of the first $8 million of profits and 6 percent of the profits in excess of that level. Graduated formulas motivate employees to strive for extraordinary profit targets by sharing even more of the incremental gain with employees.

Third, *profitability threshold formulas* fund profit sharing pools only if profits exceed a predetermined minimum level but fall below some established maximum level. Companies establish minimums to guarantee a return to shareholders before they distribute profits to employees. They establish maximums because they attribute any profits beyond that level to factors other than employee productivity or creativity, such as technological innovation.

After management selects a funding formula for the profit sharing pool, they must consider how to distribute pool money among employees. Usually, companies make distributions in one of three ways: equal payments to all employees, proportional payments to employees on the basis of annual salary, and proportional payments to employees on the basis of their contribution to profits. *Equal payments* to all employees reflect a belief that all employees should share equally in the company's gain in order to promote cooperation among employees. But, employee contributions to profits probably vary, so most employers divide the profit sharing pool among employees on a differential basis.

Companies may disburse profits according to *proportional payments based on an employee's annual salary.* As we detail in Chapters 7 and 8, salary levels vary with both internal and external factors, and, in general, the higher the salary the greater work the company assigns to a job. Presumably, higher-paying jobs indicate the greatest potential to influence a company's competitive position. For any given job, pay will differ according to performance or seniority. Chapter 4 noted that higher performance levels and seniority result in greater worth.

Still another approach is to disburse profits *as proportional payments based on an employee's contribution to profits.* Some companies use job performance as a measure of employee contributions to profit. This approach is not very feasible, however, because it is difficult to isolate each employee's contributions to profits. For example, how does a secretary's performance (answering telephones, greeting visitors, typing memos) directly contribute to company performance?

Companies can treat profit sharing distributions either as compensation awarded in addition to an employee's base pay or as "pay at risk." In the former case, base pay is set at externally competitive levels, so any profit sharing is tantamount to a bonus. In the latter case, base pay is set below the average relative to competing employers. This approach creates a sense of risk; employees' earnings for a given period may be relatively meager or relatively sizable compared with what they could have earned elsewhere.

Advantages of profit sharing plans

The use of a profit sharing plan has two main advantages, one for employees and the other for companies. When properly designed, profit sharing plans enable employees to share in companies' fortunes. As employees benefit from profit sharing plans, they will probably be more likely to work productively to promote profits. Obviously, the upshot of enhanced employee productivity is greater profits for companies that use profit sharing plans.

Companies that use profit sharing programs gain greater financial flexibility. As we discussed, monetary payouts to employees vary with profit levels. During economic downturns, payout levels are significantly lower than during economic boom periods. This feature of profit sharing plans enables companies to use limited cash reserves where needed, such as for research and development activities.

Disadvantages of profit sharing plans

There are two main disadvantages associated with profit sharing plans. Again, one directly affects employees, and the other affects companies. Profit sharing plans may undermine the economic security of employees, particularly if profit sharing represents a sizable portion of direct compensation. Because company profits vary from year to year, so will employees' earnings. Thus, employees will find it difficult to predict their earnings, and their savings and buying behavior will be affected. If there is significant variability in earnings, companies' excellent performers will likely leave for employment with competitors. Certainly, the turnover of excellent performers represents a significant disadvantage to companies.

Employers also find profit sharing programs to be problematic under certain conditions. Profit sharing plans may fail to motivate employees because they do not see a direct link between their efforts and corporate profits. Hourly employees in particular may have trouble seeing this connection, because their efforts appear to be several steps removed from the company's performance. For instance, an assembly line worker who installs interior trim—carpeting and seats—to automobiles may not find any connection between his or her efforts and level of company profits because interior trim represents just one of several steps in the production of automobiles.

Designing incentive pay programs

When designing an incentive pay plan, HR professionals and line managers should consider five key factors:

- ✮ Whether the plan should be based on group or individual employee performance
- ✮ The level of risk employees will be willing to accept in their overall compensation package
- ✮ Whether incentive pay should replace all traditional pay or complement it
- ✮ The criteria by which performance should be judged
- ✮ The time horizon for goals—long term, short term, or some combination

Group versus individual incentives

Group incentive programs are most suitable when the nature of work is interdependent and the contributions of individual employees are difficult to measure.

Companies considering various design alternatives should choose a design that fits the structure of the company. Group incentive programs are most suitable when the nature of work is interdependent and the contributions of individual employees are difficult to measure. In such situations, companies probably require cooperative behavior among their employees. Companies may be able to encourage team behavior by linking compensation to the achievement of department or division goals and eliminating from the pay determination process factors that are outside the group's control, such as the late delivery of raw materials by an independent vendor.

On the other hand, individual incentive plans reward employees for meeting or surpassing predetermined individual goals, such as production or sales quotas. As in group incentive programs, the attainment of individual goals should be well within the control of the employees. Moreover, goals for individual incentive programs should be based on independent work rather than on interdependent work. For example, it would be appropriate to base an employee's incentive on typing accuracy because the work can be performed independently and there are probably few external constraints on an employee's ability to complete typing work. At the group level, it would be reasonable to provide incentives to the individual members of a sales team. The sale and implementation of computer hardware and networks, however, are not appropriate for individual incentive programs. These products involve a team of marketing professionals and technical experts who depend upon each other to identify the configuration of hardware and networking equipment that will best meet the client's needs and to successfully install the equipment in the client's company.

Level of risk

Careful consideration should be given to the level of risk the employees are willing to accept. As mentioned previously, incentive pay may complement base salary or be used in place of all or a portion of base salary. Clearly, the level of risk increases as incentive pay represents a greater proportion of total core compensation. The level of risk tends to be greater for higher-level employees than for those who are placed low in a company's job structure. Intuitively, it is reasonable to infer that the attainment of a first-line supervisor's goal of maintaining a packing department's level of productivity above a predetermined level is less risky than the achievement of a sales manager's goal of increasing market share by 10 percent in a market in which the competition is already quite stiff. Apart from an employee's rank, the level of risk chosen should depend on the extent to which employees control the attainment of the desired goal. The adoption of incentive pay programs makes the most sense when participants have a reasonable degree of control over the attainment of the plan's goals. Logically, incentive programs are bound to fail when the goals are simply out of reach because they are too difficult or when extraneous factors tend to hamper employees' efforts to meet goals.

Complementing or replacing base pay

When complementing base pay, a company awards incentive pay in addition to an employee's base pay and fringe compensation. Alternatively, companies may reduce base pay by placing the reduced portion at risk in an incentive plan. For instance, if a company grants its employees 10 percent raises each year as a matter of course, the company could, instead, grant its employees a 4 percent cost-of-living increase and use the remaining 6 percent as incentive by awarding none of it to below-average performers, only half of it to employees whose performance is average, and the entire 6 percent to employees whose performance is above average. In this scenario, the 6 percent that was expected by the employees to become part of their base pay is no longer guaranteed because that potential salary has been placed at risk. The introduction of risk into the pay program gives employees the potential to earn more than the 6 percent because poor performers will receive less, leaving more to be distributed to exemplary performers.

Companies in cyclical industries such as retail sales could benefit by including an incentive component in the core compensation programs they offer to employees. During slow business periods, the use of regular merit pay programs that add permanent increments to base pay can create budget problems. If incentive pay were used instead of permanent merit raises, then the level of expenditure on compensation would vary with levels of business activity. In effect, the use of incentive pay can lower payroll costs during lean periods and enhance the level of rewards when business activity picks up.

Performance criteria

Obviously—from the discussion of performance appraisal in Chapter 4—the measures used to appraise employee performance should be quantifiable and accessible. For incentive pay programs, common measures of employee performance include company profits, sales revenue, and number of units produced by a business unit. Preferably, the measures chosen should be related to the company's competitive strategy. For instance, if a company is attempting to enhance quality, its incentive plan should reward employees on the basis of customer satisfaction with quality.

In reality, more than one performance measure may be relevant. In such instances, a company is likely to employ all of the measures as a basis for awarding incentives. The weighting scheme would reflect the relative importance of each performance criterion to the company's competitive strategy. For example, company performance, 10 percent; unit performance, 40 percent; and individual performance, 50 percent, incor-

THE FLIP SIDE OF THE COIN

"On the Folly of Rewarding A, While Hoping for B"

In a classic article titled "On the Folly of Rewarding A, While Hoping for B," Steven Kerr criticized organizational reward systems that reward some behaviors while ignoring other desirable work behaviors.[32] Although the article was published more than two decades ago, follies of that kind are quite pervasive in organizations today. Case-in-point: research universities.

Historically, research universities awarded faculty members various kinds of awards based on the quality and quantity of their scholarly publications. These rewards included pay raises, promotions to the ranks of associate professor and full professor, and tenure. Unfortunately, university administrators did not place nearly as much emphasis on teaching effectiveness, which meant that faculty received rewards as long as they continued to publish scholarly articles but regardless of their performance as course instructors. Given this reality, many faculty members (but certainly not all) devoted much of their energy to research at the expense of teaching quality.

In recent years, university administrators claim to place greater emphasis on the importance of teaching effectiveness. This "emphasis" came about in response to outcries from taxpayers whose dollars fund a significant portion of public university budgets, as well as the parents of children attending both private and public universities because of the rampant increases in tuition costs. Also contributing to this "emphasis" are widely publicized criticisms of faculty in newspaper articles and in books such as *Profscam*.[33]

Certainly, emphasizing teaching effectiveness has merit. Unfortunately, the reward systems in research universities have not changed very much. In business school departments, faculty pay raises continue to be based almost exclusively on publication record rather than on teaching effectiveness.[34] University administrators have not broken out of the old ways of thinking about reward and recognition practices. This lack of change may be due to the fact that university administrators, faculty, and students have not reached consensus on the meaning of teaching effectiveness or on valid methods for measuring teaching effectiveness.

porating all of the organizational levels. Clearly, an employee would receive an incentive even if company or departmental performance were poor. In effect, the relative weights are indicative of the degree of risk to an employee that is inherent in these plans. Compared with the previous example, the following plan would be quite risky: company performance, 50 percent; departmental performance, 35 percent; and individual performance, 15 percent. Employees' earnings would depend mainly on company and departmental performance, over which they possess less control than their own performance.

Time horizon: Short term versus long term

A key feature of incentive pay plans is the time orientation. There are no definitive standards to distinguish between short and long term. Instead, industry norms determine what is considered short and long term. Nevertheless, a general rule of thumb is that short-term goals generally can be achieved in a year or less, and long-term goals may require as many as several years.

In general, incentives for lower-level employees tend to be based on short-term goals that are within the control of such employees. For example, production workers' performance is judged on periods as short as one hour. On the other hand, incentive programs for professionals and executives have a long-term orientation. For instance, rewarding an engineer's innovation in product design requires a long-term orientation because it takes an extended amount of time to move through the series of steps required to bring the innovation to the marketplace—patent approval, manufacturing, and market distribution. The incentives that executives receive are based on a long-term horizon because their success is matched against the endurance of a company over time.

Linking incentive pay with competitive strategy

How do incentive pay systems fit with the two fundamental competitive strategies—lowest-cost and differentiation? Ultimately, incentive pay systems, when properly applied, can contribute to companies' meeting the goals of lowest-cost and differentiation strategies. However, the rationale for the appropriateness of incentive pay systems differs according to the imperatives of the lowest-cost and differentiation competitive strategies.

Lowest-cost competitive strategy

Lowest-cost strategies demand reduced output costs per employee. In general, incentive pay appears to be well suited to reducing output costs per employee, and will benefit companies that are pursuing a lowest-cost strategy. Specific incentive pay programs' suitability merits comment.

In general, incentive pay appears to be well suited to reducing output costs per employee, and will benefit companies that are pursuing a lowest-cost strategy.

Individual incentive programs such as piecework systems connect core compensation costs to employee productivity. From a company's perspective, a well-designed piecework system aligns its expenditure on compensation with the level of employee output. The use of piecework plans is especially effective when it motivates employees to keep up with the demand for companies' products. When employees' output matches market demand, then the company will cover its expenditure on incentive compensation and will generate a profit.

Behavioral encouragement plans provide effective incentives for companies pursuing lowest-cost strategy if these companies suffer excessive absenteeism or poor safety records. Absenteeism poses direct fiscal costs to employers and causes disruptions in work flow that can lead to compromises in production or service delivery. Poor safety records cost employers stiff monetary penalties that arise from violations of the Occupational Safety and Health Act. In addition, employers are liable for on-the-job accidents, and they carry workers' compensation insurance (Chapter 10). The cost of workers' compensation insurance increases dramatically for companies with poor safety records.

Among the group incentives, gain sharing programs are appropriate for companies that pursue a lowest-cost strategy. Simply put, employee involvement facilitates productivity enhancements. Such improvements result from more efficient ways to conduct work and enhanced employee motivation that comes from greater participation in workplace matters.

Current profit sharing plans are probably the least likely form of incentive to support lowest-cost strategies. As mentioned earlier in this chapter, profit sharing can be an ineffective incentive when employees do not perceive links between their work contributions and company profits. If profit share awards do not motivate employees, then their productivity will unlikely be influenced in any way and the money spent on such awards will be "wasted" from the company's standpoint.

Differentiation competitive strategy

Among the incentives that we reviewed earlier, team-based incentives and gain sharing are clearly the most appropriate for companies pursuing differentiation strategies.

Differentiation strategies mandate employees who display creativity, whose minds are open to novel ways of approaching work, and who are willing to take risks. Compared with lowest-cost strategies, differentiation strategies hold a longer-term focus with regard to the attainment of preestablished objectives. Among the incentives that we reviewed earlier, team-based incentives and gain sharing are clearly the most appropriate for companies pursuing differentiation strategies. By their very nature, team-based incentives and gain sharing programs promote interaction among coworkers and some degree of autonomy to devise the "best" way to achieve the objectives set by management.

Piecework plans and current profit sharing plans provide inappropriate incentives if a company wishes to promote differentiation. Piecework plans focus on increasing employees' productivity on their existing jobs rather than on encouraging employees to offer creative ideas that may lead to product or service differentiation. As before, profit sharing plans may be ineffective if employees see no link between job performance and profits.

Summary

This chapter discussed the incentive pay concept. How incentive pay systems differ from traditional pay systems (based on seniority and merit); varieties of individual, group, and companywide incentives; issues about designing incentive pay programs; and fit with competitive strategy were covered. Companies should seriously consider adopting incentive pay programs when the conditions for using incentive pay programs are appropriate. Perhaps one of the greatest challenges for companies is to ensure that employees perceive a connection between job performance and the rewards they receive. Another challenge is for companies to balance the level of risk employees will bear, particularly given the fact that American employees are accustomed to receiving base pay and regular permanent increases according to seniority or merit pay systems.

Discussion questions

1. Indicate whether you agree or disagree with the following statement. "Individual incentive plans are less preferable than group incentives and companywide incentives." Explain your answer.
2. Nowadays, there is a tendency among business professionals to endorse the use of incentive pay plans. Identify two jobs for which individual incentive pay is appropriate and two jobs for which individual incentive pay is inappropriate. Be sure to include your justification.
3. Critics of profit sharing plans maintain that these plans do not motivate employees to perform at higher levels. Under what conditions are profit sharing plans not likely to motivate employees?
4. Unlike individual incentive programs, group and companywide incentive programs reward individuals on the basis of a group (e.g., cost savings in a department) and companywide (e.g., profits) performance standards, respectively. Under group and companywide incentive programs, it is possible for low performers to benefit without making substantial contributions to group or company goals. What can companies do to ensure that low performers do not benefit?
5. Opponents of incentive pay programs argue that these programs manipulate employees more so than do seniority and merit pay programs. Discuss your views of this statement.

Key terms

incentive pay
variable pay
individual incentive plans
piecework plans
management incentive plans
behavior encouragement plans
referral plans
group incentive programs
team based incentives

small group incentives
gain sharing
Scanlon plan
Rucker plan
Improshare
profit sharing plans
current profit sharing
deferred profit sharing

1. C. Peck, *Variable pay: Nontraditional programs for motivation and reward* (New York: The Conference Board, 1993).

2. L. R. Gòmez-Mejìa and D. B. Balkin, *Compensation, organizational strategy, and firm performance* (Cincinnati: South-Western Publishing, 1992).

3. J. R. Schuster and P .K. Zingheim, *The new pay: Linking employee and organizational performance* (New York: Lexington Books, 1992).

4. S. Caudron, Master the compensation maze, *Personnel Journal* 72 (June 1993):64a–64o.

5. F. R. Dulles and M. Dubofsky, *Labor in America: A history,* 4th ed. (Arlington Heights, Ill.: Harlan Davidson, 1984).

6. Peck, *Variable pay.*

7. E. E. Lawler III. *Strategic pay* (San Francisco: Jossey-Bass, 1990).

8. Peck, *Variable pay.*

9. P. Drucker, *The practice of management* (New York: Harper, 1954).

10. L. R. Gòmez-Mejìa, D. B. Balkin, and R. L. Cardy, *Managing human resources* (Englewood Cliffs, N.J.: Prentice Hall, 1995).

11. V. Terpstra and K. David, *The cultural environment of international business,* 3rd ed. (Cincinnati: South-Western Publishing, 1991).

12. S. E. Jackson, Team composition in organizational settings: Issues in managing an increasingly diverse work force, in S. Worchel, W. Wood, and J. A. Simpson, eds., *Group process and productivity* (Newbury Park, Calif.: Sage, 1992), pp. 138–173.

13. R. M. Kanter, When a thousand flowers bloom: Structural, collective, and social conditions for innovation in organizations, in B. M. Staw and L. L. Cummings eds., *Reasearch in organizational behavior,* vol. 10 (Greenwich, Conn.: JAI Press, 1988), pp. 169–211.

14. S. Worchel, W. Wood and J. A. Simpson, eds., *Group process and productivity* (Newbury Park, Calif.: Sage, 1992).

15. J. Kanin-Lovers and M. Cameron, Team-based reward systems, *Journal of Compensation and Benefits,* (January–February, 1993):55–60.

16. J. R. Schuster and P. K. Zingheim, Building pay environments to facilitate high-performance teams. *ACA Journal* 2 (1993):40–51.

17. C. Peck, *Variable pay.*

18. Ibid.

19. J. G. Belcher Jr., Gain sharing and variable pay: The state of the art, *Compensation & Benefits Review* (May–June 1994):50–60.

20. R. J. Doyle, *Gain sharing and productivity* (New York: American Management Association, 1983).

21. Peck, *Variable pay.*

22. G. T. Milkovich and J. M. Newman, *Compensation,* 4th ed. (Homewood, Ill.: Irwin, 1993).

23. T. Ross, Why gain sharing sometimes fails, in B. Graham-Moore and T. Ross, eds., *Gain sharing: Plans for improving performance* (Washington, D.C.: Bureau of National Affairs, 1990), pp. 100–115.

24. F. G. Lesiur, ed., *The Scanlon Plan: A frontier in labor-management cooperation* (Cambridge, Mass.: MIT Press, 1958).

25. R. J. Bullock and E. E. Lawler III, Gain sharing: A few questions and fewer answers, *Human Resource Management* Vol. 23 (1984): pp. 23–40.

26. B. T. Smith, The Scanlon plan revisited: A way to a competitive tomorrow, *Production Engineering* 33 (1986):28–31.

27. A. J. Geard, Productivity from Scanlon type plans, *Academy of Management Review* 1 (1976):99–108.

28. D. W. Myers, *Compensation management* (Chicago: Commerce Clearing House, 1989): pp. 588–589.

29. E. E. Lawler III and S. G. Cohen, Designing a pay system for teams, *American Compensation Association Journal* 1, no. 1 (1992):6–19.

30. Peck, *Variable pay.*

31. Ibid.

32. S. Kerr, On the folly of rewarding A, while hoping for B, *Academy of Management Journal* 18 (1975):769–783.

33. C. J. Syles, *Profscam: Professors and the demise of higher education* (Washington, D.C.: Regenery Gateway, 1988).

34. L. R. Gòmez-Mejìa and D. B. Balkin, The determinants of faculty pay: An agency theory perspective, *Academy of Management Journal* 35 (1992):921–955.

CHAPTER

SIX

Pay-for-knowledge and skill-based pay

LEARNING OBJECTIVES

In this chapter, you will learn about

1. Pay-for-knowledge concepts and the kinds of skills and knowledge that apply to these compensation programs
2. Usage of pay-for-knowledge and skill-based pay programs
3. Reasons that companies adopt pay-for-knowledge and skill-based pay programs
4. Pay-for-knowledge plan and skill-based pay variations
5. Contrasts between pay-for-knowledge systems and incentive (variable) pay or merit pay concepts
6. Advantages and disadvantages of using pay-for-knowledge plans and skill-based pay plans
7. How pay-for-knowledge plans and skill-based pay plans fit with differentiation and lowest cost competitive strategies

TELECORP, a producer of telecommunications components, implemented a skill-based pay program in 1994 for its installation department employees. Briefly, skill-based pay programs reward employees for successfully learning new job-related skills. Compensation, training, and new product development professionals teamed up to develop this program because the technology used to make telecommunications equipment evolves rapidly. For example, the technology used to establish communications systems has evolved from analog to digital to fiber optics. Training programs designed to keep TELECORP technicians abreast of the new technology help them serve their clients more effectively. Businesses expect to have a reliable telecommunications system that carries sound clearly and quickly with minimal errors, and these are advantages of fiber optics technology over digital and analog technologies. By becoming knowledgeable about fiber optics technology, TELECORP's field technicians are able to serve their clients more effectively. Also, by staying abreast of telecommunications technology, field technicians contribute to TELECORP's competitive advantage by offering differentiated service, that is, the most up-to-date service relative to the competition's service. Rewarding employees should motivate them to become more skilled and knowledgeable.

The use of pay-for-knowledge programs is on the rise. According to the American Compensation Association, pay-for-knowledge presently is one of the fastest-growing personnel innovations in the United States.

Clearly, technological changes have influenced TELECORP's decision to adopt pay-for-knowledge programs. The use of pay-for-knowledge programs is on the rise. According to the American Compensation Association, pay-for-knowledge presently is one of the fastest-growing personnel innovations in the United States. In 1990, more than half of all Fortune 500 corporations such as General Electric and Chrysler Corporation used skill-based pay with some of their employee groups. Companies applied pay-for-knowledge programs to a wide variety of employee groups including direct labor (for example, employees who maintain inventories of goods such as furniture in warehouses), skilled tradespeople (for example, plumbers and carpenters), clerical workers (for example, secretaries), and supervisory and managerial employees.[1]

Defining pay-for-knowledge and skill-based pay

Pay-for-Knowledge plans reward managerial, service, or professional workers for successfully learning specific curricula. Federal Express Corporation's pay-for-knowledge program rewards its customer service employees who successfully learn how to calculate delivery rates and how to document packages for shipment from the United States to various foreign countries.[2] **Skill-based pay,** used mostly for employees who do physical work, increases these workers' pay as they master new skills. For example, both unions and contractors who employ carpenters use skill-based pay plans. As carpenters master more-advanced woodworking skills such as cabinetmaking, they earn additional pay.

Both skill- and knowledge-based pay programs reward employees for the range, depth, and types of skills or knowledge they are capable of applying productively to their jobs. This feature distinguishes pay-for-knowledge plans from merit pay, which rewards employees' job performance. Said another way, pay-for-knowledge programs reward employees for their *potential* to make meaningful contributions on the job. Northern Telecom's Meridian PBX Plant in Santa Ana, California, awarded a $0.50 per hour pay increase to employees for each of the first three skills they learned as evidenced by their successfully completing designated training programs. After that, employees earned an additional $0.65 per hour pay increase for each of the next four skills they successfully learned.[3]

In this chapter, we use the term *pay-for-knowledge* to refer to both pay-for-knowledge and skill-based pay programs. Although we noted differences between the two earlier, the basic principles underlying these programs are similar. As an aside, compensation professionals use the terms *competency-based pay* and *pay-for-knowledge* interchangeably.

Human resource professionals can design pay-for-knowledge plans to reward employees for acquiring new horizontal skills, vertical skills, or a greater depth of knowledge or skills. Employees can earn rewards for developing skills in one or more of these dimensions depending on the kind of skills the company wants to foster. **Horizontal skills** (or **horizontal knowledge**) are similar skills or knowledge. For example, clerical employees of a retail store might be trained to perform several kinds of recordkeeping tasks. They may maintain employee attendance records, schedule salespeople's work shifts, and monitor the use of office supplies (for example, paper clips, toner cartridges for laser printers) for reordering. Although focused on different aspects of a store's operations, all three of these tasks are based on employees' fundamental knowledge of record keeping.

Vertical skills (or **vertical knowledge**) are those skills traditionally considered supervisory skills such as scheduling, coordinating, training, and leading others. These types of supervisory skills are often emphasized in pay-for-knowledge plans designed for self-managed work teams, since team members often need to learn how to manage one another.[4] Such work teams—referred to as self-regulating work groups, autonomous work groups, or semiautonomous work groups—typically bring employees together from various functional areas to plan, design, and complete one product or service. At Chrysler Corporation, teams of skilled employees from a variety of functions—marketing, finance, engineering, and purchasing—redesign and manufacture Chrysler vehicle models. One of the most recent innovations resulting from this team approach is the redesigned Jeep Grand Cherokee, which is a very popular sports utility vehicle. The popularity of the Jeep Grand Cherokee can be attributed to the ingenuity of the work teams. These teams capitalized on the unique talents—both knowledge and skills—of different employees who together produced a reasonably priced sports utility vehicle with features (for example, four-wheel drive, leather seats) that have met market demand.

Depth of skills (or **depth of knowledge**) refers to the level of specialization or expertise an employee brings to a particular job. Some pay-for-knowledge plans reward employees for increasing their depth of skills or knowledge. Human resource professionals may choose to specialize in managing a particular aspect of the HR function, such as compensation, benefits administration, training evaluation, and new employee orientation. To be considered a compensation specialist, HR professionals must develop a depth of knowledge by taking courses offered by the American Compensation Association on job evaluation, salary survey analysis, principles of pay-for-knowledge system design, merit pay system design, and incentive pay system design, among others. The more compensation topics HR professionals master, the greater their depth of knowledge about compensation.

Usage of pay-for-knowledge programs

A wide variety of employers have established pay-for-knowledge programs[5]; however, there is no systematic survey research that documents the actual number. Companies of various sizes use pay-for-knowledge programs. More than half of the companies using this kind of pay system employ between 150 and 2,000 people. The absence of detailed evaluative data makes it impossible to conclude whether size is related to the success of these programs.

These programs are most commonly found in continuous process settings such as in manufacturing companies that use assembly lines where one employee's job depends upon the work of at least one other employee. At Bell Sports, manufacturer of motorcycle safety helmets, several steps constitute the assembly process, such as applying enamel to the helmets and attaching the visors to the helmets. Clearly, the two tasks require different sets of skills. Applying enamel requires an ability to use automated sprayers. Specifically, this skill demands that workers possess strong literacy skills so that they can interpret read-outs from the sprayers that suggest possible problems. Attaching visors to the helmets requires proficient motor skills that involve eye-hand coordination. When employees learn how to perform different jobs, they can cover for absent coworkers. In the event of absenteeism, Bell Sports benefits from having cross-trained employees because it will more likely meet its production schedules.

Pay-for-knowledge programs that emphasize vertical skills work well at manufacturing companies that organize work flow around high-performance work teams in which employees are expected to learn both functional and managerial tasks such as work scheduling, budgeting, and quality control. This means that groups of employees work together to assemble entire products such as cellular telephones (Motorola) and furniture (Steelcase, a manufacturer of office furniture), and each team member learns how to perform the jobs of other team members.

Survey evidence indicates that skill-based pay programs are employed in both manufacturing and service companies.[6] According to 1992 data, production workers in manufacturing settings participate in pay-for-knowledge programs more often than do other kinds of workers. Pay-for-knowledge programs also represent a prevalent basis for pay among clerical and skilled trades employees such as carpenters and electricians.

Reasons to adopt pay-for-knowledge programs

Pay-for-knowledge programs represent important innovations in the compensation field. Pay-for-knowledge systems imply that employees must move away from viewing pay as an entitlement. Instead, these systems treat compensation as a reward earned for successfully acquiring and, often, implementing, job-relevant knowledge and skills. For instance, support personnel may earn pay increases for learning how to use the Windows 95 software program. Advocates of pay-for-knowledge offer two key reasons that firms seeking competitive advantage should adopt this form of compensation: technological innovation and increased global competition.[7]

Technological innovation

First, in an age of technological innovation in which robots, telecommunications, artificial intelligence, software, and lasers perform routine tasks, some skills soon become obsolete.[8] Now jobs require new and different worker skills. The skills needed by automobile mechanics have changed dramatically. Previously, competent automobile mechanics were adept at manually assembling and disassembling carburetors. Now, electronic fuel injection systems, which are regulated by on-board computers, have replaced carburetors, necessitating that auto mechanics possess different kinds of skills. Specifically, automobile mechanics must now possess the skills to use computerized diagnostic systems to assess the functioning of fuel injectors.

As technology leads to the automation of more tasks, employers combine jobs and confer broader responsibilities on remaining workers. For example, the technology of advanced automated manufacturing such as in the automobile industry began doing the jobs of employees, including the laborer, the materials handler, the operator-assembler, and the maintenance person. Nowadays, a single employee performs all of those tasks in a position called manufacturing technician. The expanding range of tasks and responsibilities in this job demands higher levels of reading, writing, and computation skills than its predecessors, which required employees to possess strong hand-to-eye coordination. Most employees must possess higher levels of reading skills than before because they must be able to read the operating and troubleshooting manuals (when problems arise) of automated manufacturing equipment that is based on computer technology. Previously, manufacturing equipment was relatively simple and easy to operate and was based on simple mechanical principles such as pulleys.

These technological changes have fostered increased autonomy and team-oriented workplaces, which also demand different job-related skills than employees needed previously.[10] The manufacturing technician's job mentioned previously is generally more autonomous than its predecessor. Thus, technicians must be able to manage themselves and their time.

Employers now rely on working teams' technical and interpersonal skills to drive efficiency and to improve quality. Today's consumers often expect customized products and applications, which require that employees possess sufficient technical skill to tailor products and services to customers' needs, as well as the interpersonal skills necessary to determine client needs and customer service.[10] Long-distance telephone service providers such as AT&T, MCI, and Sprint seek competitive advantages by serving clients' present needs as well as anticipating possible changes in customers' long distance service needs. As a result, these companies offer programs such as The "I" Plan, Friends and Families, and The Most to provide clients the most favorable

> Pay-for-knowledge systems imply that employees must move away from viewing pay as an entitlement. Instead, these systems treat compensation as a reward earned for successfully acquiring and, often, implementing, job-relevant knowledge and skills.

long distance telephone rates based on their particular calling patterns. To be successful, these companies must have customer service associates who maintain current knowledge of these programs as well as the skills needed to match service plans to clients' long distance service requirements.

Increased global competition

Increased global competition has forced companies in the United States to become more productive. Now more than ever, to sustain competitive advantage, companies must provide their employees with leading-edge skills and encourage employees to apply their skills proficiently. Evidence clearly shows that foreign workers are better skilled and are able to work more productively than U.S. employees in at least two ways.

First, employers in both the European Common Market and some Pacific Rim economies emphasize learning. In both cases, employers use classes and instruction as proactive tools for responding to strategic change. In Ireland, the private sector offers graduate employment programs to employees in particular skill areas such as science, marketing, and technology.[11] An example of a marketing skill is the application of inferential statistics to a market analysis. Marketing professionals use inferential statistics to draw conclusions about whether the level of satisfaction with Brand A tennis shoes among a small sample of Brand A tennis shoe owners represents the level of satisfaction among all persons who have purchased Brand A tennis shoes.

Second, both Western European and some Pacific Rim cultures provide better academic preparation and continuing workplace instruction for noncollege-bound portions of their work forces. Although the United States is well-regarded for the quality of education its colleges and universities provide to skilled professionals such as engineers, the Europeans are much better at educating their "vocational" segment of the work force. Western European workplaces emphasize applied rather than theoretical instruction for vocational employees. The European apprenticeship structure mixes academic and applied learning both in "high schools" and in continuing education for employees.

The Norwegian government offers a guarantee of training or apprenticeship in a public or private enterprise for every person under 20 years of age who has not been accepted into a college and is unemployed. The U.S. government offers no such guarantees to its citizens.[12] Possibly owing to the Norwegian government's efforts, Norwegians worked an average of 39.9 hours per week in 1992, whereas Americans worked an average of only 34.9 hours per week. For the same year, unemployment in Norway was 5.9 percent; in the United States, unemployment was 7.3 percent.[13] Although these unemployment rates do not seem very different, they are indeed quite different. Specifically, the 7.3 percent unemployment rate for the United States translated into approximately 9,384,000 unemployed workers. If the unemployment rate in the United States were only 5.9 percent, approximately 2,375,000 fewer workers would have been unemployed.

To establish and maintain competitive advantages, companies should carefully consider the adoption of pay-for-knowledge systems. As discussed earlier, many companies already compensate employees on this basis because they have discovered the advantages of such plans. Of course, as companies consider adopting pay-for-knowledge systems, they must tailor compensation programs to the particular kinds of skills they wish to foster. Human resource professionals can guide employee development through a variety of pay-for-knowledge systems.

Varieties of pay-for-knowledge programs

A **stair-step model** actually resembles a flight of stairs, much like the arrangement illustrated in Exhibit 6-1 for an assembly technician. The steps represent jobs from a particular job family that differ in terms of complexity. Jobs that require a greater number of skills are more complex than jobs with fewer skills. For example, an assembly technician 1 job requires employees to possess two skills—line restocking and pallet breakdown. An assembly technician 3 job requires employees to possess six skills—line restocking, pallet breakdown, burr removal, line jockey, major assembly, and soldering. In terms of the stairs, higher steps represent jobs that require more skills than lower steps. Compensation specialists develop separate stair-step models for individual job families, for example, clerks and accountants. Thus, a company may have more than one stair-step model, each corresponding to a particular job family such as accounting, finance, or clerical. No stair-step model should include both skilled trade workers—such as carpenters, electricians, and plumbers—and clerical workers.

How do employees earn increases in hourly pay based on a stair-step model? Let us use the model in Exhibit 6-1. Howard Jones wants to become an Assembly

Exhibit 6-1
A Stair-Step Model at ABC Company

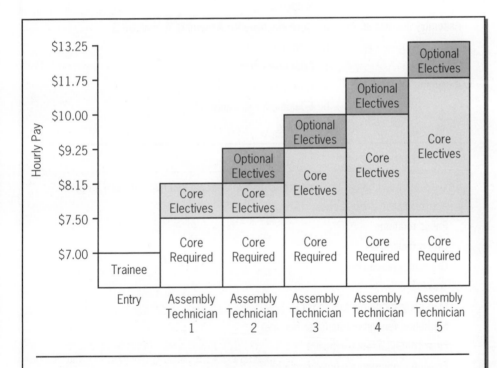

CORE REQUIRED

Employees must complete all three workshops.

1. Orientation Workshop: The goal of this workshop is to familiarize employees with ABC's pay schedule, offerings of employee benefits, work hours, holiday and vacation policies, and grievance procedures.

2. Safety Workshop: The goal of this workshop is to educate employees about the procedures for ensuring the health and safety of themselves and coworkers while using and being around the machinery.

continued on next page

Exhibit 6-1
A Stair-Step Model at ABC Company (continued)

CORE REQUIRED (CONT.)

---

3. Quality Workshop: The goal of this workshop is to acquaint employees with ABC's procedures for maintaining quality standards for parts assembly.

CORE ELECTIVES

Employees must complete all core elective courses for the designated job before they assume the commensurate duties and responsibilities.

Assembly Technician 1:	a. Line restocking
	b. Pallet breakdown
Assembly Technician 2:	a. Core electives for Assembly Technician 1
	b. Burr removal
	c. Line jockey
Assembly Technician 3:	a. Core electives for Assembly Technician 2
	b. Major assembly
	c. Soldering
Assembly Technician 4:	a. Core electives for Assembly Technician 3
	b. Acid bath
	c. Final inspection
Assembly Technician 5:	a. Core electives for Assembly Technician 4
	b. Equipment calibration
	c. Training

OPTIONAL ELECTIVES

Employees may choose to complete up to two optional electives at each step.

Administrative procedures

Public relations

Group facilitation

Grievance resolution

Training

Marketing fundamentals (basic)

Marketing fundamentals (intermediate)

Finance fundamentals (basic)

Finance fundamentals (intermediate)

Accounting fundamentals (basic)

Accounting fundamentals (intermediate)

Human resource management fundamentals (basic)

Human resource management fundamentals (intermediate)

Technician. ABC Manufacturing Company hires Howard as assembly technician trainee at $7.00 per hour. Howard starts by completing three core required workshops designed for assembly technician 1—a company orientation, a safety workshop, and a quality workshop. After successfully completing all three courses, as evidenced by his earning greater than the minimum scores on tests for each subject, Howard receives a $0.50 per hour pay increase, making his total hourly pay $7.50. In addition, Howard completes the core electives designated for his assembly technician 1 job—he learns how to restock lines and break down pallets. Upon successfully completing both courses, he receives a $0.65 per hour pay raise, making his total hourly pay $8.15 and earning him the Assembly Technician 1 title. Howard may continue to learn more skills for an assembly technician by completing the curriculum for the Assembly Technician 2 level. Afterward, if he chooses, Howard can complete the curricula to move to Level 3.

Training courses may be offered in-house by the company, at a local vocational school, or at a local community or four-year college. Usually, companies offer specialized courses in-house for skills that pertain to highly specialized work or for work that bears upon companies' competitive advantage. Federal Express sponsors customer service training internally because the skills and knowledge required to be an effective Federal Express customer service employee distinguish its service from other express mail companies including DHL and UPS. For more common skills or skills that do not bear upon competitive advantage, companies typically arrange to have their employees take training courses offered by external agents such as community colleges. Most companies require clerical employees to be able to effectively use word processing programs. Thus, it is common for companies to sponsor their employees' training in word processing courses at local community colleges.

The **skill blocks model** also applies to jobs from within the same job family. Just as in the stair-step model, employees progress to increasingly complex jobs. However, in a skill blocks program, skills do not necessarily build on each other. Thus, an employee may progress to higher steps by taking double or more steps, earning the pay that corresponds with that step. Although similar, the stair-step model and the skill blocks model differ in an important way. The stair-step model addresses the development of knowledge or skills depth. In particular, Howard Jones could develop his skills depth as an assembly technician by taking the five separate curricula. With the successful completion of each curriculum, Howard will enhance the depth of his skills as an assembly technician. As we will see shortly, the skill blocks model emphasizes both horizontal and vertical skills.

Look at Exhibit 6-2. Pro Company hired Bobby Smith as a Clerk 1 because her employment tests demonstrated her proficiency in the skills and knowledge that she needs for that level job. The required skills correspond to Clerk 1 core requirements—filing, typing, and working knowledge of one word processing program. Moreover, Bobby knows how to take transcription and shorthand, which are Level 1 core electives. During employee orientation for new clerical hires, an HR representative explained the pay-for-knowledge program available to this employee group. In particular, Bobby knows that she can advance to any level in the clerical pay structure by successfully completing the corresponding curriculum. To make her goal of becoming a Clerk 4, Bobby simply needs to complete the Level 4 curriculum. She need not take the curricula for the Clerk 2 and Clerk 3 jobs. Taking the Clerk 2, 3, or 4 curriculum will enhance Bobby's horizontal skills. The Clerk 3 curriculum provides the knowl-

Exhibit 6-2
**A Skill Blocks Model at
Pro Company**

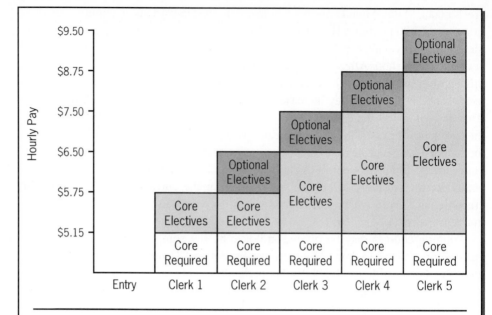

CORE REQUIRED

All employees must be proficient in all of the following skills or take the necessary courses that are offered by Pro Company in order to become proficient.

Principles of filing

Typing skill, 40 words per minute minimum speed

Working knowledge of one word processing program such as *Word for Windows* or *Wordperfect for Windows.*

CORE ELECTIVES

Employees must complete all core elective courses for the designated job before they assume the commensurate duties and responsibilities.

Clerk 1:   a. Transcription

           b. Shorthand

Clerk 2:   a. Maintaining office supplies inventory

           b. Ordering office supplies from local vendor

Clerk 3:   a. Accounts receivable ledgers

           b. Accounts payable ledgers

           c. Working knowledge of one spreadsheet program, for example, *Lotus 1-2-3* or *Excel*

Clerk 4:   a. Payroll records

           b. Maintaining records of sick pay usage, vacation usage, and performance bonus awards based on company policy

Clerk 5:   a. Project scheduling

           b. Assigning personnel to projects

Exhibit 6-2
A Skill Blocks Model at
Pro Company (continued)

OPTIONAL ELECTIVES

Employees may choose to complete up to two optional electives at each step.

Public relations (basic, intermediate, advanced)

Supervisory skills

Resolving minor employee conflicts

Effective written communication skills (basic, intermediate, advanced)

Effective oral communication skills (basic, intermediate, advanced)

edge required to successfully manage different types of ledgers. Taking the Clerk 5 curriculum will increase Bobby's vertical skills, including project scheduling and assigning personnel to projects.

A **job-point accrual model** encourages employees to develop skills and learn to perform jobs from different job families. A company would benefit if its employees were proficient in a small subset of jobs. Employees generally are not free to learn as many jobs as they would like to learn. Companies limit the number of jobs employees are allowed to learn in order to avoid having them become "jacks of all trades." Job-point accrual methods create organizational flexibility and promote company goals by assigning a relatively greater number of points to skills that address key company concerns—such as customer relations. The more points employees accrue, then the higher their core compensation level will be.

For example, let's assume that ZIP-MAIL is a new company that competes in the express mail delivery service against established firms in the business—DHL, Federal Express, and UPS. ZIP-MAIL couriers must meet the company's delivery promise of 7:30 A.M., which is at least a half-hour earlier than the promised delivery time for some of the competitors. They also must convey a professional image and establish an open rapport with individual customers and company representatives to encourage them to choose ZIP-MAIL over its competitors. In other words, customer relations skills are essential to ZIP-MAIL's success. ZIP-MAIL stands to benefit from a pay-for-knowledge program, particularly one that follows the job-point accrual model. Under this system, employees who successfully complete customer relations training courses would earn more points relative to other kinds of training offered by ZIP-MAIL, creating an incentive for employees to learn customer relations skills over other kinds of skills.

Although the job-point accrual model and the cross-departmental model are similar, the intended purpose of the two programs differs. The job-point accrual model encourages employees to learn skills and acquire knowledge that bear directly on companies' attainment of competitive advantage, as in the case of ZIP-MAIL. **Cross-departmental models** promote staffing flexibility by training employees in one department in some of the critical skills they would need to perform effectively in other departments. If the shipping department experienced a temporary staffing shortage, a production department supervisor who has been trained in distribution methods can be "loaned out" to the shipping department. The cross-departmental model can help production environments manage sporadic, short-term staffing shortages. Such

Judging Pay-for-Knowledge Program Effectiveness

You may be thinking, "The rationale for rewarding employees for gaining new skills and knowledge is clear, but, ultimately, how employees *apply* these skills in the workplace matters the most for competitive advantage." This comment is very astute. Indeed, employers who adopt any of these pay-for-knowledge variations must ensure that employees are applying the skills they have learned to jobs in the workplace. To ensure this transfer of theoretical skills to actual performance, companies that use pay-for-knowledge systems often combine them with pay-for-performance programs such as merit or incentive pay.[14] Thus, not all companies award increases to employees solely on the basis of whether they completed training successfully. In fact, some companies that use pay-for-knowledge programs defer awarding pay increases until after employees have successfully applied their knowledge or skills to the job. McDonnell Douglas Helicopter Company links pay-for-knowledge and pay-for-performance programs. Specifically, assembly workers do not receive a pay increase just for successfully completing training. Instead, they must demonstrate that they have successfully acquired their new skills by applying them to their jobs. Employees receive pay increases only after quality control inspectors verify that employees have appropriately applied their knowledge or skills to the job.

The previous example illustrates that McDonnell Douglas bases pay-for-knowledge increases according to whether employees successfully apply knowledge to their jobs. Another model that ties pay-for-knowledge increases to subsequent performance is the **skill level–performance matrix,** which rewards employees according to *how well* they have applied skills and knowledge to their jobs. This model mixes pay-for-performance compensation systems—merit pay—with the pay-for-knowledge approach. Under this approach, employee compensation depends not only on learned skill level, but also on how well employees apply that instruction according to their supervisors' subjective assessments. Exhibit 6-3 illustrates the skill-level performance matrix method. Holding skill level constant, hourly pay increases with performance, and holding performance rating constant, an employee's hourly pay rises with skill level.

Exhibit 6-3
Skill Level–Performance Matrix

SKILL LEVEL[1]	HOURLY PAY FOR PERFORMANCE RATING		
	BELOW AVERAGE	**AVERAGE**	**ABOVE AVERAGE**
Clerk I	$5.25	$5.75	$6.25
Clerk II	$5.50	$6.00	$6.75
Clerk III	$5.70	$6.30	$7.25
Clerk IV	$5.95	$6.60	$7.45
Clerk V	$6.20	$6.85	$8.25

[1] Skill level defined according to a skill blocks model (as in Exhibit 6-2).

cross-training can also help companies meet seasonal fluctuations in demand for their products or services.

Sears Roebuck & Company could train its vinyl-siding installers to install central air conditioning systems. Much of the vinyl-siding installation business activity takes place during the fall and winter, and much of the central air conditioning installation takes place during the spring and summer. Therefore, vinyl-siding installers trained in air conditioning installation could be available to meet the spike in demand for air conditioning systems installation during the spring and summer, when the demand for vinyl-siding installation is relatively lower. Rather than hiring additional staff members or laying off workers in the off-season, a company can shift employees from departments or functional areas where staffing requirements are relatively low to departments or functional areas where staffing requirements are high.

The holiday shopping rush represents an excellent context in which a company can benefit from cross-departmental training systems. Retail business activity varies widely with enhanced volume during the holiday shopping season in the fall. For several months following this period, business activity tends to subside dramatically.[15] Let's consider a company that manufactures and distributes custom-made shoes. For weeks before the holidays, the workers in the production department are working rapidly to complete all the telephone gift orders that must be shipped before Chanukah and Christmas day. Within a few days of the holidays, the company will probably receive fewer orders because purchasers of custom-made shoes recognize that they need to place orders well in advance of the date they expect to receive their shoes. As orders drop off, many workers in both sales and production departments will be less busy than workers in the distribution department. Under the cross-departmental pay-for-knowledge system, sales and production department workers will be rewarded for learning how to properly package shoes and how to complete express mail invoices so that they can assist the shipping department during its peak activity periods.

Contrasting pay-for-knowledge with job-based pay—merit pay and incentive pay

Companies institute job-based pay plans or pay-for-knowledge plans on the basis of very different fundamental principles and goals. Exhibit 6-4 lists the key differences between these two pay programs. **Job-based pay** compensates employees for jobs they currently perform. Human resource staff establishes a minimum and maximum acceptable amount of pay for each job. In the case of merit pay, managers evaluate employees' performance according to how well they fulfilled their designated roles as specified in their job descriptions and periodic objectives. Managers then award a permanent merit addition to base pay, based on employee performance.

With incentive pay, managers award one-time additions to base pay. Pay raise amounts are based on the attainment of work goals, and managers communicate both pay raise amounts and work goals to employees in advance. The executives of ACME Manufacturing Company are dissatisfied with the level of defective disk drives for computers, which is significantly higher than that of their competitor DO-RITE Manufacturing Company. ACME's monthly defect rate is 6,500 disk drives per employee, and DO-RITE's monthly defect rate is significantly less, at 3,000 disk drives per employee. ACME executives decided to implement an incentive system to en-

Exhibit 6-4
**Skill-Based and Job-Based
Pay: A Comparison**

FEATURE	SKILL-BASED	JOB-BASED
Pay level determination	Market basis for skill valuation	Market basis for job valuation
Base pay	Awarded on how much an employee knows or on skill level	Awarded on the value of compensable factors
Base pay increases	Awarded on an employee's gain in knowledge or skills	Awarded on attaining a job-defined goal or seniority
Job promotion	Awarded on an employee's skills base and proficiency on past work	Awarded on exceeding job performance standards
Key advantage to employees	Job variety and enrichment	Perform work and receive pay for a defined job
Key advantage to employers	Work scheduling flexibility	Easy pay system administration

courage employees to make fewer defective disk drives, with the ultimate goal of having a lower defect rate than DO-RITE. At the end of every month, ACME employees receive a monetary award based on their defect rate for that month. Exhibit 6-5 displays the incentive plan for ACME. As you can see, employees earn a larger incentive award as the defect rate decreases.

Pay-for-knowledge compensates employees for developing the flexibility and skills to perform a number of jobs effectively. Moreover, these programs reward employees on their potential to make positive contributions to the workplace, based on their suc-

Exhibit 6-5

**ACME's Incentive Plan for
Reductions in Monthly
Defect Rates**

ACME's goal is to achieve a monthly defect rate of 3,000 disk drives per employee to match DO-RITE's (the competition's) per employee defect rate. Employees whose monthly defect rates exceed 3,000 disk drives will receive an incentive award that is commensurate with the following schedule:

REDUCTION IN ERROR RATE	MONTHLY INCENTIVE AWARD
91–100%	$500
81–90%	$450
71–80%	$400
61–70%	$350
51–60%	$300
41–50%	$250
31–40%	$200
21–30%	$150
11–20%	$100
1–10%	$50

Exhibit 6-6
Job Description for a Toll Collector

Collects toll charged for use of bridges, highways, or tunnels by motor vehicles, or fare for vehicle and passengers on ferryboats: Collects money and gives customer change. Accepts toll and fare tickets previously purchased. At end of shift balances cash and records money and tickets received. May sell round-trip booklets. May be designated according to place of employment as Toll-Bridge Attendant (government service), or type of fare as Vehicle-Fare Collector (motor trans.; water trans.). May admit passengers through turnstile and be designated Turnstile Collector (water trans.).

Source: Reprinted from *Dictionary of occupational titles,* vol. 1, 4th ed. (Washington, D.C.: U.S. Government Printing Office, 1991).

cessful acquisition of work-related skills or knowledge. Job-based pay plans reward employees for the work they have done as specified in their job descriptions or periodic goals: that is, for how well they have fulfilled their potential to make positive contributions in the workplace.

Finally, job-based pay programs apply to an organization-wide context since employees earn base pay rates for the jobs they perform (Chapter 8 addresses how management establishes these pay rates). Pay-for-knowledge plans apply in more-limited contexts because not all jobs can be assessed on the basis of skill or knowledge. Exhibit 6-6 describes the duties that toll booth operators perform. This position would clearly not be appropriate in a pay-for-knowledge system, since the job is narrowly defined and the skills are very basic. Toll booth operators probably master these required skills and knowledge within a short period after assuming their responsibilities.

Advantages of pay-for-knowledge programs

Although no large-scale studies have clearly demonstrated these benefits, case studies suggest that employees and companies enjoy advantages from pay-for-knowledge programs. Well designed pay-for-knowledge systems, which we will discuss in Chapter 9, *can* provide employees and employers with distinct advantages over traditional pay systems.

Advantages to employees

Employees usually like pay-for-knowledge systems for at least two reasons. First, pay-for-knowledge can provide employees with both job enrichment and job security. As you probably know, job enrichment refers to a job design approach that creates more intrinsically motivating and interesting work environments. Companies can enrich jobs by combining narrowly designed tasks so that an employee is responsible for producing an entire product or service.[16]

According to job characteristics theory, employees will be more motivated to perform jobs that contain a high degree of core characteristics, such as:[17]

Pay-for-knowledge can provide employees with both job enrichment and job security.

1. **Skill variety.** The degree to which the job requires the person to do different tasks and involves the use of a number of different skills, abilities, and talents.

2. **Task identity.** The degree to which the job is important to others—both inside and outside the company.

3. **Autonomy.** The amount of freedom, independence, and discretion the employee enjoys in determining how to do the job.

4. **Feedback.** The degree to which the job or employer provides the employee with clear and direct information about job outcomes and performance.

At Volvo's Uddevalla manufacturing facility in Sweden, teams of seven to ten hourly workers produced entire vehicles rather than focusing solely on certain aspects such as drivetrain assembly or attaching upholstery to a car's interior.[18] Contributing to all aspects of manufacturing automobiles expands the horizontal dimensions (skill variety) of workers' jobs. In some cases, an employer empowers teams to manage themselves and the work they do. These managing duties, including controlling schedules, dividing up tasks, learning multiple jobs, and training one another, represent the vertical dimensions (autonomy) of work. Pay-for-knowledge programs can help companies design such intrinsically motivating jobs, especially with regard to skill variety and autonomy. Both pay-for-knowledge and job enrichment programs expand both horizontal and vertical work dimensions.

So far, evidence does suggest that pay-for-knowledge plans lead to increased employee commitment, enhanced work motivation, and improved employee satisfaction.[19] These results are probably due to the fact that well-designed pay-for-knowledge plans promote skill variety and autonomy. Some experts attribute these positive outcomes of pay-for-knowledge programs to the fact that employees can increase their skills and be paid for doing so.[20]

The second advantage for employees is that, since pay-for-knowledge programs make them more flexible, they can actually represent better job security for employees. Rather than being laid off during periods of low product demand, flexible employees can perform a variety of jobs that draw upon the skills they have attained through pay-for-knowledge programs. During periods of slow sales, it is common for many companies to conduct inventories of their products. Customer service employees who also have learned inventory accounting techniques are less likely to be laid off during periods of low sales than are customer service employees who have not

THE FLIP SIDE OF THE COIN

Pay-for-Knowledge Programs Help the Competition

The flip side of the coin is that pay-for-knowledge programs, which companies implement to promote their own competitive advantage, can actually promote their competitors' competitive advantage. Clearly, employees who acquire knowledge and skills through companies' pay-for-knowledge programs will probably increase their employment alternatives with other companies. Competitors may hire recently trained employees away by offering them higher compensation than can be offered by the present employer, who has already invested money in the employee by providing a pay-for-knowledge program. Competitors can offer higher pay because they do not have to pay for training. In effect, companies capitalize on the training offered by competitors to hire highly skilled workers. This problem may be salient to companies that pay employees who have learned how to use word processing and spreadsheet programs because these skills are easily applied to work in a large number of companies.

The flip side of the coin is that pay-for-knowledge programs, which companies implement to promote their own competitive advantage, can actually promote their competitors' competitive advantage.

learned inventory techniques. Further, employees who update their skills will be more attractive applicants to other employers as well. Very definitely, clerical employees who become proficient in the use of Windows-based computer software will have more employment opportunities available to them than clerical employees who have resisted learning these recent programs. Likewise, human resource professionals who become familiar with the constraints placed on compensation practice by recent laws (Civil Rights Act of 1991 and the Americans with Disabilities Act) will probably have more employment opportunities available to them than human resource professionals who choose not to become familiar with those pertinent laws.

Advantages to employers

Employers like pay-for-knowledge systems because, properly designed and implemented, these programs can lead to enhanced job performance, reduced staffing, and greater flexibility. First, pay-for-knowledge programs have a lot of potential influence on both the quantity and the quality of an employee's work. Employees who participate in a pay-for-knowledge program often exhibit higher productivity levels because employees who know more about an entire process may also be able to identify production shortcuts that result in increased productivity. For example, electrical wiring in an automobile runs along the vehicle's interior beneath the seats and carpeting. Members of auto assembly teams familiar with all aspects of the automobile manufacturing process could potentially identify and fix problems with the wiring before the seats and carpeting were installed. If such problems were identified after the seats and carpeting were installed, completion of the vehicle would be delayed, and fewer automobiles could be counted as finished.

> *Employers like pay-for-knowledge systems because, properly designed and implemented, these programs can lead to enhanced job performance, reduced staffing, and greater flexibility.*

Product or service quality should also gain from these programs. As employees learn more about the entire production process, quality of both the product and its delivery often improve. Schott Transformers, a supplier of magnetic components and power systems to the computer and telecommunications industries, which instituted a pay-for-knowledge program, experienced a significant increase in the quality of their service as measured by customer satisfaction surveys.[21] Such customer satisfaction increases usually follow a company's implementation of self-directed work teams in which employees develop both horizontal and vertical skills. If employees feel responsible for entire products, they take more care to ensure that customers are satisfied.

Second, companies that use pay-for-knowledge systems can usually rely on leaner staffing because multiskilled employees are better able to cover for unexpected absenteeism, family or medical leave, or training sessions that take individual employees away from their work. The successful operation of a restaurant depends upon coordinated efforts from bus persons, waitstaff, chefs, and other food preparers. When one or two buspeople are absent, the restaurant will not be able to serve its reservations customers on time. If employees are cross-trained in a number of jobs, fewer employees will have to be on hand to provide backup for absent buspeople.

Third, pay-for-knowledge systems provide companies with greater flexibility in meeting staffing demands at any particular time. Quite simply, because participants of pay-for-knowledge plans have acquired a variety of skills, they can perform a wider range of tasks. This kind of staffing flexibility helps companies when unexpected changes in demand occur. After a tornado devastated a densely populated area in Illinois, the municipal water supply was not fit for drinking because areawide power outages disabled the pumps that purify the water. As a result, residents living in the affected areas rushed to grocery stores to purchase bottled water. Because this sudden demand exceeded the normal inventories of bottled water in grocery stores, wholesale distributors such as SuperValu had to respond quickly by moving bottled water inventories from their warehouses to the retail grocery stores. This spike in demand for bottled water overwhelmed the usual number of distribution and shipping staff.

Disadvantages of pay-for-knowledge programs

Although pay-for-knowledge programs present many advantages, they have at least two limitations. First, employers feel that the main drawback of pay-for-knowledge systems is that hourly labor costs, training costs, and overhead costs can all increase. Hourly labor costs often increase because greater skills should translate into higher pay levels for the majority of workers. Since training is an integral component of pay-for-knowledge systems, training costs are generally higher than at companies with job-based pay programs. These costs can be especially high during initial startup periods as HR professionals attempt to standardize employee backgrounds. This process begins with assessing the skill levels of employees. Federal Express tests its 35,000 employees twice each year.[22]

Second, pay-for-knowledge systems may not mesh well with existing incentive pay systems.[23] Where both pay-for-knowledge and incentive pay systems are in operation, employees may not want to learn new skills when the pay increase associated with learning a new skill is less than an incentive award employees could earn using skills they already possess. Often, employees place greater emphasis on maximizing rewards in the short term rather than on preparing themselves to maximize the level of rewards over time, which can be facilitated through pay-for-knowledge programs.

An assembly line worker chooses to focus on his work because he receives monetary incentives for meeting weekly production goals set by management rather than taking skills training in inventory control for which he will earn additional pay upon successful completion of the training (although the pay increase he receives for successfully completing training is much less than the incentive awards he can earn). In the short term, this worker is earning a relatively large sum of money; however, in the long term, he may be jeopardizing his earnings potential and job security. In the future, the company may experience reduced demand for its product, which would result in the company's eliminating the incentive program. Also, when demand goes down, the company might place production workers in other jobs, such as in the warehouse, until the demand for the product returns to normal. Without the skills required to work in the warehouse, this employee may be targeted for a layoff or a reduced work schedule, either of which clearly would lead to lower earnings.

Linking pay-for-knowledge with competitive strategy

How do pay-for-knowledge systems fit with the two fundamental competitive strategies—lowest-cost and differentiation? Ultimately, pay-for-knowledge systems, when properly applied, can contribute to companies' meeting the goals of lowest-cost and differentiation strategies. However, the rationale for the appropriateness of pay-for-knowledge systems differs according to the imperatives of the lowest-cost and differentiation competitive strategies.

Lowest-cost competitive strategy

Lowest-cost strategies require firms to reduce output costs per employee. Pay-for-knowledge systems are appropriate when the training employees receive enables them to work more productively on the job with fewer errors. Pay-for-knowledge plans may seem to contradict the lowest-cost imperative because of several factors in the short term. The cost of providing training, "down time" while employees are participating in training, and inefficiencies that may result back on the job while employees work on mastering new skills can easily increase costs in the short term. Recall that Federal Express tests its 35,000 employees twice each year.[24] The company pays for four hours of study time and two hours of actual test time, which is bound to be quite expensive.

However, a longer-term perspective may well lead to the conclusion that pay-for-knowledge programs support the lowest cost imperative. Over time, productivity enhancements and increased flexibility should far outweigh the short-run costs if a company ultimately provides exemplary service to its customers. That is, Federal Express is renowned for its worldwide express mail service because of its remarkable track record in consistently meeting delivery promises in a timely fashion for a reasonable price. Much of Federal Express's success can be attributed to its knowledgeable customer service employees because these individuals play a key role in determining how to best manage the delivery of packages across time zones and through international customs check points.

Differentiation competitive strategy

A differentiation strategy requires creative, open-minded, risk-taking employees. Compared with lowest-cost strategies, companies that pursue differentiation strategies must take a longer-term focus to attain their preestablished objectives. Pay-for-knowledge compensation is appropriate when employees are organized into teams that possess some degree of autonomy over how work will be performed. Employers that pursue differentiation strategies often rely on employees' technical and interpersonal skills in working teams to drive efficiency, quality improvements, and new applications for existing products and services. As discussed earlier, at Chrysler Corporation, teams of skilled employees from a variety of functions—marketing, finance, engineering, and purchasing—redesign and manufacture Chrysler vehicle models. One of the most recent innovations resulting from this team approach is the redesigned Jeep Grand Cherokee. The popularity of the Jeep Grand Cherokee can be attributed to the ingenuity of the work teams. Such "cutting edge" companies often focus on new technology that employees must learn—a goal consistent with pay-for-knowledge programs.

New technology also allows customization of products, which requires employees with sufficient technical skill and imagination to tailor products and services to customers' needs, as well as the interpersonal skills necessary to provide good customer service. Clearly, TELECORP is an exemplar of a telecommunications company that continually provides differentiated service to its customers—both technically and interpersonally—because of its investment in pay-for-knowledge compensation programs.

Summary

This chapter discussed the pay-for-knowledge concept, reasons companies should adopt pay-for-knowledge programs, varieties of pay-for-knowledge programs, how pay-for-knowledge is related to merit pay and incentive pay programs, advantages and disadvantages of pay-for-knowledge programs, and fit with competitive strategy. Companies should seriously consider adopting pay-for-knowledge programs in order to keep up with technological innovation and to compete internationally. Perhaps the greatest challenge for companies is to ensure that employees are given the opportunity to apply newly learned skills in productive ways.

Discussion questions

1. "Pay-for-knowledge plans are less preferable than individual incentive pay programs" (Chapter 5). Indicate whether you agree or disagree with that statement. Detail your arguments to support your position.

2. Pay-for-knowledge is becoming a more prevalent basis of pay in companies. However, pay-for-knowledge is not always an appropriate basis for compensation. Discuss the conditions under which incentive pay (Chapter 5) is more appropriate than pay-for-knowledge programs. Be sure to include your justification.

3. Name at least three jobs that have been influenced by such technological advances as robotics, word processing software, fax machines, or electronic mail. Describe the jobs prior to the technological advances (see the *Dictionary of Occupational Titles* for descriptions), and explain how these jobs have changed or will change because of the technological changes. For each job, list the new skills that you feel are relevant for pay-for-knowledge programs.

4. Discuss your reaction to the following statement. "Companies should not provide training to employees because it is the responsibility of individuals to possess the necessary knowledge and skills before becoming employed."

5. As we discussed in the chapter, pay-for-knowledge programs are not suitable for all kinds of jobs. On the basis of your understanding of pay-for-knowledge concepts, identify at least three jobs for which this basis for pay is inappropriate. Be sure to provide your rationale given the information in this chapter.

Key terms

pay-for-knowledge
skill-based-pay
horizontal skills
horizontal knowledge
vertical skills
vertical knowledge
depth of skills

depth of knowledge
stair-step model
skill blocks model
job-point accrual model
cross-departmental models
skill level–performance matrix
job-based pay

Endnotes

[1] S. Caudron, Master the compensation maze, *Personnel Journal* 72 (June 1993):64a–64o.

[2] D. Filipowski, How Federal Express makes your package its most important, *Personnel Journal* 71 (February 1992):40–46.

[3] S. Caudron, Master the compensation maze.

[4] Bureau of National Affairs, Skill-based pay, in *BNA's Library on Compensation and Benefits on CD* [CD-ROM] (Washington, D.C.: Bureau of National Affairs, 1995).

[5] G. D. Jenkins Jr., G. E. Ledford Jr., N. Gupta, and D. H. Doty, *Skill-based pay: Practices, payoffs, pitfalls, and prescriptions* (Scottsdale, Ariz.: American Compensation Association, 1992).

[6] N. Gupta, G. D. Jenkins Jr., and W. P. Curington, Paying for knowledge: Myths and realities, *National Productivity Review* 5 (1986): 106–123; and Jenkins, Ledford, Gupta, and Doty, *Skill-based pay.*

[7] J. R. Schuster and P. K. Zingheim, *The new pay: Linking employee and organizational performance* (New York: Lexington Books, 1992).

[8] American Society for Training and Development, *Training America: Learning to work for the twenty-first century* (Alexandria, Virg.: American Society for Training and Development, 1989).

[9] P. B. Doeringer, *Turbulence in the American workplace* (New York: Oxford University Press, 1991).

[10] C. C. Manz and H. P. Sims Jr., *Business without bosses: How self-managing work teams are building high performance companies* (New York: Wiley, 1993).

[11] A. P. Carnevale and J. W. Johnston, *Training in America: Strategies for the nation* (Alexandria, Virg.: National Center on Education and the Economy and The American Society for Training and Development, 1989).

[12] Carnevale and Johnston, *Training in America.*

[13] International Labour Organization, *Yearbook of Labor Statistics,* 52nd ed. (Geneva, Switzerland: International Labour Organization, 1993).

[14] U.S. Department of Commerce, *Statistical abstracts of the United States,* 114th ed. (Washington, D.C.: U.S. Government Printing Office, 1994); and S.E. Haugen, The employment expansion in retail trade, 1973–85, *Monthly Labor Review* 109 (1986): 9–16.

[15] Schuster and Zingheim, *The new pay.*

[16] E. E. Lawler III, *High involvement management* (San Francisco: Jossey-Bass, 1986).

[17] D. A. Nadler, J. R. Hackman, and E. E. Lawler III, *Managing organizational behavior* (Boston: Little, Brown, 1979).

[18] M. R. Carrell, N.F. Elbert, and R. D. Hatfield, *Human resource management: Global strategies for managing a diverse workforce,* 5th ed. (Englewood Cliffs, N.J.: Prentice Hall, 1995).

[19] N. Gupta, T. P. Schweizer, and G. D. Jenkins Jr., Pay-for-knowledge compensation plans: hypotheses and survey results, *Monthly Labor Review* 110 (October 1987):40–43.

[20] Caudron, Master the compensation maze.

[21] J. Schilder, Work teams boost productivity, *Personnel Journal* 72 (February 1992): 64–71.

[22] Filipowski, How Federal Express makes your package its most important.

[23] G. D. Jenkins Jr. and N. Gupta, The payoffs of paying for knowledge, *National Productivity Review* 4 (1985):121–130.

[24] Filipowski, How Federal Express makes your package its most important.

CHAPTER

SEVEN

Building internally consistent compensation systems

CHAPTER OUTLINE

In this chapter, you will learn about

1. The importance of building internally consistent compensation systems
2. The process of job analysis
3. Job descriptions
4. The Department of Labor job analysis methodology
5. The process of job evaluation
6. A variety of job evaluation techniques
7. Alternatives to job evaluation
8. Internally consistent compensation systems and competitive strategy

Bill Allendale has worked nearly 15 years as a compensation professional. Recently, Bill joined Software Development Incorporated (SDI) as Director of Compensation. He has a significant challenge before him. Here's why.

Three software development engineers established SDI seven years ago, immediately upon completing master's degrees in computer science. None of these scientists had work experience before creating SDI. They staffed their company with 10 employees—some with technical and others with nontechnical work backgrounds. Initially, SDI was quite successful. The company's success led to rapid growth in staffing levels. In seven years, SDI's staffing levels increased from 13 (including the three founders) to 190 employees.

SDI's annual turnover rate has varied between 40 and 75 percent since its founding. With SDI's increased business activity, turnover has prevented SDI from delivering software to clients on a timely basis, and many of the clients are dissatisfied because the software has bugs in it. In fact, SDI lost a $10 million contract. How are these problems related to compensation?

Bill's review of SDI's former and current employees' annual pay raised a red flag. He immediately set a meeting with SDI's founders. Bill said, "In a nutshell, the pay structure lacks internal consistency." One founder replied, "What does that mean?"

Bill explained, "Let me explain by example. Software engineer Anne Brown earns $38,000 and administrative aide Joan Rhodes earns $46,000 a year. The software engineer job requires significantly greater educational attainment than the administrative aide job. Also, the software engineer job is tied more directly to SDI's core business activity—software development. Unfortunately, there are many more pay differences like these, which probably account for SDI's turnover problem."

Another founder asked, "What is the solution?" Bill replied, "SDI must develop an internally consistent compensation system. Annual pay rates should vary consistently with the complexity of job duties and necessary worker characteristics (for example, education)."

The third founder said, "You have our complete support. Please proceed with building an internally consistent compensation system."

Internally consistent compensation systems clearly define the relative value of each job among all jobs within a company. This ordered set of jobs represents the job structure, or the hierarchy, of the company. Companies rely on a simple, yet fundamental principle for building internally consistent compensation systems: Employees with greater qualifications, more responsibilities, and more-complex job duties should

Companies rely on a simple, yet fundamental principle for building internally consistent compensation systems: Employees with greater qualifications, more responsibilities, and more complex job duties should receive higher pay than employees with lesser qualifications, fewer responsibilities, and less complex job duties.

receive higher pay than employees with lesser qualifications, fewer responsibilities, and less-complex job duties. **Internally consistent job structures** formally recognize differences in job characteristics, and thereby enable compensation managers to set pay accordingly. Exhibit 7-1 illustrates an internally consistent compensation structure

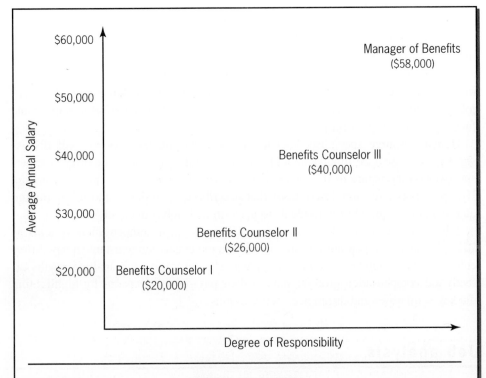

Exhibit 7-1
*Internally Consistent
Compensation Structure*

BENEFITS COUNSELOR I

Provides basic counseling services to employees and assistance to higher-level personnel in more-complex benefits activities. Works under general supervision of higher-level counselors or other personnel.

BENEFITS COUNSELOR II

Provides skilled counseling services to employees concerning specialized benefits programs or complex areas of other programs. Also completes special projects or carries out assigned phases of the benefits counseling service operations. Works under general supervision from Benefits Counselor IIIs or other personnel.

BENEFITS COUNSELOR III

Coordinates the daily activities of an employee benefits counseling service and supervises its staff. Works under direction from higher-level personnel.

MANAGER OF BENEFITS

Responsible for managing the entire benefits function from evaluating benefits programs to ensuring that Benefits Counselors are adequately trained. Reports to the Director of Compensation and Benefits.

for employee benefits professionals. As Exhibit 7-1 indicates, Benefits Managers should earn substantially more than Benefits Counselor Is: Benefits Managers have far greater responsibility for ensuring effective benefits practices than the entry-level counselor. The difference in average pay rates between Benefits Counselor II and Benefits Counselor I jobs should be far less than the difference in average pay rates between Benefits Manager and Benefits Counselor I jobs. Why? The differences in responsibility between Benefits Counselor II and Benefits Counselor I are far less than the differences between Benefits Manager and Benefits Counselor I.

Compensation experts and HR professionals create internally consistent job structures through two processes—job analysis followed by job evaluation. Job analysis is almost purely a descriptive procedure, whereas job evaluation reflects value judgments. Effective job analysis identifies and defines job content. Job content describes job duties and tasks as well as pertinent factors such as skill and effort (compensable factors) needed to perform the job adequately.

Human resource specialists lead the job analysis process. As we will discuss shortly, they solicit the involvement of employees and supervisors who offer their perspectives on the nature of the jobs being analyzed. On the basis of this information, HR specialists write job descriptions that describe the job duties and the minimum qualifications required of individuals to perform their jobs effectively.

Job evaluation is key for casting internally consistent compensation systems as strategic tools. Compensation professionals use job evaluation to establish pay differentials among employees within a company. The descriptive job analysis results directly aid compensation professionals in their pay-setting decisions by highlighting the key similarities and differences between jobs.

Job analysis

Competent compensation professionals are familiar with job analysis concepts, the process of conducting job analysis, and the fundamentals of job analysis techniques. **Job analysis** is a systematic process for gathering, documenting, and analyzing information in order to describe jobs. Job analyses describe content or job duties, worker requirements, and, sometimes, the job context or working conditions.

Job content refers to the actual activities that employees must perform in the job. Job content descriptions may be broad, general statements of job activities or detailed descriptions of duties and tasks performed in the job. Greeting clients is common to receptionist jobs. The job activity of greeting clients represents a broad statement. Describing the particular activities associated with greeting clients represents a detailed statement—for example, saying "Hello," asking the clients' names, using the telephone to notify the employees of their clients' arrival, and offering a beverage.

Worker requirements represent the minimum qualifications and skills that people must have to perform a particular job. Such requirements usually include education, experience, licenses, permits, and specific abilities, such as typing, drafting, or editing. For example, the minimum educational qualification for a lead research scientist in a jet propulsion laboratory is a Ph.D. in physics.

Working conditions include the social context or physical environment where work will be performed. For instance, social context is a key factor for jobs in the hospitality industry. Hospitality industry managers emphasize the importance of employees' interactions with guests. Hotel registration desk clerks should convey an air of enthusiasm toward guests and be willing to accommodate each guest's specific requests for a nonsmoking room or an early check-in time.

Physical environments vary along several dimensions based on the degree of noise, possible exposure to hazardous factors including hazardous chemicals. Work equipment also defines the character of the physical environment. Nuclear power plant employees work in rather hazardous physical environments because of possible exposure to dangerous radiation levels. Accountants perform their jobs in relatively safe working environments because office buildings must meet local building safety standards.

Steps in the job analysis process

The job analysis process consists of five main activities:

- ★ Determine a job analysis program
- ★ Select and train analysts
- ★ Conduct job analyst orientation
- ★ Conduct the study: Determine data collection methods and sources of data
- ★ Summarize the results: Write job descriptions

DETERMINE A JOB ANALYSIS PROGRAM Companies must determine a job analysis program by deciding between using an established system or developing their own system tailored to specific requirements. Job analysis programs vary in the method of data gathering for both established and custom job analysis programs. The most typical methods for collecting job analysis information include questionnaires, interviews, observation, and participation. Often, administrative costs represent a major consideration in selecting a job analysis method.

SELECT AND TRAIN ANALYSTS In general, job analysts must be able to collect job-related information through various methods, relate to a wide variety of employees, analyze the information, and write clearly and succinctly. Ideally, a task force comprising representatives throughout the company conducts the analysis and human resource staff members coordinate it. Although some companies rely on HR professionals to coordinate and conduct job analysis, many use teams to represent varying perspectives on work because virtually all employees interact with coworkers and supervisors.

Before the task force embarks on a job analysis, members need to be taught about the basic assumptions of the model and the procedures they must follow. The training should include discussions of the study's objectives, how the information will be used, methodology overviews, and discussions and demonstrations of the various information-gathering techniques. Analysts also should be trained to minimize the chance that they will conduct ineffective job analyses. For example, analysts should involve as many job incumbents as possible within the constraints of staff time to have representative samples of job incumbents' perceptions.

Finally, job analysts must be familiar with the structure of pertinent job data. Job analysis data are configured in levels, hierarchically from specific bits of information to progressively broader categories that include the prior specific pieces. Exhibit 7-2 defines representative analysis levels and examples of each one. The most specific information is a job element, and the broadest element is an occupation.

Exhibit 7-2
Units of Analysis in the Job Analysis Process

1. An **element** is the smallest step into which it is practical to subdivide any work activity without analyzing separate motions, movements, and mental processes involved. Inserting a diskette into floppy disk drive is an example of a job element.

2. A **task** is one or more elements and is one of the distinct activities that constitute logical and necessary steps in the performance of work by the worker. A task is created whenever human effort, physical or mental, is exerted to accomplish a specific purpose. Keyboarding text into memo format represents a job task.

3. A **position** is a collection of tasks constituting the total work assignment of a single worker. There are as many positions as there are workers. John Smith's position in the company is clerk typist. His tasks, which include keyboarding text into memo format, running a spell check on the text, and printing the text on company letterhead, combine to represent John Smith's position.

4. A **job** is a group of positions within a company that are identical with respect to their major or significant tasks and sufficiently alike to justify their being covered by a single analysis. There may be one or many persons employed in the same job. For example, Bob Arnold, John Smith, and Jason Colbert are clerk typists. With minor variations, they essentially perform the same tasks.

5. A **job family** is a group of two or more jobs that call for either similar worker characteristics or similar work tasks. File clerk, clerk typist, and administrative clerk represent a clerical job family because each job mainly requires employees to perform clerical tasks.

6. An **occupation** is a group of jobs, found at more than one establishment, in which a common set of tasks are performed or are related in terms of similar objectives, methodologies, materials, products, worker actions, or worker characteristics. File clerk, clerk typist, administrative clerk, staff secretary, and administrative secretary represent an office support occupation. Compensation analyst, training and development specialist, recruiter, and benefits counselor represent jobs from the human resources management occupation.

Source: U.S. Department of Labor, *The revised handbook for analyzing jobs* (Washington, D.C.: U.S. Government Printing Office, 1991).

These concepts are relevant for making compensation decisions. Ultimately, the units of analysis may influence compensation professionals' judgments about whether work is dissimilar or similar. Director of Compensation, Job Evaluation Specialist, and Payroll Clerk are dissimilar jobs because employees in these jobs perform different duties. However, these jobs are similar at the occupational level because they fall under the human resource management occupation. Distinguishing among jobs at the occupational level would lead to similar pay among dissimilar jobs within an occupation— Director of Compensation versus Payroll Clerk.

CONDUCT JOB ANALYST ORIENTATION Before analysts start specific job analysis techniques, they must analyze the context in which employees perform their work to better understand some of the factors that influence employees. In addition, analysts should obtain and review such internal information as organizational charts, listings of job titles, the classification of each position to be analyzed, job incumbent names and pay rates, and any instructional booklets or handbooks for operating equipment. Job analysts may also find pertinent job information in such external sources as the *Dictionary of Occupational Titles (DOT)*, trade associations, professional societies, and trade unions. We discuss the *DOT* later in this chapter.

CONDUCT THE STUDY: DETERMINE DATA COLLECTION METHODS AND SOURCES OF DATA Once analysts have gathered and made sense of these preliminary data, they can begin gathering and recording information for each job in the company. Analysts should carefully choose the method of data collection and the sources of data. The most common methods of data collection include questionnaires and observation. Questionnaires direct job incumbents' and supervisors' descriptions of the incumbents' work through a series of questions and statements, for example:

- ✰ Describe the task you perform most frequently.

- ✰ How often do you perform this task?

- ✰ List any licenses, permits, or certifications required to perform duties assigned to your position.

- ✰ List any equipment, machines, or tools you normally operate as part of your position's duties.

- ✰ Does your job require any contacts with other department personnel, other departments, outside companies, or agencies? If yes, please describe.

- ✰ Does your job require supervisory responsibilities? If yes, for which jobs and for how many employees?

Observation requires job analysts to record perceptions formed while watching employees perform their jobs.

The most common sources of job analysis data are job incumbents, supervisors, and the job analysts. Job incumbents should provide the most extensive and detailed information about how they perform job duties. Experienced job incumbents will probably offer the greatest details and insights. Supervisors also should provide extensive and detailed information, but with a different focus. Specifically, supervisors are most familiar with the interrelationship among jobs within their departments. They are probably in the best position to describe how employees performing different jobs interact. Job analysts also should involve as many job incumbents and supervisors as possible because employees with the same job titles may have different experiences.

For example, parts assembler John Smith's report indicates that a higher level of manual dexterity is required than parts assembler Barbara Bleen's report describes. Parts assembler supervisor Jan Johnson indicates that assemblers interact several times a day to help each other solve unexpected problems, but supervisor Bill Black reports no interaction among parts assemblers. Including as many job incumbents and supervisors as possible will provide a truer assessment of the parts assembler job duties than would only one report.

Of course, job analysts represent a source of information. In the case of observation, job analysts write descriptions. When using questionnaires, job analysts often ask follow-up questions to get clarification of job incumbents' and supervisors' answers. In either case, job analysts' HR expertise should guide the selection of pertinent follow-up questions.

Ultimately, companies strive to conduct job analyses that lead to reliable and valid job evaluation results. A **reliable job analysis** yields consistent results under similar conditions. For example, let's assume that two job analysts independently observe Betty Green perform her job as a retail store manager. The method is reliable if the two analysts reach similar conclusions about the duties that constitute the retail store manager job. Although important, reliable job analysis methods are not enough. Job analyses also must be valid.

A **valid job analysis** method accurately assesses each job's duties. Unfortunately, neither researchers nor practitioners possess ways to demonstrate whether job analysis results are definitively accurate. Presently, the "best" approach to producing valid job descriptions requires that results among multiple sources of job data (job incumbents, analysts, supervisors, customers) and multiple methods (interview, questionnaire, observation) converge.[1]

Reliable and valid job analysis methods are essential to building internally consistent compensation systems. The factors that describe a particular job should indeed reflect the actual work. Failure to accurately match compensable factors with the work employees perform may result in either inadequate or excessive pay rates. Both cases are detrimental to the company. Inadequate pay may lead to dysfunctional turnover—the departure of quality employees. Excessive pay represents a cost burden to the company that can ultimately undermine its competitive position. Moreover, basing pay on factors that are not related to job duties leaves a company vulnerable to allegations of illegal discrimination.

What can compensation professionals do to increase the chance that they will use reliable and valid job analysis methods? Whenever time and budgetary constraints permit, job analysts should use more than one data collection method, and they should collect data from more than one source. Including multiple data collection methods and sources minimizes the inherent biases associated with any particular one. For example, a job incumbent may think her work has a greater impact on the effectiveness of the company than her supervisor thinks it has. Observation techniques do not readily indicate the reasons why an employee performs a task in a specific way, but the interview method provides analysts with an opportunity to make probing inquiries.

SUMMARIZE THE RESULTS: WRITE JOB DESCRIPTIONS **Job descriptions** summarize a job's purpose and list its tasks, duties, and responsibilities, as well as the skills, knowledge, and abilities necessary to perform the job at a minimum level. Effective job descriptions generally explain:

✮ What the employee must do to perform the job

✮ How the employee performs the job

✮ Why the employee performs the job in terms of its contribution to the functioning of the company

✮ Supervisory responsibilities, if any

✮ Contacts (and purpose of these contacts) with other employees inside or outside the company

✮ The skills, knowledge, and abilities the employee should have or must have to perform the job duties

✮ The physical and social conditions under which the employee must perform the job

Job descriptions usually contain four sections:

✮ Job title

☆ Job summary

☆ Job duties

☆ Worker specifications

Exhibit 7-3 contains a job description for a training and development specialist.

Job titles indicate job designations. In Exhibit 7-3, the job title is Training and Development Specialist. The **job summary** statement contains a concise summary of the job based on two to four descriptive statements. This section usually indicates whether the job incumbent receives supervision and by whom. The Training and Development Specialist works under general supervision from higher-level training and development professionals or other designated administrators.

The **job duties** section describes the major work activities and, if pertinent, supervisory responsibilities. For instance, the Training and Development Specialist evaluates training needs of employees and departments by conducting personal interviews, questionnaires, and statistical studies.

Exhibit 7-3
Job Description: Training and Development Specialist

TRAINING AND DEVELOPMENT SPECIALIST

JOB SUMMARY

Training and Development Specialists perform training and development activities for supervisors, managers, and staff to improve efficiency, effectiveness, and productivity. They work under general supervision from higher-level training and development professionals.

JOB DUTIES

A Training and Development Specialist typically:

1. Recommends, plans, and implements training seminars and workshops for administrators and supervisors, and evaluates program effectiveness.

2. Evaluates training needs of employees and departments by conducting personal interviews, questionnaires, and statistical studies.

3. Researches, writes, and develops instructional materials for career, staff, and supervisor workshops and seminars.

4. Counsels supervisors and employees on policies and rules.

5. Performs related duties as assigned.

WORKER SPECIFICATIONS

1. Any one or any combination of the following types of preparation:

    (a) credit for college training leading to a major or concentration in education or other fields closely related to training and development (such as human resource management or vocational education).

    –or–

    (b) two years of work experience as a professional staff member in a human resource management department.

2. Two years of professional work experience in the training and development area in addition to the training and experience required in item 1 above.

The **worker specification** section lists the education, skills, abilities, knowledge, and other qualifications individuals must possess to perform the job adequately. **Education** refers to formal training. Minimum educational levels generally include a high school diploma or a general equivalency diploma through such advanced levels as master's degrees or doctorates.

The Equal Employment Opportunity Commission (EEOC) guidelines distinguish among the terms *knowledge, skills,* and *abilities.* **Skill** refers to an observable competence to perform a learned psychomotor act. Typing 50 words per minute with fewer than five errors is an example of a psychomotor act because it requires knowledge of the keyboard layout and manual dexterity. According to the EEOC, **ability** refers to a present competence to perform an observable behavior or a behavior that results in an observable product. For example, possessing the competence to successfully mediate a dispute between labor and management reflects an ability. **Knowledge** refers to a body of information applied directly to the performance of a function. Companies measure knowledge with tests, or they infer that employees have knowledge on the basis of formal education completed. For instance, compensation professionals should know about the Fair Labor Standards Act's overtime pay requirements.

Legal considerations for job analysis

The government does not require companies to conduct job analysis. However, conducting job analysis increases the chance that employment decisions are based solely on pertinent job requirements. Under the Equal Pay Act (Chapter 3), companies must justify pay differences between men and women who perform equal work. Different job titles do not suffice as justification. Instead, companies must demonstrate substantive differences in job functions. Job analysis helps HR professionals discern whether substantive differences in job functions exist.

Job analyses are also useful for determining whether a job is exempt or nonexempt under the Fair Labor Standards Act (FLSA). As we discussed in Chapter 3, failure to pay nonexempt employees an overtime hourly pay rate violates the FLSA. Exhibit 7-4 lists the FLSA criteria that distinguish between exempt and nonexempt jobs. Job analyses can provide job descriptions to be judged on those criteria.

Companies may perform job analyses to see if they comply with the Americans with Disabilities Act (ADA), also discussed Chapter 3. As long as disabled applicants can perform the essential functions of a job with reasonable accommodation, companies may not discriminate against these applicants by paying them less than nondisabled employees performing the same job. Human Resource professionals use job analysis to systematically define essential job functions. Companies may consult the EEOC's interpretive guidelines to determine whether a job function is essential. Exhibit 7-5 lists these guidelines.

Many of the established job analysis techniques apply to a wide variety of jobs, and both researchers and practitioners have already tested and refined them.

Job analysis techniques

Human Resource professionals either can choose from a variety of established job analysis techniques or they can custom-design them. Most companies generally choose to use established job analysis techniques because the costs of custom-made job analysis techniques often outweigh the benefits. Besides, many of the established job analysis techniques apply to a wide variety of jobs, and both researchers and practitioners have already tested and refined them.

Exhibit 7-4
FLSA Exemption Criteria for Executive, Administrative, and Professional Employees

EXECUTIVE EMPLOYEES

- Primary duties include managing the organization
- Regularly supervise the work of two or more full-time employees
- Authority to hire, promote, and discharge employees
- Regularly use discretion as part of typical work duties
- Devote at least 80 percent of work time to fulfilling the previous activities

ADMINISTRATIVE EMPLOYEES

- Perform nonmanual work directly related to management operations
- Regularly use discretion beyond clerical duties
- Perform specialized or technical work, or perform special assignments with only general supervision
- Devote at least 80 percent of work time to fulfilling the previous activities

PROFESSIONAL EMPLOYEES

- Primary work requires advanced knowledge in a field of science or learning, including work that requires regular use of discretion and independent judgment, or
- Primary work requires inventiveness, imagination, or talent in a recognized field or artistic endeavor

Source: 29 Code of Federal Regulations, Sec. 541.3. 29; Sec. 541.1.

Choosing one established plan over another depends upon two considerations—applicability and cost. Some job analysis techniques apply only to particular job families, such as managerial jobs; others can be applied to more than one job family. Also, some methods are proprietary and others are available to the public at no charge. Private consultants or consulting firms charge substantial fees to companies that use their methods, but the U.S. Department of Labor does not charge fees to use its job analysis method. We review the U.S. Department of Labor (DOL) job analysis method in detail because it is used widely in both the public and private sectors, and it applies to most jobs.

Exhibit 7-5
EEOC Interpretive Guidelines for Essential Job Functions under the American's with Disabilities Act

- The reason the position exists is to perform the function.
- The function is essential or possibly essential. If other employees are available to perform the function, the function probably is not essential.
- A high degree of expertise or skill is required to perform the function.
- The function is probably essential; and,
- Whether a particular job function is essential is a determination that must be made on a case-by-case basis and should be addressed during job analysis. Any job functions that are not essential are determined to be marginal. Marginal job functions could be traded to another position or not done at all.

Source: From the text of the Americans with Disabilities Act, Federal Register 35734 (July 26, 1991).

U.S. Department of Labor (DOL) job analysis method

The U.S. Department of Labor developed a comprehensive job analysis methodology to provide basic job information for such human resource management programs as recruitment, performance evaluation, compensation, and training. The DOL method applies to virtually all jobs in both the public and private sectors of the economy. Private sector companies often use the DOL method because of its applicability to so many jobs and its cost— it's virtually free!

The DOL method is comprehensive because it incorporates information about both jobs and workers. Specifically, this method distinguishes between work performed and worker traits. **Work performed** contains the job analysis components that are related to the actual work activities of a job and constitute information that HR professionals should include in the job summary and job duties sections of job descriptions. **Worker traits** represent characteristics of employees that contribute to successful job performance.

WORK PERFORMED Work performed includes:

- ✯ Worker functions
- ✯ Work fields
- ✯ Materials, products, subject matter, and services

Worker Function information describes what the worker does in relation to data, people, and things, as expressed by mental, interpersonal, and physical worker actions. Every job is described by data, people, and things. Exhibit 7-6 lists the 24 DOL worker functions. The Department of Labor defines these terms as follows:[2]

- ✯ *Data functions* are different kinds of activities involving information, knowledge, or concepts. In the Department of Labor, for example, synthesizing is defined as integrating analyses of data to discover facts or develop knowledge concepts or interpretations. The function "Formulates editorial policies of newspapers and originates plans for special features or projects" is an example of synthesizing. Some data functions are broad in scope and others are narrow.

Exhibit 7-6
Department of Labor Worker Functions

REF NO.	DATA	REF NO.	PEOPLE	REF NO.	THINGS
0	Synthesizing	0	Mentoring	0	Setting up
1	Coordinating	1	Negotiating	1	Precision Working
2	Analyzing	2	Instructing	2	Operating-controlling
3	Compiling	3	Supervising	3	Driving-operating
4	Computing	4	Diverting	4	Manipulating
5	Copying	5	Persuading	5	Tending
6	Comparing	6	Speaking-signaling	6	Feeding-offbearing
		7	Serving	7	Handling
		8	Taking instructions-helping		

Source: U.S. Department of Labor, *The revised handbook for analyzing jobs* (Washington, D.C.: U.S. Government Printing Office, 1991).

Computing and copying are more specialized functional activities than are the other data functions.

★ *People Functions* refer to fundamental interactions workers engage in. Taking Instructions-helping is the least complex among the people functions. The remaining people functions have no specific order denoting complexity or specificity. For instance, supervising entails determining or interpreting work procedures for a group of workers, assigning specific duties to them, maintaining harmonious relations among them, and promoting efficiency. Assigning duties to typists and examining typed material for accuracy, neatness, and conformance to standards is an example of supervising.

★ *Things functions* can be divided into relationships based upon the worker's involvement with either machines and equipment *(machine-related levels)* or with tools and work aids (nonmachine related levels). Machine-related levels include setting up (0), operating-controlling (2), driving-operating (3), tending (5), and feeding-offbearing (6). Levels 5 and 6 require little or no latitude for judgment; levels 2 and 3 require some latitude for judgment, and 0 requires considerable judgment. Nonmachine-related levels include precision working, manipulating, and handling. Handling requires little or no latitude for judgment; manipulating requires some latitude for judgment, and precision working requires considerable judgment. For instance, feeding-offbearing entails inserting, throwing, dumping, or placing materials in or removing them from machines or equipment that is automatic or tended or operated by other workers. Removing cartons of bottles from conveyor belts and stacking them on pallets is an example of feeding-offbearing.

Work fields represent the technologies and socioeconomic objectives that are related to how work gets done and what gets done as a result of the work activities of a job. In short, work fields summarize and classify the overall objectives of work, such as fabricating products (technology) and providing services (socioeconomic objective). The Department of Labor uses three-digit codes to identify work fields. There are 96 work fields in all. Exhibit 7-7 lists examples of work fields.

Exhibit 7-7
Department of Labor Work Fields

071 Bolting-Screwing, 072 Nailing, 073 Riveting

Assembling parts and materials, usually of metal, wood, and plastics, by means of screws, nails, rivets, or other fasteners.

211 Appraising, 212 Inspecting-Measuring-Testing

Evaluating and estimating the quality, quantity, and value of things and data; ascertaining the physical characteristics of materials and objects.

281 System Communicating, 282 Information Giving

Obtaining and evaluating data for purposes of completing business and legal procedures.

251 Researching

Controlled exploration of fundamental areas of knowledge, by means of critical and exhaustive investigation and experimentation.

Source: U.S. Department of Labor, *The revised handbook for analyzing jobs* (Washington, D.C.: U.S Government Printing Office, 1991).

Materials and Products

300   Plant farm crops

400   Tobacco products

500   Petroleum and related products

600   Measuring, analyzing, and controlling instruments: photographic, medical, and optical goods; watches and clocks

Subject Matter

700   Architecture and engineering

720   Mathematics and physical science

740   Arts and literature

Services

850   Transportation services

860   Communication services

920   Medical and other health services

930   Educational, legal, museum, library, and archival services

Source: U.S. Department of Labor, *The revised handbook for analyzing jobs* (Washington, D.C.: U.S. Government Printing Office, 1991).

Materials, products, subject matter, and services (MPSMS) includes:

✪ Basic *materials* processed, such as fabric, metal, or wood

✪ Final *products* made, such as automobiles; cultivated, such as field crops; harvested, such as sponges; or captured, such as wild animals

✪ *Subject matter* or data gathered or applied, such as astronomy or journalism

✪ *Services* rendered, such as barbering or janitorial

The MPSMS component contains 48 groups subdivided into 336 categories. The Department of Labor uses three-digit identification codes to denote MPSMS. Exhibit 7-8 lists examples of MPSMS.

WORKER TRAITS Worker traits include:

✪ General educational development

✪ Specific vocational preparation

✪ Aptitudes

✪ Temperaments

✪ Interests

✪ Physical demands and environmental conditions

General educational development (GED) refers to education of a general nature that contributes to reasoning development and to the acquisition of mathematical and language skills. The GED has three components—reasoning development, mathematical development, and language development. Six levels represent the entire range of development. Exhibit 7-9 describes the lowest GED level (Level 1) and the highest GED level (Level 6) for the three components.

Exhibit 7-9
*Department of Labor
General Educational
Development Scale*

LEVEL 1

Reasoning Development. Apply commonsense understanding to carry out simple one- or two-step instructions. Deal with standardized situations with occasional or no variables in or from these situations encountered on the job.

Mathematical Development. Add and subtract two-digit numbers. Multiply and divide 10s and 100s by 2, 3, 4, 5. Perform the four basic arithmetic operations with coins. Perform operations with units such as cup, pint, and quart; inch, foot, and yard; and, ounce and pound.

Language Development. Reading: Recognize meaning of 2,500 two- or three-syllable words. Read at a rate of 95–120 words per minute. Writing: Print simple sentences containing subject, verb, and object, and series of numbers, names, and addresses. Speaking: Speak simple sentences, using normal word order and present and past tenses.

LEVEL 6

Reasoning Development. Apply principles of logical or scientific thinking to a wide range of intellectual and practical problems. Deal with nonverbal symbolism (formulas, scientific equations, graphs, musical notes, etc.) in its most difficult phases. Deal with a variety of abstract and concrete variables. Apprehend the most abstruse classes of concepts.

Mathematical Development. Advanced calculus: Work with limits, continuity, real number systems, mean value theorems, and implicit function theorems. Statistics: Work with mathematical statistics, mathematical probability and applications, experimental design, statistical inference, and econometrics.

Language Development. Reading: Read literature, book and play reviews, scientific and technical journals, abstracts, financial reports, and legal documents. Writing: Write novels, plays, editorials, journals, speeches, manuals, critiques, poetry, and songs. Speaking: Be conversant in theory, principles, and methods of effective and persuasive speaking, voice and diction, phonetics, and discussion and debate.

Source: U.S. Department of Labor, *The revised handbook for analyzing jobs* (Washington, D.C.: U.S. Government Printing Office, 1991).

Specific vocational preparation is defined as the amount of lapsed time required by a typical worker to learn the techniques, acquire the information, and develop the facility needed for average performance in a specific job situation. The training may be acquired in a school, work, military, institutional, or vocational environment. Nine levels represent the entire range of specific vocational preparation. Exhibit 7-10 displays representative samples of these levels.

Aptitudes represent individuals' capacities to learn how to perform specific jobs. There are 11 aptitudes, listed in Exhibit 7-11. Human resource professionals consider aptitudes to be important worker characteristics, particularly in companies that incorporate on-the-job training as a component of workers' employment experiences.

Temperaments are adaptability requirements made on the worker by the situation. This category is important because different job situations require different traits. The Department of Labor recognizes 11 temperaments. Exhibit 7-12 lists these temperaments. Temperaments represent an important characteristic because most companies continually restructure jobs and work relationships to promote competitive advantage and improve operating efficiency. Employees who do not adapt well to changing work situations are not likely to meet their employers' performance expectations. For ex-

Exhibit 7-10
**Department of Labor
Specific Vocational
Preparation Scale**

LEVEL 1: SHORT DEMONSTRATION ONLY

Example: Fills glasses with tap beer and hands them to waiters who serve patrons. Inserts taps in unopened barrels.

LEVEL 3: OVER 30 DAYS UP TO AND INCLUDING 3 MONTHS

Example: Types letters, reports, stencils, forms, addresses, or other straight copy materials from rough draft or corrected copy.

LEVEL 5: OVER 6 MONTHS UP TO AND INCLUDING 1 YEAR

Example: Sells men's furnishings, such as neckties, shirts, belts, hats, and accessories. Advises customers on coordination of accessories.

LEVEL 7: OVER 2 YEARS UP TO AND INCLUDING 4 YEARS

Example: Supervises and coordinates activities of pantry, storeroom, and noncooking kitchen workers and purchases or requisitions foodstuffs, kitchen supplies, and equipment.

LEVEL 9: OVER 10 YEARS

Example: Develops and administers policies of organization in accordance with corporation character. Establishes operating objectives and policies for firm. Reviews progress and makes necessary changes in company plans. Directs preparation of major financial programs, such as pricing policies and salary and wage schedules, to ensure operating efficiency and adequate investment and dividend returns.

Source: U.S. Department of Labor, *The revised handbook for analyzing jobs* (Washington, D.C.: U.S. Government Printing Office, 1991).

Exhibit 7-11
**Department of Labor
Aptitudes**

G — General learning ability

V — Verbal aptitude

N — Numerical aptitude

S — Spatial aptitude

P — Form perception

Q — Clerical perception

K — Motor coordination

F — Finger dexterity

M — Manual dexterity

E — Eye-hand-foot coordination

C — Color discrimination

Source: U.S. Department of Labor, *The revised handbook for analyzing jobs* (Washington, D.C.: U.S. Government Printing Office, 1991).

Exhibit 7-12
Department of Labor
Temperaments

D. Directing, controlling, or planning activities of others. Involves accepting responsibility for formulating plans, designs, practices, policies, methods, regulations, and procedures for operations or projects; negotiating with individuals or groups for agreements or contracts; and supervising subordinate workers to implement plans and control activities.

R. Performing *repetitive* or short-cycle work. Involves performing a few routine and uninvolved tasks over and over again according to set procedures, sequence, or pace with little opportunity for diversion or interruption. Interaction with people is included when it is routine, continual, or prescribed.

I. Influencing people in their opinions, attitudes, and judgments. Involves writing, demonstrating, or speaking to persuade and motivate people to change their attitudes or opinions, participate in a particular activity, or purchase a specific commodity or service.

V. Performing a *variety* of duties. Involves frequent changes of tasks involving different aptitudes, technologies, techniques, procedures, working conditions, physical demands, or degrees of attentiveness without loss of efficiency or composure. The involvement of the worker in two or more work fields may be a clue that this temperament is required.

E. Expressing personal feelings. Involves creativity and self-expression in interpreting feelings, ideas, or facts in terms of a personal viewpoint; treating a subject imaginatively rather than literally; reflecting original ideas or feelings in writing, painting, composing, sculpting, decorating, or inventing; or interpreting works of others by arranging, conducting, playing musical instruments, choreographing, acting, directing, critiquing, or editorializing.

A. Working *alone* or apart in physical isolation from others. Involves working in an environment that regularly precludes face-to-face interpersonal relationships for extended periods of time owing to physical barriers or distances involved.

S. Performing effectively under *stress.* Involves coping with circumstances dangerous to worker or others.

T. Attaining precisely set limits, *tolerances,* and standards. Involves adhering to and achieving exact levels of performance, using precision measuring instruments, tools, and machines to attain precise dimensions; preparing exact verbal and numerical records; and complying with precise instruments and specifications for materials, methods, procedures, and techniques to attain specified standards.

U. Working *under* specific instructions. Performing tasks only under specific instructions, allowing little or no room for independent action or judgment in working out job problems.

P. Dealing with *people.* Involves interpersonal relationships in job situations beyond receiving work instructions.

J. Making *judgments* and decisions. Involves solving problems, making evaluations, or reaching conclusions based on subjective or objective criteria, such as the five senses, knowledge, past experiences, or quantifiable or factual data.

Source: U.S. Department of Labor, *The revised handbook for analyzing jobs* (Washington, D.C.: U.S. Government Printing Office, 1991).

ample, companies that use knowledge-based pay programs expect employees to perform a variety of duties rather than limited, similar duties.

Interests represent individuals' liking or preference for performing specific jobs. The Department of Labor recognizes 12 general interests. Each general interest comprises specific related interests. A two-digit code denotes the general interest. A four-digit code (that is, the general interest code followed by a decimal point and two additional digits) denotes specific interests. Exhibit 7-13 lists the 12 general interests and

Exhibit 7-13
Department of Labor
General Interest Areas

01	Artistic
02	Scientific
03	Plants and animals
04	Protective
05	Mechanical
06	Industrial
07	Business detail
08	Selling
09	Accommodating
10	Humanitarian
11	Leading-influencing
12	Physical performing

Source: U.S. Department of Labor, *The revised handbook for analyzing jobs* (Washington, D.C.: U.S. Government Printing Office, 1991).

the associated two-digit codes. Exhibit 7-14 describes the general interest business detail and its related specific interests.

Physical demands represent the physical requirements made on the worker by the specific situation, and **environmental conditions** describe the surroundings in which workers perform their jobs. The Department of Labor recognizes 20 physical demands and 14 environmental condition factors. Exhibit 7-15 lists the 20 physical demands, and Exhibit 7-16 displays the 14 environmental conditions.

USING THE DOL METHOD Human resource professionals use the DOL method by consulting two key sources: *The Revised Handbook for Analyzing Jobs (RHAJ)* and the *Dictionary of Occupational Titles (DOT)*. Academic (college or university) and public libraries designated as government depositories keep these items. Alternatively, companies can purchase these publications for nominal fees from the U.S. Government Printing Office.

Exhibit 7-14
Department of Labor
Business Detail Interest Area

07 Business Detail

An interest in organized, clearly defined activities requiring accuracy and attention to details, primarily in an office setting.

07.01	Administrative detail
07.02	Mathematical detail
07.03	Financial detail
07.04	Oral communications
07.05	Records processing
07.06	Clerical machine operation
07.07	Clerical handling

Source: U.S. Department of Labor, *The revised handbook for analyzing jobs* (Washington, D.C.: U.S. Government Printing Office, 1991).

Exhibit 7-15
***Department of Labor
Physical Demands Factors***

Strength	Climbing	Balancing
Stooping	Kneeling	Crouching
Crawling	Reaching	Handling
Fingering	Feeling	Talking
Hearing	Tasting/smelling	Near acuity
Far acuity	Depth perception	Accommodation
Color vision	Field of vision	

Illustration: Far acuity refers to clarity of vision at 20 feet or more.

For example:

FA:1   Watches for landmarks when taking off and landing airplane.

FA:2   Reads traffic signs at distances up to 200 feet while driving taxi.

FA:3   Identifies machine jams at distances of 20 to 35 feet.

FA:4   Observes forests from remote fire-lookout station to locate forest fires, and reports fires using radio or telephone.

Source: U.S. Department of Labor, *The revised handbook for analyzing jobs* (Washington, D.C.: U.S. Government Printing Office, 1991).

Exhibit 7-16
***Department of Labor
Environmental Conditions***

Exposure to weather	Extreme cold
Extreme heat	Wet and/or humid
Noise intensity level	Vibration
Atmospheric conditions	Proximity to moving mechanical parts
Exposure to electrical shocks	Working in high exposed places
Exposure to radiation	Working with explosives
Exposure to toxic or caustic chemicals	Other environmental conditions

Illustration: Exposure to radiation represents possible bodily injury from radiation.

For example:

RE:1   Prepares, administers, and measures radioactive isotopes in therapeutic, diagnostic, and trace studies, utilizing a variety of radioisotope equipment. Worker is subject to possible bodily injury from exposure to radiation.

RE:2   Operates x-ray equipment. Worker is subject to possible bodily injury from exposure to radiation.

RE:3   Operates and maintains nuclear reactor. Worker is subject to possible bodily injury from exposure to gamma and neutron radiation.

RE:4   Monitors radiation in work environment where radioactive material is used. Worker is subject to possible bodily injury from exposure to radiation.

Source: U.S. Department of Labor, *The revised handbook for analyzing jobs* (Washington, D.C.: U.S. Government Printing Office, 1991).

The U.S. federal government began the development of job analysis methodology during the 1930s in response to the passage of the **Wagner-Peyser Act.** This act established a federal-state employment service system. The sheer size of this system required standardized occupational information to support job placement activities, employment counseling, occupational and career guidance, and labor market information service. Private sector companies adopted most of the terminology found in the government's methods, making it useful in both the private and public sectors.

The *Revised Handbook for Analyzing Jobs (RHAJ)* documents the DOL method. Over time, the government revised this methodology. The U.S. Department of Labor used this job analysis method to develop the job descriptions contained in the *DOT.* The *Dictionary of Occupational Titles (DOT)* includes over 20,000 private and public sector job descriptions.

The Employment and Training Administration of the U.S. Department of Labor publishes the *DOT,* and has revised it periodically to reflect changes in occupational content and job characteristics due to technological advance. The fourth edition of the *DOT,* published in 1991, is the most recent edition. The Department of Labor does not have immediate plans to revise the *DOT* in the near future.

The *DOT* uses a coding scheme known as the *DOT Job Code* to organize jobs into coherent categories. Exhibit 7-17 illustrates the five parts of the nine-digit *DOT* job codes:[3]

★ Occupational category (first digit)

★ Occupational division (first and second digits)

★ Occupational group (first, second, and third digits)

★ Worker functions (fourth, fifth, and sixth digits) —the worker's relationship to people, data, and things as listed previously in Exhibit 7-6.

★ A unique three-digit code (seventh, eighth, and ninth digits) that distinguishes each job from others within the same category, division, group, and worker functions.

REFLECTIONS

Relevance of the DOL Method in the 1990s

We've stressed the importance of selecting characteristics that adequately describe job duties, worker characteristics, and job context. The previous discussion reveals that the DOL method represents a detailed and comprehensive job analysis method. However, do the factors associated with such methods fit well with companies' efforts to gain competitive advantage? After all, job analysis techniques like the DOL method were developed during the 1940s, before the impact of technological change and global competition on U.S. companies' competitive positions.

Although the DOL method has been revised since the 1940s, the relationships between job duties, worker characteristics, and competitive advantage are not readily apparent. This condition does not necessarily mean that existing job analysis techniques are irrelevant. Rather, HR and compensation professionals should give careful consideration to the relevance of traditional compensable factors to the attainment of competitive advantage. Discussion Question 1 should promote your thinking about the relevance of traditional job characteristics to competitive advantage.

THE FIRST THREE DIGITS IDENTIFY A PARTICULAR OCCUPATIONAL GROUP.

Occupational category (first digit)

0/1 Professional, technical, and managerial occupations

2 Clerical and sales occupations

3 Service occupations

4 Agricultural, fishery, forestry, and related occupations

5 Processing occupations

6 Machine trade occupations

7 Benchwork operations

8 Structural work occupations

9 Miscellaneous occupations

Occupational division within occupational category (first and second digits)

For service occupations:

30 Domestic service occupations

31 Food and beverage preparation and service occupations

32 Lodging and related service occupations

33 Barbering, cosmetology, and related service occupations

34 Amusement and recreation service occupations

35 Miscellaneous personal service occupations

36 Apparel and furnishings service occupations

37 Protective service occupations

38 Building and related service occupations

Occupational group within the occupational division (first, second, and third digits)

For domestic service occupations (30)

301 Household and related work

302 Launderers, private family

305 Cooks, domestic

309 Domestic service occupations, N.E.C. (not elsewhere classified)

For protective service occupations (37)

371 Crossing tenders and bridge operators

372 Security guards and corrections officers, except crossing tenders

373 Firefighters, fire department

375 Police officers and detectives in public service

376 Police officers and detectives except in public service

377 Sheriffs and bailiffs

378 Armed forces enlisted personnel

379 Protective service occupations, N.E.C. (not elsewhere classified)

(continued on next page)

THE MIDDLE THREE DIGITS (FOURTH, FIFTH, AND SIXTH DIGITS) REPRESENT WORKER FUNCTION RATINGS OF THE TASKS PERFORMED IN THE OCCUPATION.

Every job requires a worker to function to some extent in relation to data, people, and things.

DATA (4TH DIGIT)	PEOPLE (5TH DIGIT)	THINGS (6TH DIGIT)
0 Synthesizing	0 Mentoring	0 Setting up
1 Coordinating	1 Negotiating	1 Precision working
2 Analyzing	2 Instructing	2 Operating-controlling
3 Compiling	3 Supervising	3 Drive-operating
4 Computing	4 Diverting	4 Manipulating
5 Copying	5 Persuading	5 Tending
6 Comparing	6 Speaking-signaling	6 Feeding-offbearing
	7 Serving	7 Handling
	8 Taking instructions-helping	

THE LAST THREE DIGITS DIFFERENTIATE A PARTICULAR JOB WITHIN AN OCCUPATION FROM ALL OTHER JOBS WITHIN THE SAME OCCUPATION.

375.167-010	Commanding officer, homicide squad
375.167-014	Commanding officer, investigating division
375.167-018	Commanding office, motor equipment
375.167-022	Chief detective

Source: U.S. Department of Labor, *Dictionary of occupational titles,* (vol. 1), 4th ed. (Washington D.C.: U.S. Government Printing Office, 1991).

Job evaluation

Compensation professionals use **job evaluation** to systematically recognize differences in the relative worth among a set of jobs and establish pay differentials accordingly. Whereas job analysis is almost purely descriptive, job evaluation partly reflects the values and priorities that management places on various positions. On the basis of job content and the priorities of the firm, managers establish pay differentials for virtually all positions within the company.

Compensable factors

Compensation professionals generally base job evaluations on compensable factors, that is, salient job characteristics by which companies establish relative pay rates. Most companies consider skill, effort, responsibility, and working conditions, which were derived from the Equal Pay Act. These four dimensions help managers determine whether dissimilar jobs are "equal."

Skill, effort, responsibility, and working conditions are universal compensable factors because virtually every job contains these four factors. So how can meaningful distinctions regarding the value of jobs be made with such broad factors? Many companies break these general factors into more-specific factors. For example, responsibility required could be further classified as responsibility for financial matters and responsibility for personnel matters.

Compensation professionals should choose compensable factors on the basis of two considerations. First, factors must be job-related. The factors that describe a particular job should indeed reflect the actual work that is performed: Failure to accurately match compensable factors with the actual work may result in either inadequate or excessive pay rates. Both cases are detrimental to the company, since inadequate pay may lead to dysfunctional turnover.

Second, compensation professionals should select compensable factors that further the company's strategies. For example, companies that value product differentiation probably consider innovativeness to be an important compensable factor for research scientist and marketing manager jobs. Companies that distinguish themselves through high-quality customer relations are likely to place great value on such compensable factors as product knowledge and interpersonal skills. Lowest cost strategies may emphasize different kinds of compensable factors such as efficiency and timeliness.

Compensation professionals should choose compensable factors on the basis of two considerations. First, factors must be job-related.

Second, compensation professionals should select compensable factors that further the company's strategies.

The job evaluation process

The job evaluation process entails six steps:

- ★ Single versus multiple job evaluation techniques
- ★ Choosing the job evaluation committee
- ★ Training employees to conduct job evaluations
- ★ Documenting the job evaluation plan
- ★ Communicating with employees
- ★ The appeals process

SINGLE VERSUS MULTIPLE JOB EVALUATION TECHNIQUES Compensation professionals must determine whether a single job evaluation technique is sufficiently broad to assess a diverse set of jobs. In particular, the decision is prompted by such questions as, "Can we use the same compensable factors to evaluate a fork lift operator's job and the plant manager's job?" If the answer is Yes, then a single job evaluation technique is appropriate. If not, then more than one job evaluation approach should be employed. It is not reasonable to expect that a single job evaluation technique, based on a single set of compensable factors, can adequately assess diverse sets of jobs—operative, clerical, administrative, managerial, professional, technical, and executive. Clearly, a carpenter's job is distinct from a certified public accountant's position because manual dexterity is an important compensable factor in carpentry work, but it is not central to accounting positions. The decision to use a single versus multiple plans is a key issue in the comparable-worth debate, which we take up in Chapter 8's "Reflections" feature.

CHOOSING THE JOB EVALUATION COMMITTEE Human resource professionals help put together a committee of rank-and-file employees, supervisors, managers, and union representatives to design, oversee, and evaluate job evaluation results. The functions, duties, responsibilities, and authority of job evaluation committees vary considerably from company to company. In general, committees simply review job descriptions and analyses and evaluate jobs. Larger companies with a multitude of jobs often establish separate committees to evaluate particular job classifications such as nonexempt, exempt, managerial, and executive jobs. The immense number of jobs in large companies would preclude committee members from performing their regular duties.

Job evaluation is an important determinant of a job's worth within many companies. All employees, regardless of their functions, wish to be compensated and valued for their efforts. All employees strive for a reasonable pay-effort bargain—a compensation level consistent with their contributions. Managers strive to balance employee motivation with cost control since they have limited resources for operating their departments. Union representatives strive to ensure that members enjoy quality standards of living. Therefore, unions try to prevent the undervaluation of jobs.

Job evaluation procedures are not scientifically accurate because evaluation decisions are based on ordinary human judgment.

Job evaluation committees help ensure commitment from employees throughout companies. They also provide a check and balances system. Job evaluation procedures are not scientifically accurate because evaluation decisions are based on ordinary human judgment. So a consensus of several employees helps to minimize biases of individual job evaluators.

TRAINING EMPLOYEES TO CONDUCT JOB EVALUATIONS Individuals should understand process objectives. Besides knowing company objectives, evaluators also should practice applying the chosen job evaluation criteria before applying them to actual jobs. In a manner similar to the approach in job analysis procedures, evaluators should base their decisions on sound job and business-related rationales to ensure legal compliance.

DOCUMENTING THE JOB EVALUATION PLAN Documenting the job evaluation plan is useful for legal and training purposes. From an employer's perspective, a well-documented evaluation plan clearly specifies job and business-related criteria against which jobs are evaluated. Well-documented plans can allow employees to understand clearly how their jobs were evaluated and the outcome of the process. In addition, well-documented plans provide guidelines for clarifying ambiguities in the event of employee appeals or legal challenges.

COMMUNICATING WITH EMPLOYEES Job evaluation results matter personally to all employees. Companies must formally communicate with employees throughout the job analysis and evaluation processes to ensure employees' understanding and acceptance of the job evaluation process and results. Information sessions and memoranda are useful media. Not only should employers share basic information, but employees also should be given the opportunity to respond to what they believe are unsatisfactory procedures or outcomes of the job evaluation process.

THE APPEALS PROCESS Companies should set up appeals procedures that permit reviews on a case-by-case basis to provide a check on the process through reexamination. Such appeals reduce charges of illegal discrimination that would be more likely to occur if employees were not given a voice. Usually, compensation professionals review employees' appeals. Increasingly, companies process appeals through committees made up of compensation professionals and a representative sample of employees and supervisors. Grievants are more likely to judge appeals decisions as fair when committees are involved: Committee decisions should reflect the varied perspectives of participants rather than the judgment of one individual.

Job evaluation techniques

Compensation professionals categorize job evaluation methods as either market-based evaluation or job-content evaluation techniques. **Market-based evaluation** plans use market data to determine differences in job worth. Many companies choose market-based evaluation methods because they wish to assign job pay rates that are neither too low nor too high relative to the market. Setting pay rates too low will make it difficult to recruit talented candidates, and setting pay rates too high will result in an excessive cost burden for the employer. Compensation professionals rely on compensation surveys to determine prevailing pay rates of jobs in the relevant labor market. We address that issue in Chapter 8.

Job-content evaluation plans emphasize the company's internal value system, establishing a hierarchy of internal job worth based on each job's role in company strategy. Compensation professionals review preliminary structures for consistency with market pay rates on a representative sample of jobs known as benchmark jobs.

Ultimately, compensation professionals must balance external market considerations with internal consistency objectives. In practice, compensation professionals judge the adequacy of pay differentials by comparing both market rates and pay differences among jobs within their companies. They consult with the top HR official and chief financial officer when discrepancies arise, particularly when company pay rates are generally lower than the market rates. Upon careful consideration of the company's financial resources and the strategic value of the jobs in question, these individuals decide whether to adjust internal pay rates for the jobs with the below-market pay rates.

> Ultimately, compensation professionals must balance external market considerations with internal consistency objectives.

Neither a market-based nor a job-content evaluation approach alone enables compensation professionals to balance internal and external considerations. Therefore, most companies rely on both approaches. The point method is the most popular job-content method because it provides compensation professionals better control over balancing internal and market considerations. Chapter 8 fully addresses how compensation professionals combine point method results with market approaches. However, a brief overview follows our review of the point method in this chapter.

The point method

The **point method** is a job-content valuation technique that uses quantitative methodology. Quantitative methods assign numerical values to compensable factors that describe jobs, and these values are summed as an indicator of the overall value for the job. The relative worth of jobs is established by the magnitude of the overall numeric value for the jobs.

The point method evaluates jobs by comparing compensable factors. Each factor is defined and assigned a range of points based on the factor's relative value to the company. Compensable factors are weighted to represent the relative importance of each factor to the company. Job evaluation committees follow seven steps to complete the point method.

STEP 1: SELECT BENCHMARK JOBS Point method job evaluations use benchmark jobs to develop factors and their definitions to select jobs to represent the entire range of jobs in the company. **Benchmark jobs,** found outside the company, provide reference points against which jobs within the company are judged. Exhibit 7-18 lists the characteristics of benchmark jobs.[4]

1. The contents are well known, relatively stable over time, and agreed upon by the employees involved.

2. The jobs are common across a number of different employers.

3. The jobs represent the entire range of jobs that are being evaluated within a company.

4. The jobs are generally accepted in the labor market for the purposes of setting pay levels.

Source: G. T. Milkovich and J. M. Newman, *Compensation,* 5th ed. (Homewood, Ill: Richard D. Irwin, 1996).

STEP 2: CHOOSE COMPENSABLE FACTORS BASED ON BENCHMARK JOBS Managers must define compensable factors that adequately represent the scope of jobs slated for evaluation. Each benchmark job should be described by these factors that help distinguish it from the value of all other jobs. Besides the "universal" factors—skill, effort, responsibility, and working conditions—additional factors may be developed to the extent that they are job- and business-related.

Compensable factor categories may be broken down further into specific related factors or subfactors. For example, skill may include job knowledge, education, mental ability, physical ability, accuracy, and dexterity. Effort may include factors relating to both physical and mental exertion. Responsibility may include considerations related to fiscal, material, or personnel responsibilities. Working conditions may be unpleasant because of extreme temperatures or possible exposure to hazardous chemicals.

How many compensable factors should companies use? The answer is, "It depends." Compensation professionals should select as many compensable factors as are needed to adequately describe the range of benchmark jobs.

STEP 3: DEFINE FACTOR DEGREES Although compensable factors describe the range of benchmark jobs, individual jobs will vary in scope and content. So evaluators must divide each factor into a sufficient number of degrees to identify the level of a factor present in each job. Exhibit 7-19 illustrates a factor definition for writing ability and its degree statements. Degree definitions should set forth and limit the meaning of each degree so that evaluators can uniformly interpret job descriptions. It is generally helpful to include a few actual work examples as anchors.

The number of degrees will vary according to the comprehensiveness of the plan. For example, if the plan covers only a limited segment of jobs such as clerical employees, fewer degrees will be required than if the plan were to cover every group of employees. Take education as an example. Only two degrees may be necessary to describe the educational requirements for clerical jobs—high school diploma or equivalent and an associate's degree. More than two degrees would be required to adequately describe the educational requirements for clerical, production, managerial, and professionals jobs—high school diploma or equivalent, associate's degree, bachelor's degree, master's degree, and doctorate. Most analyses anchor minimum and maximum degrees, with specific jobs representing these points.

STEP 4: DETERMINE THE WEIGHT OF EACH FACTOR Weighting compensable factors represents the importance of the factor to the overall value of the job. The weights of compensable factors usually are expressed as percentages. Weighting often is done by management or by job evaluation committee decision. All of the factors are ranked according to their relative importance, and final weights are assigned after discussion

Exhibit 7-19
Writing Ability: Factor Definition and Degree Statements

Definition	Capacity to communicate with others in written form.
First Degree	Print simple phrases and sentences, using normal word order and present and past tenses.
Sample Anchor	Prints shipping labels for packages, indicating the destination and the contents of the packages.
Second Degree	Write compound and complex sentences, using proper end punctuation and adjectives and adverbs.
Sample Anchor	Fills requisitions, work orders, or requests for materials, tools, or other stock items.
Third Degree	Write reports and essays with proper format, punctuation, spelling, and grammar, using all parts of speech.
Sample Anchor	Types letters, reports, or straight-copy materials from rough draft or corrected copy.
Fourth Degree	Prepare business letters, expositions, summaries, and reports, using prescribed format and conforming to all rules of punctuation, grammar, diction, and style.
Sample Anchor	Composes letters in reply to correspondence concerning such items as request for merchandise, damage claims, credit information, delinquent accounts, or to request information.
Fifth Degree	Write manuals or speeches.
Sample Anchor	Writes service manuals and related technical publications concerned with installation, operation, and maintenance of electronic, electrical, mechanical, and other equipment.

and consensus. For example, let's assume the relative importance of skill, effort, responsibility, and working conditions to ABC Manufacturing Corporation:

✯ Skill is the most highly valued compensable factor, weighted at 60 percent.

✯ Responsibility is the next important factor, weighted at 25 percent.

✯ Effort is weighted at 10 percent.

✯ Working conditions is least important, weighted at 5 percent.

STEP 5: DETERMINE POINT VALUES FOR EACH COMPENSABLE FACTOR Compensation professionals set point values for each compensable factor in three stages. First, they must establish the maximum possible point values for the complete set of compensable factors. This total number is arbitrary, but it represents the possible maximum value jobs can possess. As a rule of thumb, the total point value for a set of compensable factors should be determined by a simple formula—the number of compensable factors times 250. ABC Manufacturing sets 1,000 (4 compensable factors × 250) as the possible maximum number of points.

Second, the maximum possible point value for each compensable factor is based on its weight as described in step 4. Again, for ABC Manufacturing, skill = 60%, responsibility = 25%, effort = 10%, and working conditions = 5%:

✯ The maximum possible total points for skills equals 600 points (60% × 1,000 points).

☆ The maximum possible total points for responsibility equals 250 points (25% × 1,000 points).

☆ The maximum possible total points for effort equals 100 points (10% × 1,000 points).

☆ The maximum possible total points for working conditions equals 50 points (5% × 1,000 points).

Third, compensation professionals distribute these points across degree statements within each compensable factor. The point progression by degrees from the lowest to the highest point value advances arithmetically: that is, on a scale of even incremental values. This characteristic is essential for conducting regression analysis—a statistical analysis method that we address in Chapter 8 in the discussion of integrating internal job structures (based on job evaluation points) with external pay rates for benchmark jobs.

How do compensation professionals assign point values to each degree? Let's illustrate this procedure by example, using the skill compensable factor. Let's also assume that the skill factor has five degree statements. Degree 1 represents the most basic skill level, and degree 5 represents the most advanced skill level. The increment from one degree to the next highest is 120 points (600 point maximum ÷ 5 degree statements).

☆ Degree 1 = 120 points (120 points × 1)

☆ Degree 2 = 240 points (120 points × 2)

☆ Degree 3 = 360 points (120 points × 3)

☆ Degree 4 = 480 points (120 points × 4)

☆ Degree 5 = 600 points (120 points × 5)

STEP 6: VERIFY FACTOR DEGREES AND POINT VALUES Committee members should independently calculate the point values for a random sample of jobs. Exhibit 7-20 shows a sample job evaluation worksheet. After calculating the point values for this sample, committee members should review the point totals for each job. Committee members give careful consideration to whether the hierarchy of jobs makes sense in the context of the company's strategic plan as well as the inherent content of the jobs. For instance, sales jobs should rank relatively high on the job hierarchy of jobs within a sales-oriented company such as in the pharmaceuticals industry. Research scientist jobs ought to rank relatively high for a company that pursues a differentiation strategy. Messenger jobs should not rank more highly than claims analyst jobs in an insurance company. In short, where peculiarities are apparent, committee members reconsider compensable factor definitions, weights, and actual ratings of the benchmark jobs.

STEP 7: EVALUATE ALL JOBS Committee members evaluate all jobs in the company once the evaluation system has been tested and refined. Each job then is evaluated by determining which degree definition best fits the job and assigning the corresponding point factors. All points are totaled for each job, and all jobs are ranked according to their point values.

BALANCING INTERNAL AND MARKET CONSIDERATIONS USING THE POINT METHOD
How do compensation professionals balance internal and market considerations with point method results? Compensation professionals convert point values into the mar-

Exhibit 7-20
Sample Job Evaluation Worksheet

Job Title: _____

Evaluation Date: _____

Name of Evaluator: _____

COMPENSABLE FACTOR	DEGREE					TOTAL
	1	2	3	4	5	
Skill						
Mental skill	60	120	180	240	(300)	300
Manual skill	60	(120)	180	240	300	120
Effort						
Mental effort	10	20	30	40	(50)	50
Physical effort	10	20	(30)	40	50	30
Responsibility						
Supervisory	25	50	(75)	100	125	75
Department budgeting	(25)	50	75	100	125	25
Working Conditions						
Hazards	10	20	30	(40)	50	40
Total job value						640

ket value of jobs through regression analysis, a statistical technique. As we discuss in Chapter 8, regression analysis enables compensation professionals to set base pay rates in line with market rates for benchmark or representative jobs. Companies identify market pay rates through compensation surveys. Of course, a company's value structure for jobs based on the point method will probably differ somewhat from the market pay rates for similar jobs. Regression analysis indicates base pay rates that minimize the differences between the company's point method results and the market pay rates.

Alternative job content evaluation approaches

Most other job content approaches use qualitative methods. Qualitative methods evaluate whole jobs and typically compare jobs with each other or against some general criteria. Usually, these criteria are vague—for example, importance of job to departmental effectiveness. The prevalent kinds of qualitative job evaluation techniques include:

* ☆ Simple ranking plans
* ☆ Paired comparisons
* ☆ Alternation ranking
* ☆ Classification plans

SIMPLE RANKING PLAN **Simple ranking plans** order all jobs from lowest to highest according to a single criterion such as job complexity or the centrality of the job to the company's competitive strategy. This approach considers each job in its entirety, usually in small companies that have relatively few employees. In large companies that classify many jobs, members of job evaluation committees independently rank jobs on a departmental basis. Different rankings will likely result. When they do, job evaluation committees discuss the differences in rankings and choose one set of rankings by consensus.

PAIRED COMPARISON AND ALTERNATION RANKING Two common variations of the ranking plan are called paired comparison and alternation ranking. The **paired comparison** technique is useful if there are many jobs to rate, usually more than 20. Job evaluation committees generate every possible pair of jobs. For each pair, committee members assign a point to the job with the highest value, and the lowest-value job does not receive a point. After evaluating each pair, the evaluator sums the points for each job. Jobs with higher points are more valuable than jobs with fewer points. The job with the most points becomes the highest-ranked job; the job with the least points becomes the lowest ranked job.

The **alternation ranking** method orders jobs by extremes. Yet, again, committee members judge the relative value of jobs according to a single criterion such as job complexity or the centrality of the job to the company's competitive strategy. This ranking process begins by first determining which job is the most valuable and then determining which job is the least valuable. Committee members then judge the next most valuable jobs and the next least valuable jobs. This process continues until all jobs have been evaluated.

Despite the simplicity of ranking plans, they exhibit three limitations. First, ranking results rely on purely subjective data; the process lacks objective standards, guidelines, and principles that would aid in resolving differences of opinion among committee members. Companies usually do not fully define their ranking criteria. For example, the criterion job complexity can be defined as level of education or as number of distinct tasks that the workers must perform daily.

Second, because ranking methods use neither job analyses nor job descriptions, they are difficult to defend legally. Committee members rely on their own impressions of the jobs.

Third, ranking approaches do not incorporate objective scales that indicate how different in value one job is from another. For instance, let's assume that a committee decides on the following ranking for training and development professionals (listed from most valuable to least valuable):

★ Director of Training and Development

★ Manager of Training and Development

★ Senior Training and Development Specialist

★ Training and Development Specialist

★ Training and Development Assistant

Rankings do not offer standards for compensation professionals to facilitate answering such questions as, "Is the Director of Training and Development job worth four times as much as the Training and Development Assistant job?" Compensation professionals' inability to answer such questions makes it difficult to establish pay levels according to job content differences.

CLASSIFICATION PLANS Companies use **classification plans** to place jobs into categories on the basis of compensable factors. Public sector organizations, such as civil service systems, use classification systems most prevalently. The federal government's classification system is a well-known example. As we discussed in Chapter 4, the General Schedule classifies federal government jobs into 15 classifications (GS-1 through GS-15) based on such factors as skill, education, and experience levels. In addition, jobs that require high levels of specialized education (for example, a physicist), significantly influence public policy (for example, law judges), or require executive decision making are classified in separate categories: Senior Level (SL), Scientific and Professional (ST) positions, and the Senior Executive Service (SES).

The federal government uses its Factor Evaluation System (FES) job evaluation methodology to classify most government jobs in the General Schedule. Jobs are evaluated on the basis of nine general compensable factors. Five of the compensable factors have subfactors. Exhibit 7-21 lists these factors and subfactors.

The GS classification system enables the federal government to set pay rates for thousands of unique jobs based on 18 classes. Pay administration is relatively simple because pay rates depend on GS level and the employees' relevant work seniority, as we discussed in Chapter 4. The most noteworthy disadvantage is the absence of regu-

---

Exhibit 7-21
Federal Government Factor Evaluation System

1. Knowledge required by the position
   a. Nature or kind of knowledge and skills needed
   b. How the skills and knowledge are used in doing the work
2. Supervisory controls
   a. How the work is assigned
   b. The employee's responsibility for carrying out the work
   c. How the work is reviewed
3. Guidelines
   a. The nature of guidelines for performing the work
   b. The judgment needed to apply the guidelines or develop new guides
4. Complexity
   a. The nature of the assignment
   b. The difficulty in identifying what needs to be done
   c. The difficulty and originality involved in performing the work
5. Scope and effect
   a. The purpose of the work
   b. The impact of the work product or service
6. Personal contacts
7. Purpose of contacts
8. Physical demands
9. Work environment

Source: U.S. Civil Service Commission, *Instructions for the factor evaluation system* (Washington, D.C.: U.S. Government Printing Office, 1977).

lar procedures for rewarding exceptional performance, which, ultimately, discourages employees from working as productively as possible.

THE HAY PLAN Edward Hay developed the *Hay Guide Chart-Profile Method of Job Evaluation* (the Hay Plan) in the 1950s, and the Hay Group, a consulting firm, applies the Hay Plan to a wide range of jobs including nonexempt and exempt jobs as well as executive positions. The evaluation of all jobs with the **Hay Plan** centers on four compensable factors. The first, **know-how,** is the total of all skills and knowledge required to do the job. The know-how factor contains three subfactors—specialized and technical knowledge, managerial relations, and human relations. The second factor, **problem solving,** is the amount of original thinking required to arrive at decisions in the job. Problem solving includes two subfactors—thinking environment and thinking challenge. The third factor, **accountability,** is the answerability for actions taken on the job. It is composed of three subfactors—freedom to act, impact on end results, and magnitude of impact. The fourth factor, **additional compensable elements,** addresses exceptional conditions in the context in which the jobs are performed.

Alternatives to job evaluation

Compensation professionals assign pay rates to jobs in numerous ways other than through the job evaluation process as previously defined. These alternative methods include the reliance on market pay rates, pay incentives, individual rates, and collective bargaining. Many companies determine the value of jobs by paying about the average rate found in the external labor market. The procedures for assessing market rates are addressed fully in Chapter 8.

Besides the market pay rate, pay incentives may also be the basis for establishing the core compensation for jobs. As we discussed extensively in Chapter 5, incentives tie part or all of an employee's core compensation to the attainment of a predetermined performance objective. Next, both core and fringe compensation may be determined through negotiations between an individual and an employer. Typically, the employer uses the market rate as a basis for negotiations, agreeing to a greater amount to the extent that the supply of talented individuals is scarce and the individual has an established track record of performance. Finally, when unions are present, pay rates are established through the collective bargaining process, which we already considered in Chapter 3.

Internally consistent compensation systems and competitive strategy

Internally consistent pay systems may reduce a company's flexibility to respond to changes in competitors' pay practices because job analysis leads to structured job descriptions and jobs.

To this point, we have examined the principles of internally consistent compensation systems and the rationale for building them. Moreover, we reviewed the key processes—job analysis and job evaluation—that lead to internally consistent compensation systems. Although we made the case for building internally consistent pay systems, these systems do have some limitations. Internally consistent pay systems may reduce a company's flexibility to respond to changes in competitors' pay practices because job analysis leads to structured job descriptions and jobs. In addition, job evaluation establishes the relative worth of jobs *within* the company. Responding to the competition may require employees to engage in duties that extend beyond what's

Job Evaluation Hinders Competitive Advantage

Earlier, we indicated that job evaluation has strategic value. However, not everybody holds that view. Opponents of job evaluation argue that the development of internally consistent pay systems may be detrimental to the attainment of competitive advantage:[6]

> The primary focus in traditional point-factor plans [that is, point plans] is internal equity across all jobs in the organization. It is difficult to determine what is internal equity beyond functional areas with consistent agreement among employees and managers. The "line of sight" for internal equity among employees, who need to believe the program is credible, is within functional areas (e.g., within marketing, within manufacturing, within human resources, within engineering), rather than between them. Trying to create internal equity across functions is subject to individual interpretation and potential disagreement and therefore reduces the likelihood of program acceptance.

> Often organizations complain that employees are too focused on internal equity and cannot be refocused. As long as the organization keeps a job evaluation system that attempts to create internal equity across the entire organization, however, the organization is communicating to employees to focus on internal equity. In this case, the job evaluation system and the focus of pay need to change so that they are able to refocus on what is important to the organization— results and organizational success.

written in their job descriptions whenever competitive pressures demand. In the process, the definitions of jobs become more fluid, and equity assessments become more difficult.

Another potential limitation of internally consistent compensation structures is the resultant bureaucracy. Companies that establish job hierarchies tend to create narrowly defined jobs that lead to greater numbers of jobs and staffing levels.[5] Such structures promote heavy compensation burdens. Employees' core compensation depends upon the jobs they perform, how well they perform their jobs, or the skills they possess. However, employee benefits (Chapters 10 and 11) represent fixed costs that typically do not vary with employees' job duties, their performance, or the skills they possess.

Summary

This chapter discussed internally consistent pay systems and described two important tools HR and compensation professionals use to build them—job analysis and job evaluation. Job analysis is a descriptive process that enables HR professionals to systematically describe job duties, worker specifications, and job context. Compensation professionals use job evaluation to assess the relative worth of jobs within companies. Job analysis and job evaluation are an art because they require the HR and compensation professionals' sound judgment. We discussed the strategic role job analysis and job evaluation play in companies' quest for competitive advantage. However, we also pointed out some of the shortcomings of these approaches. Compensation professionals must carefully weigh the possible benefits and consequences of these methods on attaining competitive advantage.

Discussion questions

1. The following questions are based on the "Reflections" feature and are related to the relevance of traditional compensable factors for competitive advantage. A useful starting point is the competitive strategies. What are the priorities of lowest-cost and differentiation competitive strategies? How are traditional compensable factors from such job analysis techniques as the DOL method related to these priorities? Discuss a few examples for each competitive strategy.

2. Conduct a job analysis for a person you know, and write a complete job description (no longer than one page) according to the principles described in this chapter. In class, be prepared to discuss the method you used for conducting the job analysis and some of the challenges you encountered.

3. This chapter provided the rationale for conducting job analysis, and it indicated some of the limitations. Take a stand for or against the use of job analysis, and provide convincing arguments for your position.

4. Respond to the statement, "Building an internally consistent job structure is burdensome to companies. Instead, it is best to simply define and evaluate the worth of jobs by surveying the market."

5. Do you consider performing job evaluation to be an art or a science? Please explain.

Key terms

internally consistent compensation
 systems
internally consistent job structures
job analysis
job content
worker requirements
reliable job analysis
valid job analysis
job descriptions
job titles
job summary
job duties
worker specification
education
skill
ability

knowledge
work performed
worker traits
worker function
work fields
materials, products, subject matter,
 and services (MPSMS)
general educational development
 (GED)
specific vocational preparation
aptitudes
temperaments
interests
physical demands
environmental conditions
Wagner-Peyser Act

Revised Handbook for Analyzing Jobs (RHAJ)

Dictionary of Occupational Titles (DOT)

job evaluation

market-based evaluation

job content evaluation

point method

benchmark jobs

simple ranking plans

paired comparison

alternation ranking

classification plans

Hay Plan

know-how

problem solving

accountability

additional compensable elements

Endnotes

[1] R. J. Harvey, Job analysis, in M. D. Dunnette and L. M. Hough, eds, *Handbook of industrial and organizational psychology,* vol. 2 (Palo Alto, Calif.: Consulting Psychologists Press, 1991).

[2] U.S. Department of Labor, *The Revised Handbook for Analyzing Jobs* (Washington, D.C.: U.S. Government Printing Office, 1991).

[3] U.S. Department of Labor, *The Dictionary of Occupational Titles* (Washington D.C.: U.S. Government Printing Office, 1991).

[4] G. T. Milkovich and J. M. Newman, *Compensation,* 5th ed. (Homewood, Ill.: Richard D. Irwin, 1996).

[5] E. E. Lawler III, What's wrong with point-factor job evaluation? *Compensation and Benefits Review* 18 (1986):20–28.

[6] J. R. Schuster and P. K. Zingheim, *The new pay: Linking employee and organizational performance* (New York: Lexington Books, 1992), pp. 121–122.

CHAPTER

EIGHT

Building market-competitive compensation systems

In this chapter, you will learn about

1. Market-competitive compensation systems
2. Strategic analysis factors
3. Compensation surveys
4. Integrating the internal job structure with external market pay rates
5. Compensation policies and strategic mandates

SURGIMED manufactures surgical and medical instruments. SURGIMED's surgical line includes internal stapling devices and endoscopic instruments. Their medical instruments line includes blood pressure cuffs, oxygen tents, and stethoscopes. SURGIMED, located in Cleveland, Ohio, is pursuing a differentiation strategy. Its goal is to be the number one or two manufacturer of lightest-weight surgical instruments worldwide by the year 2003. Innovative engineering is key to SURGIMED's attainment of this differentiation strategy.

The company was founded five years ago, and its work force and sales are growing rapidly. During these five years, SURGIMED has paid extraordinarily high salaries to attract the best-qualified employees. Although SURGIMED continues to prosper, it cannot afford to pay exceptionally high salaries to its growing work force.

Barbara Browning has just joined SURGIMED as the company's first compensation director. Before joining SURGIMED, Barbara served as a successful compensation manager for one of SURGIMED's main competitors. Barbara's first task is to prepare an overview of the competitiveness of SURGIMED's compensation program. Then she must recommend compensation policies to SURGIMED's CEO.

Market-competitive pay systems play a significant role in attracting and retaining the best-qualified employees.

Market-competitive pay systems represent companies' compensation policies designed to fit the imperatives of competitive advantage. Market-competitive pay systems play a significant role in attracting and retaining the best-qualified employees. Well-designed pay systems should promote companies' attainment of competitive strategies. Paying more than necessary can undermine lowest-cost strategies: Excess pay levels represent an undue burden. Also, excessive pay restricts companies' ability to invest in other important strategic activities—for example, research and development and training—because money is a limited resource. Companies that pursue differentiation strategies must strike a balance between offering sufficiently high salaries to attract and retain talented candidates and providing sufficient resources to enable them to be productively creative.

Market-competitive pay systems: The basic building blocks

Compensation professionals create market-competitive pay systems on the basis of four activities:

✯ Conducting strategic analyses

✯ Assessing competitors' pay practices with compensation surveys

✯ Integrating the internal job structure with external market pay rates

✯ Determining compensation policies

First, a **strategic analysis** entails an examination of a company's external market context and internal factors. Examples of external market factors include industry profile, information about competitors, and long-term growth prospects. Internal factors encompass financial condition and functional capabilities—for example, marketing and human resources. Strategic analyses permit business professionals to see where they stand in the market in terms of both external and internal factors. Companies with strong potential to increase sales levels tend to be in better standing than companies with weak potential to maintain or increase sales. Companies in strong standing should be able to devote more financial resources to fund compensation programs than companies in weak standing.

Second, **compensation surveys** involve the collection and subsequent analysis of competitors' compensation data. Compensation surveys traditionally focused on competitors' wage and salary practices. Most recently, fringe compensation is also a target of surveys because benefits are a key element of market-competitive pay systems. Compensation surveys are important because they enable compensation professionals to obtain realistic views of competitors' pay practices. Compensation professionals would have to use guesswork to build market-competitive compensation systems in the absence of compensation survey data. Making too many wrong guesses could lead to noncompetitive compensation systems, undermining competitive advantage in the end.

Third, compensation professionals integrate the internal job structure (Chapter 7) with the external market pay rates identified through compensation surveys. This integration results in pay rates that reflect both the company's and the external market's valuation of jobs. Most often, compensation professionals rely on regression analysis, a statistical method, to achieve this integration.

Finally, compensation professionals recommend pay policies that fit with their companies' standing and competitive strategies. As we discuss later in this chapter, compensation professionals must strike a balance between managing costs and attracting and retaining the best-qualified employees. Ultimately, top management makes compensation policy decisions after careful consideration of compensation professionals' interpretation of the data.

Ultimately, top management makes compensation policy decisions after careful consideration of compensation professionals' interpretation of the data.

Strategic analysis

We illustrate a strategic analysis for the hypothetical company SURGIMED, mentioned in the opening vignette. SURGIMED manufactures surgical and medical instruments. SURGIMED's surgical line includes internal stapling devices and endoscopic instruments. Their medical instruments line includes blood pressure cuffs, oxygen tents, and stethoscopes. The company is located in Cleveland, Ohio.

Strategic analyses begin with the identification of a company's industry classification because companies within a given classification compete for the same customers' business. For example, McDonald's and Burger King compete for consumers of fast foods. Motorola and Nokia are product competitors because each company seeks to be the premier manufacturer of cellular telephones. The federal government's *Standard Industrial Classification Manual* classifies industries according to the

Standard Industrial Classification (SIC) system. SIC codes represent keys to pertinent information for strategic analyses: As we'll see shortly, the federal government publishes many bulletins that contain information about industry and employment outlooks based on the SIC system. These bulletins permit compensation professionals and top managers to answer such questions as: "Will consumer demand increase for commercial airline travel over the next five years?" "Are there sufficient numbers of well-trained commercial pilots?" "How much do commercial airline pilots typically earn?"

The SIC system provides an excellent starting point because it enables companies to identify direct product or service market competitors. The SIC system is the classification system for industries used in all federal government economic statistics. Many private sector companies also rely on the SIC system to conduct strategic analyses. The federal government publishes SIC codes in the *Standard Industrial Classification Manual.*[1] The federal government created the SIC system to cover the entire field of general economic activities—11 general activities in all. Exhibit 8-1 lists these activities. SURGIMED falls in the manufacturing division.

The SIC system uses four-digit classification codes. Exhibit 8-2 shows the elements of SIC codes and a sample code—8244. The first two digits represent the **major group,** which is the broadest classification of industries: 82 denotes educational services. The first three digits stand for the **industry group number,** classifying broad categories of educational services: 824 represents vocational education; 821 (not shown in Exhibit 8-2) stands for universities, colleges, and junior colleges. The entire four-digit code denotes the specific **industry group:** 8244 represents business and secretarial schools. 8243 (not shown in Exhibit 8-2) stands for data processing schools. Both business and secretarial schools and data processing schools offer specific kinds of vocational education.

SURGIMED's SIC code is 3841. The digits 38 represent the major group—measuring, analyzing, and controlling instruments; photographic, medical and optical goods; watches and clocks:

Exhibit 8-1
Economic Activities Indexed by the Federal Government's Standard Industrial Classification Manual

- Agriculture, forestry, fishing, hunting, and trapping
- Mining
- Construction
- Manufacturing
- Transportation, communications, electric, gas, and sanitary services
- Wholesale trade
- Retail trade
- Finance, insurance, and real estate
- Personal, business, professional, repair, recreation, and other services
- Public administration
- Nonclassifiable establishments

Source: U.S. Office of Management and Budget, *Standard industrial classification manual* (Washington, D.C.: U.S. Office of Management and Budget, 1987).

Exhibit 8-2
**Standard Industrial
Classification** *Code
Elements*

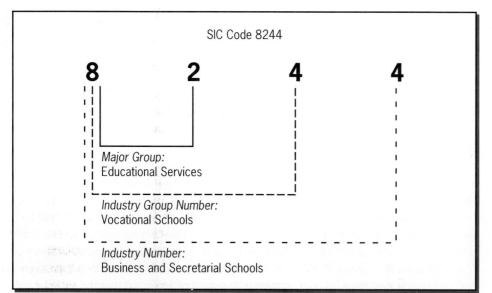

SIC Code 8244

8   2   4   4

Major Group:
Educational Services

Industry Group Number:
Vocational Schools

Industry Number:
Business and Secretarial Schools

This major group includes establishments engaged in manufacturing instruments (including professional and scientific) for measuring, testing, analyzing, and controlling, and their associated sensors and accessories; optical instruments and lenses; surveying and drafting instruments; hydrological, hydrographic, meteorological, and geophysical equipment; search detection, navigation, and guidance systems and equipment; surgical, medical, and dental instruments, equipment, and supplies; ophthalmic goods; photographic equipment and supplies; and watches and clocks.[2]

SURGIMED's industry group number is 384—surgical, medical, and dental instruments and supplies. This industry group includes five industries (that is, four-digit classifications):

✩ Manufacturers of surgical and medical instruments and apparatus (3841)

✩ Surgical appliances and supplies (3842)

✩ Dental equipment and supplies (3843)

✩ X-ray apparatus and tubes (3844)

✩ Electromedical equipment (3845)

SURGIMED's industry number is 3841—manufacturers of surgical and medical instruments and apparatus.

External Market Environment

Compensation professionals, top management, and consultants examine five elements of the external environment as they conduct strategic analyses:

✩ Industry profile

✩ Competition

✩ Foreign demand

✩ Industry's long-term prospects

✩ Labor market assessment

The U.S. Department of Commerce's *U.S. Industrial Outlook* is an invaluable information source for facts about the external environment.

INDUSTRY PROFILE **Industry profiles** describe such basic industry characteristics as sales volume, the impact of relevant government regulation on competitive strategies, and the impact of recent technological advancements on business activity. Compensation professionals use industry profile information to determine the kinds of compensation practices they should recommend to top management. For example, pay-for-knowledge programs may be appropriate where employees must learn to use new technology. In the case of sales stagnation, companies might choose to use incentive pay plans geared toward rewarding employees for contributing to increased sales activity.

The most recent edition available of the *U.S. Industrial Outlook,* published in 1994, made the following assessment of and prediction for manufacturers of surgical, medical, and dental instruments and supplies (SIC 384). Sales growth increased steadily— 6 percent annually—since 1990. In 1993, sales growth increased by 7 percent to $11.1 billion.[3] In addition, the U.S. Department of Commerce predicted that the surgical and medical instruments industry will experience growth in business activity through the year 2005.[4] Three factors support this prediction. First, medical care providers' demand for surgical and medical instruments will increase dramatically as the baby boom cohort ages and becomes more susceptible to illness. Second, there has been a strong political focus on health services and health-related industries in the United States. Third, foreign demand for U.S. medical equipment is on the rise because it generally represents state-of-the-art technology.

Companies in this industry group face strict federal government regulation. Some view government regulation as an impediment to global competitiveness because they cannot sell products until the U.S. Food and Drug Administration (FDA) grants approval. FDA approval certifies that new products are safe and free of harmful side effects. The FDA undertakes lengthy reviews and tests of newly developed medical equipment. The FDA attempts to complete reviews within a six-month period, but review cycles have been known to exceed that period.[5]

The FDA's policy has implications for U.S. manufacturers' competitive advantage domestically and internationally. U.S. manufacturers invest millions of dollars every year to develop and test surgical and medical equipment. This monetary investment represents a substantial cost burden to companies because they cannot make up these costs until they receive FDA approval. U.S. manufacturers stand to lose sales in foreign countries. Most foreign governments impose fewer restrictions than the FDA, giving them competitive advantage over U.S. manufacturers in foreign markets.

The Global Harmonization Task Force has undertaken an initiative to level the competitive playing field by developing an internationally accepted quality standard for medical devices. Members of this task force include representatives from the United States, the European Community, Japan, and Canada. A single quality inspection would promote U.S. companies' competitive advantage by giving them easier access to foreign markets.

COMPETITION Companies take stock of competitors' business activities to help position themselves in the market. Companies can distinguish themselves from the competition in different ways (for example, top-notch customer service or state-of-the-art products), and they can achieve lowest-cost objectives in various ways (for example, reducing advertising expenditures or minimizing staffing levels). Compensation professionals play a role by recommending pay systems (Chapters 4, 5, and 6) and setting pay levels—discussed later in this chapter—that support differentiation or cost objectives.

SURGIMED competes mainly with four companies in the surgical and medical instruments and apparatus industry—Pfizer, Johnson & Johnson, Medtronic, and Baxter. These companies possess sound reputations worldwide. Thus, SURGIMED must carefully establish a competitive strategy that distinguishes it from those competitors. In practice, SURGIMED's compensation professionals would give careful consideration to the specific factors that make their competitors successful and would investigate how compensation practices could be used to create competitive advantages for their own company.

FOREIGN DEMAND Companies are interested in foreign demand for their products or service: Such demand is an indicator of potential additional sales revenue. Compensation professionals factor the impact of foreign demand when making their pay policy recommendations. In general, compensation professionals may feel that higher base pay rates or incentive awards are warranted in the presence of higher foreign demand. In addition, the anticipated level of demand over time is important. It is unlikely that compensation professionals would alter pay policy recommendations for short-term increases (or decreases, for that matter) in foreign demand.

Exports to foreign countries account for nearly 25 percent of shipments in the surgical, medical, and dental instruments and supplies industry group. Three factors have contributed to this level of demand: the aging population worldwide, upgrading of health care systems worldwide, and the creation of a single comprehensive European market.

Exports to Canada and Mexico are on the rise. The reduction of trade barriers due to the *North American Free Trade Agreement* (NAFTA) is a key reason. In 1995, Canada ranked as the second largest importer of U.S. medical equipment, and Mexico ranked as the seventh largest importer. The Mexican government's effort to improve health care is also responsible for the growth in exports. These factors represent a reasonable basis to predict increased opportunities to gain additional market share.

U.S. manufacturers have a presence in Japan, but there has been little growth since the mid-1980s. The trade imbalance between these countries has limited U.S. companies' access to Japanese markets. The Japanese Ministry of Health and Welfare (JMHW) is the main obstacle to accessing Japanese markets. The JMHW regulates medical equipment purchases and limits imports from the United States. U.S. manufacturers' future access to Japanese markets looks promising because the U.S. and Japanese governments are developing agreements to improve U.S. companies' access to Japanese markets.

U.S. companies are finding export opportunities in Central Europe and the former Soviet Union. Historically, Communist rule limited U.S. companies' access. However, the weakening of Communist influence has increased U.S. companies' access. Export opportunities for U.S. companies should continue to increase: The U.S. Government-Health Industry Partnership Program and the U.S.-Russia Business Development Committee's medical work group have identified business opportunities for U.S. companies in the former Soviet Union. In Central Europe, the privatization of business—movement from government ownership to private ownership—should promote U.S. manufacturers' opportunities.

INDUSTRY'S LONG-TERM PROSPECTS Long-term prospects set the backdrop for strategic planning because these prospects are indicators of companies' futures. Companies establish strategic plans that fit with their industries' long-term prospects. For example, the cost of paper used in book printing has increased dramatically in recent years. Publishing companies will contain costs in other areas to limit substantial price increases: Consumers probably will not purchase as many books if book prices increase commensurably with paper costs. In this type of situation, compensation professionals employed by publishing companies are apt to recommend pay policies that contribute to cost containment objectives.

Long-term prospects for companies in the surgical supplies industry are promising: Health care cost-containment initiatives are swiftly changing the nature of health care delivery in the United States. Insurance companies are pressuring doctors and surgeons to use less-invasive surgical procedures to minimize the risk of complications and to reduce hospital stays. As a result, demand for such surgical equipment as stapling devices—common to less-invasive procedures—should be on the rise. Manufacturers should do well in many foreign locations for the reasons discussed earlier—NAFTA, initiatives to increase U.S. access to Japanese markets, and the opening up of former Soviet and Central European markets.

SURGIMED should fare well in the future given this optimistic industrial outlook. In addition, SURGIMED is well positioned because it specializes in the manufacture of devices for less-invasive surgical procedures. Further, SURGIMED's competitiveness should increase even more when they manufacture lightest-weight surgical instruments in the year 2003.

LABOR-MARKET ASSESSMENT

General considerations. **Labor market assessments** represent key activities. Companies should carefully assess the labor market to determine the availability of qualified employees. In the future, such growth industries as surgical and medical instruments and apparatus will find staffing to be more challenging:[6] The U.S. Bureau of Labor Statistics (BLS) expects that the growth in the U.S. labor force will slow down substantially between the years 1990 and 2005. In addition, there will be fewer new workforce entrants (that is, individuals aged 16 to 24 years) but significantly more older workers (that is, individuals aged 55 and over) in the labor force.

These labor force trends have direct implications for compensation practice. In general, there will be greater competition among companies for fewer qualified individuals. Higher labor demand relative to labor supply should lead to higher wages. Companies will have to increase wages to entice the best individuals to choose employment in their companies rather than in competitors' companies. The greater prevalence of older employees also should increase the typical wage levels. On the basis of our previous discussions of seniority and merit pay (Chapter 4), older workers will probably have higher wages than younger workers. The prevalence of older workers relative to younger workers should translate into higher compensation costs to companies.

Occupation-specific considerations. Companies should keep tabs on the occupational mix of their work forces and the relative importance of those occupations to maintaining competitive advantage. Compensation levels generally increase with the importance of jobs to companies' strategic values and, as mentioned previously, with the relative supply of labor.

U.S. manufacturers of surgical and medical instruments and apparatus employed 89,000 in 1993. Production workers make up the majority (61 percent). The remaining 39 percent includes administrative (for example, office managers), professional (for example, accountants), managerial (for example, HR department head), and executive staff. Worldwide industry employment in 1993, estimated at 287,000,[7] is projected to increase at an annual growth rate of 1.3 percent.[8]

For illustrative purposes, let's consider the labor market status of accountants. Every company needs accountants to set up their financial statements, prepare their taxes, and provide management advice. An excellent starting point is the BLS *Occupational Outlook Handbook*. This handbook contains pertinent information for conducting effective strategic analyses:

★ Qualifications and training necessary to perform jobs

★ Job outlook

★ Typical earnings range

First, information about qualifications and training helps companies focus recruitment efforts on individuals with the necessary qualifications. Accountants possess either an undergraduate or graduate degree in accounting, and they possess state licensure (for example, CPA, certified public accountant licensure). In addition, information about training helps companies determine whether they must bear the responsibility and cost for training. Colleges and universities with degree programs in accounting help by granting degrees, and the American Institute of Certified Public Accountants prepares and evaluates CPA candidates' performance on an exam.

Second, job outlook provides companies an indication of job prospects. Three scenarios describe possible job outlooks—retrenchment, status quo, and growth. Retrenchment means that fewer jobs will be available for a designated period. Status quo suggests that the present level of job opportunities will remain constant for a designated period. Under the growth scenario, job opportunities will be higher than present levels for a designated period. The BLS predicts that accountants will experience job growth:

> As the economy grows, the number of business establishments increases, requiring more accountants and auditors to set up their books, prepare their taxes, and provide management advice. As these businesses grow, the volume and complexity of information developed by accountants and auditors on costs, expenditures, and taxes will increase as well. More complex requirements for accountants and auditors also arise from changes in legislation related to taxes, financial reporting standards, business investments, mergers, and other financial matters. In addition, businesses will increasingly need quick, accurate, and individually tailored financial information due to the demands of growing international competition.[9]

Third, typical earnings range helps companies establish competitive pay levels. Companies would find it difficult to attract well-qualified candidates if they set pay levels too low. As we discussed earlier, paying well above the market may present a cost burden to companies. According to the BLS:

> accountants with limited experience had median earnings of $25,400 in 1993, with the middle half earning between $23,000 and $28,200. The most experienced accountants had median earnings of $77,200, with the middle half earning between $70,300 and $85,400.

> According to a salary survey conducted by Robert Half International, a staffing services firm specializing in accounting and finance, accountants and auditors with up to 1 year of experi-

ence earned between $23,000 and $33,500 in 1995. Those with 1 to 3 years of experience earned between $26,000 and $39,000. Senior accountants and auditors earned between $31,000 and $47,600; managers earned between $39,900 and $68,800; and directors of accounting and auditing earned between $50,300 and $84,500 a year. The variation in salaries [base pay] reflects differences in location, level of education, and credentials.[10]

In sum, labor market assessments are key elements of strategic analyses. Our analysis of SURGIMED's situation indicates that their compensation professionals should include a labor market assessment of metallurgical engineers and precision assemblers: Metallurgical engineers are key to SURGIMED's plan to differentiate itself from the competition. Only these engineers have the knowledge of metallurgical engineering theories and principles to develop lightest-weight surgical instruments. Precision assemblers are also important because they represent a significant percentage of industry employment, and their skills are essential to manufacturing high-quality surgical instruments.

Internal Capabilities

Compensation professionals, top management members, and consultants should examine three internal capabilities as part of strategic analyses:

- ✭ Functional capabilities
- ✭ Human resource capabilities
- ✭ Financial condition

FUNCTIONAL CAPABILITIES Companies must determine which functional capabilities are most crucial to maintaining competitive advantage. **Functional capabilities** are manufacturing, engineering, research and development, management information systems, human resources, and marketing. The rapid advances that are moving medical science toward less-invasive surgical procedures require special surgical instruments. One noteworthy example is arthroscopic surgery. Arthroscopes enable surgeons to perform knee surgeries without massive incisions. SURGIMED's competitive advantage depends largely on developing and manufacturing leading-edge surgical instruments for these new, less-invasive surgical procedures. Thus, research and development is essential to SURGIMED's success.

Research and development is not the critical function for all companies. For example, companies such as McDonald's Corporation rely on marketing savvy to remain competitive. McDonald's has had the reputation of catering to young children. McDonald's recent introduction of the Arch Deluxe™ hamburger represents the corporation's attempt to increase sales and market share by identifying with an older crowd: "The Arch Deluxe™ is the hamburger with the grown-up taste."

HUMAN RESOURCES CAPABILITIES State-of-the-art research equipment, manufacturing systems, or efficient marketing distribution systems do not provide companies competitive advantage unless staffed with knowledgeable and productive employees. Pay-for-performance and pay-for-knowledge programs promote productive and knowledgeable employees. Merit pay programs (Chapter 4) reinforce prior excellent job performance with permanent base pay increases. Incentive pay programs (Chapter 5) reward employees for attaining predetermined performance standards. Employees generally know in advance that rewards increase with higher performance attainments, and they know how much they will earn for achieving particular performance goals. Companies design pay-for-knowledge programs (Chapter 6) to reward self-improvement, and these programs are essential when technology advances rapidly.

FINANCIAL CONDITION A company's *financial condition* is a key consideration for top management officials and HR professionals. Financial condition has implications for companies' ability to compete. Sound financial conditions enable companies to meet operating requirements and capital requirements. Poor financial conditions prevent companies from adequately meeting operating and capital requirements.

Operating requirements encompass all human resources programs. Top management limits funding increases for compensation programs when financial conditions are poor. As a result, employees' salaries stagnate, and job offers to potential employees will probably not be competitive. Salary stagnation leads to turnover, particularly among highly qualified employees, because they will have job opportunities elsewhere.

Capital requirements include automated manufacturing technology and office and plant facilities. Companies that pursue differentiation strategies require state-of-the-art instruments and work facilities to conduct leading-edge research. Lowest cost companies need efficient equipment that keep cost per unit as low as possible.

SURGIMED must have sufficient money to invest in equipment for research and development projects. It must also have the ability to reward innovators for their unique contributions to the company's success. Barbara Browning (SURGIMED's first compensation director) should convince SURGIMED's top management of compensation's strategic role. Ultimately, they have to strike a balance among the strate-

THE FLIP SIDE OF THE COIN

The Peril of Strategic Analyses

Decision makers should keep in mind that strategic analyses represent a means to an end not an end itself. One study indicates that business decision makers devote more than 75 percent of competitive analyses to data planning, collection, and analysis.[11] "Obsessive data collection results from the poor definition of industry boundary or misspecification of rivals and their competence; an overreliance on elaborate statistical analyses to impress senior executives of the rigor of the process; and a lack of clarity about the ultimate use of the results of the analysis."[12]

The quotation indicates that decision makers should decide in advance the questions they plan to answer with strategic analyses. These questions can serve as effective guideposts through the data planning, collection, and analysis stages.

For example, labor market assessments are useful for all HR professionals. They help HR professionals target recruitment efforts and plan necessary training in situations which job candidates generally do not possess knowledge about company-specific procedures. Compensation professionals should use labor market assessments to promote the development of strategic compensation systems rather than getting caught up with the idea that labor market assessments represent an end in themselves. In short, compensation professionals must guard against the tendency to lose sight of the forest for the trees.

gic imperatives of functional capabilities, human resource capabilities, and financial condition because funds are a limited resource.

Compensation surveys

The second step compensation professionals undertake to assure external competitiveness is to consult or develop compensation surveys. Compensation surveys contain data about competing companies' compensation practices.

Preliminary Considerations

There are two important preliminary considerations compensation professionals take under advisement before investing time and money into compensation surveys:

  ★ What companies hope to gain from compensation surveys
  ★ Custom development versus use of an existing compensation survey

WHAT COMPANIES HOPE TO GAIN FROM COMPENSATION SURVEYS Compensation professionals wish to make sound decisions about pay levels on the basis of what the competition pays their employees. Sound pay decisions promote companies' efforts to sustain competitive advantage, and poor pay decisions compromise competitive advantage. Compensation surveys enable compensation professionals to make sound judgments about how much to pay employees. Offering too little will limit companies' abilities to recruit and retain high-quality employees. Offering too much will incur an opportunity cost because it is money companies could have spent on such other important matters as research and development, training and development programs, and so on. Financial resources are limited. Therefore, companies cannot afford to spend money on everything they wish.

CUSTOM DEVELOPMENT VERSUS USE OF AN EXISTING COMPENSATION SURVEY Managers must decide whether to develop their own survey instruments and administer them or to rely on the results of surveys conducted by others. In theory, customized surveys are preferable because the survey taker can tailor the questions and select respondent companies to provide the most useful and informative data. Custom survey development should enable employers to monitor the quality of the survey developers' methodology.

In practice, companies choose not to develop and implement their own surveys for three reasons. First, most companies lack qualified employees to undertake this task. Developing and implementing valid surveys requires specialized knowledge and expertise of sound questionnaire design, sampling methods, and statistical methods.

Second, rival companies are understandably reluctant to surrender information about their compensation packages to competitors since compensation systems are instrumental to competitive advantage issues. If companies are willing to cooperate, the information may be incomplete or inaccurate. For example, rival companies may choose to report the salaries for their company's lowest-paid accountants instead of the typical salary levels. Such information may lead the surveying company to set accountants' salaries much lower than if they had accurate, complete information about typical salary levels. Setting accountants' salaries too low may hinder recruitment efforts. Thus, custom development is potentially risky.

Third, custom survey development can be costly. Although cost figures are not readily available, it is reasonable to conclude that most companies use published survey data to minimize costs. The main costs include staff salaries and benefits (for those involved in developing the compensation survey and in analyzing and interpreting the data), telephone and mail charges (depending upon the data collection method), and computers for data analyses.

Using published compensation survey data

So, companies usually rely on existing compensation surveys rather than creating their own. Using published compensation survey data starts with two important considerations:

* ☆ Survey focus: core or fringe compensation
* ☆ Sources of published survey data

SURVEY FOCUS: CORE OR FRINGE COMPENSATION Human resource professionals should decide whether to obtain survey information about base pay, employee benefits, or both. Historically, companies competed for employees mainly on the basis of base pay. Many companies offered similar, substantial benefits packages to employees without regard to the costs. Companies typically did not use benefits offerings to compete for the best employees.

Times have changed. Because benefit costs are extremely high, there is now a greater variability in benefits offerings among companies as companies seek to achieve a balance between paying too much for benefits (and thereby weakening their financial condition) and paying too little (and thereby losing human resource capabilities). In 1994, U.S. companies spent an average of $11,506 per year per employee to provide discretionary benefits—for example, vacation and medical insurance coverage.[13] Such discretionary benefits accounted for approximately one-third of employers' total payroll costs. That is a huge cost to employers, but one that cannot be avoided; benefits have become a basis for attracting and retaining the best employees. Consequently, employers are likely to use compensation surveys to obtain information about competitors' base pay and benefits practices so that they can compete effectively for the best candidates.

SOURCES OF PUBLISHED COMPENSATION SURVEYS Companies can obtain published survey data from various sources—professional associations, industry associations, consulting firms, and the federal government. Exhibit 8-3 lists examples of professional associations, industry associations, and consulting firms that conduct compensation surveys. Professional and industry associations survey members regarding salaries, compile the information in summary form, and disseminate the results to members. The survey data tend to be accurate because participants—also association members— benefit from the survey results. In addition, membership fees often entitle members to obtain survey information at no additional cost.

For example, the Academy of Management's primary membership includes college and university faculty members who specialize in such management-related fields as human resource management, business policy, and international management. The Academy of Management periodically provides to its members salary information for U.S. college and university faculty. The information is broken out into geographic regions (for example, Northeast, Southwest), area of specialization (for example, human

Exhibit 8-3
Sources of Compensation
Survey Information

PROFESSIONAL ASSOCIATIONS

- The American Compensation Association publishes the *Salary Budget Survey,* reported by region and industry.
- The Society for Human Resource Management publishes information on salaries in the human resources field.

INDUSTRY ASSOCIATIONS

- Administration Management Society
- American Association of University Professors
- American Banker's Association
- American Bar Association
- American Electronics Association
- American Mathematical Society
- American Society of Association Executives
- Association of General Contractors
- National Institute of Business Management
- National Restaurant Association
- National Retail Federation
- National Society of Engineers

CONSULTING FIRMS

- Abbott, Langer & Associates
- Coopers & Lybrand
- Dietrich Associates Inc.
- Executive Compensation Service
- Hay Management Consultants
- Hewitt Associates
- Mercer-Meidinger-Hanson
- Robert Half Associates
- Towers & Perrin
- Wyatt Co.

resource management, international management), and academic rank (lecturer, assistant professor, associate professor, professor). University and college deans use the survey results to judge whether they are paying faculty too much or too little relative to the market and to determine how much to pay new hires. Faculty use the survey results to ask their deans for pay raises when their salaries fall below the market rates and to judge the adequacy of job offers.

Consulting firms represent another source of compensation survey information. Some firms specialize on particular occupations (for example, engineers) or industries (for example, financial services); other firms do not. Clients may have two choices. First, consulting firms may provide survey data from recently completed surveys. Second, these firms may literally conduct surveys from scratch exclusively for clients' use. In most cases, the first option is less expensive than the second option. But the quality of the second option may be superior because the survey was custom-designed to answer clients' specific compensation questions.

The federal government is an invaluable source of compensation survey information. The BLS provides free salary surveys to the public. Highly qualified survey takers and statisticians are responsible for producing these surveys. Many factors contributed to the implementation of BLS pay and benefits surveys. The government began collecting compensation data in the 1890s to assess the effects of tariff legislation on wages and prices. Ever since, the government's survey programs have been rooted in competitive concerns.

Nowadays, the BLS conducts five surveys containing compensation information:

☆ Area Wage Surveys

☆ White-Collar Pay Survey

☆ Employee Benefits in Small Private Establishments

☆ Employee Benefits in Medium and Large Private Establishments

☆ Employee Benefits in State and Local Governments

The BLS conducts separate *Area Wage Surveys* for 90 metropolitan areas (for example, Seattle, Washington) annually or every other year depending on the size of the area. Larger areas are surveyed every year, and smaller areas are surveyed every other year. The survey contains pay and benefits information for blue- and white-collar workers based on broad industry groups as defined in the *Standard Industrial Classification Manual.* In many instances, these surveys further distinguish between employees on the basis of experience and responsibility levels (low versus high for each category). The BLS includes hourly wage rate information for blue-collar workers, and weekly salaries for white-collar employees. Benefits data include paid holiday and vacation practices, medical insurance offerings, and retirement plans. Exhibit 8-4 shows information about engineers' pay from the Area Wage Survey for Cleveland, Ohio.

The White-Collar Pay (WCP) Survey provides detailed salary information for various white collar professional fields including accounting, law, personnel management (a BLS term, not mine), nursing, and computer science. The main focus is on annual average salaries for seven SIC major economic activities—mining; construction; manufacturing; transportation, communications, electric, gas, and sanitary services; wholesale trade; retail trade; finance, insurance, and real estate; and personal, business, professional, repair, recreation, and other services.

Employee Benefits in Small Private Establishments provides representative data for full-time and part-time employees in U.S. private establishments that have fewer than 100 employees. Participating establishments provide data for a sample of three occupational groups—professional, technical, and related; clerical and sales; blue-collar and service—in such benefits as medical insurance coverage, vacation practices, and retirement plans. The survey is based on a sample of approximately 2,500 establishments. The BLS conducts this survey in even-numbered years.

Exhibit 8-4
Engineers' Pay for
Cleveland, Ohio,
Metropolitan Area

LEVEL	NUMBER OF WORKERS SURVEYED	AVERAGE WEEKLY HOURS WORKED	WEEKLY PAY[1]		
			MEAN	MEDIAN	MIDDLE RANGE
Level I	232	40.0	$ 649	$ 626	$ 598–$ 712
Level II	753	40.0	$ 752	$ 741	$ 667–$ 827
Level III	1,559	40.0	$ 924	$ 930	$ 827–$1,020
Level IV	1,332	39.9	$1,077	$1,080	$ 989–$1,165
Level V	479	39.9	$1,257	$1,254	$1,156–$1,337
Level VI	188	40.0	$1,479	$1,478	$1,377–$1,569

Source: U.S. Bureau of Labor Statistics, *Occupational compensation survey: Pay only. Cleveland, Ohio, Metropolitan Area, August 1995* (Washington, D.C.: U.S. Government Printing Office, February 1996).

[1] The mean is calculated as $\frac{\sum_{j=1}^{n} X_j}{n}$ where X_j represents the individual weekly pay amounts, and n equals the total number of weekly salaries in the survey. The median is calculated as the $\frac{n+1}{2}$ ordered observation (from smallest to highest) where n equals the total number of weekly salaries. The middle range is calculated as the 50th percentile $\pm \left(\frac{X_{smallest} + X_{largest}}{2} \right)$.

Employee Benefits in Medium and Large Private Establishments reports on benefits provided to full-time and part-time employees in U.S. private establishments with 100 or more employees. The survey is based on a sample of approximately 2,300 establishments. The scope of coverage is similar to the survey for small private establishments. The BLS conducts this survey in odd-numbered years.

The Employee Benefits in State and Local Governments follows the same format as the previous two surveys, but it applies to benefits practices in state and local governments. This survey is based on a sample of about 1,000 establishments. The BLS conducts this survey in even-numbered years. This and the previous two surveys report information using similar formats. Exhibit 8-5 contains an example from the *Employee Benefits in Medium and Large Private Establishments* survey.

Exhibit 8-5
Summary: Participation in
Selected Employee Benefits
Programs for Full-Time
Employees by Geographic
Region

BENEFIT	NORTHEAST	SOUTH	NORTH-CENTRAL	WEST
Paid time off:				
Holidays	94%	92%	93%	87%
Vacations	98%	96%	98%	96%
Personal leave	40%	16%	18%	13%
Survivor benefits:				
Life insurance	93%	88%	95%	88%
Survivor income	5%	4%	7%	5%
Health care benefits:				
Medical care	83%	80%	84%	79%
Dental care	62%	52%	65%	72%
Vision care	31%	17%	24%	40%

Source: U.S. Bureau of Labor Statistics, *Employee benefits in medium and large private establishments, 1993* (Washington, D.C.: U.S. Government Printing Office, 1994).

Compensation Surveys: Strategic Considerations

Two essential strategic considerations are:

✯ Defining the relevant labor market

✯ Choosing benchmark jobs

DEFINING RELEVANT LABOR MARKET **Relevant labor markets** are the fields of potentially qualified candidates for particular jobs. Companies collect compensation survey data from the relevant labor markets. Relevant labor markets are defined on the basis of job families, geography, and product or service market competitors.

Job family refers to a group of two or more jobs that either have similar worker characteristics (for example, job-related work experience, skill, formal education) or contain similar work tasks.[14] Accountants and auditors, engineers, HR managers, physicians, and assemblers are examples of distinct job families. Companies that plan to hire accountants and auditors should consider accountants and auditors only rather than individuals from such other job families as engineers because the worker characteristics and work tasks are clearly different:[15] Accountants and auditors prepare, analyze, and verify financial reports and taxes, and they monitor information systems that furnish that information to managers in business, industrial, and government organizations. Engineers apply the theories and principles of science and mathematics to the economical solution of practical technical problems. For example, civil engineers design, plan, and supervise the construction of buildings, highways, and rapid transit systems.

Companies search over a wider geographic area for candidates for jobs that require specialized skills or skills that are low in supply relative to the demand for those skills by employers. For instance, hospitals are likely to search nationwide for neurosurgeons because their specialized skills are scarce. Companies are likely to limit searches for clerical employees to more-confined local areas because clerical employees' skills are relatively common, and their supply tends to be higher relative to companies' demand for them. An insurance company based in Hartford, Connecticut, restricts its search for clerical employees to the Hartford area.

Companies use product or service market competitors to define the relevant labor market when industry-specific knowledge is a key worker qualification and competition for market share is keen. For example, such long-distance telephone companies as Sprint, MCI, and AT&T probably prefer to steal away marketing managers from industry competitors rather than from such unrelated industries as snack foods or medical and surgical supplies. Knowledge about snack foods and customer food preferences has little to do with long-distance telephone service and customers' preferences for long-distance telephone service.

Job family, geographic scope, and product or service market competitors are not necessarily independent dimensions. For example, a company defines product or service market competitors as the basis for defining the relevant labor market for product managers. However, this dimension overlaps with geographic scope because competitors' companies are located throughout the country (for example, Boston, San Francisco, Dallas, and Miami).

With many professional, technical, and management positions, all three factors—job family, geographic scope, and companies that compete on the basis of product or service—can be applicable. For more information about relevant labor markets for various occupations, employers can consult professional and industrial associations and consulting firms (see Exhibit 8-3).

CHOOSING BENCHMARK JOBS As we discussed in Chapter 7, benchmark jobs are key to conducting effective job evaluations. Benchmark jobs also play an important role in compensation surveys. Human resource professionals determine the pay levels for jobs on the basis of typical market pay rates for similar jobs. In other words, HR professionals rely on benchmark jobs as reference points for setting pay levels. As we discussed in Chapter 7, benchmark jobs have four characteristics:[16]

- ✩ The contents are well-known, relatively stable over time, and agreed upon by the employees involved.
- ✩ The jobs are common across a number of different employers.
- ✩ The jobs represent the entire range of jobs that are being evaluated within a company.
- ✩ The jobs are generally accepted in the labor market for the purposes of setting pay levels.

Why are benchmark jobs necessary? Ideally, HR professionals would match each job within their companies to a job contained in compensation surveys. In reality, however, one-to-one matches are not feasible for two reasons. First, large companies may have hundreds of unique jobs, making one-to-one matches tedious, time-consuming, and expensive in terms of salary and benefits paid to staff members responsible for making these matches. Second, it is highly unlikely that HR professionals will find perfect or close matches between their companies' jobs and jobs contained in the compensation surveys: Companies adapt job duties and scope to fit their particular situations. In other words, jobs with identical titles may differ somewhat in the degrees of compensable factors. Perfect matches are the exception rather than the rule. For example, Company A's Secretary I job may require only a high school education or general equivalency diploma. Company B's Secretary I job may require higher educational credentials such as an associate's degree in office administration.

Companies can make corrections for differences between their jobs and external benchmark jobs. These corrections are based on subjective judgment rather than on objective criteria. Job incumbents and compensation professionals should independently compare compensable factors for the companies' jobs with the compensable factors for the external benchmark jobs. Exhibit 8-6 illustrates a rating scale for that purpose. Job incumbents and supervisors should complete this questionnaire separately to minimize rater biases (see Chapter 4, "Performance Appraisal"). Differences in ratings can be reconciled through discussion.

Compensation Survey Data

Compensation professionals should be aware of three compensation survey data characteristics. First, compensation surveys contain immense amounts of information. A perusal of every datum point would be mind-boggling even to the most mathematically inclined individuals. In addition, there is bound to be wide variation in pay rates across companies, making it difficult to build market-competitive pay systems. Thus, compensation professionals should use statistics to efficiently describe large sets of data. Second, compensation survey data are outdated because there is a lag between when

Exhibit 8-6

Comparing Companies'
Jobs with Benchmark Jobs

INSTRUCTIONS TO JOB INCUMBENTS: Compare elements of your job with elements of the survey benchmark job.

INSTRUCTIONS TO SUPERVISORS: Compare elements of your employee's job with elements of the survey benchmark job.

		ADJUST PAY
SKILL (Check the statement that most applies.)		
My (employee's) job requires substantially more skill than the benchmark job.	☐	+4%
My (employee's) job requires somewhat more skill than the benchmark job.	☐	+2%
My (employee's) job and benchmark job require equal skill.	☐	0%
My (employee's) job requires somewhat less skill than the benchmark job.	☐	−2%
My (employee's) job requires substantially less skill than the benchmark job.	☐	−4%
EFFORT (Check the statement that most applies.)		
My (employee's) job requires substantially more effort than the benchmark job.	☐	+2%
My (employee's) job requires somewhat more effort than the benchmark job.	☐	+1%
My (employee's) job and benchmark job require equal effort.	☐	0%
My (employee's) job requires somewhat less effort than the benchmark job.	☐	−1%
My (employee's) job requires substantially less effort than the benchmark job.	☐	−2%
RESPONSIBILITY (Check the statement that most applies.)		
My (employee's) job requires substantially more responsibility than the benchmark job.	☐	+4%
My (employee's) job requires somewhat more responsibility than the benchmark job.	☐	+2%
My (employee's) job and benchmark job require equal responsibility.	☐	0%
My (employee's) job requires somewhat less responsibility than the benchmark job.	☐	−2%
My (employee's) job requires substantially less responsibility than the benchmark job.	☐	−4%

Pay adjustment calculation: Total the percentages for the three checked items. Possible range is from +10% to −10%.

☐ **Pay adjustment (For example, a total of 0% means no adjustment is required; +3% indicates that the job's pay rate be increased by 3%, and −3% indicates that the job's pay rate be decreased by 3%.)**

the data were collected and when employers implement compensation plans based on the survey data. Third, compensation professionals must use statistical analyses to integrate their internal job structures (based on job evaluation points—Chapter 7) with the external market on the basis of the survey data. We discuss that matter in detail later in this chapter.

Exhibit 8-7 contains sample salary information collected from a salary survey of 35 engineering jobs according to seniority. Engineer I incumbents possess less than two years of engineering work experience. Engineer II incumbents have two to less than four years of engineering work experience. Engineer III incumbents possess four to six years of work experience as engineers. Seven companies (A–G) from Cleveland, Ohio, participated in the survey, and most have more than one incumbent at each level. Company B has 3 Engineer I incumbents, 3 Engineer II incumbents, and 2 Engineer III incumbents.

As a starting point, let's begin with basic tabulation of the survey data. Basic tabulation helps organize data, promotes decision makers' familiarization with the data, and reveals possible extreme observations *(outliers).* Exhibit 8-8 displays a *percentage distribution table,* and Exhibit 8-9 displays a histogram. Both indicate the number of job incumbents whose salaries fall within the specified intervals. For example, 11 engineers' annual salaries range between $30,000 to $35,000. The fact that only one job incumbent falls in the $45,001 and above interval qualifies that salary as an outlier. We'll discuss the importance of outliers shortly.

USING THE APPROPRIATE STATISTICS TO SUMMARIZE SURVEY DATA Two properties describe numerical data sets:

☆ Central tendency

☆ Variation

Central tendency represents the fact that a set of data cluster or center around a central point. Central tendency is a number that represents the typical numerical value in the data set. What is the typical annual salary for engineers in our data set? Two types of central tendency measures are pertinent to compensation—arithmetic mean (often called mean or average) and median.

We calculate the *mean* annual salary for engineers by adding all the annual salaries in our data set and then dividing the total by the number of annual salaries in the data set. The sum of the 35 salaries in our example is $1,337,500. Thus, the mean is $38,214.29 (that is, $1,337,500 divided by 35). In this example, the mean informs compensation professionals about the "typical" salary or going market rate for the group of Engineers I, II, and III. Compensation professionals often use the mean as a reference point to judge whether employees' compensation is below or above the market.

We use every data point to calculate the mean. Consequently, having one or more outliers would lead to a distorted representation of the typical value. The mean understates the true typical value when there is one or more extremely small value. The mean overstates the true typical value when there is one or more extremely large value. The mean's shortcoming has implications for compensation professionals.

Understated mean salaries may cause employers to set starting salaries too low to attract the best-qualified job candidates. Overstated mean salaries probably promote recruitment efforts because employers may set starting salaries higher than necessary. But, this condition creates a cost burden to companies.

COMPANY	JOB TITLE	1996 ANNUAL SALARY
A	Engineer I	$33,000
A	Engineer I	34,500
A	Engineer II	36,000
A	Engineer III	43,500
B	Engineer I	33,000
B	Engineer I	33,000
B	Engineer I	36,000
B	Engineer II	37,500
B	Engineer II	36,000
B	Engineer II	37,500
B	Engineer III	45,000
B	Engineer III	43,500
C	Engineer I	34,500
C	Engineer II	37,500
C	Engineer III	43,500
D	Engineer I	36,000
D	Engineer I	36,000
D	Engineer III	55,000
E	Engineer I	33,000
E	Engineer I	33,000
E	Engineer I	34,500
E	Engineer II	36,000
E	Engineer II	36,000
E	Engineer II	37,500
E	Engineer III	45,000
F	Engineer I	34,500
F	Engineer II	37,500
F	Engineer III	45,000
F	Engineer III	45,000
F	Engineer III	43,500
G	Engineer I	34,500
G	Engineer I	33,000
G	Engineer II	37,500
G	Engineer II	37,500
G	Engineer III	43,500

Exhibit 8-7
Raw Compensation Survey Data for Engineers in Cleveland, Ohio

Exhibit 8-8
Frequency Table for Engineers

SALARY INTERVAL	NUMBER OF SALARIES FROM SURVEY
$30,000–$35,000	11
$35,001–$40,000	14
$40,001–$45,000	9
$45,001 & above	1

The *median* is the middle value in an ordered sequence of numerical data. If there is an odd number of data points, the median literally is the middle observation. Our data set contains an odd number of observations. The median is $36,000. Exhibit 8-10 illustrates the calculation of the median.

If there is an even number of data points, the median is the mean of the values of the two middle numbers. Let's assume that we have four salaries, ordered from the smallest value to the highest value:

$25,000 $28,000 $29,500 $33,000

The median is $28,750:

$$\frac{\$28,000 + \$29,500}{2}$$

The median does not create distorted representations as the mean does because its calculation is independent of the magnitude of the values that surround it.

Variation is the second property used to describe data sets. **Variation** is the amount of spread or dispersion in a set of data. Compensation professionals find three measures of dispersion to be useful—standard deviation, quartile, and percentile.

Exhibit 8-9
Histogram of Survey Data for Engineers

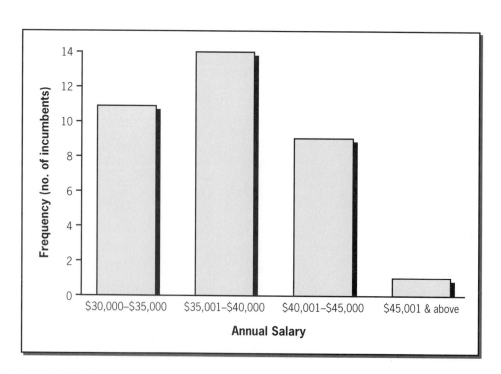

Exhibit 8-10
**Calculation of the Median
for Engineer Survey Data**

The salary data are arranged in ascending order. The median is $(n + 1)/2$, where n equals the number of salaries. The median is item 18 ([35 + 1]/2). Thus, the median value is $36,000.

1. 33000
2. 33000
3. 33000
4. 33000
5. 33000
6. 33000
7. 34500
8. 34500
9. 34500
10. 34500
11. 34500
12. 36000
13. 36000
14. 36000
15. 36000
16. 36000
17. 36000
18. 36000 ⟵——— median
19. 37500
20. 37500
21. 37500
22. 37500
23. 37500
24. 37500
25. 37500
26. 43500
27. 43500
28. 43500
29. 43500
30. 43500
31. 45000
32. 45000
33. 45000
34. 45000
35. 55000

Standard deviation refers to the average distance of each salary figure from the mean—the amount that large observations rise above the mean and the amount that small observations dip below the mean. Exhibit 8-11 demonstrates the calculation of the standard deviation for our data set.

The standard deviation equals $5,074.86. Compensation professionals find standard deviation to be useful for two reasons. First, as we noted previously, compensation professionals often use the mean as a reference point to judge whether employees' compensation is below or above the market. *The standard deviation indicates whether an individual salary's departure below or above the mean is "typical" for the market.* For example, Irwin Katz's annual salary is $27,500. His salary falls substantially below the typical salary: The difference between the mean salary and Irwin Katz's salary is $10,715.29 (that is, $38,214.29 − $27,500). This difference is much greater than the typical departure from the mean; the standard deviation is just $5,074.86.

Second, the standard deviation indicates the range for the majority of salaries. The majority of salaries fall between $33,139.43 ($38,214.29 − $5,074.86) and $43,289.15 ($38,214.29 + $5,074.86). Remember, $38,214.29 is the mean and $5,074.86 is the standard deviation. Compensation professionals can use this range to judge whether their companies' salary ranges are similar to the markets' salary ranges. A company's salary range is not typical of the market if most of its salaries fall below or above the market range. Companies will probably find it difficult to retain quality employees when most salaries fall below the typical market range.

Both **quartiles** and **percentiles** describe dispersion by indicating the percentage of figures that fall below certain points. Exhibit 8-12 illustrates the use of quartiles and percentiles for our survey data. There are three quartiles. The first quartile is $34,500. In other words, 25 percent of the salary figures are less than or equal to $34,500. The second quartile is $36,000. Fifty percent of the salary figures are less than or equal to $36,000. The third quartile is $43,500. Seventy-five percent of the salary figures are less than or equal to $43,500. There are 100 percentiles ranging from the first per-

---

Exhibit 8-11
Calculation of the Standard Deviation (S.D.) for Engineer Survey Data

$$S.D. = \sqrt{\frac{\sum_{i=1}^{n} X_i^2 - nM^2}{n-1}}$$

where:

$\sum_{i=1}^{n} X_i^2$ = the sum of the squares of the individual salary observations.

nM^2 = the square of the sample size (n; that is, 35 salaries) multiplied by the mean for the 35 salaries.

$$S.D. = \frac{(\$33,000^2 + \$33,000^2 + \ldots + \$55,000^2) - 35(\$38,214.29)^2}{35 - 1}$$

$$S.D. = \sqrt{\frac{51,987,260,000 - 51,111,618,000}{34}}$$

$$S.D. = \$5,074.86$$

Exhibit 8-12
Percentile and Quartile
Rank for Engineer Survey
Data

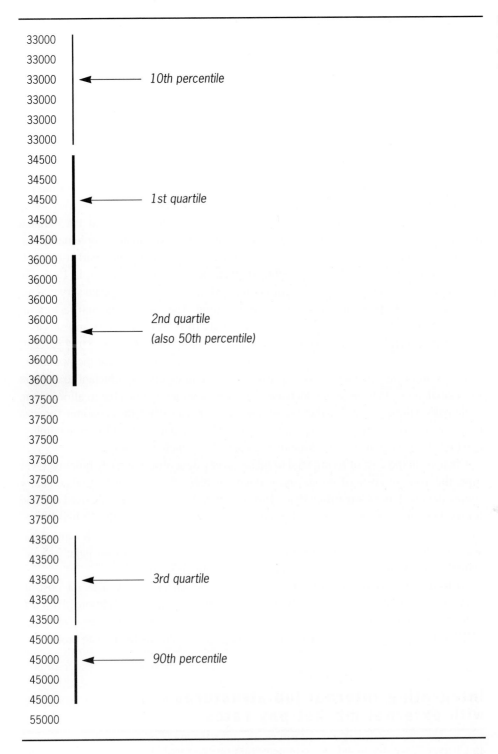

33000	
33000	
33000	◄─────── 10th percentile
33000	
33000	
33000	
34500	
34500	
34500	◄─────── 1st quartile
34500	
34500	
36000	
36000	
36000	
36000	2nd quartile
36000	◄─────── (also 50th percentile)
36000	
36000	
37500	
37500	
37500	
37500	
37500	
37500	
37500	
43500	
43500	
43500	◄─────── 3rd quartile
43500	
43500	
45000	
45000	◄─────── 90th percentile
45000	
45000	
55000	

centile to the hundredth percentile. For our data, the tenth percentile equals $33,000 and the ninetieth percentile equals $45,000.

Quartiles and percentiles complement standard deviations by indicating the percentage of observations that fall below particular figures. Compensation professionals' review of percentiles and quartiles can enhance their insights into the dispersion of salary data. For example, compensation professionals want to know the percentage of engineers earning a particular salary level or less. If $25,000 represents the tenth percentile for engineers' annual salaries, then only 10 percent earn $25,000 or less. Compensation professionals are not likely to recommend similar pay for new engineer hires. Although paying at this level represents a cost savings to companies, companies will likely experience retention problems because 90 percent of engineers earn more than $25,000.

UPDATING THE SURVEY DATA Companies establish pay structures for future periods. SURGIMED's compensation professionals wish to develop a pay structure for the period January 1, 1997, through December 31, 1997. For this illustration, it is May 1996. The salary survey data were collected in early January 1996 to represent 1995 annual pay averages. These data will be one year old at the pay plan's implementation. Compensation professionals typically use historical salary data to build market-competitive pay systems because it is impossible to obtain actual 1997 salary data in 1996. So, companies use simple techniques to correct for such lags when they update survey data.

Several factors play an important role in updating. The most influential factors include economic forecasts and changes in the costs of consumer goods and services. Employers generally award small permanent pay increases (for example, 3 to 4 percent) when the economic forecast is pessimistic. Pessimistic forecasts suggest the possibility of recession or higher unemployment levels. Thus, employers are reluctant to commit substantial amounts to fund pay increases because they may not be able to afford them. Employers typically award higher permanent pay increases when the economic forecast is optimistic. Optimistic forecasts imply enhanced business activity or lower unemployment levels. Management discretion dictates actual pay increase amounts.

Changes in the cost of living tend to make survey data obsolete fairly quickly. Over time, the average costs of goods and services increase. So companies update salary survey data with the **Consumer Price Index (CPI),** the most commonly used method for tracking changes in the costs of goods and services throughout the United States. The BLS reports the CPI every month in *The CPI Detailed Report.* Each January issue provides annual averages for the preceding year. Exhibit 8-13 on page 215 describes some basic facts about the CPI and how to interpret it.

SURGIMED's Barbara Browning will update the salary survey data for cost-of-living only because she expects no short-term changes in economic conditions. The CPI-U for Cleveland, Ohio, is most appropriate because it is most representative of where SURGIMED's employees live. Exhibit 8-14 on page 216 details the update process.

Integrating internal job structures with external market pay rates

In Chapter 7, we discussed that compensation professionals use job evaluation methods to establish internally consistent job structures. In other words, companies value jobs that possess higher degrees of compensable factors (for example, 10 years of relevant work experience) than jobs with fewer degrees of compensable factors (for example, 1 year of relevant work experience). Ultimately, these valuation differences should correspond to pay differences based on compensation survey data.

BASIC FACTS

The CPI indexes monthly price changes of goods and services that people buy for day-to-day living. The index is based on a representative sample of goods and services, because obtaining information about all goods and services would not be feasible. The BLS gathers price information from about 21,000 retail and service establishments—for example, gasoline stations, grocery stores, and department stores. Approximately 40,000 landlords provide information about rental costs, and about 20,000 home owners give cost information pertaining to home ownership.

The CPI represents the average of the price changes for the representative sample of goods and services within each of the following areas:

- Urban United States

- 4 regions

- 4 class sizes

- 13 groups cross-classified by region and population size

- 29 local metropolitan statistical areas

The BLS publishes CPI for two population groups: a CPI for All Urban Consumers (CPI-U) and the CPI for Urban Wage Earners and Clerical Workers (CPI-W). The CPI-U represents the spending habits of 80 percent of the population of the United States. The CPI-U covers wage earners; clerical, professional, managerial, and technical workers; short-term and self-employed workers; unemployed persons; retirees; and others not in the labor force. The CPI-W represents the spending habits of 32 percent of the population, and it applies to consumers who earn more than one-half of their income from clerical or wage occupations. The distinction between the CPI-U and CPI-W is important because the CPI-U is most representative of all consumers, whereas unions and management use the CPI-W during negotiations to establish effective cost-of-living adjustments; most unionized jobs are clerical or wage jobs rather than salaried professional, managerial or executive jobs.

INTERPRETING THE CPI: PERCENTAGE CHANGES VS. POINT CHANGES

The span 1982–1984 is the base period for the CPI-U and CPI-W, which is 100. Compensation professionals use the base period to determine the change in prices over time. How much did consumer prices increase in Cleveland, Ohio, between the base period and 1995?

The *CPI Detailed Report* indicates that the 1995 CPI-U for Cleveland was 147.9 We know that the base period CPI is 100. Consumer prices in Cleveland increased 47.9 percent between 1995 and the base period. We determine price change with the formula:

$$\frac{(\text{Current CPI} - \text{Previous CPI})}{\text{Previous CPI}} \times 100\%$$

For this example:

$$\frac{(147.9 - 100)}{100} \times 100\% = 47.9\%$$

Compensation professionals are most concerned with annual CPI changes because they are updating recently collected survey data. The same formula yields price changes between periods other than the base period. How much did prices increase in Cleveland between 1994 and 1995? The *CPI Detailed Report* (January 1995) indicates that the 1994 annual CPI-U for Cleveland was 144.5, and we know that the 1995 annual average is 147.9:

$$\frac{(147.9 - 144.5)}{144.5} \times 100\% = 2.4\%$$

Consumer prices in Cleveland increased 2.4 percent between 1994 and 1995.

Source: U.S. Bureau of Labor Statistics, *CPI detailed report* (Washington, D.C.: U.S. Government Printing Office, 1996), p. 185.

Exhibit 8-14
Updating Salary Survey,
Using CPI-U, Cleveland, Ohio

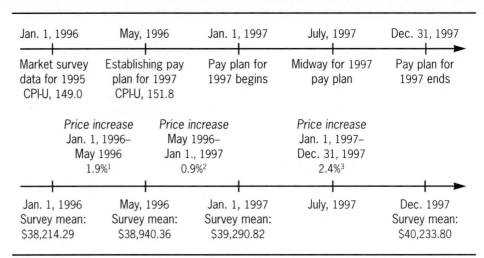

Jan. 1, 1996	May, 1996	Jan. 1, 1997	July, 1997	Dec. 31, 1997
Market survey data for 1995 CPI-U, 149.0	Establishing pay plan for 1997 CPI-U, 151.8	Pay plan for 1997 begins	Midway for 1997 pay plan	Pay plan for 1997 ends

| | Price increase Jan. 1, 1996– May 1996 1.9%[1] | Price increase May 1996– Jan 1., 1997 0.9%[2] | Price increase Jan. 1, 1997– Dec. 31, 1997 2.4%[3] | |

| Jan. 1, 1996 Survey mean: $38,214.29 | May, 1996 Survey mean: $38,940.36 | Jan. 1, 1997 Survey mean: $39,290.82 | July, 1997 | Dec. 1997 Survey mean: $40,233.80 |

[1] [(Current CPI − Previous CPI)/Previous CPI] × 100%.

[2] Estimate based on the increase in prices for Cleveland, Ohio, for the second half of 1995.

[3] Estimate based on the 1995 annual increase for Cleveland, Ohio.

We also indicated earlier that paying well below or well above the typical market rate for jobs can create competitive disadvantages for companies. Thus, it is important that companies use market pay rates as reference points for setting pay rates. To that end, we use *regression analysis,* which is a statistical analysis technique. Regression analyses enable compensation professionals to establish pay rates for a set of jobs that are consistent with typical pay rates for jobs in the external market.

We'll apply regression analysis to determine pay rates for SURGIMED's Engineer I, Engineer II, and Engineer III jobs. Before presenting the regression analysis technique, we need two sets of information: the job evaluation point totals for each engineer job based on SURGIMED's job evaluation and the updated salary survey data. SURGIMED's engineer jobs have the following job evaluation points: Engineer I (100 points), Engineer II (500 points), and Engineer III (1,000) points.

Regression analysis enables decision makers to predict the value of one variable from the value of another. Compensation professionals' goal is to predict salary levels for each job on the basis of job evaluation points. Why not simply "eyeball" the listing of salaries contained in the survey to identify the market rates? There are two reasons. First, companies pay different rates to employees who are performing the same (or very similar) jobs. Our salary survey indicates that Engineer III pay rates vary between $43,500 and $55,000. Eyeballing the typical rate from the raw data is difficult when surveys contain large numbers of salaries.

Second, we wish to determine pay rates for a set of SURGIMED's jobs—Engineer I, Engineer II, and Engineer III—on the basis of their relation to typical market pay rates for the corresponding jobs contained in the salary survey. Our focus is on pricing a job *structure* not on pricing one job in isolation.

How does regression analysis work? Regression analysis finds the best-fitting line between two variables. Compensation professionals use job evaluation points assigned to benchmark jobs (based on the matching process discussed earlier) and the salary survey data for the benchmark jobs. They refer to the best-fitting line as the

Exhibit 8-15
Regression Analysis Results for the Engineer Survey Data

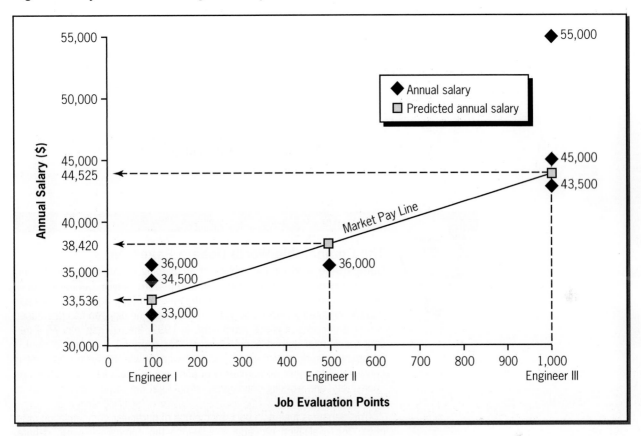

market pay line. The **market pay line** is representative of typical market pay rates relative to a company's job structure. Pay levels that correspond with the market pay line are market-competitive pay rates. Exhibit 8-15 displays the regression results.

The following equation models the prediction.

$$\hat{Y} = a + bX$$

where

$\hat{Y}$ = predicted salary
X = job evaluation points
a = the $\hat{Y}$ intercept. This is the Y value at which $X = 0$.
b = the slope

The slope represents the change in Y for every change in job evaluation points. In other words, the slope represents the dollar value of each job evaluation point. For example, let's assume that the slope is 26. A job consisting of 301 job evaluation points is worth $26 more than a job consisting of 300 job evaluation points.

For our data, the equation is:*

---

* Compensation professionals use statistical analysis programs to conduct regression analyses. There are many programs to choose from including (*SPSS*) and (*SAS*).

$$\hat{Y} = \$32{,}315.66 + \$12.21X$$

Thus, this market policy line indicates the following market pay rates:

★ Engineer I: $33,536.66

$$\hat{Y} = \$32{,}315.66 + \$12.21(100 \text{ job evaluation points})$$

★ Engineer II: $38,420.66

$$\hat{Y} = \$32{,}315.66 + \$12.21(500 \text{ job evaluation points})$$

★ Engineer III: $44,525.66

$$\hat{Y} = \$32{,}315.66 + \$12.21(1{,}000 \text{ job evaluation points})$$

REFLECTIONS

The Comparable-Worth Debate Rages On

Comparable worth is the subject of an ongoing debate regarding the pay differentials between men and women who perform similar, but not identical, work. Women earn substantially less than men. In fact, a gender-based pay gap has endured for over 150 years.[17] Although the pay gap has decreased in recent decades, it is still substantial. In 1992, the pay gap was 75.4 percent, or women earned about 75 cents for every $1 that men earned.[18] Comparable-worth advocates argue that women who perform work that is comparable to men's work in terms of compensable factors—skill, effort, responsibility, and working conditions—should get the same compensation as the men.

This debate is fueled, in part, by the use of particular compensation practices. Job evaluation procedures influence the comparable-worth debate. Using market wage or "typical" wage rates from compensation surveys also contributes to this continuing issue. Paula England, a renowned sociologist, has written a book that contains a thorough theoretical analysis and review of the research on the comparable-worth debate.[19] For the purposes of this discussion, only a brief summary of the key issues based on her work are presented.

An important question in the comparable-worth debate is, "Why are jobs that are typically held by women paid substantially less than comparable jobs held by men?" Many comparable-worth advocates argue that discrimination against women explains this pay differential. Two contextual factors contribute to this discrimination:

- Increase in employment among women

- Segregation of women from men in the workplace on the basis of jobs and industry

An important question in the comparable-worth debate is, "Why are jobs that are typically held by women paid substantially less than comparable jobs held by men?"

Since World War II, women have joined the U.S. work force in increasing numbers, because of both economic need and increased opportunities for jobs and higher wages. Single or divorced mothers have had to support themselves financially, and many women entered the work force during the 1970s, when economic recessions resulted in the temporary layoffs for their husbands. The growth in the number of employment opportunities for women resulted from a restructuring of the economy that produced declining employment in both agriculture and manufacturing and increases in service industries such as food service, retail sales, and the health industry.

Job segregation also influences comparable worth. Few jobs in the United States are substantially integrated by gender. In other words, men are the predominant incumbents of certain jobs, and women are the predominant incumbents of others. Presently, men dominate high-status occupations in American society such as medical doctors, lawyers, and college or university professors, and women dominate lower-status occupations such as housekeepers, clerical workers, and elementary school teachers. Even when women become doctors, engineers, lawyers, or university professors, pay differences still exist. Although women are beginning to move into male-dominated occupations, the majority still remain in their traditional roles (see "The Flip Side of the Coin," Chapter 3).

Many comparable-worth advocates believe that certain compensation practices—job evaluation and compensation surveys—are the media through which discrimination against women operates. Job evaluation per se is not discriminatory. In fact, many comparable-worth advocates argue that the use of a single job evaluation system that reflects the complete range of female- and male-dominated jobs can establish the "true" worth of jobs on the basis of content.[20] However, the use of multiple job evaluation systems to evaluate jobs may be discriminatory if one system is applied to male-dominated jobs and another system is applied to female-dominated jobs.

Take the point rating system for example. Let's assume that two point rating programs are developed, one for service jobs that are generally held by women—maid service, food service—and the other for service jobs that are generally held by men—janitorial, maintenance. In addition, both systems are based on the universal compensable factors—skill, effort, responsibility, and working conditions—and the same descriptions for these compensable factors apply to each group of jobs. Job evaluators may consciously or unconsciously underrate the degree of compensable factors for the female-dominated jobs relative to the male-dominated jobs.

Compensation surveys also have been implicated as culprits in disparities in the pay of men and women who hold jobs of comparable worth. Specifically, comparable-worth advocates (among others) argue that market rates are biased against women. In **Lemons v. The City and County of Denver,**[21] Lemons claimed that her job as a nurse—a female-dominated job—was illegally paid less than comparable jobs (for instance, animal keeper) held predominantly by men. In fact, Lemons argued that nursing required more education and skill than some of the male-dominated jobs that are designated as comparable and so should be paid at a higher rate despite market factors—the fact that the male-dominated jobs generally earned higher rates in the local labor market. She also argued that local labor markets were inherently biased against women and therefore should not be a legitimate basis for establishing pay rates. The court disagreed with her charge on the basis that Title VII (Chapter 3) did not focus on equalizing market disparities.

In summary, the courts treat the market as a reality that allows companies little room for discretion in terms of gender-based salary differentials. Specifically, the courts hold that no single company should be held accountable for any pay-related biases against women. They have chosen not to interfere with companies' reliance on market pricing because doing so could potentially undermine companies' ability to compete. Mandating that companies increase some female employees' pay would represent a substantial cost burden, hindering ability to compete. Today, the comparable-worth debate continues. Advocates and opponents still debate about the possible impact of job evaluation and compensation surveys on the pay differential.

Compensation policies and strategic mandates

Companies can choose from three pay level policies:

☆ Market lead

☆ Market lag

☆ Market match

The **market lead policy** distinguishes companies from the competition by compensating employees more highly than most competitors. Leading the market denotes paying at levels that are above the market pay line (Exhibit 8-15). The **market lag policy** also distinguishes companies from the competition, but by compensating employees less than most competitors. Lagging the market indicates that pay levels fall below the market pay line (Exhibit 8-15). The **market match policy** most closely follows the typical market pay rates because companies pay according to the market pay line. Thus, pay rates fall along the market pay line (Exhibit 8-15).

The market lead policy is clearly most appropriate for companies that pursue differentiation strategies. SURGIMED may choose a market lead pay policy for its engineers because this company needs the very best engineers to promote its competitive strategy of being the top manufacturer of lightest-weight surgical instruments by the year 2003.

Barbara Browning and top management officials must decide *how much* to lead the market: for example, 5 percent, 10 percent, 25 percent, or more. The "how much" depends on two factors. First, how much pay differential above the market is sufficient to attract and retain the most highly qualified engineers? Second, are there other funding needs for activities that promote differentiation strategies such as research and development? Past experience and knowledge of the industry norms should provide useful information.

The market lag policy appears to fit well with lowest-cost strategies because companies realize cost savings by paying lower than the market pay line. Paying well below the market will yield short-term cost savings. However, these short-term savings will probably be offset by long-term costs. Companies that use the market lag policy may experience difficulties recruiting and retaining highly qualified employees. Too much turnover will undercut companies' abilities to operate efficiently and to market goods and services on a timely basis. Thus, companies that adopt market lag policies need to balance cost-savings with productivity and quality concerns.

A market lag policy is inconsistent with SURGIMED's differentiation strategy. SURGIMED's attainment of competitive advantage depends largely on its ability to employ a creative team of metallurgical engineers.

The market match policy represents a safe approach for companies because they generally are spending no more or less on compensation (per employee) than competitors are paying. This pay policy does not fit with the lowest cost strategy for obvious reasons. It fits better with differentiation strategies. This statement appears to contradict previous ones about differentiation strategies, such as pay "high" salaries to attract and retain the best talent. Some companies that pursue differentiation strategies follow a market match policy to fund expensive operating or capital needs that support differentiation—for example, research equipment, research laboratories.

A "one size fits all" approach to policy selection is inappropriate. Most companies use more than one pay policy simultaneously. For example, companies generally use market match or market lead policies for professional and managerial talent because these employees contribute most directly to companies' competitive advantage. Companies typically apply market match or market lag policies to clerical, administrative, and unskilled employees (for example, janitorial): Companies' demand for these employees relative to supply in the relevant labor markets is low, and these employees' contributions to attainment of competitive advantage is less direct.

Summary

This chapter discussed market-competitive pay systems and described two important compensation tools: strategic analyses and compensation surveys. Strategic analyses enable compensation professionals to better understand the internal and external contexts of their companies, giving them a better sense of how much they can afford to compensate employees. Compensation surveys provide "snapshots" of competitors' pay practices. Survey information provides the reference points for establishing pay level policies. Students should realize that conducting both strategic analyses and compensation surveys is an art, not a science. These practices require compensation professionals' sound judgment for making recommendations that fit well with competitive strategies. Careful thought about the meaning underlying the facts and statistics is the key to successfully building market-competitive pay systems.

Discussion questions

1. You are a compensation analyst for WORRY-NOT Insurance Company, which is located in Hartford, Connecticut. Define the relevant labor market for insurance claims adjusters. Do the same for data entry clerks. Describe the rationale for your definitions.
2. Discuss your views of comparable worth, building upon the discussion presented in this chapter.
3. Discuss the relationship between the choice of having multiple pay structures and the concerns inherent in the comparable-worth debate.
4. Refer to the regression equation presented earlier in this chapter. When $b = 0$, the market pay line is parallel to the x-axis (that is, job evaluation points). Provide your interpretation.
5. Refer to Exhibit 8-10. Cross out salaries 26 through 35. Calculate the mean and median for this reduced data set.

Key terms

market-competitive pay systems
strategic analysis
compensation surveys
Standard Industrial Classification Manual

Standard Industrial Classification (SIC)
major group
industry group
industry profiles

labor market assessments
functional capabilities
operating requirements
capital requirements
relevant labor markets
job family
central tendency
variation
standard deviation
quartiles

percentiles
Consumer Price Index (CPI)
market pay line
comparable worth
Lemons v. The City and County of
  Denver
market lead policy
market lag policy
market match policy

Endnotes

[1] U.S. Office of Management and Budget, *Standard industrial classification manual* (Washington, D.C.: U.S. Office of Management and Budget, 1987).

[2] U.S. Office of Management and Budget, *Standard industrial classification manual,* p. 243.

[3] U.S. Department of Commerce, *U.S. industrial outlook* (Washington, D.C.: U.S. Department of Commerce, 1994), p. 44-1.

[4] H. N. Fullerton Jr., Labor force projections: The baby boom moves on, *Monthly Labor Review* 116, No. 11 (1993):29–42.

[5] Back that innovation, *Forbes,* January 18, 1993, p. 48.

[6] Fullerton, Labor force projections.

[7] U.S. Department of Commerce, *U.S. industrial outlook.*

[8] J. Franklin, Industry output and employment, *Monthly Labor Review* 116, No. 11 (1993):41.

[9] U.S. Bureau of Labor Statistics, Occupational outlook handbook, 1996–97, Bulletin 2470 (Washington, D.C.: U.S. Bureau of Labor Statistics, 1996), p. 23.

[10] Ibid.

[11] J. Prescott and C. Fleisher, *Professionals: Who we are and what we do* (Pittsburgh: University of Pittsburgh, 1991, cited in S. A. Zahra and S. S. Chaples, Blind spots in competitive analysis, *Academy of Management Executive* 7 (1993):7–28.

[12] Zahra and Chaples, Blind spots in competitive analysis.

[13] U.S. Chamber of Commerce, *Employee benefits 1995 edition: Survey data from benefit year 1994* (Washington, D.C.: U.S. Chamber of Commerce Research Center, 1995).

[14] E. J. McCormick, *Job analysis: Methods and applications* (New York: AMACOM, 1979).

[15] U.S. Bureau of Labor Statistics, *Occupational outlook handbook, 1996–97.*

[16] G. T. Milkovich and J. M. Newman, *Compensation,* 5th ed. (Homewood, Ill.: Richard D. Irwin, 1996).

[17] C. Goldin, *Understanding the gender gap: An economic history of American women* (New York: Oxford University Press, 1990).

[18] Women's Bureau of the U.S. Department of Labor, *Facts on working women* (Washington, D.C.: U.S. Government Printing Office, 1993).

[19] P. England, *Comparable worth: Theories and evidence* (New York: Aldine De Gruyter, 1992).

[20] National Committee on Pay Equity, *Job evaluation: A tool for pay equity* (Washington, D.C.: National Committee on Pay Equity, 1987).

[21] *Lemons v. The City and County of Denver,* 22 FEP Cases 959, 620 F.2d 228 (1980).

CHAPTER

NINE

Building pay structures that recognize individual contributions

CHAPTER OUTLINE

In this chapter, you will learn about

1. Fundamental principles of pay structure design
2. Merit pay system structures
3. Sales incentive pay structures
4. Pay-for-knowledge structures
5. Pay structure variations: broadbanding and two-tier wage plans

Anne Jenkins and Sylvia Tanner are systems analysts for DATAMAX SYSTEMS, INC. Anne joined DATAMAX SYSTEMS eight years ago as a systems analyst right after completing her bachelor's degree in computer programming and applications. Sylvia has worked as a systems analyst for five years—the first three years for a competitor and the last two for DATAMAX SYSTEMS.

DATAMAX SYSTEMS employees just received notification of their annual merit pay increases. Anne received an 8 percent pay increase of $4,720, raising her annual salary to $63,720. Sylvia received an 11 percent pay raise of $6,820, increasing her annual salary to $68,820.

During lunch, Anne and Sylvia talked about their pay increases and adjusted annual salaries. In addition, they discussed their overall performance evaluations. Although Anne and Sylvia work as systems analysts in the same department, they have different supervisors. Anne expressed dismay because her smaller pay raise was based on an "exemplary, exceeds performance standards" performance rating; Sylvia's larger pay raise was based on an "acceptable, meets performance standards" rating. About two weeks later, Anne handed her supervisor a letter of resignation, indicating that she had secured a comparable position elsewhere at substantially higher pay.

Pay structures should define the boundaries for recognizing employee contributions.

Pay structures assign different pay rates for jobs of unequal worth *and* provide the framework for recognizing differences in individual employee contributions. No two employees possess identical credentials, nor do they perform the same jobs equally well. Companies recognize these differences by paying individuals according to their credentials, knowledge, or job performance. When completed, pay structures should define the boundaries for recognizing employee contributions. Furthermore, pay structures have strategic value. Well-designed structures should promote the retention of valued employees.

Employee contributions in this context correspond to the pay bases that we addressed in previous chapters—seniority, merit, incentive pay, and knowledge-based pay. In this chapter, we address how companies structure these pay bases with the exception of seniority, which is typically not the main basis for pay in companies. We start out by considering the fundamental process of constructing pay structures. Next, we examine the design elements of merit pay structures. Then, we move on to specific pay structures including merit pay, sales incentive pay, and pay-for-knowledge.

Constructing a pay structure

Compensation specialists develop pay structures based on five steps:

✮ Deciding on how many pay structures to construct

* Determining a market pay line
* Defining pay grades
* Calculating pay ranges for each pay grade
* Evaluating the results

Step 1: Deciding on the number of pay structures

Companies often establish more than one pay structure, depending upon market rates and the company's job structure. Common pay structures include exempt and nonexempt structures, pay structures based on job families, and pay structures based on geography.

EXEMPT AND NONEXEMPT PAY STRUCTURES As you will recall, the categories exempt and nonexempt reflect a distinction in the Fair Labor Standards Act. Exempt jobs are not subject to the overtime pay provisions of the act, although some companies, such as Anheuser-Busch, pay certain exempt employees overtime compensation in keeping with union contracts. Core compensation terms for exempt jobs are usually expressed as an annual salary. Nonexempt jobs are subject to the overtime pay provision of the act. Accordingly, the core compensation for nonexempt jobs is expressed as an hourly pay rate. Companies establish these pay structures for administrative ease. Some broadly consistent features distinguish exempt from nonexempt jobs: Exempt jobs, by definition of the Fair Labor Standards Act, are generally supervisory, professional, managerial, or executive jobs that each contain a wide variety of duties. On the other hand, nonexempt jobs are generally nonsupervisory in nature, and the duties tend to be narrowly defined.

PAY STRUCTURES BASED ON JOB FAMILY Executive, managerial, professional, technical, clerical, and craft represent distinct job families. Pay structures are also defined on the basis of job family, each of which shows a distinct salary pattern in the market. For example, the Davis-Bacon Act requires contractors and subcontractors to pay wages at least equal to those prevailing in the area where work is performed. This act applies only to employers with federal or federally financed contracts worth more than $2,000 for the construction, alteration, or repair of public works or buildings. Moreover, the Davis-Bacon Act also applies only to laborers and mechanics, excluding clerical, professional, and managerial employees. Thus, companies holding federal contracts meeting these criteria have limited latitude for setting pay; however, the latitude for setting pay rates for other jobs is greater.

PAY STRUCTURES BASED ON GEOGRAPHY Companies with multiple, geographically dispersed locations such as sales offices, manufacturing plants, service centers, and corporate offices may establish pay structures based on going rates in different geographic regions since local conditions may influence pay levels. The cost of living is substantially higher in the Northeast region than in the South and Southeast regions of the United States. For example, in 1995, the minimum annual salary needed to meet expenses (goods and services and taxes) in Boston, Massachusetts, was $26,556. The minimum requirement for Houston, Texas, was much lower—$19,831. Consequently, companies that employ administrative assistants in each location may choose to establish separate pay structures.

Step 2: Determining a market pay line

We discussed how to determine the market pay line in Chapter 8. Again, the market pay line is representative of typical market pay rates relative to a company's job structure. Pay levels that correspond with the market pay line are market-competitive pay rates. Exhibit 9-1 illustrates a market pay line for a series of clerical jobs. Pay rates

Exhibit 9-1
**Pay Structure for
Clerk Jobs**

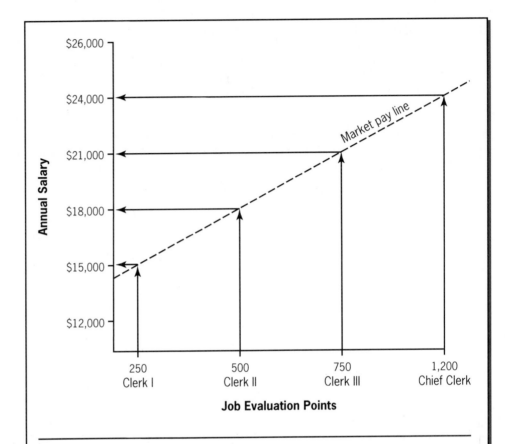

CLERK I

Employees receive training in basic office support procedures, the operation of office equipment, and the specific activities of the unit. Tasks assigned are simple and repetitive in nature and are performed in accordance with explicit instructions and clearly established guidelines. Sample duties include: Files materials in established alphabetical order and prepares new file folders and affixes labels. Clerk Is must possess a high school diploma or equivalent.

CLERK II

Employees work under general supervision in support of an office. They perform routine office support tasks that require a knowledge of standard office procedures and the ability to operate a variety of office equipment. Sample duties include: Prepares simple factual statements or reports involving computations such as totals or subtotals and composes memos requesting or transmitting factual information. Clerk IIs must possess a high school diploma or equivalent and one year work experience performing simple clerical tasks.

continued on next page

Exhibit 9-1
Pay Structure for
Clerk Jobs (continued)

CLERK III

Employees work under general supervision in support of an office. They perform office support tasks requiring knowledge of general office and departmental procedures and methods and ability to operate a variety of office equipment. Sample duties include: Reconciles discrepancies between unit records and those of other departments and assigns and reviews work performed by Clerks I and II. Clerk IIIs must possess a high school diploma or equivalent, two years work experience performing moderately complex clerical tasks, and completed coursework (five in all) in such related topics as word processing and basic accounting principles.

CHIEF CLERK

Employees work under direction in support of an office. They perform a wide variety of office support tasks that require the use of judgment and initiative. A knowledge of the organization, programs, practices, and procedures of the unit is central to the performance of the duties. Chief clerks must possess a high school diploma or equivalent, four years work experience performing moderately difficult clerical tasks, and an associate's degree in office management.

---

that fall along the market pay line represent competitive pay rates based on the company's selection of a relevant labor market, and these rates promote internal consistency because they increase with the value of jobs. The values of the jobs are based on job evaluation points. The Clerk I job has the least complex and least demanding duties and has fewer worker requirements than the remaining clerk jobs (Clerk II, Clerk III, and Chief Clerk).

Step 3: Defining pay grades

Pay grades group jobs for pay policy application. Human resource professionals typically group jobs into pay grades based on similar compensable factors and value. These criteria are not precise. In fact, no one formula determines what is sufficiently similar in terms of content and value to warrant grouping into a pay grade.

Ultimately, job groupings are influenced by other factors such as management's philosophy, as discussed earlier. Wider pay grades—that is, ones that include a relatively large number of jobs—minimize hierarchy and social distance between employees. Narrower pay grades tend to promote hierarchy and social distance. Exhibit 9-2 illustrates pay grade definitions based on the jobs used in Exhibit 9-1.

Human resource professionals can develop pay grade widths as either "absolute" job evaluation point spreads or as percentage-based job evaluation point spreads. When absolute point spreads are used, grades are based on a set number of job evaluation points for each grade. For example, a compensation professional establishes pay grades equal to 200 points each. Grade 1 includes jobs that range from 1 to 200 job evaluation points, grade 2 contains jobs that range from 201 to 400 points, and so on.

Companies may choose to vary the absolute point spread by increasing the point spread as they move up the pay structure, in recognition of the broader range of skills that higher pay grades represent. For example, certified public accounting jobs require a broader range of skills—knowledge of financial accounting principles and both state and federal tax codes—than do mailroom clerk jobs. Often, companies assign trainee positions to the lower, narrower pay grades because trainees generally have limited job-relevant skills. For instance, Grade 1 may contain trainee positions with job evaluation scores that range from 1 to 150; Grade 2 may contain basic jobs beyond traineeships with scores of 151 to 400, and Grade 3 may include advanced jobs with scores of 401 to 1,000.

Step 4: Calculating pay ranges for each pay grade

Pay ranges build upon pay grades. Pay grades represent the horizontal dimension of pay structures (job evaluation points). **Pay ranges** represent the vertical dimension (pay rates). Pay ranges include midpoint, minimum, and maximum pay rates. The minimum and maximum values denote the acceptable lower and upper bounds of pay for the jobs contained within particular pay grades. Exhibit 9-3 illustrates pay ranges.

Human resource professionals establish midpoints first; then they establish minimum and maximum values. The **midpoint pay value** is the halfway mark between the range minimum and maximum rates. Midpoints generally match values along the mar-

Exhibit 9-2
Pay Grade Definitions

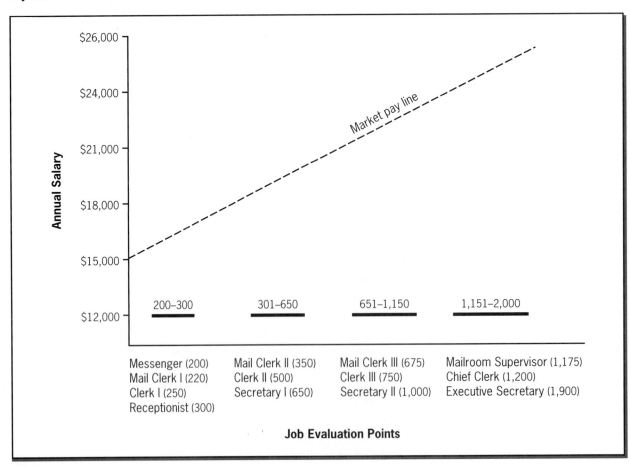

Exhibit 9-3
Pay Range Definitions

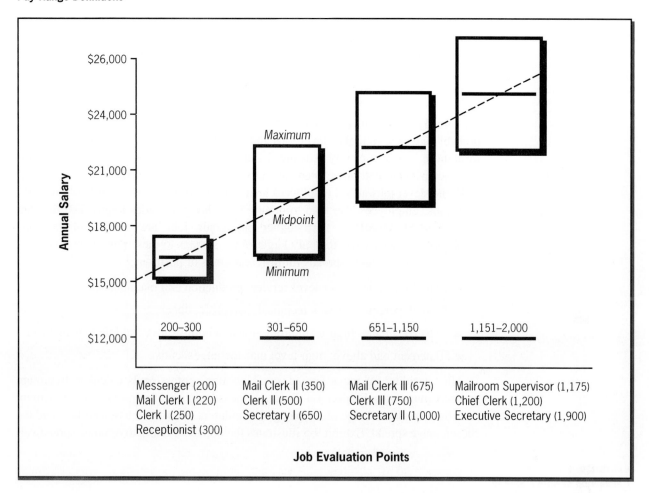

ket pay line, representing the competitive market rate determined by the analysis of compensation survey data. Thus, the midpoint may reflect the market average or median (Chapter 8).

A company sets the midpoints for its pay ranges according to its competitive pay policy, as we discussed in Chapter 8. If the company wants to lead the market with respect to pay offerings (market lead policy), it sets the midpoint of the ranges higher than the average for similar jobs at other companies. If the company wants to pay in accord with the market norm (market match policy), midpoints should equal average midpoints. If the company were interested in lagging the market (market lag policy), it would set the midpoints below the market average. A company's base-pay policy line graphically connects midpoints of each pay grade.

How do compensation professionals calculate pay grade minimums and maximums? They may fashion pay grade minimums and maximums after the minimums and maximums for pay grades that competitors have established. An alternative approach is to set the pay grade minimums and maximums on the basis of range spread. A **range spread** is the difference between the maximum and the minimum pay rates of a given pay grade. It is expressed as a percentage of the difference between the minimum and maximum divided by the minimum.

Companies generally apply different range spreads across pay grades. Most commonly, they use progressively higher range spreads for pay grades that contain more-valuable jobs in terms of the companies' criteria. Smaller range spreads characterize pay grades that contain relatively narrowly defined jobs that require simple skills with relatively low responsibility. Entry-level clerical employees perform limited duties, ranging from filing folders alphabetically to preparing file folders and affixing labels. Presumably, these jobs represent bottom-floor opportunities for employees who will probably advance to higher-level jobs and who will acquire the skills needed to perform those jobs proficiently. Advanced clerical employees review and analyze forms and documents to determine adequacy and acceptability of information.

Higher-level jobs afford employees greater promotion opportunities than do entry-level jobs. Employees also tend to remain in higher pay grades longer, and the specialized skills associated with higher pay grade jobs are considered valuable. Therefore, it makes sense to apply larger range spreads to these pay grades. The following are typical range spreads for different kinds of positions:[1]

- ★ 20 to 25 percent: lower-level service, production and maintenance
- ★ 30 to 40 percent: clerical, technical, paraprofessional
- ★ 40 to 50 percent: high-level professional, administrative, middle management
- ★ 50 percent and above: high-level managerial, executive

After deciding on range spread, compensation professionals calculate minimum and maximum rates. Exhibit 9-4 illustrates the calculation of minimum and maximum rates based on knowledge of the pay grade midpoint (step 1 discussed earlier) and the chosen range spread. Exhibit 9-5 illustrates the impact of alternative range spread val-

Exhibit 9-4
Calculation of Range Spread

Steps		
1. Identify the midpoint:	$20,000	Maximum = $23,333.33
2. Determine the range spread:	40%	Range spread = 40%
3. Calculate the minimum: $\dfrac{\text{midpoint}}{100\% + (\text{range spread}/2)}$	$= \dfrac{\$20,000}{100\% + (40\%/2)}$ $= \$16,666.67$	Midpoint = $20,000
4. Calculate the maximum: minimum + (range spread x minimum)	$= \$16,666.67 + (40\% \times \$16,666.67)$ $= \$23,333.33$	Minimum = $16,666.67

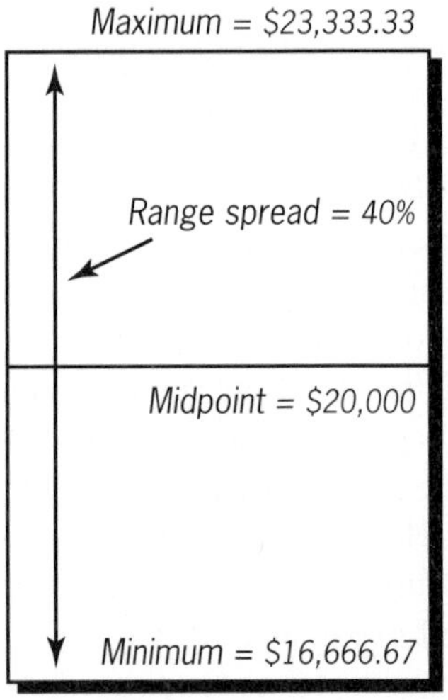

	RANGE SPREAD			
	20%	**50%**	**80%**	**120%**
Minimum:				
$\dfrac{\text{midpoint}}{100\% + (\text{range spread}/2)}$	$22,727	$20,000	$17,857	$15,625
Maximum:				
minimum + (range spread × minimum)	$27,272	$30,000	$32,143	$34,375
Difference between maximum and minimum values	$4,545	$10,000	$14,286	$18,750

ues on minimum and maximum values. This approach is typically applied when a company chooses to base the minimum and maximum rates on budgetary constraints. We discuss budgeting issues later in this chapter (see "The Flip Side of the Coin").

Adjacent pay ranges usually overlap with other pay ranges so that the highest rate paid in one is greater than the lowest rate of the successive pay grade. Exhibit 9-6 illustrates how to calculate pay range overlap. Overlapping pay ranges allow companies to promote employees to the next level without adding to their pay. Nonoverlapping pay ranges require pay increases for job promotions. Compensation professionals ex-

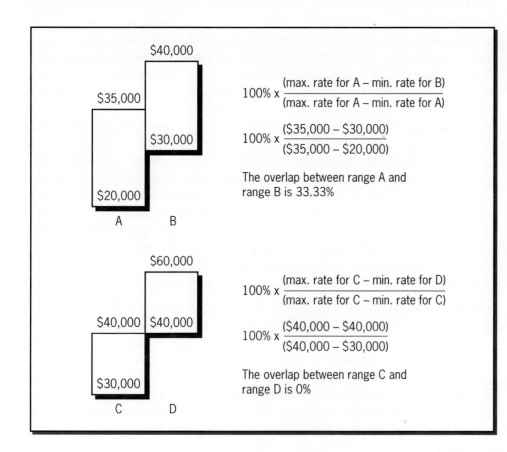

Exhibit 9-6
Calculating Pay Range Overlap

$40,000
$35,000
$30,000
$20,000
A   B

$$100\% \times \frac{(\text{max. rate for A} - \text{min. rate for B})}{(\text{max. rate for A} - \text{min. rate for A})}$$

$$100\% \times \frac{(\$35,000 - \$30,000)}{(\$35,000 - \$20,000)}$$

The overlap between range A and range B is 33.33%

$60,000
$40,000 $40,000
$30,000
C   D

$$100\% \times \frac{(\text{max. rate for C} - \text{min. rate for D})}{(\text{max. rate for C} - \text{min. rate for C})}$$

$$100\% \times \frac{(\$40,000 - \$40,000)}{(\$40,000 - \$30,000)}$$

The overlap between range C and range D is 0%

press overlap as a percentage. For example, the degree of overlap between pay range A and pay range B is about 33 percent.

PAY COMPRESSION The minimum pay rate for a range usually is the lowest pay rate that the company will pay for jobs that fall within that particular pay grade. In theory, newly hired employees receive pay that is at or near the minimum. In practice, new employees often receive well above minimum pay rates, sometimes only slightly below or even higher than the pay moderately tenured employees receive. **Pay compression** occurs whenever a company's pay spread between newly hired or less-qualified employees and more-qualified job incumbents is small.[2]

Two situations result in pay compression. The first is a company's failure to raise pay range minimums and maximums. Companies that retain set range maximums over time limit increase amounts. For example, let's assume that the entry-level starting salaries for newly hired certified public accountants have increased 7 percent annually for the last five years. TAX-IT, a small accounting firm, did not increase its pay range minimums and maximums for entry-level accountants during the same period because of lackluster profits. Nevertheless, TAX-IT hired several new accountants at the prevailing market rate. Failure to pay competitive pay rates would hinder TAX-IT's ability to recruit talented accountants. As a result, many of the TAX-IT accountants with five or fewer years' experience will have lower salaries (or slightly higher salaries at best) than newly hired accountants without work experience. The second situation that results in pay compression is scarcity of qualified job candidates for particular jobs. When the supply of such candidates falls behind a company's demand, wages for newly hired employees rise, reflecting a bidding process among companies for qualified candidates.

Pay compression can threaten companies' competitive advantage. Dysfunctional employee turnover is a likely consequence of pay compression. Dysfunctional turnover represents high-performing employees' voluntary termination of their employment. High-performing employees will probably perceive their pay as inequitable because they are receiving lower pay relative to their positive contributions (that is, experience, demonstrated performance) than newly hired employees who are receiving similar pay.

How can companies minimize pay compression? Maximum pay rates represent the most that a company is willing to pay an individual for jobs that fall in that particular range. Maximum pay rates should be set close to the maximum paid by other companies in the labor market for similar jobs. Setting competitive maximum rates enables a company to raise pay rates for high-quality employees who may consider employment opportunities with a competitor. However, maximum rates should not exceed maximum rates offered by competitors for comparable jobs because high maximums represent costs to the company over and above what are needed to be competitive.

GREEN CIRCLE PAY RATES Employees sometimes receive below-minimum pay rates for their pay range, especially when they assume jobs for which they do not meet every minimum requirement as specified in the worker specification section of the job description. Below-minimum pay range rates are known as **green circle rates.** The pay rates of employees who are paid at green circle rates should be brought within the normal pay range as quickly as possible. Doing so requires that both the employer and the employee take the necessary steps to eliminate whatever deficiencies in skill or experience warranted paying below the pay range minimum.

RED CIRCLE PAY RATES On occasion, companies must pay certain employees greater than maximum rates for their pay ranges. Known as **red circle rates,** these higher pay rates help retain valued employees who have lucrative job offers from competitors. Alternatively, exemplary employees may receive red circle rates for exceptional job performance, particularly when a promotion to a higher pay grade is not granted. Red circle rates also apply to employees who receive job demotions to pay grades with lower maximum rates than the employees' current pay. Companies usually reduce demoted employees' pay over time until they receive pay that is consistent with their new jobs. In this case, red circle rates allow employees a chance to adjust to pay decreases.

Step 5: Evaluating the results

After compensation professionals establish pay structures according to the previous steps, they must evaluate the results. Specifically, they must analyze significant differences between the company's internal values for jobs and the market's value for the same jobs. If discrepancies are evident, the company must reconsider the internal values they have placed on jobs. If their valuation of particular jobs exceeds the market's valuation of the same jobs, they must decide whether higher-than-market pay rates will undermine attainment of competitive advantage. If a company undervalues jobs relative to the market, managers must consider whether these discrepancies will limit the company's ability to recruit and retain highly qualified individuals.

Compensation professionals must also consider each employee's pay level relative to the midpoint of its pay grade. Again, the midpoint represents a company's competitive stance relative to the market. **Compa-ratios** index the relative competitiveness of internal pay rates on the basis of pay range midpoints. Compa-ratios are calculated as follows:

$$\frac{\text{Employee's pay rate}}{\text{Pay range midpoint}}$$

Compa-ratios are interpreted as follows. A compa-ratio of 1 means that the employee's pay rate equals the pay range midpoint. Companies with market match policies strive for compa-ratios that equal 1. A compa-ratio of less than 1 means that the employee's pay rate falls below the competitive pay rate for the job. Companies with market lag policies strive for compa-ratios of less than 1. A compa-ratio that is greater than 1 means that an employee's pay rate exceeds the competitive pay rate for the job. Companies with market lead policies strive for compa-ratios greater than 1.

Human resource professionals also can use compa-ratios to index job groups that fall within a particular pay grade. Specifically, compa-ratios may be calculated to index the competitive position of a job by averaging the pay rates for each job incumbent. Moreover, compa-ratios may be calculated for all jobs that are included in a pay grade, a department, or a functional area such as accounting.

Compa-ratios provide invaluable information about the competitiveness of companies' pay rates. Compensation professionals can use compa-ratios as diagnostic tools to judge the competitiveness of their companies' pay rates. Compa-ratios that exceed 1 tell compensation professionals that pay is highly competitive with the market. Compa-ratios that fall below 1 tell compensation professionals that pay is not competitive with the market, and they should consider another course of action to increase pay over a reasonable period.

In sum, we have reviewed the elements of pay structures and the steps compensation professionals follow to construct them. Next, we consider three popular pay structures with which compensation professionals should be familiar: merit pay structure, sales incentive compensation structure, and pay-for-knowledge structure.

Designing merit pay systems

Establishing an effective merit pay program that recognizes employee contributions requires that compensation professionals avoid such pitfalls as ineffective performance appraisal methods and poor communication regarding the link between pay and performance.

As we noted in Chapter 4, companies that use merit pay systems must ensure that employees see definite links between pay and performance. We also reviewed the rationale for using merit pay systems as well as the possible limitations of this kind of pay system. Establishing an effective merit pay program that recognizes employee contributions requires that compensation professionals avoid such pitfalls as ineffective performance appraisal methods and poor communication regarding the link between pay and performance. Besides these considerations, managers interested in establishing a merit pay system must determine merit increase amounts, increase timing, and the type of merit pay increase employees will receive—permanent or recurring increases versus one-time or nonrecurring additions to base pay. They must also settle on base pay levels relative to the base pay of functionally similar jobs.[3]

Merit increase amounts

Merit pay increases should reflect prior job performance levels, and they should motivate employees to perform their best. As managers establish merit increase amounts, they must not only consider past performance levels, but they must also establish rates that will motivate employees even after the impact of inflation and other payroll deductions. Updating compensation survey data should account for increases in consumer prices (Chapter 8). As we noted in Chapter 4, just-meaningful pay increases refer to minimum increase amounts employees will see as making a meaningful change in their compensation.[4] Trivial pay increases for average or better employees will not reinforce their performance or motivate enhanced future performance.

No precise mathematical formula determines the minimum merit increase that will positively affect performance; managers must consider three research findings.[5] First, boosting the merit increase amount will not necessarily improve productivity since research has shown diminishing marginal returns on each additional dollar allocated to merit increases.[6] In other words, each additional merit increase dollar was associated with smaller increases in production.

Second, employees' perceptions of just-meaningful differences from merit increases depends on individuals' cost of living, their attitude toward the job, and their expectations of rewards from the job. For employees who value pay for meeting economic necessity, a just-meaningful difference in pay increase tends to depend upon changes in the cost of living. On the other hand, for employees who value pay as a form of recognition, the size of the expected pay raise (versus cost-of-living) affects a just-meaningful difference.[7]

Third, for the pay increase to be considered meaningful, the employee must see the size of the increase as substantive in a relative sense as well as in an absolute sense.[8] **Equity theory** suggests that an employee must regard his or her own ratio of merit increase pay to performance as similar to the ratio for other comparably performing people in the company. In practical terms, managers should award the largest merit pay increases to employees with the best performance, and they should award the smallest increases to employees with the lowest acceptable performance. The difference between these merit increases should be approximately proportional to the differences in performance.

Timing

The vast majority of companies allocate merit increases, as well as cost-of-living and other increases, annually.[9] Presently, companies typically take one of two approaches in timing these pay raises. Companies may establish a **common review date,** or **common review period,** so that all employees' performance is evaluated on the same date or during the same period, for example, the month of June, which immediately follows a company's peak activity period. Best suited for smaller companies, common review dates reduce the administrative burden of the plan by concentrating staff members' efforts to limited periods.

Alternatively, companies may review employee performance and award merit increases on the **employee's anniversary date**—the day on which the employee began to work for the company. Most employees will thus have different evaluation dates. These staggered review dates may not monopolize supervisors' time, but this approach can be administratively burdensome because reviews must be conducted regularly throughout the year.

Recurring versus nonrecurring merit pay increases

Companies have traditionally awarded merit pay increases permanently, and permanent increases are sometimes associated with some undesirable side effects such as placing excessive cost burdens on the employer. In terms of costs, U.S. companies are increasingly concerned with containing costs as just one initiative in their quest to establish and sustain competitive advantages in the marketplace. Companies may advocate **nonrecurring merit increases**—lump sum bonuses—which lend themselves well to cost containment and have recently begun to gain some favor among unions including the International Brotherhood of Electrical Workers.[10] Lump sum bonuses strengthen the pay-for-performance link and minimize costs because these increases are not permanent. Thus, subsequent percentage increases are not based on higher base pay levels.

> *Companies have traditionally awarded merit pay increases permanently, and permanent increases are sometimes associated with some undesirable side effects such as placing excessive cost burdens on the employer.*

Present level of base pay

Pay structures specify acceptable pay ranges for jobs within each pay grade. Thus, each job's base pay level should fall within the minimum and maximum rates for its respective pay grade. In addition, compensation professionals should encourage managers to offer similar base pay to new employees performing similar jobs unless employee qualifications—education, relevant work experience—justify pay differences. This practice is consistent with the mandates of several laws (Chapter 3)—Title VII of the Civil Rights Act of 1964, the Equal Pay Act of 1963, and the Age Discrimination in Employment Act of 1967. Of course, employees' merit pay increases should vary with their performance.

Rewarding performance: the merit pay grid

Exhibit 9-7 illustrates a typical merit pay grid that managers use to assign merit increases to employees. Managers determine pay raise amounts by two factors jointly:

Exhibit 9-7
Merit Pay Grid

Performance Rating

		Excellent	Above Average	Average	Below Average	Poor
Q3	$60,000 $55,000 $50,000	7%	5%	3%	0%	0%
Q2	$45,000 $40,000 $35,000	9%	7%	6%	2%	0%
Q1	$30,000 $25,000 $20,000	12%	10%	8%	4%	0%

Current Annual Salary

employees' performance ratings and the position of employees' present base pay rates within pay ranges. Pay raise amounts are expressed as percentages of base pay. For instance, let's say that two employees will each receive a 5 percent merit pay increase. One employee is paid on an hourly basis, earning $8.50 per hour, and the other is paid on an annual basis, earning $32,000 a year. The employee whose pay is based on an hourly rate (usually nonexempt in accord with the Fair Labor Standards Act, that is, one who must be paid overtime for time in excess of 40 hours per week) receives a pay raise of 43 cents per hour (5 percent of $8.50), increasing her hourly pay to $8.93. The employee whose pay is based on an annual rate, typically exempt from the Fair Labor Standards Act provisions, receives a pay increase of $1,600 (5 percent of $32,000), boosting her annual pay to $33,600.

In Exhibit 9-7, employees whose current annual salary falls in the second quartile of the pay range and whose performance rates an average score receive a 6 percent increase. Employees whose current annual salary falls in the first quartile of the pay range and whose job performance is excellent receive a 12 percent increase.

EMPLOYEES' PERFORMANCE RATINGS As you know, merit pay systems use performance appraisals to determine employees' performance. Where merit pay systems are in place, an overall performance rating guides the pay raise decision. In Exhibit 9-7, an employee receives any one of five performance ratings ranging from Poor to Excellent. As you can see, when we hold position in pay range constant, pay raise amounts increase with level of performance. This pattern fits well with the logic underlying pay-for-performance principles: Recognize higher performance with greater rewards.

EMPLOYEES' POSITION WITHIN THE PAY RANGE Employee's position within the pay range is indexed by quartile ranking, which, in Chapter 8, we described as a measure of dispersion. Again, quartiles describe the distribution of data, in this case, hourly or annual base pay amount, by identifying the percentage of figures that fall below certain points. There are three quartiles. In Exhibit 9-7, the first quartile is the point below which 25 percent of the salary data lie, which is $35,000. In other words, for this array of salary figures, 25 percent of these figures are less than or equal to $35,000. The second quartile is the point below which 50 percent of the salary data lie; $50,000 for this example. The third quartile is the point below which 75 percent of the salary data lie; $60,000 for this example. The lower a person's pay falls within its designated pay grade—for example, the first quartile versus the third quartile—the higher the percentage pay raise, all else equal. Similarly, the higher a person's pay within its grade, the lower the percentage pay raise, all else equal.

Holding performance ratings constant, compensation professionals reduce merit pay increase percentages as quartile ranks increase to control employees' progression through their pay ranges. Pay grade minimums and maximums are determined not only by corporate criteria about the value of various groups of unlike jobs; budgeting also may dictate such minimums and maximums. Let's take the case of two employees whose performance ratings are identical but whose base pay places them in dif-

FLIP SIDE OF THE COIN

Best-Laid Plans Fail because of Insufficient Funding

Compensation professionals possess skills and knowledge to conceive well-designed merit pay plans that reinforce employees' motivation to perform well with just-meaningful pay increases and merit increase percentages that clearly distinguish among employees on the basis of their performance. However, the best laid plans don't always lead to the desired results. Well-designed merit pay structures (and others that we discuss shortly) will fail without adequate funding.

Compensation budgets are blueprints that describe the allocation of monetary resources to fund pay structures. Compensation professionals index budget increases that fund merit pay programs in percentage terms. For example, a 10 percent increase for next year's budget means that it will be 10 percent as great as the current year's budget. Often, this value is an indicator of the average pay increase employees will receive. Obviously, the greater the increases in compensation budgets, the greater flexibility compensation professionals will have in developing innovative systems with substantial motivating potential.

Unfortunately, the magnitude of the increases in compensation budgets in recent years has been minuscule. For example, the average earnings for all production or nonsupervisory employees in the United States increased only 2.6 percent between 1993 and 1994.[11] The average annual increases were approximately the same for the prior two-year period. Although this value varies by occupation, industry, and region of the country, it does reflect a trend in the United States of stagnant growth in compensation budgets. The picture becomes even bleaker because the increase in cost of living for the same period was, coincidentally, 2.6 percent.[12] This means that, on average, annual pay raises matched the increase in cost of living, taking the motivational value out of pay increases.

ferent quartiles of the pay grade—one in the third quartile and the other in the first quartile. If these employees were to receive the same pay raise percentage, the base pay rate for the employee in the third quartile most likely would exceed the maximum pay rate for their range more quickly than would the base pay rate for the employee in the first quartile.

Pay structures based on merit will differ from sales compensation in at least two key ways. First, whereas sales compensation programs center on incentives that specify rewards that an employee will receive for meeting a preestablished—often objective—level of performance, merit pay programs generally base an employee's reward on someone else's (most often the employee's supervisor) subjective evaluation of the employee's past performance. Second, in most instances, a sales employee's compensation is variable to the extent that it is composed of incentives. Under a merit pay system, an employee earns a base pay, appropriate for the job (as discussed earlier in this chapter), that is augmented periodically with permanent pay raises or one-time bonuses.

Designing sales incentive compensation plans

Sales compensation programs can help businesses meet their objectives by aligning the financial self-interest of sales professionals with the company's marketing objectives.

Compensation programs for salespeople rely on incentives.[13] Sales compensation programs can help businesses meet their objectives by aligning the financial self-interest of sales professionals with the company's marketing objectives.[14] By extension, sales compensation programs can help companies achieve strategic objectives by linking sales professional's compensation to fulfilling customer needs or other marketing objectives, such as increasing market share. Thus, sales compensation plans derive their objectives more or less directly from strategic marketing objectives, which, in turn, derive from company competitive strategy. Several particular sales objectives include:[15]

- ✫ **Sales volume** indicates the amount of sales that should be achieved for a specified period.
- ✫ **New business** refers to making sales from customers who have not made purchases from the company before.
- ✫ **Retaining sales** simply targets a level of sales from existing customers.
- ✫ **Product mix** rewards sales professionals for selling a preestablished mix of the company's product goods or services. The rationale for the product mix objective is to help the company increase its competitiveness by promoting new products and services. Said another way, successfully meeting this sales objective rewards sales professionals for helping the company stay viable by not putting "all its eggs into one basket."
- ✫ **Win-back sales** is an objective that is designed to motivate sales professionals to regain business from former clients who are now buying from a competing company.

Alternative sales compensation plans

Companies usually use one of five kinds of sales incentive plans. The type of plan appropriate for any given company will depend on the company's competitive strategy, as we indicate following the discussion of the five plans. The order of presentation roughly represents the degree of risk (from lowest to highest) to employees.

- ✯ Salary-only plans
- ✯ Salary-plus-bonus plans
- ✯ Salary-plus-commission plans
- ✯ Commission-plus-draw plans
- ✯ Commission-only plans

SALARY-ONLY PLANS Under a **salary-only plan,** sales professionals receive fixed base compensation, which does not vary with the level of units sold, increase in market share, or any other indicator of sales performance. From employees' perspective, salary-only plans are relatively risk free because they can expect a certain amount of income. From a company's perspective, salary-only plans are burdensome because the company must compensate its sales employees regardless of their achievement levels. Thus, salary-only plans do not fit well with the directive to link pay with performance through at-risk pay. Nevertheless, salary-only plans may be appropriate for particular kinds of selling situations:

- ✯ Sales of high-priced products and services or technical products with long lead times for sales
- ✯ Situations in which sales representatives are primarily responsible for generating demand while other employees actually close the sales
- ✯ Situations in which it is impossible to follow sales results for each salesperson, that is, where sales are accomplished through team efforts
- ✯ Training and other periods during which sales representatives are unlikely to make sales on their own

SALARY-PLUS-BONUS PLANS **Salary-plus-bonus plans** offer a set salary coupled with a bonus. Bonuses usually are single payments that reward employees for achievement of specific, exceptional goals. For a real estate agent, generating in excess of $2 million dollars in residential sales for a one-year period may earn a bonus totaling several thousands of dollars.

SALARY-PLUS-COMMISSION PLANS **Commission** is a form of incentive compensation based on a percentage of the product or service selling price. **Salary-plus-commission plans** spread the risk of selling between the company and the sales professional. The salary component presumably enhances a company's ability to attract quality employees and allows a company to direct its employees' efforts to nonselling tasks that do not lead directly to commissions, such as participating in further training or servicing accounts. The commission component serves as the employees' share in the gain they generated for the company.

COMMISSION-PLUS-DRAW PLANS **Commission-plus-draw plans** award sales professionals with subsistence pay—money to cover basic living expenses—yet provides them with a strong incentive to excel. The subsistence pay component is known as a **draw.** However, unlike salaries, companies award draws as advances, which are charged against commissions that sales professionals are expected to earn. Companies use two types of draws. **Recoverable draws** act as company loans to employees that are carried forward indefinitely until employees sell enough to repay their draws. **Nonrecoverable draws** act as salary because employees are not obligated to repay the loans if they do not sell enough. Clearly, nonrecoverable draws represent risks to companies because these expenses are not repaid if employees' sales performance is lackluster. Companies that adopt nonrecoverable draws may stipulate that employees cannot continue in the employment of the company if they fail to cover their draw for a specified number of months or sales periods during the year. This arrangement is quite common among car salespeople.

COMMISSION-ONLY PLANS Under **commission-only plans,** salespeople derive their entire income through commissions. Three particular types of commissions warrant mention. **Straight commission** is based on the fixed percentage of the sales price of the product or service. For instance, a 10 percent commission would generate a $10 incentive for a product or service sold that is priced at $100 and $55 for a product or service sold that is priced at $550.

Graduated commissions increase percentage pay rates for progressively higher sales volume. For example, a sales professional may earn a 5 percent commission per unit for sales volume up to 100 units, 8 percent for each unit in excess of the hundredth unit sold but fewer than 500 units, and 12 percent for each unit in excess of the five hundredth unit sold during each sales period.

Finally, **multiple-tiered commissions** are similar to graduated commissions but with one exception. Employees earn a higher rate of commission for all sales made in a given period if the sales level exceeds a predetermined level. For instance, employees might earn only 8 percent for each item if total sales volume falls short of 1,000 units. However, if total sales volume exceeds 1,000 units, then employees might earn a per item commission equal to 12 percent for every item sold. Commission-only plans are well suited for situations in which:

☆ The salesperson has substantial influence over the sales

☆ Low to moderate training or expertise is required

☆ The sales cycle—the time between identifying the prospect and closing the sale—is short

In contrast to salespeople on salary-only plans, commission-only salespeople shoulder all the risk: Employees earn nothing until they sell. Despite this risk, potential rewards are substantial, particularly when graduated and multiple-tiered commission plans are used.

Although commissions may fit well with cost-cutting measures, these incentives are not always the best tactic for compensating sales professionals. In fact, commission structures probably suffer from many of the same limitations of individual incentive plans that we discussed in Chapter 5, such as competitive behaviors among employees. Moreover, some sales experts argue that commissions undermine employees' intrinsic motivation to sell, that is, their genuine interest in the challenge and enjoyment that selling brings. These experts argue that once salespeople have lost that intrinsic motivation, commissions act essentially as controls to maintain sales professionals' performance levels. Said another way, such professionals may simply go through the motions in order to earn money without regard to quality and customer satisfaction.[16]

Some sales experts argue that commissions undermine employees' intrinsic motivation to sell, that is, their genuine interest in the challenge and enjoyment that selling brings.

Sales compensation plans and competitive strategy

Sales plans with salary components are most appropriate for differentiation strategies. Under salary-based sales plans, employees can count on receiving income. By design, salary plans do not require employees to focus on attaining sales volume goals or other volume indicators (for example, market share). Sales professionals who receive salary can turn their attention to addressing clients' needs during the presale and servicing phases of the relationship. Salary-based sales compensation applies to the sale and servicing of such technical equipment as computer networks, including the hardware (that is, the individual computer and network server) as well as the software (that is, such applications programs as Microsoft Excel or the Windows 95 operating system).

Commission-oriented sales compensation plans are best suited for lowest-cost strategies because compensation expenditures vary with sales revenue. As a result, only the most productive employees earn the best salaries. Essentially, commissions represent awards for "making the sale." For example, real estate sales agents' earnings depend upon two factors—number of houses sold and selling price. Similarly, new car salespersons' earnings depend upon the number of cars sold and selling price. In either situation, customers are likely to have questions and concerns after the sales transaction. Many real estate companies employ real estate assistants at low salaries—not much more than the minimum wage—who mediate such buyers' queries of the sellers as "What grade of rock salt is most appropriate for the water softener apparatus?" Often, real estate assistants are training to be full-fledged real estate agents, and they view low pay as a necessary tradeoff for learning the ropes.

Determining fixed pay and the compensation mix

Managers must balance fixed and incentive pay elements to bear directly on employee motivation. The mix depends mainly upon four factors:

- ✯ Influence of the salesperson on the buying decision
- ✯ Competitive pay standards within the industry
- ✯ Amount of nonsales activities required
- ✯ Noncash incentives

INFLUENCE OF THE SALESPERSON ON THE BUYING DECISION For the most part, the more influence sales professionals have on "buying" decisions, the more the compensation mix will feature incentive pay. Salespeople's influence over sales varies greatly with specific product or service marketed and the way they are sold. Many sales professionals assume an order taker role, with little influence over purchase decisions. For example, salespeople in such large department stores as the Federated Stores, Inc. have little influence over the merchandise for sale, since these stores send their buyers to foreign countries to purchase lines of clothing that will be sold in their stores throughout the United States. Product display and promotional efforts—television or newspaper advertisement campaigns—are determined by store management. Although a salesclerk with a bad attitude may prevent sales from occurring, these workers control very little of the marketing effort.

On the other end of the spectrum, some employees serve as consultants to the client. For instance, when a company decides to invest in computerizing its entire worldwide operations, it may approach a computer manufacturer such as IBM to purchase the necessary equipment. Given the technical complexity of computerizing a company's worldwide operations, the client would depend on IBM to translate its networking needs into the appropriate configuration of hardware and software. Ultimately, these IBM sales professionals influence the purchaser's decision to buy.

COMPETITIVE PAY STANDARDS WITHIN THE INDUSTRY A company's compensation mix must be as enticing as that offered by competitors if the company wants to recruit quality sales professionals. Industry norms and the selling situation are among the key determinants of compensation mix. For instance, competitive standards may dictate that the company give greater weight to either incentive or fixed pay, which we addressed earlier. Incentive (commission) pay weighs heavily in highly competitive retail industries including furniture, home electronics, and auto sales. Salary represents a significant salary component in such high-entry-barrier industries as pharmaceuticals. In the case of pharmaceuticals, barriers to entry include the vast amount of U.S. Food and Drug Administration regulation regarding procedures for testing new products that significantly extends the time from product conception through testing to marketing for general use. Salary is an appropriate compensation choice because pharmaceutical companies face little risk of new competition.

AMOUNT OF NONSALES ACTIVITIES REQUIRED In general, the more nonsales duties salespeople must fulfill, the more their compensation package should tend toward fixed pay. Some companies and products, for instance, require extensive technical training or customer-servicing activities. An excellent example can be found in the pharmaceuticals industry. Pharmaceutical sales professionals must maintain a comprehensive understanding of their products' chemical composition, clinical use, and contraindications.

NONCASH INCENTIVES So far, we have emphasized cash or monetary incentives—commissions and bonuses for salespeople. Companies may also use **noncash incentives** to complement compensation components. Such noncash incentives as contests, recognition programs, expense reimbursement, and benefits policies can encourage sales performance and attract sales talent. Luxury ocean cruises and trips to exotic locations are common contest prizes.

Noncash incentives are especially useful to accent employees' exemplary performance and to convey how highly the company values their contributions. Moreover, noncash incentives may work well to encourage such short-term efforts as new product line introductions or the establishment of new sales territories. Noncash incentives can be less expensive for an employer to provide than cash incentives, making them a feasible form of sales incentive. However, awarding employees too often with noncash incentives could potentially undermine the intended effects of accenting superior achievements. Presumably, noncash incentives derive value by distinguishing exemplary performers from others in creative ways.

Designing pay-for-knowledge programs

As indicated in Chapters 4 and 5, merit pay and incentive pay represent job-based approaches to compensating employees. In Chapter 6, we discussed that many companies recognize the importance of paying for knowledge. For this discussion, we use the terms *knowledge* and *skills* interchangeably, as the design features for both knowledge-based and skill-based pay structures are virtually the same. In their purest form, pay-for-knowledge programs reward employees for the acquisition of job-related knowledge (or skills, in the case of skill-based pay plans). In practice, companies are concerned with how well employees' performance improves as a result of their newly acquired knowledge. Our focus in this section is on the latter.

Ethics of Incentive Pay

Most short-term incentive awards are tied to the achievement of goals established . . . at the beginning of the plan year.[17] While goal setting in most businesses is more an art than a science, an appropriate ethical stance would be that once approved and announced, a goal is a goal unless extraordinary circumstances occurred during the course of the year which negatively impacted goal achievement. The ethical challenge is often related to the definition of "extraordinary." Some CEOs [chief executive officers] have gone to great lengths to convince their directors that events which would otherwise be considered routine were in fact "extraordinary" and not subject to management control in order that otherwise unearned management bonuses could be paid.

The human resources executive usually is responsible for the design and administration of top management incentive plans and often has input into the annual goal-setting process. In addition, the HR executive is enlisted in drafting (and sometimes presenting) the recommendations for the forthcoming year's goals and for justifying bonus targets that sometimes are not reflective of business conditions.

A common rationalization presented to the HR executive, when asked to bend the rules by drafting a supportive argument to the compensation committee, is management's fear that outstanding executives will leave if adequate bonuses are not paid. In some cases this occurs. In most cases this doesn't happen until several years of payouts have been skipped by the firm in question, while competitors have continued to award bonuses to their executives.

While goal setting in most businesses is more an art than a science, an appropriate ethical stance would be that once approved and announced, a goal is a goal unless extraordinary circumstances occurred during the course of the year which negatively impacted goal achievement.

Establishing skill blocks

Skill (knowledge) blocks are sets of skills (knowledge) necessary to perform a specific job (for example, typing skills versus analytical reasoning) or group of similar jobs (for example, junior accounting clerk, intermediate accounting clerk, and senior accounting clerk). Exhibit 9-8 contains an example of a knowledge block with which we are familiar—building market competitive compensation systems (Chapter 8).

The number of skill blocks included in a pay-for-knowledge structure can range from two to several. Current plans average about 10 skill blocks.[18] The appropriate number of blocks will vary according to the variety of jobs within a company. The development of skill blocks should occur with three considerations in mind.

First, before anything can be done, it is essential that the company develop job descriptions, which we discussed in Chapter 7. Job descriptions should be treated as blueprints for the creation of a pay-for-knowledge system. Well-crafted job descriptions should facilitate the identification of major skills, the required training programs to help employees acquire horizontal and vertical skills, and the development of accurate measures of performance.

Second, individual jobs should be organized into job families or groups of similar jobs such as clerical, technical, accounting. The information conveyed within a job description should enable the plan developers to identify skills that are common to all jobs in the family and skills that are unique for individual jobs in the family. On the basis of these groupings, all tasks necessary to perform the jobs in a job family should be listed to facilitate the identification of the skills necessary to perform the tasks.

1. Strategic analyses
   A. External market environment
      a. Industry profile
      b. Foreign demand
      c. Competition
      d. Long-term prospects
      e. Labor-market assessment
   B. Internal capabilities
      a. Financial condition
      b. Functional capabilities
      c. Human resource capabilities
2. Compensation surveys
   A. Using published compensation survey data
      a. Survey focus: Core or fringe compensation
      b. Sources of published compensation surveys
   B. Compensation surveys: Strategic considerations
      a. Defining relevant labor market
      b. Choosing benchmark jobs
   C. Compensation survey data: Summary, analysis, and interpretation
      a. Using the appropriate statistics to summarize survey data
         i. Central tendency
         ii. Variation
      b. Updating the survey data
      c. Statistical analysis

Third, skills should be grouped into blocks. There are no hard and fast rules compensation professionals can follow to determine skill blocks. A general guideline is that the blocked knowledge should be related to specific job tasks and duties. For example, in Exhibit 9-8, knowledge about the external environment and a company's internal capabilities—two distinct sets of knowledge—together form the foundation of strategic analyses.

Transition matters

A number of initial considerations arise when making a transition from using job-based pay exclusively to using pay-for-knowledge programs as well. These issues include assessment of skills, alignment of pay with the knowledge structure, and access to training.[19]

SKILLS ASSESSMENT The skills assessment issue centers on who should assess whether employees possess skills at levels that justify a pay raise, on what basis assessments should be made; and when assessments should be conducted. Gaining employee trust is critical during the transition period, since employees may view new systems as threats to job security. Therefore, some combination of peer and self-assessments as well as input from known "experts" such as supervisors may be essential. The important ingredients here are employee input and the expertise of supervisors and managers. In the case of knowledge assessment, paper-and-pencil tests are useful tools.

Having established who should conduct assessments, on what basis should assessments be made? During the transition, companies use conventional performance measures that reflect employees' proficiency of skill use, complemented by employees' self-assessments. The use of both types of data will likely increase an employee's understanding of the new system as well as build faith in it, particularly when the comparison of testimony and the more conventional performance measures converge.

A final assessment matter concerns timing. During transition phases, managers should assess employees' performance more frequently to keep employees informed of how well they are doing under the new system. In addition, more frequent assessments should reinforce the key aim of pay-for-knowledge—to encourage employees to learn more. The use of performance feedback is essential for this process.[20]

ALIGNING PAY WITH THE KNOWLEDGE STRUCTURE One of the most difficult tasks that managers face as they guide employees toward a pay-for-knowledge system is aligning pay with the knowledge structure. Upon implementation of pay-for-knowledge, employees' core compensation must reflect the knowledge or skills the company incorporates into its pay-for knowledge structure. If employees' actual earnings are more than the pay-for-knowledge system indicates, managers must develop a reasonable course of action for employees so that they can acquire skills that are commensurate with current pay. If employees are underpaid, the company must provide pay adjustments as quickly as possible. The length of time required to make these necessary adjustments will depend upon two factors—the number of employees and the extent to which these employees are underpaid. Obviously, with limited budgets, companies will require more-extended periods as either the number of underpaid employees or the pay deficit increases.

ACCESS TO TRAINING A final transition matter is access to training. Pay-for-knowledge systems make training necessary rather than optional for those employees who are motivated for self-improvement. Accordingly, companies that adopt pay-for-knowledge must ensure that all employees have equal access to the needed training for acquiring higher-level skills. They must do so not only to meet the intended aim of pay-for-knowledge programs—to reward employees for enhancing their skills—but also to address legal imperatives. Restricting access to training can lead to a violation of key laws (Chapter 3)—Title VII of the Civil Rights Act of 1964 and the Age Discrimination in Employment Act of 1967. Companies must also educate employees about what their training options are and how successful training will lead to increased pay and advancement opportunities within the company. In other words, employers should not assume that employees will necessarily recognize the opportunities that are available to them. Those opportunities must be clearly communicated. Written memos and informational meetings conducted by HR representatives are effective communication media.

Training and certification

Successful pay-for-knowledge programs depend upon a company's ability to develop and implement systematic training programs. For many of the reasons that we cited in

Chapter 1—intense domestic and global competition, rapid technological advancement, and educational deficits of new workforce entrants—progressive companies in the United States have adopted a continuous learning philosophy, which, like pay-for-knowledge, encourages employees to take responsibility for enhancing their skills and knowledge.[21] Clearly, training is a key component of continuous learning.

Because employees are required to constantly learn new skills, training becomes an ongoing process. Companies implementing pay-for-knowledge plans typically increase the amount of classroom and on-the-job training.[22] When training is well designed, employees should be able to learn the skills needed to increase their pay as well as the skills necessary to teach and coach other employees at lower skill levels. Accurate job descriptions will be useful in determining training needs and focusing training efforts.

Employers must make necessary training available to their employees so they can progress through the pay-for-knowledge system. A systematic method for ensuring adequate training coverage involves matching training programs with each skill block. Accessibility does not require that employers develop and deliver training themselves. Training that is developed and delivered by an agency that is not directly affiliated with the company—community college, vocational training institute, university, private consultant—can be just as accessible when the employer integrates the offering of these other sources with its pay-for-knowledge program.

IN-HOUSE OR OUTSOURCING TRAINING The following criteria should be used to determine whether to develop and deliver training within the workplace or to outsource:[23]

☆ **Expertise.** Specialized training topics require greater expertise, and more-generic topics require less expertise. Employers generally turn to in-house resources if they can draw on existing expertise. If in-house expertise is lacking, employers often seek an outside provider either to fill the need directly or to train individuals who become instructors. Employers usually rely on in-house expertise for employer- and product-specific training. Such training is governed by employer philosophies and procedures and is, therefore, not readily available in the external market.

☆ **Timeliness.** Employers often seek outside services if the in-house staff does not have adequate time to develop and deliver the program within the time frame requested. For example, ABC Corporation is replacing its IBM-compatible AT models with IBM-compatible computers with Pentium processors. The new machines use Microsoft Windows 95 as the operating system rather than Microsoft DOS. The Windows interface differs significantly from the DOS interface, and the Windows system possesses additional functions.

☆ **Size of the employee population to be trained.** Employers will typically rely on in-house resources for larger groups of employees. The major impetus behind this decision is economics. If there is a large demand for training, the chance increases that the program will be delivered more than once, resulting in economies of scale.

☆ **Sensitivity or proprietary nature of the subject matter.** Sensitive or proprietary training is defined as training used to gain a competitive advantage or training that gives access to proprietary, product, or strategic knowledge.

Employers rarely issue security clearances to outside resources to provide training of this nature. If the area of the training is sensitive or proprietary, the training is likely to be done in-house regardless of the other factors just discussed.

CERTIFICATION AND RECERTIFICATION **Certification** ensures that employees possess at least a minimally acceptable level of skill proficiency upon completion of a training unit. Quite simply, if employees do not possess an acceptable level or degree of skill proficiency, then the company wastes any skill-based compensation expenditure. Usually, supervisors and coworkers, who are presumably most familiar with the intricacies of the work with which they are involved, certify workers. Certification methods can include work samples, oral questioning, and written tests.

Recertification, under which employees periodically must demonstrate mastery of all the jobs they have learned or risk losing their pay rates, are necessary to maintain the workforce flexibility offered by a pay-for-knowledge plan.[24] The recertification process typically is handled by retesting employees, retraining employees, or requiring employees to occasionally perform jobs in which they will use previously acquired skills.

Pay structure variations

The principles of pay structure development just reviewed apply to most of the established pay structures in companies throughout the United States. Broadbanding and two-tier pay structures represent variations to those pay structure principles.

Broadbanding

DESCRIBING THE BROADBANDING CONCEPT AND ADVANTAGES Companies may choose **broadbanding** to consolidate existing pay grades and ranges into fewer, wider pay grades. Exhibit 9-9 illustrates a broadbanding structure and its relationship to traditional pay grades and ranges. Broadbanding represents the increasing organizational trend toward flatter, less hierarchical corporate structures that emphasize teamwork over individual contributions alone.[25] Some federal government agencies including

Broadbanding represents the increasing organizational trend toward flatter, less hierarchical corporate structures that emphasize teamwork over individual contributions alone.

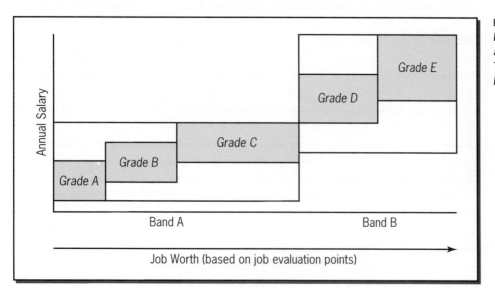

Exhibit 9-9
Broadbanding Structure and Its Relationship to Traditional Pay Grades and Ranges

the Navy, the General Accounting Office, and the Central Intelligence Agency began experimenting with the broadbanding concept in the 1980s to introduce greater flexibility to their pay structures. Some private sector companies began using broadbanding in the late 1980s for the same reason. General Electric Corporation's plastics business is a noteworthy adopter of broadbanding. Because broadbanding is relatively new, little research describes these structures or documents their effectiveness in establishing flatter organizational structures.

Broadbanding uses only a few, large salary ranges spanning levels within the organization previously covered by several pay grades. Thus, HR professionals place jobs that were separated by one or more pay grades in old pay structures into the same band under broadbanding systems. For example, condensing three consecutive grades into a single broadband eliminates the hierarchical differences among the jobs evident in the original, narrower pay grade configuration. Now, employees holding jobs in a single broadband have more-equal pay potential than under a multiple pay grade configuration. In addition, elimination of narrow bands broadens employees' job duties and responsibilities.

Some companies establish broadbands for distinct employee groups within the organizational hierarchy—upper management, middle management, professionals, staff. This approach reduces management layers dramatically, and it should promote quicker decisionmaking cycles. Other companies may create broadbands on the basis of job families—clerical, technical, administrative. Bands based on job families should give employees broader duties within their job classes. Still others may set broadbands according to functional areas, collapsing across job families. For example, a broadband may be established for all human resource specialists—training, compensation, recruitment, performance appraisal. These bands should encourage employees to expand their knowledge and skills in several HR functions.

Broadbanding shifts greater responsibility to supervisors and managers for administering each employee's compensation within the confines of the broadbands. Because broadbands include a wider range of jobs from prior narrowly defined pay grades, supervisors have greater latitude in setting employees' pay on the basis of the tasks and duties they perform. Under traditional pay grades, employees receive pay and pay increases based on a limited set of duties stated in their job descriptions.

LIMITATIONS OF BROADBANDING Notwithstanding the benefits of broadbanding, it does have some limitations. Broadbanding is not a cure-all for all compensation-related dysfunctions that exist within companies. For instance, broadbanding changes *how* compensation dollars are allocated but not *how much* is allocated. Managers often think that flatter organizational structures reduce costs. To the contrary, the use of broadbanding may lead to higher compensation expenses because managers have greater latitude in assigning pay to their employees. In fact, the federal government's limited experience showed that broadbanding structures were associated with more rapid increases in compensation costs than were traditional pay structures.[26]

Broadbanding also necessitates a tradeoff between the flexibility to reward employees for their unique contributions and a perception among employees that fewer promotional opportunities are available. This transition from multiple, narrowly defined pay grades to fewer broadbands reduces organizational hierarchies that support job promotions. Employers and employees alike need to rethink the idea of promotions as a positive step through the job hierarchy.

Two-tier pay structures

DESCRIBING THE TWO-TIER PAY SYSTEM CONCEPT AND ADVANTAGES **Two-tier pay structures** reward newly hired employees less than established employees on either a temporary or a permanent basis. Under a temporary basis, employees have the opportunity to progress from lower entry-level pay rates to the higher rates enjoyed by more-senior employees. Permanent two-tier systems reinforce the pay rate distinction by retaining separate pay scales: Lower-paying scales apply to newly hired employees, and current employees enjoy higher-paying scales. Although pay progresses within each scale, the maximum rates to which newly hired employees can progress are always lower than more-senior employees' pay scales. Exhibit 9-10 illustrates a typical two-tier wage structure.

Two-tier wage systems are most prevalent in unionized companies. Labor representatives have reluctantly agreed to two-tier wage plans as a cost control measure. In exchange for reduced compensation costs, companies have promised to limit layoffs. These plans represent a departure from unions' traditional stance of single base pay rates for all employees within job classifications. Approximately one out of every three collective bargaining agreements contained a two-tier wage provision between 1989 and 1995.[27]

Two-tier pay structures enable companies to reward long-service employees while keeping costs down by paying lower rates to newly hired employees who do not have an established performance record within the company. Usually, as senior employees terminate their employment—taking jobs elsewhere or retiring—they are replaced by workers who are compensated according to the lower-paying scale.

Two-tier pay structures enable companies to reward long-service employees while keeping costs down by paying lower rates to newly hired employees who do not have an established performance record within the company.

Exhibit 9-10
Two-Tier Wage Structure

The following pay rates apply to the 1998 calendar year. Employees hired on or after January 1, 1998 will be paid according to Schedule A below. Employees hired before January 1, 1998 will be paid according to Schedule B below.

SCHEDULE A

JOB CLASSIFICATION	HOURLY PAY RATE	COST-OF-LIVING ADJUSTMENT	TOTAL HOURLY PAY RATE
Shop floor laborers	$12.10	$1.36	$13.46
Assemblers	$14.05	$1.36	$15.41
Carpenters	$16.50	$1.36	$17.86
Plumbers	$16.90	$1.36	$18.26

SCHEDULE B

JOB CLASSIFICATION	HOURLY PAY RATE	COST-OF-LIVING ADJUSTMENT	TOTAL HOURLY PAY RATE
Shop floor laborers	$14.10	$1.36	$15.46
Assemblers	$16.05	$1.36	$17.41
Carpenters	$18.50	$1.36	$19.86
Plumbers	$18.90	$1.36	$20.26

LIMITATIONS OF TWO-TIER PAY STRUCTURES A potentially serious limitation of two-tier plans is that the lower pay scale applied to newly hired workers may restrict a company's ability to recruit and retain the most highly qualified individuals. Resentment can build among employees on the lower tier toward their counterparts on the upper tier, which may lead to lower-tier employees' refusal to perform work that extends in any way beyond their respective job descriptions. Such resentment may lead employees on the upper tier to scale back their willingness to take on additional work to the extent that they perceive that pay premiums are not large enough to compensate for extra duties. In addition, opponents of two-tier wage systems contend that pay differentials cause lower employee morale. Finally, conflict between the tiers may lead to excessive turnover. When high performers leave, the turnover is dysfunctional to the company and can have long-term implications for productivity and quality.

Summary

In this chapter, we reviewed the pay structure concept as well as the building blocks needed to establish pay structures. Compensation professionals develop pay structures for the various pay bases. Pay structure development generally entails linking the internal job structure with the external market's pricing structure for jobs, knowledge, or skills. Once developed, pay structures recognize individual differences in employee contributions, and these structures represent operational plans for implementing and administering pay programs.

Discussion questions

1. Respond to the following statement. "Pay grades limit a company's ability to achieve competitive advantage." Do you agree? Provide a rationale for your position.
2. Two employees perform the same job, and each received an exemplary performance rating. Is it fair to give one employee a smaller percentage merit increase because his pay falls within the third quartile, while giving a larger percentage merit increase to the other because his pay falls within the first quartile? Please explain your answer.
3. Describe some ethical dilemmas sales professionals may encounter. How can sales compensation programs be modified to minimize ethical dilemmas?
4. React to this statement: "Merit pay grids have the potential to undermine employee motivation." Please discuss your views.
5. Compression represents a serious dysfunction of pay structures. Discuss some of the major ramifications of compression. Also discuss how companies can minimize or avoid these ramifications.

Key terms

pay structure

pay grade

pay range

midpoint pay value

range spread

pay compression

green circle rate

red circle rate

compa-ratio

equity theory

common review date

common review period

employee's anniversary date

nonrecurring merit increase

compensation budget

salary-only plan

salary-plus-bonus plan

commission

salary-plus-commission plan

commission-plus-draw plan

draw

recoverable draw

nonrecoverable draw

commission-only plan

straight commission

graduated commission

multiple-tiered commission

noncash incentive

skill (knowledge) block

certification

recertification

broadbanding

two-tier pay structure

Endnotes

[1] The Bureau of National Affairs, Pay structures, in *BNA's Library on Compensation & Benefits on CD* [CD-ROM] (Washington, D.C.: The Bureau of National Affairs, 1995).

[2] D. W. Myers, *Compensation management* (Chicago: Commerce Clearing House, 1989).

[3] R. L. Heneman, *Merit pay: Linking pay increases to performance* (Reading, Mass.: Addison-Wesley, 1992).

[4] L. A. Krefting and T.A. Mahoney, Determining the size of a meaningful pay increase, *Industrial Relations* 16 (1977):83–93.

[5] Heneman, *Merit pay.*

[6] W. W. Rambo and J. N. Pinto, Employees' perceptions of pay increases, *Journal of Occupational Psychology* 62 (1989): 135–145.

[7] L. A. Krefting, J. M. Newman, and F. Krzystofiak, What is a meaningful pay increase? in D. B. Balkin and L. R. Gómez-Mejía, eds., *New perspectives on compensation* (Englewood Cliffs, N.J.: Prentice Hall, 1987), pp. 135–140.

[8] Heneman, *Merit pay.*

[9] Wyatt Company, *Salary management practices in the private sector* (Philadelphia: U.S. Advisory Committee on Federal Pay in co-operation with the American Compensation Association, 1987).

[10] C. L. Erickson, and A. C. Ichino, Lump-sum bonuses in union contracts, *Advances in Industrial and Labor Relations* 6 (1994): 183–218.

[11] U.S. Bureau of Labor Statistics, *Employment and earnings* (Washington, D.C.: U.S. Government Printing Office, January, 1995).

[12] U.S. Bureau of Labor Statistics, *CPI detailed report* (Washington, D.C.: U.S. Government Printing Office, April, 1995).

[13] J. F. Carey, *Complete guide to sales force compensation* (Homewood, Ill.: Business One Irwin, 1992).

[14] D. C. Kuhlman, Implementing business strategy through sales compensation, in W. Keenan Jr., ed., *Commissions, bonuses, and beyond* (Chicago: Probus Publishing, 1994), pp. 1–26.

[15] Myers, *Compensation management.*

[16] W. Keenan Jr. The case against commissions, in W. Keenan Jr., ed., *Commissions, bonuses, and beyond* (Chicago: Probus Publishing, 1994), pp. 257–270.

[17] Passage quoted from S. D. Rosen and H. A. Juris, Ethical issues in human resource man-

agement, pages 197–216 in G. R. Ferris, S. D. Rosen, and D. T. Barnum, eds., *Handbook of human resource management* (Cambridge, Mass.: Blackwell Publishers, 1995), p. 205.

[18] The Bureau of National Affairs, Skill-based pay, in *BNA's Library on Compensation & Benefits on CD* [CD-ROM] (Washington, D.C.: The Bureau of National Affairs, 1995).

[19] B. J. Dewey, Changing to skill-based pay: Disarming the transition landmines, *Compensation & Benefits Review* 26 (1994): 38–43.

[20] K. Karl, A. M. O'Leary-Kelly, and J. J. Martocchio, The impact of feedback and self-efficacy on performance in training, *Journal of Organizational Behavior* 14 (1993):379–394.

[21] J. Rosow, and R. Zager, *Training—The competitive edge* (San Francisco: Jossey-Bass, 1988).

[22] G. D. Jenkins Jr. and N. Gupta, The payoffs of paying for knowledge, *National Productivity Review* 4 (1985): 121–130.

[23] A. P. Carnevale and J. W. Johnston, *Training in America: Strategies for the nation* (Alexandria, Virg.: National Center on Education and the Economy and The American Society for Training and Development, 1989).

[24] G. D. Jenkins Jr., G. E. Ledford Jr., N. Gupta, and D. H. Doty, *Skill-based pay* (Scottsdale, Ariz.: American Compensation Association, 1992).

[25] H. H. Risher and R. J. Butler, Salary banding: An alternative salary-management concept, *ACA Journal* 2 (Winter 1993/94): 48–57.

[26] B. W. Schay, K. C. Simons, E. Guerra, and J. Caldwell, *Broad-banding in the federal government—Technical report* (Washington, D.C.: U.S. Office of Personnel Management, 1992).

[27] The Bureau of National Affairs (1995). *Collective bargaining negotiations and contracts,* No. 1302 (Washington, D.C.: The Bureau of National Affairs, 1995), p. 93:1.

CHAPTER

TEN

Legally required benefits

CHAPTER OUTLINE

In this chapter, you will learn about

1. Which employee benefits are legally required
2. The Social Security Act of 1935 and its mandated protection programs—unemployment insurance, benefits for dependents, and Medicare
3. Compulsory state disability laws (workers' compensation)
4. The Family and Medical Leave Act of 1993
5. Some of the implications for strategic compensation and possible employer approaches to managing legally required benefits

The U.S. government established programs to protect individuals from catastrophic events such as disability and unemployment. Legally required benefits are protection programs that attempt to promote worker safety and health, maintain family income streams, and assist families in crisis. The cost of legally required benefits to employers is quite high. In 1994, employers spent an annual average of $3,079 for each full-time nonunion employee and $4,784 for each full-time employee who is a member of a union.[1] Human resource staffs and compensation professionals in particular must follow a variety of laws as they develop and implement programs.

Historically, legally required benefits provided a form of social insurance.[2] Prompted largely by the rapid growth of industrialization in the United States during the early part of the twentieth century and the Great Depression of the 1930s, social insurance programs were initially designed to minimize the possibility that individuals who became severely injured while working or unemployed would become destitute. In addition, social insurance programs aimed to stabilize the well-being of dependent family members of injured or unemployed individuals. Further, early social insurance programs were designed to enable retirees to maintain subsistence income levels. These intents of legally required benefits remain intact today.

Legally required benefits may indirectly promote competitive advantage for all companies by enabling unemployed individuals, disabled employees, and dependent family members of deceased or disabled employees to participate in the economy as consumers of products and services.

Since then, legally required benefits apply to virtually all U.S. companies, and they "level the playing field," so to speak. It is unlikely that these programs will *directly* lead to a competitive advantage for one company over another. However, legally required benefits may *indirectly* promote competitive advantage for all companies by enabling unemployed individuals, disabled employees, and dependent family members of deceased or disabled employees to participate in the economy as consumers of products and services. As we discussed in Chapter 3, the government has a vested interest in promoting a vigorous economy. A vigorous economy is one that exhibits regular buying and selling such that the demand for goods and services does not substantially outpace or fall below the supply of those goods and services. Clearly, the participation of individuals as consumers of the products and services sold in the marketplace is key to maintaining a vigorous economy. In this and the next chapter, it will become evident that many elements of fringe compensation serve this end.

Components of legally required benefits

The key legally required benefits are mandated by the following laws—the *Social Security Act of 1935,* various state workers' compensation laws, and the *Family and Medical Leave Act of 1993.* All provide protection programs to employees and their dependents.

Social Security Act of 1935

HISTORICAL BACKGROUND Income discontinuity caused by the Great Depression led to the Social Security Act as a means to protect families from financial devastation in the event of unemployment. The Great Depression of the 1930s was a time during which scores of businesses failed and masses of people became chronically unemployed. During this period, employers shifted their focus from maximizing profits to simply staying in business. Overall, ensuring the financial solvency of employees during periods of temporary unemployment and after work-related injuries promoted the well-being of the economy and contributed to some companies' ability to remain in business. Specifically, these subsistence payments contributed to the viability of the economy by providing temporarily unemployed or injured individuals with the means to contribute to economic activity by making purchases that result in demand for products and services.

Income discontinuity caused by the Great Depression led to the Social Security Act as a means to protect families from financial devastation in the event of unemployment. The Great Depression of the 1930s was a time during which scores of businesses failed and masses of people became chronically unemployed.

The **Social Security Act of 1935** also addresses retirement income and the health and welfare of employees and their families. Most employees could not afford to meet their financial obligations (for example, housing expenses and food) on a daily basis. Clearly, then, most employees could not afford to retire because they were unable to save sufficient funds to support themselves in retirement. Further, employees' poor financial situations left them unable to afford medical treatment for themselves and their families.

Four programs within the act aim to relieve some of the consequences of these social problems. They are

- ✯ Unemployment insurance

- ✯ Retirement insurance

- ✯ Benefits for dependents

- ✯ Disability benefits

- ✯ Medicare

Each of those programs will be reviewed in turn.

UNEMPLOYMENT INSURANCE The Social Security Act founded a national federal-state unemployment insurance program for individuals who become unemployed through no fault of their own. Each state administers its own program and develops guidelines within parameters set by the federal government. States pay into a central unemployment tax fund administered by the federal government. The federal government invests these payments, and it disburses funds to states as needed.[3] The unemployment insurance program applies to virtually all employees in the United States with the exception of most agricultural and domestic workers (for example, housekeepers).

Individuals must meet several criteria in order to qualify for unemployment benefits. Unemployment itself does not necessarily qualify an individual for these benefits, although criteria vary somewhat by state. Individuals applying for unemployment insurance benefits must have been employed for a minimum period of time. This **base period** tends to be the first four of the last five completed calendar quarters immediately preceding the individual's benefits year. In addition, all states require sufficient previous earnings, typically $1,000 during the last four quarter periods combined. Further, individuals eligible for unemployment insurance benefits must meet several other criteria, which are listed in Exhibit 10-1.

Individuals who meet the eligibility criteria receive weekly benefits. Because the federal government places no limits on a maximum allowable amount, the benefits amount varies widely from state to state. Most states calculate the weekly benefits as a specified fraction of an employee's average wages during the highest calendar quarter of the base period.

The majority of states pay regular unemployment benefits for a maximum of 26 weeks. A 1970 amendment to this act established a permanent program of extended unemployment benefits, usually for an additional 13 weeks. The extended program in any state is triggered when the state's unemployment exceeds a predetermined level. Besides this statutory requirement for extended benefits is another type of program that offers extended unemployment insurance benefits. This extended program is known as a **supplemental unemployment benefit (SUB),** and it is most common in industries in which employment conditions are cyclical such as in the steel industry. Virtually all SUB benefits are part of collective bargaining agreements. Exhibit 10-2 illustrates the unemployment insurance benefits for selected states in 1995.

Unemployment insurance benefits are financed by federal and state taxes levied on employers under the **Federal Unemployment Tax Act (FUTA).** Employee tax contributions are automatically deducted from gross pay and listed on the employee's pay stub. In general, state and local governments as well as nonprofit companies are exempt from FUTA. Employer contributions amount to 6.2 percent of the first $7,000 earned by each employee ($434). The 6.2 percent is divided between state and federal agencies; 5.4 percent is disbursed to state unemployment commissions ($378), and the remaining 0.8 percent covers administrative costs at the federal level ($56).

Although this 6.2 percent figure represents the typical tax burden, each company pays an actual rate depending upon its prior experience with unemployment. Accordingly, a company that lays off a large percentage of employees will have a higher tax rate than a company that lays off none or relatively few of its employees. This **experience rating** system implies that a company can manage its unemployment

---

Exhibit 10-1
Eligibility Criteria for Unemployment Insurance Benefits

To be eligible for unemployment insurance benefits, an individual must:

1. Not have left a job voluntarily
2. Be able and available for work
3. Be actively seeking work
4. Not have refused an offer of suitable employment
5. Not be unemployed because of a labor dispute (exception in a few states)
6. Not have had employment terminated because of gross violations of conduct within the workplace

---

Exhibit 10-2
Unemployment Benefit Amounts for Selected States

STATE	WEEKLY BENEFIT AMOUNT (WBA)	MAXIMUM TOTAL BENEFIT INCLUDING EXTENDED BENEFITS	MINIMUM BASE PERIOD AND QUALIFYING WAGES	WAITING PERIOD
Alabama	$22 min., $180 max. effective 7/3/94	Lesser of 26 times WBA or $1/3$ base period wages	$1 1/2$ times high-quarter wages; at least $774.02	None
Alaska	$44 min., $212 max., plus $24 for each dependent, up to $72 per week, to max. of $284	16 to 26 weeks, depending on earnings ratio	$1,000 in 2 quarters of base period; at least $100 in other than high quarter	One week
California	$40 min., $230 max.	26 times WBA, up to $1/2$ base period wages	$1,300 in high quarter, or $900 in high quarter and total base period wages of $1 1/4$ times high-quarter wages	One week
Delaware	$20 min., $265 max.	Lesser of 26 times WBA or $1/2$ base period wages	36 times WBA; reduced benefits payable with base period wages of at least $720 if difference between base period wages and 36 times WBA is no more than $180	None
Florida	$10 min., $250 max.	$1/2$ of weeks worked in base period	20 times claimant's average weekly wages (at least $20)	One week
Hawaii	$5 min., $345 max., for claims effective on or after 1/1/95	26 times WBA	26 times WBA; wages in 2 quarters of base period	One week
Illinois	$51 min.; maximums: $235 no dependents; $278 nonworking spouse; $311 one or more dependents	Lesser of 26 times WBA or total wages paid during base period	$1,600; $440 in other than high quarter	One week
Kansas	$63 min., $255 max. effective 7/1/94	Lesser of 26 times WBA or $1/3$ base period wages	30 times WBA; wages in more than 1 quarter	One week
Louisiana	$10 min., $181 max.	Lesser of 26 times WBA or 27 percent base period wages	$1,200; $1 1/2$ times high-quarter wages	One week
Minnesota	$38 min., $304 max., effective 7/3/94	Lesser of 26 times WBA or 70 percent of credit weeks	1.25 times high-quarter wages; high-quarter wages of $1,000; wages in 15 calendar weeks and 2 calendar quarters	One week

(continued p.258)

Exhibit 10-2
Unemployment Benefit Amounts for Selected States (continued)

STATE	WEEKLY BENEFIT AMOUNT (WBA)	MAXIMUM TOTAL BENEFIT INCLUDING EXTENDED BENEFITS	MINIMUM BASE PERIOD AND QUALIFYING WAGES	WAITING PERIOD
Montana	$54 min., $223 max., effective 7/3/94	Duration depends on ratio of total base period wages to high quarter wages	7 percent of average annual wage ($1,271, effective 7/1/92	One week
New Mexico	$39 min., $197 max., effective for 1994	Lesser of 26 times WBA or 60 percent base period wages	$1\,1/4$ times high-quarter wages	One week
New York	$40 min., $300 max., effective 2/4/92	26 times WBA	Covered employment for 20 weeks of previous 52 with weekly wages of at least $80	One week
Oregon	$66 min., $285 max., effective 7/5/93	Lesser of 26 times WBA or $1/3$ base period wages	$1,000 and 18 weeks of work	One week
South Carolina	$20 min., $203 max., effective 7/1/93	Lesser of 26 times WBA or $1/3$ base period wages	$1\,1/2$ times high-quarter wages; $540 in high quarter and total base period wages of at least $900	One week
Tennessee	$30 min., $200 max., effective 7/4/94	26 times WBA or $1/4$ of base period wages	40 times WBA, with lesser of 6 times WBA or $900 in 3 quarters outside high quarter	One week
Texas	$41 min., $245 max., effective 10/1/93 through 9/30/94	Lesser of 26 times WBA or 27 percent of base period wages	37 times WBA; wage credits in 2 quarters	One week

tax burden. In practice, the tax rate on companies varies between a small fraction of a percentage to as high as 10 percent.

RETIREMENT INSURANCE The retirement insurance program contains a number of benefits that were amended to the act after its enactment in 1935. Besides providing retirement income, the amendments include survivors' insurance (1939) and disability insurance (1965). Virtually all U.S. workers are eligible for protections under the Social Security Act, except for three exempt classes. First, civilian employees of the federal government and railroad employees who were hired before 1984 are exempt from the retirement program; however, these individuals are not exempt from the Medicare program, which we discuss later in this chapter. Second, employees of state and local governments who are already covered under other retirement plans are exempt from Social Security retirement contributions. Third, American citizens working overseas for foreign affiliates of U.S. employers who own less than 10 percent of interest in the foreign affiliate are exempt from the retirement program.

Individuals may receive various benefit levels upon retirement, or under survivors' and disability programs, based on how much credit they have earned through eligible payroll contributions. They earn credit based on **quarters of coverage.** For example, in 1995, an employee earns credit for one quarter of coverage for each $630 dollars in annual earnings on which Social Security taxes are paid.[4] This figure is based on the average total wages of all workers as determined by the Social Security Administration (SSA). Of course, employees may earn up to four quarters of coverage credit each. Individuals become **fully insured** when they earn credit for 40 quarters of coverage, or 10 years of employment, and remain fully insured for life. Other eligibility criteria concerning quarters of coverage are based on more-complex formulas.[5]

Once an individual has become fully insured, he or she must meet additional requirements before receiving benefits under the particular programs. Under the retirement program, fully insured individuals may choose to receive benefits as early as age 62, though their benefit amounts will be permanently reduced if they begin receiving them before age 65. Individuals who are 65 years of age or older will receive their full benefits. In the year 2003, the minimum age for full benefits will rise slowly from age 65 to age 67 in the year 2027. Exhibit 10-3 displays examples of the number of retirees and average monthly retirement benefits for selected years between 1970 and 1993. The monthly retirement benefits are stated in current dollar amounts as well as in constant dollar amounts with 1993 as the base year. The number of retiree beneficiaries has risen steadily since 1970 and the average monthly benefits based on current and constant dollars have increased. However, the actual increase in purchasing power has increased more slowly, as reflected in the constant dollar figures. For example, although the average monthly benefits based on constant dollars increased by 471 percent between 1970 and 1993, the actual purchasing power of the retirement benefits increased much less, by only 56 percent.[6]

BENEFITS FOR DEPENDENTS Employees' dependents may also earn Social Security benefits if the employees are currently insured or disability insured. **Currently insured** status determines whether survivors will be eligible if a worker dies. Currently

Exhibit 10-3
Social Security Retirement Benefits in Current-Payment Status (end of year), 1970 to 1993

TYPE OF BENEFICIARY	1970	1980	1985	1987	1988	1989	1990	1991	1992	1993
Retired workers (thousands)	13,349	19,582	22,432	23,440	23,858	24,327	24,838	25,289	25,758	26,104
Average monthly benefit, current dollars										
Retired worker	118	341	479	513	537	567	603	629	653	674
Retired worker and wife	199	567	814	873	914	966	1,027	1,072	1,111	1,145
Average monthly benefit, constant (1993) dollars										
Retired worker	432	576	639	648	650	656	657	665	671	674
Retired worker and wife	729	958	1,086	1,103	1,106	1,117	1,119	1,133	1,142	1,145

Source: U.S. Social Security Administration, *Annual Statistical Supplement* to the *Social Security Bulletin* and unpublished data.

insured status is not as strict as fully insured status: An employee need only have worked and contributed to Social Security during at least six quarters of coverage out of the 13-quarter period ending with the quarter in which death occurs. Meeting currently insured status entitles a beneficiary of a deceased employee to survivors' benefits only.

The SSA calculates survivors' benefits on the basis of the insureds' employment status and the survivors' relationship to the deceased. Dependent, unmarried children of the deceased and a spouse of the deceased who is caring for a child or children may receive survivors' benefits if the deceased worker was either fully insured or currently insured. A widow or widower at least age 60 or parents at least age 62 who were dependent on the deceased employee are entitled to survivors' benefits if the deceased worker was fully insured. The average monthly benefit in 1993 was $173 for children of disabled workers to $630 for widows and widowers.[7]

DISABILITY BENEFITS To receive disability benefits, an individual must meet the requirements of **disability insured** status. Disability insured status requires that a worker be fully insured and have a minimum amount of work under Social Security

REFLECTIONS

Inadequacy of Social Security Funding

Consider the following: The funding for Social Security programs in the future may be inadequate. In 1992, a report on the financial status of Social Security indicated that the financing for the retirement and survivors' benefits programs is sufficient to make timely payments of benefits roughly through the year 2037.[8] Creators of the 1935 act were unaware of demographic trends. Specifically, the baby boom generation, or baby boomers, born roughly between 1942 and 1964, represents a swell in the American population. By the year 2010, the baby boom generation will approach retirement, and the number of beneficiaries will probably exceed the number of individuals making contributions to fund these programs. The U.S. Census Bureau predicts that the elderly population—individuals aged 65 and over—will increase from about 32 million in 1992 (12.6 percent of the population) to about 70 million (20.7 percent of the population) by 2030 and will reach 79 million (20.6 percent of the population) by 2050.[9]

Apart from the baby boom phenomenon, other factors may make the funding base for Social Security programs inadequate. For example, recent advances in medical practice have extended peoples' life spans. The U.S. Census Bureau predicts that the very old—individuals aged 85, which is the age group with the greatest need for health and social services—will increase from approximately 3.3 million in 1992 to 8.4 million in 2030 and will reach 18 million in 2050.[10] In the case of survivors' benefits and retirement benefits, the longer the beneficiary survives, the greater the strain on the system.

Some analysts are alarmed by those predictions, which paint a bleak future for many Social Security programs. Others believe that the Social Security programs will meet their obligations. For example, former Social Security Commissioner Robert Ball argues that, as with all large systems, problems will arise, but the federal government will take whatever action is needed to ensure the well-being of U.S. citizens.[11]

- ✯ All premiums currently due for enrollees included in the formal payment program will be paid.

- ✯ Premium liability will be assumed by the organization through the month in which it notifies the SSA that it is dropping an individual from its rolls, or through the month of death, whichever occurs first.

Anyone eligible for the Medicare hospital insurance plan Part A is automatically enrolled for supplementary Part B medical insurance. An individual who already is receiving monthly Social Security or railroad retirement benefits is considered to have enrolled for Part B insurance the month before the month he or she became entitled to hospital insurance. Those over age 65 not eligible for Social Security benefits are considered to have enrolled for Part B insurance in the month they file an application for Part A. A Social Security beneficiary can decline medical insurance coverage.

In general, the Medicare voluntary medical insurance plan pays for the following physicians' bills:

- ✯ Diagnosis, therapy, and surgery

- ✯ Consultation during home, office, and institutional calls

- ✯ Medical services and supplies ordinarily furnished in a doctor's office, such as services of an office nurse

- ✯ Medications that cannot be self-administered

Part B also covers out-patient hospital services, including diagnosis and treatment in an emergency room or out-patient clinic, other out-patient services such as surgery, physical therapy, and speech pathology, and those furnished in a comprehensive outside rehabilitation facility. Moreover, Part B provides coverage for home health services for an unlimited number of medically necessary visits as stipulated by a doctor.

Part B Medicare does not cover the following services and items:

- ✯ Eye examinations to determine need for eyeglasses or the eyeglasses themselves

- ✯ Cost of hearing aids or fitting expenses

- ✯ Injuries covered by workers' compensation law

State compulsory disability laws (workers' compensation)

HISTORICAL BACKGROUND Workers' compensation insurance came into existence during the early decades of the twentieth century, when industrial accidents were very common and workers suffered from occupational illnesses at alarming rates.[14] The first constitutionally acceptable workers' compensation law was enacted in 1911. By 1920, all but six states had instituted workers' compensation laws.[15] State **workers' compensation laws** are based on the principle of liability without fault.[16] That is, an employer is absolutely liable for providing benefits to employees that result from occupational disabilities or injuries regardless of fault.[17] Another key principle of workers' compensation laws is that employers should assume costs of occupational injuries and accidents. Presumably, these expenses represent costs of production that employers are able to recoup through setting higher prices.

Workers' compensation insurance programs, run by states individually, are designed to cover expenses incurred in employees' work-related accidents. Maritime workers within U.S. borders and federal civilian employees are covered by their own

Workers' compensation insurance came into existence during the early decades of the twentieth century, when industrial accidents were very common and workers suffered from occupational illnesses at alarming rates.

workers' compensation programs. The maritime workers' compensation program is mandated by the **Longshore and Harborworkers' Compensation Act,** and federal civilian employees receive workers' compensation protection under the **Federal Employees' Compensation Act.** Thus, workers' compensation laws cover virtually all employees in the United States, except for domestic workers, some agricultural workers, and small businesses with fewer than one dozen regular employees.[18]

WORKERS' COMPENSATION OBJECTIVES AND OBLIGATIONS TO THE PUBLIC Six basic objectives underlie workers' compensation laws:[19]

☆ Provide sure, prompt, and reasonable income and medical benefits to work-accident victims, or income benefits to their dependents, regardless of fault.

☆ Provide a single remedy and reduce court delays, costs, and workloads arising out of personal injury litigation.

☆ Relieve public and private charities of financial drains.

☆ Eliminate payment of fees to lawyers and witnesses as well as time-consuming trials and appeals.

☆ Encourage maximum employer interest in safety and rehabilitation through appropriate experience-rating mechanisms.

☆ Promote frank study of causes of accidents (rather than concealment of fault)—reducing preventable accidents and human suffering.

Employers must fund workers' compensation programs according to state guidelines. Participation in workers' compensation programs is compulsive in 47 states and elective in the remaining three states (New Jersey, South Carolina, and Texas). In general, these states require that employers subscribe to workers' compensation insurance through private carriers or, in some instances, through state funds. Self-insurance, another funding option allowed in the majority of states, requires companies to deposit a surety bond, enabling them to pay their own workers' claims directly.[20] Many companies select self-insurance because it gives employers a greater discretion in administering their own risks. Nevertheless, self-insured companies must pay their workers the same benefits as those paid by state funds or private insurance carriers.

The National Commission on State Workmen's Compensation Laws specified six primary obligations of state workers' compensation programs. This commission has established these obligations in order to ensure prompt and just remedy for workers injured on the job.[21] Exhibit 10-5 lists these obligations.

CLAIMS UNDER WORKERS' COMPENSATION PROGRAMS Employees can incur three kinds of workers' compensation claims. The first, **injury claims,** are usually defined as claims for disabilities that have resulted from accidents such as falls, injuries from equipment use, or physical strains from heavy lifting. Employees who work long hours at computer keyboards or assembly lines, performing the same task over and over again, frequently complain of numbness in the fingers and neck as well as severe wrist pain. This type of injury is known as repetitive strain injury. A 1992 Bureau of Labor Statistics survey indicates that repetitive strain injuries represent 62 percent of all occupational injuries.

The second kind of claim, **occupational disease claims,** results from disabilities caused by ailments associated with particular industrial trades or processes. For example, black lung, a chronic respiratory disease, is a common ailment among coal

1. Take initiative in administering the law.

2. Continually review performance of the program and be willing to change procedures and to request the state legislature to make needed amendments.

3. Advise workers of their rights and obligations and assure that they receive the benefits to which they are entitled.

4. Apprise employers and insurance carriers of their rights and obligations; inform other parties in the delivery system such as health care providers of their obligations and privileges.

5. Assist in voluntary and informal resolution of disputes that are consistent with law.

6. Adjudicate claims that cannot be resolved voluntarily.

Source: J. V. Nackley, *Primer on workers' compensation* (Washington, D.C.: The Bureau of National Affairs, 1987).

miners. In older office buildings, lung disease from prolonged exposure to asbestos is another kind of ailment. In general, the following occupational diseases are covered under workers' compensation programs:

☆ Pneumoconioses, which are associated with exposure to dusts

☆ Silicosis from exposure to silica

☆ Asbestos poisoning

☆ Radiation illness

The third kind, **death claims,** asks for compensation for deaths that occur in the course of employment or that are caused by compensable injuries or occupational diseases. The particular injuries and illnesses covered by workers' compensation programs vary by state.

Workers file claims to the state commission charged with administering the workers' compensation program. The names of these agencies vary by state. Examples include bureaus of workers' compensation and industrial accident boards. Typically, one state agency oversees the administration of the program and disburses benefits to the individuals whose claims have been deemed meritorious. Another agency within the state, such as the board of workers' compensation appeal, resolves conflicts that may arise, such as claim denials with which claimants are dissatisfied.

Depending upon the claim, workers' compensation laws specify four kinds of benefits. The first, *medical benefits,* are provided without regard to the amount or time over which the benefits will be paid. The second, *disability income,* compensates individuals whose work-related accident or illness has at least partially limited their ability to perform the regular duties of their jobs. The amount of disability income varies by state; the norm is two-thirds of the employees' average weekly wage for a predetermined period prior to the incident leading to disability. One exception is Michigan, where the weekly disability payment is calculated as 80 percent of spendable earnings.

Third, *death benefits* are awarded in two forms—burial allowances and survivors' benefits. Burial allowances reflect a fixed amount, varying by state. In 1995, the maximum burial allowance ranged from $1,400 in Montana to $7,500 in Minnesota.[22] Survivors' benefits are paid to deceased employees' spouses and to any dependent children. The amounts, based on different criteria vary widely by state. For example, assuming no dependent children, the minimum allowable weekly payment to a spouse living in Florida is $20, and to a spouse living in Oregon it is $326.32.

The fourth kind of benefit, **rehabilitative services,** covers physical and vocational rehabilitation. Claims for this benefit must usually be made within six months to two years of the accident. For instance, in Kansas, the rehabilitative benefits require the employer to pay reasonable board, lodging, and travel up to $3,500 for a 36-week period and may require the employer to pay up to $2,000 more, if necessary.[23]

RECENT TRENDS IN WORKERS' COMPENSATION In recent years, workers' compensation claims have risen dramatically in terms of both numbers and amounts of claims. The increase in prevalence of repetitive strain injuries resulting from the use of keyboards has contributed to this trend. In 1980, $13.6 billion was paid in workers' compensation claims.[24] In 1992, workers' compensation cost nearly 25 per cent of all legally-required benefits for companies in the private sector, and 20 per cent for state and local government institutions.[25] Exhibit 10-6 illustrates total premiums paid into workers' compensation programs and the total annual benefits paid for selected years between 1980 and 1993 by type of claim. Disability benefits represented the greatest amount of paid workers' compensation claims for each year listed in Exhibit 10-6. Survivor benefits represented the least amount.

Exhibit 10-6
Workers' Compensation Premiums and Benefits Paid, 1980 to 1993 (in billions of dollars)

ITEM	1980	1984	1985	1986	1987	1988	1989	1990	1991	1992	1993
Workers covered (mil.)	79	82	84	86	88	91	94	95	94	95	96
Premium amounts paid	22.3	25.1	29.2	34.0	38.1	43.3	48.0	53.1	55.2	55.5	57.3
Private carriers	15.7	16.6	19.5	22.8	25.4	28.5	31.9	35.1	35.7	32.8	33.6
State funds	3.0	3.0	3.5	4.5	5.3	6.7	7.2	8.0	8.7	9.6	10.9
Federal programs	1.1	1.6	1.7	1.8	1.8	1.9	2.0	2.2	2.1	2.2	2.3
Self-insurers	2.4	3.9	4.5	4.9	5.5	6.2	6.9	7.9	8.7	10.4	10.6
Annual benefits paid	13.6	19.7	22.2	24.6	27.3	30.7	34.3	38.2	42.2	44.7	42.9
By private carriers	7.0	10.6	12.3	13.8	15.5	17.5	19.9	22.2	24.5	24.0	21.8
From State funds	4.3	5.4	5.7	6.2	6.8	7.5	8.0	8.7	9.7	11.0	11.3
Employers' self-insurance	2.3	3.7	4.1	4.5	5.1	5.7	6.4	7.4	7.9	9.6	9.7
Type of benefit:											
Medical/hospital-ization	3.9	6.4	7.5	8.6	9.9	11.5	13.4	15.2	16.8	18.3	17.5
Compensation payments	9.7	13.3	14.7	16.0	17.4	19.2	20.9	23.1	25.3	26.4	25.4
Disability	8.4	11.7	13.1	14.3	15.8	17.6	19.2	21.2	23.3	24.4	23.5
Survivor	1.3	1.6	1.7	1.6	1.6	1.6	1.7	1.8	2.0	2.0	2.0

Source: U.S. Social Security Administration, *Annual Statistical Supplement* to the *Social Security Bulletin.*

Family and Medical Leave Act of 1993

The Family and Medical Leave Act (FMLA) of 1993 aims to provide employees with job protection in cases of family or medical emergency. The basic thrust of the act is guaranteed leave, and a key element of that guarantee is the right of the employee to return either to the position he or she left when the leave began or to an equivalent position with the same benefits, pay, and other terms and conditions of employment. The passage of the FMLA reflects growing recognition that many employees' parents are becoming elderly, rendering them susceptible to a serious illness or medical condition. These elderly parents will likely require frequent (if not constant) attention for an extended period while ill, which places a burden on their adult children.

The passage of the FMLA also recognizes the increasing prevalence of two-income families and the changing roles of men regarding child care. Moreover, increasingly, both partners in a marriage work full time and share the family responsibilities including child rearing. The number of families with two earners increased from 12,990,000 in 1980 to 16,349,000 in 1993, representing a 25.8 percent increase.[26] Much like elderly parents, children can become seriously ill, requiring parents' attention. Also, the FMLA enables fathers to take a "paternity" leave to care for their newborn babies. Until the passage of the FMLA, men had not had comparable protection that women receive under the Pregnancy Discrimination Act (Chapter 3).

Title I of the FMLA states that

> An eligible employee is entitled to 12 unpaid work weeks of leave during any 12-month period for three reasons: because of the birth or placement for adoption or foster care of a child; because of the serious health condition of a spouse, child, or parent; or because of the employee's own serious health condition. Leave may be taken for birth or placement of a child only within 12 months of that birth or placement.

> Family leave provisions apply equally to male and female employees: "A father, as well as a mother, can take family leave because of the birth or serious health condition of his child; a son as well as a daughter is eligible for leave to care for a parent."

The minimum criteria for eligibility under this act include the following: Eligible workers must be employed by a private employer or by a civilian unit of the federal government. Also, eligible workers must have been employed for at least 12 months by a given employer. Finally, eligible workers must have provided at least 1,250 hours of service during the 12 months prior to making a request for a leave. Employees who do not meet these criteria are excluded, as are those who work for an employer with fewer than 50 employees within a 75-mile radius of the employee's home.

Employers may require employees to use paid personal, sick, or vacation leave first as part of the 12-week period. If an employee's paid leave falls short of the 12-week mandated period, then the employer must provide further leave, unpaid, to total 12 weeks. While on leave, employees retain all previously earned seniority or employment benefits, though employees do not have the right to add such benefits while on leave. Further, while on leave, employees are entitled to receive health insurance benefits. Finally, employees may be entitled to receive health benefits if they do not return from leave because of a serious health condition or some other factor beyond their control.

Human resource professionals along with department managers should develop proactive plans that will enable companies to effectively manage work loads of employees who take leave. One approach is to cross-train workers, who will then have the knowledge and skills to cover vacant jobs while their coworkers are on leave. Pay-

The basic thrust of the act is guaranteed leave, and a key element of that guarantee is the right of the employee to return either to the position he or she left when the leave began or to an equivalent position with the same benefits, pay, and other terms and conditions of employment.

for-knowledge programs (Chapter 6) lend themselves well to enabling employers to meet this objective, particularly when vacant jobs require company-specific knowledge, as in the case of customer service representatives, or highly specialized skills, as in the case of quality assurance inspectors. Alternatively, companies can staff temporarily vacant jobs with temporary workers. This approach is reasonable for jobs that do not require company-specific knowledge, as in the case of many clerical jobs such as filing clerks and word processor operators.

The implications of legally required benefits for strategic compensation

Fringe compensation is unlike most bases for core compensation—merit, pay-for-knowledge, incentives. Under those core programs, the amount of compensation employees receive varies with their level of contribution to the company. Instead, fringe benefits tend to emphasize social adequacy. Under the principle of social adequacy, benefits are designed to provide subsistence income to all beneficiaries regardless of their performance in the workplace.[27] Thus, although humanitarian, legally required benefits do not *directly* meet the imperatives of competitive strategy. However, legally required benefits may contribute *indirectly* to competitive advantage by enabling individuals to remain as participants in the economy.

Nevertheless, legally required benefits may be a hindrance to companies in the short term because these offerings require substantial employee expenditures such as contributions mandated by the Social Security Act and various state workers' compensation laws. Without these mandated expenditures on compensation, companies could choose to invest those funds in direct compensation programs designed to boost productivity and product or service quality. Alternatively, companies could choose investments in research and development activities essential for product differentiation. Finally, for companies pursuing lowest-cost strategies, management may simply choose to place the funds in reserve, representing a reduction in the overall cost to conceive, develop, and deliver a product or service.

How can HR managers and other business professionals minimize the cost burden associated with legally required benefits? Let's consider this issue for both workers' compensation and unemployment insurance benefits. In the case of workers' compensation, employers can respond in two ways. The first response is to reduce the likelihood of workers' compensation claims. The implementation of workplace safety programs is one strategy for reducing workers' compensation claims. Effective safety programs include teaching employees and supervisors safest work procedures and safety awareness. Another strategy for reducing workers' compensation claims is the use of health promotion programs that include inspections of the workplace to identify health risks such as high levels of exposure to toxic substances and then eliminating those risks.

The second employer response is to integrate workers' compensation benefits into the rest of the benefits program. Because of the rampant cost increases associated with workers' compensation, several state legislatures have considered integrating employer-sponsored medical insurance and workers' compensation programs. Specifically, this "twenty-four-hour" coverage would roll the medical component of workers' compensation into traditional employer-provided health insurance. Some

FMLA May Create Cost Burden

Earlier, we discussed that the FMLA was passed to enable employees to take time off from work while meeting family and medical needs. Perhaps the hottest issue of debate preceding the passage of the act centered on its possible negative effects on companies' ability to compete. Opponents argued that granting 12 weeks unpaid leave while maintaining an employee's health and medical insurance coverage would create a cost disadvantage for U.S. companies relative to foreign competition. Continuing to pay for fringe compensation is costly, especially when there is no productivity return from the beneficiary, that is, the employee who is taking leave. Ideally, filling the vacancy with temporary workers should compensate for the productivity loss associated with employees on leave. In some cases, temporary replacements do not possess as much experience as permanent employees. By the time the temporary employee has become proficient, it is likely that the permanent employees will be returning from leave.

Although this argument is plausible, the jury is still out on the impact of the act. A representative period of time is needed that takes into account fluctuations in the American and global economies as well as particular business cycles. Unfortunately, the passage of the FMLA was sufficiently recent to preclude such a determination.

companies have already experimented with twenty-four-hour coverage. For instance, Polaroid Corporation has found that there are some cost advantages associated with integrating medical insurance and workers' compensation—reduced administrative expense through integration of the coverages, better access to all employee medical records, and a decrease in litigation.[28]

Use of twenty-four-hour coverage is not widespread for a number of reasons.[29] Many insurance companies view this approach as complicated. In addition, some companies are concerned that this coverage would cost them in unanticipated ways.

Employers also can contain their costs for unemployment insurance. As discussed earlier, the amount of tax employers contribute to providing unemployment insurance depends partly on their experience rating. Thus, employers can contain costs by systematically monitoring the reasons they terminate workers' employment and avoiding terminations that lead to unemployment insurance claims whenever possible. For example, it is not uncommon for companies to employ workers on a full-time basis when they experience increases in demands for their products or services. Adding full-time workers is reasonable when companies expect that the higher demand will last for an extended period of time such as more than two years. However, if the increase in demand is short term, when the demand goes back down, companies usually reduce their work force through layoffs. Unless the laid-off employees immediately find employment, they will file claims with their local employment security office for unemployment insurance. Their claims contribute to the companies' unemployment experience rating and, thus, cost expenditures.

Summary

This chapter discussed the legally required benefits concept, the rationale for legally required benefits, varieties of legally required benefits, and the implications of benefits for strategic compensation. Although companies have little choice with regard to the implementation of these benefits, management can proactively manage the costs of these legally required benefits to some extent. In the coming years, employees, employers, unions, and the government will pay greater attention to the adequacy of Social Security benefits for the succeeding generations. Likewise, these groups will closely monitor the effectiveness of the FMLA.

Discussion questions

1. Except for the Family and Medical Leave Act, the remaining legally required benefits were conceived decades ago. What changes in the business environment and society might affect the relevance or perhaps the viability of any of these benefits? Please discuss.

2. Provide your reaction to this statement: "Fringe compensation is seen by employees as an entitlement derived from their membership in companies." Explain the rationale for your reaction.

3. Conduct some research on the future of the Social Security programs. On the basis of your research, prepare a statement not to exceed 250 words that describes your view of the Social Security programs (for example, whether they are necessary, their viability, or whether there should be changes in how the programs are funded). Refer to the information obtained from your research efforts, indicating how it influenced your views.

Key terms

Social Security Act of 1935
base period
supplemental unemployment benefit (SUB)
Federal Unemployment Tax Act (FUTA)
experience rating
quarters of coverage
fully insured
currently insured
disability insured
Medicare

Part A
Part B
workers' compensation laws
Longshore and Harborworkers' Compensation Act
Federal Employees' Compensation Act
injury claims
occupational disease claims
death claims
rehabilitative services

Endnotes

1. U.S. Department of Commerce, *Statistical abstracts of the United States,* 115th ed. (Washington, D.C.: U.S. Government Printing Office, 1995).

2. The Bureau of National Affairs, *Employee benefits law* (Washington, D.C.: The Bureau of National Affairs, 1991).

3. G. E. Rejda, *Social insurance and economic security* (Englewood Cliffs, N.J.: Prentice Hall, 1994).

4. The Bureau of National Affairs, *Labor relations expediter,* vol. 710, no. 737 (Washington, D.C.: The Bureau of National Affairs, 1994), p. 206.

5. B. T. Beam Jr. and J. J. McFadden, *Employee benefits,* 5th ed. (Chicago: Dearborn Financial Publishing, 1996).

6. U.S. Department of Commerce, *Statistical abstracts of the United States,* 115th ed.

7. Ibid.

8. Board of Trustees, Federal Old-Age and Survivors Insurance and Disability Insurance Trust Funds, *Annual report of the Federal Old-Age and Survivors Insurance and Disability Insurance Trust Funds* (Washington, D.C.: U.S. Government Printing Office, 1992).

9. G. Spencer, Projection of the population of the United States, by age, sex, race, and Hispanic origin: 1992 to 2050, in *Current Population Reports,* P-25, No. 1092 (Washington, D.C.: U.S. Government Printing Office, November 1992).

10. Ibid.

11. R. M. Ball, Social security across the generations, pages 24–25 in J. R. Gist, ed., *Social Security and the economic well-being across generations* (Washington, D.C.: Public Policy Institute of the American Association of Retired Persons, 1988).

12. Beam and McFadden, *Employee benefits,* 5th ed.

13. U.S. Department of Commerce, *Statistical abstracts of the United States,* 115th ed.

14. F. R. Dulles and M. Dubofsky, *Labor in America: A history* (Arlington Heights, Ill.: Harlan Davidson, 1993).

15. Rejda, *Social insurance and economic security.*

16. U.S. Chamber of Commerce, *1995 analysis of workers' compensation laws* (Washington, D.C.: U.S. Chamber of Commerce, 1995).

17. Beam and McFadden, *Employee benefits,* 5th ed.

18. U.S. Chamber of Commerce, *1995 analysis of workers' compensation laws.*

19. Ibid.

20. J. V. Nackley, *Primer on workers' compensation* (Washington, D.C.: The Bureau of National Affairs, 1987).

21. Ibid.

22. U.S. Chamber of Commerce, *1995 analysis of workers' compensation laws.*

23. Ibid.

24. U.S. Department of Commerce, *Statistical abstracts of the United States,* 115th ed.

25. U.S. Bureau of Labor Statistics, *Employee benefits survey: A BLS reader* (Washington, D.C.: U.S. Government Printing Office, 1995).

26. U.S. Department of Commerce, *Statistical abstracts of the United States,* 115th ed.

27. Beam and McFadden, *Employee benefits,* 5th. ed.

28. N. C. Tompkins, Around-the-clock medical coverage, *HR Magazine,* 37 (1992): pp. 66–72.

29. L. C. Baker and A. B. Krueger, Twenty-four-hour coverage and workers' compensation insurance. Working paper, Princeton University Industrial Relations Section, 1993.

CHAPTER

ELEVEN

Discretionary benefits

In this chapter, you will learn about

1. The role of discretionary benefits in strategic compensation
2. The various kinds of protection programs
3. The different types of pay for time-not-worked
4. A variety of employee services
5. The considerations that go along with designing and planning discretionary benefits programs
6. How discretionary benefits fit with differentiation and lowest-cost competitive strategies

Today, discretionary benefits represent a significant fiscal cost to companies. In 1994, U.S. companies spent an average $11,506 per year per employee to provide discretionary benefits.[1] Such discretionary benefits accounted for approximately one-third of employers' total payroll costs (that is, the sum of core compensation and all fringe compensation costs).

Traditionally, many companies offered an array of discretionary benefits to employees without regard to the costs. Often, companies competed for the best individuals partly through the number and kinds of benefits, making no adjustments later for the quality of employees' job performance. Nowadays, employers recognize that employees must *earn* discretionary fringe compensation if their companies are to sustain competitive advantages.[2] Companies' costs to provide medical insurance have risen at a phenomenal rate in recent years. For example, the dollar cost of medical insurance premiums for employees increased from $2,579 per employee per year in 1992 to $2,851 in 1993: an increase of 10.5 percent in just one year. Medical insurance costs often amount to one-third of companies' total expenditures on discretionary fringe compensation. Contemporary benefits strategies focus on cost containment and cost sharing.[3] Exhibit 11-1 illustrates the employer costs for employee compensation per hour worked in 1994.

Increasing workforce diversity has challenged companies' quest to reduce their discretionary benefits costs. The greater workforce diversity has lead to the creation of additional benefits as well as greater uses of more-traditional benefits.

Increasing workforce diversity has challenged companies' quest to reduce their discretionary benefits costs.[4] The greater workforce diversity has lead to the creation of additional benefits as well as greater uses of more-traditional benefits. For example, the number of one-earner families maintained by women has risen dramatically from 5,690,000 in 1980 to 7,792,000 in 1993, representing a 37 percent increase.[5] This particular workforce trend has created a need for family assistance benefits. Offering child care benefits can be costly because of the staff time to coordinate and run these programs. For example, in the case of offering referrals only, staff must spend considerable time identifying local child care providers and carefully checking the credentials and references of those providers.

Companies are responding to increased workforce diversity through the adoption of *flexible benefits plans,* or *cafeteria plans,* which allow employees to choose between two or more types of benefits. Unfortunately, flexible benefits plans are costly. A company that adopts a cafeteria plan will incur development and administrative costs over and above more-traditional benefits program costs. For instance, a company of 10,000 employees could expect initial development costs of approximately

Exhibit 11-1
Employer Costs for Private Industry Employee Compensation per Hour Worked, as of March 1994 (in dollars)

COMPENSATION COMPONENT	TOTAL	GOODS PRODUC-ING[1]	SERVICE PRODUC-ING[2]	MANUFAC-TURING	NON-MANUFAC-TURING	UNION MEMBERS	NON-UNION MEMBERS
Total compensation	17.08	20.80	15.82	20.72	16.19	23.27	16.04
Wages and salaries	12.14	13.87	11.56	13.69	11.76	14.76	11.70
Total benefits	4.94	6.96	4.26	7.03	4.43	8.51	4.34
Paid leave	1.11	1.38	1.02	1.55	1.00	1.66	1.02
Vacation	0.54	0.72	0.48	0.79	0.48	0.90	0.48
Holiday	0.38	0.50	0.34	0.57	0.33	0.53	0.36
Sick	0.14	0.11	0.15	0.13	0.14	0.16	0.14
Other	0.05	0.05	0.05	0.06	0.05	0.08	0.04
Supplemental pay	0.44	0.71	0.36	0.72	0.38	0.75	0.39
Premium pay	0.19	0.40	0.12	0.40	0.14	0.50	0.14
Nonproduction bonuses	0.20	0.23	0.19	0.22	0.19	0.11	0.21
Shift pay	0.06	0.06	0.05	0.10	0.04	0.14	0.04
Insurance	1.23	1.85	1.03	1.96	1.06	2.46	1.03
Health insurance	1.14	1.70	0.95	1.79	0.98	2.28	0.94
Retirement and savings	0.52	0.85	0.41	0.81	0.45	1.23	0.40
Pensions	0.41	0.68	0.32	0.63	0.35	1.12	0.29
Savings and thrift	0.11	0.17	0.09	0.17	0.09	0.12	0.11
Legally required[3]	1.60	2.08	1.44	1.87	1.53	2.30	1.48
Social Security	1.02	1.20	0.95	1.20	0.97	1.27	0.97
Federal unemployment	0.03	0.03	0.03	0.03	0.03	0.03	0.03
State unemployment	0.13	0.17	0.11	0.16	0.12	0.17	0.12
Workers' compensation	0.41	0.68	0.32	0.48	0.39	0.75	0.35
Other benefits[4]	0.04	0.11	0.02	0.12	0.02	0.11	0.03

Source: Based on a sample of establishments; U.S. Bureau of Labor Statistics, *News, Employer costs for employee compensation,* U.S. Department of Labor Publication 94-290.

[1] Mining, construction, and manufacturing.

[2] Transportation, communications, public utilities, wholesale trade, retail trade, finance, insurance, real estate, and services.

[3] Includes railroad retirement, railroad unemployment, railroad supplemental unemployment, and other legally required benefits, not shown separately.

[4] Includes severance pay and supplemental unemployment benefits.

$500,000.[6] Two main factors contribute to the incremental costs of flexible benefits programs. The first factor is the value of employee hours that would be spent in preparing the program for implementation. The second factor is the cost of repro-gramming the organization's computer system to include necessary information and to accept the employees' benefit choices.

An overview of discretionary benefits

Discretionary benefits fall into three broad categories: protection programs, pay for time not worked, and services. Protection programs provide family benefits, promote health, and guard against income loss caused by catastrophic factors such as unemployment, disability, or serious illnesses. Not surprisingly, pay for time not worked provides employees time off with pay such as vacation. Services provide enhancements such as tuition reimbursement and daycare assistance to employees and their families.

In the past several decades, firms have offered a tremendous number of both legally required and discretionary benefits. In Chapter 10, we discussed how the growth in legally required benefits from a select body of federal and state legislation developed out of social welfare philosophies. Quite different from those reasons are several factors that have contributed to the rise in discretionary benefits.

Discretionary benefits originated in the 1940s and 1950s. During both World War II and the Korean War, the federal government mandated that companies not increase employees' core compensation, but it did not place restrictions on companies' fringe compensation expenditures. Companies invested in expanding their offerings of discretionary benefits as an alternative to pay hikes as a motivational tool. As a result, many companies began to offer welfare practices. **Welfare practices** were "anything for the comfort and improvement, intellectual or social, of the employees, over and above wages paid, which is not a necessity of the industry nor required by law."[7] Moreover, companies offered employees welfare benefits to promote good management and to enhance worker productivity.

The opportunities to employees through welfare practices varied. For example, some employers offered libraries and recreational areas; others provided financial assistance for education, home purchases, and home improvements. In addition, employers' sponsorship of medical insurance coverage became common.

Quite apart from the benevolence of employers, employee unions also directly contributed to the increase in employee welfare practices owing to the National Labor Relations Act of 1935 (NLRA), which legitimized bargaining for employee benefits. Union workers tend to participate more in benefits plans than do nonunion employees.[8] Exhibit 11-2 illustrates some of the differences in participation in benefits programs between nonunion and union employees. For example, in 1993, union workers were more likely to receive health care benefits and retirement income benefits than were nonunion workers.

Unions also indirectly contributed to the rise in benefits offerings. As we discussed in Chapter 3, nonunion companies often fashion their employment practices after union companies as a tactic to minimize the chance that their employees will seek union representation.[9] Nonunion companies tend to minimize the likelihood of unionization by offering their employees benefits that are comparable to the benefits received by employees in union shops.

Since the turn of this century, employees generally viewed both legally required benefits and discretionary benefits as entitlements. Anecdotal evidence suggests that most employees still do: From their perspective, company membership entitles them to fringe compensation. Until recently, companies have also treated virtually all elements of fringe compensation as entitlements. They have not questioned their role as social welfare mediators. However, both rising benefit costs and increased foreign

Exhibit 11-2
Percent of Full-time
Employees Participating in
Selected Employee Benefit
Programs, by Union Status,
Medium and Large Private
Establishments, 1993

BENEFIT	UNION EMPLOYEES	NONUNION EMPLOYEES
Paid time off		
Holidays	95	90
Vacations	97	97
Personal leave	20	22
Lunch period	11	8
Rest period	74	68
Funeral leave	90	81
Jury duty leave	92	89
Military leave	55	52
Maternity leave	2	3
Paternity leave	1	1
Unpaid time off		
Maternity leave	65	59
Paternity leave	59	51
Disability benefits		
Short-term disability protection	95	84
Paid sick leave	50	69
Sickness and accident insurance	72	36
Long-term disability insurance	28	45
Survivor benefits		
Life insurance	95	90
Accidental death and dismemberment	77	67
Survivor income benefits	9	4
Health care benefits		
Medical care	90	79
Dental care	73	58
Vision care	48	20
Out-patient prescription drug coverage	89	78
Retirement income benefits		
All retirement	88	76
Defined benefit	81	48
Defined contribution	35	53
Savings and thrift	15	33
Deferred profit sharing	5	16
Employee stock ownership	2	3
Money purchase pension	7	8
Cash or deferred arrangements		
With employer contributions	18	41
No employer contributions	9	6

Source: U.S. Bureau of Labor Statistics, *Employee benefits in medium and large private establishments, 1993*
(Washington D.C.: U.S. Government Printing Office, 1994).

competition have led companies to question this entitlement ethic. For instance, according to the U.S. Bureau of Labor Statistics in 1994, U.S. companies spent as much as $22,000 per employee to provide discretionary benefits.

A more recent phenomenon that gives rise to discretionary benefits is the federal government's institution of tax laws that allow companies to lower their tax liability on the basis of the amount of money they allocate to providing employees with particular discretionary benefits. These tax laws permit companies to deduct from their pretaxable income the cost of certain benefits, thereby lowering companies' tax liabilities.

Components of discretionary benefits

Protection programs

INCOME PROTECTION PROGRAMS

Disability insurance. Disability insurance replaces income for employees who become unable to work because of sickness or accident. Unfortunately, employees need this kind of protection. At all working ages, the probability of being disabled for at least 90 consecutive days is much greater than the chance of dying while performing one's job; one out of every three employees will have a disability that lasts at least 90 days.[10]

Employer-sponsored or group disability insurance typically takes two forms. The first, **short-term disability insurance,** provides benefits for limited periods of time, usually less than six months. The second, **long-term disability insurance,** provides benefits for extended periods of time anywhere from six months to life. Disability criteria differ between short-term and long-term plans.[11] Short-term plans usually consider disability as an inability to perform any and every duty of one's (the disabled's) occupation. Long-term plans use a more stringent definition, specifying disability as an inability to engage in any occupation for which the individual is qualified by reason of training, education, or experience.

Most short-term disability plans pay employees 50 to 100 percent of their pretax salary; long-term disability plans pay 50 to 70 percent of pretax salary.[12] In general, long-term benefits are subject to a waiting period of anywhere from six months to one year, and usually they become active only after an employee's sick leave and short-term disability benefits have been exhausted.

Long-term disability insurance provides a monthly benefit to employees who, owing to illness or injury, are unable to work for an extended period of time. Payments of long-term disability benefits usually begin after three to six months of disability and continue until retirement or for a specified number of months. Payments generally equal a fixed percentage of predisability earnings.

Both short- and long-term disability plans may duplicate disability benefits mandated by the Social Security Act and state workers' compensation laws (discussed in Chapter 10). These employer-sponsored plans generally supplement legally required benefits established by the *Employee Retirement Income Security Act of 1974 (ERISA),* which we will discuss later in this chapter. Employer-sponsored plans do not replace disability benefits mandated by law.

Life insurance. Employer-provided **life insurance** protects employees' families by paying a specified amount to an employee's beneficiaries upon the employee's death.

Most policies pay some multiple of the employee's salary: for instance, benefits paid at twice the employee's annual salary. Frequently, employer-sponsored life insurance plans also include accidental death and dismemberment claims, which pay additional benefits if death was the result of an accident or if the insured incurs accidental loss of a limb.[13]

Companies typically offer employees life insurance. In 1992, they provided life insurance to 78 percent of full-time private sector employees and to 89 percent of full-time public sector employees.[14] On average, manufacturing industries spent $168 per employee in 1994 to provide life insurance, and nonmanufacturing industries spent only $130 per employee.[15]

There are two kinds of life insurance: term coverage and life coverage. **Term coverage,** the most common type of life insurance offered by companies, provides protection to employees' beneficiaries only during employees' employment. **Life coverage,** on the other hand, extends coverage into the retirement years.

Individuals can subscribe to life insurance on an individual basis by purchasing policies from independent insurance agents or representatives of insurance companies. Alternatively, they can subscribe to group life insurance through their employers. Group plans have clear benefits.[16] First, group plans allow all participants covered by the policy to benefit from coverage while employers assume the burden of financing the plan either partly or entirely. Second, group policies permit a larger set of individuals to participate in a plan at a lower cost per person than if each person had to purchase life insurance on an individual basis.

Pension programs. **Pension programs** provide income to individuals throughout their retirement. Individuals may participate in more than one pension program simultaneously. It is not uncommon for employees to participate in pension plans sponsored by their companies as well as in pension plans that they establish themselves such as the 401(k) plan. In 1994, employers' contributions to pension plans on behalf of their employees were substantial, averaging $1,968 per employee per year.[17]

Pension program design and implementation are quite complex, largely because of the many laws that govern their operations, particularly the Employee Retirement Income Security Act of 1974 (ERISA).

Three sets of terms broadly characterize pension plans:

✯ Contributory versus noncontributory plans

✯ Qualified versus nonqualified plans

✯ Defined contribution plans versus defined benefit plans

Contributory pension plans require contributions by the employee who will benefit from the income upon retirement. **Noncontributory pension plans** do not require any contributions by employees. Noncontributory pension plans are the most popular for two reasons.[18] First, employees do not receive tax breaks on current earnings for the contributions they make. Second, a variety of complex tax laws create administrative burdens for companies that permit employee contributions to pension plans.

Qualified pension plans entitle employers to receive tax benefits from their contributions to pension plans. In general, this means that employers may take current tax deductions for contributions to fund future retirement income. Employees may also receive some favorable tax treatment (that is, a lower tax rate). A qualified plan generally entitles employees to favorable tax treatment on the benefits they receive upon

Exhibit 11-3
The General Characteristics of Qualified Pension Plans

ELIGIBILITY

Employers may impose any initial eligibility requirement but for those that pertain to age or service. No minimum age over 21 can be required, nor can more than one year of service be required for eligibility.

NONDISCRIMINATION

Employers cannot provide highly compensated employees (for example, vice presidents, chief executive officers) with preferential treatment with regard to employer contributions to the plans or the level of benefits received *unless* the employer contributions or benefit levels are based solely on employees' compensation level or years of service.

VESTING REQUIREMENTS

Employers must provide employees with a nonforfeitable right to the funds they contribute to the plans on behalf of their employees after a specified period, commonly five years. For example, employees who terminate their employment after five years maintain the right to the funds contributed on their behalf by the employer. However, employees who terminate their employment before the five-year period forfeit the right to the funds contributed on their behalf by the employer.

PAYOUT RESTRICTIONS

Employees generally pay a penalty (usually 10 percent) on withdrawal of funds from any qualified plan before early retirement age (59 $1/2$ years).

---

retirement. Any investment income that is generated in the pension program is not taxed until the employee retires. **Nonqualified pension plans** provide less-favorable tax treatments for employers and employees. Exhibit 11-3 lists the defining characteristics of qualified plans.

Finally, companies may establish their retirement plans as either defined contribution plans or defined benefit plans. Under **defined contribution plans,** employers and employees make annual contributions to separate accounts established for each participating employee, based on a formula contained in the plan document. Typically, formulas call for employers to contribute a given percentage of each participant's compensation annually. Employers invest these funds on behalf of the employee in any one of a number of ways, such as company stocks, diversified stock market funds, or federal government bond funds. In 1994, companies contributed an average $543 per employee to defined contribution pension plans.[19]

The most common types of defined contribution plans are profit sharing plans, employee stock ownership plans (ESOPs), deferred 401(k) plans, and savings and thrift plans. Regarding profit sharing plans, employers might use allocation formulas that divide contributions among participants in proportion to their relative compensation paid during the plan year, or the employer might disburse the share of profits equally among employees regardless of their earnings. A recent survey indicates that most employers allocate shares of profit proportional to employee earnings.[20] Once employers make contributions, the funds are invested and held until distribution. In recent years, profit sharing plans have grown phenomenally. In 1993, 3,777,000 deferred profit sharing plans were in effect within companies located in the United States.[21]

Employee stock ownership plans are governed by rules similar to the rules for profit sharing plans, except that benefits generally are distributed in the form of stock in the employer corporation. These plans are unique because they may involve the use of borrowed funds, whereas profit sharing plans base distributions on earned profits. Typically, the employer guarantees the ESOP's loan from an outside lender. Employers typically award stock to employees in proportion to their earnings. Another critical difference between profit sharing and ESOPs is the level of investment risk. Profit sharing plans carry less risk than ESOPs because employers generally use more than one investment vehicle. Employee stock ownership plans are riskier because employers use only one investment vehicle—company stock. Nevertheless, the use of ESOPs is on the rise. In 1975, 1,601 ESOPs covered 248,000 employees; in 1992, 9,764 plans covered 11,153,000 employees.[22]

Deferred 401(k) plans, named after the section of the Internal Revenue Code that established them, are deferred profit sharing plans that permit participating employees to determine contribution amounts within set limits. The portion of salary that is deducted reduces employees' taxable income, thus lowering income tax liability. 401(k) plans differ from deferred profit sharing plans in that employees can decide how much of their compensation is deferred. The Internal Revenue Service sets dollar limits on the maximum allowable pretax contribution to a 401(k) plan, and it comes out of current salary, adjusted for increases in the cost of living. In 1995, the amount was $9,240. Between 1991 and 1994, the percentage of companies that offered employees 401(k) plans has remained steady, ranging between 70 and 74 percent.[23]

Savings and thrift plans are savings plans that employers set up on behalf of employees. Savings and thrift plans feature employee contributions matched by the employer. In 1993, the typical employee contribution ranged between 10 and 20 percent of annual income.[24] Employees make contributions to savings and thrift plans on a pretax basis. Also, employees cannot withdraw their contributions from their accounts before their retirement without a substantial monetary penalty. The contributions by employers vary widely, usually between 1 and 50 percent of employees' annual contributions.[25] The prevalence of savings and thrift plans diminished from 27 percent in 1991 to 16 percent in 1994.[26]

Stock bonus plans are governed by rules similar to those that apply to profit sharing plans, except that benefits generally are distributed in the form of stock in the employer corporation. Both employees and employers make regular contributions to these plans. The employer then invests both contributions in an investment vehicle selected by the employees—stocks, bonds, or money market funds.

Defined benefit plans guarantee retirement benefits specified in the plan document. This benefit usually is expressed in terms of a monthly sum equal to a percentage of a participant's preretirement pay multiplied by the number of years he or she has worked for the employer. Although the benefit in such a plan is fixed by a formula, the level of required employer contributions fluctuates from year to year. The level depends on the amount necessary to make certain that benefits promised will be available when participants and beneficiaries are eligible to receive them. As a result, companies find defined benefit plans more burdensome to administer than defined contribution plans. From employees' perspectives, defined benefit plans are advantageous because they guarantee the amount of benefits the employees will receive upon retirement.

Exhibit 11-4
U.S. Health Care
Expenditures, 1960 to 1993

HEALTH PROTECTION PROGRAMS Health protection has become a major concern of both employees and employers for several years. From the employees' perspective, health coverage is valuable, particularly as the costs of health care have increased dramatically. Exhibit 11-4 charts the rise in national health care expenditures between 1960 and 1993: Total expenditures rose by more than 3,000 percent, from $27.1 billion in 1960 to $884.2 billion in 1993. The expenditure amounts from private sources were substantially higher than the expenditure amounts from public sources.

YEAR	TOTAL[1]		TOTAL HEALTH SERVICES AND SUPPLIES (BILLIONS OF DOLLARS)	
	TOTAL (BILLIONS OF DOLLARS)	PER CAPITA (DOLLARS)	PRIVATE	PUBLIC
1960	27.1	143	19.8	5.7
1965	41.6	204	29.9	8.3
1970	74.3	346	44.0	25.0
1971	82.2	379	48.1	28.2
1972	92.3	421	53.9	31.8
1973	102.4	464	59.7	35.9
1974	115.9	521	65.9	42.8
1975	132.6	591	74.1	50.2
1976	151.9	671	85.7	56.9
1977	172.6	755	96.6	64.7
1978	193.2	836	109.7	73.6
1979	218.3	937	124.0	84.0
1980	251.1	1,068	141.3	96.1
1981	291.4	1,227	164.3	113.9
1982	328.2	1,369	186.5	126.9
1983	360.8	1,490	205.3	139.5
1984	396.0	1,620	228.0	151.6
1985	434.5	1,761	252.9	165.2
1986	466.0	1,871	268.7	180.4
1987	506.2	2,013	291.3	196.6
1988	562.3	2,214	327.5	213.7
1989	623.9	2,433	361.7	240.1
1990	696.6	2,686	399.8	272.5
1991	755.6	2,882	422.8	306.0
1992	820.3	3,094	451.7	341.2
1993	884.2	3,299	484.3	370.9

Source: U. S. Health Care Financing Administration, *Health Care Financing Review* (Winter 1994); table 150.

[1] The total is more than the sum of private and public expenditures because it includes medical research and medical facilities construction.

Companies can choose from varieties of health protection including commercial insurance, self-funded insurance, health maintenance organizations (HMOs), and preferred provider organizations (PPOs). Most companies offer more than one kind of medical and health protection coverage. In 1994, 53 percent of companies used commercial insurance plans, 60 percent used self-funded coverage, 63 percent used HMOs, and 57 percent used PPOs.[27]

Commercial insurance (also known as fee-for-service plans) **Commercial insurance plans** provide protection for three types of medical expenses: hospital expenses, surgical expenses, and physicians' charges. Hospital expense coverage pays for room and board charges and other in-hospital services agreed upon in the contract, such as laboratory fees and x-ray charges.

Surgical expense benefits pay for medically necessary surgical procedures but usually not for elective surgeries such as cosmetic surgical procedures. In general, commercial insurance pays expenses according to a schedule of usual, customary, and reasonable charges. The **usual, customary, and reasonable charge** is defined as being not more than the physician's usual charge; within the customary range of fees charged in the locality; and reasonable, based on the medical circumstances.[28] Whenever actual surgical expenses exceed the usual, customary, and reasonable level, the patient must pay the difference. Finally, such policies cover physicians' charges for services rendered in the hospital on in- or out-patient bases as well as office visits.

Under commercial insurance plans, policy holders (employees) may generally select any licensed physician, surgeon, or medical facility for treatment, and the insurance plan reimburses the policy holders after medical services are rendered. The insurance policy, or contract between the insurance company and the employees, specifies the expenses that are covered and at what rate. A common feature of commercial insurance plans is the deductible. Each year, employees must meet a **deductible,** or out-of-pocket expense, that they must pay before insurance benefits become active. The purpose of the out-of-pocket expense provision is to protect individuals from catastrophic medical expenses. Single individuals often have annual deductibles of $800, and family deductibles are as high as $2,000 per year. The insurance plan then pays covered expenses in excess of the deductible.

Commercial insurance plans also feature coinsurance, which becomes relevant after the insured pays his or her annual deductible. **Coinsurance** refers to the percentage of covered expenses not paid by the medical plan. Most commercial plans stipulate 20 percent coinsurance. This means that the policy holder must pay 20 percent of covered expenses and the insurance plan will pay the remaining 80 percent. Just as deductibles vary, so do coinsurance provisions. Exhibit 11-5 lists the coverage of a standard commercial medical insurance program.

Upon deciding to offer health protection benefits to employees, companies must decide between offering these benefits through an individual or a group policy. Individual policies typically require evaluation of each employee's health. Group health insurance plans are negotiated by an employer to cover all employees for specific benefits. Premiums are determined by an actuarial analysis of plan participants rather than on an actual evaluation of each employee's health. Employers may choose either to pay for the entire policy premium or to share the cost with employees. Group plans offer advantages to both employees and employers. For employers, group plans are generally less expensive because underwriting these plans involves less risk to the

Exhibit 11-5
A Sample Fee-for-Service Plan

Benefit Summary

The benefits described in this summary represent the major areas of coverage. For detailed information, see the specific covered benefits section. The annual plan deductible and other updated information for each plan year will appear annually in your Benefit Choice Options booklet.

EFFECTIVE DATE   July 1, 1994

PLAN YEAR   July 1–June 30 of each year

PLAN YEAR MAXIMUM   Unlimited

LIFETIME MAXIMUM   Unlimited

ANNUAL PLAN DEDUCTIBLE   (July 1, 1994)

Member Annual Plan Deductible

Annual Salary	Deductible
$44,100 or less	$150
$44,101–$55,200	$250
$55,201 and over	$300
Retiree/Annuitant/Survivor	$100
Dependent Annual Plan Deductible	$100

Family Deductible Cap

Annual Salary	Family Cap
$44,100 or less	$300
$44,101–$55,200	$400
$55,201 and over	$450
Retiree/Annuitant/Survivor	$300

COVERAGE AFTER ANNUAL PLAN DEDUCTIBLES

Physician & Surgeon Services	In-patient or office visits	• 80% of R&C [reasonable and customary] after deductible
Out-patient Services	Diagnostic lab/x-ray	• 100% of R&C after deductible
	Durable medical equipment & prosthetics	• 80% of R&C after deductible
	Surgical facility charges	• 90% after deductible

	PPO Hospitals	**Non-PPO Hospital**
In-patient Hospital	90% after annual plan deductible	65% after annual plan deductible and $100 admission deductible, if member resides within 25 miles of PPO hospital. Annual non-PPO out-of-pocket maximum applies.
		80% after annual plan deductible and $100 admission deductible, if member does not reside within 25 miles of PPO hospital. General out-of-pocket maximum applies.

Exhibit 11-5
A Sample Fee-for-Service Plan (continued)

	General	Non-PPO Hospital
OUT-OF-POCKET MAXIMUM	Plan pays 100% of R&C after you pay $800 per individual or $2,000 per family in deductibles and coinsurance.	Plan pays 100% of R&C after you pay $3000 per individual or $7000 per family in non-PPO deductibles and coinsurance.

All charges are subject to the benefit administrators' determinations of medical necessity and reasonable and customary (R&C) fees.

---

insurer. For employees, insurance companies impose fewer restrictions on the terms of coverage such as waiving physical examinations as a condition for enrollment.

Self-funded insurance. Self-funded insurance and commercial insurance programs appear superficially to be the same. **Self-funded insurance plans** specify areas of coverage, deductibles, and coinsurance rates just as commercial policies do. Differences between commercial insurance plans and self-funded insurance plans center on how benefits provided to policy holders are financed. When companies elect commercial insurance plans, they establish a contract with an independent insurance company such as the Hartford. Commercial insurance companies pay benefits from their financial reserves, which are based on the premiums companies and employees pay to receive insurance. Companies may choose to self-fund employee insurance, an alternative to commercial insurance. Such companies pay benefits directly from their own assets, either current cash flow or funds set aside in advance for potential claims.

The decision to self-fund is based on financial considerations. Self-funding makes sense when a company's financial burden associated with covering medical expenses for its employees is less than the cost to subscribe to a commercial insurance company for coverage. By not paying premiums in advance to a commercial carrier, a company retains these funds for current cash flow. A recent survey indicates that self-funding is on the rise, with approximately two out of every three companies surveyed using this method.[29]

Health maintenance organization (HMO) and preferred provider organization (PPO). HMOs and PPOs are popular systems that organize, deliver, and finance health care. **Health maintenance organizations (HMOs)** are sometimes described as providing "prepaid medical services," since fixed periodic enrollment fees cover HMO members for all medically necessary services, provided that the services are delivered or approved by the HMO. HMOs generally provide in-patient and out-patient care as well as services from physicians, surgeons, and other health care professionals. Most medical services are either fully covered or some HMOs require participants to make nominal **copayments.** Common copayments are $5 or $10 per doctor's office visit and $5 or $10 per drug prescription.

HMOs are regulated at both federal and state levels. At the federal level, HMOs are governed by the **Health Maintenance Organization Act of 1973,**[30] amended in 1988 to encourage their use: The federal government believes that HMOs are a viable alternative method of financing and delivering health care. Companies must offer HMOs if they are subject to the minimum wage provisions of the Fair Labor Standards Act (Chapter 3). The Health Maintenance Organization Act spurred the growth of HMOs by making development funds available to qualifying HMOs and imposing a "dual choice" requirement on employers that sponsored health benefits programs. Under the dual choice requirement, employers with at least 25 employees had to offer at least one HMO as an alternative to a traditional commercial insurance plan.

In 1995, the dual choice requirement was eliminated to allow HMOs and other types of health care programs to compete on a more equal footing in two ways. First, employers now can negotiate rates on the basis of the expected experience of their employee population. That is, the premium amount varies with the extent to which employees use HMO services. Employers whose employees tend to use HMO services extensively pay higher premiums than employers whose employees tend to use HMO services less extensively.

The second way employers now can compete more equally is the result of replacing the requirement that employer contributions not financially discriminate against employees choosing an HMO option. In other words, companies must make the same percentage contribution toward an HMO's premium as is made toward premiums of other medical plans.

HMOs differ according to where service is rendered, how medical care is delivered, and how contractual relationships between medical providers and the HMOs are structured. **Prepaid group practices** provide medical care for a set premium rather than on a fee-for-service basis. A set of physicians who have contracted to share facilities, equipment, and support staff provide services to HMO members. A group HMO usually operates on a 24-hour basis, covering emergency phones and sometimes emergency rooms around the clock.

Individual practice associations are partnerships or other legal entities that arrange health care services by entering into service agreements with independent physicians, health professionals, and group practices. Physicians who participate in this type of HMO practice out of their own facilities and continue to see HMO enrollees and patients who are not HMO enrollees. Participating physicians base fees on a capped fee schedule. This means that the HMO establishes the amount it will reimburse physicians for each procedure. If physicians charge more than the fee set by the HMO, then they must bill the difference to the patients. For example, an HMO sets a cap of $40 for an annual physical examination. If the physician charges $55 for the annual examination, then the physician bills the HMO for $40 and the patient for the remaining $15.

Under a **preferred provider organization (PPO),** a select group of health care providers agree to provide health care services to a given population at a higher level of reimbursement than under fee-for-service plans. Physicians qualify as PPO preferred providers by meeting quality standards, agreeing to follow cost containment procedures implemented by the PPO, and accepting the PPO's reimbursement structure. In return, the employer, insurance company, or third-party administrator helps guarantee provider physicians with certain patient loads by furnishing employees with financial incentives to use the preferred providers.

What are the key differences between HMOs and PPOs? There are two major differences. First, PPOs do not provide benefits on a prepaid basis. Health care providers receive payment after they render services to patients. Second, employees who subscribe to PPOs are generally free to select any physician or health care facility of their choice.

Dental insurance. **Dental insurance** is now a relatively common component of fringe compensation packages. In 1994, approximately 75 percent of companies in the United States offered dental insurance to their employees.[31] The likelihood of

Covering Uninsureds' Health Care Costs

You or your employer must pay more for your health protection coverage because so many individuals do not possess health protection coverage. The number without protection is staggering—nearly 40 million persons in 1993![32] Although many individuals do not receive health protection coverage of any kind, health care providers deliver health care services at no charge or a reduced charge. Physicians and hospitals offset the expenses associated with providing health care coverage by charging individuals who have health insurance higher fees than they typically charge individuals who do not have insurance. This practice is known as **cost shifting.** Many insurance companies necessarily increase their premiums to cover the higher claims costs, which means that you or your employer may be paying more for your health protection coverage.

employers offering dental insurance plans increased with company size.[33] Union employees are more likely to have dental insurance coverage than are nonunion employees. In 1991, 70 percent of union employees received dental coverage, compared with only 57 percent of nonunion employees.[34] Employers have several options to choose from, including commercial dental insurance, self-insurance, dental service corporations, and dental maintenance organizations. In 1993, commercial dental insurance was the most widely used option: 87 percent of all employees within medium and large companies that offered dental care used commercial dental insurance.[35]

Commercial dental insurance plans provide cash benefits by reimbursing patients for out-of-pocket costs or by paying dentists directly for patient costs. Deductibles and coinsurance are common, and plans typically pay 50 to 80 percent of fees after deductibles are paid. With **self-insured dental plans,** employers directly finance dental benefits using their general assets or pay into a trust from which benefits are paid. Self-insured plans often involve the services of third-party administrators. **Dental service corporations,** owned and administered by state dental associations, are nonprofit corporations of dentists. Participating dentists register their fees, and patients usually are required to pay the difference between the fixed fee established by the corporations and the dentist's actual fee, which is often higher. **Dental maintenance organizations** deliver dental services through the comprehensive health care plans of many HMOs and PPOs. Some independent networks of dentists, also known as dental maintenance organizations, give employers access to providers who will offer discounted services; in effect, they are dental PPOs.

Vision insurance Fewer companies offer their employees **vision insurance** than dental insurance. In 1994, only 34 percent of companies in the United States offered vision insurance to their employees.[36] Consequently, little data exist regarding the costs companies incur that result from offering vision insurance to employees. The most common types of plans are commercial insurance and managed care plans that are akin to dental maintenance organizations.

Pay for time-not-worked

The second type of discretionary benefits is pay for time not worked. This category of benefits is relatively straightforward. As the name implies, these benefits pay employees for time-not-worked. The major kinds of pay for time-not-worked are

- ✭ Holiday
- ✭ Vacation
- ✭ Sick leave
- ✭ Personal leave
- ✭ Jury duty
- ✭ Funeral leave
- ✭ Military leave
- ✭ Cleanup, preparation, travel time

Companies offer most pay for time-not-worked as a matter of custom, particularly paid holidays, vacations, and sick leave. In unionized settings, the particulars about pay for time-not-worked are contained within the collective bargaining agreement. The pay for time-not-worked practices that are most typically found in unionized settings are jury duty; funeral leave; military leave; cleanup, preparation, and travel time.

Exhibits 11-6, 11-7, and 11-8 illustrate pay for time-not-worked practices in medium and large private companies, small private companies, and state and local governments, respectively. Such practices varied widely. In general, full-time em-

Companies offer most pay for time-not-worked as a matter of custom, particularly paid holidays, vacations, and sick leave. In unionized settings, the particulars about pay for time-not-worked are contained within the collective bargaining agreement.

THE FLIP SIDE OF THE COIN

Sick Leave Benefits Extend Vacation

Many U.S. companies offer paid sick leave benefits. Although companies may differ regarding the number of paid days they provide to employees each year, most of these policies share in common a noteworthy feature: They prohibit the accrual of unused sick leave days from year to year.

For instance, an employee receives 10 paid sick leave days per calendar year. During 1997, the employee takes six paid sick leave days. With a nonaccrual provision, this employee would forfeit having four days off with pay in 1997. Consequently, paid sick leave and personal day policies with this feature create an incentive for employees to remain out of work for the maximum number of days allowed by the policies. In the case of sick leave, it is easy for employees to take leave for reasons other than illness: Most employers do not require that employees provide proof of illness such as doctor notes because the staff time to manage checking can be substantial.

The bottom line is that employees may use paid sick leave days for reasons other than illness. All absences are likely to lead to disruptions in the workplace in the form of lower productivity and, possibly, lower morale among those who may be required to cover for absent coworkers. But the nonaccrual provision of these plans may contribute unnecessarily to such disruptions in the workplace. Thus, what companies intend as a benefit for employees may actually be a detriment to companywide productivity.

BENEFIT	PERCENT OF FULL-TIME EMPLOYEE RECIPIENTS	AVERAGE AMOUNT
Holidays	76	≤ 11 days per year
Vacation	100	Depends on tenure
Personal leave	62	≤ 3 days per year
Jury duty	87	No stated maximum
Funeral leave	77	≤ 3 days per year
Military leave	53	≤ 10 days per year

Source: U.S. Bureau of Labor Statistics, *Employee benefits in medium and large private establishments, 1993* (Washington, D.C.: U.S. Government Printing Office, 1994).

Exhibit 11-6
Pay for Time-Not-Worked Practices in Medium and Large Private Establishments, 1993

BENEFIT	PERCENT OF FULL-TIME EMPLOYEE RECIPIENTS	AVERAGE AMOUNT
Holidays	75	≤ 11 days per year
Vacation	88	Depends on tenure
Personal leave	9	≤ 3 days per year
Jury duty	50	No stated maximum
Funeral leave	37	≤ 3 days per year
Military leave	10	≤ 10 days per year

Source: U.S. Bureau of Labor Statistics, *Employee benefits in small private establishments, 1992* (Washington, D.C.: U.S. Government Printing Office, 1994).

Exhibit 11-7
Pay for Time-Not-Worked Practices in Small Private Establishments, 1992

BENEFIT	PERCENT OF FULL-TIME EMPLOYEE RECIPIENTS	AVERAGE AMOUNT
Holidays	38	≤ 11 days per year
Vacation	67	Depends on tenure
Personal leave	30	≤ 3 days per year
Jury duty	96	No stated maximum
Funeral leave	35	≤ 3 days per year
Military leave	14	≤ 10 days per year

Source: U.S. Bureau of Labor Statistics, *Employee benefits in state and local governments, 1992* (Washington, D.C.: U.S. Government Printing Office, 1994).

Exhibit 11-8
Pay for Time-Not-Worked Practices in State and Local Governments, 1992

ployees of small private establishments were less likely to receive pay for time-not-worked than were full-time employees of medium and large private establishments. Full-time employees of state and local governments were less likely to receive paid time off for holidays than were full-time employees of private establishments.

Medium and large establishments were more likely to provide full-time employees paid vacations than were either small private establishments or state and local governments.

Services

EMPLOYEE ASSISTANCE PROGRAMS (EAPS) **Employee assistance programs (EAPs)** help employees cope with personal problems that may impair their job performance, such as alcohol or drug abuse, domestic violence, the emotional impact of AIDS and other diseases, clinical depression, and eating disorders.[37] In 1993, more than 60 percent of all full-time workers employed in medium and large private establishments had the opportunity to participate in EAPs.[38] In 1993, approximately the same percentage of full-time workers employed in state and local governments could participate in EAPs.[39] Only 17 percent of all full-time workers employed in small private establishments had the chance to participate in EAPs in 1993.[40]

Companies offer EAPs because at any given time, an estimated 10 to 15 percent of any company's employees experience difficulties that interfere with their job performance.[41] Although EAP costs are substantial, the benefits seem to outweigh the costs. For example, the annual cost per employee of an EAP is approximately $30 to $40. However, employers' gains outweigh their out-of-pocket expenses for EAPs: They save in terms of reduced employee turnover, absenteeism, medical costs, unemployment insurance rates, workers' compensation rates, accident costs, and disability insurance costs.[42] In fact, one analysis of EAP effectiveness demonstrated that 78 percent of EAP users found resolutions to their problems.[43]

EAPs provide a range of services and are organized in various ways, depending on the employer. In some companies, EAPs are informal programs developed and run on-site by in-house staff. Other employers contract with outside firms to administer their EAPs, or they rely on a combination of their own resources and help from an outside firm.

FAMILY ASSISTANCE PROGRAMS **Family assistance programs** help employees provide elder care and child care. Elder care provides physical, emotional, or financial assistance for aging parents, spouses, or other relatives who are not fully self-sufficient because they are too frail or disabled. Child care programs focus on supervising preschool-aged dependent children whose parents work outside the home. Many employees now rely on elder care programs because of their parents' increasing longevity[44] and because of the growing number of families in which both spouses work outside the home.[45] Child care needs arise from the growing number of single parents and dual-career households with children. Despite the need for elder and child care programs, only 5 percent of private sector employees and 13 percent of public sector employees were eligible for elder care benefits in 1992 according to The Bureau of National Affairs.

A variety of employer programs and benefits can help employees cope with their family assistance responsibilities. The programs range from making referrals to on-site child or elder care centers to providing company-sponsored daycare programs, and they vary in the amount of financial and human resources needed to administer them. In general, the least expensive and least labor intensive programs are referral services. Referral services are designed to help workers identify and take advantage of available community resources, conveyed through media such as educational workshops, videos, employee newsletters and magazines, and EAPs.

Flexible scheduling and leave allows employees the leeway to take time off during work hours to care for relatives or to respond to emergencies (see Chapter 14). Flexible scheduling, which includes programs such as compressed work weeks (such as four 10-hour days or three 12-hour days), flextime, and job sharing enable companies to help employees balance the demands of work and family.[46] Besides flexible work scheduling, some companies allow employees to extend their legally mandated leave sanctioned by the Family and Medical Leave Act (see Chapter 10). Under extended leave, employers typically continue to provide fringe compensation such as insurance and they promise to secure individuals comparable jobs upon their return.[47]

Day care is another possible benefit. Some companies subsidize child or elder day care in community-based centers. Elder care programs usually provide self-help, meals, and entertainment activities for the participants. Child care programs typically offer supervision, preschool preparation, and meals. Facilities must usually maintain state or local licenses. Other companies, such as Stride Rite Corporation, choose to sponsor on-site daycare centers, offering services that are similar to those offered by community-based centers.

TUITION REIMBURSEMENT Companies offer **tuition reimbursement programs** to promote their employees' education. Under a tuition reimbursement program, an employer fully or partially reimburses an employee for expenses incurred for education or training. A survey on tuition reimbursement programs showed that 43 percent of these plans reimbursed less than 100 percent of tuition; however, some companies vary the percentage of tuition reimbursed according to the relevance of the course to the company's goals or the grades employees earn.[48]

Tuition reimbursement programs are not synonymous with pay-for-knowledge programs (Chapter 6). Tuition reimbursement programs fall under the category of fringe compensation. Under these programs, employees choose the courses they wish to take and when they want to take them. In addition, employees may enroll in courses that are not directly related to their work. As we discussed in Chapter 6, pay-for-knowledge is one kind of core compensation. Companies establish set curricula that employees take, and they generally award pay increases to employees upon successfully completing courses within the curricula. Pay increases are not directly associated with tuition reimbursement programs.

TRANSPORTATION SERVICES Some employers sponsor programs that help bring employees to the workplace and back home again using energy-efficient forms of transportation. They may sponsor public transportation or vanpools: employer-sponsored vans or buses that transport employees between their homes and the workplace.

Employers provide transit subsidies to employees working in metropolitan and suburban areas served by various forms of mass transportation such as buses, subways, and trains. Companies may offer transit passes, tokens, or vouchers. Practices vary from partial subsidy to full subsidy.

Many employers must offer **transportation services** to comply with the law. Increasingly, local and state governments request that companies reduce the number of single-passenger automobiles commuting to their workplace each day because of government mandates for cleaner air. The *Clean Air Act Amendments of 1990* require employers in large metropolitan areas such as Los Angeles to comply with state and local commuter-trip-reduction laws. Employers may also offer transportation services in order to recruit individuals who do not care to drive themselves in rush-hour traffic. Further, transportation services enable companies to offset for deficits in parking space availability, particularly in congested metropolitan areas.

Employees obviously stand to benefit from transportation services. For example, using public transportation or joining a vanpool often saves money by eliminating commuting costs such as gas, insurance, car maintenance and repairs, and parking fees. Moreover, commuting time can be quite lengthy for some employees. By leaving the driving to others, employees can use the time more productively, for instance, reading, completing paperwork, or "unwinding."

Some companies provide outplacement assistance (technical and emotional support) to employees who are being laid off or terminated.

OUTPLACEMENT ASSISTANCE Some companies provide outplacement assistance (technical and emotional support) to employees who are being laid off or terminated. They do so through a variety of career and personal programs designed to develop employees' job-hunting skills and strategies and to boost employees' self-confidence.[49] A variety of factors lead to employee termination, factors to which outplacement assistance programs are best suited, including:

✯ Layoffs due to economic hardship

✯ Mergers and acquisitions

✯ Company reorganizations

✯ Changes in management

✯ Plant closings or relocation

✯ Elimination of specific positions, often the result of changes in technology

Outplacement assistance provides such services as personal counseling, career assessments and evaluations, training in job search techniques, résumé and cover letter preparation, interviewing techniques, and training in the use of basic workplace technology such as computers.[50] Beneficial to employees, outplacement assistance programs hold possible benefits for companies as well. Outplacement assistance programs may promote a positive image of the company among those being terminated, their families, and friends by helping these employees prepare for employment opportunities.

WELLNESS PROGRAMS In the 1980s, employers began sponsoring **wellness programs** to promote and maintain employees' physical and psychological health. Wellness programs vary in scope. They may emphasize weight loss only, or they may emphasize a range of activities, for instance, weight loss, smoking cessation, and cardiovascular fitness. Programs may be offered on- or off-site. Some companies may invest in staffing professionals for wellness programs; others contract with external vendors such as community health agencies or private health clubs.

Although wellness programs are relatively new, some evidence already indicates that these innovations can save companies money and reduce employees' need for health care. For every $1 invested in preventive health care programs, companies can expect to save as much as $6 in medical insurance costs.[51] Mesa Oil Company's wellness program yielded a cost savings of $200,000 that was attributable to reduced spending on health care (by as much as 50 percent) for employees who participated in the program compared with those who did not participate.[52] A study of 15,000 Control Data employees showed a strong relationship between health habits such as smoking and health care costs.[53]

Among workplace wellness programs, smoking cessation, stress reduction, nutrition and weight loss, exercise and fitness activities, and health screening programs are most common. **Smoking cessation** plans range from simple campaigns that stress the negative aspects of smoking to intensive programs directed at helping individuals stop smoking. Many employers offer courses and treatment to help and encourage smokers to quit. Other options include offering nicotine replacement therapy, such as nicotine gum and patches, and self-help services. Many companies sponsor antismoking events, such as the "Great American Smoke-Out," during which companies distribute T-shirts, buttons, and literature that discredit smoking.

Stress management programs can help employees cope with many factors inside and outside work that contribute to stress. For instance, job conditions, health and personal problems, and personal and professional relationships can make employees anxious and thus less productive. Symptoms of stressful workplaces include low morale, chronic absenteeism, low productivity, and high turnover rates. Employers offer stress management programs to teach workers to cope with conditions and situations that cause stress. Seminars focus on recognizing signs of stress and burnout and how to handle family- and business-related stress. Stress reduction techniques can improve quality of life inside and outside the workplace. Employers benefit from increased employee productivity, reduced absenteeism, and lower health care costs.

Weight control and nutrition programs are designed to educate employees about proper nutrition and weight loss, both of which are critical to good health. Information from the medical community has clearly indicated that excess weight and poor nutrition are significant risk factors in cardiovascular disease, diabetes, high blood pressure, and cholesterol levels. Over time, these employee programs should yield better health, increased morale, and improved appearance. For employers, these programs should result in improved employee productivity and lower health care costs.

Companies can contribute to employees' weight control and proper nutrition by sponsoring memberships in weight loss programs such as Weight Watchers and Jenny Craig. Sponsoring companies may also reinforce weight loss programs' positive results through support groups, intensive counseling, competitions, and other incentives. Companies sometimes actively attempt to influence employee food choices by stocking vending machines with nutritional food.

Laws that guide discretionary fringe compensation

Many laws guide discretionary fringe compensation practices. We review only the major laws on this topic. These include the *Employee Retirement Income Security Act of 1974 (ERISA)*, the *Consolidated Omnibus Budget Reconciliation Act of 1985 (COBRA)*, key antidiscrimination laws, and the *Fair Labor Standards Act*.

Employee Retirement Income Security Act of 1974 (ERISA)

The **Employee Retirement Income Security Act of 1974 (ERISA)** was established to regulate the establishment and implementation of various fringe compensation programs. These include medical, life, and disability programs as well as pension programs. The essence of ERISA is to provide protection of employee benefits rights.

ERISA addresses matters of employers' reporting and disclosure duties, funding of benefits, the fiduciary responsibilities for these plans, and vesting rights. Companies must provide their employees with straightforward descriptions of their employee benefits plans, updates when substantive changes to the plan are implemented, annual synopses on the financing and operation of the plans, and advance notification if the company intends to terminate the benefits plan. The funding requirement mandates that companies meet strict guidelines to ensure having sufficient funds when employees reach retirement. Similarly, the fiduciary responsibilities require that companies not engage in transactions with parties having interests adverse to those of the recipients of the plan and refrain from dealing with the income or assets of the employee benefits plan in their own interest.

Vesting refers to employees' acquisition of nonforfeitable rights to pension benefits. Specifically, employees must either be 100 percent vested after no more than five years of service or partially vested after no more than three years of service and 100 percent vested after no more than seven years of service. One hundred percent vested means that an employee cannot lose pension benefits even if he or she leaves the job before retirement.

There are two minimum criteria for eligibility under ERISA. First, employees must be allowed to participate in a pension plan after they reach age 21. Second, employees must have completed one year of service based on at least 1,000 hours of work. There is no maximum age limit for eligibility.

Since the passage of ERISA, there have been a number of amendments to the act. The impetus for these amendments has been the ever-changing laws relating to the tax treatment of employees' contributions to pension plans. For example, the tax laws do offer employees the opportunity to deduct a limited amount of their gross income (that is, income before any federal, state, or local taxes are assessed) for investment into a pension plan. Such deductions reduce the taxable gross pay amount on which taxes are assessed, clearly lowering employees' tax burden. The amendments are quite complex and technical, requiring familiarity with the Internal Revenue Code, the tax code administered by the Internal Revenue Service. The key amendments include the *Tax Equity and Fiscal Responsibility Act of 1982, Deficit Reduction Act of 1984,* and the *Tax Reform Act of 1986.*

Consolidated Omnibus Budget Reconciliation Act of 1985 (COBRA)

The **Consolidated Omnibus Budget Reconciliation Act of 1985 (COBRA)** was enacted to provide employees with the opportunity to temporarily continue receiving their employer-sponsored medical care insurance under their employer's plan if their coverage otherwise would cease owing to termination, layoff, or other change in employment status. COBRA applies to a wide variety of employers, with exemptions available only for companies that normally employ fewer than 20 workers, church plans, and plans maintained by the U.S. government.

Under COBRA, individuals may continue their coverage for up to 18 months, as well as for their spouses and dependents. Coverage may extend for up to 36 months for spouses and dependents facing a loss of employer-provided coverage because of an employee's death, a divorce or legal separation, or certain other qualifying events. Employee termination, retirement, layoff, and death are examples of qualifying events. Exhibit 11-9 displays the maximum continuation period for particular qualifying events.

Companies are permitted to charge COBRA beneficiaries a premium for continuation of coverage of up to 102 percent of the cost of the coverage to the plan. The 2 per-

Exhibit 11-9
*Continuation of Coverage
under COBRA*

The following information applies to health, vision and dental coverage only. If you are interested in continuing life insurance when your employment terminates, please refer to the materials provided which describe your life coverage.

COBRA (Consolidated Omnibus Budget Reconciliation Act) was signed into law on April 7, 1986 as P.L. 99-272. Under COBRA, the employer must provide covered members and their dependents who would lose coverage under the plan the option to continue coverage. The mandate is restricted to certain conditions under which coverage is lost, and the election to continue must be made within a specified election period. COBRA went into effect for members and their dependents on July 1, 1986.

A. COBRA Requirements

Qualifying Events	Maximum Continuation Period
Member	
a) Termination of employment for any reason, including termination of disability benefits and layoff, except for gross misconduct.	18 months
b) Loss of eligibility due to reduction in work hours.	18 months
c) Determination by the Social Security Administration (SSA) of disability that existed at time of qualifying event.	29 months
Dependent	
a) Member's termination of employment as stated above.	18 months
b) Member's loss of eligibility due to reduction in work hours.	18 months
c) Member's death, divorce, or legal separation.	
1) spouse or ex-spouse, under age 55.	36 months
2) spouse or ex-spouse age 55 or older.	The date spouse or ex-spouse becomes entitled to Medicare.
d) Member's Medicare entitlement. (Under certain conditions, this could be 36 months.)	18 months
e) Ceases to satisfy plan's eligibility requirements for dependent status.	36 months
f) Determination by the Social Security Administration (SSA) of disability that existed at time of qualifying event. Must have been covered under member's insurance at time of qualifying event.	29 months

If your are covered under COBRA and have been determined to be disabled by the federal Social Security Administration (SSA), you may be eligible to extend your coverage time from 18 months to 29. You must submit a copy of the SSA determination to the State's COBRA Administrator within 60 days of the date of the SSA determination letter and before the end of the original 18-month COBRA coverage period. Failure to notify the administrator and submit the required documentation within the 60-day period will disqualify you for the extension.

To be eligible for the extension of time, members must have been determined by the SSA to be disabled at the time of the event which qualified them for COBRA. Dependents must have been determined by the SSA to be disabled at the time of the event which qualified the member for COBRA and must have been covered by the member for insurance at that time.

cent markup reflects a charge for administering COBRA. Employers that violate the COBRA requirements are subject to an excise tax for each affected employee for each day that the violation continues. In addition, plan administrators who fail to provide required COBRA notices to employees may be personally liable for a civil penalty for each day the notice is not provided.

Additional pertinent legislation

As we discussed in Chapter 3, the Civil Rights Act of 1964, 1991, the Age Discrimination in Employment Act, and the Pregnancy Discrimination Act prohibit discrimination in both core and fringe compensation. This means that employers provide members of protected classes (for example, women, or all individuals at least age 40) with equal opportunity to receive the same benefits as members of the majority. In addition, we discussed the Fair Labor Standards Act, which applies to fringe compensation as well as to core compensation. Employees who are covered by this law are entitled to pay at a rate of one and one-half times their normal hourly rate for hours worked in excess of 40 during a work week. Fringe benefits that are linked to pay, as in the case of unemployment insurance (Chapter 10), increase correspondingly during those overtime hours.

Unions and fringe compensation

In Chapter 3, we reviewed the National Labor Relations Act of 1935 (NLRA), which gives rights to employees to self-organize, form, join, or assist labor unions, bargain collectively through representatives of their own choosing, and engage in other concerted activities for the purpose of collective bargaining. In 1993, workers covered by collective bargaining agreements were more likely to receive life insurance coverage, retirement benefits, and health protection coverage than were workers not covered by collective bargaining agreements.[54]

Under the NLRA, the possible subjects for bargaining fall under three categories: mandatory, permissive, or illegal. Only the lists of mandatory and permissive subjects include compensation issues. To date, the National Labor Relations Board (NLRB) has declared no compensation subjects as illegal. **Mandatory bargaining subjects** are those that employers and unions must bargain on if either constituent makes proposals about them. In the domain of fringe compensation, the following items are mandatory subjects of bargaining:

- ✩ Disability pay (supplemental to what is mandated by Social Security and the various state workers' compensation laws)
- ✩ Employer-provided health insurance
- ✩ Pay for time-not-worked
- ✩ Pension and retirement plans

The NLRA strictly limits management discretion in unionized firms to establish major elements of the fringe compensation program. For example, the NLRB held that an employer committed an unfair labor practice when it unilaterally switched insurance carriers and changed the health protection benefits provided under its collective bargaining agreement. The NLRB held that the collective bargaining agreement contemplated that the same insurance carrier would be retained while the contract was in effect and that benefits would remain as agreed upon during negotiations.[55]

Although employee health care benefits plans are mandatory subjects for bargaining, under certain circumstances, the change in the identity of the plan's insurance carrier or third-party administrator is not a compulsory bargaining subject. For example, a federal appeals court ruled that an employer's unilateral change to a new insurance carrier that was substantively the same as the old carrier was lawful.[56] The employer had proposed that it unilaterally be able to change insurance carriers. The union countered by saying that change could be made only after both parties had agreed on the terms and conditions of the health care coverage. When the parties could not agree on the terms, an interim contract provision was inserted that stated that the employer could not unilaterally adopt an alternative delivery system. Subsequently, the employer changed carriers without first consulting the union. The union sued to prevent the company from switching carriers, but the court held that the change of carriers was lawful for two reasons: First, the coverage under the new carrier remained substantially the same. Second, the provision restricting the unilateral adoption of an alternative delivery system was so ambiguous that it did not prevent the employer from switching insurance carriers.

Permissive bargaining subjects are those subjects on which neither the employer nor union is obligated to bargain. The following are fringe compensation items that fall in the permissive subjects category:

★ Administration of funds for fringe compensation programs

★ Retiree benefits (such as medical insurance)

★ Workers' compensation, within the scope of state workers' compensation laws

Designing and planning the benefits program

Discretionary benefits can work strategically by offering protection programs, pay for time not worked, and services that promote a company's goals of, for example, cost containment and employee motivation. As they plan and manage fringe compensation programs, human resource professionals should keep these functions in mind. Probably no company expects its fringe compensation program to meet all its objectives. Company management, along with union representatives, must determine which objectives are the most important for their particular work forces.

Many experts argue that employee input is key to developing a "successful" program.[57] Such input helps companies target the limited resources they have available for fringe compensation to those areas that best meet employees' needs. For example, if a company's work force includes mostly married couples who are raising young children, family assistance programs would likely be a priority. Employees involved in program development are most likely to accept and appreciate the benefits they receive. Companies can involve employees in the benefits determination process in a variety of ways such as surveys, interviews, and focus groups.

Human resource professionals must address fundamental issues as they design fringe programs, including:

★ Who receives coverage

Probably no company expects its fringe compensation program to meet all its objectives. Company management, along with union representatives, must determine which objectives are the most important for their particular work forces.

Exhibit 11-10

Types of Employee Input for Designing Benefits Programs

Ask employees:

- What they know about existing benefits
- What they perceive to be the value of possible benefit changes
- What they think about the quality and timeliness of benefits communications and administration
- What they perceive to be the value of existing benefits, compared with those provided by other employers

Source: Adapted from J. A. Haslinger and D. Sheering, Employee input: The key to successful benefits programs, *Compensation & Benefits Review* (May–June 1994):61–70.

✯ Whether to include retirees in the plan

✯ Whether to deny benefits to employees during their probationary periods

✯ How to finance benefits

✯ The degree of employee choice in determining benefits

✯ Cost containment

✯ Communication

Employers can ascertain key information from employees that can be useful in designing these programs. Exhibit 11-10 lists examples of the kinds of information employers may wish to obtain from their employees. The areas of input emphasize employees' beliefs about other employers' benefits offerings and employees' thoughts about the value of the benefits they receive.

Determining who receives coverage

Companies decide whether to extend benefits coverage to full-time and part-time employees or to full-time employees only. The trend is toward offering part-time employees no benefits. For example, in 1991, 92 percent of full-time private sector employees working received paid vacation, but only 39 percent of part-time private sector employees received any paid vacation. And 60 percent of full-time employees received retirement benefits, whereas only 21 percent of part-time employees received any retirement benefits.[58]

Deciding whether to include retirees in the plan

The decision of whether to include retirees in the benefits plan centers on whether to extend medical insurance coverage to employees beyond the COBRA-mandated coverage period, which we discussed earlier. In 1993, only 26 percent of medium and large private companies offered medical insurance to retirees,[59] and only 18 percent of small private companies offered medical insurance to retirees.[60] Offering medical coverage to retirees benefits them in obvious ways because employers usually finance these benefits either wholly or partly, enabling many retirees on limited earnings to receive adequate medical protection. Until recently, extending medical insurance coverage to retirees also benefited employers: The money they spent to extend coverage to retirees was tax deductible. In 1997, however, employers' contributions to extend medical coverage to retirees will not be tax deductible, which means that such expenses will reduce company earnings.[61] Consequently, it is expected that in the future fewer employers will finance medical insurance coverage for retirees.

Probationary period

Another scope issue companies must address is employees' status. In many companies, employees' initial term of employment (usually fewer than six months) is deemed the **probationary period,** and companies view such periods as an opportunity to ensure that they have made sound hiring decisions. Many companies choose to withhold discretionary fringe compensation for all probationary employees. Companies benefit directly through lower administration-of-benefits costs for these employees during the probationary period. However, probationary employees may find themselves experiencing financial hardships if they require medical attention.

Financing

Human resource managers must consider how to finance benefits. In fact, the available resources and financial goals may influence, to some extent, who will receive coverage. Managers may decide on noncontributory, contributory, or employee-financed programs or some combination thereof. **Noncontributory financing** implies that the company assumes total costs for each discretionary benefit. Under **contributory financing,** the company and its employees share the costs. Under **employee-financed benefits,** employers do not contribute to the financing of discretionary benefits. The majority of benefit plans today are contributory, largely because the cost of benefits has risen so dramatically.

Employee choice

Human resource professionals must decide on the degree of choice employees should have in determining the set of benefits they will receive. If employees within a company can choose from among a set of benefits, as opposed to all employees receiving the same set of benefits, the company is using a **flexible benefits,** or **cafeteria, plan.** Companies implement cafeteria plans to meet the challenges of diversity as we discussed earlier. Although there is limited evidence regarding employees' reactions to flexible benefits, the existing information indicates benefit satisfaction, overall job satisfaction, pay satisfaction, and understanding of benefits increased after the implementation of the flexible benefits plan.[62] Many of these outcomes are desirable as they are known to lead to reduced absenteeism and turnover.

Cafeteria plans vary.[63] The two most common cafeteria plans are discussed here. **Flexible spending accounts** permit employees to pay for certain benefits expenses (such as child care) with pretax dollars. Before each plan year, employees elect the amount of salary-reduction dollars they wish to allocate to this kind of plan. Employers then use those moneys to reimburse employees for expenses incurred during the plan year that qualify for repayment. Exhibit 11-11 illustrates the features of a flexible spending account for State of Illinois employees. These features are typical for flexible spending accounts used in private and public sector companies.

Core plus option plans extend a preestablished set of benefits, such as medical insurance, as a program core, usually, mandatory for all employees. Beyond the core, employees may choose from an array of benefits options that suit their personal needs. Companies establish upper limits of benefits values available to each employee. If em-

Exhibit 11-11
Flexible Spending Accounts

How the FSA Program Works

The Flexible Spending Accounts (FSA) Program lets you use tax-free dollars to pay for medical expenses and/or dependent care expenses, increasing your take-home pay and giving you more spendable income. Through convenient payroll deductions, you may contribute up to $5,000 tax-free to a spending account for either one or both plans.

Spending accounts are like getting a tax rebate every time you pay for eligible health and child (dependent) care expenses. The FSA Program is simple to use:

- You sign up during one of the enrollment periods and determine how much pretax earnings you wish to put into your FSA account.

- You put pretax money into your spending accounts. (The amount you choose is taken out of your paycheck through payroll deduction and deposited into your FSA account before taxes are calculated.)

- When you have an eligible expense, you send in a claim form with the required documentation.

- Then you get a check back from your account.

When you are reimbursed from your spending accounts, you recieve that money tax-free. This amount doesn't appear on your W-2 Form as taxable income—and a lower taxable income means you pay less taxes.

Employees have two types of FSAs available: the Medical Care Assistance Plan (MCAP) for eligible health-related expenses and the Dependent Care Assistance Plan (DCAP) for eligible child or other dependent care expenses.

Important Notes

- **Federal Tax Deductions:** Expenses reimbursed through a FSA may not also be used as itemized deductions on your federal tax return.

- **Forfeitures:** Money contributed to your FSA in any plan year can only be used to reimburse eligible expenses incurred during that same plan year. Per IRS regulations, any amounts not claimed by the end of the filing deadlines are forfeited.

- **FSA Accounts Are Separate:** The IRS requires that amounts contributed for reimbursement of health care expenses be accounted for separately from those for day care. In other words, you cannot use amounts deposited in your MCAP Account to cover DCAP expenses, or vice versa.

- **Tax Savings:** The employer does not guarantee any specific tax consequences from participation in the FSA program. You are responsible for understanding the effects on your individual situation as a result of directing earnings into tax-free spending accounts. You are also responsible for the validity and eligibility of your claims. You may wish to consult with your personal tax adviser regarding your participation.

- **Changing Your FSA Midyear:** Unless your are newly hired or experience a qualifying change of family status, you may not enroll in, withdraw from, or change your contribution to a FSA account outside of the annual Benefit Choice Period.

Dependent Care Assistance Plan (DCAP)

Who Is Eligible to Participate in DCAP?

Eligible employees include:

- Employees who are actively at work and are receiving a paycheck from which deductions can be taken.

- If you are married, your spouse must be either gainfully employed or looking for work (but must have earned income for the year); a full-time student for at least five months during the year; or disabled and unable to provide for his or her own care.

Eligible dependents for DCAP are defined by the IRS and include:

- Your spouse;
- Children or other individuals you are eligible to claim as dependents on your federal income tax return; and,
- Individuals who could have been claimed as dependents on your income tax except that the person had income which exceeded the amount allowable to be claimed as a dependent.

What Expenses Are Eligible for Reimbursement under DCAP?

- Nursery schools and preschools;
- Schooling prior to the first grade if the amount you pay for schooling is incident to and cannot be separated from the cost of care;
- Day care centers that comply with all applicable state and local laws and regulations;
- Work-related baby sitters—whether in or out of your home;
- Before and after-school care;
- Housekeepers in your home if part of their work provides for the well-being and protection of your eligible dependents;
- Adult day care facilities (but not expenses for overnight nursing home facilities);
- Disabled dependent care at centers that comply with state and local laws and regulations;
- Employment taxes you pay on wages for qualifying child and dependent care services; and,
- Other expenses which meet program and IRS criteria.

How Much Can I Contribute to My DCAP Account?

You must contribute at least $10 per paycheck if you are paid semimonthly or $20 per paycheck for monthly payrolls. You may contribute a maximum of $208.33 for semimonthly payrolls or $416.66 for monthly payrolls ($4,999.92 annually). Special contribution limits apply for DCAP contributions.

Medical Care Assistance Plan (MCAP)

Who Is Eligible to Participate in MCAP?

- Employees who are working full-time or not less than half-time, are receiving a paycheck from which deductions can be taken, and are participating in one of the state's health plans are eligible.

What Expenses Are Eligible for Reimbursement under MCAP?

- Health and dental care costs not fully covered by the insurance plans in which you or your family members participate, for example:

  deductibles,

  copayments,

  amounts in excess of the maximum benefit, or

  amounts in excess of the reasonable and customary charge limits of the health or dental plans;

- Health and dental care not considered as covered services by the insurance plans in which you or your family members participate; and,
- Other expenses which meet program and IRS criteria.

Exhibit 11-11
Flexible Spending Accounts (continued)

Exhibit 11-11
Flexible Spending Accounts (continued)

How Much Can I Contribute to My MCAP Account?

You must contribute at least $10 per paycheck if you are paid semimonthly or $20 per paycheck for monthly payrolls. You may contribute a maximum of $208.53 for semimonthly payrolls or $416.66 for monthly payrolls.

For more detailed information on FSA program requirements, contact your Group Insurance Representative for a program booklet. It is important that you read the materials carefully and consult with your personal tax adviser to determine whether MCAP and/or DCAP accounts are beneficial for your particular situation.

ployees do not choose the maximum amount of benefits, employers may offer an option of trading extra benefits credits for cash. Exhibit 11-12 illustrates the choices of a typical core-plus plan.

Cost containment

In 1965, fringe compensation accounted for 21.5 percent of total compensation expenditures; in 1993, it totaled 39.3 percent of compensation expenditures.

Overall, human resource managers today seek to contain costs. As indicated earlier, the rise in health care costs is phenomenal, so fringe compensation now accounts for a higher percentage of total compensation costs incurred by companies than it used to. In 1965, fringe compensation accounted for 21.5 percent of total compensation expenditures; in 1993, it totaled 39.3 percent of compensation expenditures.[64] This change would not necessarily raise concerns if total compensation budgets were increasing commensurably. As we discussed in Chapter 9 (see "The Flip Side of the Coin"), the growth in funds available to support all compensation programs has stagnated. As a consequence, employers face difficult tradeoffs between fringe compensation offerings and core compensation.

Communication

Earlier, we discussed the fact that employees often regard fringe compensation as an entitlement. Thus, it is reasonable to infer that employees are not aware of the value

Exhibit 11-12
A Sample Core Plus Option Plan

The core plus option plan contains two sets of benefits: *core benefits* and *optional benefits*.

All employees receive a minimum level of *core benefits*:

- Term life insurance equal to 1 times annual salary
- Health protection coverage (commercial plan, self-funded, HMO, PPO) for the employee and dependents
- Disability insurance

All employees receive credits equal to 4 to 7 percent of salary, which can be used to purchase *optional benefits*:

- Dental insurance for employee and dependents
- Vision insurance for employee and dependents
- Additional life insurance coverage
- Paid vacation time up to 10 days per year

If an employee has insufficient credits to purchase the desired optional benefits, he or she can purchase these credits through payroll deduction.

of receiving fringe compensation. In fact, research that supports that inference suggests that employees either are not aware of or undervalue the fringe compensation they receive.[65] Given the significant costs associated with offering fringe compensation, companies should try to convey the value employees are likely to derive from having such benefits. Accordingly, a benefits communication plan is essential. An effective communication program should have three primary objectives:[66]

- ✯ To create an awareness of and appreciation for the way current benefits improve the financial security as well as the physical and mental well-being of employees

- ✯ To provide a high level of understanding about available benefits

- ✯ To encourage the wise use of benefits

A variety of media can be used to communicate such information to employees. Printed brochures that abstract the key features of the benefits program are useful for conveying the "big picture" and for helping potential employees compare benefits offerings with those of other companies they may be considering. The company should hold initial group meetings with benefits administrators or give audiovisual presentations to new hires. The meetings and presentations should detail the elements of the company's benefits program. Shortly after the group meetings or audiovisual presentations (usually within a month), new employees should meet individually with benefits administrators, sometimes known as counselors, to select benefits options. After the employee has selected benefits, the company should provide a personal benefits statement that details the scope of coverage and value of each component. Exhibit 11-13 illustrates a personal statement of benefits. Beyond these particulars, companies may update employees on changes in benefits—reductions in or additions to benefits choices or coverage—by means of periodic newsletters.

The implications of discretionary benefits for strategic compensation

Not unlike core compensation, discretionary benefits can contribute to a company's competitive advantage for the reasons we discussed earlier, such as tax advantage and recruiting the best-qualified candidates. Discretionary benefits can also undermine the imperatives of strategic compensation. Ultimately, companies that provide discretionary benefits as entitlements to employees are less likely to promote competitive advantage than companies that design discretionary fringe compensation programs to "fit" the situation.

Management can use discretionary benefit offerings to promote particular employee behaviors that have strategic value. For instance, when employees take advantage of tuition reimbursement programs, they are more likely to contribute to the strategic imperatives of product or service differentiation or cost reduction. Knowledge acquired from job-relevant education may enhance the creative potential of employees as well as their ability to implement more cost-effective modes of work. Alternatively, ESOPs may contribute to companies' strategic imperatives by instilling a sense of ownership in employees. Having a financial stake in the company should lead employees to behave in ways that will promote the company's objectives.

Management can use discretionary benefit offerings to promote particular employee behaviors that have strategic value.

Exhibit 11-13
Example of a Personal Statement of Benefits

A PERSONAL BENEFIT STATEMENT FOR:

John Doe

SSN: *xxx-xx-xxxx*   Date of Birth: *09/06/62*

Marital status: *Single*

REVIEW OF YOUR CURRENT BENEFIT CHOICES

As of March 1995, our records indicate you have chosen the following benefits (Rates may change July 1, 1995):

MEDICAL

For you:

PERSONAL CARE HMO

For your dependent(s):

NONE

State's monthly contribution:	
For you:	*$151.00*
For your dependent(s):	*None*
Your monthly contribution:	*$10.00*

DENTAL

QUALITY CARE DENTAL PLAN

Your monthly contribution:	*$5.00*
State's annual contribution:	
For you:	*$84.00*
For your dependent(s):	*None*

LIFE INSURANCE

As a full-time employee you receive state-paid life insurance equal to your annual salary. If you work part-time, your state-paid amount is less. When you retire at age 60 or older, you still receive $5,000 worth of state-paid life insurance.

State's monthly contribution for your state-paid life insurance:

Basic life	*($61,100):*	*$26.89*

Your monthly contribution for the following optional coverage:

For you	*(None):*	*None*
Spouse life	*(None):*	*None*
Child life	*(None):*	*None*
Accidental Death and Dismemberment:	*(None):*	*None*

FLEXIBLE SPENDING ACCOUNTS

You are enrolled in the following plan(s):

Dependent Care Assistance Plan	
Annual deduction:	*Not Enrolled*
Medical Care Assistance Plan	
Annual deduction:	*Not Enrolled*

DEPENDENTS

You have chosen to cover the following dependents under your Health Plan:

No Dependents

NOTE: Any corrections for either premium paid or insurance coverage may only be applied retroactively for up to six months from the month in which the change was reported to the Group Insurance Representative. Be sure to review your paycheck for proper deductions and report any concerns to your Group Insurance Representative immediately.

DOLLAR VALUE OF YOUR BENEFITS

Your total annual compensation is your salary or retirement payment plus the value of state-paid medical, dental, and life insurance coverage.

State-paid medical insurance coverage for you:	*$1,812.00*
State contribution for medical insurance coverage for your dependent(s):	*None*
State-paid dental insurance coverage for you and your dependent(s):	*$84.00*
State-paid life insurance coverage for you:	*$322.68*
TOTAL VALUE OF YOUR STATE PAID BENEFITS:	*$2,218.68*

A company can use its offering of discretionary benefits to distinguish itself from the competition. In effect, competitive benefits programs potentially convey the message that the company is a good place to work because it invests in the well-being of its employees. Presumably, lucrative benefits programs will attract a large pool of applicants that includes high-quality candidates, positioning a company to hire the best-possible employees.

Discretionary benefits also serve a strategic purpose by accommodating the needs of a diverse work force. As we discussed previously, companies choose between offering one standard set of benefits to all employees or a flexible benefits program that permits each employee to have some control over the kinds of discretionary benefits coverage. For example, with an increase of dual-career couples with children, there comes a strong need for some form of child care for preschool age children. However, not all employees require child care because they do not have children or their children are old enough not to require this kind of supervision. If a company were to offer a standard fixed plan of discretionary fringe compensation, then only one segment of the work force would benefit—obviously, those with very young children. Employees not needing child care assistance would be receiving a benefit of no value to them, which, in effect, reduces the entire value of the benefits program for those employees. On the other hand, a company that did not offer child care could expect to see evidence of absenteeism and turnover as employees with young children struggled to cope with child care. In either case, a standard benefits plan would not be helpful. However, a cafeteria plan would enable employees to receive benefits that are useful to their situation, minimizing the possible problems just mentioned. In the long run, accommodating the diverse needs of the work force has strategic value by minimizing dysfunctional behaviors—absenteeism and turnover—which are disruptive to a company's operations.

Finally, the tax advantage afforded companies from offering particular discretionary benefits has strategic value. In effect, the tax advantage translates into cost savings to companies. These savings can be applied to promote competitive advantage. For example, companies pursuing differentiation strategies may invest these savings into research and development programs. Also, companies pursuing lowest-cost strategies may be in a better position to compete because these savings may enable the companies to lower the prices of their products and services without cutting into profits.

Summary

This chapter described the major kinds of discretionary benefits and reviewed the role of discretionary benefits in strategic compensation. Presently, there appears to be wide variation in the kinds of fringe compensation practices that companies offer. Increasingly, companies are investing in protection programs and services that are designed to enhance the well-being of employees in a cost-efficient manner. As competition increases, placing greater pressures on cost containment strategies, companies have already faced hard choices about the benefits they have been able to offer their employees. It is likely that this trend will continue in the foreseeable future.

Discussion questions

1. Many compensation professionals are faced with making choices about which discretionary benefits to drop because funds are limited and the costs of these benefits continually increase. Assume that you must make such choices. Rank order discretionary benefits, starting with the ones you would *most likely drop* and ending with the ones you would *least likely drop*. Explain your rationale. Do factors such as the demographic composition of the work force of the company matter? Explain.

2. Discuss your views about whether discretionary fringe compensation should be an entitlement or something earned on the basis of job performance.

3. What role can flexible benefits programs play in alleviating the potential dissatisfaction that goes along with cutting benefits? Should companies move to a flexible benefits approach to "get the most bang for the buck"? Explain.

4. Assume that you are an HRM professional whose responsibility is to develop a brochure for the purpose of conveying the value of your company's benefits program to potential employees. Your company has asked you to showcase the benefits program in a manner that will encourage recruits to join the company. Develop a brochure (of no more than two pages) that meets that objective. Conduct research on companies' benefits practices (in a journal such as *Personnel Journal*) as a basis for developing your brochure.

5. Your instructor will assign you an industry. Conduct some research in order to identify the prevalent fringe compensation practices for that industry. Also, what factors (for example, technology, competition, government regulation) might influence the present practices? How will these practices change?

Key terms

welfare practices
short-term disability insurance
long-term disability insurance
life insurance
term coverage
life coverage
pension programs
contributory pension plans
noncontributory pension plans
qualified pension plans
nonqualified pension plans
defined contribution plans
defined benefit plans

commercial insurance plans
usual, customary, and reasonable
  charge
deductible
coinsurance
self-funded insurance plans
health maintenance organizations
  (HMOs)
copayments
Health Maintenance Organization
  Act of 1973
prepaid group practices
individual practice associations

preferred provider organization (PPO)

dental insurance

cost shifting

commercial dental insurance

self-insured dental plans

dental service corporations

dental maintenance organizations

vision insurance

employee assistance programs (EAPs)

family assistance programs

flexible scheduling and leave

day care

tuition reimbursement programs

transportation services

outplacement assistance

wellness programs

smoking cessation

stress management

weight control and nutrition programs

Employee Retirement Income Security Act of 1974 (ERISA)

vesting

Consolidated Omnibus Budget Reconciliation Act of 1985 (COBRA)

mandatory bargaining subjects

permissive bargaining subjects

probationary period

noncontributory financing

contributory financing

employee-financed benefits

flexible benefits plan

cafeteria plan

flexible spending accounts

core plus option plans

Endnotes

[1] U.S. Chamber of Commerce, *Employee benefits 1995 edition: Survey data from benefit year 1994* (Washington, D.C.: U.S. Chamber of Commerce Research Center, 1995).

[2] J. R. Schuster and J. K. Zingheim, *The new pay* (New York: Lexington Books, 1990).

[3] L. K. Beatty, Pay and benefits break away from tradition, *HR Magazine* 39 (1994): 63–68.

[4] W. B. Johnston, *Workforce 2000: Work and workers for the 21st century* (Indianapolis: Hudson Institute, 1991).

[5] U.S. Department of Commerce, *Statistical abstracts of the United States,* 115th ed. (Washington, D.C.: U.S. Government Printing Office, 1995).

[6] B. T. Beam Jr. and J. J. McFadden, *Employee benefits,* 5th ed. (Chicago: Dearborn Financial Publishing, 1996).

[7] U.S. Bureau of Labor Statistics, *Welfare work for employees in industrial establishments in the United States,* Bulletin No. 250 (Washington, D.C.: U.S. Government Printing Office, 1919), pp. 119–123.

[8] U.S. Bureau of Labor Statistics, *Employee benefits survey: A BLS reader* (Washington, D.C.: U.S. Government Printing Office, 1995).

[9] L. Solnick, The effect of the blue collar unions on white collar wages and benefits, *Industrial and Labor Relations Review* 38 (1985): 23–35.

[10] Beam and McFadden *Employee benefits,* 5th ed.

[11] Ibid.

[12] Ibid.

[13] U.S. Bureau of Labor Statistics, *Employee benefits survey.*

[14] Ibid.

[15] U.S. Chamber of Commerce, *Employee benefits 1995 edition.*

[16] M. Bucci, Growth of employer-sponsored group life insurance, *Monthly Labor Review* 114 (1991):25–32.

[17] U.S. Chamber of Commerce, *Employee benefits 1995 edition.*

[18] Beam and McFadden, *Employee benefits,* 5th ed.

[19] U.S. Chamber of Commerce, *Employee benefits 1995 edition.*

[20] E. M. Coates III, Profit sharing today: Plans and provisions, *Monthly Labor Review* 114 (1991):19–25.

[21] U.S. Bureau of Labor Statistics, *Employee benefits in medium and large private establishments, 1993* (Washington, D.C.: U.S. Government Printing Office, 1994).

22 U.S. Chamber of Commerce, *Employee benefits 1995 edition.*

23 Ibid.

24 U.S. Bureau of Labor Statistics, *Employee benefits in medium and large private establishments, 1993* (Washington, D.C.: U.S. Government Printing Office, 1995).

25 Ibid.

26 U.S. Chamber of Commerce, *Employee benefits 1995 edition.*

27 Ibid.

28 U.S. Bureau of Labor Statistics, *Employee benefits in medium and large private establishments, 1993.*

29 U.S. Chamber of Commerce, *Employee benefits 1995 edition.*

30 Health Maintenance Organizations, 42 U.S.C. 88 300e–330e-17 (1973).

31 U.S. Chamber of Commerce, *Employee benefits 1994 edition: Survey data from benefit year 1994* (Washington, D.C.: U.S. Chamber of Commerce Research Center, 1995).

32 U.S. Department of Commerce, *Statistical abstracts of the United States,* 115th ed.

33 U.S. Bureau of Labor Statistics, *Employee benefits in medium and large private establishments, 1993.*

34 U.S. Bureau of Labor Statistics, *Employee benefits survey.*

35 U.S. Bureau of Labor Statistics, *Employee benefits in medium and large private establishments, 1993.*

36 U.S. Chamber of Commerce, *Employee benefits 1995 edition.*

37 D. Kirrane, EAPs: Dawning of a new age, *HR Magazine* 35 (1990):30–34.

38 U.S. Bureau of Labor Statistics, *Employee benefits in medium and large private establishments, 1993.* (Washington, D.C.: U.S. Government Printing Office, 1994).

39 U.S. Bureau of Labor Statistics, *Employee benefits in state and local governments, 1992.* (Washington, D.C.: U.S. Government Printing Office, 1994).

40 U.S. Bureau of Labor Statistics, *Employee benefits in small private establishments, 1992.* (Washington, D.C.: U.S. Government Printing Office, 1994).

41 The Bureau of National Affairs, Employee assistance programs, in *Compensation and benefits.* [Compact disc] (Washington, D.C.: U.S. Bureau of National Affairs, 1995).

42 W. F. Cascio, *Costing human resources: The financial impact of behavior in organizations,* 3rd ed. (Boston: PWS-Kent, 1991).

43 F. Luthans and R. Waldersee, What do we really know about EAPs? *Human Resource Management* 28 (1989):385–401.

44 G. Spencer, Projection of the population of the United States, by age, sex, race, and Hispanic origin: 1992 to 2050, in *Current Population Reports,* P-25, No. 1092 (Washington, D.C.: U.S. Government Printing Office, November 1992).

45 Johnston, *Workforce 2000.*

46 J. D. Goodstein, Institutional pressures and strategic responsiveness: Employer involvement in work-family issues, *Academy of Management Journal* 37 (1994):350–382.

47 Ibid.

48 L. R. Gómez-Mejía, D. B. Balkin, and R. L. Cardy, *Managing human resources* (Englwood Cliffs, N.J.: Prentice Hall, 1995).

49 L. Newman, Good bye is not enough, *Personnel Administrator* 33 (1988):84–86.

50 V. M. Gibson, The ins and outs of outplacement, *Management Review* 80 (1991): 59–61.

51 S. Tully, America's healthiest companies, *Fortune,* June 15, 1995, pp. 98–100+.

52 Gómez-Mejía, Balkin, and Cardy, *Managing human resources.*

53 K. R. Parkes, Relative weight, smoking, and mental health as predictors of sickness and absence from work, *Journal of Applied Psychology* 72 (1987):275–286.

54 U.S. Bureau of Labor Statistics, *Employee benefits in medium and large private establishments, 1993.*

55 *Wisconsin Southern Gas Co.,* 69 L.R.R.M. 1374, 173 N.L.R.B. No. 79 (1968).

56 *UAW v. Mack Trucks Inc.,* 135 L.R.R.M. 2833 (3rd Cir. 1990).

57 J. A. Haslinger and D. Sheering, Employee input: The key to successful benefits programs, *Compensation & Benefits Review* (May–June 1994):61–70.

58 U.S. Bureau of Labor Statistics, *Employee benefits survey.*

59 U.S. Chamber of Commerce, *Employee benefits 1994 edition.*

60 U.S. Bureau of Labor Statistics, *Employee benefits in small private establishments, 1992.*

61 Beam and McFadden, *Employee benefits,* 5th ed.

62 A. E. Barber, R. B. Dunham, and R. Formisano, The impact of flexible benefit plans on employee benefit satisfaction.

Paper presented at the 50th annual meeting of the Academy of Management, San Francisco, 1990.

[63] Beam and McFadden, *Employee benefits,* 5th ed.

[64] U.S. Chamber of Commerce, *Employee benefits 1994 edition.*

[65] R. Huseman, J. Hatfield, and R. Robinson, The MBA and fringe benefits, *Personnel Administration* 23 (1978):57–60.

[66] Beam and McFadden, *Employee benefits,* 5th ed.

CHAPTER

TWELVE

International compensation

CHAPTER OUTLINE

Continued on next page

311

LEARNING OBJECTIVES

In this chapter, you will learn about

1. Competitive strategies and how international activities fit in
2. How globalization affects human resource departments
3. Methods for setting expatriates' base pay
4. Incentive compensation for expatriates
5. Fringe compensation for expatriates
6. The balance sheet approach
7. Repatriation issues
8. Compensation issues for host country nationals and third country nationals

Compensation for global managers can directly influence the strategic direction and, to some degree, the successful accomplishment of strategies of multinational corporations (MNCs) competing in the world marketplace. Without superior international managers that are motivated to succeed, the probability of successfully accomplishing global corporate plans is diminished. The reward system in an organization strongly influences the culture of the company and plays an important role in fostering successful goal attainment. To successfully compete in the global marketplace, managers assigned to foreign positions must maintain motivation and willingness to sustain productivity sometimes beyond the level of their domestic counterparts.[1]

[Unfortunately], it's a familiar scenario: An HR executive at a major corporation identifies an excellent candidate for an overseas assignment—an upper-level manager with the specific skills needed to open a new overseas office and meet the strategic objectives for the region. No doubt about it, this individual is the best talent for the job.

The problem? The manager reluctantly turns down the offer because an overseas stint would interrupt a spouse or partner's career. The HR executive, with no policies in place to address this increasingly common issue, scrambles to fill the post with the second- or third-best candidate.[2]

International compensation programs have strategic value. U.S. businesses continue to establish operations in foreign countries.

International compensation programs have strategic value. U.S. businesses continue to establish operations in foreign countries. The establishment of operations in Pacific Rim countries, Eastern European countries, and Mexico is on the rise. The general trend for expanding operations overseas serves as just one indicator of the "globalization" of the economy. U.S. companies place professional and managerial U.S. (citizen) employees overseas to establish and operate satellite plants and offices. Although there are many glamorous aspects about working overseas, the glamor comes at a price of personal and, sometimes, professional sacrifices. Compensation takes on strategic value by providing employees assigned to jobs in foreign countries minimal financial risk associated with working overseas and lifestyles for them and their families comparable to their lifestyles in the United States. Multinational companies—that is, companies with operations in more than one country—develop special compensation packages to help make up for the personal sacrifices international assignees and their immediate families make while fulfilling international assignments. These sacrifices are associated with cultural variations that affect lifestyle—dealing with an unfamiliar culture, enhanced responsibilities, and higher living expenses.

Competitive strategies and how international activities fit in

U.S. companies' presence in foreign countries is on the rise. You might forget that you are in China while taking a taxi ride through the streets of Beijing: Billboards and establishments for such U.S. companies as Baskin Robbins, McDonald's, Pizza Hut, Pepsi, Coca-Cola, and Motorola are common sights. In fact, the Golden Arches™ stand tall in Tiananmen Square!

Several factors have contributed to the expansion of global markets. These include such free trade agreements as the *North American Free Trade Agreement* (NAFTA; see "The Flip Side of the Coin"), the unification of the European market, and the gradual weakening of Communist influence in Eastern Europe and Asia. Likewise, foreign companies have greater opportunities to invest in the United States. According to the U.S. Department of Congress Statistical abstracts of the United States, 115th edition, U.S. exports of goods and services increased by 135 percent between 1984 and 1994, from $217.9 billion to $512.7 billion. U.S. imports of goods and services from foreign countries also increased substantially during the same period: 103 percent, from $325.7 billion to $663.8 billion.

Lowest-cost producers' relocation to cheaper production areas

Many U.S. businesses have established manufacturing and production facilities in Asian countries and in Mexico because labor is significantly cheaper than in the United States. There are two key reasons for the cost difference. First, labor unions generally do not have much bargaining power in developing Asian countries or in Mexico, where the government possesses extensive control over workplace affairs. Second, Asian governments do not value individual employee rights as much as the U.S. government does. As we discussed in Chapter 3, the Fair Labor Standards Act of 1938 provides employees a minimum hourly wage rate, limits exploitation of child labor, and mandates overtime pay.

Differentiation and the search for new global markets

Coca-Cola and Pepsi products are well known worldwide because these companies aggressively introduced their soft drink products throughout numerous countries. Establishing Coke and Pepsi products worldwide does not represent a differentiation

NAFTA: Job Gain or Job Loss?

The **North American Free Trade Agreement (NAFTA)** became effective on January 1, 1994. NAFTA has two main goals. First, NAFTA was designed to reduce trade barriers among Mexico, Canada, and the United States. The most formidable trade barriers are customs taxes and import quotas. Before NAFTA, Mexico assessed hefty tariffs on U.S.- and Canadian-made goods. In addition, Mexico imposed quotas on the amount of imports from the U.S. and Canada. These restrictions protected Mexico's economy by enabling Mexican businesses to operate with limited competition from foreign manufacturers. In addition, Mexico benefited from the revenue gained from assessing substantial customs tariffs.

Second, the NAFTA agreement set out to remove barriers to investment among the three countries. Before NAFTA was implemented, the Mexican government carefully controlled the influx of U.S. and Canadian business operations in Mexico. Many U.S. and Canadian business leaders considered Mexico to be an attractive location for manufacturing plants because Mexican labor is substantially cheaper than either U.S. or Canadian labor. Again, Mexico established these barriers to protect its economic interests.

In the United States, intense debate among politicians, workers, and business leaders preceded NAFTA's enactment. The debate centered on whether NAFTA would lead to a substantial loss or gain in U.S. jobs. Proponents argued that NAFTA would stimulate U.S. job growth because of greater access to Mexican product markets. Opponents argued that NAFTA would end in substantial U.S. job loss because U.S. corporations would find it difficult to justify paying hefty wages (particularly in the unionized sector) when Mexican labor is much cheaper. Some economists predicted that NAFTA would lead to a loss of 17,000 U.S. jobs in 1994, and 219,000 U.S. jobs would be lost in 1995.[3] Others predicted that NAFTA would result in a net creation of approximately 170,000 U.S. jobs in 1994.[4]

The U.S. Department of Labor certified that nearly 40,000 workers lost their jobs to NAFTA within the first 18 months of its enactment. More-pessimistic reports suggested that as many as 70,000 additional workers became unemployed during that period.[5] Reliable, updated information on job loss is lacking. Nevertheless, the preliminary statistics suggest that enhanced trade freedom among countries may come at a price—loss of jobs.

strategy. However, Coke and Pepsi could distinguish themselves from competing companies by taking on new business initiatives that depart from "business as usual" and meet specific market needs.

For Coke and Pepsi, business as usual means marketing soft drink products—carbonated water with artificial colors and flavors. Coke and Pepsi's marketing bottled spring water would clearly be a departure from business as usual. The People's Republic of China (PRC) possesses a definite need for bottled spring water: The Chinese government is unable to provide its citizens and visitors drinkable water because the country does not maintain adequate water purification plants. Coke and Pepsi could distinguish themselves from other soft drink companies by marketing spring water along with their regular soft drink products. Coke and Pepsi would be known as companies that serve necessary (bottled water) and recreational (soft drinks) beverage needs.

How globalization is affecting HR departments

The globalization of business requires that companies send employees overseas to establish and operate satellite plants and offices. Naturally, companies must invest in the development of appropriate HR practices. International business operations are destined to fail without the "right" people. Human resource professionals must be certain to identify the selection criteria that are most related to successful international work assignments. For example, do candidates possess adequate cultural sensitivity? Do they believe that U.S. customs are the only appropriate way to approach problems? Are candidates' families willing to adjust to foreign lifestyles?

Training is another key HR function. Expatriates must understand the cultural values that predominate in foreign countries; otherwise, they risk hindering business. For example, one of Procter and Gamble's Camay soap commercials was successful in the United States, but the Japanese perceived the very same commercial that aired in Japan to be rude. The commercial depicted a man barging into the bathroom on his wife while she was using Camay soap. Japanese cultural values led Japanese viewers to judge this commercial as offensive. The Japanese deemed the commercial as acceptable after Procter and Gamble modified the commercial to include a woman using Camay soap in privacy.

Companies' investment in cross-cultural training varies. Some companies provide release time from work to take foreign language courses at local colleges or universities. Highly progressive companies such as Motorola run corporate universities that offer cross-cultural training courses.

The complexity of international compensation programs

The development and implementation of international compensation programs typically pose four challenges to companies that U.S. compensation programs do not have to consider. First, successful international compensation programs further corporate interests abroad and encourage employees to take foreign assignments. Second, well-designed compensation programs minimize financial risk to employees and make their and their families' experiences as pleasant as possible. Third, international compensation programs promote a smooth transition back to life in the United States upon completion of the international assignment. **Repatriation** is the process of making the transition from an international assignment and living abroad to a domestic assignment and living in the home country. Fourth, sound international compensation programs promote U.S. businesses' lowest cost and differentiation strategies in foreign markets.

Preliminary considerations

We must take some basic issues under advisement before examining the elements of international compensation programs. Compensation professionals must distinguish among host country nationals, third country nationals, and expatriates as compensation recipients with their own unique issues. In addition, compensation professionals should consider such matters as term of the international assignment, staff mobility, and equity, because those factors pertain directly to the design elements of international compensation programs.

Host country nationals, third country nationals, and expatriates: definitions and relevance

There are three kinds of recipients of international compensation:

✯ Host country nationals (HCNs)

✯ Third country nationals (TCNs)

✯ Expatriates

We will define these recipients as employees of U.S. companies doing business in foreign countries. However, these definitions also apply to employees of non-U.S. companies doing business in foreign countries.

Host country nationals (HCNs) are foreign national citizens who work in U.S. companies' branch offices or manufacturing plants in their home countries. Japanese citizens working for General Electric Company in Japan are HCNs.

Third country nationals (TCNs) are foreign national citizens who work in U.S. companies' branch offices or manufacturing plants in foreign countries—excluding the United States and their home countries. Australian citizens working for General Motors Company in the People's Republic of China are TCNs.

Expatriates are U.S. citizens employed in U.S. companies with work assignments outside the United States. U.S. citizens employed in CitiBank's London, England, office are expatriates.

Our primary focus is on compensation for expatriates. Following the extensive discussion of expatriate compensation, we consider some of the challenges compensation professionals face when compensating HCNs and TCNs.

As a reminder, our focus is on U.S. companies, and these definitions reflect that focus. Other countries can be the focus as well. For example, let's define HCN, TCN, and expatriate from the Australian perspective. BHP, an Australian company, conducts business worldwide in such countries as the People's Republic of China and the United States. A Chinese citizen who works for BHP in Shanghai is an HCN. A U.S. citizen who works for BHP in Shanghai is a TCN. An Australian citizen who works for BHP in Shanghai is an expatriate.

Human resource professionals construct international compensation packages on the basis of three main factors:

✯ Term of international assignment

✯ Staff mobility

✯ Equity: Pay referent groups

Term of international assignment

The term of the international assignment is central in determining compensation policy.

The term of the international assignment is central in determining compensation policy.[6] Short-term assignments—usually less than one year in duration—generally do not require substantial modifications to domestic compensation packages. However, extended assignments necessitate features that promote a sense of stability and comfort overseas. These features include housing allowances, educational expenses for children, and adjustments to protect expatriates from paying "double" income taxes—U.S. federal and state taxes and applicable foreign taxes.[7]

Staff mobility

Companies must also consider whether foreign assignments necessitate employees' moving from one foreign location to another—from Beijing, China, to the Special Economic Zone in China, or from England to Japan. Such moves within and across foreign cultures can disrupt expatriates' and their families' lives. Staff mobility comes at a price to companies in the form of monetary incentives and measures to make employees' moves as comfortable as possible.

Equity: pay referent groups

Well-designed U.S. compensation programs promote equity among employees: Employees' pay is commensurate with performance or knowledge attainments. Expatriates are likely to evaluate compensation, in part, according to equity considerations. Many U.S. companies use domestic employees as the pay referent groups when developing international compensation packages because virtually all expatriate employees eventually return to the United States.

Some companies use local employees as the pay referent groups for long-term assignments because they wish to facilitate expatriates' integration into foreign cultures. As we discuss later, large components of Mexican managerial employees' compensation packages include base pay and such cash allowances as Christmas bonuses. On the other hand, the main components of U.S. managerial employees' compensation packages include base pay and long-term incentives. U.S. expatriates working in Mexico on long-term assignments are likely to have compensation packages that are similar to Mexican managerial employees' compensation packages.

Components of international compensation programs

The basic structure of international compensation programs is similar to the structure of domestic compensation programs. The main components include base pay and fringe compensation. The inclusion of non-performance-based incentives and allowances distinguishes international compensation packages from domestic compensation packages. Exhibit 12-1 lists the main components of international compensation programs.

Setting base pay for U.S. expatriates

U.S. companies must determine the method for setting expatriates' base pay. Final determination should come only after companies carefully weigh the strengths and limitations of alternative methods. In addition, the purchasing power of base pay is an important consideration. Purchasing power affects standard of living. The following quotation captures the essence of purchasing power for expatriates. In this example, the U.S. expatriate is stationed in Italy. "Does an Italian lira purchase as much macaroni today as it did yesterday?" Two key factors influence purchasing power—the stability of local currency and inflation.

Exhibit 12-1
U.S. Expatriates'
Compensation Package
Components

Core Compensation
  Base pay
  Incentive compensation
    Foreign service premium
    Hardship allowance
    Mobility premium
Fringe Compensation
  Standard Benefits
    Protection programs
    Pay for time-not-worked
  Enhanced Benefits
    Relocation assistance
    Educational reimbursement for expatriates' children
    Home leave and travel reimbursement
    Rest and relaxation leave allowance

Methods for setting base pay

U.S. companies use one of the following three methods to calculate expatriates' base pay:

- ✰ Home-country-based method
- ✰ Host-country-based method
- ✰ Headquarters-based method

HOME-COUNTRY-BASED METHOD The **home-country-based method** compensates expatriates the amount they would receive if they were performing similar work in the United States. Job evaluation procedures enable employers to determine whether jobs at home are equivalent to comparable jobs in foreign locations on the basis of compensable factors. How does location lead to differences in apparently equal jobs? For example, foreign language skills are probably essential outside English-speaking countries. Adjustments to expatriates' pay should reflect additional skills.

The home-country-based pay method is most appropriate for expatriates: Equity problems are not very likely to arise because expatriates' assignments are too short to establish local national employees as pay referents. Instead, expatriates will base pay comparisons on their home country standards. In general, the home-country-based pay method is most suitable when expatriate assignments are short in duration and local nationals performing comparable jobs receive substantially higher pay. As we discussed earlier, expatriates may rely on local cultural norms over extended periods as the standard for judging the equitableness of their compensation.

HOST-COUNTRY-BASED METHOD The **host-country-based method** compensates expatriates on the basis of the host countries' pay scales. Companies use various standards for determining base pay including market pricing, job evaluation techniques, and job holders' past relevant work experience. Other countries use different standards. As we discuss later in this chapter, the Japanese emphasize seniority. Expatriates' base pay will be competitive with other employees' base pay in the host countries. The host-country-based method is most suitable when assignments are of long duration. As we noted previously, expatriates will be more likely to judge the adequacy of their pay relative to their local coworkers rather than to their counterparts at home.

HEADQUARTERS-BASED METHOD The **headquarters-based method** compensates all employees according to the pay scales used at the headquarters. Neither the location of the international work assignment nor the home country influences base pay. This method makes the most sense for expatriates who move from one foreign assignment to another and rarely, if ever, work in their home countries. Administratively, this system is simple because it applies the pay standard of one country to all employees regardless of the location of their foreign assignment or their country of citizenship.

Purchasing power

Decreases in purchasing power lead to lower standards of living. Quite simply, expatriates cannot afford to purchase as many goods and services as before, or they must settle for lower quality. Diminished purchasing power undermines the strategic value of expatriates' compensation because top-notch employees are probably not willing to settle for lower standards of living while stationed at foreign posts. In addition, changes in the factors that immediately influence standard of living—the stability of currency and inflation—are somewhat unpredictable. This unpredictability creates a sense of uncertainty and risk. As we discuss later in this section, most U.S. companies use the balance sheet approach to minimize this risk.

CURRENCY STABILIZATION Most U.S. companies award expatriates' base pay in U.S. currency not in the local foreign currency. However, foreign countries as a rule do not recognize U.S. currency as legal tender. Therefore, expatriates must exchange U.S. currency for local foreign currency in accordance with daily exchange rates. An **exchange rate** is the price at which one country's currency can be swapped for another.[8] Exchange rates are expressed in terms of units of foreign currency per U.S. dollar or in terms of U.S. dollars per unit of foreign currency. For example, on May 30, 1996, the exchange rate for French francs was 4.97 francs for each U.S. $1.

Government policies and complex market forces cause exchange rates to fluctuate daily. Exchange rate fluctuations have direct implications for expatriates' purchasing power. For example, let's start with the previous exchange rate of 4.97 francs per U.S. $1. Also, let's assume that the exchange rate is 4.55 francs per U.S. $1 on December 31, 1996. This example illustrates a decline in the exchange rate for French francs. U.S. expatriates experience lower purchasing power because they receive fewer francs for every U.S. $1 they exchange. Case in point (based on my recent experience in Paris): For an 8-ounce soft drink, I paid 39.76 francs which equals U.S. $8 (39.76 francs/4.97 francs per $1 U.S.)! If the exchange rate had declined to 4.50 francs per U.S. $1, the soft drink would have cost U.S. $8.83 (39.76 francs/4.50 francs per U.S. $1).

INFLATION **Inflation** is the increase in prices for consumer goods and services. Inflation erodes the purchasing power of currency. Let's assume that ABC Corporation does not award pay increases to its expatriates stationed in Japan in 1991.

Exhibit 12-2
Annual Inflation Rates (%)
for Selected Countries,
1991–1994

COUNTRY	1991	1992	1993	1994	5-YEAR RATE[1] (1990–1994)
Egypt	19.7	13.7	12.0	8.1	65.0
France	3.2	2.4	2.1	1.7	9.7
Japan	3.3	1.7	1.2	0.7	7.1
Mexico	22.7	15.5	8.7	6.9	64.7

Source: International Monetary Fund Statistics Department, *International financial statistics yearbook* (Washington D.C.: International Financial Statistics, Publications Services, 1995).

[1] The base year equals 1990.

Expatriates' purchasing power remains unaffected as long as there isn't any inflation (and reduced exchange rate) during the same period. However, these expatriates had lower purchasing power in 1991 because inflation averaged 3.3 percent in Japan. In other words, the average costs of consumer goods and services increased 3.3 percent between 1990 and 1991. Exhibit 12-2 shows the annual inflation rates for various countries between 1991 and 1994.

Incentive compensation for U.S. expatriates

International compensation plans include a variety of unique incentives to encourage expatriates to accept and remain on international assignments.

In the United States, U.S. companies offer incentives to promote higher job performance and to minimize dysfunctional turnover (when high performers quit their jobs). International compensation plans include a variety of unique incentives to encourage expatriates to accept and remain on international assignments. These incentives also compensate expatriates for their willingness to tolerate less-desirable living and working conditions. The main incentives are foreign services premiums, hardship allowances, and mobility premiums.

Foreign service premiums

Foreign service premiums are monetary payments above and beyond regular base pay. Companies offer foreign service premiums to encourage employees to accept expatriate assignments. These premiums generally apply to assignments that extend beyond one year. The use of foreign service premiums is widespread.

Companies calculate foreign service premiums as a percentage of base pay. Foreign service premiums range between 10 and 30 percent of base pay.[9] The percentage amount increases with the length of assignment. Sometimes it is necessary to award larger amounts when there is a shortage of available candidates. Companies disburse payment of the foreign service premium over several installments to manage costs and to "remind" expatriates about the incentive throughout their assignments.[10]

Employers that use foreign service premiums should consider the possible drawbacks. First, if employees misconstrue this premium as a regular permanent increase to base pay, resentments toward the employer may develop after the last installment. Second, foreign service premiums may not have incentive value when employers make several small installments rather than fewer large installments. Third, employees may feel as if their standard of living has declined upon returning to the United States because they no longer receive this extra money.

Hardship allowances

The **hardship allowance** compensates expatriates for their sacrifices while on assignment. Specifically, these allowances are designed to recognize exceptionally hard living and working conditions at foreign locations. Employers disburse hardship allowances in small amounts throughout the duration of expatriates' assignments. It is easy for expatriates to lose sight of the foreign service premiums and hardship allowances because they appear as relatively small increments to their paychecks. Companies should take care to communicate the role of these payments.

Companies offer hardship allowances only at exceptionally severe locations. The U.S. Department of State established a list of hardship posts where the living conditions are considered unusually harsh.[11] Most multinational companies award hardship allowances to executive, managerial, and supervisory employees.[12] Hardship allowances range from 5 to 25 percent of base pay—the greater the hardship, the higher the premium. The U.S. Department of State uses three criteria to identify hardship locations:

- ✪ Extraordinarily difficult living conditions, such as inadequate housing, lack of recreational facilities, isolation, inadequate transportation facilities, and lack of food or consumer services

- ✪ Excessive physical hardship including severe climates or high altitudes and the presence of dangerous conditions affecting physical and mental well-being

- ✪ Notably unhealthy conditions, such as diseases and epidemics, lack of public sanitation, and inadequate health facilities

The U.S. Department of State has deemed over 150 places as hardship locations. Exhibit 12-3 lists examples of hardship locations and recommended hardship differentials.

COUNTRY: CITY	DIFFERENTIAL (%)
Afghanistan: Kabul	25
Belarus: Minsk	20
Brunei: Bandar Seri Begawan	10
Cape Verde: Praia	15
Dominican Republic: Santo Domingo	10
Estonia: Tallinn	5
Greece: Athens	5
India: Bombay	20
Madagascar: Antananarivo	15
Mexico: Guadalajar	5
Poland: Warsaw	10
Russia: Moscow	15
Sierra Leone: Freetown	25
Venezuela: Caracas	5
Zaire: Bukavu	20

Exhibit 12-3
Hardship Locations and Differentials

Source: U.S. Department of State, *The U.S. Department of State indexes of living costs abroad, quarters allowances, and hardship differentials—January 1996*, Department of State Publication 10197 (Washington, D.C.: U.S. Government Printing Office, 1996).

Mobility premiums

Mobility premiums reward employees for moving from one assignment to another. Companies use these premiums to encourage employees to accept, leave, or change assignments—usually between foreign posts or from a domestic position to one in a foreign country. Expatriates typically receive mobility premiums as single lump sum payments.

Establishing fringe compensation for U.S. expatriates

Benefits represent an important component of expatriates' compensation packages. Companies design benefits programs to attract and retain the best expatriates. In addition, companies design these programs to promote a sense of security for expatriates and their families. Further, well-designed programs should help expatriates and their families maintain regular contact with other family members and friends in the United States.

Benefits fall into three broad categories—protection programs, pay for time-not-worked, and services. Protection programs provide family benefits, promote health, and guard against income loss caused by catastrophic factors such as unemployment, disability, or serious illnesses. Pay for time-not-worked provides employees such paid time off as vacation. Service practices vary widely. Services provide enhancements such as tuition reimbursement and daycare assistance to employees and their families.

Just like domestic fringe compensation packages, international fringe compensation plans include such protection programs as medical insurance[13] and retirement programs.[14] In most cases, U.S. citizens working overseas continue to receive medical insurance and participate in their retirement programs.

International and domestic plans are also similar in that they offer pay for time-not-worked; however, international packages tend to incorporate more-extensive benefits of this kind, which we discuss later. Moreover, international fringe compensation differs from domestic compensation with regard to the types of allowances and reimbursements. For international assignees, these payments are designed to compensate for higher costs of living and housing, relocation allowances, and education allowances for expatriates' children.

Employers should take several considerations into account when designing international fringe benefits programs, including:[15]

* **Total remuneration.** What is included in the total employee pay structure—cash wages, benefits, mandated social programs, and other perquisites? How much can the business afford?

* **Benefit adequacy.** To what extent must the employer enhance mandated programs to achieve desired staffing levels? Programs already in place and employees' utilization of them should be critically examined before determining what supplementary programs are needed and desirable.

* **Tax effectiveness.** What is the tax deductibility of these programs for the employer and employee in each country, and how does the U.S. tax law treat expenditures in this area?

★ **Recognition of local customs and practices.** Companies often provide benefits and services to employees on the basis of those extended by other businesses in the locality, independent of their own attitude toward these same benefits and services.

International fringe compensation packages contain the same components as domestic fringe compensation packages and enhancements.[16] U.S. expatriates receive many of the same standard benefits as their counterparts working in the United States. Expatriates also receive enhanced benefits for taking overseas assignments.

Standard benefits for U.S. expatriates

Protection programs and pay for time-not-worked are the most pertinent standard benefits.

PROTECTION PROGRAMS Previously, we discussed legally required protection programs (Chapter 10) and discretionary protection programs (Chapter 11). Let's consider the application of each kind to the international context.

The key legally required protection programs are mandated by the following laws—the Social Security Act of 1935, various state workers' compensation laws, and the Family and Medical Leave Act of 1993. All provide protection programs to employees and their dependents. Expatriates continue to participate in the main Social Security programs—retirement insurance, benefits for dependents, and Medicare. The Family and Medical Leave Act also applies to expatriates. However, state workers' compensation laws generally do not apply to expatriates. Instead, U.S. companies can elect private insurance that provides equivalent protection.

Discretionary protection programs provide family benefits, promote health, and guard against income loss caused by catastrophic factors such as unemployment, disability, or serious illnesses. U.S. companies provide these protection programs to expatriates for the same reasons they do in the United States—as a strategic response to workforce diversity and to retain the best-performing employees. Withholding these benefits from expatriates would create a disincentive for employees to take international assignments.

PAY FOR TIME-NOT-WORKED Standard pay for time-not-worked benefits include annual vacation, holidays, and emergency leave. Expatriates typically receive the same annual vacation benefits as their domestic counterparts. These benefits are particularly common among expatriates with relatively short-term assignments: Companies do not provide expatriates extended regular vacation leave because expatriates are likely to perceive the removal of these benefits upon return to domestic assignments as punitive. However, U.S. companies must comply with foreign laws that govern the amount of vacation. For example, Mexican law entitles employees to 14 days vacation per year, and Swedish law mandates 30 days!

Expatriates generally receive paid time off for foreign national or local holidays that apply to their foreign locations. Foreign holiday schedules may provide fewer or more holidays than the United States. Also, some countries require employers to provide all employees paid time off for recognized holidays. In the United States, companies offer paid holidays as a discretionary benefit or as set in collective bargaining agreements.

Paid leave for personal or family emergencies also is a component of most expatriate compensation packages. Such emergencies may include critically ill family members or their deaths in the United States or in the foreign posts. Most companies provide paid emergency leave, but some companies provide unpaid leaves of absence. In either case, companies cover travel expenses between the foreign post and the United States.

Enhanced benefits for U.S. expatriates

Enhanced benefits for U.S. expatriates include:

- ✯ Relocation assistance
- ✯ Education reimbursements for expatriates' children
- ✯ Home leave and travel reimbursements
- ✯ Rest and relaxation leave and allowance

RELOCATION ASSISTANCE **Relocation assistance payments** cover expatriates' expenses to relocate to foreign posts. Exhibit 12-4 lists the items most commonly covered under relocation assistance programs. Relocation assistance is generally large enough to pay for major expenses. Companies usually base these payment amounts on three main factors: Payments increase with distance, length of assignment, and rank in the company.

EDUCATION REIMBURSEMENTS FOR EXPATRIATES' CHILDREN Expatriates typically place their children in private schools designed for English-speaking students. Tuition in foreign countries is often more expensive than tuition for private U.S. schools. Approximately 70 percent of companies offer **education reimbursements** for expatriate children.[17] These companies choose to reimburse expatriate children's education for two reasons. First, some foreign public schools are generally not comparable to U.S. public schools. Some are better and others are below the U.S. standard. Companies make generous educational reimbursements where public school quality is low. Second, most U.S. children do not speak foreign languages fluently. Thus, they cannot enroll in foreign public schools.

HOME LEAVE BENEFITS AND TRAVEL REIMBURSEMENTS Companies offer **home leave benefits** to help expatriates manage the adjustment to foreign cultures and to maintain direct personal contact with family and friends. As the name implies, home leave benefits enable expatriates to take paid time off in the United States. Home leave benefits vary considerably from company to company. The length and frequency of these

---

Exhibit 12-4
Relocation Assistance Payments

The relocation allowance or reimbursement provides employees with money for:

- Temporary quarters prior to departure because the expatriate's house has been sold or rented
- Transportation to the foreign post for employees and their families
- Reasonable expenses incurred by the family during travel
- Temporary quarters while waiting for delivery of household goods or while looking for suitable housing
- Moving household goods to the foreign post
- Storing household goods in the United States

---

leaves usually depend on the expected duration of expatriates' assignments—longer assignments justify longer home leaves. Also, expatriates must serve a minimum period at the foreign post before they are eligible for home leave benefits—anywhere from 6 to 12 months. Companies offer these extended benefits along with the standard pay for time-not-worked benefits.

Companies compensate expatriates while they are away on home leave. In addition, most companies reimburse expatriates for expenses associated with travel between the foreign post and the United States. These reimbursements apply to expatriates and family members who live with expatriates at foreign posts. Companies typically make reimbursements for the cost of round-trip airfare, ground transportation, and accommodations while traveling to and from the foreign post.

REST AND RELAXATION LEAVE AND ALLOWANCE Expatriates who work in designated hardship foreign locations receive **rest and relaxation leave benefits.** Rest and relaxation leave represents additional paid time off. Progressive employers recognize that expatriates working in hardship locations may need extra time away from the unpleasant conditions to "recharge their batteries." Rest and relaxation leave benefits differ from standard vacation benefits because companies designate where expatriates may spend their time. For example, many U.S. companies with operations in China's Special Economic Zone designate Hong Kong as an acceptable retreat because it is relatively close by, and Hong Kong has many amenities not present in the Special Economic Zone. These include diverse ethnic restaurants and Western-style entertainment.

Rest and relaxation leave programs include allowances to cover travel expenses between the foreign post and retreat locations. Companies determine allowance amounts on the basis of such factors as the cost of round-trip transportation, food, and lodging associated with the designated locations. Allowances usually cover the majority of the costs. The U.S. Department of State publishes per diem schedules for various cities. Location and family size determine per diem amounts.

Balance sheet approach for U.S. expatriates' compensation packages

Most U.S. multinational companies use the balance sheet approach to determine expatriates' compensation packages. The **balance sheet approach** provides expatriates the standard of living they normally enjoy in the United States. Thus, the United States is the standard for all payments.

The balance sheet approach has strategic value to companies for two important reasons. First, this approach protects expatriates' standards of living. Without it, companies would have a difficult time placing qualified employees in international assignments. Second, the balance sheet approach enables companies to control costs because it relies on objective indexes that measure cost differences between the U.S. and foreign countries. We discuss those indexes shortly.

The use of the balance sheet approach is most appropriate when:

☆ The home country is an appropriate reference point for economic comparisons.

☆ Expatriates are likely to maintain psychological and cultural ties with the home or base country.

★ Expatriates prefer not to assimilate into the local foreign culture.

★ The assignment is of limited duration.

★ The assignment following the international assignment will be in the home country.

★ The company promises employees that they will not lose financially while on foreign assignment.[18]

Companies that use the balance sheet approach compare the costs of four major expenditures in the United States and the foreign post.

★ Housing and utilities

★ Goods and services

★ Discretionary income

★ Taxes

Employees receive allowances whenever the costs in the foreign country exceed the costs in the United States. Allowance amounts vary according to the lifestyle enjoyed in the United States. In general, individuals with higher incomes tend to live in more-expensive homes, and they are in better positions to enjoy more-expensive goods and services (for example, designer labels versus off-brand labels). Higher income also means higher taxes.

Where do U.S. companies obtain pertinent information about costs for foreign countries? U.S. companies may rely on three information sources. First, they can rely on expatriates who have spent considerable time on assignment or foreign government contacts. Second, private consulting companies (for example, Deloitte & Touche) or research companies (for example, The Bureau of National Affairs Plus) can conduct custom surveys. Third, most U.S. companies consult the *U.S. Department of State Indexes of Living Costs Abroad, Quarters Allowances, and Hardship Differentials,* which is published quarterly. The *U.S. Department of the State Indexes* is the most cost-effective source because it is available at no charge in libraries that have government depositories.

Housing and utilities

Employers provide expatriate employees with **housing and utilities allowances** to cover the difference between housing and utilities costs in the United States and in the foreign post. The U.S. Department of State uses the term **quarters allowances.** Exhibit 12-5 displays pertinent information from the U.S. Department of State's Quarters Allowances.

The quarters allowances table contains three main sections—the survey date, exchange rate, and annual allowance by family status and salary range. The survey date is the month when the Office of Allowances received housing expenditure reports.

The exchange rate section includes three pieces of information—foreign unit and number per U.S. dollar. We reviewed the concept of exchange rate earlier. It is expressed as the number of foreign currency units given in exchange for U.S. $1. The U.S. Department of State uses the exchange to compute the quarters allowances. In the Netherlands, expatriates receive 1.61 guilders for every U.S. $1 exchanged, and expatriates in Japan receive 102 Japanese yen for every U.S. $1.

Exhibit 12-5
Quarters Allowances, January 1996

COUNTRY: CITY	SURVEY DATE	FOREIGN UNIT	NO. OF FOREIGN UNITS PER U.S. $	FAMILY STATUS	ANNUAL INCOME		
					LESS THAN $31,000	$31,000 TO $55,000	$55,000 & OVER
Australia: Melbourne	Jan. 1995	Dollar	1.34	Family	$14,100	$15,400	$16,400
				Single	$12,900	$14,700	$15,400
Belgium: Brussels	Nov. 1994	Franc	29.60	Family	$27,500	$28,800	$32,600
				Single	$23,700	$27,500	$28,800
France: Paris	Dec. 1994	Franc	4.85	Family	$29,300	$35,100	$35,100
				Single	$26,500	$31,300	$31,300
Germany: Berlin	May 1995	Mark	1.41	Family	$24,800	$29,700	$30,500
				Single	$22,700	$24,800	$30,500
Italy: Rome	July 1995	Lira	1,571.00	Family	$21,400	$24,800	$35,900
				Single	$20,000	$22,400	$35,900
Japan: Tokyo	Feb. 1995	Yen	102.00	Family	$65,600	$81,000	$81,000
				Single	$60,200	$76,400	$78,000
Thailand: Bangkok	May 1994	Baht	24.70	Family	$17,400	$21,000	$21,900
				Single	$15,900	$17,400	$19,600
England: London	Mar. 1995	Pound	0.6263	Family	$26,300	$29,100	$31,400
				Single	$23,100	$28,900	$30,000
Netherlands: The Hague	Mar. 1995	Guilder	1.61	Family	$30,000	$32,800	$36,500
				Single	$26,500	$29,600	$31,100

Source: U.S. Department of State, *The U.S. Department of State indexes of living costs abroad, quarters allowances, and hardship differentials—January 1996,* Department of State Publication 10197 (Washington, D.C.: U.S. Government Printing Office, 1996).

The category family status distinguishes between singles and families. Single person is self-explanatory. The term *family* refers to two-person families. For example, in Bangkok, the quarters allowance is $19,600 for single expatriates with annual incomes of $56,000 and over. In Tokyo, the allowance is $78,000!

Employees with larger families living with them at the foreign posts receive supplements. Families of three to four persons receive a 10 percent supplement, families of five to six persons receive a 20 percent supplement, and families of seven or more persons receive a 30 percent supplement. In Berlin, the quarters allowance is $38,160 for a seven-member expatriate family earning $50,000 per year (that is, $29,700 regular family allowance × 1.30—a 30 percent supplement).

Goods and services

Expatriates receive **goods and services allowances** where the cost of living is higher than in the United States. Employers base these allowances on **indexes of living costs abroad.**[19] The indexes of living costs abroad compare the costs (in U.S. dollars) of representative goods and services (excluding education) expatriates purchase at the

Exhibit 12-6
Indexes of Living Costs Abroad, January 1996

COUNTRY: CITY	SURVEY DATE	FOREIGN UNIT	NO. OF FOREIGN UNITS PER U.S. $	LOCAL INDEX
Argentina: Buenos Aires	July 1995	Peso	1.00	151
Azerbaijan: Baku	Apr. 1994	Manat	800.00	109
Belgium: Brussels	May 1994	Franc	34.70	158
Brazil: Brasilia	Sept. 1994	Real	0.84	136
Bulgaria: Sofia	July 1994	Leva	53.90	84
China: Beijing	Jan. 1995	Yuan	8.44	123
Egypt: Cairo	July 1994	Pound	3.40	95
Finland: Helsinki	Aug. 1995	Markka	4.27	160
Japan: Tokyo	May 1995	Yen	81.00	233
Mexico: Monterrey	Jan. 1994	Peso	3.10	112
Russia: Moscow	Feb. 1994	Rubles	1,560.00	155
Spain: Madrid	July 1995	Peseta	121.00	148
Sweden: Stockholm	May 1994	Kroner	7.70	168
England: London	July 1995	Pound	0.61	148
Vietnam: Hanoi	Nov. 1994	N Dong	11,000.00	107

Source: U.S. Department of State, *The U.S. Department of State indexes of living costs abroad, quarters allowances, and hardship differentials—January 1996,* Department of State Publication 10197 (Washington, D.C.: U.S. Government Printing Office, 1996).

Note: The indexes exclude housing and education.

foreign location and the cost of comparable goods and services purchased in the Washington, D.C., area. The indexes are place-to-place cost comparisons at specific times and currency exchange rates.

Exhibit 12-6 displays pertinent information from the Department of State's indexes of living costs abroad table. The table contains three pertinent sections—the survey date, the exchange rate, and the local index. The survey date represents the month the Department of State received the cost data. We already reviewed the exchange rate concept. The local index is a measure of the cost of living for expatriates at their foreign posts relative to the cost of living in Washington, D.C.

The index for Washington, D.C., is 100, representing the base comparison. The local index for Stockholm is 168: On average, the costs for goods and services in Stockholm are 68 percent higher than in Washington, D.C.: [(168 − 100)/100] × 100. The local index for Cairo is 95. On average, the costs for goods and services in Cairo are 5 percent lower than in Washington, D.C.: [(95 − 100)/100] × 100. Companies should provide allowances to compensate for the higher costs in Stockholm. Allowances are not needed for Cairo because the cost of living is lower there than in the United States.

Discretionary income

Discretionary income covers a variety of financial obligations in the United States for which expatriates remain responsible. These expenditures are usually of a long-term nature. Companies typically do not provide allowances because expatriates re-

Exhibit 12-7
*Discretionary Income
Expenditures*

- Pension contributions
- Savings and investment
- Insurance payments
- Equity portion of mortgage payments
- Alimony payments
- Child support
- Student loan payments
- Car payments

main responsible for them despite international assignments. Exhibit 12-7 lists examples of discretionary income expenditures.

Tax considerations

U.S. citizens working overseas for U.S. corporations are subject to the Federal Unemployment Tax Act (FUTA). Expatriates continue to pay U.S. income taxes and Social Security taxes while on assignment. The Internal Revenue Service (IRS) taxes U.S. citizens' income regardless of whether they earn income in the United States or while on foreign assignment. Expatriates also must pay income taxes to local foreign governments according to the applicable income tax laws. Paying taxes to both the U.S. government and foreign governments is known as "double" taxation.[20] The Internal Revenue Code (IRC) includes two rules that enable expatriates to minimize double taxation by reducing their U.S. federal income tax obligations:

- ✯ IRC Section 901
- ✯ IRC Section 911

EXPATRIATE CONSIDERATIONS: IRC SECTION 901 AND IRC SECTION 911 Expatriates can minimize double taxation by claiming a tax credit under IRC Section 901. **IRC Section 901** allows expatriates to credit foreign income taxes against the U.S. income tax liability:

- ✯ If the U.S. federal income tax is greater than the foreign tax amount, then expatriates need pay only the difference to the federal government.

or,

- ✯ If the foreign tax exceeds the U.S. federal income tax amount, expatriates can apply the foreign tax excess—the difference between the foreign income tax and the U.S. federal income tax—as a deduction from future federal taxable income for up to five years.

IRC Section 911 permits "eligible" expatriates to exclude as much as $70,000 of foreign earned income from taxation, plus a housing allowance. Let's look at the income exclusion and housing allowance elements separately.

Exhibit 12-8 lists specific types of income that are eligible for exclusion under IRC Section 911. IRC Section 911 requires that expatriates pay U.S. federal income taxes only on the income amount above $70,000. For example, an expatriate whose foreign earned income totaled $150,000 in 1996 had to pay taxes on only $80,000 (that is, $150,000 − $70,000 exclusion).

Exhibit 12-8
*Cash and Noncash Income
Exclusions: IRC Section 911*

CASH

- Salaries and wages
- Bonuses
- Sales commissions
- Incentives
- Professional fees

NONCASH

- Housing
- Meals
- Cars
- Allowances for cost of living differentials, education, home leave, tax reimbursements, children's education, and moving expenses

To qualify for the foreign income exclusion, expatriates must have a *tax home.* In addition, expatriates must meet either a bona fide foreign residence test or a physical foreign presence test.[21]

Under IRC Section 911, a **tax home** is an expatriate's foreign residence while on assignment and the expatriate's only place of residence. The IRS generally uses two criteria to determine whether foreign residences qualify as tax homes. First, the foreign residence must be the expatriate's only residence. Second, length of assignment determines whether an expatriate's foreign residence qualifies as a tax home. The IRS classifies foreign residences as tax homes when expatriates accept indefinite assignments expected to last at least two years.[22]

Expatriates whose foreign residences do not qualify as tax homes are ineligible for IRC Section 911 protection. However, establishing a tax home does not automatically qualify expatriates for protection under IRC Section 911. Once the IRS has established an expatriate's residence as a tax home, the expatriate must meet either the **bona fide foreign residence criterion** or the **physical foreign presence criterion.** Expatriates must meet the criteria specified in either the bona fide foreign residence test (Exhibit 12-9) or the physical foreign presence criterion (Exhibit 12-10).

Expatriates who qualify for the foreign earned income exclusion are entitled to exclude foreign housing expenses. Exclusions are limited only to the portion of the foreign housing expense that exceeds reasonable housing expenses of approximately $9,000 in the United States.[23] Exhibit 12-11 lists the eligible housing expenses for IRC Section 911.

CHOOSING BETWEEN IRC SECTION 901 AND IRC SECTION 911 Expatriates must choose between the foreign tax credit (IRC Section 901) and income exclusion (IRC Section 911) because they cannot benefit from both provisions. Certified tax advice is the best source of information. As a general rule, the difference between U.S. income tax rates and foreign income tax rates is a reasonable guide. IRC Section 911 typically leads to lower U.S. income tax liability where the U.S. income tax rate is greater than the foreign income tax rate. IRC 901 usually results in lower U.S. income tax liability

Exhibit 12-9
***Bona Fide Foreign
Residence Test***

An expatriate must have established a home or permanent living quarters in a foreign country for at least an entire tax year, usually January 1 to December 31, and demonstrate intent to take residency in a foreign country.

TAX YEAR

For example, Anna Greenspan arrives in Stockholm on January 3, 1996, to begin her expatriate assignment. She completes her assignment on December 22, 1997, and leaves Stockholm that same day to return to the United States. Although Anna lived in Stockholm for nearly 23 months, she does not meet the bona fide foreign residence test because she did not live in Stockholm for at least *one full tax year* (January 1 to December 31 in any year). The periods January 3, 1996, to December 31, 1996, and January 1, 1997, to December 22, 1997, both fall short of complete tax years.

Bona fide residency status continues until an expatriate completes an assignment. For instance, Joan Bleen arrives in Shanghai on December 30, 1995, to begin her expatriate assignment. She completes her assignment on March 15, 1998. Joan meets the bona fide foreign residence criterion test because she lived in Shanghai for at least one full tax year. Thus, she may exclude as much as $70,000 of her annual income each full tax year—1996 and 1997. She also qualifies to apply part of the $70,000 income exclusion to her 1998 tax returns on the basis of the amount of time spent on assignment in 1998—January 1, 1998, to March 15, 1998.

Residency is not restricted to a single foreign country. An expatriate can live in more than one country as long as the total time outside the United States is spent in foreign territories. For example, Otis Martin meets the tax year standard for 1996 because he spent the entire year on assignment in Brussels, Paris, and Lisbon.

INTENT TO TAKE FOREIGN RESIDENCY

In general, demonstrating one or more of the following criteria qualifies as intent to take foreign residency:

- The acquisition of a home or long-term lease
- The presence of family in the foreign country
- The intent to become involved in the social life and culture of the foreign country

Source: Treasury Regulations 1.911-2(d)(2).

Exhibit 12-10
***Physical Foreign Presence
Test***

An expatriate must be physically present in a foreign country or countries for 330 full days during a period of 12 consecutive months.

- The 330 qualifying days do not have to be consecutive.
- The 12-month period may begin on any day of any month.
- Presence in a foreign country includes time spent on vacation or for any other purpose not just for employment-related purposes.
- If the 12-month period used to satisfy the physical foreign presence test crosses over two tax years, the foreign income exclusion must be prorated.

Source: Int. Rev. Code of 1986, § 911(d)(1).

Exhibit 12-11
**Eligible Housing Expenses
for IRC Section 911**

- Rent or the fair rental value of housing provided by the employer
- Repairs, utilities other than telephone
- Personal property insurance
- Costs of renting furniture
- Residential parking fees

Exhibit 12-12
**Choosing between IRC
Section 901 and IRC
Section 911**

Maria Hernandez earned $150,000 during 1996 for AJAX Corporation while on an overseas assignment. Let's consider whether Maria should elect IRC Section 901 or IRC Section 911 for two scenarios:

- U.S. income tax rate (32%) > Foreign income tax rate (15%)
- U.S. income tax rate (32%) < Foreign income tax rate (50%)

	IRC SECTION 901 (TAX CREDIT)	IRC SECTION 911 (TAX DEDUCTION)
U.S. income tax rate (32%) > Foreign income tax rate (15%)		
(A) Gross Income	$150,000	$150,000
(B) IRC Section 911 Exclusion		$ 70,000
(C) Adjusted Gross Income (A – B)	$150,000	$ 80,000
(D) Foreign Income Tax (C × 15%)		$12,000
(E) Taxable Income (C – D)	$ 150,000	$ 68,000
(F) U.S. Income Tax (E × 32%)	$ 48,000	$ 21,760
(G) Foreign Tax Credit	$ 12,000	$ 0
(H) U.S. Tax Due (F – G)	$ 36,000	$ 21,760
U.S. income tax rate (32%) < Foreign income tax rate (50%)		
(A) Gross Income	$150,000	$150,000
(B) IRC Section 911 Exclusion		$ 70,000
(C) Adjusted Gross Income (A – B)	$150,000	$ 80,000
(D) Foreign Income Tax (C × 50%)		$ 40,000
(E) Taxable Income (C – D)	$ 150,000	$ 40,000
(F) U.S. Income Tax (E × 32%)	$ 48,000	$ 12,800
(G) Foreign Tax Credit	$ 40,000	$ 0
(H) U.S. Tax Due (F – G)	$ 8,000	$ 12,800

where the U.S. income tax rate is less than the foreign income tax rate. Exhibit 12-12 illustrates these points.

EMPLOYER CONSIDERATIONS: TAX PROTECTION AND TAX EQUALIZATION Although IRC Sections 901 and 911 substantially reduce expatriates' double taxation burdens, neither generally eliminates double taxation. Under the balance sheet approach, companies choose between two approaches to provide expatriates tax allowances: tax protection and tax equalization.

A key element of tax protection and tax equalization methods is the hypothetical tax. Employers calculate the **hypothetical tax** as the U.S. income tax based on the same salary level, excluding all foreign allowances. Under **tax protection** employers reimburse expatriates for the difference between the sum of the actual U.S. and foreign income tax amounts and the hypothetical tax when the actual income tax amount—based on tax returns filed with the IRS—is greater. When the taxes are less than or equal to the hypothetical tax, however, expatriates simply pay the entire income tax bill. Expatriates realize a tax benefit whenever actual taxes amount to less than the hypothetical tax because they will have paid lower income taxes on their overseas assignments than on assignments in the United States. Exhibit 12-13 illustrates income tax reimbursements under tax protection.

Under **tax equalization,** employers take the responsibility for paying income taxes to the U.S. and foreign governments on behalf of the expatriates. Tax equalization starts with the calculation of the hypothetical tax. On the basis of this hypothetical tax amount, employers deduct income from expatriates' paychecks that totals the hypothetical tax amounts at year-end. Employers reimburse expatriates for the difference

---

Exhibit 12-13
Tax Protection: An Illustration

Under tax protection, expatriates' reimbursement for income taxes equals:

Reimbursement amount = (Actual U.S. taxes + Actual foreign taxes) − Hypothetical tax

- When the reimbursement amount is positive, expatriates receive that amount as their tax reimbursement.

- When the reimbursement amount is negative, the amount is ignored. The expatriate does not receive a tax reimbursement because actual U.S. and foreign taxes paid total to less than the hypothetical tax. Under tax protection, expatriates keep the unexpected gain.

For example, Jerry Johnson accepted a foreign assignment beginning April 1, 1997. His total annual income for 1997 was $120,000. Jerry earned $30,000 of his total income while in the United States (January 1, 1997–March 31, 1997). He earned the remaining $90,000 while on his foreign assignment.

Jerry owes the U.S. government $8,400 in taxes, and he owes the foreign government $26,000 in foreign taxes. His hypothetical tax is $38,400 based on a 32 percent U.S. income tax rate. Jerry would have paid $38,400 ($120,000 × 32%) if he had earned his entire 1997 annual salary in the United States.

Reimbursement amount = (Actual U.S. taxes + Actual foreign taxes) − Hypothetical tax
  − $4,000   ($8,400   + $26,000) − $38,400

Jerry paid $4,000 less than he would have if he had worked the entire year in the United States. Under tax protection, he is not required to pay the additional $4,000 in taxes to either government.

Exhibit 12-14
Tax Equalization: An Illustration

Under tax equalization, employers take the responsibility for paying income taxes to the U.S. and foreign governments on behalf of the expatriates. Let's apply tax equalization to the scenario presented in Exhibit 12-13:

Jerry Johnson accepted a foreign assignment beginning April 1, 1997. His total annual income for 1997 was $120,000. Jerry earned $30,000 of his total income while in the United States (January 1, 1997–March 31, 1997). He earned the remaining $90,000 while on his foreign assignment.

Jerry owes the U.S. government $8,400 in taxes, and he owes the foreign government $26,000 in foreign taxes. His hypothetical tax is $38,400 based on a 32 percent U.S. income tax rate. Jerry would have paid $38,400 ($120,000 × 32%) if he had earned his entire 1997 salary in the United States.

- Tax equalization starts with the calculation of the hypothetical tax. Jerry's hypothetical tax is $38,400.

- Jerry's employer deducts the hypothetical tax in portions from each of Jerry's paychecks.

- Jerry's employer uses the hypothetical tax deduction to cover Jerry's U.S. and foreign income taxes.

Two possibilities exist:

1. If total actual taxes amount to less than the hypothetical tax amount, the employer must reimburse Jerry on the basis of the following formula:

   Reimbursement amount = (Actual U.S. taxes + Actual foreign taxes) – Hypothetical Tax
   – $4,000   ($8,400   + $26,000) – $38,400

   In this case, the employer owes Jerry $4,000, because Jerry paid the employer $4,000 too much in hypothetical tax.

2. If total actual taxes amount to more than the hypothetical tax amount, the expatriate must reimburse the employer on the basis of the following formula (these numbers depart from the previous example to illustrate the point):

   Reimbursement amount = (Actual U.S. taxes + Actual foreign taxes) – Hypothetical tax
   $3,000   ($15,400   + $26,000) – $38,400

   In this case, Jerry would owe the employer $3,000, because the employer paid $3,000 more than the hypothetical tax collected. In other words, the hypothetical tax was an underestimate of Jerry's actual tax liability.

---

between the hypothetical tax and actual income tax whenever the actual income tax amount is less. Expatriates reimburse their employers whenever the actual income tax amount exceeds the hypothetical income tax amounts. Exhibit 12-14 illustrates income tax reimbursements under tax equalization.

Tax equalization offers employers two important advantages over tax protection. First, expatriates receive equitable treatment regardless of their locations, and they do not keep the unexpected tax gain from being posted in countries with income tax rates lower than in the United States. As a result, employers should have an easier time motivating expatriates to move from one foreign post to another. Second, companies save money by not allowing expatriates to keep tax windfalls.

Illustration of the balance sheet approach

Exhibit 12-15 illustrates the balance sheet approach. The following example illustrates the necessary annual allowances for Susan Chung, who left her position at XYZ

Exhibit 12-15
*The Balance Sheet
Approach*

ANNUAL EXPENSE	CHICAGO, U.S.A.	BRUSSELS, BELGIUM (U.S. $ EQUIVALENT)	ALLOWANCE
Housing and utilities	$35,000	$ 67,600	$32,600
Goods and services	$ 6,000	$ 9,500	$ 3,500
Taxes	$22,400	$ 56,000	$33,600
Discretionary income	$10,000	$ 10,000	$ 0
Total	$73,400	$143,100	$69,700

Corporation's headquarters in Chicago for a temporary assignment in Brussels. Susan's annual earnings are $80,000. The U.S. income tax rate is 28 percent, and the Belgian income tax rate is 70 percent. The housing and utilities and the goods and services categories for Brussels are based on the index of living costs abroad published in the *U.S. Department of State's Indexes of Living Costs Abroad, Quarters Allowances, and Hardship Differentials—January 1996.* The discretionary income item is zero because this category represents Susan's ongoing financial commitments in the United States— student loan payments and car payments. XYZ Corporation provides Susan a $69,700 total allowance to protect her standard of living while in Belgium.

Repatriation compensation issues

Special compensation considerations should not end with the completion of international assignments. Effective expatriate compensation programs promote employees' integration into their companies' domestic work forces. Persons returning from for-

Special compensation considerations should not end with the completion of international assignments. Effective expatriate compensation programs promote employees' integration into their companies' domestic work forces.

REFLECTIONS

Gaining Control of International Compensation Programs

As one international compensation professional admitted at an International Personnel Association meeting in Chicago in November 1994:

> I am really confused at this point about what I am supposed to be doing with our present expatriate compensation program. A clear signal from the top is lacking, and there are different viewpoints being bandied about at different levels of the organization. Cost is important—they say—but damn cost if there is an immediate business requirement to send someone overseas. You wonder who is calling the shots. And, most important, what is my role and my responsibility to assist the corporation to become and/or remain globally competitive?[24]

The speaker has a point. His statement reflects the concern of many international compensation specialists suddenly facing a new set of rules for developing, implementing, managing, administering, and interpreting expatriate compensation programs. Compensation practitioners, who like things neat and tidy—that is, organized and institutionalized—must now make sense of new developments and rapidly changing business requirements that contradict traditional practices that have dominated the field of international compensation.

eign assignment may initially view their domestic assignments as punishment because their total compensation decreases. Upon return, former expatriates forfeit special pay incentives and extended leave allowances. Although most former expatriates understand the purpose of these incentives and allowances, it often takes a while for them to adjust to "normal" compensation practices.

Many expatriates may not adjust very well to compensation-as-usual because they feel their international experiences have made them substantially more valuable to their employers than they were before their international assignment. The heightened sense of value may intensify when former expatriates compare themselves with colleagues who have never taken international assignments. Two consequences are likely. First, former expatriates may find it difficult to work collaboratively with colleagues, undermining differentiation objectives. Second, strong resentments may lead former expatriates to find employment with competitors. Adding insult to injury, competitors stand to benefit from former expatriates' international experience.

Companies can actively prevent many of these problems by taking two measures. First, companies should invest in former expatriates' career development. Career development programs signal that companies value returnees. In addition, former expatriates may view their employers' investments in career development as a form of compensation, reducing the equity problems described earlier. Second, companies should capitalize on expatriates' experiences to gain a better understanding of foreign business environments. Also, former expatriates can contribute to the quality of international assignments by conveying what did and did not work well during their assignments.

Host country national and third country national compensation issues

Compensating host country nationals (HCNs) and third country nationals (TCNs) poses special challenges. In Chapter 2, we recognized that variations in national culture play a role in shaping compensation practices. Specifically, national culture creates normative expectations. Expatriates responsible for managing the compensation programs may find that cultural differences reduce the effectiveness of U.S. compensation practices. Three examples illustrate this point.

A striking contrast exists between U.S. and Japanese culture. In U.S. businesses, strategic business decisions generally originate from top management. Japanese business leaders cultivate consensus on business decisions, or *nemawashi*. U.S. culture promotes a sense of individualism, which translates into high career mobility. Japanese culture promotes a sense of collectivism, which leads to heightened loyalty for employers.

These cultural values are apparent in compensation systems. As we discussed previously (Chapters 4, 5, and 6), the predominant bases for pay in the United States are performance and knowledge, which represent equity. In Japan, the predominant basis for pay is seniority, which represents equality. As a result, pay differences among the Japanese tend to be smaller than pay differences among U.S. employees.

Another noteworthy cultural contrast exists between the U.S. and the People's Republic of China (PRC). The differences between the U.S. market economy and the PRC's centralized government-controlled economy sets the stage for cultural clashes. For decades, the Chinese government owned and operated virtually all business organizations. The Communist party places substantial emphasis on equal contributions to society, group welfare, and the concern for interpersonal relationships. In addition, the Communist party calls for greater emotional dependence of Chinese citizens on their employers. Further, it expects employers to assume a broad responsibility for their members.

These ideals are evident in the Chinese workplace and in compensation practices. Employers provide housing and modest wages for food and clothing. The Chinese receive health care under government-sponsored protection programs. Because of Communist ethic, the Chinese do not identify very well with pay-for-performance programs.

Our third example involves the compensation packages for U.S. and Mexican managerial employees, which differ substantially. The most important elements of U.S. managers' compensation are base pay and long-term incentives. Base pay and cash allowances represent the lion's share of Mexican managerial employees' compensation packages. In fact, the Mexican government mandates that employers award Christmas bonuses, profit sharing, and a minimum 20 percent vacation pay premium (that is, employers must pay employees at least an additional 20 percent of the regular pay while on vacation). U.S. employers offer these allowances at their discretion, not by government mandate.

The most noteworthy difference is Mexico's acquired right law: Employees possess the right to benefit from compensation practices that were in effect for at least two years. For example, let's assume that an employer institutes the practice of 40 paid vacation days per year. Employees acquire the right to 40 paid vacation days per year *every year* if the company instituted this practice for at least two consecutive years. Although U.S. companies never operated under an acquired right law, U.S. employees viewed benefits as an entitlement. Nowadays, U.S. companies discourage that view because benefits represent a significant cost.

The illustrations represent only some of the challenges U.S. companies are bound to face when compensating TCNs and HCNs. Compensation professionals need to understand the cultural contexts before they can develop effective international compensation programs. Pay-for-performance and pay-for-knowledge plans represent the foundation of U.S. compensation programs. Business leaders should not abandon these programs because they are inconsistent with cultural norms. Instead, it will be necessary for U.S. companies to work closely with their international partners to convey the importance of these approaches.

Summary

This chapter discussed international compensation and its strategic role. The globalization of the economy necessitates U.S. companies' investments overseas. Well-designed expatriate compensation programs support strategic initiatives by attracting and maintaining the best performers. Effective expatriate compensation programs reduce risk and promote the comfort of expatriate families stationed at foreign posts. The balance sheet approach minimizes financial risk to expatriates, and various incentives and allowances promote comfort. We also discussed that successful expatriate compensation programs facilitate returnees' transition to domestic assignments.

1. Discuss the strengths and weaknesses of the following methods for establishing base pay in international contexts—home-country-based pay, headquarters-based pay, and host-country-based pay.

2. For a country of your choice, conduct research into the cultural characteristics that you believe should be important considerations in establishing a core compensation program for a U.S. company that plans to locate there. Discuss these characteristics. Also, discuss whether you feel that pay-for-performance programs are compatible. If they are compatible in any way, what course of action would you take to promote this compatibility?

3. Discuss your reaction to the following statement: "U.S. companies should increase *base pay* (beyond the level that would be paid in the United States) to motivate employees to accept foreign assignments."

4. Allowances and reimbursements for international assignments are costly. Should companies avoid international business activities? Explain your answer. If you answer No, what can companies do to minimize costs?

5. Of the many reimbursements and allowances that U.S. companies make for employees who take foreign assignments, please indicate which one is the most essential. Discuss your reasons.

Key terms

North American Free Trade
  Agreement (NAFTA)
repatriation
host country nationals (HCNs)
third country nationals (TCNs)
expatriates
home-country-based method
host-country-based method
headquarters-based method
exchange rate
inflation
foreign service premiums
hardship allowance
mobility premiums
relocation assistance payments
education reimbursements

home leave benefits
rest and relaxation leave benefits
balance sheet approach
housing and utilities allowances
quarters allowances
goods and services allowances
indexes of living costs abroad
discretionary income
IRC Section 901
IRC Section 911
tax home
bona fide foreign residence criterion
physical foreign presence criterion
hypothetical tax
tax protection
tax equalization

Endnotes

[1] M. Harvey, Designing a global compensation system: The logic and a model, *The Columbia Journal of World Business* 28 (Winter 1993):56–72.

[2] R. A. Swaak, Today's expatriate family: Dual careers and other obstacles, *Compensation & Benefits Review* (January–February 1995):21–26.

[3] R. E. Scott, *1994 and 1995 U.S.-Mexico Trade Data: NAFTA impacts,* Occasional Paper No. 56 (Center for International Education and Research, College of Business Management, University of Maryland at College Park, May 1995).

[4] G. Hufbauer, and J. L. Schott, *NAFTA: An assessment* (Washington, D.C.: Economic Policy Institute, 1993).

[5] P. Cooper and L. Wallach, *NAFTA's broken promises: Job creation under NAFTA* (Washington, D.C.: Public Citizen Publications, September 1995).

[6] T. M. Wederspahn, Costing failures in expatriate human resources management, *Human Resource Planning* 15 (1992):27–35.

[7] S. M. Kates and C. Speilman, Reducing the cost of sending employees overseas, *The Practical Accountant* 28 (1995):50–55.

[8] G. G. Munn, F. L. Garcia, and C. J. Woelfel, *Encyclopedia of banking and finance* (Chicago: St. James Press, 1991).

[9] R. J. Stone, Compensation: Pay and perks for overseas executives, *Personnel Journal* (January 1986):67.

[10] D. W. Myers, *Compensation management* (Chicago: Commerce Clearing House, 1989).

[11] U.S. Department of State, *The U.S. Department of State indexes of living costs abroad, quarters, allowances, and hardship differentials—January 1996,* Department of State Publication 10197 (Washington, D.C.: U.S. Government Printing Office, 1996).

[12] M. Harvey, Empirical evidence of recurring international compensation problems, *Journal of International Business Studies,* (Fourth quarter, 1993):785–799.

[13] W. A. Glaser, Health insurance in practice: International variations in financing, benefits, and problems (San Francisco: Jossey-Bass, 1991).

[14] J. McKay, International benefits policy: A U.S. multinationals perspective, *Employee Benefits Journal* (December 1994):22–25.

[15] M. E. Horn, *International employee benefits: An overview* (Brookfield, Wisc.: International Foundation of Employee Benefit Plans, 1992).

[16] Myers, *Compensation management.*

[17] Harvey, Empirical evidence of recurring international compensation problems.

[18] W. R. Sheridan and P. T. Hansen, Linking international business and expatriate compensation strategies, *American Compensation Association Journal* (Spring 1996): 66–81.

[19] U.S. Department of State, *The U.S. Department of State indexes of living costs abroad, quarters allowances, and hardship differentials.*

[20] S. M. Kates and C. Spielman, Reducing the cost of sending employees overseas, *Practical Accountant* 28 (1995):50–55.

[21] I.R.C. §911 (b)(d); Treas. Reg. §1.911 (d)(2).

[22] Rev. Rul. 83–82, 1983-1 C.B. 45.

[23] I.R.C. § 911(c).

[24] R. A. Swaak, Expatriate management: The search for best practices, *Compensation & Benefits Review* (March–April 1995): 21–29.

CHAPTER

THIRTEEN

Compensating executives

In this chapter, you will learn about

1. Components of executive core compensation
2. Components of executive fringe compensation
3. Principles and processes of setting executive compensation
4. Executive compensation disclosure rules
5. The executive compensation controversy: Are U.S. executives paid too much?

From an economic standpoint, the CEO is the seller of his/her services, and the compensation committee is the buyer of these services. Under classic economic theory, a reasonable price is obtained through negotiations that are arm's length between an informed seller and an informed buyer. An awkward situation can result when the CEO hires a professional compensation director and/or compensation consultant. In this case, the compensation consultant that makes the recommendation to the compensation committee works for the CEO. In theory, the CEO hires the consultant to perform an objective analysis of the company's executive pay package and to make whatever recommendations the consultant feels are appropriate. This relationship has potential to promote a conflict of interest because of the perceived pressure for the consultant to protect the CEO's financial interests. The irony is that the consultant is often viewed as representing the shareholders' interests. In a sense, the buyers of the CEO's services are the shareholders and their representatives, the compensation committee of the board of directors. They tend to act upon the compensation consultant's recommendation.[1]

The income disparity between executives and other employees is astounding.

This passage illustrates just one of the main differences between compensating executives and compensating other employees. There are many other contrasts. The income disparity between executives and other employees is astounding. The median annual earnings for nonexecutives was $24,908 in 1995.[2] Chief executive officers (CEOs) earned an average $1,653,670 in annual salary and bonuses during 1995.[3]

Principles of executive compensation: implications for competitive strategy

Executives are the top leaders in their companies. Intuitively, it seems reasonable that executives should earn substantial compensation packages. After all, their skills and experiences enable them to develop and direct the implementation of competitive strategies. Few dispute the key role executives play in promoting competitive advantage. However, public scrutiny of executive compensation packages has intensified during the 1990s because of heightened concerns of global competitiveness and rampant corporate downsizing initiatives leaving thousands of employees jobless. We take up the executive compensation controversy later in this chapter. Next, we review fundamental concepts—defining executive status and the components of executive compensation packages.

Defining executive status: key employees and highly paid employees

Virtually all the components of executive compensation plans provide favorable tax treatment for both the executive and the company. Who are executives? The term *executive* applies to two designations—highly paid employees and key employees.

Highly paid employees and key employees hold positions of substantial responsibility. Exhibit 13-1 illustrates the placement of highly paid and key employees in a typical organizational structure. Although titles vary among companies and pay structures, chief executive officers (CEOs), presidents, and executive vice presidents generally meet the criteria for key employees. As Exhibit 13-1 shows, the CEO often is the top company executive. Vice presidents of functional areas (for example, human resources) and directors below them usually meet the criteria for highly paid employees.

Key employees (IRS guidelines)

The Internal Revenue Service (IRS) defines a **key employee** as an employee who, at any time during the current year or any of the four preceding years, is:[4]

* ✯ One of 10 employees owning the largest percentages of the company

* ✯ An employee who owns more than 5 percent of the company

* ✯ An employee who earns more than $150,000 per year and owns more than 1 percent of the company

* ✯ The IRS definition of key employee excludes any officer whose pay falls below $45,000 per year.

Highly paid employees (IRS Guidelines)

The Internal Revenue Service (IRS) defines a **highly paid employee** as one of the following:[5]

* ✯ An employee who owns at least 5 percent of the business

* ✯ An employee earning over $75,000 annually in either the current or the preceding calendar year

* ✯ An employee who earned over $50,000 either last year or this year whose salary is in the top 20 percent of all salaries paid to active employees

* ✯ An officer who earned over 150 percent either last year or this year of the dollar limit for annual additions to a defined contribution plan (Chapter 11). The defined contribution plan must apply to at least one officer up to a maximum of 50 officers.

Executive compensation packages

Executive compensation comprises both core and fringe compensation elements much as compensation packages for other employees do. However, one noteworthy feature distinguishes executive compensation packages from nonexecutive compensation packages. Executive compensation packages emphasize long-term or deferred rewards over short-term rewards. The main components of executive compensation include:

Exhibit 13-1
Examples of Highly Paid and Key Employees

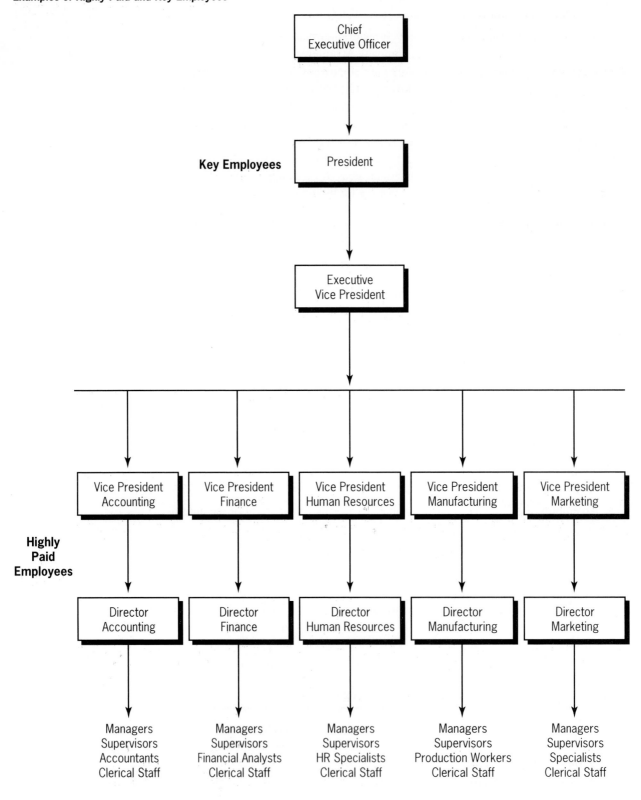

* Current or annual core compensation

* Deferred core compensation: stock compensation

* Deferred core compensation: golden parachutes

* Fringe compensation: enhanced benefits and perquisites

Components of current core compensation

Executive current core compensation packages contain three components—annual base pay, annual bonuses, and short-term incentives. In 1995, CEOs received an average of $1,653,670 in base pay and bonuses.[6] This 1995 figure rose slightly more than 18 percent from 1994, when CEOs received an average of $1,399,698 in base pay and bonuses,[7] and was more than 32 percent as high as 1993 levels; in 1993, CEOs received an approximate average of $1,259,728 in base pay and bonuses.[8] Information on short-term incentives earnings was not readily available.

BASE PAY Base pay is the fixed element of annual cash compensation. Companies that use formal salary structures may have specific pay grades and pay ranges (Chapter 9) for nonexempt employees and exempt employees including supervisory, management, professional, and executive jobs with the exception of the CEO.

As discussed in Chapter 9, compensation professionals generally apply different range spreads across pay grades. Most commonly, they use progressively higher range spreads for pay grades that contain more-valuable jobs in terms of the company's competitive strategies. Higher-level jobs afford employees fewer promotion opportunities than do entry-level jobs. Employees also tend to remain in higher pay grades longer, and the specialized skills associated with higher pay grade jobs are considered valuable. Therefore, it makes sense to apply larger range spreads to these pay grades.

CEO jobs do not fall within formal pay structures for two reasons. First, CEOs' work is highly complex and unpredictable. It is not possible to specify discrete responsibilities and duties. Two things make it impossible to describe CEOs' jobs: First is the choice of competitive strategy by CEOs and other executives and the influence of external and internal market factors (Chapter 8) on the implementation of competitive strategy. Second, setting CEO compensation differs dramatically from the rational processes compensation professionals use to build market-competitive pay systems (Chapter 8). We discuss agency theory, tournament theory, and social comparison theory later as explanations for setting CEO compensation.

BONUSES Bonuses represent single pay-for-performance payments companies use to reward employees for achievement of specific, exceptional goals. As discussed in previous chapters, compensation professionals design bonuses for merit pay programs (Chapter 4), gain sharing plans and referral plans (Chapter 5), and sales incentive compensation programs (Chapter 9). Bonuses also represent a key component of executive compensation packages.

Companies' compensation committees recommend bonus awards to boards of directors for their approval (we discuss the role of compensation committees and boards of directors later in this chapter). Four types of bonuses are common in executive compensation:

* Discretionary bonus

* Performance-contingent bonus

✯ Predetermined allocation bonus

✯ Target plan bonus

As the term implies, boards of directors award **discretionary bonuses** to executives on an elective basis. They weigh four factors in determining the amount of discretionary bonus— company profits, the financial condition of the company, business conditions, and prospects for the future. For example, boards of directors may award discretionary bonuses to executives for sound decisions leading to strong annual profits or substantial increases in market share.

Executives receive **performance-contingent bonuses** based on the attainment of such specific performance criteria as growth in profits or market penetration which are communicated in advance. The performance appraisal system for determining bonus awards is often the same goal-oriented appraisal system used for determining merit increases or general performance reviews for salary (Chapter 4).

Unlike the previous executive bonuses, the total bonus pool for the **predetermined allocation bonus** is based on a fixed formula. Company profit is the central factor in determining the size of the total bonus pool and bonus amounts.

The **target plan bonus** ties bonuses to corporate performance. The bonus amount increases commensurably with performance based on company profit or market share. Executives do not receive bonuses when performance falls below minimally acceptable standards. The target plan bonus differs from the predetermined allocation bonus in an important way: Predetermined allocation bonus amounts are fixed, regardless of corporate performance. Board of directors members set the bonus pool each year on their assessment of fair payment for achieving that performance level.

SHORT-TERM INCENTIVES Companies award short-term incentive compensation to executives to recognize their progress toward fulfilling competitive strategy goals. Executives may participate in current profit sharing plans and gain sharing plans. Exhibit 13-2 describes these plans. We already discussed, in Chapter 5, the use of current profit sharing plans and gain sharing plans for nonexecutive employees. Whereas short-term incentives reward nonexempt and lower-level management employees for achieving major milestone work objectives, short-term incentives applied to executives are designed to reward them for meeting intermediate performance criteria. The performance criteria are related to the performance of a company as dictated by competitive strategy. Change in the company's earnings per share over a one-year period, growth in profits, and annual cost savings are criteria that may be used in executives' short-term incentive plans.

Short-term incentive compensation programs usually apply to a group of select executives within a company. The plan applies to more than one executive because the synergy that results from the efforts and expertise of top executives influences corporate performance. The board of directors distribute short-term incentive awards to each executive on the basis of rank and compensation level. Thus, the CEO will receive a larger performance award than the executive vice president, whose position is under the CEO's position.

For example, let's assume that the CEO and executive vice president of a chain of general merchandise retail stores have agreed to lead the corporation as the lowest-cost chain of stores in the general merchandise retail industry. The CEO and her executive vice president establish a five-year plan to meet this lowest-cost competitive strategy. The vice president of compensation recommends that the company adopt a

---

CURRENT PROFIT SHARING PLANS

As we discussed in Chapter 5, profit sharing plans pay a portion of company profits to employees, separate from base pay, cost-of-living adjustments, or permanent merit pay increases. Two basic kinds of profit sharing plans are used widely today. First, current profit sharing plans award cash to employees, typically on a quarterly or annual basis. Second, deferred profit sharing plans place cash awards in trust accounts for employees. These trusts are set aside on employees' behalf as a source of retirement income. Current profit sharing plans provide cash to employees as part of their regular core compensation; thus, these payments are subject to IRS taxation when they are earned. Deferred profit sharing plans are not taxed until the employee begins to make withdrawals during retirement.

GAIN SHARING PLANS

As we discussed in Chapter 5, gain sharing describes group incentive systems that provide participating employees with an incentive payment based on improved company performance whether it be increased productivity, increased customer satisfaction, lower costs, or better safety records. Gain sharing was developed so that all employees could benefit financially from productivity improvements resulting from the suggestion system. Besides serving as a compensation tool, most gain sharing reflects a management philosophy that emphasizes employee involvement.

---

gain sharing program to reward top executives for contributing to the cost reduction objective. After one year, the complementary decisions made by the CEO, executive vice president, and vice president of compensation have enabled the corporation to save $10,000,000. The board of directors agree that the executives' collaborative decisions led to noteworthy progress toward meeting the lowest-cost strategy. They award the CEO 2 percent of the annual cost savings ($200,000) and the executive vice president 1 percent ($100,000).

Components of deferred core compensation: stock compensation

Deferred compensation refers to an agreement between an employee and a company to render payments to an employee at a future date. Deferred compensation is a hallmark of executive compensation packages. As an incentive, deferred compensation is supposed to create a sense of ownership, aligning the interests of the executive with those of the owners or shareholders of the company over the long term. CEOs earned an average of $2,092,722 in long-term compensation during 1995. The 10 highest paid CEOs earned an average $17,026,200 in long-term compensation during 1995.[9]

Apart from the incentive value, deferred compensation provides tax advantages to executives. In particular, deferring payment until retirement should lead to lower taxation. Why does deferment create a tax advantage? Executives do not pay tax on deferred compensation until they receive it. Presumably, executives' income tax rates will be substantially lower during retirement, when their total income is lower than while they were employed.

Company stock shares are the main form of executives' deferred compensation. **Company stock** represents total equity of the firm. **Company stock shares** represent equity segments of equal value. Equity interest increases positively with the number

Deferred compensation is a hallmark of executive compensation packages.

Exhibit 13-3
Employee Stock Terminology

Stock option. A right granted by a company to an employee to purchase a number of stocks at a designated price within a specified period of time.

Stock grant. A company's offering of stock to an employee.

Exercise of stock grant. An employee's purchase of stock using stock options.

Disposition. Sale of stock by the stockholder.

Fair market value. The average value between the highest and lowest reported sales price of a stock on the New York Stock Exchange on any given date. The Internal Revenue Service specifies whether an option has a readily ascertainable fair market value at grant. An option has a readily ascertainable fair market value if the option is actively traded on an established stock exchange at the time the option is granted.

of stock shares. Stocks are bought and sold every business day in public stock exchanges. The New York Stock Exchange is among the best-known stock exchanges. Exhibit 13-3 lists basic terminology pertaining to stocks.

Companies design executive stock compensation plans to promote an executive's sense of ownership of the company. Presumably, a sense of ownership should motivate executives to strive for excellent performance. In general, stock value increases with gains in company performance. In particular, a company's stock value rises in response to reports of profit gains. However, factors outside executives' control often influence stock prices despite executives' performance. For example, forecasts of economy-wide recession, increases in the national unemployment rate, and threats of war (as in the case of the Gulf War in 1990) often lead to declines in stock value.

Six particular forms of deferred (stock) compensation are:

> *Companies design executive stock compensation plans to promote an executive's sense of ownership of the company.*

☆ Incentive stock options

☆ Nonstatutory stock options

☆ Restricted stocks

☆ Phantom stock options

☆ Discount stock options

☆ Stock appreciation rights

INCENTIVE STOCK OPTIONS **Incentive stock options** entitle executives to purchase their companies' stock in the future at a predetermined price. Usually, the predetermined price equals the stock price at the time an executive receives the stock option. In effect, executives are purchasing the stocks at a discounted price. Executives generally purchase the stock after the price has increased dramatically. **Capital gains** is the difference between the stock price at the time of purchase and the lower stock price at the time an executive receives the stock option. Executives receive income tax benefits by participating in incentive stock options. The federal government does not tax capital gains until the disposition of the stock.

NONSTATUTORY STOCK OPTIONS Much like incentive stock options, stock options are awarded to executives at discounted prices. In contrast to incentive stock options, **nonstatutory stock options** do not qualify for favorable tax treatment. Executives pay income taxes on the difference between the discounted price and the stock's fair market value at the time of the stock grant. They do not pay taxes in the future when they choose to exercise their nonstatutory stock options.

Nonstatutory stock options do provide executives an advantage. Ultimately, executives' tax liability is lower over the long term: Stock prices generally increase over time. As a result, the capital gains will likely be much greater in the future when executives exercise their options rather than when their companies grant those options.

RESTRICTED STOCK Restricted stock is a common type of long-term executive compensation. In 1995, the median restricted stock grant ranged from a low of $200,000 (that is, 42 percent of base pay) in manufacturing industries to a high of $222,000 (that is, 54 percent of salary) in the diversified service industry.[10] Boards of directors award restricted stock to executives at considerable discounts. The term **restricted stock** means that executives do not have any ownership control over the disposition of the stock for a predetermined period, often, five to 10 years. Executives must sell the stock back to the company for exactly the same discounted price at the time of purchase if they terminate their employment before the end of the designated restriction period.[11] In addition, restricted stock grants provide executives tax incentives. They do not pay tax on any income resulting from an increase in stock price until after the restriction period ends.[12]

PHANTOM STOCK A **phantom stock** plan is a compensation arrangement whereby boards of directors compensate executives with hypothetical company stocks rather than actual shares of company stock.[13] Phantom stock plans are similar to restricted stock plans because executives must meet specific conditions before they can convert these phantom shares into real shares of company stock. There generally are two conditions. First, executives must remain employed for a specified period, anywhere between five and 20 years. Second, executives must retire from the company. Upon meeting these conditions, executives receive income equal to the increase in the value of company stock from the date the company granted the phantom stock to the conversion date. Phantom stock plans provide executives tax advantages. Executives pay taxes on the capital gains after they convert their phantom shares to real shares of company stock during retirement. Executives' retirement income will probably be significantly less than their income before retirement. Thus, the retirees' income tax rates will be lower.

DISCOUNT STOCK OPTION PLANS **Discount stock option**[14] plans are similar to nonstatutory stock option plans with one exception. Companies grant stock options at rates far below the stock's fair market value on the date the option is granted. This means that the participating executive immediately receives a benefit equal to the difference between the exercise price and the fair market value of the employer's stock.

STOCK APPRECIATION RIGHTS **Stock appreciation rights** provide executives income at the end of a designated period, much as with restricted stock options. However, executives never have to exercise their stock rights to receive income. The company simply awards payment to executives on the basis of the difference in stock price between the time the company granted the stock rights at fair market value and the end of the designated period, permitting the executives to keep the stock. Executives pay tax on any income from gains in stock value when they exercise their stock rights, presumably after retirement when their tax rates are lower.[15]

Components of deferred core compensation: the golden parachute

Most executives' employment agreements contain a *golden parachute* clause. **Golden parachutes** provide pay and benefits to executives after their termination resulting from a change in ownership, or corporate takeover. Golden parachutes extend pay and benefits anywhere between one and five years, depending upon the agreement. Planned retirement, resignation, and disability do not trigger golden parachute benefits. Boards of directors include golden parachute clauses for two reasons. First, golden parachutes limit executives' risks in the event of an unforeseen takeover. Second, golden parachutes promote recruitment and retention of talented executives.

Companies benefit from golden parachute payments because they can treat these payments as business expenses. This means that companies can reduce their tax liability by increasing the parachute amount. In the heyday of corporate takeovers during the 1980s, the total value of golden parachutes far exceeded the total value of executives' annual incomes. Public outcry that companies were abusing a tax break led to government-imposed intervention that limited tax benefits to companies. In general, companies may receive tax deductions on golden parachutes that amount to less than three times an executive's average annual compensation for the preceding five years.

Components of fringe compensation: enhanced protection program benefits and perquisites

Executives receive discretionary benefits that are like the benefits of other employees—protection program benefits, pay for time-not-worked, and employee services. But, executives' discretionary benefits differ in two ways. First, protection programs include supplemental coverage that provides enhanced benefit levels. Second, the services component contains benefits exclusively for executives. These exclusive executive benefits are known as **perquisites,** or **perks.** Legally required benefits apply to executives, with the exception of one provision of the Family and Medical Leave Act of 1993, which we discuss later.

ENHANCED PROTECTION PROGRAM BENEFITS Supplemental life insurance and supplemental executive retirement plans distinguish protection programs for executive employees from protection programs for nonexecutive employees. As discussed in Chapter 11, employer-provided life insurance protects employees' families by paying a specified amount to employees' beneficiaries upon employees' death. Most policies pay some multiple of the employee's salary; for instance, benefits paid at twice the employee's annual salary. Besides regular life insurance, executives receive supplemental life insurance protection that pays an additional monetary benefit. Companies design executives' supplemental life insurance protection to meet two objectives.[16] First, **supplemental life insurance** increases the value of an executive's estate, bequeathed to designated beneficiaries (usually, family members) upon the executive's death. Life insurance programs may be designed to provide greater benefits than standard plans usually allow. Second, these programs provide executives favorable tax treatments. Exhibit 13-4 summarizes the main features of alternative life insurance plans for executives.

Supplemental retirement plans are designed to restore benefits restricted under qualified pension plans. As discussed in Chapter 11, qualified pension plans entitle employers to receive tax benefits from their contributions to pension plans. In general, this means that employers may take current tax deductions for contributions to fund

Exhibit 13-4
*Alternative Life Insurance
Plans for Executives*

SPLIT-DOLLAR PLANS

The death benefit is divided or split between the employer and the employee's designated beneficiary. The premium can be paid entirely by the employer, or premium costs can be shared between the employer and employee. The employer does not receive a tax deduction for its share of the premium payments. However, employers are reimbursed for their premium payments by their share of the death benefit, which they receive tax free.

DEATH BENEFIT ONLY PLANS

Death benefit only plans pay benefits only to a designated beneficiary upon the death of the employee. This arrangement avoids federal estate taxes on the death benefit. According to federal estate tax laws, death benefits are included in an employee's estate if he or she held the right to receive payment from the life insurance plan while alive (some life insurance plans do allow employees to receive payments under limited conditions while alive). Because the employee was never eligible to receive payment on the plan while alive, the death benefit only plan payments are not considered part of the estate and thus are not subject to estate taxes.

GROUP TERM LIFE INSURANCE PLANS

As we discussed in Chapter 11, term life insurance coverage is the most common type of life insurance offered by companies. These plans provide protection to employees' beneficiaries only during employees' employment. Group term life insurance plans provide greater amounts of insurance coverage to executives than to other employees.

Source: Adapted from B. T. Beam Jr. and J. J. McFadden, *Employee benefits,* 5th. ed. (Chicago: Dearborn Financial Publishing, 1996).

future retirement income. Employees may also receive some favorable tax treatment (that is, a lower tax rate) because any investment income that is generated in the pension program is not taxed until the employee retires.

Annual benefits of a qualified plan may not exceed the lesser of $90,000 (adjusted for inflation) or 100 percent of the participants' average annual compensation based on the three highest annual compensation levels.[17] For example, an executive's three highest annual salaries are $690,000, $775,000, and $1,100,000. The average of these three highest salaries is $855,000. Of course, $90,000 is less than $855,000. Thus, an executive's retirement income based on her company's qualified pension plan cannot exceed $90,000 adjusted for inflation.

A supplemental retirement plan can make up the difference. For illustrative purposes, let's assume that the annual benefit under a qualified pension plan is 60 percent of the final average salary for the past 15 years of service. In our example, the final average salary is $240,000. On the basis of this formula, the executive should receive an annual retirement benefit of $144,000 ($240,000 × 60%). That annual benefit exceeds $90,000—the statutory limit for qualified retirement plans. Because of the statutory limit, companies may offer a supplemental executive retirement plan that provides the difference between the value derived from the pension formula ($144,000) and the statutory limit ($90,000). In this example, the executive would receive a supplemental annual retirement benefit of $54,000.

PERQUISITES Executive perquisites are an integral part of executive compensation. Perquisites cover a broad range of benefits, from free lunches to free use of corporate

Exhibit 13-5
Common Executive Perks

- Company cars
- Financial services
- Legal services (for example, income tax preparation)
- Recreational facilities (for example, country club and athletic club memberships)
- Travel perks (for example, first-class airfare)
- Residential security
- Tickets to sporting events

jets. Exhibit 13-5 lists common executive perks. Perquisites serve two purposes. First, these benefits recognize executives' attained status. Membership to an exclusive country club reinforces executives' attained social status. Second, executives use perks for personal comfort or as a business tool. For example, a company may own a well-appointed cabin in the Rocky Mountains of Vail, Colorado. Executives may use the cabin for rest and relaxation or as a place to court new clients or close a lucrative business deal. Arranging relaxing weekends in Vail not only benefits executives and their families but also provides executives opportunities to develop rapport with prospective clients.

A POSSIBLE EXCEPTION TO THE FAMILY AND MEDICAL LEAVE ACT OF 1993 Executives are entitled to take FMLA leaves and to receive continuing health benefits during such leaves. However, the FMLA does not guarantee the same job to the highest-paid 10 percent of the company's salaried employees when they return from FMLA leave. Of course, the criterion "highest-paid 10 percent" includes CEOs and other top executives. An employer may deny job restoration to such employees if:[18]

- ✯ The denial is necessary to prevent substantial and grievous economic injury to the employer's operations
- ✯ The employer has notified the employee of its intent to deny restoration
- ✯ An employee already on leave elects not to return to employment after receiving such notice

Principles and processes for setting executive compensation

We discussed the processes compensation professionals use to reward performance (merit pay and alternative incentive pay methods) and the acquisition of job-related knowledge and skills (pay-for-knowledge and skilled-based pay) in previous chapters. Although pay-for-performance is the public rationale for setting executive compensation, reality often is quite different. Three alternative theories explain the principles and processes for setting executive compensation. These include agency theory, tournament theory, and social comparison theory. We begin by discussing the key players in setting executive compensation.

The key players in setting executive compensation

Different individuals and groups participate in setting executive compensation. These individuals and groups include compensation consultants, board of directors members, and compensation committees. Each plays a different role in setting executive compensation.

EXECUTIVE COMPENSATION CONSULTANTS **Executive compensation consultants** usually propose several recommendations for pay packages. Often, executive compensation consultants are employed by large consulting firms that specialize in executive compensation or that advise company management on a wide variety of business issues. For example, Hay Associates, Hewitt Associates, Towers Perrin, and William M. Mercer are four widely known consulting firms that specialize in executive compensation.

Their recommendations about what and how much to include in executive compensation packages are based on strategic analyses, much like the analyses we discussed in Chapter 8. As you recall, a strategic analysis entails an examination of a company's external market context and internal factors. External market factors include industry profile, information about competitors, and long-term growth prospects. Financial condition is the most pertinent internal factor regarding executive compensation. Strategic analyses permit compensation consultants to see where their client company stands in the market. Companies in strong standing should be able to devote more financial resources to fund lucrative executive compensation programs than can companies in weaker standing.

More often than not, executive compensation consultants find themselves in conflict-of-interest situations:

> Ostensibly, compensation consultants were hired by the CEO to perform an objective analysis of the company's executive pay package and to make whatever recommendations the consultant felt were appropriate. In reality, if those recommendations did not cause the CEO to earn more money than he was earning before the compensation consultant appeared on the scene, the latter was rapidly shown the door.[19]

Executive compensation consultants find themselves in conflict-of-interest situations.

Executive compensation consultants' professional survival may depend on recommending lucrative compensation packages. Recommending the most lucrative compensation packages will quickly promote a favorable impression of the consultant among CEOs, leading to future consulting engagements.

BOARD OF DIRECTORS A **board of directors** represents shareholders' interests by weighing the pros and cons of top executives' decisions. Boards of directors usually contain about 15 members. These members include CEOs and top executives of other successful companies, distinguished community leaders, well-regarded professionals (for example, physicians, attorneys), and possibly a few top-level executives from within the company.

Boards of directors give final approval of the recommendations. Some critics of a compensation committee (discussed below) have argued that CEOs use compensation to co-opt board independence.[20] CEOs often nominate candidates for board membership, and their nominations usually lead to candidates' placement on the board. Board members receive compensation for their service to the boards. In 1994, the average compensation for service on boards of Fortune 500 companies was $60,000,[21] having risen 50 percent since 1991, when average board member compensation was

$40,000.[22] Increasingly, companies are using such benefits as medical insurance, retirement programs, and company stock to attract top-notch individuals. In 1994, board members received an average of $37,000 in cash compensation and $23,000 in benefits.[23]

Board members' failure to cooperate with CEOs may lead either to fewer benefits or to their removal.

> The . . . board . . . determines the pay of the CEO. But who determines the pay of the outside directors? Here, a sort of formal Japanese Kabuki has developed . . . . The board of directors determines the pay of the CEO, and for all practical purposes, the CEO determines the pay of the board of directors. Is it any accident, then, that there is a statistical relationship between how highly the CEO is paid and how highly his outside directors are paid?[24]

As we discuss shortly, recent changes in Securities and Exchange Commission rulings have increased board members' accountability for approving executive compensation packages. Boards are held responsible for being supportive of shareholders' best interests.

COMPENSATION COMMITTEE Board members from the company's board and from the boards of other companies constitute a **compensation committee.** Outside board members serve on compensation committees to minimize conflicts of interest. Thus, outside directors usually make up the committee's membership majority.

Compensation committees perform three duties. First, compensation committees review consultants' recommendations for compensation packages. Second, they discuss the assets and liabilities of the recommendations. The complex tax laws require compensation committees to consult compensation experts, legal counsel, and tax advisers. Third, on the basis of their deliberations, the committee recommends the consultant's best proposal to the board of directors for their consideration.

Theoretical explanations for setting executive compensation

Three prominent theories describe the processes related to setting executive compensation—*agency theory, tournament theory,* and *social comparison theory.* The following discussion provides concrete interpretations of those theories. (In addition to the works cited throughout this chapter, several excellent scholarly journal articles provide full explanations of these theoretical frames as applied to executive compensation.[25])

AGENCY THEORY Ownership is distributed among thousands of shareholders in such large companies as Ford Motor Company, General Electric, General Motors, and IBM. For example, owning at least one share of stock in Ford Motor Company bestows ownership rights in Ford Motor Company, although each shareholder's ownership is quite small, amounting to less than 1 percent. Inability to communicate frequently or directly is a major problem confronting thousands of shareholders. According to **agency theory,** shareholders solve that problem by choosing top executives to act as their agents.

Shareholders delegate control to top executives to represent their ownership interests. However, top executives usually do not own majority shares of their companies' stocks. Consequently, executives usually do not share the same interests as the collective shareholders. These features make it possible for executives to pursue activities that benefit themselves rather than the shareholders. Executives' acting in their own self-interest is known as the *agency problem.*[26] Specifically, executives may emphasize the attainment of short-term gains (increasing market share through lower costs)

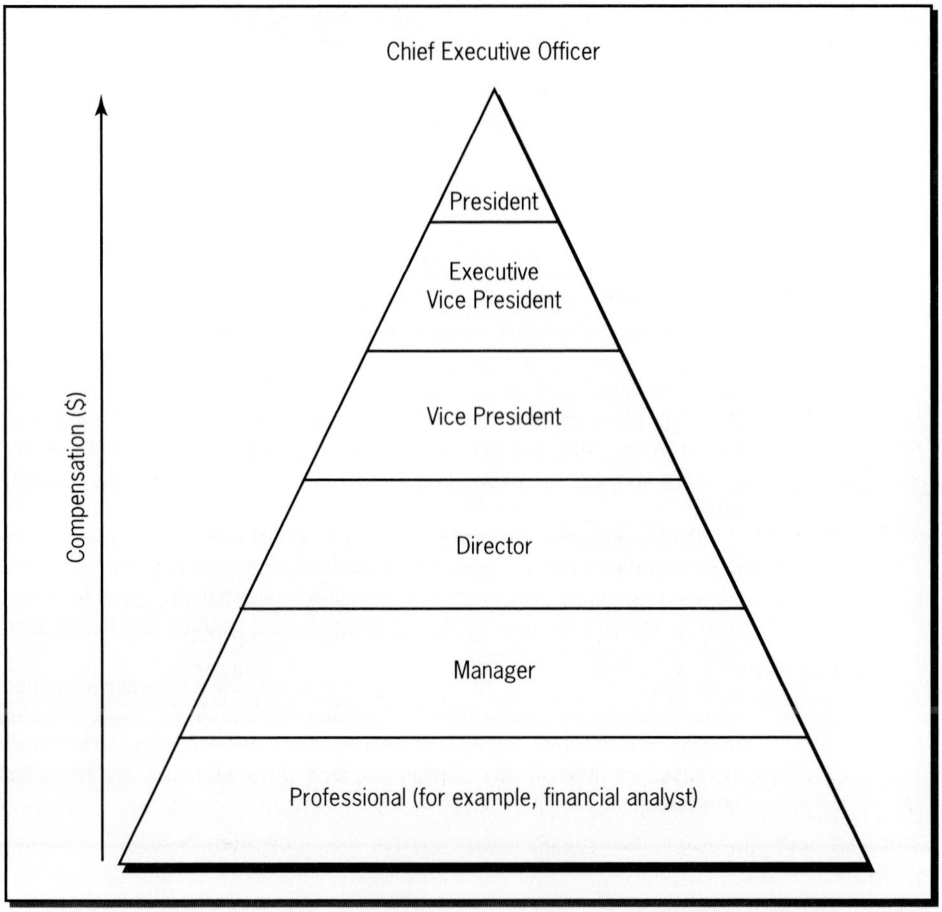

Exhibit 13-6
*CEO Compensation as a
Tournament*

Chief Executive Officer

President

Executive
Vice President

Vice President

Director

Manager

Professional (for example, financial analyst)

Compensation ($)

at the expense of long-term objectives (for example, product differentiation). Boards of directors may be willing to provide executives generous annual bonuses for attaining short-term gains.

Shareholders negotiate executive employment contracts with executives to minimize loss of control. Executive employment contracts define terms of employment pertaining to performance standards and compensation. These contracts specify current and deferred compensation and benefits. The main objective of shareholders is to protect the companies' competitive interests. Shareholders use compensation to align executives' interests with shareholders' interests. As discussed earlier, awarding company stocks to executives is one way of doing that.

TOURNAMENT THEORY **Tournament theory** casts lucrative executive compensation as the prize in a series of tournaments or contests among middle- and top-level managers who aspire to become CEO.[27] Winners of the tournament at one level enter the next tournament. In other words, an employee's promotion to a higher rank signifies a win, and more-lucrative compensation (higher base pay, incentives, enhanced benefits, and perks) represents the prize. The ultimate prize is promotion to CEO and a lucrative executive compensation package. Obviously, the chances of winning competitions decrease dramatically as employees rise through the ranks, because there are fewer positions at higher levels in corporate hierarchical structures. Exhibit 13-6 depicts CEO compensation as a tournament.

Should Tax Laws Drive Executive Compensation Programs?

Companies benefit from paying high salaries to executives. U.S. tax laws permit companies to deduct executives' annual salaries as a business expense, substantially reducing corporate tax bills. The tax laws essentially create an incentive for companies to award lucrative annual salaries. The more money executives earn, the more money companies save in taxes.

In 1993, President Clinton signed into effect a law that imposes a $1 million cap on the amount of executive compensation that companies can deduct as a business expense. The purpose of this law was to slow the growth in executives' annual salaries by removing the corporate tax break. (Although the average annual executive salary and bonus have exceeded $1 million since 1993, a substantial number of CEOs earn annual salaries and bonuses less than $1 million.) As it turns out, this law has had the opposite effect.

Some companies increased executives' annual salary to $1 million in order to get the maximum possible tax deduction. Establishing the tax cap at $1 million signaled companies that annual executive salaries equal to or less than $1 million were reasonable. Anything above $1 million was less reasonable, thus, subject to taxation.

In short, a law designed to limit growth in executive compensation inadvertently promoted growth in executive compensation. In this case, a law led to substantially higher pay without clear evidence that executive performance increased commensurably. Should tax laws drive executive compensation programs?

SOCIAL COMPARISON THEORY According to **social comparison theory,** individuals need to evaluate their accomplishments, and they do so by comparing themselves with similar individuals.[28] Demographic characteristics (for example, age, race) and occupation are common comparative bases. Individuals tend to select social comparisons whom they view as slightly better than themselves.[29] Researchers have applied social comparison theory to explain the processes for setting executive compensation.[30]

As we discussed earlier, compensation committees play an important role in setting executive compensation. Compensation committees often include CEOs from other companies of equal or greater stature. Social comparison theory purports that compensation committee members rely on their own compensation packages and the compensation packages of CEOs in companies of equal or greater stature to determine executive compensation.

Executive compensation disclosure rules

Companies that sell and exchange securities (for example, company stock and bonds) on public stock exchanges are required to file a wide variety of information with the Securities and Exchange Commission, including executive compensation practices. The **Securities and Exchange Commission (SEC)** is a nonpartisan, quasijudicial federal government agency with responsibility for administering federal securities laws.

- Stock option and stock appreciation right tables
- Long-term incentive plan table
- Pension plan table
- Performance graph comparing the company's stock price performance against a market index and a peer group
- Report from the compensation committee of the board of directors explaining compensation levels and policies
- Description of the directors' compensation, disclosing all amounts paid or payable
- Disclosure of certain employment contracts and golden parachutes

The **Securities Exchange Act of 1934** applies to the disclosure of executive compensation. Companies' board of directors members may be subject to personal liability for paying excessive compensation. Under securities law, publicly held corporations are required to disclose detailed information on executive compensation to shareholders and the public. Shareholders can bring **derivative lawsuits** on behalf of a corporation, claiming that executive compensation is excessive. Thus far, the courts are generally unwilling to substitute their judgment for the business judgment of a board of directors or compensation committee. Nevertheless, these SEC rulings suggest that directors should exercise more independent judgment in approving executive compensation plans. Apparently, the SEC decided directors were too heavily influenced by executives' wishes and so instituted the new rulings, which they hoped would make directors think more carefully about the consequences to shareholders of their decisions.

SEC rulings suggest that directors should exercise more independent judgment in approving executive compensation plans.

In 1992 and 1993, the SEC modified its rules pertaining to the disclosure of executive pay.[31] Exhibit 13-7 lists types of information about executive compensation that companies should disclose. The main objective of the SEC rulings is to clarify the presentation of the compensation paid to the CEO and the four most highly paid executives.

The SEC rules are presented in tabular and graphic forms, making information more accessible to the public at large than before the 1992 and 1993 modifications. These rules indirectly regulate compensation levels through enhanced public access to information by discouraging corporations from granting potentially embarrassing executive pay, especially when corporate performance is weak. There are several tables, but the most central table is titled the *Summary Compensation Table.*[32] The **Summary Compensation Table** discloses compensation information for the CEO and the four most highly paid executives over a three-year period. Exhibit 13-8 contains an excerpt of the Summary Compensation Table.

As you can see in Exhibit 13-8, the Summary Compensation Table covers the compensation paid to the named executive officers during the last completed fiscal year and the two preceding fiscal years. The table contains two main subheadings: annual compensation and long-term compensation. Annual compensation includes salary (base pay), bonus, and other annual compensation. Long-term compensation includes restricted stock awards, stock appreciation rights, and long-term incentive payouts. The last column titled "All Other Compensation ($)" is a catch-all column to record other forms of compensation. Information contained in this column must be described in a footnote.

Exhibit 13-8
Excerpt from the SEC Summary Compensation Table

NAME AND PRINCIPAL POSITION	YEAR	ANNUAL COMPENSATION			LONG-TERM COMPENSATION			ALL OTHER COMPENSATION ($)
					AWARDS			
		SALARY ($)	BONUS ($)	OTHER ANNUAL COMPENSATION ($)	Restricted Stock Award(s) ($)	No. of Securities Underlying Options/ No. of SARs[1]	LTIP Payouts[2] ($)	
CEO	1997							
	1996							
	1995							
Four highest paid officers								
A	1997							
	1996							
	1995							
B	1997							
	1996							
	1995							
C	1997							
	1996							
	1995							
D	1997							
	1996							
	1995							

[1] SAR: stock appreciation rights.

[2] LTIP: long-term incentive plan.

Are U.S. executives paid too much?

Are U.S. executives paid too much? Popular press and newspaper accounts generally suggest that executives are overpaid. Of course, you should form your own opinion. Some pertinent information to be considered includes comparison between executive compensation and compensation for other worker groups; strategic questions such as, Is pay commensurate with performance?; ethical considerations, such as, Is executive compensation fair?; and international competitiveness.

Comparison between executive compensation and compensation for other worker groups

The median annual earnings of all full-time nonexecutive U.S. workers was $24,908 in 1995.[33] Child care workers earned the least (median income, $9,360), and physicians earned the most (median income, $59,280). In 1995, CEOs earned an average salary and bonus totaling $1,653,670 and deferred compensation amounting to $2,092,722.[34] CEO annual salary and bonus ranged from a low of $306,000 to a high of $65,580,000!

A strategic question: is pay commensurate with performance?

There are several measures of corporate performance (Exhibit 13-9). Are CEOs compensated commensurably with their companies' performance? It is difficult to answer just Yes or just No because the evidence is mixed.[35] A recent study of the relationship between Fortune 500 companies' CEO compensation and corporate performance found:[36]

Are CEOs compensated commensurably with their companies' performance? It is difficult to answer just Yes or just No because the evidence is mixed.

☆ CEO annual base pay and annual bonuses showed strong positive relationships with pretax profit margins and return on equity. As company performance (as measured by pretax profit margins and return on equity) increased, so did CEO annual base pay and bonuses.

☆ All long-term CEO compensation components (for example, restricted stock, incentive stock options) were not significantly related to company performance (again, as measured by pretax profit margins and return on equity).

An ethical consideration: is executive compensation fair?

Is executive compensation fair? Three considerations drive this question—companies' ability to attract and retain top executives, income disparities between executives and nonexecutive employees, and layoffs of thousands of nonexecutive employees.

ATTRACT AND RETAIN TOP EXECUTIVES Many compensation professionals and board of director members argue that the trends in executive compensation are absolutely necessary for attracting and retaining top executives. Presumably, executives' decisions directly promote competitive advantage by positioning companies to achieve lowest-cost and differentiation strategies effectively. We discussed many examples, including the successful repositioning of The Victor Company (JVC) and American Express Company ("Reflections," Chapter 2). In Chapter 3, we indicated that competitive advantage invigorates the economy by increasing business activity, employment levels, and individuals' abilities to participate in the economy as consumers of companies' products and services.

INCOME DISPARITIES Exhibit 13-10 illustrates the marked income disparity between annual pay for various nonexecutive jobs and CEOs. The typical annual earnings for lowest-paid occupation (child care workers) amounted to a mere 0.5 percent (yes, one-half of 1 percent) of the average annual CEO salary and bonus. The ratio of highest-paid occupation (physicians) to the average annual CEO salary and bonus was not much better—3.6 percent. Said differently, the typical CEO's annual salary and bonus was 176 times as great as the typical child care worker's annual pay and 28 times as great as the typical physician's annual pay!

The typical CEO's annual salary and bonus was 176 times as great as the typical child care worker's annual pay and 28 times as great as the typical physician's annual pay!

The income disparity between executives and nonexecutive employees is increasing. The median annual earnings for nonexecutives rose only 2.6 percent between 1994 and 1995—from $24,284 to $24,908.[37] Executives' earnings in annual pay and bonuses increased by 18.1 percent during the same period—from $1,399,698 to $1,653,670.[38] CEO annual pay and bonuses rose nearly seven times as fast as nonexecutive earnings.

Exhibit 13-9
*Corporate Performance
Measures*

SIZE

- Sales
- Assets
- Profits
- Market value
- Number of employees

GROWTH

- Sales
- Assets
- Profits
- Market value
- Number of employees

PROFITABILITY

- Profit margin
- Return on assets (ROA)
- Return on equity (ROE)

CAPITAL MARKETS

- Dividend yield
- Total return to shareholders
- Price/earnings ratio
- Payout

LIQUIDITY

- Current ratio
- Quick ratio
- Working capital from operations
- Cash flow from operations

LEVERAGE

- Debt-to-equity ratio
- Short-term vs. long-term debt
- Cash flow vs. interest payments

LAYOFFS BORNE BY WORKERS BUT NOT BY EXECUTIVES Thousands of workers have been laid off since 1990. The rate of worker layoffs increased dramatically—39 percent—between 1990 and 1995.[39] In both 1990 and 1995 alone, more than 750,000 employees lost their jobs. Top management typically advances several reasons that ne-

OCCUPATION	ANNUAL EARNINGS ($)	INCOME DISPARITY (%)[1]
Physicians	59,280	3.6
Lawyers	58,500	3.5
Aerospace engineers	50,804	3.1
College and university teachers	43,836	2.7
Personnel and labor relations managers	36,192	2.2
Elementary school teachers	33,280	2.0
Firefighters	32,552	2.0
Accountants and auditors	32,188	1.9
Electricians	30,992	1.9
General office supervisors	26,780	1.6
Correctional institution officers	25,948	1.6
Automobile mechanics	24,232	1.5
Bus drivers	21,788	1.3
Secretaries	20,952	1.2
Machine operators, assemblers, and inspectors	19,136	1.1
Laborers	17,108	1.0
File clerks	16,796	1.0
Bank tellers	15,600	0.9
Janitors and cleaners	15,236	0.9
Nursing aides, orderlies, and attendants	14,612	0.8
Teachers' aides	14,144	0.8
Waiters and waitresses	14,092	0.8
Farm workers	13,416	0.8
Child care workers	9,360	0.5

Sources: U.S. Bureau of Labor Statistics, *Employment and earnings* (Washington, D.C.: U.S. Government Printing Office, January 1996). J. A. Byrne, How high can CEO pay go? *Business Week*, April 22, 1996, pp. 100–106.

[1] Nonexecutives' 1995 median income divided by the 1995 average CEO salary plus bonus. For example: $32,188/$1,653,670 = 1.9%. The nonexecutive earnings were based on the 1995 weekly median earnings reported in *Employment and Earnings* (January 1996). Annual median earnings equal weekly median earnings multiplied by 52 (weeks/year). The 1995 average CEO salary and bonus ($1,653,670) was reported in *Business Week*'s annual survey of executive compensation.

cessitate these layoffs—global competition, reductions in product demand, technological advances that perform many jobs more efficiently than employees, mergers and acquisitions, and establishing production operations in foreign countries with lower labor costs. Virtually none of the executives of any of the companies involved lost their jobs. As millions of workers lost their jobs between 1990 and 1995, corporate profits increased an average 75 percent and CEO pay rose an average 92 percent.[40]

International competitiveness

Increased global competition has forced companies in the United States to become more productive. Excessive expenditures on compensation can threaten competitive

In Defense of U.S. Executive Compensation Practices

Popular press accounts of U.S. executive compensation practices generally advance two criticisms. First, executive compensation levels are unwarranted when the relationship between executive compensation and company performance is tenuous. Second, executives do not deserve to earn as much as they do, particularly when they authorize mass layoffs to promote competitiveness. Consider these responses in defense of U.S. executive compensation practices.

Criticism 1: Executive compensation levels are unwarranted when the relationship between executive compensation and company performance is tenuous. This criticism is consistent with basic pay-for-performance principles: Reward employees commensurably with their performance. Critics should adopt a multiyear view of corporate performance when judging the appropriateness of executive pay levels. Consistent with competitive strategies, it may be several years before the fruits of sound strategic planning are realized. In addition, factors beyond executives' control (for example, the economic recession due to the Gulf War) may result in lackluster short-term corporate performance.

Criticism 2: Executives do not deserve to earn as much as they do, particularly when they authorize mass layoffs to promote competitiveness. Some basic facts and assumptions are necessary before providing a response to this criticism:

- In 1994, the median annual nonexecutive earnings was $24,284, and CEOs earned an average $1,399,698 in annual pay and bonuses.

- Let's assume that U.S. CEO compensation should be similar to typical Japanese CEO compensation—$312,000 a year.[41] Japanese CEOs typically earn a total of $480,000 a year 65 percent of which is awarded as salary and annual bonuses ($480,000 × 65% = $312,000).

- U.S. CEOs earned an average excess totaling $1,087,698 (that is, $1,399,698 – $312,000).

On the basis of those facts and assumption, approximately 45 employees, on average, would retain their jobs ($1,087,698/$24,284) for one year if the compensation of the company's CEO were reduced by $1,087,698. Although the livelihood of 45 employees is important, a broader perspective is necessary. Saving 45 jobs in one year may lead to dire future consequences if the company is unable to retain a highly qualified CEO. Losing a highly qualified CEO may result in hindered corporate performance which, in turn, may lead to permanent job loss among thousands.

---

advantage. Compensation expenditures are excessive when they outpace the quality and quantity of employees' contributions. In addition, compensation expenditures may be excessive when they are substantially higher than competitors' compensation outlays. Concerns about U.S. companies' competitiveness in global markets are common because of the vast differences in compensation levels between CEOs of U.S. and foreign companies.

INTERNATIONAL COMPENSATION COMPARISONS Comparisons between U.S. executive compensation and foreign executives' compensation can be made on two dimensions—total compensation amount and components. Securities and Exchange Commission (SEC) rules require the disclosure of executive compensation in U.S. companies. However, comparable rules do not exist in foreign countries. Consequently, it is difficult to make detailed comparisons between U.S. and foreign executive compensation.

Research indicates that U.S. CEOs earn significantly more than their foreign counterparts.[42] Total 1994 CEO compensation in six countries averaged $389,711,[43] lagging far behind U.S. CEOs' 1994 average compensation—$4,280,673.[44] Typical foreign CEO pay (salary and annual bonus, deferred compensation, benefits, and perks) amounted close to:[45]

- ★ Japan: $480,000 (about $312,000 in annual salary and bonus)
- ★ France: $475,000 (about $275,500 in annual salary and bonus)
- ★ Italy: $425,000 (about $276,250 in annual salary and bonus)
- ★ Germany: $410,000 (about $323,900 in annual salary and bonus)
- ★ United Kingdom: $395,000 (about $225,150 in annual salary and bonus)
- ★ Spain: $350,000 (about $276,500 in annual salary and bonus)
- ★ Thailand: $116,790 (annual salary and bonus)
- ★ Singapore: $113,740 (annual salary and bonus)
- ★ Indonesia: $96,340 (annual salary and bonus)
- ★ Australia: $87,120 (annual salary and bonus)
- ★ Philippines: $72,850 (annual salary and bonus)

Although executive compensation packages consist of similar basic components (salary and annual bonus, deferred compensation, benefits, and perks), there appear to be differences in the relative mix of those components among countries.[46]

- ★ Japan: Salary and annual bonus, 65%; deferred compensation, 17%; benefits and perks, 18%
- ★ France: Salary and annual bonus, 58%; deferred compensation, 16%; benefits and perks, 26%
- ★ Italy: Salary and annual bonus, 65%; deferred compensation, 5%; benefits and perks, 30%
- ★ Germany: Salary and annual bonus, 79%; deferred compensation, 9%; benefits and perks, 12%
- ★ United Kingdom: Salary and annual bonus, 57%; deferred compensation, 13%; benefits and perks, 30%
- ★ Spain: Salary and annual bonus, 79%; deferred compensation, 7%; benefits and perks, 14%

UNDERMINING U.S. COMPANIES' ABILITY TO COMPETE? Presently, there is no evidence showing that U.S. executive compensation pay practices have undermined U.S. companies' ability to compete. CEO pay has risen commensurably with corporate profits in recent years. Corporate profits increased an average 75 percent, while CEO pay rose an average 92 percent between 1990 and 1995.[47] Might executive compensation practices undermine U.S. companies' ability to compete in the future?

On one hand, it is reasonable to predict that CEO pay will not undermine U.S. companies' ability to compete because CEO pay increased as company profits increased. On the other hand, the current wave of widespread layoffs may hinder U.S. companies' ability to compete. As you recall from Chapter 2, U.S. companies use layoffs to maintain profits and cut costs, heightening workers' job insecurities. The remaining workers may lose faith in pay-for-performance systems and trust in their employers as colleagues lose their jobs; yet CEOs continue to receive high compensation. Workers may not feel that their working hard will lead to higher pay or to job security. For example, Caterpillar Inc.'s CEO Donald Fites received a 75 percent raise in total compensation between 1994 and 1995. During the same period, the bonus pool for hourly and salaried workers decreased by 25 percent.[48] Workers faced with such disparities may choose not to work proficiently. Consequently, reduced individual performance and destabilized work forces may make it difficult for U.S. companies to compete against foreign companies.

Summary

In this chapter, we reviewed the components and principles of executive compensation. The components include base pay, bonuses, short-term incentives, stock and stock option plans, enhanced benefits, and perquisites. Next, we examined the principles and processes underlying executive compensation. Finally, we addressed whether U.S. executive compensation is excessive. Although popular press accounts suggest that executive compensation is excessive, you will have to form your own opinion, particularly as you assume compensation management responsibilities for your employer. As compensation professionals, you will likely face many difficult questions from employees regarding the rationale for and the fairness of lucrative executive compensation packages.

Discussion questions

1. What can be done to make compensation committees function consistently with shareholders' interests? Please explain.
2. Which component of compensation is most essential to motivate executives to lead companies toward competitive advantage? Discuss your rationale.
3. Is executive compensation excessive, or is it appropriate? Discuss your position.
4. Discuss the differences between enhanced benefits and perquisites.
5. Consult the three most recent *Business Week* special reports on executive compensation. These reports appear in the issues published during the third week of April each year. Pick a company that appears in the survey each year, noting the information about annual and long-term compensation. Next, review some recent materials that describe the industry and future prospects (for example, consult newspapers, business periodicals,

trade magazines, or the U.S. Department of Commerce's *U.S. Industrial Outlook*, which we discussed in Chapter 8). Finally, write a one-page report summarizing your selected industry's current condition and future prospects. Then comment on whether you believe that the three-year trend in executive compensation is appropriate. Explain your rationale.

Key terms

key employee
highly paid employee
discretionary bonuses
performance-contingent bonuses
predetermined allocation bonus
target plan bonus
deferred compensation
company stock
company stock shares
incentive stock options
capital gains
nonstatutory stock options
restricted stock
phantom stock
discount stock option
stock appreciation rights

golden parachute
perquisites
perks
supplemental life insurance
supplemental retirement plans
executive compensation consultants
board of directors
compensation committee
agency theory
tournament theory
social comparison theory
Securities and Exchange
  Commission (SEC)
Securities Exchange Act of 1934
derivative lawsuits
Summary Compensation Table

Endnotes

[1] B. Walters, T. Hardin, and J. Schick, Top executive compensation: Equity or excess? Implications for regaining American competitiveness, *Journal of Business Ethics* 14 (1995):227–234.

[2] U.S. Bureau of Labor Statistics, *Employment and earnings* (Washington, D.C.: U.S. Government Printing Office, January 1996).

[3] J. A. Byrne, How high can CEO pay go? *Business Week,* April 22, 1996, pp. 100–106.

[4] I.R.C. § 416 (i).

[5] Ibid.

[6] Byrne, How high can CEO pay go?

[7] J. A. Byrne, with L. Bongiorno, CEO pay: Ready for takeoff, *Business Week,* April 25, 1995, pp. 88–94.

[8] J. A. Byrne, with L. Bongiorno, That eye-popping executive pay, *Business Week,* April 25, 1994, pp. 52–58.

[9] Byrne, with Bongiorno, CEO pay.

[10] M. Andreas-Klein, *Top executive compensation in 1995: An advance report* (New York: The Conference Board, 1996).

[11] I.R.C. § 83; Treas. Reg., §§ 1.83-1(b)(2), 1.83-1(e), 1.83-2(a).

[12] I.R.C. § 83; Treas. Reg., §§ 1.83-1(b)(1), 1.83-1(c).

[13] I.R.C. §§ 61, 83, 162; Treas. Reg. § 1.83.

[14] I.R.C. §§ 61, 83, 162, 451; Treas. Reg. § 1.83.

[15] Ibid.

[16] B. T. Beam Jr. and J. J. McFadden, *Employee benefits,* 5th ed. (Chicago: Dearborn Financial Publishing, 1996).

[17] Treas. Reg. § 1.415-3(a)(1).

[18] Family and Medical Leave Act of 1993 § 104(b).

[19] G. S. Crystal, Why CEO compensation is so high, *California Management Review* 34 (1991):9–29.

[20] Ibid.

[21] A. G. Perkins, Director compensation: The growth of benefits, *Harvard Business Review* 73 (January–February 1995):12–14.

[22] P. Hempel and C. Fay, Outside director compensation and firm performance, *Human Resource Management* 33 (1994):111–133.

[23] Perkins, Director compensation.

[24] G. S. Crystal, *In search of excess: The over-compensation of American executives* (New York: W. W. Norton, 1991).

[25] For further information on agency theory, see: K. M. Eisenhardt, Agency theory: An assessment and review, *Academy of Management Review* 14 (1989):57–74; M. Jensen and W. H. Meckling, Theory of the firm: Managerial behavior, agency costs, and ownership structure, *Journal of Financial Economics* 3 (1976):305–360; and H. L. Tosi Jr. and L. R. Gómez-Mejía, The decoupling of CEO pay and performance: An agency theory perspective, *Administrative Science Quarterly* 34 (1989):169–189. For further information on tournament theory and social comparison theory, see: P. S. Goodman, An examination of referents used in the evaluation of pay, *Organizational Behavior and Human Performance* 12 (1974):170–195; E. Lazear and S. Rosen, Rank-order tournaments as optimum labor contracts, *Journal of Political Economy* 89 (1981):841–864; and C. A. O'Reilly III, B. G. Main, and G. S. Crystal, CEO compensation as tournament and social comparison: A tale of two theories, *Administrative Science Quarterly* 33 (1988):257–274.

[26] Jensen and Meckling, Theory of the firm.

[27] Lazear and Rosen, Rank-order tournaments as optimum labor contracts.

[28] L. Festinger, A theory of social comparison processes, *Human Relations* 7 (1954): 117–140.

[29] A. Tversky and D. Kahneman, Judgment and uncertainty: Heuristics and biases, *Science* 185 (1974):1124–1131.

[30] O'Reilly, Main, and Crystal, CEO compensation as tournament and social comparison.

[31] SEC Release No. 33-6962 (Oct. 16, 1992); SEC Release No. 33-6940 (July 10, 1992); SEC Release No. 34-33229 (Nov. 29, 1993).

[32] Summary Compensation Table: 17 C.F.R. 229.402(b), as amended Nov. 29, 1993, effective Jan. 1, 1994.

[33] U.S. Bureau of Labor Statistics, *Employment and Earnings.*

[34] Byrne, How high can CEO pay go?

[35] L. R. Gómez-Mejía and D. B. Balkin, *Compensation, organizational strategy, and firm performance* (Cincinnati: South-Western Publishing, 1992).

[36] M. Andreas-Klein, *Top executive pay for performance* (New York: The Conference Board, 1995).

[37] U.S. Bureau of Labor Statistics, *Employment and earnings* (January 1996); and U.S. Bureau of Labor Statistics, *Employment and earnings* (Washington, D.C.: U.S. Government Printing Office, January 1995).

[38] Byrne, How high can CEO pay go?; and Byrne, with Bongiorno, CEO pay.

[39] Byrne, How high can CEO pay go?

[40] Ibid.

[41] R. Morais, G. Eisenstodt, and S. Kichen, with Y. Anezaki, M. Baumann, B. Bierach, K. Kure, H. Onozuka, and S. Puhler, The global boss' pay: Where (and how) the money is, *Forbes,* June 7, 1993, pp. 90–98.

[42] Ibid.

[43] J. Flynn, with F. Nayeri, Continental divide over executive pay, *Business Week,* July 3, 1995, pp. 40–41.

[44] Byrne, with Bongiorno, CEO pay.

[45] Special Report: Asia lifestyles, *Far Eastern Economic Review* 159 (August 8, 1996): 35–44; Flynn, with Nayeri, Continental divide over executive pay (Japan and European countries); and L. Mazur, Europay, *Across the Board* 32 (January 1995):40–43.

[46] Flynn, with Nayeri, Continental divide over executive pay; and Mazur, Europay.

[47] Byrne, How high can CEO pay go?

[48] J. G. Belcher Jr., Gain sharing and variable pay: The state of the art, *Compensation & Benefits Review* (May–June 1994):50–60.

CHAPTER

FOURTEEN

Compensating the flexible work force: Contingent employees and flexible work schedules

CHAPTER OUTLINE

In this chapter, you will learn about

1. Various groups of contingent workers and the reasons for U.S. employers' increased reliance on them
2. Core and fringe compensation issues for contingent workers
3. Key features of flexible work schedules, compressed work weeks, and telecommuting
4. Core and fringe compensation issues for flexible work schedules, compressed work weeks, and telecommuting
5. Unions' reactions to contingent workers and flexible work schedules
6. Strategic issues and choices in using contingent workers

Employers are still very concerned about the prospect of another downturn in the economy that may leave them with high overhead costs. Instead of having that problem, they are moving more to [contingent] workers. They can keep their costs, especially fringe costs, down with the use of temps. In short, the major reason for growth has to do with maintaining a lean payroll.

. . . Temporary work is also growing because of the increase in job dissatisfaction. Workers are not staying with employers as long as they used to. They are more willing than ever before to move across the street or town for small change. Automation has exacerbated this trend. Mechanization and automation have reduced the skill content of many occupations and turned more positions into boring ones. . . . The temporary help industry helps workers because they get a chance to job-hop and break up the monotony of everyday work life.[1]

Bill and Mary met while pursuing doctoral degrees in computer science. They were married during their third year of graduate studies. Upon completing their degrees, both Bill and Mary received dream job offers as software engineers. Bill's offer would place him in San Francisco; Mary's offer would place her in Boston. Both are very committed to their careers and to their marriage. Wouldn't it be great if Bill could perform his job for the San Francisco company while living in Boston, where Mary works?

The complexities of employees' personal lives—dependent children and elderly relatives, dual-career couples, disabilities—make working standard eight-hour days for five consecutive days every week difficult.

Changing business conditions and personal preferences have led to an increase in the use of contingent workers and flexible work schedules in the United States; companies employed as many as 6 million contingent workers in February 1995.[2] Likewise, the complexities of employees' personal lives—dependent children and elderly relatives, dual-career couples, disabilities—make working standard eight-hour days for five consecutive days every week difficult. Nearly 5 million employees worked on flexible work schedules during 1993.[3] Altogether, contingent and flexible schedule employees represent approximately 10 percent of the U.S. civilian labor force.

The preceding chapters addressed compensation issues for **core employees,** also known as permanent, full-time employees. Core employees possess full-time jobs, and they generally plan long-term or indefinite relationships with their employers.[4] In addition, we operated under the assumption that all core employees work standard schedules—fixed eight-hour work shifts, five days a week. Compensation practices differ somewhat between core employees and the flexible work force. Thus, we will consider the main differences in compensation.

The contingent work force

One study maintains that the contingent work force segment is growing faster than the work force as whole.[5] **Contingent workers** engage in explicitly tentative employment relationships with companies. The duration of their employment varies according to convenience needs and employers' business needs.

Groups of contingent workers

There are four distinct groups of contingent workers:

★ Part-time employees

★ Temporary employees

★ Leased employees

★ Independent contractors, free-lancers, and consultants

PART-TIME EMPLOYEES Part-time employment makes up a growing share of jobs in the United States.[6] The Bureau of Labor Statistics distinguishes between two kinds of part-time employees—voluntary and involuntary. A **voluntary part-time employee** chooses to work fewer than 35 hours per regularly scheduled work week. In some cases, individuals supplement full-time employment with part-time employment to meet financial obligations.

Some workers, including a small but growing number of professionals, elect to work part-time as a lifestyle choice. These part-timers sacrifice pay, and possibly career advancement, in exchange for more free time to devote to family, hobbies, and personal interests. These part-time workers often have working spouses whose benefits extend coverage to family members. Such benefits generally include medical and dental insurance coverage.

Involuntary part-time employees work fewer than 35 hours per week because they are unable to find full-time employment. Involuntary part-time work represents the lion's share of all part-time employment.[7] Most involuntary part-time jobs are low-skilled, and these job holders possess very little interest in career advancement.[8]

Exhibit 14-1 lists some specific reasons for part-time work and the percentage of individuals who work part-time for each reason. Some individuals who usually work full-time also hold part-time jobs. Others typically work part-time jobs only. This exhibit displays the reasons for both groups.

Companies may experience a number of advantages and disadvantages from employing part-time workers. Flexibility is the key advantage. Most companies realize a substantial cost savings because they offer part-time workers few or no discretionary benefits. Exhibit 14-2 shows employers' costs for providing various discretionary benefits and legally required benefits to full-time and part-time employees. Employers save considerable money in the areas of paid leave, insurance, and legally required benefits.

Companies also save on overtime pay expenses. Hiring part-time workers during peak business periods minimizes overtime pay costs. As we discussed in Chapter 3, the Fair Labor Standards Act of 1938 (FLSA) requires that companies pay nonexempt employees at a rate equaling one and one-half times their regular hourly pay rates. Retail businesses save considerable amounts by employing part-time sales associates during the peak holiday shopping season.

> *Companies may experience a number of advantages and disadvantages from employing part-time workers. Flexibility is the key advantage.*

	USUALLY WORK	
	FULL-TIME (%)	PART-TIME (%)
Slack work or business conditions	3.6	10.4
Could find only part-time work	Not applicable	6.0
Seasonal work	<1	<1
Job started or ended during the week	<1	0
Child care problems	<1	2.4
Other family or personal obligations	2.3	15.6
Health or medical limitations	0	2.1
In school or training	<1	19.2
Retired, Social Security limit on earnings	<1	5.9
Vacation or personal day	9.6	0
Holiday, legal, or religious	3.5	0
Weather-related curtailment	3.2	0
Other	8.6	11.8

Source: U.S. Department of Commerce, *Statistical abstracts of the United States,* 115th ed. (Washington, D.C.: U.S. Government Printing Office, 1995).

Note: Percentages total to more than 100% because some individuals work part-time for more than one reason.

BENEFIT	FULL-TIME	PART-TIME
Paid leave	$1.33	$0.25
Supplemental pay	$0.57	$0.14
Insurance	$1.40	$0.28
Retirement and savings	$0.63	$0.10
Other benefits	$0.04	<$ .01
Legally required benefits	$1.76	$1.02
Total hourly benefits costs	$5.73	$1.80

Source: U.S. Bureau of Labor Statistics, *Employer costs for employee compensation—March 1995,* USDL 95-225 (Washington, D.C.: U.S. Government Printing Office, June 22, 1995).

Job sharing is a special kind of part-time employment agreement. Two or more part-time employees perform a single full-time job. These employees may perform all job duties or share the responsibility for particular tasks. Some job sharers meet regularly to coordinate their efforts. Job sharing represents a compromise between employees' needs or desires not to work full-time and employers' need to staff jobs on a full-time basis. Both employers and employees benefit from the use of job sharing. Exhibit 14-3 lists some of the benefits of job sharing to employers and employees.

TEMPORARY EMPLOYEES Companies traditionally hire temporary employees for two reasons. First, temporary workers fill in for permanent workers who are on approved

Exhibit 14-3
Benefits of Job Sharing

BENEFITS TO EMPLOYERS

- Maintenance of productivity because of higher morale and maintenance of employee skills
- Retention of skilled workers
- Reduction or elimination of the training costs that result from retraining laid-off employees
- Greater flexibility in deploying workers to keep operations going
- Minimization of postrecession costs of hiring and training new workers to replace those who found other jobs during layoff
- Strengthening employees' loyalty to the company

BENEFITS TO EMPLOYEES

- Continued fringe benefits protection
- Continued employment when the likelihood of unemployment is high
- Maintenance of family income
- Continued participation in qualified retirement programs

---

leaves of absence including sick leave, vacation, bereavement leave, jury duty, or military leave. Second, temporary workers offer extra sets of hands when companies' business activities are high during such times as the holiday season for retail businesses or summer for amusement parks. Temporary employees perform jobs on a short-term basis usually measured in days, weeks, or months.[9]

More recently, companies have started to hire temporary workers for three additional reasons. First, temporary employment arrangements provide employers the opportunity to evaluate whether legitimate needs exist for creating new positions. Second, temporary employment arrangements give employers the opportunity to decide whether to retain workers on a permanent basis. "The temp job is often what one university placement director calls the 'three-month interview'—and a gateway to a full-time job and perhaps a new career." [10] In effect, the temporary arrangement represents a probationary period when employers observe whether workers are meeting job performance standards. As a corollary, such temporary arrangements provide workers the chance to decide whether to accept employment on a full-time basis after they have had time to "check things out." Third, employing temporary workers is generally less costly than hiring permanent workers because temporary workers do not receive such costly discretionary benefits as medical insurance coverage.

Companies hire temporary employees from a variety of sources. The most common source is **temporary employment agencies.** In 1993 alone, companies employed nearly 1.6 million temporary workers.[11] Traditionally, most temporary employment agencies placed clerical and administrative workers.[12] Nowadays, some temporary agencies also place workers with specialized skills, for example, auditors, computer systems analysts, and lawyers. This type of agency is becoming more common.[13]

Companies generally consider two main factors when establishing relationships with temporary employment agencies. First, companies consider agencies' reputation as an important factor, judging reputation by how well agencies' placements work out. Some agencies place a wide range of employees; others specialize in one type of placement (for example, financial services professionals). When companies plan to hire a variety of temporary workers, it is often more convenient to work with agencies that do not specialize. Ultimately, companies should judge these agencies' placement records for each type of employee.

Second, companies also should consider agencies' fees. Cost is a paramount consideration for companies pursuing lowest-cost competitive strategies. Temporary agencies base fees as a percentage of their placements' pay rates. The percentage varies from agency to agency. Fortunately, the competition among temporary agencies keeps these rates in check.

Although temporary employees perform work in a variety of companies, their legal employer is the temporary employment agency. Temporary employment agencies take full responsibility for selecting temporary employee candidates. These agencies also determine candidates' qualifications through interviews and testing. Particularly for clerical and administrative jobs, many temporary agencies train candidates to use such office equipment as fax machines, electronic mail, and spreadsheet and word processing software programs. Temporary employees receive compensation directly from the agency.

Companies may hire temporary employees through other means. For example, some companies hire individuals directly as temporary workers. Under **direct hire arrangements,** temporary employees typically do not work for more than one year. In addition, the hiring companies are the temporary workers' legal employers. Thus, companies take full responsibility for all HRM functions that affect temporary employees, including recruitment, performance evaluation, compensation, and training.

On-call arrangements are another method for employing temporary workers. On-call employees work sporadically throughout the year when companies require their services. Some unionized skilled trade workers are available as on-call employees when they are unable to secure permanent, full-time employment. These employees' unions maintain rosters of unemployed members who are available for work. When employed, on-call workers are employees of the hiring companies. Thus, the hiring companies are responsible for managing and implementing HRM policies including compensation.

LEASED EMPLOYEE ARRANGEMENTS **Lease companies** employ qualified individuals whom they place in client companies on a long-term, presumably permanent basis. Lease companies place employees within client companies in exchange for fees. Most leasing companies bill the client for the direct costs of employing the workers—such as payroll, benefits, and payroll taxes—and then charge a fixed fee. Lease companies base these fees on either a fixed percentage of the client's payroll or a fixed fee per employee.

Leasing arrangements are common in the food service industry. ARAMARK Food Services is an example of a leasing company that provides cafeteria services to client companies. ARAMARK staffs these companies' in-house cafeterias with cooks, food preparers, and check-out clerks. These cafeteria workers are employees of the leasing company not of the client company. Lease companies also operate in other industries, including security services, building maintenance, and administrative services.

Lease companies and temporary employment agencies are similar because both manage all HRM activities. Thus, lease companies provide both wages and benefits to their employees. Lease companies and temporary employment agencies differ in an important respect. Lease company placements tend to be permanent rather than temporary.

Independent Contracting: The Best of Both Worlds

Mary Johnson turned 65 years old two weeks ago. Mary worked as a tax accountant at XYZ Manufacturing Company for 41 years. Today—Friday afternoon—is her last day as a permanent, full-time employee, and her colleagues have thrown her a retirement party. XYZ's chief accountant recognized Mary with a gold watch, and he asked her to make a few remarks to her colleagues. After speaking warmly about her tenure with XYZ, Mary concluded with, "Thank, you. I'll see all of you in the office bright and early on Monday morning."

Scenarios like this one are becoming more common in U.S. businesses. Many businesses rehire retirees as independent contractors. These independent contractors teach permanent replacements the ropes. Companies benefit most when retirees possess specialized, company-specific knowledge. After all, who knows a job better than the longtime incumbent? In addition, companies invite retirees back to help out during peak business periods rather than hiring permanent employees. Further, independent contractors are cost effective because they do not participate in company-sponsored benefits programs.

INDEPENDENT CONTRACTORS, FREE-LANCERS, AND CONSULTANTS **Independent contractors, free-lancers,** and **consultants** (the term *independent contractor* will be used in this discussion) establish working relationships with companies on their own rather than through temporary employment agencies or lease companies.[14] Independent contractors typically possess specialized skills that are in short supply in the labor market. Companies select independent contractors to complete particular projects of short-term duration—usually a year or less. Adjunct faculty members represent a specific example of independent contractors. Colleges and universities hire adjunct faculty members to cover for permanent faculty members who are on sabbatical leave. Colleges and universities also employ adjunct faculty members until they hire permanent replacements. In addition, some companies staff segments of their work forces with independent contractors to contain discretionary benefits costs.

Reasons for U.S. employers' increased reliance on contingent workers

Structural changes in the U.S. economy have contributed to the rise of contingent employment:

- ☆ Economic recessions
- ☆ International competition
- ☆ The shift from manufacturing to service economies
- ☆ Rise in female labor force participation

ECONOMIC RECESSIONS Many companies lay off segments of their work forces during economic recessions as a cost control measure. After economic recessions, some companies restore staffing levels with permanent employees. Increasingly, many companies restore staffing levels with contingent workers.[15] Since the early 1970s, the U.S. economy has experienced several economic recessions. These repeated recessions have shaken employers' confidence about future economic prosperity. Staffing segments of work forces with contingent workers represents a form of risk control because employers save on most discretionary benefits costs. In addition, companies can terminate contingent workers' services easily: These employment relationships are explicitly tentative. Both the host employer and workers understand that these engagements are of limited duration.

INTERNATIONAL COMPETITION International competition is another pertinent structural change. American companies no longer compete just against each other. Many foreign businesses have demonstrated the ability to manufacture goods at lower costs than their American competitors. As a result, successful American companies have streamlined operations to control costs.[16] These companies are saving costs by reducing the numbers of permanent employees and using contingent workers as an alternative.[17]

THE SHIFT FROM MANUFACTURING TO SERVICE ECONOMIES Manufacturing companies' employment declined nearly 11 percent between 1980 and 1994.[18] During this period, a steady decrease in employment in manufacturing industries was offset by a substantial rise in employment in both the retail trade and service sectors.[19] Service sector employment rose nearly 80 percent between 1980 and 1994.[20] Contingent workers typically find employment in service businesses rather than manufacturing businesses because service businesses are more labor intensive than capital (for example, heavy manufacturing equipment) intensive. Many companies in the service industries rely on contingent workers to adjust staffing levels in line with business activity. So the shift to service economies contributed to a surge in contingent employment.

RISE IN FEMALE LABOR FORCE PARTICIPATION The increase in female participation in the labor force has promoted growth in the use of contingent workers. One-income families were commonplace until the early 1970s, and males headed these households. Since then, several economic recessions in the United States left large numbers of individuals unemployed.

Many wives entered the labor force temporarily to supplement families' incomes during husbands' unemployment spells.[21] The majority took low-paying jobs as clerical or service workers because they did not have sufficient education to attain high-paying jobs. Even educated women could not find high-paying jobs because the recessions limited such opportunities. As a result, many well-educated women also assumed low-paying clerical or service positions.[22]

A large segment of these women remained in the contingent labor force after these economic recessions ended because husbands' salaries did not keep up with inflation. Contingent employment enabled women to balance the demands of home and work. Although men have been taking greater responsibility for child rearing, women still bear the brunt of these duties.[23] Thus, contingent employment, compared with permanent, full-time employment, affords women the opportunity to balance the demands of home and work. Consequently, contingent workers are disproportionately female.[24]

The rise in single-parent households also contributed to the rise in contingent employment. Many single female parents possess low levels of education, so their job opportunities are limited. As a result, single female parents accept such low-paying contingent jobs as domestic work, retail sales, and low-level clerical positions. Apart from low educational attainment, single female parents accept contingent work because it enables them to spend more time with their children. As an aside, these women generally cannot afford to pay for regular daycare services.

Nowadays, a large segment of well-educated females enters the contingent work force because of dual-career pressures. In many areas of the country, employers have the luxury of large pools of educated, skilled workers who have followed a spouse pursuing job opportunities. These areas typically have few large employers. For example, in Ft. Collins, Colorado, and Champaign-Urbana, Illinois, universities are the main employers. Many spouses with professional credentials take low-paying, part-time jobs because there are few good job opportunities.

THE FLIP SIDE OF THE COIN

Contingent Employment Compromises Employee Loyalty

Employers easily can justify increased contingent employment as a business necessity—cost containment, flexibility, and so on. However, companies may be trading employee loyalty for reduced costs and greater flexibility. Employees used to expect to maintain employment within their choice companies for as long as they wished. Indeed, many employees remained with a single company for decades. A retirement bash and receipt of a "gold watch" for longtime service had become a cliché. Such companies as Ford Motor Company, General Motors, IBM, and Lincoln Electric exemplified extended employment.

Workers presently in the labor force are not likely to forget past practices that once led to job security and sound retirement nest eggs. It is probably not unreasonable to expect that workers will take personal interest in companies' performance as the employment relationship becomes more tentative. Instead, more workers will probably be alert to better and possibly more-secure employment alternatives: that is, they will be less loyal to their employers. As more employees assume contingent worker status, companies may become victim to reduced employee loyalty, heightened job insecurity among core employees, lower control over product or service quality, higher turnover, higher compliance burdens and costs, and greater training costs.

First, both core and contingent workers may develop less loyalty for their employers. Hiring contingent workers may lead core employees to feel less secure about their status. Consequently, core employees' loyalty may be diminished, which can translate into lower worker dependability and work quality.

Second, employers can lose control over product or service quality when employing contingent workers. This problem is most likely to occur when companies engage contingent workers on short-term bases: It takes contingent workers time to learn company-specific procedures and work processes. Thus, companies that do not employ contingent workers long enough for them to learn their jobs will not maintain sufficient control over quality.

Third, turnover rates among core workers will probably increase when companies employ contingent workers. As noted earlier, core employees may feel uncertain about their job status, and this uncertainty will probably lead to lower loyalty. The absence of job security and diminished loyalty will increase core employees' job search activities. Over time, the best-qualified core employees will receive competitive job offers that lead to dysfunctional turnover.

Fourth, as we will see shortly, companies must carefully determine whether particular workers qualify as contingent employees or core employees. The staff time required to make such determinations represents a significant cost. Misclassification can lead to hefty fines.

Fifth, companies must bear the costs of training contingent workers. In many cases, employing contingent workers can be as costly as employing core workers. That is, the savings from not offering contingent workers discretionary benefits is offset by training costs. These costs become less significant for companies that employ contingent workers long enough to realize returns on the training investment through higher productivity and work quality.

Core and fringe compensation for contingent workers

Compensation practices for contingent workers vary. Nevertheless, all parties involved in employing contingent workers possess liability under federal and state laws, including:

✩ Overtime and minimum wages required under the Fair Labor Standards Act of 1938 (FLSA)

✩ Paying insurance premiums required under state workers' compensation laws

✩ Nondiscriminatory compensation and employment practices under:

✩ Employee Retirement Income Security Act of 1974 (ERISA)

✩ National Labor Relations Act of 1935 (NLRA)

✩ Title VII of the Civil Rights Act of 1964

✩ Americans with Disabilities Act of 1990 (ADA)

✩ Age Discrimination in Employment Act of 1967 (ADEA)

Temporary employment agencies and leasing companies that place workers in clients' firms are liable under these laws. In addition, the client company may also be liable. "The fact that a worker is somebody else's employee while he or she is on your premises, or performing services for the business, is not necessarily a defense to alleged violations of federal and state labor laws including Title VII of the Civil Rights Act, the Fair Labor Standards Act, and the Americans with Disabilities Act." [25] As we discussed in Chapter 3, each of these laws applies to compensation practice.

Part-time employees

Companies that employ part-time workers are the legal employers, as is the case for permanent, full-time employees. Compensating part-time employees poses the following challenges for employers:

✩ Should companies pay part-time workers on an hourly or a salary basis?

✩ Do equity problems arise between permanent full-time employees and part-time employees?

✩ Do companies offer part-time workers benefits?

CORE COMPENSATION Part-time employees earn less, on average, than core employ-ees. In 1995, part-time workers earned an average $7.17 per hour, whereas full-time employees earned $13.71 per hour. Full-time white-collar employees earned $16.49 per hour; part-time white-collar employees earned $9.05 per hour. Full-time blue-collar workers earned substantially more than their part-time counterparts ($11.74 ver-sus $7.06 per hour). Similarly, full-time service employees earned more than part-timers ($7.60 versus $5.08 per hour).[26]

Companies often expect salaried part-time employees to do much more than their fair share of the work because the effective hourly pay rate decreases as the number of hours worked increases. An explicit agreement pertaining to work-hour limits can minimize this problem. Similarly, an agreement may specify explicit work goals. Alternatively, companies may avoid this problem by paying part-time employees on an hourly basis.

Part-time and full-time employees may perceive the situation as inequitable under certain circumstances. For example, equity problems may arise when salaried full-time employees and hourly part-time employees work together. It is possible that highly skilled full-time employees might effectively be underpaid relative to less-skilled part-time employees performing the same work. That is, full-time employees' "hourly" pay rate will be lower when they perform more and better work in a shorter period than less-skilled part-time workers.

FRINGE COMPENSATION Companies generally do not provide part-time employees discretionary benefits. However, benefits practices for part-time workers vary widely according to company size as well as between the private and public sectors.* In 1993, approximately half of part-time employees working in medium and large private com-panies earned pay for time-not-worked benefits. In 1992, fewer received medical in-surance coverage (24 percent) or retirement benefits (40 percent).[27] Small private companies were less likely to offer part-time employees fringe compensation. Approximately one-third earned pay for time-not-worked benefits, and even fewer re-ceived medical insurance (5 percent) or retirement benefits (12 percent).[28]

Employers are not required to offer protective insurance (that is, medical, dental, vision, or life insurance) to part-time employees. However, part-time employees who do receive health insurance coverage under employer-sponsored plans are entitled to protection under the Consolidated Omnibus Budget Reconciliation Act (COBRA). As discussed in Chapter 11, COBRA provides employees the opportunity to continue re-ceiving employer-sponsored health care insurance coverage temporarily following ter-mination or layoff. Employees who qualify for COBRA protection receive insurance coverage that matches the coverage level during employment.

Employers may be required to provide part-time employees qualified retirement programs.[29] Part-time employees who meet the following two criteria are eligible to participate in qualified retirement programs:

✯ Minimum age of 21 years

and

> *Part-time employees earn less, on average, than core employees. In 1995, part-time workers earned an average $7.17 per hour, whereas full-time employees earned $13.71 per hour.*

---

* The terms used in this discussion were defined by the U.S. Bureau of Labor Statistics. The term *large private establishments* refers to companies that employ 100 or more workers in all private nonfarm industries. The term *small private establishments* refers to companies that employ fewer than 100 workers in all private nonfarm industries. State and local (county, city) govern-ments included in this survey employ 50 employees or more.

☆ Completed at least 1,000 hours of work in a 12-month period (that is, "year of service")

Special considerations apply to seasonal employees' eligibility for qualified retirement benefits because most seasonal employees do not meet the annual service pension eligibility criterion. Maritime industries such as fishing represent seasonal employment, and fishermen are seasonal employees. The Secretary of Labor defines 125 service days as the "year of service" for maritime workers.[30] Part-time and seasonal employees cannot be excluded from pension plans if they meet the Secretary of Labor's "year of service" criterion.

Temporary employees

The temporary employment agencies are the legal employers for temporary employees. Thus, temporary employment agencies are responsible for complying with federal employment legislation with one exception that we will address shortly—workers' compensation. Compensating temporary employees poses challenges for companies.

☆ Do equity problems arise between permanent employees and temporary employees?

☆ How do the FLSA overtime provisions affect temporary employees?

☆ Do companies offer temporary workers benefits?

☆ Who is responsible for providing workers' compensation protection: the temporary employment agency or the client company?

CORE COMPENSATION Temporary workers in the United States earned an average $7.74 in November 1994. Average hourly earnings ranged from $6.05 in Tampa-St. Petersburg-Clearwater, Florida, to $11.46 in Boston, Massachusetts.[31] Hourly pay rates varied widely by occupation and workers' particular qualifications. Exhibit 14-4 compares hourly wage rates for permanent employees and temporary employees. Temporary employees earned significantly lower wage rates than permanent workers. In fact, temporary employees earned 35.3 percent less, on average, than permanent employees.

Exhibit 14-4
Permanent Employees' vs. Temporary Employees' Hourly Earnings: Occupational Averages for the United States

	TEMPORARY	PERMANENT	DIFFERENCE (%)
All employees	$ 7.74	$11.97	35.3
Janitors and cleaners	$ 5.67	$ 7.32	22.5
Maids and housekeepers	$ 5.26	$ 6.18	14.8
Receptionists	$ 7.07	$ 8.20	13.7
Accountants and auditors	$13.96	$15.47	9.7
Secretaries	$ 9.49	$ 9.90	4.1
Computer operators	$10.63	$10.95	2.9

Sources: U.S. Bureau of Labor Statistics, *Occupational compensation survey: temporary help supply services in the United States and selected metropolitan areas* (Washington, D.C.: U.S. Government Printing Office, May 1995). U.S. Bureau of Labor Statistics, *Employment and earnings* (Washington, D.C.: U.S. Government Printing Office, January 1996).

Note: The data for temporary workers represent November 1994 averages, and the data for permanent workers represent 1995 annual averages.

Equity problems may (or may not) arise where permanent and temporary employees work together. On one hand, temporary employees may work diligently because they know that their assignments in client companies are explicitly of limited duration. In addition, frequent moves from one company to the next may limit workers' opportunities or desires to build careers with any of these companies. Further, temporary workers may neither take the time nor have the time to scope out pay differences because their engagements are brief—anywhere from one day to a few weeks. Thus, these temporary employees are not likely to perceive inequitable pay situations.

On the other hand, some temporary employees may not work diligently because they did not choose temporary employment arrangements. Individuals who lose their jobs because of sudden layoff and few permanent job alternatives are most susceptible. Pay differences between these temporary employees and permanent employees are likely to intensify perceptions of inequity.

It is important to distinguish between temporary employees and seasonal employees for determining eligibility under the FLSA minimum wage and overtime pay provisions. Companies hire temporary employees to fill in as needed. This means that companies may hire temporary employees at any time throughout a calendar year. However, seasonal employees work during set regular periods every year. Life guards on New England beaches are seasonal employees because they work only during the summer, when people visit beaches to swim. Summer camp counselors also are seasonal employees.

The FLSA extends coverage to temporary employees. Thus, temporary employment agencies must pay temporary workers at least the federal minimum wage rate. Also, the FLSA requires employers to provide overtime pay at one and one-half times the normal hourly rate for each hour worked beyond 40 hours per week. Host companies are responsible for FLSA compliance where temporary employment agencies are not involved, as in the case of direct hire or on-call arrangements.

Some seasonal employees are exempt from the FLSA's minimum wage and overtime pay provisions.[32] The FLSA does not explicitly address minimum wage and overtime pay practices for seasonal employees. However, professional legal opinions were added as needed to resolve ambiguities and to guide practice. The opinions pertain to specific employers' questions about the act's scope of coverage: for example, the applicability of FLSA overtime and minimum wage provisions to seasonal amusement park workers. All amusement or recreational establishment employees are covered by the FLSA's minimum wage and overtime pay provisions when the establishments operate at least seven months per year. However, youth counselors employed at summer camps are generally exempt from the FLSA minimum wage and overtime pay provisions. Professional opinions do not automatically generalize to all seasonal employees.

FRINGE COMPENSATION Anecdotal evidence indicates that companies typically do not provide discretionary benefits to temporary employees. This information should not be surprising. As we discussed earlier, many companies employ temporary workers to minimize discretionary benefits costs. However, temporary employees (and seasonal workers) are eligible for qualified pension benefits if they meet ERISA's minimum service requirements for seasonal and part-time employees as discussed earlier.

The **dual employer common law doctrine** establishes temporary workers' rights to receive workers' compensation.[33] According to this doctrine, temporary workers are employees of both temporary employment agencies and the client companies. The written contract between the employment agency and the client company specifies which organization's workers' compensation policy applies in the event of injuries.

Leased employees

Designating leased employees' legal employers is less clear than for part-time and temporary employees. Leasing companies are the legal employers regarding wage issues and legally required benefits. However, both leasing companies and client companies are the legal employers regarding particular discretionary benefits. Thus, compensating leased employees is complex.

> ✮ Do leased employees receive discretionary benefits?

> ✮ Who is responsible for providing discretionary benefits: the leasing company or the client company?

CORE COMPENSATION Presently, systematic compensation data for leased employees are lacking. Thus, it is not possible to compare leased employees' and core employees' wages and salaries.

FRINGE COMPENSATION Both pension eligibility and discretionary benefits are key issues. Leased employees are generally entitled to participation in the client companies' qualified retirement programs. However, the leasing company becomes responsible for leased employees' retirement benefits when the **safe harbor rule**[34] requirements are met. Exhibit 14-5 lists the safe harbor rule requirements.

Another section of the Internal Revenue Code influences companies' discretionary benefits policies (excluding retirement benefits) for leased employees.[35] Under this rule, client companies are responsible for providing leased employees group medical insurance, group life insurance, educational assistance programs, and continuation coverage requirements for group health plans under COBRA.

Independent contractors, free-lancers, and consultants

The Bureau of Labor Statistics does not monitor pay levels for independent contractors. Companies are not obligated to pay the following on behalf of independent contractors, free-lancers, and consultants:

Exhibit 14-5
Safe Harbor Rule Requirements

- The leased employee must be covered by the leasing company's pension plan, which must (1) be a money purchase pension plan with a nonintegrated employer contribution rate for each participant of at least 10 percent of compensation, (2) provide for full and immediate vesting, and (3) allow each employee of the leasing organization to immediately participate in such a plan;

and

- Leased employees cannot constitute more than 20 percent of the recipient's "nonhighly compensated work force." Nonhighly compensated work force means the total number of (1) nonhighly compensated individuals who are employees of the recipient and who have performed services for the recipient for at least a year or (2) individuals who are leased employees of the recipient (determined without regard to the leasing rules).

Source: I.R.C. § 414(n)(5).

★ Federal income tax withholding

★ Overtime and minimum wages required under the FLSA. However, employers are obligated to pay *financially dependent workers* overtime and minimum wages.

★ Insurance premiums required under state workers' compensation laws, except where states explicitly require that companies maintain workers' compensation coverage for all workers regardless of whether they are independent contractors. Missouri's workers' compensation laws require coverage of *all* individuals.

★ Protection under Employee Retirement Income Security Act of 1974 (ERISA), the National Labor Relations Act (NLRA), Title VII of the Civil Rights Act of 1964, and the Americans with Disabilities Act (ADA)

To determine whether employees are financially dependent on them, employers must apply the **economic reality test.** Exhibit 14-6 lists the criteria for the economic reality test, which is the basis for establishing an employer's obligation to pay overtime and minimum wages. For example, are topless night club dancers entitled to minimum wage under FLSA? A night club's owners claimed that the dancers were not eligible because they were independent contractors:

★ The dancers could perform whenever and wherever they wanted.

★ The club had no control over the manner of performance.

★ The dancers had to furnish their own costumes.

A federal district court ruled that the night club's topless dancers were entitled to minimum wage because they were economically dependent on the night club.[36] The dancers were economically dependent on the night club for the following reasons:

★ The club owners set hours in which the dancers could perform.

★ The club owners issued guidelines on dancers' behavior at the club.

★ The club owners deducted 20 percent from the credit card tips of each dancer to cover administrative costs.

---

1. The extent to which the worker has the right to control the result of the work and the manner in which the work is performed

2. The degree to which the individual is "economically dependent" on the employer's business or, in other words, the amount of control the employer has over the individual's opportunity to realize a profit or sustain a loss

3. The extent to which the services are an integral part of the employer's business operations

4. The amount of initiative or level of skill required for the worker to perform the job

5. The permanency, exclusivity, or duration of the relationship between the employer and the worker

6. The extent of the worker's investment in equipment or materials required for the job

---

Exhibit 14-6
Economic Reality Test: Six Criteria to Determine Whether Workers Are Financially Dependent on the Employer

Employers' obligations under many federal and state employment laws depend on whether workers are employees or independent contractors. Companies must use the Internal Revenue Code's **right to control test** to determine whether employed individuals are employees or independent contractors. If an employer has the right to control the work activities, then the individuals hired are classified as employees rather than independent contractors. Exhibit 14-7 lists 20 criteria of the right to control test.

Exhibit 14-7

Right to Control Test: 20 Factors to Determine Whether an Employer Has the Right to Control a Worker

1. **Instructions.** Requiring a worker to comply with another person's instructions about when, where, and how he or she is to work ordinarily indicates an employer-employee relationship.

2. **Training.** Training a worker indicates that the employer wants the services performed in a particular manner and demonstrates the employer's control over the means by which the result is reached.

3. **Integration.** Integration of the worker's services into the business operations and the dependence of success or continuation of the business on the worker's services generally indicate that the worker is subject to a certain amount of direction and control by the employer.

4. **Services rendered personally.** If the services must be rendered personally, presumably the employer is interested in the methods used to accomplish the work as well as the results, and control is indicated.

5. **Hiring, supervising, and paying assistants.** The employer's hiring, supervising, and paying the worker's assistants generally indicates control over the worker. However, if it is the worker who hires, supervises, and pays his or her assistants and is ultimately responsible for their work, then the worker has an independent contractor status.

6. **Continuing relationship.** A continuing relationship between the worker and the employer indicates that an employer-employee relationship exists.

7. **Set hours of work.** The establishment of set hours of work by the employer indicates control.

8. **Full time required.** If the worker must devote full time to the employer's business, the employer has control over the worker's time. An independent contractor, on the other hand, is free to work when and for whom he or she chooses.

9. **Doing work on employer's premises.** If the work is performed on the employer's premises, control is suggested, especially if the work could be performed elsewhere.

10. **Order or sequence set.** If a worker must perform services in the order or sequence set by the employer, control is indicated because the worker is unable to follow his or her own pattern of work.

11. **Oral or written reports.** Requiring the worker to submit regular or written reports to the employer suggests control.

12. **Payment by hour, week, month.** Payment by the hour, week, or month suggests an employer-employee relationship unless it is just a convenient way of paying a lump sum agreed upon as the cost of a job. Payment by the job or on commission generally indicates an independent contractor status.

13. **Payment of business and/or traveling expenses.** If the employer ordinarily pays the worker's business or traveling expenses, the worker is an employee.

14. **Furnishing of tools and materials.** If the employer furnishes significant tools, materials, and other equipment, an employer-employee relationship usually exists.

Exhibit 14-7
*Right to Control Test: 20
Factors to Determine
Whether an Employer Has
the Right to Control a
Worker (continued)*

15. **Significant investment by worker.** If a worker invests in facilities that he or she uses to perform services and that are not typically maintained by an employee (such as rental of office space), an independent contractor status usually is indicated. Lack of investment in facilities tends to indicate that the worker depends on the employer for such facilities.

16. **Realization of profit or loss.** A worker who cannot realize a profit or suffer a loss as a result of his or her services generally is an employee.

17. **Working for more than one firm at a time.** If a worker performs more than *de minimis* services for a multiple of unrelated persons or firms at the same time, independent contractor status is generally indicated.

18. **Making services available to general public.** If a worker makes his or her services available to the general public on a regular and consistent basis, independent contractor status is indicated.

19. **Right to discharge.** The employer's right to discharge a worker indicates employee status.

20. **Right to terminate.** If a worker can terminate his or her relationship with the employer at any time without incurring liability, employee status is indicated.

Source: Rev. Rul. 87-41, 1987-1 C.B. 296.

Flexible work schedules: flextime, compressed work weeks, and telecommuting

Many companies now offer employees flexible work schedules to help them balance work and family demands. Flextime and compressed work week schedules are the most prominent flexible work schedules used in companies. Flexible work schedules practices generally apply to permanent, full-time employees rather than to contingent employees.

Flextime schedules

Flextime schedules allow employees to modify work schedules within specified limits set by the employer. Employees adjust when they will start work and when they will leave. However, flextime generally does not lead to reduced work hours. For instance, an employee may choose to work between 10 A.M. and 6 P.M., 9 A.M. and 5 P.M. or 8 A.M. and 4 P.M.

All workers must be present during certain workday hours when business activity is regularly high. This period is known as **core hours.** The number of core hours may vary from company to company, by departments within companies, or by season. Although employees are relatively free to choose start and completion times that fall outside core hours, management must carefully coordinate these times to avoid understaffing. Some flextime programs incorporate a **banking hours** feature. This feature enables employees to vary the number of work hours daily as long as they maintain the regular number of work hours on a weekly basis.

Employers can expect three possible benefits from using flextime schedules. First, flextime schedules lead to lower tardiness and absenteeism. Flexibly defining the work week better enables employees to schedule medical and other appointments outside work hours. As a result, workers are less likely to be late or miss work altogether.

Second, flexible work schedules should lead to higher work productivity. Employees have greater choice about when to work during the day. Individuals who work best during the morning hours may schedule morning hours, and individuals who work best during the afternoons or evenings will choose those times. In addition, possessing the flexibility to attend to personal matters outside work should help employees focus on doing better jobs.

Third, flexible work schedules benefit employers by creating longer business hours and better service. Staggering employees' schedules should enable businesses to stay open longer hours without incurring overtime pay expenses. Also, customers should perceive better service because of expanded business hours. Companies that conduct business by telephone on national and international bases will more likely be open during customers' normal operating hours in other time zones.

Two possible limitations of flexible work schedules include increased overhead costs and coordination problems. Maintaining extended operations leads to higher overhead costs including support staff and utilities. In addition, flexible work schedules may lead to work coordination problems when some employees are not present at the same time.

Compressed work week schedules

Compressed work week schedules enable employees to perform their work in fewer days than a regular five-day work week. As a result, employees may work four 10-hour days or three 12-hour days. These schedules can promote companies' recruitment and retention successes by:

- ✯ Reducing the number of times employees must commute between home and work

- ✯ Providing more time together for dual-career couples who live apart

Telecommuting

Telecommuting is an alternative work arrangement in which employees perform work at home or some other location besides the office. Telecommuters generally spend part of their time working in the office and other times working at home. This alternative work arrangement is appropriate for work that does not require regular direct interpersonal interactions with other workers. Examples include accounting, systems analysis, and telephone sales. Telecommuters stay in touch with coworkers and superiors through electronic mail, telephone, and faxes. There are several possible telecommuting arrangements. Exhibit 14-8 summarizes these alternatives.

Potential benefits for employers include increased productivity and lower overhead costs for office space and supplies. Telecommuting also serves as an effective recruiting and retention practice for employees who strongly desire to perform their jobs away from the office. Employers may also increase the retention of valued employees who choose not to move when their companies relocate.

Employees find telecommuting beneficial. Telecommuting enables parents to be near their infants or preschool-aged children and to be home when older children finish their school days. In addition, telecommuting arrangements minimize commuting time and expense, which are exceptional in such congested metropolitan areas as Boston, Los Angeles, and New York City. Travel time may increase three-fold during peak rush-hour traffic periods. Parking and toll costs can be hefty. Monthly parking

Exhibit 14-8
Alternative Telecommuting Arrangements

- **Satellite work center.** Employees work from a remote extension of the employer's office that includes a clerical staff and a full-time manager.

- **Neighborhood work center.** Employees work from a satellite office shared by several employers.

- **Nomadic executive office.** Executives who travel extensively maintain control over projects through use of telephone, fax, and electronic mail.

- Employees sometimes work entirely outside the office. Others might work off-site only once a month or two to three days a week.

- Telecommuters can be full- or part-time employees.

- Telecommuting arrangements can be temporary or permanent. A temporarily disabled employee may work at home until fully recovered. A permanently disabled employee may work at home exclusively.

Source: Adapted from The Bureau of National Affairs, Telecommuting, in *Compensation & Benefits* [CD-ROM] (Washington, D.C.: The Bureau of National Affairs, 1996).

rates alone often exceed a few hundred dollars per car. Finally, the reduction of employees' involvement in office politics should promote higher job performance.

Telecommuting programs may also lead to disadvantages for employers and employees. Some employers are concerned about the lack of direct contact with employees, which makes conducting performance appraisals more difficult. Employees sometimes feel that work-at-home arrangements are disruptive to their personal lives. In addition, some employees feel isolated because they do not personally interact as often with coworkers and superiors.

Balancing the demands of work life and home life

U.S. companies use flexible work schedules to help employees balance the demands of work life and home life. Flextime, compressed work weeks, and telecommuting should provide single parents or dual-career parents the opportunity to spend more time with children. Flextime gives parents the opportunity to schedule work around special events at their children's schools. Compressed work weeks enable parents on limited incomes to save on daycare costs by limiting the number of days at the office. Parents can benefit from telecommuting in a similar fashion. Likewise, dual-career couples living apart also benefit from flexible work schedules. Compressed work weeks and telecommuting reduce the time spouses have to spend away from each other.

U.S. companies use flexible work schedules to help employees balance the demands of work life and home life.

Core and fringe compensation for flexible employees

The key core compensation issue for flexible work schedules is overtime pay. The main fringe compensation issues are pay for time-not-worked benefits and working condition fringe benefits.

Core compensation

In many cases, "flexible" employees work more than 40 hours during some weeks and fewer hours during other weeks. The FLSA requires that companies compensate nonexempt employees at an overtime rate equal to one and one-half times the normal hourly rate for each hour worked in excess of 40 hours per week. The overtime provisions are based on employees' working set hours during fixed work periods. How do FLSA overtime provisions apply to flexible work schedules?

Let's assume the following flexible work schedule. An employee works 40 hours during one week, 30 hours during a second week, and 50 hours during a third week. This employee worked 40 hours per week, on average, for the three-week period, but is she entitled to overtime pay for the additional 10 hours worked during the third week?

Some employees' weekly flexible schedules may fluctuate frequently and unpredictably according to such nonwork demands as chronically ill family members. Unpredictable flexible schedules make overtime pay calculations difficult. It is possible that companies may make inadequate or excessive overtime payments. A Supreme Court ruling *(Walling v. A. H. Belo Corp.)*[37] requires that employers guarantee fixed weekly pay for employees whose work hours vary from week to week, when

⭐ the employer typically cannot determine the number of hours employees will work each week

and

⭐ the work week period fluctuates both above and below 40 hours per week

This pay provision guarantees employees fixed weekly pay regardless of how many hours worked, and it enables employers to control weekly labor cost expenditures.

The use of compressed work week schedules may lead to differences in overtime practices in some states. Whereas the federal government bases overtime pay on a weekly basis, some states use other time bases to determine eligibility for overtime pay. Exhibit 14-9 lists maximum hour provisions for selected states. As you can see, there is wide variation in daily overtime practices.

Fringe compensation

Flexible work week schedules have the greatest impact on pay for time-not-worked benefits. Many companies determine employees' sick leave benefits and vacation on the basis of the number of hours they work each month. The determination of paid vacation and sick leave for employees on standard work schedules is relatively straightforward. However, flexible employees work fewer hours some months and more hours during other months. This variability complicates companies' calculations of pay for time-not-worked benefits.

Another issue is the treatment of paid time off for holidays. Under standard work schedules, the vast majority of employees work five eight-hour days from Monday through Friday. For example, all employees take Thanksgiving Day off (a Thursday) with pay. Under flexible schedules, some employees may not be scheduled to work on Thursdays. Consequently, standard-schedule employees receive one day off with pay during Thanksgiving week, and some flexible employees work their regular schedules, missing a paid day off from work. Companies must establish policies that provide flexible workers with comparable paid-time-off benefits or alternative holidays. Such policies are necessary to maintain equity among employees. However, scheduling alternative holidays may lead to coordination problems for small companies: Companies with small staffs may not have enough employees to cover for flexible workers during their alternative holiday time off from work.

Exhibit 14-9
Maximum Hours before Overtime for Selected States

ARKANSAS

- 10-hour day, 40-hour week for workers with flexible work hour plan if part of collective bargaining agreement or signed employer-employee agreement filed with state Department of Labor

---

CONNECTICUT

- Nine-hour day, 48-hour week in manufacturing/mechanical establishments for workers under 18 or over 66, handicapped persons, and disabled veterans
- Ten-hour day, 55-hour week during emergencies or peak demand, with commissioner's permission
- Six-day, 48-hour week for employees under 18 or over 66, handicapped persons, and disabled veterans in public restaurant, cafe, dining room, barber shop, hairdressing, or manicuring establishment; amusement or recreational establishment; bowling alley; shoe shining establishment; billiard or pool room, or photographic gallery

---

MICHIGAN

- 10 hours a day in factories, workshops, salt blocks, sawmills, logging or lumber camps, booms or drivers, mines or other places used for mechanical or manufacturing purposes

---

NEVADA

- 8-hour day, 40-hour week, unless mutually agreed 10-hour day 4-day week

---

A fringe compensation issue known as **working condition fringe benefits** applies to telecommuters. Employers are likely to provide telecommuters the necessary equipment to perform their jobs effectively while off-site—microcomputers, modems, printers, photocopy machines, sundry office supplies, and telex machines. In addition, some employers provide similar equipment to employees who wish to work additional hours outside their regular work schedules—during the evenings or weekends. This arrangement does not qualify as telecommuting.

The Internal Revenue Service treats the home use of office equipment and supplies as employees' taxable income when the use falls outside established telecommuting relationships. However, employees are not taxed when the home use of employer-provided equipment falls within established telecommuting relationships. Under this condition, the Internal Revenue Service treats the home use of employer-provided equipment as a working condition fringe benefit.

Unions' reactions to contingent workers and flexible work schedules

Unions generally do not support companies' use of contingent workers and flexible work schedules. Most union leaders believe that alternative work arrangements threaten members' job security and are prone to unfair and inequitable treatment. The most common concerns include:

Unions generally do not support companies' use of contingent workers and flexibile work schedules. Most union leaders believe that alternative work arrangements threaten members' job security and are prone to unfair and inequitable treatment.

* Employers exploit contingent workers by paying them lower wages and benefits than permanent employees.

* Employers' efforts to get cheap labor will lead to a poorly trained and less-skilled work force that will hamper competitiveness.

* Part-time employees are difficult to organize because their interests are centered on activities outside the workplace. Thus, part-time workers probably are not good union members.

* Part-time employment erodes labor standards: Part-time workers are often denied fringe benefits, job security, and promotion opportunities. Increasing part-time employment would promote inequitable treatment.

* Union leaders believe that temporary employees generally have little concern about improving the productivity of a company for which they will work for only a brief period.

* Unions' bargaining power is weakened when a company demonstrates its ability to perform effectively with temporaries.

* The long days of compressed work weeks or flextime could endanger workers' safety and health, even if the workers choose these long days themselves.

* Concerns about employee isolation, uncompensated overtime, and company monitoring in the home are among the reasons unions have been reluctant to permit telecommuting by their members.

Unions' position against contingent employment is unlikely to change because this practice undermines efforts to secure high wages and job security for members. However, some unions, particularly in the public sector, have begun to accept the use of flexible work schedules. The benefits of these arrangements—increased productivity, lower absenteeism, and lower tardiness—strengthen unions' bargaining power.

Strategic issues and choices in using contingent and flexible workers

How does employing contingent workers and using flexible work schedules fit with the two fundamental competitive strategies—lowest-cost and differentiation? Ultimately, these innovations, when properly applied, can contribute to companies' meeting the goals of lowest-cost and differentiation strategies. However, the rationale for the appropriateness of contingent employment and flexible work schedules differs according to the imperatives of the lowest-cost and differentiation competitive strategies.

Lowest-cost competitive strategy

Lowest-cost strategies require firms to reduce output costs per employee. Contingent employment saves companies considerable amounts of money because they do not provide these workers most discretionary benefits. Discretionary benefits represent a significant fiscal cost to companies. In 1994, U.S. companies spent an average $11,506 per employee to provide discretionary benefits.[38] Such discretionary benefits accounted for approximately one-third of employers' total payroll costs (that is, the sum of core compensation and all fringe compensation costs).

Employers' use of well-trained contingent workers also contributes through reduced training costs. However, not all contingent workers possess company knowledge of company-specific work practices and procedures. Company-specific training represents a significant cost to companies. Companies that do not employ contingent workers long enough to realize the productivity benefits from training undermine lowest-cost objectives. Company-sponsored training may seem to contradict the lowest-cost imperative in the short-term. The following factors can increase short-term costs:

⭐ Costs of training materials and instructors' professional fees

⭐ Down time while employees are participating in training

⭐ Inefficiencies that may result until employees master new skills

However, a longer-term perspective may lead to the conclusion that contingent work arrangements support the lowest-cost imperatives. Over time, productivity enhancements and increased flexibility should far outweigh the short-run costs if companies establish track records of high productivity, quality, and exemplary customer service.

Flexible schedules should also contribute to lowest-cost imperatives. Limited evidence suggests that flexible employees demonstrate lower absenteeism than employees with fixed work schedules.

Differentiation competitive strategy

A differentiation strategy requires creative, open-minded, risk-taking employees. Compared with lowest cost strategies, companies that pursue differentiation strategies must take a longer-term focus to attain their preestablished objectives. Contingent workers and flexible schedules both should contribute to innovation; however, systematic studies demonstrating their contribution are lacking. Contingent employment probably is appropriate because companies will benefit from the influx of "new" employees from time to time who bring fresh ideas with them. Over the long run, contingent employment should minimize problems of *groupthink:* **Groupthink** occurs when all group members agree on mistaken solutions because they share the same mindset and view issues through the lens of conformity.[39]

Flexible work schedules also should promote differentiation strategies for two reasons. First, flexible work schedules enable employees to work when they are at their physical or mental best. Second, flexible work schedules allow employees to work with fewer distractions and worries about personal matters: The inherent flexibility of these schedules allows employees to attend to personal matters as needed.

Summary

This chapter discussed the contingent workers and flexible work arrangements, reasons companies rely on contingent employment arrangements and flexible work schedules, special compensation issues, unions' reactions to contingent employment and flexible work schedules, and fit with competitive strategy. Companies that choose to employ contingent workers must give serious consideration to the possible long-term benefits and consequences. Flexible work schedules seem to accommodate the changing workers' needs well. Given the possible limitations of contingent employment and flexible work schedules, companies should strike a balance between the use of core employment and contingent employment and a balance between standard work schedules and flexible work schedules.

Discussion questions

1. Discuss some of the problems that companies are likely to face when both contingent workers and permanent, full-time employees are employed in the same location. Does it matter whether contingent workers and permanent, full-time employees are performing the same jobs? Please explain.

2. Companies generally pay temporary employees lower wages and offer them fewer benefits than their permanent, full-time counterparts. Nevertheless, what are some of the possible drawbacks for companies that employ temporary workers? Do you believe that these drawbacks outweigh the cost savings? Please explain.

3. What arguments can be made in favor of using compressed work week schedules for companies that pursue lowest cost strategies? What are the arguments against using compressed work week schedules in such situations?

4. What impact will flexible work schedules have on employees' commitment to their employers? On employee productivity? On company effectiveness?

5. Provide your reactions to the following statement: "Contingent workers should be compensated on a pay-for-knowledge system."

Key terms

core employees
contingent workers
voluntary part-time employee
involuntary part-time employee
job sharing
temporary employment agencies
direct hire arrangements
on-call arrangements
lease companies
independent contractors
free-lancers
consultants

dual employer common law doctrine
safe harbor rule
economic reality test
right to control test
flextime schedules
core hours
banking hours
compressed work week schedules
telecommuting
working condition fringe benefits
groupthink

Endnotes

[1] R. E. Parker, *Flesh peddlers and warm bodies: The temporary help industry and its workers* (New Burnswick, N.J.: Rutgers University Press, 1994), pp. 38, 39.

[2] U.S. Bureau of National Affairs, New survey examines contingent workers, *Bulletin to Management Datagraph* (September 1995): 284–286.

[3] U.S. Bureau of Labor Statistics, *Employee benefits in medium and large private establishments, 1993* (Washington, D.C.: U.S. Government Printing Office, 1994).

[4] L. R. Gómez-Mejía, D. B. Balkin, and R. L. Cardy, *Managing human resources* (Englewood Cliffs, N.J.: Prentice Hall, 1995).

[5] P. Callaghan and H. Hartmann, *Contingent work: A chart book on part-time and temporary employment* (Washington, D.C.: Economic Policy Institute, 1991).

[6] C. Tilly, *Short hours, short shrift: Causes and consequences of part-time work* (Washington, D.C.: Economic Policy Institute, 1990).

[7] Ibid.

[8] M. J. Piore, Notes for the theory of labor market stratification, in R. Edwards, ed. *Labor market segmentation* (Lexington, Mass.: D.C. Heath, 1975).

[9] Callaghan and Hartmann, *Contingent work.*

[10] P. M. Burgess, Making it in America's new economy. Commencement Address, University of Toledo, June 11, 1994.

[11] F. Gillian, Contingent staffing requires serious strategy, *Personnel Journal* (April 1995):50–58.

[12] Callaghan and Hartmann, *Contingent work.*

[13] S. Caudron, Contingent work force spurs HR planning, *Personnel Journal* (July 1994):52–60.

[14] J. Pearce, Toward an organizational behavior of contract laborers: Their psychological involvement and effects on employee coworkers, *Academy of Management Journal* 36 (1993):1082–1096.

[15] J. J. Simonetti, N. Nykodym, and L. M. Sell, Temporary employees: A permanent boom? *Personnel* (August 1988):50–56.

[16] U.S. Department of Labor, *Flexible workstyles: A look at contingent labor* (Washington, D.C.: U.S. Government Printing Office, 1988).

[17] Caudron, Contingent work force spurs HR planning.

[18] U.S. Department of Commerce, *Statistical abstracts of the United States,* 115th ed. (Washington, D.C.: U.S. Government Printing Office, 1995).

[19] Callaghan and Hartmann, *Contingent work.*

[20] U.S. Department of Commerce, *Statistical abstracts of the United States,* 115th ed.

[21] P. England, *Comparable worth: Theories and evidence* (New York: Aldine De Gruyter, 1992).

[22] R. Belous, *The contingent economy: The growth of the temporary, part-time and subcontracted workforce* (McLean, Virg.: National Planning Association, 1989).

[23] H. V. Hayghe, Family members in the work force, *Monthly Labor Review* 113 (1990): 14–19.

[24] Callaghan and Hartmann, *Contingent work.*

[25] S. F. Cooper, The expanding use of contingent workers in the American economy: New opportunities and dangers for employers, *Employee Relations Law Journal* 20 (1995):525–539.

[26] U.S. Bureau of Labor Statistics, *Employer costs for employee compensation—March 1995,* USDL 95-225 (Washington, D.C.: U.S. Government Printing Office, June 22, 1995).

[27] U.S. Bureau of Labor Statistics, *Employee benefits in medium and large private establishments, 1993.*

[28] U.S. Bureau of Labor Statistics, *Employee benefits in small private establishments, 1992* (Washington, D.C.: U.S. Government Printing Office, 1994).

[29] I.R.C. § 410(a)(1).

[30] B. J. Coleman, *Primer on ERISA,* 4th ed. (Washington, D.C.: The Bureau of National Affairs, 1993).

[31] U.S. Bureau of Labor Statistics, *Occupational compensation survey: Temporary help supply services in the United States and selected metropolitan areas* (Washington, D.C.: U.S. Government Printing Office, May 1995).

[32] I.R.C. § 411(b)(4)(c).

[33] The Bureau of National Affairs, *Employee Relations Weekly,* October 24, 1994.

[34] I.R.C. § 414(n)(5).

[35] I.R.C. § 414(n)(1)(2)(3).

[36] *Martin v. Priba Corp.* (USDC N. Texas, No. 3:91-CV-2786-G, 11/6/92).

[37] *Walling v. A. H. Belo Corp.,* 316 U.S. 624, 2 WH Cases 39 (1942).

[38] U.S. Chamber of Commerce, *Employee benefits 1995 edition: Survey data from benefit year 1994* (Washington, D.C.: U.S. Chamber of Commerce Research Center, 1995).

[39] C. R. Sheppard, *Small groups* (San Francisco: Chandler, 1964).

GLOSSARY OF KEY TERMS

Aaron v. City of Wichita, Kansas, a court ruling, offered several criteria to determine whether City of Wichita fire chiefs are exempt employees, including the relative importance of management as opposed to other duties, frequency with which they exercise discretionary powers, relative freedom from supervision, and the relationship between their salaries and wages paid to other employees for similar nonexempt work.

Ability, based on Equal Employment Opportunity Commission guidelines, refers to a present competence to perform an observable behavior or a behavior that results in an observable product.

Accountability, a compensable factor in the Hay Plan, is the answerability for actions taken on the job. This factor contains three subfactors—freedom to act, impact on end results, and magnitude of impact.

Additional Compensable Elements, a compensable factor in the Hay Plan, addresses exceptional conditions in the context in which the jobs are performed.

Age Discrimination in Employment Act of 1967 (ADEA) protects workers age 40 and older from illegal discrimination.

Agency theory provides an explanation of executive compensation determination based on the relationship between company owners (shareholders) and agents (executives).

Alternation ranking, a variation of simple ranking job evaluation plans, orders all jobs from lowest to highest based on alternately identifying the jobs of lowest and highest worth.

Americans with Disabilities Act of 1990 (ADA) prohibits discrimination against individuals with mental or physical disabilities within and outside employment settings including public services and transportation, public accommodations, and employment.

Andrews v. DuBois, a district court ruling, determined that the following activities at employees'

home associated with the care of dogs used for law enforcement are compensable under the Fair Labor Standards Act of 1938 (FLSA)—feeding, grooming, and walking the dogs. The court reasoned that these activities are indispensable to maintaining dogs as a critical law enforcement tool, are part of officers' principal activities, and are of benefit to the employer.

Aptitudes represent individuals' capacities to learn how to perform specific jobs.

Atonio v. Wards Cove Packing, a Supreme Court case, ruled that plaintiffs (that is, employees) in employment discrimination suits must indicate which employment practice created disparate impact, and demonstrate how the employment practice created disparate impact (intentional discrimination).

Balance sheet approach provides expatriates the standard of living they normally enjoy in the United States.

Banking hours refers to a feature of flextime schedules that allows employees to vary the number of hours they work each day as long as they work a set number of hours each week.

Base pay represents the monetary compensation employees earn on a regular basis for performing their jobs. Hourly pay and salary are the main forms of base pay.

Base period is the minimum period of time an individual must be employed before becoming eligible to receive unemployment insurance under the Social Security Act of 1935.

Behavior encouragement plans are individual incentive pay plans that reward employees for specific behavioral accomplishments, such as good attendance or safety records.

Behavioral observation scale (BOS), a specific kind of behavioral system, displays illustrations of positive incidents (or behaviors) of job performance for various job dimensions. The evaluator rates the employee on each behavior according to the extent to which the employee performs in a manner consistent with each behavioral description.

Behavioral systems, a type of performance appraisal method, requires that raters (for example, supervisors) judge the extent to which employees display successful job performance behaviors.

Behaviorally-anchored rating scale (BARS), a specific kind of behavioral system, is based on the critical incident technique (CIT), and these scales are developed in the same fashion with one exception. For the CIT, a critical incident would be written as "the incumbent completed the task in a timely fashion." For the BARS format, this incident would be written as "the incumbent is expected to complete the task in a timely fashion."

Benchmark jobs, found outside the company, provide reference points against which the value of jobs within the company are judged.

Bennett Amendment allows employees to charge employers with Title VII violations regarding pay only when the employer has violated the Equal Pay Act of 1963.

Board of directors represents shareholders' interests by weighing the pros and cons of top executives' decisions. Members include chief executive officers and top executives of other successful companies, distinguished community leaders, well-regarded professionals (for example, physicians, attorneys), and a few of the company's top-level executives.

Bona fide foreign residence criterion or the physical foreign presence criterion must be met to qualify for the IRC Section 911 income exclusion.

Boureslan v. Aramco, a Supreme Court case in which the Supreme Court ruled that federal job discrimination laws do not apply to U.S. citizens working for U.S. companies in foreign countries.

Brito v. Zia Company, a Supreme Court ruling, deemed that the Zia Company violated Title VII of the Civil Rights Act of 1964 when a disproportionate number of protected class individuals were laid off on the basis of low performance appraisal scores. Zia Company's action was a violation of Title VII because the use of the performance appraisal system in determining layoffs was indeed an employment test. In addition, the court ruled that the Zia Company had not demonstrated that its performance appraisal instrument was valid.

Broadbanding is a pay structure form that leads to the consolidation of existing pay grades and pay ranges into fewer wider pay grades.

Cafeteria plan (*see* flexible benefits plan).

Capital gains is the difference between the company stock price at the time of purchase and the lower stock price at the time an executive receives the stock options.

Capital requirements include automated manufacturing technology, and office and plant facilities.

Capital-intensity refers to the extent to which companies' operations are based on the use of large-scale equipment. On average, capital-intensive industries (for example, manufacturing) pay more than less capital-intensive industries (service industries).

Career development is a cooperative effort between employees and their employers to promote rewarding work experiences throughout employees' work lives.

Central tendency represents the fact that a set of data cluster or center around a central point. Central tendency is a number that represents the typical numerical value in a data set.

Certification ensures that employees possess at least a minimally acceptable level of skill proficiency upon completion of a training unit. Certification methods can include work samples, oral questioning, and written tests.

Civil Rights Act of 1964 is a major piece of federal legislation designed to protect the rights of underrepresented minorities.

Civil Rights Act of 1991 shifted the burden of proof of disparate impact from employees to employers, overturning several 1989 Supreme Court rulings.

Classification plan, a particular method of job evaluation, places jobs into categories based on compensable factors.

Coinsurance refers to the percentage of covered medical expenses paid by the medical insurance policy holder than by the medical insurance plan.

Collective bargaining agreements are written documents that describe the terms of employment reached between management and unions.

Commercial dental plans provide cash benefits by reimbursing patients for out-of-pocket costs for particular dental care procedures, or by paying dentists directly for patient costs.

Commercial insurance plans provide protection for three types of medical expenses: hospital expenses, surgical expenses, and physicians' charges.

Commission is a form of incentive compensation, based upon a percentage of the product or service selling price and the number of units sold.

Commission-only plan is a specific kind of sales compensation plan. Some salespeople derive their entire income through commissions.

Commission-plus-draw plans award sales professionals commissions and draws.

Common review date is the designated date when all employees receive performance evaluations.

Common review period is the designated period (for example, the month of June) when all employees receive performance evaluations.

Compa-ratios index the relative competitiveness of internal pay rates based on pay range midpoints.

Company stock represents total equity or worth of the company.

Company stock shares represent equity segments of equal value. Equity interest increases with the number of stock shares.

Comparable worth represents an ongoing debate in society regarding pay differentials between men and women who perform similar, but not identical work.

Comparison systems, a type of performance appraisal method, requires that raters (for example, supervisors) evaluate a given employee's performance against other employees' performance attainments. Employees are ranked from the best performer to the poorest performer.

Compensable factors are job attributes (for example, skill, effort, responsibility, and working conditions) that compensation professionals use to determine the value of jobs.

Compensation budgets are blueprints that describe the allocation of monetary resources to fund pay structures.

Compensation committee is comprised of board of directors members within and outside a company. Compensation committees review executive compensation consultants' alternate recommendations for compensation packages, discuss the assets and liabilities of the recommendations, and recommend the consultant's

best proposal to the board of directors for their consideration.

Compensation strategies describe the use of compensation practices that support human resource and competitive strategies.

Compensation surveys involve the collection and subsequent analysis of competitors' compensation data.

Competitive advantage describes a company's success based on employees' efforts to maintain market share and profitability over a sustained period of several years.

Competitive strategy refers to the planned use of company resources—technology, capital, and human resources—to promote and sustain competitive advantage.

Compressed work week schedules enable employees to perform their full-time weekly work obligations in fewer days than a regular five-day work week.

Concessionary bargaining focuses on unions promoting job security over large wage increases in negotiations with management.

Consolidated Omnibus Budget Reconciliation Act of 1985 (COBRA) was enacted to provide employees the opportunity to temporarily continue receiving their employer-sponsored medical care insurance under their employer's plan if their coverage otherwise would cease due to termination, layoff, or other change in employment status.

Consultants (*see* independent contractors).

Consumer Price Index (CPI) indexes monthly price changes of goods and services that people buy for day-to-day living.

Contingent workers engage in explicitly tentative employment relationships with companies.

Continuous learning is a philosophy that underlies most training efforts in companies. Progressive companies encourage employees to continuously develop their skills, knowledge, and abilities through formal training programs.

Contrast errors occur when a rater (for example, a supervisor) compares an employee to other employees rather than to specific, explicit performance standards.

Contributory financing implies that the company and its employees share the costs for discretionary benefits.

Contributory pension plans require monetary contributions by the employee who will benefit from the income upon retirement.

Copayments represent nominal payments individuals make for office visits to their doctors or for prescription drugs.

Core compensation describes the monetary rewards employees receive. There are six types of core compensation: base pay, seniority pay, merit pay, incentive pay, cost-of-living adjustments (COLAs), and pay-for-knowledge and skill-based pay.

Core employees possess full-time jobs, and they generally plan long-term or indefinite relationships with their employers.

Core hours applies to flextime schedule, namely, the hours when all workers must be present.

Core plus option plans establish a set of benefits, such as medical insurance, as mandatory for all employees who participate in flexible benefits plans.

Cost leadership strategy focuses on gaining competitive advantage by being the lowest cost producer of a good or service within the marketplace, while selling the good or service at a price advantage relative to the industry average.

Cost shifting refers to the practice used by physicians and hospitals to offset health care expenses for individuals who are unable to pay by charging higher fees to individuals with health insurance.

Cost-of-living-adjustments (COLAs) represent periodic base pay increases that are based on changes in prices, as indexed by the consumer price index (CPI). COLAs enable workers to maintain their purchasing power and standards of living by adjusting base pay for inflation.

Critical incident technique (CIT), a specific kind of behavioral system, requires job incumbents and their supervisors to identify performance incidents—on-the-job behaviors and behavioral outcomes—that distinguish successful performance from unsuccessful performance. The supervisor then observes the employees and records their performance on these critical job aspects.

Cross-departmental model, a kind of pay-for-knowledge program, promotes staffing flexibility by training employees in one department with some of the critical skills they would need to perform effectively in other departments.

Current profit sharing plans award cash to employees typically on a quarterly or annual basis.

Currently insured status refers to designated survivors' eligibility to receive benefits under the Social Security Act in the event of a worker's death. A worker need only have worked and contributed to Social Security during at least six quarters of coverage out of the 13-quarter period ending with the quarter in which death occurs.

Davis-Bacon Act of 1931 established employment standards for construction contractors holding federal government contracts valued at more than $2,000. Such contractors must pay laborers and mechanics at least the prevailing wage in the local area.

Day care refers to programs that supervise and care for young children and elderly relatives when their regular caretakers are at work.

Death claims are workers' compensation claims for deaths that occur in the course of employment or that are caused by compensable injuries or occupational diseases.

Deductible refers to the out-of-pocket expenses that employees must pay before dental, medical, or vision insurance benefits become active.

Deferred compensation refers to an agreement between an employee and a company to render payments to an employee at a future date. Deferred compensation is a hallmark of executive compensation packages.

Deferred profit sharing plans place cash awards in trust accounts for employees. These trusts are set aside on employees' behalf as a source of retirement income.

Defined benefit plans guarantee retirement benefits specified in the plan document. This benefit is usually expressed in terms of a monthly sum equal to a percentage of a participant's pre-retirement pay multiplied by the number of years he or she has worked for the employer.

Defined contribution plans require that employers and employees make annual contributions to separate retirement fund accounts established for each participating employee, based on a formula contained in the plan document.

Dental insurance provides reimbursement for routine dental checkups and particular corrective procedures.

Dental maintenance organizations deliver dental services through the comprehensive health care plans of many health maintenance organizations (HMOs) and preferred provider organizations (PPOs).

Dental service corporations, owned and administered by state dental associations, are nonprofit corporations of dentists.

Depth of knowledge refers to the level of specialization, based on job-related knowledge, that an employee brings to a particular job.

Depth of skills refers to the level of specialization, based on skills, that an employee brings to a particular job.

Derivative lawsuits represent legal action that is initiated by company shareholders claiming that executive compensation is excessive.

Dictionary of Occupational Titles (DOT) includes over 20,000 private and public sector job descriptions.

Differentiation strategy focuses on product or service development that is unique from those of its competitors. Differentiation can take many forms including design or brand image, technology, features, customer service, or price.

Direct hire arrangements refer to companies' recruitment and selection of temporary workers without assistance from employment agencies.

Disability insured refers to an employee's eligibility to receive disability benefits under the Social Security Act of 1935. Eligibility depends upon the worker's age and the type of disability.

Discharge represents involuntary termination specifically for poor job performance, insubordination, or gross violation of work rules.

Discount stock options, a kind of executive deferred compensation, entitle executives to purchase their companies' stock at a future time for a predetermined price. Discount stock options are similar to nonstatutory stock options with one exception. Companies grant stock options at rates far below the stock's fair market value on the date the option is granted.

Discretionary benefits are benefits that employers offer at their own choice. These benefits fall into three broad categories—protection programs, pay for time-not-worked, and services.

Discretionary bonuses are awarded to executives on an elective basis by boards of directors. Boards of directors weigh four factors in determining discretionary bonus amounts: company profits, the financial condition of the company, business conditions, and prospects for the future.

Discretionary income covers a variety of financial obligations in the United States for which expatriates remain responsible.

Disparate impact represents unintentional employment discrimination. It occurs whenever an employer applies an employment practice to all employees, but the practice leads to unequal treatment of protected employee groups.

Disparate treatment represents intentional employment discrimination, occurring whenever employers intentionally treat some workers less favorably than others because of their race, color, sex, national origin, or religion.

Distributive fairness, as applied to compensation, refers to employees' beliefs about the appropriateness of the actual pay and pay-increase amounts.

Draw is a subsistence pay component (that is, to cover basic living expenses) in sales compensation plans. Companies usually charge draws against commissions that sales professionals are expected to earn.

Dual employer common law doctrine establishes temporary workers' rights to receive workers' compensation.

Dysfunctional turnover occurs whenever high-performing employees voluntarily terminate their employment, particularly when these high-performing employees take jobs in competitor companies.

Early retirement programs contain incentives designed to encourage highly paid employees with substantial seniority to retire earlier than planned. These incentives expedite senior employees' retirement eligibility and increase retirement income. In addition, many companies include continuation of medical benefits.

Economic reality test helps companies determine whether employees are financially dependent on them.

Education reimbursements apply to expatriates' children. Companies generally reimburse expatriates for the cost of children's private-school tuition in foreign posts.

Education, based on Equal Employment Opportunity Commission guidelines, refers to formal training.

EEOC v. Chrysler, a district court ruling, deemed that early retirement programs are permissible when companies offer them to employees on a voluntary basis. Forcing early retirement upon older workers represents age discrimination.

EEOC v. Madison Community Unit School District No. 12, a circuit court ruling, shed light on judging whether jobs are equal based on four compensable factors—skill, effort, responsibility, and working conditions.

Employee's anniversary date represents the date an employee began working for his or her present employer. Often, employees receive performance reviews on their anniversary dates.

Employee assistance programs (EAPs) help employees cope with personal problems, such as alcohol or drug abuse, domestic violence, the emotional impact of AIDS and other diseases, clinical depression, and eating disorders, that may impair their job performance.

Employee benefits include any variety of programs that provide for pay for time-not-worked (for example, vacation), employee services (for example, transportation services), and protection programs (for example, life insurance).

Employee Retirement Income Security Act of 1974 (ERISA) was established to regulate the establishment and implementation of various fringe compensation programs. These include medical, life and disability insurance programs as well as pension programs. The essence of ERISA is the protection of employee benefits rights.

Employee-financed benefits mean that employers do not contribute to the financing of discretionary benefits.

Employment termination takes place when employees' agreement to perform work is ended. Employment terminations are voluntary or involuntary.

Environmental conditions describe the surroundings in which workers perform their jobs.

Equal benefit or equal cost principle contained within the Older Workers Benefit Protection Act (OWBPA) generally requires employers to offer benefits to older workers that are of equal or greater value than the benefits offered to young workers.

Equal Pay Act of 1963 requires that men and women must receive equal pay for performing equal work.

Equity theory suggests an employee must regard his or her own ratio of merit increase pay to performance as similar to the ratio for other comparably performing people in the company.

Errors of central tendency occur when raters (for example, supervisors) judge all employees as average or close to average.

Exchange rate is the price at which one country's currency can be swapped for another.

Executive Branch enforces the laws of various quasi-legislative and judicial agencies, and executive orders.

Executive compensation consultants propose recommendations to chief executive officers and board of director members for alternate executive compensation packages.

Executive Order 11141 prohibits companies holding contracts with the federal government from discriminating against employees on the basis of age.

Executive Order 11246 requires companies holding contracts (worth more than $50,000 per year and employing 50 or more employees) with the federal government to develop written affirmative action plans each year.

Executive orders influence the operation of the federal government and companies that are engaged in business relationships with the federal government.

Exempt refers to an employee's status regarding the overtime pay provision of the Fair Labor Standards Act of 1938 (FLSA). Generally, administrative, professional, and executive employees are exempt from the FLSA overtime and minimum wage provisions.

Expatriates are U.S. citizens employed in U.S. companies with work assignments outside the United States.

Experience rating system establishes higher contributions (to fund unemployment insurance programs) for employers with higher incidences of unemployment.

Extrinsic compensation includes both monetary and nonmonetary rewards.

Fair Labor Standards Act of 1938 (FLSA) addresses major abuses that intensified during the Great Depression and the transition from agricultural to industrial enterprises. These include substandard pay, excessive work hours, and the employment of children in oppressive working conditions.

Family and Medical Leave Act of 1993 (FMLA) requires employers to provide employees 12 weeks of unpaid leave per year in cases of family or medical emergency.

Family assistance programs help employees provide elder care and child care. Elder care provides physical, emotional, or financial assistance for aging parents, spouses, or other relatives who are not fully self-sufficient because they are too frail or disabled. Child care programs focus on supervising preschool-aged dependent children whose parents work outside the home.

Federal Employees' Compensation Act mandates workers' compensation insurance protection for federal civilian employees.

Federal government oversees the entire United States and its territories. The vast majority of laws that influence compensation were established at the federal level.

Federal Unemployment Tax Act (FUTA) specifies employees' and employers' tax or contribution to unemployment insurance programs required by the Social Security Act of 1935.

First-impression effect occurs when a rater (for example, a supervisor) makes an initial favorable or unfavorable judgment about an employee, and then ignores or distorts the employee's actual performance based on this impression.

Flexible benefits plan allows employees to choose a portion of their discretionary benefits based on a company's discretionary benefits options.

Flexible scheduling and leave allows employees to take time off during work hours to care for relatives or react to emergencies.

Flexible spending accounts permit employees to pay for certain benefits expenses (such as childcare) with pre-tax dollars.

Flextime schedules allow employees to modify work schedules within specified limits set by the employer.

Forced distribution is a specific kind of comparison performance appraisal system in which raters (for example, supervisors) assign employees to groups that represent the entire range of performance.

Foreign service premiums are monetary payments awarded to expatriates above their regular base pay.

Free-lancers (*see* independent contractors).

Fringe compensation (*see* employee benefits).

Fully insured refers to an employee's status in the retirement income program under the Social Security Act of 1935. Forty quarters of coverage lead to fully insured status.

Functional capabilities include manufacturing, engineering, research and development, management information systems, human resources, and marketing. These are crucial to maintaining competitive advantage.

Gain sharing describes group incentive systems that provide participating employees an incentive payment based on improved company performance whether it be for increased productivity, increased customer satisfaction, lower costs, or better safety records.

General educational development (GED) refers to education of a general nature that contributes to reasoning development and to the acquisition of mathematical and language skills. The GED has three components—reasoning development, mathematical development, and language development.

General Schedule classifies federal government jobs into 15 classifications (GS-1 through GS-15) based on such factors as skill, education, and experience levels. In addition, jobs that require high levels of specialized education (for example, a physicist), influence significantly on public policy (for example, law judges), or require executive decision making are classified in three additional categories: Senior level (SL), Scientific & Professional (ST) positions, and the Senior Executive Service (SES).

Glass Ceiling Act established the Glass Ceiling Commission—a 21-member bipartisan body appointed by President Bush and congressional leaders and chaired by the Secretary of Labor. The committee conducted a study of opportunities for, and artificial barriers to, the advancement of minority men and all women into management and decision making positions in U.S. businesses. The committee prepared and submitted to the President of the United States and Congress written reports containing the findings and conclusions resulting from the study and the recommendations based on those findings and conclusions.

Golden parachutes, a kind of executive deferred compensation, provide pay and benefits to executives following their termination resulting from a change in ownership, or corporate takeover.

Goods and service allowances compensate expatriates for the difference between goods and service costs in the United States and in the foreign post.

Graduated commission increases percentage pay rates for progressively higher sales volume in a given period.

Great Depression refers to the period during the 1930s when scores of businesses failed and most workers became chronically unemployed.

Green circle rates represent pay rates for jobs that fall below the designated pay range minimums.

Group incentive programs reward employees for their collective performance, rather than for each employee's individual performance.

Groupthink occurs when all group members agree on mistaken solutions because they share the same mindset and view issues through the lens of conformity.

Hardship allowance compensates expatriates for their sacrifices while on assignment.

Hay Plan (The Hay Guide Chart-Profile Method of Job Evaluation) establishes the worth of jobs based on four compensable factors—Know-How, Problem Solving, Accountability, and Additional Compensable Elements.

Headquarters based method compensates all employees according to the pay scales used at the headquarters.

Health Maintenance Organizations (HMOs) are sometimes described as providing "prepaid medical services," since fixed periodic enrollment fees cover HMO members for all medically necessary services, provided that the services are delivered or approved by the HMO. HMOs represent an alternative to commercial and self-funded insurance plans.

Highly paid employee, as defined by the Internal Revenue Service, is an employee who owns at least 5 percent of the business, an employee earning over $75,000 annually in either the current or preceding calendar year, an employee who earned over $50,000 either last year or this year whose salary is in the top 20 percent of all salaries paid to active employees, or an officer who earned over 150 percent either last year or this year of the dollar limit for annual additions to a defined contribution plan. The defined contribution plan must apply to at least one officer up to a maximum of 50 officers.

Home leave benefits enable expatriates to take paid time off in the United States.

Home-country based pay method compensates expatriates the amount they would receive if they were performing similar work in the United States.

Horizontal knowledge refers to similar knowledge (for example, record keeping applied to payroll applications and record keeping applied to employee benefits).

Horizontal skills refer to similar skills (for example, assembly skills applied to lawn mowers and assembly skills applied to snow blowers).

Host country nationals are foreign national citizens who work in U.S. companies' branch offices or manufacturing plants in their home countries.

Host-country based method compensates expatriates based on the host countries' pay scales.

Hourly pay is one type of base pay. Employees earn hourly pay for each hour worked.

Housing and utilities allowances compensate expatriates for the difference between housing and utilities costs in the United States and in the foreign post.

Human capital refers to employees' knowledge and skills, enabling them to be productive (*see* human capital theory).

Human capital theory states that employees' knowledge and skills generate productive capital known as human capital. Employees can develop knowledge and skills from formal education or on-the-job experiences.

Human resource strategies specify the particular use of HR practices to be consistent with competitive strategy.

Hypothetical tax is the U.S. income tax based on the same salary level, excluding all foreign allowances.

Illegal discriminatory bias occurs when a supervisor rates members of his or her race, gender, nationality, or religion more favorably than members of other classes.

Improshare is a specific kind of gain sharing program that awards employees based on a labor hour ratio formula. A standard is determined by analyzing historical accounting data to find a relationship between the number of labor hours needed to complete a product. Productivity is then measured as a ratio of standard labor hours and actual labor hours.

Incentive pay or variable pay is defined as compensation, other than base wages or salaries, that fluctuates according to employees' attainment of some standard such as a preestablished formula, individual or group goals, or company earnings.

Incentive stock options entitle executives to purchase their companies' stock in the future at a predetermined price. Usually, the predetermined price equals the stock price at the time an executive receives the stock options. Incentive stock options entitle executives to favorable tax treatment.

Independent contractors are contingent workers who typically possess specialized skills that are in short supply in the labor market. Companies select independent contractors to complete particular projects of short-term duration—usually a year or less.

Indexes of living costs abroad compare the costs (U.S. dollars) of representative goods and services (excluding education) expatriates purchase at the foreign location and the cost of comparable goods and services purchased in the Washington, D. C. area. Companies use these indexes to determine appropriate goods and service allowances.

Individual incentive plans reward employees for meeting work-related performance standards such as quality, productivity, customer satisfaction, safety, or attendance. Any one or a combination of these standards may be used.

Individual practice associations, a particular kind of HMO, are partnerships or other legal entities that arrange health care services by entering into service agreements with independent physicians, health professionals, and group practices.

Individualism–collectivism, a dimension of national culture, is the extent to which individuals value personal independence versus group membership.

Industry group is the second most broad classification of industries within the Standard Industrial Classification system.

Industry profiles describe such basic industry characteristics as sales volume, the impact of relevant government regulation on competitive strategies, and the impact of recent technological advancements on business activity.

Industry represents the least broad (that is, the most specific) classification of an industry within the Standard Industrial Classification system.

Inflation is the increase in prices for consumer goods and services. Inflation erodes the purchasing power of currency.

Injury claims are workers' compensation claims for disabilities that have resulted from accidents such as falls, injuries from equipment use, or physical strains from heavy lifting.

Interests represent individuals' liking or preference for performing specific jobs.

Intrinsic compensation reflects employees' psychological mindsets that they experience when performing their jobs.

Involuntary part-time employees work fewer than 35 hours per week because they are unable to find full-time employment.

Involuntary terminations are initiated by companies for a variety of reasons including poor job performance, insubordination, violation of work rules, reduced business activity due to sluggish economic conditions, or plant closings.

IRC Section 901 allows expatriates to credit foreign income taxes against their U.S. income liability.

IRC Section 911 permits eligible expatriates to exclude as much as $70,000 of foreign earned income from taxation, plus a housing allowance.

Job analysis is a systematic process for gathering, documenting, and analyzing information in order to describe jobs.

Job characteristics theory describes the critical psychological states that employees experience when they perform their jobs (that is, intrinsic compensation). According to job characteristics theory, employees experience enhanced psychological states when their jobs rate high on five core job dimensions—skill variety, task identity, task significance, autonomy, and feedback.

Job content refers to the actual activities that employees must perform in the job. Job content descriptions may be broad, general statements of job activities or detailed descriptions of duties and tasks performed in the job.

Job control unionism refers to a union's success in negotiating formal contracts with employees and establishing quasi-judicial grievance procedures to adjudicate disputes between union members and employers.

Job descriptions summarize a job's purpose and list its tasks, duties, and responsibilities, as well as the skills, knowledge, and abilities necessary to perform the job at a minimum level.

Job duties, a section in job descriptions, describe the major work activities, and, if pertinent, supervisory responsibilities.

Job evaluation systematically recognizes differences in the relative worth among a set of jobs, and establishes pay differentials accordingly.

Job family refers to a group of two or more jobs with either similar worker characteristics (for example, job-related work experience, skill, formal education) or similar work tasks.

Job sharing is a special kind of part-time employment agreement. Two or more part-time employees perform a single full-time job.

Job summary, a statement that appears in job descriptions, summarizes the job based on two to four descriptive statements.

Job titles, listed in job descriptions, indicate job designations.

Job-based pay compensates employees for jobs they currently perform.

Job-content evaluation, an approach to job evaluation, emphasizes the company's internal value system, establishing a hierarchy of internal job worth based on each job's role in company strategy.

Job-point accrual model, a type of pay-for-knowledge program, provides employees opportunities to develop skills and to learn to perform jobs from different job families.

Just-meaningful pay increase refers to the minimum pay increase that employees will see as making a substantial change in compensation.

Key employee, as defined by the Internal Revenue Service, is an employee who, at any time during the current year or any of the four preceding years, is one of ten employees owning the largest percentages of the company, an employee who owns more than five percent of the company, or an employee who earns more than $150,000 per year and owns more than one percent of the company.

Know-How, a compensable factor in the Hay Plan, is the total of all skills and knowledge required to do the job. This factor contains three subfactors— specialized and technical knowledge, managerial relations, and human relations.

Knowledge, based on Equal Employment Opportunity Commission guidelines, refers to a body of information applied directly to the performance of a function.

Labor market assessments enable companies to determine the availability of qualified employees.

Labor-management relations involve a continuous relationship between a company's HR professionals and a group of employees— members of a labor union and its bargaining unit.

Layoff represents involuntary termination that results from sluggish economic conditions or from plant closings.

Lease companies employ qualified individuals whom they place in client companies on a long-term, presumably, "permanent" basis. Lease companies place employees within client companies in exchange for fees.

Legally-required benefits are protection programs that attempt to promote worker safety and health, maintain family income streams, and assist families in crisis. The key legally required benefits are mandated by the following laws—the Social Security Act of 1935, various state workers' compensation laws, and the Family and Medical Leave Act of 1993.

Leniency errors occur when raters (for example, supervisors) appraise an employee's performance more highly than the performance actually rates when compared to objective criteria.

Life coverage is a type of life insurance that provides protection to employees' beneficiaries during employees' employment and into the retirement years.

Life insurance protects an employee's family by paying a specified amount to the employee's beneficiaries upon the employee's death. Most policies pay some multiple of the employee's salary.

Line employees are directly involved in producing companies' goods or service delivery. Assembler, production worker, and sales employee are examples of line jobs.

Local government enacts and enforces laws that are most pertinent to smaller geographic regions, for example, Champaign County in Illinois, and the city of Los Angeles.

Long-term disability insurance provides income benefits for extended periods of time, ranging from six months to life.

Longevity pay systems reward employees with permanent additions to base pay who have reached pay grade maximums and who are not likely to move into higher pay grades.

Longshore and Harborworkers' Compensation Act mandates workers' compensation insurance protection for maritime workers.

Lorance v. AT&T Technologies, a Supreme Court ruling, limited employees' rights to challenge the use of seniority systems only within 180 days from the system's implementation date.

Lowest-cost strategy (*see* cost leadership strategy).

Major group is the broadest classification of industries within the Standard Industrial Classification system.

Management by objectives (MBO), a goal-oriented performance appraisal method, requires that supervisors and employees determine objectives for employees to meet during the rating period, and the employees appraise how well they have achieved their objectives.

Management incentive plans award bonuses to managers when they meet or exceed objectives based on sales, profit, production, or other measures for their division, department, or unit.

Mandatory bargaining subjects are those that employers and unions must bargain on if either constituent makes proposals about them.

Market lag policy distinguishes companies from the competition by compensating employees less than most competitors. Lagging the market indicates that pay levels fall below the market pay line.

Market lead policy distinguishes companies from the competition by compensating employees more highly than most competitors. Leading the market denotes pay levels that place in the area above the market pay line.

Market match policy most closely follows the typical market pay rates because companies pay according to the market pay line. Thus, pay rates fall along the market pay line.

Market pay line is representative of typical market pay rates relative to a company's job structure.

Market-based evaluation, an approach to job evaluation, uses market data to determine differences in job worth.

Market-competitive pay systems represent companies' compensation policies that fit the imperatives of competitive advantage.

Masculinity–femininity, a dimension of national culture, refers to whether masculine or feminine values are dominant in society. Masculinity favors material possessions. Femininity encourages caring and nurturing behavior.

Materials, products, subject matter, and services (MPSMS), based on the U.S. Department of Labor Job Analysis Method, includes basic materials processed, such as fabric, metal, or wood; final products made, such as automobiles; cultivated, such as field crops; harvested, such as sponges; or captured, such as wild animals; subject matter or data with or applied, such as astronomy or journalism; services rendered, such as barbering or janitorial.

McNamara-O'Hara Service Contract Act of 1965 requires that all federal contractors employing service workers must pay at least the minimum wage as specified in the FLSA. In addition, contractors holding contracts with the federal government that exceed $2,500 in value must pay the local prevailing wages, and offer fringe compensation equal to the local prevailing benefits.

Medicare serves nearly all U.S. citizens aged 65 or older by providing insurance coverage for hospitalization, convalescent care, and major doctor bills. The Medicare program includes two separate plans: compulsory hospitalization insurance, Part A, and voluntary supplementary medical insurance, Part B. The Social Security Act of 1935 established Medicare.

Merit bonuses or **nonrecurring merit increases** are lump sum monetary awards based on employees' past performance. Employees do not continue to receive nonrecurring merit increases every year. Instead, employees must earn them each time.

Merit pay programs reward employees with permanent increases to base pay according to differences in job performance.

Midpoint pay value is the halfway mark between the range minimum and maximum rates. Midpoints generally match values along the market pay line, representing the competitive market rate determined by the analysis of compensation survey data.

Mobility premiums reward employees for moving from one assignment to another.

Multiple-tiered commission increases percentage pay rates for progressively higher sales volume in a given period only if sales exceed a predetermined level.

National culture refers to the set of shared norms and beliefs among individuals within national boundaries who are indigenous to that area.

National Labor Relations Act of 1935 (NLRA) establishes employees' rights to bargain collectively with employers on such issues as wages, work hours, and working conditions.

Negative halo effect occurs when a rater (for example, a supervisor) generalizes an employee's negative behavior on one aspect of the job to all aspects of the job.

Noncash incentives complement monetary sales compensation components. Such noncash incentives as contests, recognition programs, expense reimbursement, and benefits policies, can encourage sales performance and attract sales talent.

Noncontributory financing implies that the company assumes total costs for discretionary benefits.

Noncontributory pension plans do not require employee contributions to fund retirement income.

Nonexempt refers to an employee's status regarding the overtime pay provision of the Fair Labor Standards Act of 1938 (FLSA). Generally, employees whose jobs do not fall into particular categories (that is, administrative, professional, and executive employees) are covered by overtime and minimum wage provisions.

Nonqualified pension plans provide less favorable tax treatments for employers than qualified pension plans.

Nonrecoverable draws act as salary because employees are not obligated to repay the loans if they do not sell enough.

Nonrecurring merit increases or **merit bonuses** are lump sum monetary awards based on employees' past job performance. Employees do not continue to receive nonrecurring merit increases every year. Instead, employees must earn them each time.

Nonstatutory stock options, a kind of executive deferred compensation, entitle executives to purchase their companies' stock at a future date at a predetermined price. Usually, the predetermined price equals the stock price at the time an executive receives the stock options. Nonstatutory stock options do not entitle executives to favorable tax treatment.

North American Free Trade Agreement (NAFTA) became effective on January 1, 1994. NAFTA has two main goals. First, NAFTA was designed to reduce trade barriers among Mexico, Canada, and the United States. Second, NAFTA also set out to remove barriers to investment among these three countries.

Occupational disease claims are workers' compensation claims for disabilities caused by ailments associated with particular industrial trades or processes.

Older Workers Benefit Protection Act (OWBPA), the 1990 amendment to the ADEA, indicates that employers can require older employees to pay more for health care insurance coverage than younger employees. This practice is permissible when older workers collectively do not make proportionately larger contributions than the younger workers.

On-call arrangement is a method for employing temporary workers.

Operating requirements encompass all human resources programs.

Organizational and product life cycles describe the evolution of company and product change in terms of human life cycle stages. Much as people are born, grow, mature, decline, and die, such cycles can describe companies, products, and services. Business priorities including HR vary with life cycle.

Organizational culture is a system of shared values and beliefs that produce norms of behavior.

Outplacement assistance refers to company-sponsored technical and emotional support to employees who are being laid off or terminated.

Paired comparison, a variation of simple ranking job evaluation plans, orders all jobs from lowest to highest based on comparing the worth of each job in all possible job pairs. Paired comparison also refers to a specific kind of comparison method for appraising job performance. Supervisors compare each employee to every other employee, identifying the better performer in each pair.

Part A refers to compulsory hospitalization insurance under Medicare.

Part B refers to voluntary supplementary medical insurance under Medicare.

Pay compression occurs whenever a company's pay spread between newly hired or less qualified employees and more qualified job incumbents is small.

Pay for time-not-worked represents discretionary employee benefits that provide employees time off with pay (such as vacation).

Pay grades group jobs for pay policy application. HR professionals typically group jobs into pay grades based on similar compensable factors and value.

Pay ranges represent the span of possible pay rates for each pay grade. Pay ranges include midpoint, minimum, and maximum pay rates. The minimum and maximum values denote the acceptable lower and upper bounds of pay for the jobs classified within particular pay grades.

Pay structures represent pay rate differences for jobs of unequal worth and the framework for recognizing differences in employee contributions.

Pay-for-Knowledge plans reward managerial, service, or professional workers for successfully learning specific curricula.

Pension programs provide income to individuals throughout their retirement. Companies may sometimes use early retirement programs to reduce work force size and trim compensation expenditures.

Percentiles describe dispersion by indicating the percentage of figures that fall below certain points. There are 100 percentiles ranging from the first percentile to the 100th percentile.

Performance appraisal describes employees' past performance and serves as a basis to recommend how to improve future performance.

Performance-contingent bonuses, awarded to executives, are based on the attainment of such specific performance criteria as market share attainment.

Perks (*see* perquisites).

Permissive bargaining subjects are those subjects on which neither the employer nor the union is obligated to bargain.

Perquisites are benefits offered exclusively to executives, for example, country club memberships.

Phantom stock, a type of executive deferred compensation, is an arrangement whereby boards of directors compensate executives with hypothetical company stocks rather than actual shares of company stock. Phantom stock plans are similar to restricted stock plans because executives must meet specific conditions before they can convert these phantom shares into real shares of company stock.

Physical demands represent the physical requirements made on the worker by the specific situation.

Physical foreign presence criterion or the bona fide foreign residence criterion must be met to qualify for the IRC Section 911 income exclusion.

Piece work plan, an individual incentive pay program, rewards employees based on their individual hourly production against an objective output standard, determined by the pace at which manufacturing equipment operates. For each hour, workers receive piece work incentives for every item produced over the designated production standard. Workers also receive a guaranteed hourly pay rate regardless of whether they meet the designated production standard.

Point method represents a job-content evaluation technique that uses quantitative methodology. Quantitative methods assign numerical values to compensable factors that describe jobs, and these values are summed as an indicator of the overall value for the job.

Portal-to-Portal Act of 1947 defines the term "hours worked" that appears in the FLSA.

Positive halo effect occurs when a rater (for example, a supervisor) generalizes employees' positive behavior on one aspect of the job to all aspects of the job.

Poverty threshold represents the minimum annual earnings needed to afford housing and other basic necessities. The federal government determines these levels each year for families of different sizes.

Power distance, a dimension of national culture, is the extent to which people accept a hierarchical system or power structure in companies.

Predetermined allocation bonuses, awarded to executives, are based on a fixed formula. Often, company profits is the main determinant of the bonus amounts.

Preferred provider organization (PPO) is a select group of health care providers who provide health care services to a given population at a higher level of reimbursement than under commercial insurance plans.

Pregnancy Discrimination Act of 1978 (PDA) is an amendment to Title VII of the Civil Rights Act of 1964. The PDA prohibits disparate impact discrimination against pregnant women for all employment practices.

Prepaid group practices, a specific type of HMO, provide medical care for a set premium, rather than a fee-for-service basis.

Probationary period is the initial term of employment (usually six months or less) during which companies attempt to ensure that they have made sound hiring decisions. Often, employees are not entitled to participate in discretionary benefits programs during their probationary periods.

Problem Solving, a compensable factor in the Hay Plan, is the amount of original thinking required to arrive at decisions in the job. This factor contains two subfactors—thinking environment and thinking challenge.

Procedural fairness, as applied to compensation, refers to employees' beliefs about the appropriateness of the policies and practices used to determine pay and pay-increase amounts.

Production plan (*see* piece work plan).

Profit sharing plans pay a portion of company profits to employees, separate from base pay, cost-of-living adjustments, or permanent merit pay increases. Two basic kinds of profit sharing plans are used widely today—current profit sharing and deferred profit sharing.

Protection programs are either legally required or discretionary employee benefits that provide family benefits, promote health, and guard against income loss caused by catastrophic factors like unemployment, disability, or serious illnesses.

Qualified pension plans entitle employers to tax benefits from their contributions to pension plans. In general, this means that employers may take current tax deductions for contributions to fund future retirement income.

Quarters allowance is the U.S. Department of State term for housing and utilities allowances.

Quarters of coverage refers to each 3-month period of employment during which an employee contributes to the retirement income program under the Social Security Act of 1935.

Quartiles describe dispersion by indicating the percentage of figures that fall below certain points. There are three quartiles—75th quartile, 50th quartile, and 25th quartile.

Range spread is the difference between the maximum and the minimum pay rates of a given pay grade.

Rating errors in performance appraisal reflect differences between human judgment processes versus objective, accurate assessments uncolored by bias, prejudice, or other subjective, extraneous influences.

Recertification ensures that employees periodically demonstrate mastery of all the jobs they have learned.

Recoverable draws act as company loans to employees that are carried forward indefinitely until employees sell enough (that is, earn a sufficient amount in commissions) to repay their draws.

Recruitment entails identifying qualified job candidates and promoting their interest in working for a company.

Red circle rates represent pay rates that are higher than the designated pay range maximums.

Referral plans are individual incentive pay plans that reward employees for referring new customers or recruiting successful job applicants.

Relevant labor markets represent the fields of potentially qualified candidates for particular jobs.

Reliable job analysis yields consistent results under similar conditions.

Relocation assistance payments cover expatriates' expenses to relocate to foreign posts.

Repatriation is the process of making the transition from an international assignment and living abroad to a domestic assignment and living in the home country.

Rest and relaxation benefits provide expatriates assigned to hardship locations paid time off. Rest and relaxation leave benefits differ from standard vacation benefits because companies designate where expatriates may spend their time.

Restricted stock, a type of executive deferred compensation, requires that executives do not have any ownership control over the disposition of the stock for a predetermined period, generally, five to ten years.

Revised Handbook for Analyzing Jobs (**RHAJ**) documents the Department of Labor Method of job analysis, which is used to develop the job descriptions contained in the *Dictionary of Occupational Titles.*

Right to control test helps companies determine whether employed individuals are employees or independent contractors.

Rucker Plan is a particular type of gain sharing program that emphasizes employee involvement. Gain sharing awards are based on the ratio between value added less the costs of materials, supplies, and services rendered and the total cost of employment.

Salary is one type of base pay. Employees earn salaries for performing their jobs, regardless of the actual number of hours worked. Companies generally measure salary on an annual basis.

Salary-only plan is a specific type of sales compensation plan. Sales professionals receive fixed base compensation, which does not vary with the level of units sold, increase in market share, or any other indicator of sales performance.

Salary-plus-bonus plan is a specific type of sales compensation plan. Sales professionals receive fixed base compensation, coupled with a bonus. Bonuses usually are single payments that reward employees for achievement of specific, exceptional goals.

Salary-plus-commission plan is a particular type of sales compensation plan. Sales professionals receive fixed base compensation and commission.

Scanlon Plan is a specific type of gain sharing program that emphasizes employee involvement. Gain sharing awards are based on the ratio between labor costs and sales value of production.

Scientific Management practices promoted labor cost control by replacing inefficient production methods with efficient production methods.

Securities and Exchange Commission (SEC) is a nonpartisan, quasi-judicial federal government agency with responsibility for administering federal securities laws.

Securities Exchange Act of 1934 applies to the disclosure of executive compensation.

Selection is the process HR professionals employ to hire qualified candidates for job openings.

Self-funded insurance plans are similar to commercial insurance plans with one key difference: Companies typically draw from their own assets to fund claims when self-funded.

Self-insured dental plans are similar to commercial dental plans except companies fund payment for dental procedures themselves.

Seniority pay systems reward employees with permanent additions to base pay periodically according to employees' length of service performing their jobs.

Services represent discretionary employee benefits that provide enhancements to employees and their families such as tuition reimbursement and daycare assistance.

Severance pay usually includes several months pay following involuntary termination and, in some cases, continued coverage under the employers' medical insurance plan. Often, employees rely on severance pay to meet financial obligations while searching for employment.

Short-term disability insurance provides income benefits for limited periods of time, usually six months or less.

Similar-to-me effect refers to the tendency on the part of raters (for example, supervisors) to judge favorably employees whom they perceive as similar to themselves.

Simple ranking plan, a specific method of job evaluation, orders all jobs from lowest to highest according to a single criterion such as job complexity or the centrality of the job to the company's competitive strategy.

Skill blocks model, a kind of pay-for-knowledge program, applies to jobs from within the same job family. Just as in the stair-step model, employees progress to increasingly complex jobs. However, in a skill blocks program, skills do not necessarily build on each other.

Skill level-performance matrix, a type of pay-for-knowledge program, rewards employees according to how well they have applied skills and knowledge to their jobs.

Skill, based on Equal Employment Opportunity Commission guidelines, refers to an observable competence to perform a learned psychomotor act.

Skill-based pay, used mostly for employees who do physical work, increases workers' pay as they master new skills.

Smoking cessation is a particular type of wellness program that stresses the negative aspects of smoking in intensive programs directed at helping individuals stop smoking.

Social comparison theory provides an explanation for executive compensation determination based on the tendency for boards of directors to offer executive compensation packages that are similar to the executive compensation packages in peer companies.

Social Security Act of 1935 established four main types of legally-required benefits—unemployment insurance, retirement income, benefits for dependents, and medical insurance (Medicare).

Specific vocational preparation (SVP) is defined as the amount of lapsed time required by a typical worker to learn the techniques, acquire the information, and develop the facility needed for average performance in a specific job situation.

Staff functions support the functions performed by line employees. Human Resources and accounting are examples of staff functions.

Stair-step model, a type of pay-for-knowledge program, resembles a flight of stairs. The steps represent jobs from a particular job family that differ in terms of complexity. Skills at higher levels build upon previous lower-level skills.

Standard deviation refers to the mean distance of each salary figure from the mean.

Standard Industrial Classification (SIC) system. SIC codes represent keys to pertinent information for strategic analyses. The SIC codes are four digits, representing the major group (first two digits), industry group (the first three digits), and industry (all four digits).

Standard Industrial Classification Manual classifies industries based on the Standard Industrial Classification system.

State government enacts and enforces laws that pertain exclusively to their respective regions, for example, Illinois and Michigan.

Stock appreciation rights, a type of executive deferred compensation, provide executives income at the end of a designated period, much as with restricted stock options. However, executives never have to exercise their stock rights to receive income. The company simply awards payment to executives based on the difference in stock price between the time the company granted the stock rights at fair market value to the end of the designated period, permitting the executives to keep the stock.

Straight commission is based on the fixed percentage of the sales price of the product or service.

Strategic analysis entails an examination of a company's external market context and internal factors. Examples of external market factors include industry profile, information about competitors, and long-term growth prospects. Internal factors encompass financial condition and functional capabilities—for example, marketing and human resources.

Strategic decisions support business objectives.

Strategic management entails a series of judgments, under uncertainty, that companies direct toward achieving specific goals.

Stress management is a specific kind of wellness program designed to help employees cope with many factors inside and outside work that contribute to stress.

Strictness errors occur when raters (for example, supervisors) judge an employee's performance lower than the performance actually rates when compared against objective criteria.

Summary Compensation Table discloses compensation information for CEOs and the four most highly paid executives over a three-year period employed by companies whose stock is traded on public stock exchanges. The information in this table is presented in tabular and graphic forms to make information more accessible to the public.

Supplemental life insurance protection represents additional life insurance protection offered exclusively to executives. Companies design executives' supplemental life insurance protection to increase the value of executives' estates, bequeathed to designated beneficiaries (usually, family members) upon the executives' death, and to provide greater benefits than standard plans usually allow.

Supplemental retirement plans, offered to executives, are designed to restore benefits restricted under qualified plans.

Supplemental unemployment benefit (SUB) refers to unemployment insurance that is usually awarded to individuals who were employed in cyclical industries. This benefit supplements unemployment insurance that is required by the Social Security Act of 1935.

Tactical decisions support competitive strategy.

Target plan bonuses, awarded to executives, are based on executives' performance. Executives do not receive bonuses unless their performance exceeds minimally acceptable standards.

Tax equalization is one of two approaches (the other is tax protection) to provide expatriates tax allowances. Employers take the responsibility for paying income taxes to the United States and foreign governments on behalf of the expatriates.

Tax home is an expatriate's foreign residence while on assignment, and the expatriate's only place of residence.

Tax protection is one of two approaches (the other is tax equalization) to provide expatriates tax allowances. Employers reimburse expatriates for the difference between the actual income tax amount and the hypothetical tax when the actual income tax amount—based on tax returns filed with the Internal Revenue Service—is greater.

Telecommuting represents alternative work arrangements in which employees perform work at home or some other location besides the office.

Temperaments are adaptability requirements made on the worker by the situation.

Temporary employment agencies place individuals in client companies as employees on a temporary basis.

Term coverage is a type of life insurance that provides protection to employees' beneficiaries only during employees' employment.

Third country nationals are foreign national citizens who work in U.S. companies' branch offices or manufacturing plants in foreign countries—excluding the United States and the employees' home country.

Time-and-motion studies analyzed the time it took employees to complete their jobs. Factory owners used time-and-motion studies and job analysis to meet this objective.

Title I of the Americans with Disabilities Act of 1990 (ADA) requires that employers provide "reasonable accommodation" to disabled employees. Reasonable accommodation may include such efforts as making existing facilities readily accessible, job restructuring, and modifying work schedules.

Title II of the Civil Rights Act of 1991 enacted the Glass Ceiling Act.

Title VII of the Civil Rights Act of 1964 indicates that it shall be an unlawful employment practice for an employer to discriminate against any individual with respect to his compensation, terms, conditions, or privileges of employment, because of such individual's race, color, religion, sex, or national origin.

Tournament theory provides an explanation for executive compensation determination based on substantially greater competition for high ranking jobs. Lucrative chief executive compensation packages represent the prize to those who win the competition by becoming chief executives.

Training is a planned effort to facilitate employees' learning of job-related knowledge, skills, or behaviors. Effective training programs lead to desired employee learning, which translates into improved future job performance.

Trait systems, a type of performance appraisal method, requires raters (for example, supervisors or customers) to evaluate each employee's traits or characteristics such as quality of work, quantity of work, appearance, dependability, cooperation, initiative, judgment, leadership, responsibility, decision-making ability, or creativity.

Transportation services represent energy efficient ways to transport employees to and from the workplace. Employers cover part or all of the transportation costs.

Tuition reimbursement programs promote employees' education. Under a tuition reimbursement program, an employer fully or partially reimburses an employee for expenses incurred for education or training.

Two-tier pay structures reward newly hired employees less than established employees on either a temporary or permanent basis.

Uncertainty avoidance, a dimension of national culture, represents the method by which society deals with risk and instability for its members.

Usual, customary, and reasonable charge is defined as being not more than the physician's usual charge; within the customary range of fees charged in the locality; and reasonable, based on the medical circumstances. Commercial insurance plans generally do not pay more than this amount.

Valid job analysis method accurately assesses each job's duties.

Variable pay (*see* incentive pay).

Variation represents the amount of spread or dispersion in a set of data.

Vertical knowledge refers to knowledge traditionally associated with supervisory activities, for example, performance appraisal and grievance review procedures.

Vertical skills are those skills traditionally considered supervisory activities such as scheduling, coordinating, training, and leading others.

Vesting refers to employees' acquisition of nonforfeitable rights to pension benefits.

Vision insurance provides reimbursement for routine optical checkups and particular corrective procedures.

Voluntary part-time employees choose to work fewer than 35 hours per regularly scheduled work week.

Voluntary terminations are initiated by employees in order to work for other companies or to begin their retirements.

Wage (*see* hourly pay).

Wagner-Peyser Act established a federal-state employment service system.

Walling v. A. H. Belo Corp., a Supreme Court ruling, requires that employers guarantee fixed weekly pay when the following conditions prevail—the employer typically cannot determine the number of hours employees will work each week, and the work week period fluctuates both above and below 40 hours per week.

Walsh-Healey Act of 1936 mandates that contractors with federal contracts meet guidelines regarding wages and hours, child labor, convict labor, and hazardous working conditions. Contractors must observe the minimum wage and overtime provisions of the FLSA. In addition, this act prohibits the employment of individuals younger than 16, and convicted criminals. Further, this act prohibits contractors from exposing workers to any conditions that violate the Occupational Safety and Health Act.

Weight control and nutrition programs, a particular type of wellness program, are designed to educate employees about proper nutrition and weight loss, both of which are critical to good health.

Welfare practices, common prior to 1950s, is the term used to describe the predecessor of contemporary employee benefits. Welfare practices included such amenities as libraries for employees.

Wellness programs promote employees' physical and psychological health.

Work fields, based on the U.S. Department of Labor Job Analysis Method, represent the technologies and socioeconomic objectives that relate to how work gets done, and what gets done as a result of the work activities of a job.

Work Hours and Safety Standards Act of 1962 requires that all contractors pay employees one and one-half times their regular hourly rate for each hour worked in excess of 40 hours per week.

Work performed, based on the U.S. Department of Labor Job Analysis Method, contains the job analysis components that relate to the actual work activities of a job and constitute information that HR professionals should include in the job summary and job duties sections of job descriptions.

Worker function, based on the U.S. Department of Labor Job Analysis Method, describes what the worker does in relation to data, people, and things, as expressed by mental, interpersonal, and physical worker actions.

Worker requirements represent the minimum qualifications and skills that people must have to perform a particular job. Such requirements usually include education, experience, licenses, permits, and specific abilities, such as typing, drafting, or editing.

Worker specification, a section in job descriptions, lists the education, skills, abilities, knowledge, and other qualifications individuals must possess to perform the job adequately.

Worker traits, based on the U.S. Department of Labor Job Analysis Method, represent characteristics of employees that contribute to successful job performance.

Workers' compensation laws established state-run insurance programs that are designed to cover medical, rehabilitation, and disability income expenses resulting from employees' work-related accidents.

Working condition fringe benefits refer to the work equipment (for example, computer) and services (for example, an additional telephone line) employers purchase for telecommuters' use at home.

AUTHOR INDEX

SUBJECT INDEX

Flextime schedules (core hours), 383, 384
401(k) plans, 279–281
Foreign service premium, 320
Free lancers, 373, 380–383
Fringe compensation, 7, 8. *See also* Benefits;
Discretionary benefits; Legally required
benefits

G

Gain sharing, 115–120. *See also* Incentive pay;
Leadership philosophy; Employee involvement; Bonus
Gain sharing, Improshare, 119, 120
buy-back provision, 119
labor hour ratio formula, 119
Gain sharing, Rucker Plan (value-added formula), 117–119
Gain sharing, Scanlon plan, 116, 117
company-wide screening committee, 117
production-level committees, 117
sales value of production—SVOP, 117, 118
Glass Ceiling Act, 64
Glass ceiling barriers, 64
Global competition, 25
pay-for-knowledge, 136
Golden parachute, 350
Government
federal, 52, 53
influence on compensation, 52, 53
local, 52, 53
state, 52, 53
Government pay practices. *See also* Federal government employees
seniority pay, 77–79
Government's goals, 52
Great Depression, 53
Green circle rates, 232

H

Hardship allowances, 321
Hay plan, 184

Health protection, 282–287
coinsurance, 283, 284, 285, 287
commercial or fee-for-service-plans, 283–285
copayments, 285
cost shifting, 287
deductible, 283, 284, 285, 287
dental insurance, 286, 287
health maintenance organizations (HMOs),
285, 286, 287
preferred provider organizations (PPOs), 285,
286, 287
self-funded insurance, 285
usual, customary, and reasonable charges, 283,
284, 285
vision insurance, 287
Health maintenance organization (HMO), 285,
286, 287
prepaid group practices vs. individual practice
associations, 286
Health Maintenance Organization Act of 1973,
285
High-involvement organization structure, 34
Highly paid employees, 343
Holidays, 288, 289
Host country nationals, 316, 336, 337
Hourly pay (wage), 5
Human capital theory, 6, 77
Human resource strategy, 28
Human resources, 8, 10, 14

I

Incentive pay, 6, 23, 25, 32, 104–128
commissions and sales plans, 238–242
competitive strategies, 127, 128
Incentive pay, design, 124–128
complementing or replacing base pay, 125,
126
group versus individual, 124, 125
level of risk, 125
performance criteria, 126
time horizon (short-term versus long-term),
127